THE TROWENNA SEA

Witi Ihimaera is an award-winning New Zealand novelist of Maori descent. His collection of short stories, *Pounamu Pounamu*, was published in 1972, followed by *Tangi* in 1973, the first novel by a Maori. His much-loved 1987 novel, *The Whale Rider*, was made into an internationally acclaimed film in 2002. *The Trowenna Sea* is Ihimaera's twelfth novel.

OTHER FICTION BY WITI IHIMAERA

Short Stories—
Pounamu Pounamu (1972)
The New Net Goes Fishing (1977)
Dear Miss Mansfield (1989)
Kingfisher Come Home (1995)
Ihimaera: His Best Stories (2003)
Ask the Posts of the House (2007)

Novels—
Tangi (1973)
Whanau (1974)
The Matriarch (1986)
The Whale Rider (1987)
Bulibasha, King of the Gypsies (1994)
Nights in the Gardens of Spain (1995)
The Dream Swimmer (1997)
The Uncle's Story (2000)
Sky Dancer (2001)
Whanau II (2004)
The Rope of Man (2005)

WITI
IHIMAERA

THE TROWENNA SEA

a novel

RAUPO

A RAUPO BOOK
Published by the Penguin Group
Penguin Group (NZ), 67 Apollo Drive, Rosedale,
North Shore 0632, New Zealand (a division of Pearson New Zealand Ltd)
Penguin Group (USA) Inc., 375 Hudson Street,
New York, New York 10014, USA
Penguin Group (Canada), 90 Eglinton Avenue East, Suite 700, Toronto,
Ontario, M4P 2Y3, Canada (a division of Pearson Penguin Canada Inc.)
Penguin Books Ltd, 80 Strand, London, WC2R 0RL, England
Penguin Ireland, 25 St Stephen's Green,
Dublin 2, Ireland (a division of Penguin Books Ltd)
Penguin Group (Australia), 250 Camberwell Road, Camberwell,
Victoria 3124, Australia (a division of Pearson Australia Group Pty Ltd)
Penguin Books India Pvt Ltd, 11, Community Centre,
Panchsheel Park, New Delhi – 110 017, India
Penguin Books (South Africa) (Pty) Ltd, 24 Sturdee Avenue,
Rosebank, Johannesburg 2196, South Africa

Penguin Books Ltd, Registered Offices: 80 Strand, London, WC2R 0RL, England

First published by Penguin Group (NZ), 2009
1 3 5 7 9 10 8 6 4 2

Copyright © Witi Ihimaera, 2009

The right of Witi Ihimaera to be identified as the author of this work in terms of
section 96 of the Copyright Act 1994 is hereby asserted.

Designed and typeset by Pindar (NZ)
Printed in Australia by McPherson's Printing Group

ISBN 9780143202455

A catalogue record for this book is available
from the National Library of New Zealand.

www.penguin.co.nz

The Trowenna Sea is a work of fiction:

   In particular, it imagines a life for one of the characters, Hohepa Te Umuroa, as an eyewitness and participant of history, both in New Zealand and Tasmania.

The novel is dedicated with great respect to the descendants of three of the historical characters who appear in it: Hohepa Te Umuroa, whose iwi kindly gave me their permission to write about him, John Jennings Imrie and his wife Etty Bailey.

   It is further dedicated to the citizens of Tasmania, Australia, and the people of the Maramatanga, Patiarero and of the Whanganui River.

   And it is dedicated also to James Anthony Ihimaera-Pritchard, born during the writing of *The Trowenna Sea*. Haere mai, tama, ki te Ao o Tane.

CONTENTS

THE FIRST BOOK
PILGRIMS

ISMAY'S STORY

Tasmania, Australia

PROLOGUE
Tasmania, 1903

The child keeps badgering me with her questions, her moist snout poking close to my face as if she thinks I can't see or hear her. But I do both well enough, and most often I am patient.

Today, however, she hurries me along too quickly, pleading as her excuse the deadline for submission of her article for Tasmania's centenary year publication. She plays on the maudlin sentimentality of being an Australian in the same way others in fervent mood have trumpeted the event.

I will not be harried in this manner. I have lived my life at my own pace and do not desire to accelerate, however much she and her band of earnest young colleagues wish to sniff out colourful anecdotes of our state's glorious past to fill their book.

The child's name is Georgina. She is my granddaughter, and I wish she would desist. I do not need her studious eyes and false pleading voice, and there is no need for her to shout. I am not deaf, only hard of hearing, which is a different matter altogether. She has already made her intentions clear enough, speaking in her precise vowels and wheedling tone and I care not one jot that she has only a month left before she presents her article: I will not be rushed on by her.

The celebration will take place next year and while, of course, Georgina has a right to be proud that she has an aged grandmother who is able to recall Van Diemen's Land as it was last century, I am not sufficiently prepared in my spirit to visit all my memories of that time quite yet. I prefer to conserve them and keep them safe in my personal care. Such memories may indeed be hers by right of kinship, but I am still possessive of them. After all, they are very precious to me and I have never been one who believes that everything about one's past should be disclosed. A discreet veil is infinitely to be preferred; why should I bequeath them to the public gaze? Georgina will have, at my death, the jewellery and particularly the ruby necklace and earrings I have seen her covet since childhood. Is that not enough for a greedy child?

Georgina will just have to show a modicum of tolerance with an old woman approaching eighty years. And when I do begin, while I know she would like me to take a detour down to the low road, I shall stay on the high road. My days of jumping hither and yon around my memories only confuse me more. Indeed, I have never understood her generation's penchant for looking under every stone for the truth, whatever that is.

She will have to bear with me and let me come in my own time to the particular memories she so badgers me about.

Some things I will tell her.

Others I will not.

I

For instance, I will *not* tell her about the circumstances in which I grew up as a child on the other side of the world, in Wolverhampton, Staffordshire, England.

Why not? I do not wish to burden the girl with a narrative that would only cause her anguish, have her mewling her concern: 'Oh Nanna, why didn't you tell us?' While some might question this erasure of the years prior to my maturity, I have forbidden myself such disclosure for one reason: my former history is one I treat with contempt. I have consigned it and everyone in it — except for my dear mother, aunt and uncle, and female cousins — to the silence it deserves. There's another reason: Georgina already shows too indecent an interest in my life. The less I tell her the better.

For this current document, however, I shall, albeit briefly, open that door.

———

Herewith, consider as you wish, my circumstances.

I was born in 1822 to Lowthian and Selina (née Glossop) Webster. Both my parents were of the mercantile class: my mother was one of two daughters born to the well-known Glossop family, which owned cotton mills; Lowthian was the scion of Webster & Son iron foundry at Bilston (he being the son of Albion Webster, founder of a business made prosperous by armament production during the Napoleonic Wars). The large oval family portrait at the bottom of the great staircase in Webster Hall showed Lowthian to be a handsome youth. The artist was of the obsequious kind: he painted his subject in bold, striking colours, in a stylish high-buttoned coat, against the background of his iron empire. Lord of All He Surveys, Lowthian holds a riding crop in his right hand.

This symbol of power and flagellation, together with the incipient sneer of lip, suggest that the artist was attempting to convey Lowthian's real nature, and this underlies my contempt for him. I knew well, possibly more than anyone else, that it was cruelty that motivated Lowthian's relationship with his workers. They would never attain the romantic clear blue of sky the artist painted above their master's head and which presented him as a philanthropist of the masses — though that was the status to which his peers eventually elevated him. But then many towns and cities raise statues of such men in squares and parks that also bear their names; my father was no better than they were, and a lot worse than most of them.

As for my mother, she was the elder sister, gentle both as a young girl and as a woman; her aged parents, hoping to secure their dynasty, planned a merger of their cotton interests with the Webster & Son foundry. They met with no objection when they proposed her marriage to Lowthian. She was of a romantic inclination which was not to survive her traumatic and brutal wedding night.

What Selina thought of the travail of birth I shudder to imagine, but I know she welcomed me with the purity of a mother's love. My father, however, greeted my arrival as an extreme affront. Like many of his class, he regarded patriarchy as the only rule of life.

'What say you, madam?' he asked my mother when confronted with a babe who lacked the requisite and ridiculous male appendage. This, my only crime, was sufficient for Lowthian to set himself against me even when I was christened at Bilston parish and entered into the ledger of Grocott's Bradley Bridge Church. He was purposely absent from the occasion and did not even offer the excuse of a business trip abroad. What shocked the congregation more was the surname I was christened with.

'I name you Ismay Elizabeth Glossop,' the reverend intoned.

Not Webster, my father's surname; Lowthian had refused to give it. As for Ismay, it was a thirteenth-century variant of the French Esmé.

Family name or not, my father could not forbid my return to Webster Hall, where I was forever the mote in his eye, unable to be plucked out and therefore the source of his greatest displeasure. Selina, however, was able to redeem herself when she gave birth in quick and outraged succession to my two brothers, Alfred and St John, who ultimately proved equal in arrogance to Lowthian.

Three children in as many years was a burden that unfairly and unduly challenged my mother's frailty and maternal responsibilities. But she had an ulterior motive when she asked Lowthian, in seeming despair, to release me into the hands of her sister, my Aunt Eleanor. My departure, she told him, would enable her to pay better attention to two boisterous boys who savaged their wet nurse whenever they suckled.

My father complied with her request willingly, relieved to be rid of any evidence of an eldest girl child bearing his paternity: out of sight, out of mind.

'Mother, why must I leave you?' I remember asking my mother as she bundled me up against the cold and gave me to a servant to deliver to my aunt's residence.

Her face was wan and pinched with distress. 'Cease your remonstrations, child,' she reprimanded. 'This is your escape. It is for the best.'

For the best? As the carriage bore me away from Webster Hall I felt that Selina was abandoning me, making me a foundling child to be brought up by strangers. Bitterness against her found its way into my innocent heart.

Thus it was that I arrived at my Aunt Eleanor's spacious home. She may not have married as wealthily as Selina, but certainly she had wedded just as respectably, for my Uncle Rollo Springvale was a surgeon to the rich and prosperous of Wolverhampton. Uncle Rollo also showed his humanitarian sympathies by extending his practice to the poor of the city — and there were many of those. Wolverhampton was one of the fastest-growing industrial cities of the time, striving to equal Birmingham for iron, steel and other manufacturing production. The poor poured in to service that civic ambition.

I was deposited at the door like an unwanted parcel, bearing a label around my neck. I am referring cynically to the annuity that Lowthian agreed to provide for my Christian care and upkeep, and to the note he wrote (I can just see his lip curling with arrogant amusement as he did so) to my Uncle Rollo, to wit:

> Dear brother-in-law, herewith find one girl child to join your own overcrowded cave of female cubs. Care for her as if she were your own.
>> Lowthian Webster.

His reference was to Uncle Rollo's own offspring, my cousins Sybil, Isobel and Ursula. Unlike my own father, Uncle Rollo bore the preponderance of daughters with an equanimity that belied any inner disappointment he may have harboured.

Aunt Eleanor tried to peck me on both cheeks but found me wanting and unresponsive with respect to reciprocal emotion. Uncle Rollo obtained a better response when, gravely, he shook me by the hand. He was thin, tall and somewhat austere. 'Ismay, is it?' he asked. 'We shall call you May for short.'

'No, you will not,' I glared, setting my child's chin with determination.

Aunt Eleanor gasped at my rudeness. But Uncle Rollo smiled and patted me on the hair. 'Young lady, in this household it is a pleasure to meet a girl who says no to me. We will get on very well, I think.'

In Uncle Rollo I had my only male champion.

2

For the next eleven years, my intransigence and unwillingness to oblige any of my dear aunt's entreaties must have been a trial to the Springvales, but Aunt Eleanor and Uncle Rollo adopted me lovingly and I became part of their household. My grievance at being placed among them could not long prevail against their positive and embracing nature. During the harsh winter I was five I came down with pneumonia, and only by Uncle Rollo's medical skills and Aunt Eleanor's patient nursing was I able to recover. When I opened my eyes to see my aunt's dear face and my weeping cousins, I knew that they cared for me. Uncle Rollo sealed it with the words, 'Look, daughters! Your sister is back with us.'

How could any heart, even one as stubborn as mine, resist such sentimentality?

It was my good fortune, possibly the best I could have hoped for, to enter such a household in which women were affirmed. And although I was by nature more strong-headed than my cousins, a trait which persisted throughout my life, Aunt Eleanor did her best not to let this deter her from treating me as one of her own daughters.

'Imagine the difficulty if you had been a boy, Ismay!' she would tell me. 'Luckily, as you were a girl, we simply added you to our normal regime.'

My aunt, of course, glossed over the additional stresses caused by my increasingly rebellious ways. It all sounded easy enough but, oh, I must have been a trial to her! By the age of ten it was clear that I had a preternatural talent for learning and a curiosity about the world that could only be assuaged by reading. For instance, while my cousins enjoyed the latest novels of Jane Austen, or the poetry of Elizabeth Barrett Browning, I found greater fascination in the classical, philosophical, geographical and historical tomes of Uncle Rollo's capacious library.

'Doesn't your brain get tired, cousin?' Sybil asked as I hefted open another weighty volume from the shelves. Medical opinion of the time was that girls became overstrained if subjected to too much mental exertion.

'No,' I snapped, watching as she, Isobel and Ursula dutifully responded to the level of education our governesses considered more appropriate for the female sex: elocution, polite conversation, study of etiquette, deportment and neat handwriting. Nor was I at all interested in acquiring training in the rules and rituals concerning the running of the household or dinner party or ball, or how to gain perfection in needlepoint, skill in playing the pianoforte, the elegant steps required when partnered in the quadrille and, of course, the importance of wearing the latest ballroom fashions. I found it difficult, and a bore, to appreciate the niceties of manners which, to put it candidly, were designed to restrict not only one's own behaviour but also that of others.

I never really fitted into my tutor's view of what a 'lady' was supposed to be. For one thing, I was always impetuous, running when I should be walking. For another — and I will make no excuse for it — I was forthright and outspoken. Well do I remember Aunt Eleanor bemoaning, 'You will never become a lady, Ismay, unless you curb your forward tendencies, lower your voice, remember your deportment at all times and please do endeavour to moderate your speed.'

By the time I was twelve my natural curiosity had my governesses on their mettle. I even outstripped them in many subjects. They persisted in endeavouring to restrain my learning to those texts more suitable for a young woman but, happily, without success. They called my yearnings 'immoderate education beyond the natural range of female accomplishment', but their entreaties to me to return to moderation went in one ear and out the other.

Oh, I felt so restricted! Whenever Uncle Rollo invited colleagues or young male students to dinner, I hung thirstily on their every word as they discussed politics and debated economics, the state of the nation, and England's colonial accomplishments in the Americas, India and Australia. Sometimes, much to the dismay of Aunt Eleanor, my itch to become involved led me to pose questions or views of my own. After dinner, when the men adjourned to talk about politics, how I wished to follow them. Instead, I was lectured sternly on my appropriate station. 'A woman is to be

Adam's helpmate, Ismay. He has the major graces; we have the minor.'

Such lectures made me burn with fury. More vexing still, however, was my growing understanding that while I could voyage to new worlds in books, I could barely travel beyond the front door — or back door, for that matter — for a taste of the world I was reading about. A woman's sphere was the Home. Women and young girls were scrupulously chaperoned at all times, and Aunt Eleanor ensured that a cohort of watchful butlers and housemaids stood guard at the portals to freedom to prevent my delinquent curiosity. Nor could I enlist my cousins in my escapades. They preferred to stay indoors, safe from what they considered a dangerous world. Limited opportunities for escape presented themselves only when we ventured out into the Wolverhampton streets with Aunt Eleanor to visit other matrons and their female broods. How I hated being kept in check as if we were chickens under the eye of a very clucky hen.

'No, do not cross the road to look into the window of the apothecary! Where are you off to now, child? No, I do not want to see what is attracting the crowd at the corner! Ismay! What are you doing on the other side of the street? Return at once!'

We moved hastily by carriage from one henhouse to another where, having negotiated perilous streets, my aunt could relax and talk about society matters, and my cousins could discuss the latest fashions from London with the daughters of the house. I could have died from irritation.

———

From time to time my aunt took me to Webster Hall to meet my mother. I had not forgiven her for abandoning me, and my attitude must have been distressing to her. As well, there was always some subterfuge about the visits, and that confused me even more. For instance, they often were embarked upon at short notice, whenever my father Lowthian was away from Wolverhampton on business; and sometimes not even my brothers Alfred and St John were present.

One day, in a fit of pique, I ventured to Selina, 'Why you would want to see me, given the secrecy with which we meet, is beyond my comprehension. You are obviously still ashamed of me.'

My mother gave a cry, hid her face and excused herself from the room.

Aunt Eleanor was beside herself with anger. She shook me hard. 'Ismay Elizabeth Glossop,' she scolded. 'Don't you realise what a sacrifice your mother made for you? And still makes for you? Had you remained at Webster Hall, you would have been coerced and subjected to Lowthian's vindictive control. He is still against you, child.'

I was shocked at the strength of the reprimand, and was immediately chastened. When Selina returned, I embraced her.

'I'm sorry, Mother,' I said. A rush of emotion overcame me and, for the first time since that evening eleven years earlier when I had been spirited away from her, I wept in her arms.

From that moment we re-established our bond as mother and daughter. Like Aunt Eleanor, Selina conducted herself with the feminine decorum of her class but, unlike my aunt, she admired my independent spirit. My sympathy and love for her grew as I gradually discovered the ways in which her own spirit had been destroyed; even the servants at Webster Hall disdained her control.

Not while I was around. Lowthian may once have called me a female cub. In my renewed bond with my mother, I devoted myself as her protector.

Whenever my father and brothers did happen to arrive while I was with Selina, they refused to acknowledge my family connection as a Webster.

'Is your sister visiting again?' Lowthian asked her one day when I had stayed too long. As for Alfred and St John, the lack of intimate communication between us made it only too easy for them to begin to call me their aunt. I disappeared, as a sibling, before their very eyes.

I cannot understand how my mother survived their daily demands. She was like a sad ghost out of a dream: thin, pale, nervous, fearful. At the end of every visit she always pressed me to her breast, kissed both my cheeks and, as often as not, gave me a small gift from her jewel box. On one occasion I showed some interest in a lovely hatpin fashioned in the shape of a silver butterfly with gorgeous filigree wings. She gave it to me immediately, pinning it into my long unruly hair.

***

I was about fourteen when I decided to take an unusual course for young women of my class and social standing. I will not admit to scheming, but one does as one must.

I had come to appreciate the comparative freedoms enjoyed by the male sex and noted, for instance, that Uncle Rollo had carte blanche to go wherever he wished. By that age, my intellectual fascination had expanded to, and become focused on, his own profession; I had played with my dolls not as my cousins were wont to do — as surrogate children that they would one day nurse themselves — but as a medical practitioner does with his patients. Of course, when Aunt Eleanor discovered me using a rather fearsome scalpel from his medical briefcase — a box lined with red velvet and containing his surgical implements — she was scandalised.

Perhaps it was only natural that in adolescence I would advance to that section of Uncle Rollo's library which contained his notes made as a student at Edinburgh University, and textbooks such as *The Anatomy of the Human Body*, *Discourse on the Nature and Cure of Wounds* and *The Principles of Surgery*, so my scheming, as I have put it, was not without genuine interest in my uncle's medical profession. Assuredly, it was my earnest desire for adult discourse that led me to be discovered often by him in the library with one of those aforementioned medical publications and he, being of an amiable demeanour, fell easily into expanding on my innocent questioning of symptoms and surgical interventions. Had Aunt Eleanor discovered us in such conversations, she would have immediately put a stop to them. I suspect that for many years he had wished for someone in the family to pass his wisdom on to and, while he found surrogates in the youthful male students who apprenticed themselves to him, he took pleasure in the fact that he had in his female household someone who enquired about his surgical work.

For this and other reasons, Uncle Rollo became my main educator and governor and he, dear man, did not seem to mind when I fell into the habit of long discussions on the practices and principles of medicine with him in his study after dinner when the ladies of the house were otherwise occupied in music or poetry.

But, minx that I was, I so inveigled myself into his good graces that it seemed entirely natural for me to take the next step. One night, when Uncle Rollo was putting on his hat and coat to attend a medical emergency, I put a hand in his and asked if I might go with him. I followed this up by taking possession of his briefcase and waiting at the door. Mere feminine ingratiation would not have won me the consent I so desired and I was gratified, therefore, that he appreciated my maturity and capability.

However, as I went to put on my cape, Aunt Eleanor bore grimly down on us like a galleon to block the armada.

'Oh, no you don't,' she said.

Uncle Rollo took her by the arm and kissed her forehead. 'Why stand in the way of Fate!' he sighed.

Difficult as it was for me to achieve, I tried to look submissive and meek, and waited until Uncle's tender persuasions had obtained the agreement we both sought from our beloved mistress.

'Very well then, but just this once,' Aunt Eleanor said.

———

Once? From that moment on, whenever Uncle Rollo was called on to tend to the medical needs of the wealthy, I became his companion.

Most often I waited quietly in another room while my uncle went about his diagnoses and treatments. But one day I found myself being pressed into service when Uncle Rollo requested that I assist in a sensitive examination. Mrs Croyden-Barrington was a woman of a certain age, and had what seemed to me a mystifying problem involving her pelvic area.

'Could you ask the patient,' Uncle Rollo asked, 'where the pain is located?'

I followed Mrs Croyden-Barrington's pointed finger. 'The patient is indicating that the pain is below her navel in the area of the frontal nether region.'

Mrs Croyden-Barrington gasped. Like most women of her class, she could not bring herself to name those parts of her physique that were in pain. Nor would she let my uncle touch her.

Uncle Rollo coughed. 'Is the pain located within or without?'

Mrs Croyden-Barrington was mortified, but managed to recover herself. Crimsoning, she whispered in my ear a long and somewhat circumlocutory list of symptoms that I finally diagnosed as being associated with the changes that occur to women when their best years are behind them.

'Within,' I answered. 'But it is also of a more general feminine nature,' I added, smiling sweetly at Mrs Croyden-Barrington. I knew full well that appealing to Uncle Rollo's clients would best ensure my continuing to accompany him.

Very soon, my stock increased as word spread among Uncle Rollo's female clientele that he possessed a dear young female assistant who soothed them and listened sympathetically to them while the doctor treated their specific problems. I became regularly employed in the relaying of their pains, palpitations and assorted maladies to him. Sometimes, I acted as a stand-in for these women as Uncle Rollo inspected *me*, asking, 'Is the pain located here?' while they nodded and winced when he touched the correct area.

'You are earning your keep,' he said to me, his eyes twinkling.

———

Tending to the wealthy was one matter. My ambition lay further — to venture with my uncle into the realms of the city's poor.

However, I reckoned without Aunt Eleanor, who was not going to give way without a fight. Usually, my uncle's working-class patients attended the surgery, but when they were gravely ill or the victims of accidents at the factories he would attend them in person.

Time after time I would take up the medical briefcase but be stopped by my aunt from following Uncle Rollo. Oh, how furious I was! However, determination was on my side and, on the occasion of an emergency at the local colliery, I could not be stopped. I stepped past her and out the door.

'Ismay Elizabeth Glossop!' Aunt Eleanor reprimanded as I followed Uncle Rollo to the trap that was waiting to take him. 'Come inside, immediately.'

'We should hurry,' I said to Uncle Rollo.

He smiled quizzically, hesitated, and then clucked at the horse and jingled the reins, leaving Aunt Eleanor gasping like a ship stranded in the doldrums.

'I'll bring her back safe and sound,' he said.

Even so, my aunt's protesting voice followed us down the street — except that her imprecations were aimed at Uncle Rollo, not me. 'The fact that our city is named after the Lady Wulfruna,' she called, 'is no excuse for Ismay to be marked by her same wilfulness.'

'I am for the dogbox when we return,' he said.

And so began my journey into the world of the lower classes, the industrial workers who lived in the aptly named Black Country. Aunt Eleanor's fears were not without foundation. There were dangers here — not only from louts and robbers but also from the ever increasing number of worker migrants who brought typhus fever and smallpox.

Aunt Eleanor's palpable anxiety when we returned made me momentarily contrite. 'I have been at my wits' end worrying about you,' she scolded. She made me bathe twice: first, my governess scrubbed me and searched my hair for lice and other hateful vermin that might have crossed the border into polite society where they did not belong; second, she added bath salts to the water, knowing I hated that even more. When I arose from the bath I smelt like . . . lily of the valley.

Malicious girl that I was, I obtained my revenge by leaving a few of Uncle Rollo's leeches in a tiny vial on Aunt Eleanor's dresser — he used them to let blood and reduce tensions in the nervous system. Her screeches echoed satisfactorily through the house and, while I was scolded by my uncle, the reprimand was worth it.

No, not even Aunt Eleanor could stop me from my excursions. At that time of my life, danger was my desire. And happily, my cousins Sybil, Ursula and Isobel did not seem to object that I had won their father's special affections. Already indulged by him, and blossoming into young beauties, they were more than satisfied with their mother's society and the *other* world that I was so disinterested in. Sybil had arrived at that time of life when many a young woman tried to obtain from her male parent whatever she wished — a new dress, a coveted piece of jewellery — by feminine stealth; having me divert him from refusing to purchase the desired object was a blessing, given that Aunt Eleanor entirely approved of a woman's right to acquire as many baubles and garments as she could. Ursula was not as pretty, but you could see that one day she would turn heads, and Isobel was endearing with her pouting ways.

One quiet afternoon, Sybil observed my excitement as I prepared to accompany Uncle Rollo. Laughing, she embraced me and said, 'Oh, Ismay, you're the boy Father always wished he had.' It was not meant unkindly; rather, there was approval in it, and in many ways I recognised the truth of her insight. But I did not want to be a male, heaven forbid! All I wanted to do was experience the same freedoms as the masculine gender, not become one of them. Of course I also revelled in escaping the strictures of my own polite society and discovering the wider world, no matter that it confronted me with social inequities that Sybil and my cousins would never fully comprehend.

What a dichotomy: walk through the squares or along the streets of the west end of the city and you would mark the external magnificence of the buildings and picture the costly luxuries within. Enter the parks and you would behold the gorgeous equipages rolling on like a stream too large for its channel, and the lazy postures and satiated visages of those who occupied the costly carriages.

Venture to the east, however, and you were immediately within the world of the sons and daughters of misery: filthy streets and squalid dwellings in the last state of want and wretchedness. Thousands of workers had left their agricultural estates, hoping for better lives in the city, only to find themselves trapped into toiling and sweating day after day for the bare necessities of life. Theirs was the world of the coalmines and factories upon which England's economic wealth was founded. Indeed, Staffordshire was like one vast coalfield. For a period, the output of its coalmines was greater than the rest of the world combined. Twenty thousand workers toiled underground, including on Wolverhampton's famous 'Ten Yard Seam', from where the coal was shifted by a huge canal system to the wider market at home and abroad. But the mines also underpinned the local cotton, steel, glassmaking, brewing and other industries. Potbellied potentates were frequently heard to compare their workers to an army and to boast of more than ten thousand recruits coming into the city a year. The great expansion of the factory system was what minted the lives of the factory owners with gold. It was a permanent fact. It was also a permanent evil. Factory workers lived on the veritable margins of disaster.

This was the world into which I plunged with Uncle Rollo, despite Aunt Eleanor's vain entreaties — that poor lady soon realised that I had grown beyond her control. How common it was for a boy to come to the surgery in the early evening calling, 'Doctor! Doctor! My father has taken ill. Please come quickly.' No sooner was the appeal made than we would set off by trap until we could negotiate the squalid streets no longer.

'Come, Ismay, we must go the rest of the way on foot,' Uncle Rollo said. And then we would race pell-mell, he holding a lamp, following the voice of the lad who had come to fetch us, some panicky wraith already gone ahead and urging us onward.

Down through the narrow passages we would hasten. Through little courts and yards where, for lack of sewers, human excrement and piss stained the intervals between. Up straggling lanes known as guts, being only two or three feet wide and barely able to be squeezed through, further into the entrails of dirt, refuse, declivities of mud and slush, stagnant water and filth.

'Are you still with me, Ismay?' Uncle Rollo would call. 'Don't lag behind now.' I had become responsible for carrying his medical briefcase as we picked our way over the uneven and broken pavements.

Finally we would arrive at some dank worker's hovel, filled with flies, and lacking air, drainage or even a privy outside. Inside, a woman would hover in filthy skirt, rags wrapped around her feet. Uncle Rollo would put down his lamp and begin, without hesitation, his examination of the poor wretch coughing and moaning in the corner.

'What seems to be the trouble now?'

Usually, the patient was having difficulty breathing — the fluff from the cotton when it was being carded wound around the lungs and tightened them up. Asthma, colds and pneumonia were rife, too, caused by the offensive pall that cast itself over the poor.

From time to time, Uncle Rollo was called on to attempt to deliver a baby by caesarean because some hideous midwife had botched the opportunity of natural delivery. I know that he was sometimes importuned to rid women of unwanted babies; he was a moral person and would not do it, but he would often despair that the poor young woman would then fall victim to some dirty butcher's knife and herself succumb, along with her unborn child. On a few occasions I saw him close the eyes of a dying man or woman, whispering a kind word into the ears of the family and offering them a coin or two for the funeral.

But Uncle Rollo's primary work involved dealing with the horrifying consequences of industrial accidents. Burns and scalds when a boiler exploded or blast furnaces, forges or steam engines malfunctioned were legion; some explosions catapulted molten metal two hundred feet into the air, causing grievous injury to all who stood in its path.

One calamity stands in my memory. Word came that an unwary iron foundry worker had been trapped when his apron caught between the revolving cylinders of the machine on which he'd been working. He was dragged through like a heap of cotton and came out shredded and torn. Though alive when help was sent for, he had succumbed to his injuries by the time Uncle Rollo and I arrived.

'There is nothing we can do,' Uncle said, his face grim. His expression was very black indeed and, because he was not a man to let such a matter rest without complaint, I was not surprised when he added, 'Come, Ismay, let us visit the owner of the foundry. He may think the loss of a life is an insignificant matter. I do not.'

What did surprise me, however, was when Uncle Rollo turned the trap through the gateway to Webster Hall. A butler opened the door to him, but he brushed him aside and went upstairs to Lowthian's study, where my father observed our intrusion with amusement.

'I have made repeated requests to you,' Uncle Rollo began, 'to institute procedures of the kind that other, more enlightened factory owners have done, including casing all moving parts of machinery.'

'Set the law on me, brother-in-law,' Lowthian laughed. He didn't care that I was present to witness his callousness. 'I can easily pay the fine.' He well knew that human life among the working classes was not highly valued: for severe injury to a young person caused by gross neglect, colliery owners paid a mere ten pounds twelve shillings; and for killing a woman by the same act of indifference to her life and limb, the fine was less than for a similar accidental killing of a horse — so was a woman's flesh rated to horse flesh.

'Though the fine might be a small sum to you,' Uncle Rollo answered, 'it will be a large compensation for the woman you have widowed this day. And she and I, sir, will have the great satisfaction of seeing you again subjected to the court's scrutiny and shamed before the law. Good day to you, sir.'

By such acts did my uncle show his humanitarian nature and his zeal in his attempts to improve the working conditions of the poor. Whenever he walked among them he treated them with courtesy and kindliness. He was always fastidious about the cleanliness of his instruments. 'They do not distinguish between who is rich and who is not,' he said, 'and therefore, neither should I.' Taking on board this wise lesson, I became adept and meticulous in checking them and keeping the instruments spotless. They looked sinister — the knives of various sizes, saws, forceps, probes and drills — but I came to value their ability to save lives, and was critical of the apprentices who sharpened them, reprimanding them if the edges were too blunt.

'Hmmmph,' Aunt Eleanor would say as she watched me polishing and checking the instruments. 'If only you would take similar care with your toiletries.'

She was referring to those ridiculous trifles for plucking, picking, shaping and smoothing.

———

Then my mother Selina's health took a turn for the worse and Lowthian was faced with the bills for securing a succession of nurses to tend to her. Never one to spend money gladly, he realised that he could make better use of the annuity he was paying for me and recalled me home to Webster Hall. Perhaps he also entertained the idea of using me as a marital chattel to wed to some business prospect and thus recoup his investment.

Whatever the case, I returned to care for my mother. My carriage took me through the tall, ornate gateway and stopped in the gravelled courtyard. Lowthian was standing by his painting when I stepped through the door. The curl of lip had now become cruelly etched as deep lines in his jowls; the artfully stained cheeks had become ruddy from dissipation and, in his mature years, his curve of belly had become a monstrous overhanging gut.

He took one look at me. My elation knew no bounds when I realised his appraisal showed approval: after all, this was the man who had cast me out because of my gender. Although I was female, I was stamped with that authority which, I dislike to admit, he probably recognised as his sole legacy.

Indeed, I held his gaze for longer than he was able to hold mine. By such small victories was my life thereafter measured.

Then his eyes hooded over.

'Your sister is upstairs. Attend to her.'

3

Now you know why I am loath to tell Georgina, indeed *will not* tell her, of my early years. Instead, I will begin my narrative for her commemorative publication from the time I was a young woman, desperate to improve my plight and to escape the circumstances of my life.

———

I cared for my mother Selina with love and diligence. Upset and saddened by her frail condition, I realised that under Lowthian's adept tyranny she had been bullied into submission and had become increasingly fragile of mind, body and spirit. Nor did she have supporters among the servants. Thus, although I had been reluctant to return to Webster Hall, I soon became determined to support her in whatever way I could, and committed myself to ensuring that some sunlight should shine in her otherwise pitiable life.

I did not find the task onerous. My small room was opposite Selina's and, in the morning, after he had levelled at her his usual abusive tirade about her worth as his wife and mistress of Webster Hall, Lowthian departed for the day. I made short shrift of the servants — most of whom would have maintained their master's contempt of my mother — and ordered breakfast for both of us in her room. There I would read aloud to her from the weekly newspaper from London. She particularly liked to hear about Victoria, our new sovereign, crowned in 1837 as Queen of the United Kingdom of Great Britain and Ireland. For the rest of the morning she liked to stay in bed, but after lunch we would retire to the sitting room, where I would read to her or help her with her needlework. Selina had not had permanent female company in the house for quite some time and — I say this without any sense of boastfulness — my stay at Webster Hall occasioned some of the happiest moments of her life. She often told me so. Indeed, after a few months, I was able to convince her to leave her oppressive precinct away from the watchful eyes of the servants (they reported her every move to Lowthian) for the occasional excursion to the nearby park. The air put the colour of roses to her cheeks; but, always, her nervousness about Lowthian's imminent return would make her anxious to get home. His daily habit was to insist that she dine with him in the evening. I was, of course, included in these nocturnal trials at which he would either subject Selina to a mocking outburst about her appearance and belittle her about her lack of control of the servants, or submit us both to his smouldering silence.

I suppose it was too much to hope that Selina and I would find champions in my brothers Alfred and St John. After all, they visited Webster Hall only during vacation periods from college, and although they smiled and seemed to be benign, I was soon to discover that, in our father's presence, they were ineffectual.

For instance, they were home for dinner when, after a humiliating tirade from Lowthian, Selina excused herself with repeated plaintive cries for him to desist, and ran to her room. I rounded on him.

'What a great heroic man you are,' I said, 'to use your courage and strength in this way on a defenceless woman.'

Immediately, Lowthian stood up, came over to me, pulled me from my chair and threw me to the floor. I was shocked when he stood over me and raised his hand. Did my brothers intervene? No.

I looked up at Lowthian and held his gaze. His hand wavered.

'Selina may be defenceless,' I said to him, 'but I am not. Have a care, sir. You mark her or me in any way, and your brother-in-law, Rollo, will have you before a judge by the morning.' They were words said with bravado, for no court would have taken a daughter's side against her father, no matter how estranged the relationship. But they had the effect of staving off any further attack.

Not once, however, did Alfred and St John intervene.

I went up to Selina, as was my habit, to calm her down, give her the medicine she required to maintain her mental equilibrium and then a soporific to put her to sleep. Watching her close her eyes, I wondered how such a gentle soul could have stood up for so long under such a punitive regime. Obviously her husband was taking his sexual pleasures elsewhere — no doubt from the poor working-class women who worked for him and had no recourse except to let him have his way. He did not — as far as I could tell — force himself upon Selina, as would have been his conjugal right. I

31

realise that matters between one's parents must remain private but, even so, I often wondered why Lowthian kept her. There seemed to be no warrantable reason.

I had my answer some time later when one of Lowthian's partners came to Webster Hall and declared his wish to withdraw his capital from the business because of Lowthian's unscrupulous relations with his workers. My father's rage was indescribable; he struck the man across the cheek. 'You, like all my stockholders,' he shouted, 'will wait upon me, sir, and I will judge when you may depart.'

Lowthian was not a man to let people leave him. Once you were contracted to him, you were his for life.

If my anger is showing, I will not apologise for it. From the moment I returned to Webster Hall my life was yoked with my mother Selina's and subjected to Lowthian's malign attitudes. Good fortune attended us, however, by giving me the strength and defiant nature to keep him at bay. Aunt Eleanor and Uncle Rollo's regular visits and, in particular, my uncle's steadfast intervention on behalf of the Glossop women, prevented Lowthian — and, yes, the servants; my brothers may be excused by their passivity — from inflicting upon us an escalation of the physical violence we so feared.

Violence in attitude and speech was another matter. That continued unabated, because it could leave no physical mark.

I had been at Webster Hall for about three years when Aunt Eleanor, on one of her welcome regular visits, made a comment that signalled I was (though I disliked to admit it to myself) growing into womanhood.

'You will be attracting a swain or two soon, Ismay,' she said.

I remember well that chance remark and, also, the moment of vanity when I first took it seriously. After she left, I took audit of my chances with regard to matrimony. My face in the mirror was framed beneath a disposition of red hair, and I was pretty enough, although I lacked a certain sweetness. My eyes were green tinted with gold, and my nose was pert. Had I learnt to inscribe the cheeks with a dimple as I smiled, that might have drawn attention away from the otherwise stubborn set of my lips and chin. My shape, as I have mentioned before, was not slim, and I knew that as I got older I would become heavy and broad. My most serious defect, however, lay in my erect carriage, and a stiffness of bearing and demeanour which was somewhat confrontational.

I tell you this without any sense of self-pity. Such an emotion was a luxury I had never afforded myself; rather, I had always assessed my charms, if they might be called such, from the perspective of critical analysis, and based my assessments on objective evaluation. In this respect, my cousins Sybil, Ursula and Isobel were considerably advantaged with their femininity, girlish demeanour and coquettish ways. My love of them will not allow me to be critical of them, though I must admit I sometimes found them rather timid and was frequently exasperated by the limits of their conversation. I have a portrait of them somewhere: ah yes, there they are! They parlayed their prettiness to move them safely through their lives, being as silly in their heads as they wished, and being admired by foolish boys for it. But look where it got them! Sybil married to local gentry, Ursula to a German baron and Isobel with her estate in Oxford. Aunt Eleanor managed to train them to perfection, and thus they turned out as good wives and mothers, able to take their place in the social life of their chosen milieu.

But me, a coquette? Never. My entire personality and manner marked me with the kind of authority that no man desiring a more passive specimen of my sex would, in my view, want to marry. I therefore reconciled myself to spinsterhood and resisted any inquiry about my availability for matrimony.

Instead, I continued to develop a career as medical assistant to my uncle. Having given up his practice among the rich and wealthy, he became a house surgeon at Wolverhampton Dispensary at No. 46 Queen Street, the city's first hospital for the exclusive care of the medical and surgical needs of the poor. Recalling how valuable I had been to him when he had ministered among them, he asked Lowthian to permit me to vary my duties to Selina by taking up a position part-time as his assistant.

Much to my surprise, Lowthian agreed and, with my mother quickly affirming her consent — 'Go, dear Ismay, you cannot always be around to protect me' — I began to work for my uncle three days a week. Not until much later did I discover that to enable my release Uncle Rollo had to pay my father compensation so that he could employ a day nurse for Selina. Recommended by Uncle Rollo, the day nurse was a retired matron by the name of Baines who proved as diligent as I was in protecting Selina.

Aunt Eleanor still insisted on including me in the Springvale calendar, particularly Sunday parish service at Grocott's Bradley Bridge Church. It was there, one day in October 1840, that my cousins and I noted the congregation had been increased by a number of young men. 'They are intending doctors,' Ursula told me, 'taking practice with Father at the Dispensary. And one of them particularly wants to have Father's favour.' She glanced meaningfully at Sybil, who tossed her head with disdain.

The Reverend Garner was presiding, as usual, from the pulpit, and Mrs Garner was at the organ. With a brief nod, he indicated that she should begin the opening hymn:

Who would true valour see 'gainst all disaster,
Let him in constancy follow the Master,
There's no discouragement shall make him once relent,
His first avowed intent to be a pilgrim . . .

The church was full, I recall, and I was enjoying the hymn. But I have one of those voices which, while it enjoys singing, does not always do so in tune or with the most appropriate of tones. When I was younger and had aspirations to the choir, that ambition was put paid to by my errant voice which would not sing in key. On one occasion Mrs Garner, poor dear, modulated the organ to suit my singing but, oh, my voice continued hither and yon like a ship with ragged sails at the whim of the wind, and very soon there was huge disarray.

'Alas, Miss Glossop,' Mrs Garner said at last. 'When you were christened your voice was blessed with a modicum of melody. As you have matured, sad to say, the modicum has not. Your musical appreciation should be left to the listening and not to the singing of it.'

It was thus with great pleasure that I became aware of a lovely tenor voice issuing from the back of the congregation. The voice was strangely accented in some mockery of English, and very soon the whole congregation was taking surreptitious glances to ascertain its source. Aunt Eleanor gave us a reprimanding glance but I had caught a glimpse of a very large, dark-haired boy singing his heart out as if there wasn't a care to be had in the world.

Who so beset him round with dismal stories,
Do but themselves confound — His strength the more is,
No foes shall stay his might, though he with giants fight:
He will make good his right to be a pilgrim . . .

But it was not the large boy who had the tenor voice. Rather, it was his slender blond friend, handsome in his own way, who owned the surprisingly sweet voice.

'That's the one,' Ursula told me. 'Sybil's Scottish beau. He has come from Edinburgh University to complete his medical studies with Father. Apparently his father and ours are good friends and both in the medical profession.'

'If he is Sybil's beau,' Isobel added naughtily, 'he is one of many.'

'Well, he is not!' Sybil answered, tossing her head with irritation. It was well known that she had set her cap at a more suitable candidate, Marcus Wrenn, son of a Wolverhampton marquis, who was currently reading classics at Balliol.

The Rev. Garner's custom was always to invite parishioners to a cup of tea and cake in the vicarage after the service. My cousins and I were pressed into duty. The flirtatious girls fluttered over the medical students like dizzy butterflies, and the boys — including the young blond lad — were dazzled by the shiny wings that shimmered in their faces.

I was handing out cake to the Widow Elliott when I heard Uncle Rollo address him.

'Aha! Mr Gower McKissock, young sir! I hope you wield your scalpel as splendidly as you do your voice!'

'Perhaps, Father,' Isobel teased Sybil, 'Mr McKissock could join our choir?'

None of them, not even Mr McKissock, gave me a glance as they were served afternoon tea. I tried not to show any irritation. Not that I was especially interested in them anyway. As for the Scots boy, why, I could not see in him any quality other than a fine singing voice as incentive to any further interest on my part.

———

My three-days-a-week employ with Uncle Rollo coincided with two days at the Dispensary and one day I accompanied him on his weekly visit to Wolverhampton's Home for the Insane, which was a sister institution to the Dispensary. I shudder to remember those bleak walls and large wards connected by barred corridors within which congregated the mentally infirm. There, Uncle Rollo generally performed surgery on the cranium, or else bloodletting to relieve the humours and thereby the pressures which contributed to the patient's mental condition. But even then, Uncle Rollo suspected that mental infirmity had more to do with what happened in the mind than the body.

'One should pity any wretch who ends up here,' he told me sadly. 'Nonetheless, our institution is better than most and, who knows, given the tribulations these patients have endured in their normal lives, perhaps they find greater peace here, away from the cause of those troubles.'

Back at the Dispensary, Uncle Rollo was generous in allowing me to be present at consultations, and he continued — I don't think he realised he was doing it — to informally instruct me in anatomy, physiology and the treatment of diseases while he tended his patients. But the highlight was to watch him when, every Thursday morning, he presented a weekly lecture, by way of a surgical operation, to young male students observing from the wooden viewing gallery of the operating room. This was, after all, the best way a young surgeon could learn his trade: by observing a mature surgeon at work.

Women were not allowed to be present, but Uncle Rollo gave permission so long as I was able to mask my sex, lest I disturb the heartbeats of rampant males. In those days, even piano legs had to be draped to prevent their becoming too deeply disconcerting. Thus, during his lectures, I took to putting on one of Uncle Rollo's hats, one of his coats, and standing in the back where I hoped I would not be noticed.

If I may dwell on this subject, how cross it makes me to recall that medical practice was open only to the male of our species! I had all the ability and dedication to become a doctor, but that profession was unattainable. Nurses and midwives, having subordinate status, yes, those callings were available to women, but nothing could dent the exclusive male domain. I used to rail against such injustice whenever I saw a young doctor making obvious mistakes or giving the wrong diagnosis. And I simply hated it when I heard revered professors discussing women's biological endowments and altruistic and sacrificial virtues as unfit for the intellectual discipline and regimen of the medical profession.

Young women today do not know how fortunate they are! Alas, I was forty years too early in my own feminist presumptions. Even so, I applaud the accomplishments of those women who, in 1878, were finally admitted to all degrees at the University of London, including medicine; and I honour my dear cousin Sybil who, in Wolverhampton, used her by-then-powerful influence as wife of a city lord to have our university follow suit. Indeed, I had hoped that Georgina's mother — my daughter Clara — might go into medicine and, through her, I might vicariously fulfil my own ambitions as a doctor. Sadly, Clara met Georgina's father and decided to be the meek and obliging wife she has become — and thereby maintained what men have considered to be the inevitable female default. Georgina does not appear to be in any way inclined to rectify her mother's error of judgement, but at least she has excelled in the academic sphere, notably the pestilential journalism which she has now focused on my life with such unpleasantness.

It was while watching Uncle Rollo, in that invariably packed viewing gallery, usually from the back row, that I observed the major surgical operations available to patients at the time, including trepan, amputation and lichotomy. If I may say so, whereas many young male surgeons fainted at the sight of blood and still went on to graduate, I never allowed myself the slightest dizzy spell.

And, of course, I obtained practical experience born of days when word would come of an accident at one of the mills or factories.

———

One such incident occurred just as Uncle Rollo and I were about to close the Dispensary for the day. A worker, black with soot, presented himself urgently at our doorway.

'Sir, there's been a cave-in at the Bridgeside Colliery. It's very serious. Will you please come quickly?'

Uncle Rollo looked at me. 'Alas, Ismay, we shall have to delay your return to Webster Hall and make a detour. Would you mind?'

I was already reaching for my hat and affixing it with my favourite butterfly pin. 'Mind? Of course not, Uncle.'

'I didn't think you would,' he said.

The colliery was in the Bradley area of Bilston. Darkness had completely fallen when we arrived, but even from afar I could see the flaming torches as miners and their families waited either silent or weeping at the site. When our trap came to a halt, the mine owner, Mr Bridge, came forward to greet us. 'Thank you for coming,' he said. 'We have managed to get six injured out of the mine, but three men are still trapped below at the coalface and need consideration before being moved.'

'You cannot bring them up for my attention?' Uncle Rollo asked.

'I dare not,' Mr Bridge said.

'Is there any danger from gas?'

'Not at this stage. The canary was still chirping her little song. And air is managing to get through the tunnels. But time may be against us.'

Uncle Rollo looked at me. 'Well, it's not the first time I've been below ground and it certainly won't be the last. Meanwhile, Ismay, I'll leave you to attend to the injured above ground. Make them as comfortable as possible and then send them immediately to the Dispensary.'

He took his surgical kit from me and walked to the pit shaft. A loud cheer met his intention as he stepped into a large cage with a crew of three accompanying coal miners. 'God bless you, sir,' a voice called from the crowd.

On command, a couple of pit ponies began to snort and pull — and Uncle Rollo and his companions descended into the darkness.

As I busied myself with the injured I had the welcome assistance of a small slip of a girl who had detached herself from the surrounding group.

'Thank you,' I said to her as, upon my instruction, she brought water from a nearby well, and binding cloth and bandages that had been stored in the colliery manager's office for simple emergencies. 'What is your name?'

'Sally Jenkins, miss,' she answered. Her hair was streaked with dirt; she was stunted and anaemic, her thin body showing through her threadbare clothing.

Fortunately, most of the miners' injuries were not as fearful as I had expected. Two had broken limbs, three had perhaps cracked ribs, but the rest — once the water had washed away the blood — only superficial bruises, cuts and bleeding. But just as I had finished applying a tourniquet to one of the men, there was a sudden loud popping noise from underground. The surface of the earth shook, and a jet of dust and coal puffed from the pit shaft. People screamed and backed away.

'It sounds like another cave-in, miss,' Sally Jenkins said.

A rush of terror overcame me. With a cry, I ran to the shaft. Mr Bridge and some of the miners tried to restrain me, but I pushed them aside.

'Uncle Rollo! Uncle Rollo?'

Peering down made me giddy. The shaft descended into stygian gloom, and at first I could not see anything else but blackness. Uncle Rollo had been swallowed up in a premature burial by the earth.

Vertigo claimed me and I almost fainted. 'I've got you, miss,' a miner said. I shook my head to clear it. My heart was thundering. And then — was that a small square of light far below?

My heart leapt with hope. I made up my mind.

The cage which had taken Uncle Rollo down had been brought up to the surface. I stepped into it. 'Lower me, please.'

'Miss Glossop,' Mr Bridge said, 'I cannot let you go down.' His eyes were popping out of his head at my impetuousness.

'Will you oblige?' I demanded angrily.

Still none ventured to help me. Then Sally Jenkins approached. 'Miss,' she said, 'if you are intending to go down, you cannot go dressed like that.'

Indeed I was wearing too many petticoats, and my cape and bonnet were added hindrances. With Sally Jenkins' aid I was soon trimmed down.

I called to Mr Bridge. 'Now, sir, I must go to my uncle.' I raised my voice to him. 'Lower me down, I say!'

With a brief nod of his head, he relented. 'Set the ponies,' he said. And just as the cage began to descend, Sally Jenkins stepped in beside me. 'I'll come with you,' she said. 'You would lose your way otherwise.'

'You work below ground?' I asked. 'How old are you?'

'I'm ten, I think, miss. I go down the shaft at half past four in the morning and begin to work soon after. I usually leave at three o'clock but today I didn't leave until five. My dad makes his money per piece of coal delivered. He had decided to go back for one more load, and I was waiting for him at the home gate, when the mine collapsed. I told him not to go — he'd already made twenty journeys today — but we need the money. He's one of the men trapped.'

We descended. Time seemed to lose all meaning as the darkness of the underworld enveloped us. Sally lit a candle lamp and closed its window. I noted the change when the brick sides of shaft down which we travelled became a lining of cast iron.

'It's to hold back the loose sand and water, miss. Bridgeside is one of the older mines and all of the upper seams have already been worked. We mine deep coal now.'

'Deep coal?' I shivered.

'Around four hundred feet down.'

At last we grounded in a cavernous area lit by a large furnace. Despite the recent explosion, the atmosphere here was clear — thanks, Sally told me, to the furnace. Even so, I was almost overcome by heat and claustrophobia, and gasped with fear.

'You'll get used to it,' Sally said. 'Everybody has the dizziness the first time they come down. And we need the furnace, as it keeps the air circulating. It draws air from above ground into the downcast shaft, through the mine and then out with the rising heat to the surface by the upcast shaft.'

I had expected the mine to be empty. With horror I saw that it was full of people. Brawny-armed men were loading the coal for lifting to the surface; assisting them were children the same age as Sally. I could smell the stench of their sweat from where I stood. 'Don't they know about the accident?' I asked.

'It would take more than an accident in one part of the mine,' Sally answered, 'for the whole mine to be cleared. All miners have families to feed. Let's go quickly now, miss, to where the trouble is.'

A number of corridors led away into the darkness. My heart was pounding as I followed Sally out of the main cavern and along a corridor that became smaller and smaller until I had to bend low to pass along it. Very soon my dress was covered with soot, and when I smoothed my hair back from my forehead I saw that my skin was blackened with coal dust.

'Uncle Rollo? Uncle Rollo, please answer me!'

Oh, I had never been afraid of the dark, but this was different. Sensing my growing panic, Sally pressed a comforting hand in mine. 'Don't worry, miss.'

But the light, how I missed it!

In the glow from the flickering lamp I noticed that we had crawled through a series of little doors. Manning them were children, black as tinkers, of barely six tender years, their moles' eyes shining in the dark.

'I used to have their job,' Sally said proudly. 'If we don't have the doors the air doesn't stay in the tunnels and the miners at the end, where they're picking at the coal, won't be able to breathe. The children must make sure the doors are quickly opened and closed. Watch! Here comes a corf—'

At that moment there was a rumbling and rattling and a big trolley — the corf — filled with coal came into view. It was pulled by a sorry-looking wretch, crawling on all fours, half naked and dressed in a man's trousers with a belt around the waist and a chain between the legs.

The wretch was a young girl; her rudimentary breasts were the disclosure of her sex.

As the trolley passed by, I saw that a young boy was pushing it from behind. The child who stood by the door opened it and, once the wagon was through, closed it again.

'I'm a hurrier like that girl,' Sally said. 'I've been down here four years. I hurry the corves along, maybe twenty a day, as the more we deliver the more money we make, up to a shilling a day sometimes. It's heavy work, the sweat runs off me all over sometimes, but I have a good thruster boy who pushes with his head. I've never been poorly, like some of the others who have a touch of the breath now, and I get some of Saturday off and Sundays too, when I can walk about and get fresh air.'

By now the corridor was only about four feet high, and I was on all fours, following behind Sally as she scrabbled ahead. I saw that there was muddy water in the tunnel, seeping from the sides, pooling on the floor to eight inches deep. Very soon I was up to my elbows in it and my dress was clammy and heavily soaked.

The oppressive atmosphere, claustrophobic darkness, the stench and now the water made me sink into despair. In particular, I felt distressed at the depths of man's bestial nature, that he used little children of such tender age in such a malevolent manner as his beasts of burden.

'How many girls are down here?'

'We have to live,' Sally answered simply. 'I work with my father, so I have protection if the men want to feel me. My mother has nine little ones to feed. I get half an hour for breakfast, an hour for dinner and half an hour for tea — and I am not slapped about often. Some of the boys are horribly beaten with the hammer. They have awful scars.'

Sally's simple narrative made me feel ashamed of my distress. After all, I led such a privileged life and, until now, had scarce imagined the kind of life that workers led in their deep burrows below the surface of the earth.

Then, 'Look, miss!' Sally exclaimed.

A flaming torch was approaching from out of the darkness: a group of men, crawling back from the cave-in. Among them was Uncle Rollo!

With a cry I staggered towards him. He caught me in his arms. His clothes were blackened and streaked with dust and grime, and his face streamed with sweat.

'Ismay, why are you down here, you stupid, wilful, vexing, troublesome girl!' I had never seen him so cross.

'Thank God you are alive,' I sobbed.

'You should have waited above ground,' he thundered. 'Now, come along. Behind us the miners are carrying out three men who are wounded. It's bad enough that I have to worry about them as well as you. Have you lost your senses?'

But I continued to sob. 'Don't be angry with me,' and, after a while, he gave me a hug.

'All right, Ismay, don't cry any more.'

We made our way back to the pit shaft and ascended in the cage. Mr Bridge and the miners' families clapped. But Uncle Rollo was furious with Mr Bridge for letting me go down, and gave him a good tongue-lashing. And he still hadn't finished with me either.

'Ismay, *why* did you come down, you foolish girl?'

How could I explain to him? Throughout the entire ordeal I had an image of Aunt Eleanor in front of me. To have had to tell her that Uncle Rollo had been killed would have been too much for me to bear. I simply had to make sure I had done all in my power to save him.

Then Uncle Rollo relented again. 'We had better get the injured to the Dispensary and then wash before we go on home. Let's hide evidence of our adventure tonight, eh? Imagine if we arrived at the door to our house and your aunt saw us! She would faint. She must never know the terrible risk we have both taken.'

Risk?

As we started to leave the mine, I looked at Sally Jenkins — she was the one taking risks! She descended every day into the darkness.

I felt the need to reward the girl for taking me down. I gave her my hatpin, the pretty one with the silver butterfly on it. 'For you,' I said.

'I'd best not take it, miss,' she answered, stepping away. 'Someone might think I stole it. And then I would be up before the judge and sent to prison or even transported to the colonies.'

But I pressed the trinket on her and, after a while, she accepted it, twirling it so that the wings caught flame in the night.

'If ever you need my help or that of my Uncle Rollo, don't hesitate to come and see us,' I said as I scribbled our address on a piece of paper.

She nodded her head uncertainly. 'I'm sorry, miss, I can't read. I can say letters though.' Then she was gone.

'Uncle Rollo,' I asked, 'isn't there anything that we can do about her circumstances? And the gross working conditions of the children?'

He shook his head. 'Men of conscience, and women too, are already asking the same question. We must hope, Ismay, the world will better itself.'

That evening I had a horrifying dream. I dreamt of a phantasmagoric being, with many black mouths shafted by flames. Staggering through the blackness of his monstrous belly were swarthy, smoke-begrimed men, women and children with moles' eyes. And one of them was a young girl who clutched at me and cried out, 'Please, miss, please get me out of here.'

The young girl was Sally Jenkins.

———

The next day being Thursday, Uncle Rollo gave his usual weekly lecture at Wolverhampton Dispensary. I was running late and, after donning Uncle's clothing, and with the hat tipped well over half my face, slipped in at the back, where I also noted the presence of Sybil's Scots swain, Mr McKissock.

Uncle Rollo was dressed in his frockcoat. He waited in silence as two dressers — surgical assistants — carried the patient in on a makeshift stretcher. The man was writhing, racked with pain, moaning, fully conscious; a blanket covered him.

'Gentlemen, this miner was involved in an accident last evening at one of our local collieries.' Uncle Rollo removed the blanket. 'Let's see the damage.'

The miner's left leg was wrapped above the knee with a tourniquet. Below the knee cap were blood-soaked bandages; the two dressers removed them. As soon as the lower limb was exposed, we all gave a moan of sympathy: it had multiple fractures and the muscles and sinews had been crushed to pulp.

'Gentlemen,' Uncle Rollo said, 'I think we are all agreed?'

'Amputation,' came the answer.

Uncle Rollo nodded. 'Yes, it will have to come off, I'm afraid, but herewith the first lesson: no surgeon should lop off any part of a man's body unless it is necessary. And always be aware that this man, from the moment he leaves the theatre, will be forever altered.' He turned to the miner. 'Are you ready, my good man? Do I have your permission to proceed?'

The poor miner was sweating, but he nodded.

'Good,' Uncle Rollo said. 'Different surgeons have different procedures. You would all be well advised to develop a facility in a number of them and apply the one which, as you assess it, is most suitable for the surgery to hand. One rule, however, is paramount for me. This is that the amputation should be done in as quick a time as possible so as to minimise the pain to the patient and the shock to his system. Some surgeons have been able to perform an amputation of the leg in thirty seconds flat. But this is not a race, and we are not butchers. Nevertheless—'

Uncle Rollo opened his kit of instruments and laid them out on a side trolley. 'Tighten the tourniquet please,' he said to the two dressers.

The miner looked at the collection of knives, saws and needles with palpable horror.

'In removing a limb,' Uncle Rollo continued, 'hold it either vertical or allow it to be horizontal throughout. In this patient's case, we will work in the horizontal.' He clamped his left hand across the patient's thigh and picked up his favourite knife. 'Locate the place of election and then make your incision. A common man, unable to afford an expensive artificial foot, would be better off losing a leg just below the knee.'

The miner uttered a piteous question, 'Are you sure it must be done, sir?'

'There is no other recourse,' Uncle Rollo answered tenderly.

Before the miner could think further on his travail, in one rapid movement the incision was done. He gave a loud, surprised moan.

One of the dressers immediately tightened the tourniquet further to stem the blood. The other dresser fainted.

Uncle Rollo joked with the miner. 'And you are the one losing a limb, not him.' He turned to the audience, annoyed. 'Come on gentlemen, don't be tardy. One of you please come to assist.'

Oh, had I not been a woman I would have bounded down the steps to his side!

'Sir, I will volunteer,' a voice said. I recognised the Scottish lilt.

'Thank you Mr McKissock,' Uncle Rollo answered. Turning to the miner, he asked, 'Shall we continue? I apologise in advance for the pain.'

The miner nodded, his face wan. 'I am in your hands, sir.'

Uncle Rollo made another deeper cut with his knife, dividing the muscles covering the bone. Another sweep and he separated the flesh adhering to the bone. This time, the miner's shouts of pain echoed loudly throughout the lecture theatre. I was dismayed at his distress.

'Amputation is very rarely, as might be supposed,' Uncle Rollo continued, 'a matter of making one simple cut. Although some surgeons advocate making a sweeping incision around the circumference of the limb, in reality it is more complex, and depends on the circumstances prevailing at the time of the operation.'

He put the knife away and took up a saw. And this time, when Uncle Rollo began to saw through the bone, the miner screamed and began to spasm on the stretcher — 'Hold him firmly, sirs!' Uncle Rollo roared at Mr McKissock and the other dresser.

I put my fists to my ears but, resolute, watched the proceedings. Others students were looking away, holding handkerchiefs to their mouths.

Uncle Rollo kept sawing.

The miner screamed once more. 'Have mercy on me, sir,' he cried to Uncle Rollo. 'Kill me and have done with it.'

Then, thank heaven, he became senseless.

One further push of the saw through bone and Uncle Rollo was done. The dresser, giving a gasp of horror, saw that he was holding the miner's severed leg. Mr McKissock went to his aid, took hold of the limb and dropped it into a box of sawdust put nearby for the purpose.

Uncle Rollo, meanwhile, was busy tying off the main artery of the thigh with a knot and then tying off other smaller blood vessels.

'Let me help you, sir,' Mr McKissock said. Very soon he too was tying off the blood vessels, at one point holding the thread in his mouth. I admired his cool head.

'Loosen off the tourniquet,' Uncle Rollo instructed. Then, 'What is your needlework like, Mr McKissock? Would you like to complete the surgery?' He watched as Mr McKissock stitched the flesh together so that the skin could form a flap around the exposed wound.

Uncle Rollo looked at the clock. 'With the help of a good assistant, we have brought this operation to a close in . . . fifty seconds.'

Less than a minute? It had seemed much longer. Up until that moment, the entire room had taken an indrawn breath. Now all were on their feet and were able to expel it with a cheer.

Uncle Rollo's response was cool. 'For you young surgeons, eager to prove yourselves, amputation is not where you should display your impetuosity, boldness and dexterity. If I may make an analogy to the art of the violinist, do not fiddle with your bow upon the bone as if you were playing the fast movement of a Paganini concerto. Rather, gentlemen, think not of your own virtuosity and, instead, lay your bow kindly upon the strings, for the music you play is an elegy.'

There was a murmur of puzzlement.

And then the miner revived, and bitter tears flooded down his face.

Uncle Rollo put a reassuring hand on his shoulder. 'They don't realise the problem, do they?' he said to the miner. He looked at all of us, gathering us into the dilemma. 'We may save lives,' he continued, 'but what kind of life can this miner look forward to now? With one leg, will he be able to continue his employ? No.'

When I think back, I wonder at Uncle Rollo's intuitive wisdom and skill. Medical practice was not as we know it to be today. There were no modern aids such as surgical clamps to control blood loss, and no penicillin to fight infection. Horrific to relate, most operations took place without the aid of anaesthetic; not until 1847 did the first operation involving ether take place in Wolverhampton — only the third such operation to be done in all of England. In many ways the miner on whom Uncle Rollo operated that day was fortunate in having so practised and careful a surgeon attend him. He was also lucky that, in my uncle, he had a doctor who was aware that rehabilitation needed to attend upon those whose livelihoods were curtailed by surgery.

Uncle Rollo signed to Mr McKissock and the dresser to take the miner from the operating theatre. The room emptied quietly and, once everyone had left, I made my way to my small office to change my clothes. When I returned to the ward where I knew the miner would be taken, I saw Uncle Rollo speaking kind words to him and pressing some coins into his hands.

Mr McKissock was still with my uncle as he took his instruments to a washroom off the ward. Uncle Rollo was by nature a man of tidy habits, and he rinsed his instruments thoroughly before packing them away. Mr McKissock, however, kept peppering him with questions.

In the end, Uncle Rollo gave a helpless laugh. 'Sir, could you allow your inquiries to cease now? I am tired and I must be off to my home soon.' He saw me waiting; as for Mr McKissock, he scarce gave me a glance.

'I'm sorry, sir,' Mr McKissock answered, 'but I wanted to seize this opportunity. Another like this might not come again.'

'Why are you so persistent?'

'I need to know,' he kept saying.

'Why?'

'Because, where I am going, there may not be an opportunity to take advantage of the wisdom I will garner here.'

'And where might that be?'

'I have a mind to go to New Zealand.'

Uncle Rollo nodded. Then, 'All right, one last piece of advice, Mr McKissock,' he said. 'Amputation is terrible for the patient to bear, dreadful for the surgeon to behold and, even after the travail, it may still be fatal. Do not assume that Mr Jenkins or any of the patients you have in such an operation as we have done will survive. Most of them don't. The operation may be successfully concluded, but infection can set in. I have found it helpful to keep all my instruments clean. Whether it helps, I don't know. But it may.'

Mr Jenkins?

Not until then did it dawn on me that the man on whom my uncle had operated was the father of the young girl, Sally Jenkins, who had accompanied me down the mineshaft the previous evening.

———

I had the opportunity to hear more of Gower McKissock's dreams when he came with five other medical students to dinner at the house some days later. Uncle Rollo liked every now and then to have his young surgeons to dine, and I was usually asked to attend to round out the number of women present.

It was Uncle Rollo who took up the subject again. 'So, young sir,' he asked. 'New Zealand, eh?'

Mr McKissock nodded. 'Ever since the New Zealand Company began systematic colonisation of those islands, I have entertained the notion to go there. There are already settlements in Kororareka, Auckland and Wellington, I'm told, but the Company has bought land for organised settlement in Whanganui too.'

'Whongah . . . nooee?' one of his colleagues asked.

'It's a name that comes from the Maoris' lexicon,' Mr McKissock answered. 'The settlement is on a large, beautiful river.'

Uncle Rollo nodded approvingly. 'Where there are colonists, there is a need for surgeons, eh? So you mean to make your fortune in the colony?'

'Yes, sir,' Mr McKissock answered. 'The skills that I will take as a doctor will provide me with the wherewithal to begin a practice. In fact, I have already made enquiries of the New Zealand Company, and am advised that they plan a further new settlement at Nelson, which is in the South Island.'

'The situation with the Maoris does not alarm you?' Aunt Eleanor asked.

'Ma'am, I understand a treaty was signed with the Maori chiefs earlier this year. New Zealand is now a Crown colony. And the dreadful days of the *Boyd* massacre are long over. I think we should look to better days and not look back at past atrocities.' He was referring to the butchering and eating of the sailors aboard the English vessel arrived at Whangaroa in 1809. That was over thirty years ago, but the memory of it always sent a shiver through the comfortable drawing rooms of Wolverhampton.

'The Maoris are still of a warlike mind, are they not?' Sybil asked.

'Look what happened when poor Mrs Guard and her two children were ransomed by the Maoris!' one of the other students burst out. 'That such a fate should befall an Englishwoman! Had two warships not gone to her rescue, who knows what terrible atrocities might have been done to her?'

Mr McKissock nodded. 'But with honesty and goodwill one hopes that a new society can be forged that will be based on the best principles of British governance. The only trouble is . . .'

'Yes, sir?'

Mr McKissock, bold as brass, looked straight at Sybil. 'I have been advised that I should take a wife.'

Aunt Eleanor gave Uncle Rollo a look. Both were aware that Sybil had many beaux, including the frontrunner, Marcus Wrenn; Aunt Eleanor approved of the possibility of a union between them. To let Sybil go — not only out the front door but to the other side of the world where, like Mrs Guard, she might be made a captive by the Maori? Never!

Uncle Rollo gave a cough. 'Gentlemen, perhaps this is a good time to escort the ladies to the sitting room and then we will retire to the smoking room.'

Of course, once the men had left us, Sybil was the centre of attention.

'You know he is totally smitten by you,' Ursula said.

'I have never given Mr McKissock any indication that I return his interest,' Sybil answered.

'Oh, Sybil,' Isobel sighed. 'You know that is untrue. You give every swain encouragement.'

'My romantic inclinations are toward another suitor,' Sybil snapped, 'and anyway, what kind of society would I find in New Zealand?'

'In that case,' Aunt Eleanor said, 'it would be best to nip Mr McKissock's hopes in the bud.'

4

New Zealand? *New Zealand!*

The child, Georgina, wishes me to hasten on to Van Diemen's Land, pleading that New Zealand has no part in her narrative, and that stopping even for a moment upon those shaky isles would delay the delivery of her patriotic article on Tasmania.

The problem with time management is her own, not mine, and I will not be made responsible for it. I may have been English first, but I was second a New Zealander, before I became a Tasmanian — I am that rather than an Australian.

She will simply have to continue to suffer a grandmother who will not cut history according to the cloth of her fancy.

From the moment that I heard Mr McKissock talk about the Antipodean colony, my imagination was fired. I may not have been the only person who, discontented with the reality of England, turned to New Zealand — but I was certainly one of the most ardent. I made a scrapbook of every piece of information about the country, from its discovery by Captain Cook RN. Following his observation of the transit of Venus in Tahiti in 1769 (what paradisical images of the South Seas the conjunction of the words 'Venus' and 'Tahiti' engendered!), he sailed further south to try to discover what scientists assumed to exist there: a great southern continent to balance and anchor the northern hemisphere. Although New Zealand comprised only a fragment of this southern continent, and one already discovered by others like Tasman, Dufresne and d'Urville, what a sliver it was described to be!

I read everything of it I could and, even though the savagery of the native Maori could not be denied, Mr Wakefield's speech to the House of Commons only confirmed my interest: 'Very near to Australia there is a country which all testimony concurs in describing as the fittest in the world for colonisation, as the most beautiful country with the finest climate, and the most productive soil; I mean New Zealand.'

Sometimes, sleepless, I looked out at the night sky from my bedroom at Webster Hall and wondered what it would be like if I was in the southern hemisphere, where the heavens were dominated by the Southern Cross. As dawn came, I gazed across the gloomy roofs of Wolverhampton, the squalid streets, the fearful coal pits and the curtains of black smoke that formed the normal canopy of Bilston. I would conjure up a morning sea, impossibly blue and sparking, merging into a faraway sky, limitless, going on to the end of forever.

Oh, how I responded to the siren song of that sea and the clarion call to adventure! I even wondered at the possibility of going to New Zealand myself! But how could that be achieved? If a young woman might not dare to venture out of doors unaccompanied, how could I therefore ever get as far as that land at the bottom of the world? A man like Gower McKissock could take off, just like that, with a snap of his fingers. But a woman? No. Yet, was I not his equal in prospect, let alone intelligence?

I fulminated against such injustice!

Then compelling events at Webster Hall added urgency to my growing interest in New Zealand.

Whatever freedoms I enjoyed in the company of my Uncle Rollo, I was, in the end, a young woman at the mercy of my father, regarded as Lowthian's property and thus forever subject to his discipline. The more I struggled against his chains, the more that set me in direct conflict with him — and the more his bonds tightened on me.

I recall an argument I had with him about the Webster Iron Works. 'You are nothing but a slave driver,' I said to him. 'And philanthropist? You have done nothing to help the masses of the poor. Mark the poverty-stricken mother standing in a doorway with a pale-faced child in her arms. Listen to the sounds that proceed from the wretched-looking home with the broken windows: they are the everyday noises of a father swearing in his drink and ragged children crying for their supper. They are all promising candidates for the Old Bailey and thence for transportation to the colonies.'

'So you are a humanitarian now?' he laughed.

I was furious and frustrated but, most of all, I realised I was as much a slave to him as were his workers.

My conflict with my father was one matter; the relationship with my siblings Alfred and St John was another. I had thought them to be passive but, when I was faced with physical threat from them — they began to show excellent results from the tutelage of Lowthian's misogyny — I obtained a further realisation of the danger of my position.

In their eyes I became by sinister degrees not a sister at all but rather a female relative and, even more dangerously, a nurse whose status in the household was one of dependency.

Perhaps it was only to be expected, therefore, that one night, when I was leaving Selina's room for my own, my younger sibling, St John, accosted me. He was standing in the shadows of the hallway and, as I passed, he slipped one hand around my waist and pulled me in to him.

'Let's have some sport eh, aunt?'

Fortunately for me, Matron Baines, the nurse employed to look after my mother, came upon us. 'What is happening here, sir?' she asked St John.

He loosed me from his grasp and turned away. His mocking laughter made me realise that he would try again.

I had to get away. But how?

A pathway opened soon afterward.

———————

In those days, the survival of the Wolverhampton Dispensary depended on subscriptions and donations from the wealthy citizenry. It happened that that year they failed to cover the running costs, and the committee had to appeal for an increase of a permanent character in order to secure for the Dispensary an assured future. A charity ball was arranged to collect funds.

The prospect of a ball which, all agreed, would be a nonpareil put Aunt Eleanor and my cousins into an immediate frenzy of excitement. Along with every other female of quality in the city, they descended on the dressmakers, milliners, shoemakers and, in some cases, the wigmaker, with undisguised glee. Some young women were able to send away to London for the latest fashions — or even to travel there themselves. Sybil, Ursula and Isobel were not among these lucky few, but having a father who could obtain prior notice of such important social events had its advantages and they were able to engage the best designers and dressmakers Wolverhampton could offer.

As for me, my mother Selina made one of her rare trips out of the house and took me to Birmingham, a strategy that very few of the young ladies of Wolverhampton thought of. Success! After a fruitless afternoon of searching, I found a gown of emerald shot silk with a tight waist which, when I moved, flowed and revealed clever hidden hues of purple and pink. I must have looked very well in it, for Selina insisted, 'You must have it!' and purchased it at great cost. When we returned to Webster Hall she went to her jewel box and brought out a beautiful necklace of rubies and matching earrings.

I modelled the gown and jewellery together for her.

Tears sprang to her eyes. 'You are beautiful,' she said.

I must admit I couldn't believe my eyes when I saw myself — the rubies flashed, and the gown shimmered and gleamed like a shield when I moved.

———————

The night of the ball arrived. Aunt Eleanor, Uncle Rollo and my cousins collected me from Webster Hall.

'I wish you could come with me,' I said to Selina.

'Oh my dear,' she answered, 'go before your father changes his mind.'

Lowthian had been angry with her for purchasing the dress, even though it was from her own Glossop money, and Uncle Rollo had used much persuasion on him — I was his assistant and he required me to be at hand for reasons of protocol — before Lowthian would allow me to attend.

Selina kissed both my cheeks and saw me off. I think she, as much as I, appreciated the look of envy that darted from Sybil's eyes at my appearance.

I *was* beautiful!

———————

The long line of carriages waiting to deposit their impatient passengers at the entrance of the Wolverhampton Town Hall indicated that the ball was set to become the great winter event of our city.

'Everybody is here,' Aunt Eleanor whispered to Uncle Rollo with pride.

She sailed through the entrance like a galleon and we followed after her, excited and exuberant, up the stairs and into the foyer.

The major-domo pronounced our entrance: 'My lords, ladies and gentlemen, Dr Rollo and Mrs Springvale, Misses Sybil, Ursula and Isobel Springvale and Miss Ismay Glossop.'

The fashions were rich and elegant, and I was very pleased that my own appearance was equal to any of the ladies!

And never let it be said that Wolverhampton did not possess a society as gracious as any other in the whole of England! The entire ballroom had been made up in a Far Eastern theme, with artificial verdure representing towering jungle motifs, palms and huge displays of exotic flora. Boys dressed as Indian nabobs strutted through the crowd, and there was even a man with a monkey!

My cousins, of course, were quickly snapped up by their swains, and I got my first glimpse of Sybil's beau, Marcus Wrenn, who had come up from Oxford especially for the ball. No wonder they were attracted to each other: safely in each other's arms, neither looked the least capable of sustaining any kind of life outside their society. Sybil made a huge fuss of retying his cravat with a pretty, impatient gesture: 'There!'

I also caught a glimpse of Mr McKissock, standing with a group of young surgeons. He was clean-shaven, his hair slicked back, and looked very handsome in high-buttoned shirt, long black coat and pencil-slim trousers.

'Thank heavens,' Aunt Eleanor whispered as I accompanied her to a settee where, as she seated herself, the silk of her bodice stretched almost to cracking. 'I thought he might come in a kilt.'

Much to my surprise and pleasure, a young military officer, Lieutenant Harry Forsythe, on posting to Van Diemen's Land, approached me.

'Would you care to dance?' he asked.

I blushed and, I hope, declined him gracefully — and then I hastily moved up the stairway to the overlooking gallery to put myself out of the way of any further invitations.

Why? I couldn't dance the quadrille! At that moment I wished I had taken seriously my childhood governess's entreaties to acquaint myself with Alexander Strathy's *Elements of the Art of Dancing*; alas, I would never be able to show off my form with the wide variety of rapid, skimming steps in the 'Chaine anglaise' and 'Le pantalon'. The intricacies of the three chassés, a jeté and assemblé were as forever out of my reach as the sissone, échappé, temps levé and glissade. Why, I could never do even a pirouette without knocking one of my poor cousins off her carefully constructed pas de zephyr.

Better to watch from above as the women whirled about, necks arched and heads back, laughing prettily at their handsome men. From here I could appreciate the lines of couples as they wove around the ballroom in intricate patterns, and admire their decorum and deportment and carriage.

I felt a wave of affection for my cousins and the young men they danced with. Their dresses were among the finest; the light caught on their jewels as they floated by like clouds. If only those young partners knew how diligently our governess had worked on the feminine art of making even the worst of dancers believe he was the best partner on the floor. Or the art of eliciting questions, laughing at jests and encouraging discourse in one's partner, which made him think he must be the most brilliant conversationalist in the entire world. All those hard-earned lessons were now paying dividends as suitors rushed to enter their names into my cousins' engagement books.

So great a throng! I saw Mr McKissock approach Sybil in hopes of giving Marcus Wrenn a run for her hand. She was, as ever, gracious, dancing with him lightly like a swan and then, when the dance ended, playing up to him while, at the same time, pretending to have no choice when another young man came to whisk her away. I could have applauded had I not seen that little piece of acting so well tutored by our governess.

Mr McKissock's face was strained with love as Sybil took leave of him. Alone, he sought the safety of the punch bowl. His ardour irritated me; after all, he would never have any return from my cousin, whereas . . .

I have always been impetuous. Watching him, an idea formed in my head: of *course*!

————

I went down the stairs and joined Mr McKissock at the table. It was spread with chocolate and glasses of punch. Young men and women were laughing over a fruit ice or dessert.

I interposed myself in Mr McKissock's line of sight and was flattered that he cast an appreciative eye over me without realising who I was. Certainly, I deserved his appreciation — I had taken great care with my make-up and hair.

Hs eyes widened. 'Miss Glossop!' he exclaimed. 'I hardly recognised you.'

I remained cool, responding, 'That is because you have never previously paid me any attention.'

He smiled, inclining his head. 'That is true enough,' he answered, 'but may I rectify my error? Would you like to take some refreshment?'

I nodded in assent. 'A glass of punch, please.' While there was nothing more than friendly pleasure in his manner, nevertheless that was an advantage I had never had with him and one that my impetuosity, now in full flight, was inclined to press.

He handed me a glass of punch. But as we made polite conversation I saw him darting glances at Sybil. Oh, what a fool he was! Could he not see that she didn't love him?

It was now or never. I am afraid I completely contravened the manuals relating to decorum and correct behaviour between women and men in polite society.

'Mr McKissock,' I said, 'it is so hot in here. Would you like to escort me to the terrace?'

His eyebrows rose but, after all, he was a gentleman. He took my left elbow and together we walked out to the courtyard, where other couples were also taking the air.

For a moment or two we stood in silence. Then I ventured into conversation. 'How exciting it must be to contemplate emigration to New Zealand,' I began. 'Do you know when you will leave?'

'Within six months,' he answered.

'I envy you the adventure,' I continued. 'Scientific despatches by such as Joseph Banks only verify a country which, uplifted high, is of undeniable beauty. I have also seen sketches by William Hodges and others which portray it in an idealistic light as a place free of entrenched distinctions and inherited privilege, where one may build a future based on the ideals of true fraternity.'

Mr McKissock looked at me, impressed. 'You appear to be well read on the subject,' he said.

'You mentioned recently at dinner that Whanganui was a possible destination,' I continued. 'I understand that a new settlement, to be named after Lord Nelson, might afford better opportunities for the migrant?'

He gave a surprised laugh. 'That is the very place I am contemplating,' he answered. 'The location will depend upon my wife.'

'Ah,' I nodded.

'You must know I have intentions towards your cousin, Sybil Springvale,' he continued.

'Yes,' I answered. 'But what if my dear cousin is not available?'

Here Mr McKissock became ruffled. 'I don't know what you mean,' he said.

'There are others who woo her,' I continued. 'Surely you are aware that Mr Marcus Wrenn also pursues her?'

'Wrenn has no chance!' he snorted.

'But if he wins, where will that leave you, sir?'

By now, there among the camellias, my heart was thundering. There was nothing for it but to seize the moment.

'Mr McKissock, there are other women who would go with you to New Zealand.'

'Others?' He seemed to take a moment to understand what I was talking about.

I pressed on. 'The woman who stands before you is one of them.'

He looked at me, startled, his mouth opening and closing like a gasping fish.

———

54

Only then did I berate myself for being too hasty, and for lacking the subtle, coquettish skills of my cousins.

But I truly believed that Mr McKissock would get the hint and see the sense of my offer. I must have been living in a world of my own desperate fabrication because I thought that he would smile and say, 'Why, Miss Glossop, of course you should come with me to New Zealand!'

However, as the silence lengthened between us, I realised how premature my approach was.

Under the circumstances I appreciated that he took my bold invitation without betraying a hint of amusement. Even so, he took a step back, troubled.

'Miss Glossop, please do not embarrass yourself or me any further. The berth that you speak of is already taken.' Bowing stiffly, he extended his arm and escorted me back inside. I could tell from his cold attitude that he wished to be rid of me.

Our joint embarrassment was relieved when Lieutenant Harry Forsythe, whom I had politely refused earlier, tried his luck with me again. This time I accepted, even though I knew I would stumble over my feet, but I wanted to be whizzed away from Mr McKissock. At least I had the compensation of demonstrating to him that even if he did not find me attractive, others did.

When the ball ended I was in abject misery and mortified at my rash behaviour. What had I been thinking?

I couldn't wait to get away. I stood outside Wolverhampton City Hall with the Marquis Wrenn and Aunt Eleanor, Uncle Rollo and my cousins waiting for our carriages.

Aunt Eleanor saw that Mr McKissock was still paying court to Sibyl.

'Sibyl?' she called. 'Come ride with the marquis and me.'

Aunt Eleanor and the marquis were old friends; they were of the same social class and negotiations were already taking place for the marriage of their children.

In that moment, I felt a great sympathy for Mr McKissock, and myself too.

———

A week later, while visiting Uncle Rollo and Aunt Eleanor, I heard raised voices from the morning room.

'Mr McKissock is here,' Aunt Eleanor whispered. 'From the sound of things, Sibyl has rejected his marriage offer.'

'I should go,' I answered, seeking to extricate myself from the visit.

I was too late. As I was putting on my cape, Mr McKissock came to say goodbye to my aunt and uncle. He was pale and stern. His face took on an even grimmer aspect when he saw me.

'Come to gloat, Miss Glossop?' he asked. 'You knew, didn't you, when we spoke at the ball, that your cousin would reject me?'

Uncle Rollo and Aunt Eleanor looked at us both, astonished. 'Kindly do not use that tone with my niece,' Uncle Rollo warned Mr McKissock.

I answered them first. 'No, I am at fault,' I said. 'But I am afraid that Mr McKissock completely misrepresents my motives when I made a certain offer to him. Your accusation is unfair, sir,' I continued, turning to him. 'I am most sincere in regretting that my cousin Sybil does not wish to marry you.'

Aunt Eleanor was apoplectic. 'What offer! Ismay Elizabeth Glossop, what have you been up to!'

I ignored her for the moment. Then I took a deep breath — and I put myself forward again! I had been spurned once; to be turned down a second time did not seem to matter. 'My offer still stands,' I said to Mr McKissock. 'I am serious.'

'Serious?' he answered with an incredulous laugh. 'You are not even attractive to me.'

Wilfully, I carried on. 'Take me and you will not regret it. I am not without culture. My cousins prefer the romantic novels but I would rather open Macaulay's history of the Roman Empire or medical books dealing with the physique and determination of illnesses by diagnosis. Science, mathematics, political economy, Greek and Latin — these are my collateral interests.'

Uncle Rollo and Aunt Eleanor, watching us both like patrons at a theatre, were gasping at the drama.

Mr McKissock was livid. He looked at me with disbelief.

'I am totally flabbergasted, Miss Glossop,' he began, 'that you could even think of yourself as a replacement! I plan to return to Scotland to my father, who is gravely ill. While I am at home, I shall find a wife — I am perfectly capable of doing that — from among the good women of Edinburgh. 'Do you realise, Miss Glossop, the embarrassment I feel at this moment? I am frankly humiliated, madam.'

And what about my own humiliation! However, I controlled myself. 'I am sorry to have caused you any distress. That was never my intention. Good day to you, Mr McKissock. I wish you well in your search.'

Uncle Rollo turned on me as soon as he'd left. 'Well, Ismay?' he asked. 'Your explanation?'

'I told Mr McKissock at the ball that I wished to go to New Zealand.'

'As his wife?' Aunt Eleanor gasped.

'That was implied. But he rejected me.'

'Before he asked Sybil?'

'Yes,' I answered. 'I knew she would never accept him.'

Aunt Eleanor just about fainted away.

I shall admit to female weakness. Later that night, on my return to Webster Hall, I went up to my room, lit a little blue lamp, and looked across Wolverhampton from the unsheathed window. The smoke was low-hanging over the gloomy, miserable roofs and squalid streets. I felt, as any animal or slave must, a deep and utter depression about my captivity . . . and Selina's.

Why Selina's?

Oh, mad as my offer was, it had some sense in it. Had Mr McKissock accepted my offer, it would not have come unfettered: I had already resolved that my mother should accompany me to New Zealand. It had been the only solution to our joint plight at Webster Hall.

In that, too, I had failed.

God moves in mysterious ways.

Three months later, Mr McKissock returned to Wolverhampton. When he came to see me at Webster Hall, he had Uncle Rollo with him.

'Mr McKissock has farewelled his father,' my uncle told me, drawing me aside while Mr McKissock went to pay his respects to my mother. 'It was not easy for him. His father was a fine man — and a good friend of mine. As for the other matter of finding a bride, he has had difficulty. When I was attending his father's funeral in Edinburgh I asked Mr McKissock to reconsider your offer.' Uncle Rollo gave me a stern look. 'Ismay, you are not unpleasing to the eye. Your best qualities are, however, better seen at second glance than at first. I suggested that Mr McKissock take a second look. A word of advice: no matter how much you value your intellectual wares, do enlist his kindly interest by not being too forward in that department.'

I asked Mr McKissock to take a seat. Uncle Rollo excused himself and took a position outside the door — which remained open. For a long while Mr McKissock and I sat opposite each other in silence.

'I am very sorry to hear about your father, Mr McKissock,' I began.

His face changed and I saw, briefly, his vulnerability. When he spoke, he was practical and forthright, and he went straight to the point.

'Miss Glossop, I wish to go to New Zealand. No suitable candidate for female companionship has presented herself and, while I endeavoured to find such a woman in Edinburgh, wooing two, to be precise, both possibilities turned turtle on me. I therefore come to you to ascertain whether or not you are still inclined and of a mind to . . . yourself . . . travel to the colonies.'

'Mr McKissock, is that a marriage proposal?'

'A determined man,' he answered, 'may baulk at the first obstacle but, once he has had the opportunity to survey the height and challenge of it, his interest in surmounting the challenge is somewhat piqued.'

My gratification at being bold — let alone my heart — leapt at his words. But even though I felt some satisfaction that Mr McKissock had come cap in hand to me, I required some appeasement. 'Do you come to me of your own volition and not to keep in my uncle's good books?' I asked.

He was startled by my question. 'I cannot say that his words to me were not without persuasion.'

At least he was honest! 'All right, Mr McKissock,' I said finally, 'I will allow you to call again, but only when there has been an increase in your own personal willingness to want me. After all, I shall be wife to you and not to my uncle.'

'Call again?' he asked. 'But I thought you *wanted* to marry me!'

I showed him to the door, where Uncle Rollo looked at both of us with gloom. His turtle doves were not cooing at each other. However, he perked up when Mr McKissock whispered in his ear, 'Your niece changes the course and sets the bar high but I shall show willingness to jump it.'

Overhearing, I could not help feeling irritated. I noted the casual nature of his approach. 'If that is the case,' I said to him, 'do improve your dressage. I realise you are a Scotsman and thrifty, but you would make a better suit, no matter that I am your last resort, if you spend more silver coins and come bearing roses and with more of a desire to woo me. I may have made the first move but I am not about to throw myself completely into your life without some respect given on your part. I am not without pride.'

To be frank, I felt I was particularly suited to Gower McKissock's cloth. Even Sybil herself, when apprised of the situation, did not at all mind that I, her cousin, was being considered as a wife by a former suitor. 'You are just right for him,' she said.

Why, I wondered, had *he* never seen that!

It was a gamble to send Mr McKissock away — but he did return to Webster Hall. And this time he was better dressed and brought a bouquet, not of roses but of lovely summer flowers of pristine whites, bright yellows and blushes of pink.

'Will you walk with me, Miss Glossop?' he asked.

'Mother, will you chaperone?' I asked. It was time for me to introduce Selina to Mr McKissock and to advise him that she was part of my matrimonial agreement.

We put on our hats and off we went.

For the first part of our perambulation we stayed on the crowded streets and our conversation was rather stilted; Selina carefully stayed out of listening distance. I did not take the lead, but rather waited for Mr McKissock to pose his questions. I should have realised he would be practical.

'Miss Glossop, what would you bring to our marriage?'

'If you are referring to financial matters, sir,' I answered, 'I am not without means. I understand that as an investor in the New Zealand Company you have already paid for a hundred acres of farmland and one town acre; I will, of course, pay for half of that investment.'

'Will I need to speak to your father about that?'

'No,' I answered. 'The payment will come from my mother's inheritance.'

He squinted up at the sky. 'Perhaps then, Miss Glossop,' he continued, 'we may move on to discussion of the conjugal relationships that are the male expectation when one is wed.'

Well, that took the wind out of my sails. 'Mr McKissock, this is a public place. Perhaps we should adjourn to the park over the way there.'

We found a seat; he dusted it down for me, and we sat. Selina wandered across to a small fountain.

After a few minutes, I regained my breath. 'Sir, I set more store by my intelligence but I will not turn away from wifely duties.' My face was becoming red and I was flustered. Had I known that his eyes were twinkling, I would have slapped him.

'Good,' he said. 'Despite all your qualities which are usually described as virile, and normally attributed to the masculine gender, I am pleased to hear that you will allow me in some things to have the lead.'

Oh, I felt like slapping him then! 'I will do what is expected of me, but I will retain my own way. Do not presume that I will give over to you my independence, as that is not negotiable. I will proffer my opinions and criticisms even to those who are considered to be my superiors.'

'Then it is done?'

'Not quite yet. My mother is to come with me.'

He looked across at Selina. Paused. Nodded.

'Thank you,' I said, melting with gratitude.

He put his hand out. Assuming he intended to shake hands, I extended mine. With a swift gesture, he slipped his hand around my waist and pulled me in to him. 'You are taking liberties, sir, before you make due matrimonial promise and payment,' I reprimanded him.

He looked into my eyes, untangled me and looked away. How I wish I had been more accepting of his advances, because his next words were branded upon my heart for ever. 'Very well, Miss Glossop,' he said finally. 'But you understand, don't you, that I will never love you.'

5

So it was that I, Ismay Elizabeth Glossop, went to New Zealand with Gower McKissock.

When I write it like that, I omit all the tedious details attending emigration. Gower and I paid sixty pounds each as cabin passengers, and there was much paperwork — birth, baptismal and other family certificates, bank documents, bonds and other financial documents — to submit not only to the British authorities but also to the register of the New Zealand Company. And then there were the necessary tools of trade for Gower to set up his surgery. Apart from surgical implements, equipment was required also to make a home — gimlets, hammers, an axe or two, nails, hinges, latches, saws, reaping hooks, scythe blades, garden tools, seeds and plant cuttings, needles and thread, knives and forks, crockery — and, of course, a gun or two with powder or shot to protect property and family.

I focus instead on our marriage.

———

Of course, it wasn't as easy as all that to obtain my release from my father.

Knowing him, I am sure he demanded a pretty penny from the Glossop family — Uncle Rollo was executor — before he would let me go. My uncle would never tell me the details, and I expected that he had made a similar ransom payment for my mother. But eventually we were able to post the banns and were married by the Reverend Garner.

Aunt Eleanor was beside herself with anxiety. 'Oh, Ismay Elizabeth, what will become of you?'

My dear Uncle Rollo gave me a gift that I have treasured all my days — the medical briefcase, complete with instruments, I had carried as a young girl through the slum streets of Wolverhampton.

'I always wanted to leave this to my son, if I had been given such. How fortunate I was to be given a niece instead.'

We wept in each other's arms. There was a great love between my uncle and me.

The most difficult moment, however, was after the ceremony when I happily informed Selina that she was coming to New Zealand with us.

'I can't,' she said.

I was unprepared for the rejection. 'I cannot leave you here,' I cried, upset. But no matter how much I tried to persuade her, she would not budge.

'Foolish, beloved child,' she sighed. 'Your father released you, yes, but me? I am his chattel as well as his wife. Although he doesn't want or need me, he can do what he wishes of me. And he does not wish me to leave him.'

'Then I won't go to New Zealand,' I answered.

'And stay here and remain under his power also?' she asked. She caressed my face and gently kissed away my tears. 'You must slip his chains. For my sake.'

In the end Uncle Rollo persuaded me to obey Selina. 'Matron Baines and I will keep an eye on your mother and heaven help Lowthian if he continues to mistreat her.'

She gave me the beautiful ruby necklace with matching earrings which I had worn to the Wolverhampton Dispensary charity ball.

———

A week after the wedding, on 7 April 1841, somewhat exhausted from purchasing everything that we would need for resettlement and sending it on ahead of us, Gower and I went down to London.

We had a week in the capital, ostensibly on honeymoon while we waited for embarkation to New Zealand. Oh, the young, like Georgina, have such romantic notions about love and marriage! They think one simply falls into the arms of the other and violins begin to play. Nothing could have been less likely for Gower and me.

Late each evening, my husband — who I discovered was never patient in sexual matters — waited for a sign that he might initiate his conjugal expectations.

I gave him no such sign.

On the fourth night he took me to the opera. Gluck's *Orpheus and Eurydice* had always been popular in England where it was performed in both English and Italian. I had never seen the work before and was entranced by the story of the noble Orpheus who had to go down into Hades to rescue his beloved wife. What particularly enamoured me was that both the main parts were sung by women. And the music and sentiments were so noble and elevated!

However, when the opera arrived at Act Three, Scene One, I was completely undone. In the scene, Orpheus, at the piteous pleadings of Eurydice, removes her veil to look at her before they have left Hades — and he loses her.

Che faro senza Eurydice
Dove andro senza il mio ben!
Che faro dove andro
Che faro senza il mio ben
Dove andro senza il mio ben!

Oh dear — that was when I began to sob brokenly. All my life I had had to make my own way, and here I was making my own way again — this time with a man I really didn't know — and to the other side of the world. Would he ever weep for me as Orpheus did for Eurydice?

What on earth had possessed me?

Gower, in sympathy, tried to take my hand. My tears and boohooing were attracting frowns and hisses from others in the audience.

'Don't touch me,' I said to him. Embarrassed, I realised that the orchestra had stopped playing. Worse, the singers on stage had stopped singing. I got up from my seat and fled from the auditorium. Behind me, I heard the conductor addressing the audience: 'Ladies and gentlemen we will begin the aria again . . .'

That evening, Gower required all his tact and sympathy to calm me down. Eventually, I could even see the humour in the affair.

'There are not many people,' he said, 'who, without even singing, could stop an opera.'

Although I blush to reveal such things, he pressed himself upon me and, because he had been so kindly disposed to me, I allowed him to proceed. Our joint awareness of our bodies, honed by clinical observance, enabled us to seek a freedom in each other that eased the experience for me — after all, I was a virgin.

On his part, dare I say it, the male urge provided the impetus for completion of the act that lack of love could not. But, oh, there is a *look* in a man's eyes — other women who are not loved will know what I am referring to — that unmasks him at his moment of ecstasy. Surprise, regret and acceptance are all part of the look so that, even when he lies in your arms murmuring his thanks, you know that he would rather you were the woman he really loved.

I wish I had not seen that look.

———————

From London we journeyed to Gravesend for embarkation on the *Esmond Hurst*, a small sailing ship of 370 tons, bound for Adelaide and thence for New Zealand. The port was milling with emigrants. Among the luggage being loaded I spied my huge baize-lined chest in which was Uncle Rollo's medical briefcase, my best clothes, jewellery and enough linen to last us a lifetime.

Normally I was not a person to have second thoughts but seeing my luggage stowed in the hold made me realise that there was no turning back. And when I saw that all my personal effects were bundled with Gower's under a joint label — Mr & Mrs G. McKissock — I felt pangs of grief and personal loss.

Then a sailor rang a handbell. 'Oyez! Oyez! The owners of the sailing ship *Esmond Hurst* and its master, Captain William Forde, advise that the ship will set sail with the morning tide and it is ordered by the master that all passengers be on board by midnight.'

I took a deep breath. 'We had best answer the summons,' I said to Gower.

———————

We boarded with one hundred and eighty-five others. Some were investors like ourselves as cabin passengers. Most were taking free passage as emigrant mechanics, gardeners and agricultural labourers and a small number of soldiers were going out to join the 58th (Rutlandshire) Regiment of Foot in New Zealand. As we eased off the bowline and made mid-channel, I felt the tug of the current pulling us seaward. The ship left harbour; I, too, felt that I had cast off, weighed anchor, unfurled my sails and left one life, southward bound towards another.

The departure was not without its tears. Would I ever see England again? Or touch the cheek of my dear Uncle Rollo, mother Selina, and my aunt and cousins? Everything was happening so quickly and, at that moment, having given myself up to a man I hardly knew was no compensation.

I left Gower on deck with the other passengers and went down to our room. I opened one of our travel cases for my dressing gown and saw the programme for *Orpheus and Eurydice*:

What is life to me without you?
All my joy, alas, has flown
What is life, life without you?
Why remain on earth alone?
Why remain on earth alone . . .
Eurydice? Eurydice . . .

Sentimentally, I began humming the aria. Maybe, in the future Gower might address himself to me with such ardency and passion. Could I be his joy? His life?

I could hope, couldn't I, that in time . . .

No. Best be realistic. Not reach out. Not expect too much.

As I was locking the programme away, I felt a strong, insistent surge within me. I was puzzled. I felt the surge again, and my eyes widened. Surely this was much too early . . .

I sat down on the bed in a state of bewilderment. I knew with absolute certainty, as England faded behind us, that I was pregnant.

———

Our vessel kept to the east and ran down the coast of Portugal. In the distance we could make out the hills of the island of Palma, one of the Canaries. Then the land receded, and all around was uninterrupted ocean.

Gower was as startled as I to discover that I was pregnant. I doubt whether he — like myself — had pictured himself as a parent so soon. Still sexually demanding, he was also solicitous and, I think, secretly proud of proof of his manhood.

Sad to say, my early happiness was dashed when I miscarried on the open seas. The first of my babies rushed away with the blood between my legs. I was inconsolable. I had not realised how much the baby meant to me . . . to both of us. Perhaps I even thought that Gower would begin to love me if I bore him a son. 'Our baby is gone,' I wept.

He was kind, but uncomfortable dwelling on the loss. 'We shall have others,' he said, and I took that comment as an indication of deeper affection on his part.

Our fellow company was congenial. There was a clear difference in class between the investors and the passengers travelling by assisted free passage, but I have never been one to let social niceties prevent friendly discourse. Among the assisted emigrants were a young couple, John and Jane Bright, with their two daughters, Jemima and Dolly. John was a carpenter and joiner, and I was able to convince Gower that he should build our cottage on arrival in New Zealand.

One of the soldiers — oh, he was so young! — was an eleven-year-old boy, William Allen, a bugler who was excited about getting the chance to go to New Zealand. Every morning and afternoon his commanding officer would get the soldiers to their drills but, for the rest of the time, they were able to join with the rest of the passengers.

'Master Allen,' I asked him one day, 'why are you so keen to see active service?'

'I am to fight the daring Maoris,' he said proudly.

One night, lying awake, I heard him singing:

The minstrel boy to the war is gone
In the ranks of death you'll find him—

I went on deck and there he was, facing south, his profile gilded by the bright full moon. His voice had not yet broken and it was so beautiful, innocent, brimming with optimism, eagerness and excitement at being a soldier.

His father's sword he has girded on
And his wild harp slung behind him!

Very soon I was joined by other passengers. Enchantment surrounded us as we listened.

No chains shall sully thee!
Thou soul of love and bravery
Thy songs were made for the pure and free
They shall never sound in slavery—

My heart went out to him — but the enchantment did not last long! For the rest of the voyage young Allen proved to be such a nuisance, always practising on his bugle morning and night.

Grievously, we lost among the passengers Dolly, the Brights' three-year-old toddler, on the second leg of the journey. She was crushed during a storm by some huge barrels which came bursting though their sleeping quarters. I helped to wash and wrap her little body in a blanket and sew it up in a hammock. Came the time of the burial, the sails were clewed down and taken in so as to lay the ship to. The ship's company and passengers seated themselves around the quarterdeck for the funeral service. John and Jane Bright hugged their remaining daughter Jemima as the little body was launched over the ship's side and into the ocean, in which it instantly sank.

I thought of my first babe, gone.

We kept up our spirits with a debating club; recital evenings when a young man would play the violin or a matron, fancying her voice, would subject us to her version of Handel arias; and sometimes we would read from a play by William Shakespeare. Much of the day was spent on top, as the air below deck was particularly foul.

Then the *Esmond Hurst* crossed the equator. The men had such fun acting out a masquerade concerning Neptune, and holding a court in which those who were found guilty were doused with a bucket of water. Tragedy again visited the Bright family; this time John Bright, who could not keep his food or water down. He wasted away and nothing that Gower could do for him could stop the dreadful loss of weight that took him quickly from robust man to skeleton. When he died and his body was committed to the sea, he made scarcely a splash.

We continued to make good way and, as we skirted down the coast of Africa, I felt that strong insistent surge in me again. When my morning sickness began, I was very happy.

'I am with child a second time, Mr McKissock,' I told Gower.

Not long after, we doubled the Cape of Good Hope. It grew extremely cold, so that the ropes and riggings froze and the sails were stiff. The journey was always hazardous; death visited us again, with three passengers dying of pneumonic conditions and one other lost overboard.

The run, almost direct to Adelaide, Australia, began. The journey had become dreary and fatiguing. The long dark nights and never-ending roar of the sea were hard to endure, and I often felt that we would never get to our destination.

I was fearful that I might lose my second babe, so that when Gower suggested we leave the ship at Adelaide and wait out my confinement there, I said yes. We stayed in that lovely town of sunny white houses until our babe, Gower Jr, was born. He was delivered by his father. As Gower cradled him, I watched hopefully for signs of bonding.

Then New Zealand beckoned again and we boarded the *Andrew Paterson*, carrying a lesser complement of ninety-seven passengers.

The passage from Adelaide to New Zealand was dreadful, with mounting, tumbling seas that threatened to toss us forward and over the edge of the world. Were it not for the preserving care of the Almighty's hand, I fear we would have been utterly destroyed by the waves. Even so, there were deaths on board, of two elderly passengers and one bonny tyke. How preciously I held on to Gower Jr, praying that he would survive!

Indeed, I was feeding him below deck when I heard a hubbub from topside. Gower came to fetch me.

'What is it?' I asked.

'Come and see,' he answered.

It was daylight's close, but the sky was clear and of an extraordinary pallor. Ahead I saw a coronet of cloud floating on the sea. The *Andrew Paterson* had reached the bold shores of the country that lay between the parallels of 34 and 48 degrees south latitude, and between the 166th and 179th meridians of east longitude.

'New Zealand at last,' I said. I fell to my knees on the deck and thanked God.

With our stay in Adelaide, passage from England had taken over a year.

For the next few days the ship journeyed down the west coast of New Zealand's North Island, around the great Taranaki Bight with its awe-inspiring mountain capping the land. My heart quickened with anticipation as we sailed further southward, encountering other vessels hugging the coastline. By second nightfall we had arrived at the tempestuous strait between the North and South Island. The captain advised that we would come to Nelson by the following mid-morning.

I stood on deck in a bracing wind with Gower, watching the dawn come up. Ahead, snow-capped mountains reared above a haze of blue, strange and mysterious. I never saw the equal of those mountains, rising like stairways to the heavens, so grand and sublime. I was not cowed by them; rather, I lifted my face to them.

'Mark my words,' I called out. 'Although I have a son, I lost my first child to you. I have paid my price, New Zealand. Our account is settled.'

Gower smiled at my words. 'So it is mountains that you now expect to bow to you is it, Mrs McKissock?'

Then, with a rush, the mountains leapt like palisades around us and a stiff breeze sent us spinning into a bay of native coastal forest. At the base was the town of Nelson. With skill and flair the sailors of the *Andrew Paterson* piloted the ship through the inconsistent surf towards the narrow channel at the end of Boulder Bank. Safely negotiating the entrance, we dropped anchor in the sheltered water behind.

I shook out my skirts and straightened my bonnet. Other ships lay at anchor and on the morning air came the sounds of Nelson townspeople about their business. Excitement mounted inside me. 'What are we waiting for, Mr McKissock?'

Laughing with joy, I allowed myself to be handed into a rowboat. Gower gave our son into my arms and then joined us. The rowboat had no sooner scraped sand than I was out of it, wading in the glistening water to New Zealand soil. I turned to my husband. 'We are here!' I said to him. 'Oh, Gower, now our adventure begins!'

6

After our luggage came off the ship, we went on foot to the New Zealand Company's depot. Gower was warmly welcomed by Captain Wakefield, the well-liked brother of Edward Gibbon Wakefield, under whose command Nelson was being laid out: from the summit, Church Hill, where the Company depot was, having Trafalgar and Nile streets running from it.

'Sir,' Captain Wakefield said to Gower with a cheeky smile, 'I have your first patients already awaiting your inspection.' The 'patients' turned out to be a herd of pigs, somewhat worse for wear, unloaded from another vessel.

'I hope,' Gower answered, 'that future patients will be of the two-legged variety.'

But before he could attend to the pigs, a tall, thin man called to him, 'Mr McKissock!'

Coming towards us was a young couple. After much back-slapping, Gower introduced his friend to me as John Jennings Imrie, an old friend from Edinburgh. I put my hand out to the woman with him.

'I am Ismay McKissock,' I said.

'And I am Etty Imrie,' she answered.

'John Jennings and I were at university together,' Gower explained. 'It was he who encouraged me to attend a meeting that the New Zealand Company held in Edinburgh.'

'We're of the Episcopalian persuasion,' John Jennings said. 'We've come to New Zealand as missioners.' He turned to Gower. 'Perhaps, you heathen, you are ready for conversion?'

'No,' Gower answered. 'But,' he added, 'I will be visiting some new patients who may become parishioners!'

Etty Imrie and I watched with good humour. She was bright-eyed, her hair severely tied back, and appeared to brook no nonsense. 'Scotsmen,' she sighed.

We warmed to each other immediately.

———

On this agreeable note did Gower and I begin our two-year stay in Nelson. In that year of 1842 we joined over three thousand people brought to Nelson by the New Zealand Company; twenty-four vessels landed, following Captain Arthur Wakefield's expeditionary vessel, *Will-Watch*, and the *Whitby* and *Arrow* with one hundred pioneers, mostly male, from England. The roll call of ships included *Fifeshire*, *Mary Ann*, *Lloyds* and *Lord Auckland*.

Of all of them, the story of the *Lloyds* was salutary, undercutting our overall optimism. It carried the women and children of the first male pioneers but, when it landed, the husbands and fathers were greeted with the news that sixty-five of their children had died on the journey. The cries and laments were heartrending. Over the next few days nothing could lift the relentless pall of utter sadness that descended on the town. My heart went out to the womenfolk, and Etty Imrie and I immediately organised other women of the colony to offer as much sympathy and succour as we could. As for the sorrowing men, I was proud to see Gower and John Jennings lending their support; never doubt that strong-hearted men weep.

'You have good strong shoulders, Mr McKissock,' I said to him.

'I am a father, too,' he answered. 'I know how the men are feeling.'

I took that as an indication from him that he was settling into our relationship. In those days I could not help but store such signs away in my glad heart.

But folk who have travelled twelve thousand miles in search of a new home are not easily daunted, and Nelson continued to establish itself as a vigorous township. Native timber was felled for cottages and barns, and land cleared for crops. Very soon, the town boasted over two hundred and fifty good houses, most in the growing residential area known as 'The Wood'; and many whare and huts for temporary accommodation. As a settlement, we were well on the way to becoming the second largest in New Zealand.

Meanwhile I was grateful that Gower and I had found good accommodation each with the other and, certainly, I had no quarrel with the way he assumed his duties as a parent and head of the household. In all these respects, no woman could wish for a better husband. Even more impressive was how he took command of our future. We were shown our allotment in Milton Street and he contracted William Wilkie and Francis Arnott as builders to raise a small cottage — Mr Wilkie was happy for the work; he had courted and married Jane Bright, after her husband had died, and in one fell swoop acquired both a wife and a daughter to feed. As well, Gower inspected some very fine public buildings close to the depot before choosing one as his surgery. I did not disclose my hand about my medical understanding, preferring him to think he had the 'upper berth', at least in that department.

Very soon his practice was very busy; the townspeople admired him and, certainly, he caught the eye of many a woman. Whenever that happened I felt pangs of guilt that I had trapped him in a situation — namely, our marriage — that he had not wished upon himself.

One evening, after we had made love, I turned away from him. In the silence that followed, I felt alone and sad. I pulled his arms around me and tried to burrow into them. Before I could stop them, the words sprang to my lips: 'Mr McKissock, I am so sorry.'

'Sorry?' he asked.

'I know that I am not attractive to you.'

He hugged me closer into his strong arms. Kissed my shoulders. Took an intake of breath, as if to say something — but Gower Jr cried from his cradle and I had to rise and attend to him.

While I was holding him, Gower joined me. He put an arm around my waist. 'I am not unhappy,' he said. 'Our life is what it is.'

———

After that, I learnt not to ask too many questions and, instead, to live from day to day. Gower and I were happy enough. We lived fully, with a routine that found him busy at the surgery or making house calls. He was also involved in community leadership — Captain Wakefield called constantly on his opinion in town-planning matters. Through his activities we quickly made some fine friendships among the growing number of new arrivals. Among them was Major Charles Heaphy, artist and draughtsman for the New Zealand Company.

All of us who had come to Nelson — English, Scots, Irish, German and, yes, some Polish and Jews — were pilgrims with different expectations, some of which were met, and others not. We all had at heart a common bond: we had left the rigid class system, national divisions, religious intolerance and chaos of industrial Europe with hopes of a new freedom and the desire to make decent lives for ourselves at the bottom of the world.

And lest I leave that impression, please do not think our lives were without play or gaiety. Of a weekend the local men and women would gather to dance. By then the waltz and polka were the rage, and I found them much less mathematical than those terrifying dances of polite Wolverhampton society. I was more sure-footed and relaxed, even if higher opinion (thank goodness located in England, not New Zealand!) felt the polka was vulgar and the waltz would lead to the end of civilised society.

———

As for settler relationships with the Maori, I was relieved that in Nelson, at least, they were cordial. While some appeared fearsome, with their tattooed faces, if you looked past their facial and body moko you discovered a people who were intelligent and honourable in their dealings; most of them, in the universal spirit of enquiry, had converted to the Anglican faith. Savage they could be in their determination to retain their mana or power, but they were also prepared to relate on all levels politically, economically and culturally. The principal source of tension was the disputes over land sales to the 'Pakeha' (as the colonists were called) — even those of the New Zealand Company; otherwise, the relationship at the personal level was for the most part fair.

I became quite friendly with a grumpy old Maori woman, Mahuika. She came to Gower's surgery one day when I happened to be visiting with Gower Jr. Gower could not understand the stream of Maori that issued from her as she tried to indicate what the problem was. His non-comprehension turned her distress to exasperation, and Gower asked my help. 'Would you do as you did with the elderly ladies of Wolverhampton,' he began, 'and find out what the problem is?'

I had not known that Uncle Rollo had mentioned the story to him — but I did my best. Fortunately, I had already learnt a few words of Maori, filled with blowing and whistling sounds, picking it up during daily bartering with the Maori for fruit and vegetables.

'E kia nei te mate?' I asked. 'Where is the pain?'

She scowled and pointed to her shoulders.

'Ki konei?' I asked. 'Here? Kei runga? Kei raro?'

After a quick pantomime between us, in which Mahuika slapped my hands and kept up a stream of imprecations about my stupidity, I determined she had dislocated her shoulder in a fall.

Once the problem was identified, Gower was able to proceed to the appropriate, but painful, manipulation that would return her shoulder to its natural position. Mahuika was grateful, muttering and looking into her pockets for some coins to pay with.

Gower made a chance remark. Noting the number of other Maori who had begun to visit the surgery, he said to me with a sigh, 'Perhaps you should come more often to help interpret what the natives want.'

'I don't know the language,' I answered.

Mahuika pricked up her ears. 'Haere mai koe ki au apopo,' she said to me, quickly thrusting her coins back into her pocket. 'Come to me tomorrow. I will teach you. It will be my payment to the takuta, the doctor,' she said.

She thought she was getting the better deal.

———

This was how I came to take lessons, every second day, in the Maori language.

My classroom was the beach at Nelson, a most unconventional location, but this was where Mahuika lived with the group of other kuia and girls who camped on the beach, waiting for the sailors to land by dinghy from the ships which called at the port. Prostitution is not a word I would use for the services the girls offered, but they were highly sought after by the sailors. As for Mahuika and the older women, they sold Maori trinkets and, in Mahuika's case, she offered fortune-telling in return for tobacco or a shiny silver coin.

Of course, when Gower discovered that I would be mingling with riff-raff on the beach — and unaccompanied, too — he had second thoughts! But my obstinacy would not be brooked by his argument and, after all, we had already agreed that the surgery would benefit.

On the first day, how I relished the freedom of being able to go where I wished! I took Gower Jr with me. I don't think Mahuika was expecting that I would take up her offer. Her face fell and she muttered a few words to her fellow kuia but, after all, a deal was a deal.

From the very start our relationship was fractious. I introduced Gower Jr to Mahuika. She looked with distaste at his colour, 'He huhu,' she said, making reference to a white grub. I wasn't going to let her get away with that! Quick as a flash I recalled a piece of information from my New Zealand scrapbook about the Maori liking for the sweet-tasting white grub. 'He huhu pea, engari te huhu reka?' I answered her. 'A white grub perhaps but, notwithstanding his colour, don't Maori consider the huhu a delicacy?'

She gave me a quizzical glance and then began to grin. 'E koe!' she laughed. 'Get you! Challenging your teacher already!'

She slapped my hands and feet.

'Timata,' she said. 'We begin. Keep up.'

———

I attended my Maori language lessons dutifully for the next seven months. I would sit in the sand beside Mahuika while Gower Jr wandered hither and yon along the beach — there were always other Maori, sailors, elderly kuia or the sailors' girls and their children to watch over him — and very soon, because learning the language excited me, I became oblivious to the waves as they stained my dress.

What a sophisticated language it was! I would have preferred to learn from a textbook — and Mahuika often castigated me with her filthy imprecations whenever I could not retain her teaching in my memory. Acquiring a vocabulary was the most difficult step. Mahuika was not averse to using a short stick to rap my arms or legs if I was tardy or forgetful. I soon diminished my punishments, however, when I began paying for the continuation of my lessons — and then I offered also to improve her English.

Indeed, this was my way of getting even with her. I relished rapping her back for her errors, and very soon we were both trading light blows, but with love, as we grew to like each other. Like the good pupil I was, I improved my stakes with my teacher by supplementing my silver coin with an apple, a stub of foul-smelling topeka or licorice or, every now and then, a piece of cloth.

Aue, alas, I only wish I was as quick to learn her language as she was in learning English. Over time, however, my inventory of words improved — though I must admit that it did not only come from Mahuika. From helping Gower with his Maori patients, I developed a medical vocabulary, too: upoko for head, tinana for body, waewae for leg, manawa for stomach; huango for asthma, toto for bleeding, areare for abscess, he wera for burns, raumati for diarrhoea, and so on.

My close association with the girls on the beach gave me another kind of vocabulary of suggestive imprecations that had them rolling in the sand with mirth whenever I applied them to some hapless sailor who thought I was a prostitute, too.

But I was far away from any comprehensive understanding of the Maori language or fluency in it and it was only when I was one day visiting John Jennings and Etty Imrie that good fortune attended me. John Jennings himself was struggling to learn Maori so as to be better able to communicate with his parishioners. As soon as I saw his small, hundred-page book entitled *A Grammar and Vocabulary of the Language of New Zealand*, published by the Church Missionary Society for Anglican missionaries, I pounced on it.

From that moment I progressed in leaps and bounds. I discovered that the genius of the language was in the free combination of words, its flexibility and elasticity. Very soon I was so adept that Mahuika one day looked at me, suspicious, and gave me a jealous rap of her stick. 'Kei whea koe to reo? Somebody else is teaching you too!'

'No,' I assured her. 'It has become my joy to do individual study.'

'Ah,' she nodded. 'So you have grown to love the reo rangatira?'

'Yes,' I answered. I truly meant it.

She caressed my cheeks with tenderness. 'Then I have nothing further to teach you,' she said.

But I didn't want to leave her and, when Gower Jr saw me weeping, he came running. 'Mother, why are you crying?'

I looked at Mahuika and kissed her cheeks. 'I have made a good friend,' I told Gower Jr, 'and now we are saying goodbye to each other.'

'I have my destiny,' Mahuika answered. 'You have yours.'

At the time I didn't know what she was talking about.

———

So how did Gower and I happen to go to Tasmania?

In 1843, there was trouble with the Maori when we investors, promised one hundred acres each along with our one town acre, began to call for that return. Surveyors went out to the nearby Wairau Valley with their equipment but were turned away by Maori landowners. When Captain Wakefield and other settlers reacted by trying to establish their rights, they were murdered.

Rumours were rife that Nelson itself would suffer an attack.

Saddened by the turn of events, Gower and I made the decision to leave Nelson temporarily, until the troubles were over. A number of ships were setting sail from the port. Ours, the *Aldred Leith*, was the last to leave.

Our sadness soon turned to consternation when we learned we were heading, not for Wellington or any other port in New Zealand, but for Van Diemen's Land!

'We have brought very little with us,' Gower said to the captain. 'We have not sufficient money even to pay you for our safe passage. What about our house, our belongings?'

For some reason, my consternation was replaced by a great sense of — call it what you will, but I shall describe it as fatalism.

I pressed Gower's hands in mine. 'We will be all right, Mr McKissock.'

I had had the good sense to scoop up into a large hold-all the savings we kept in the house, along with important documentation — the deeds to our land, house and surgery — and, of course, my jewellery; the beautiful ruby necklace and earrings among them. 'All is not lost. We can send for our belongings once we land. I am sure the captain will, under the circumstances, wait until we obtain the money to pay him.'

'Don't you want to go back to Nelson?' Gower asked, surprised.

I took a deep breath and said, 'We had good friends and I will miss Etty Imrie and John Jennings. We were making a good life in Nelson — but let us keep going forward.'

'Do you mean, Mrs McKissock,' he continued, with greater astonishment, 'that we should become emigrants to Australia?'

I had a feeling this was meant to be. New Zealand was not our end destination. My resolve grew. 'Why not?' I said recklessly. 'It is one's follies and not one's cautious decisions that lead generally to the unexpected, the odd, the excitingly worthwhile, do you not agree?'

Gower's eyes widened. He roared with laughter, nodded, and said, 'Ismay Elizabeth Glossop, your uncle always told me that you could never be curbed!'

We hugged each other and — I couldn't help it — I grabbed him around the waist. 'Dance with me, Gower!' I cried, and with our son hopping between us like a little chick, we spun in an impromptu polka all the way from one side of the deck to the other and back again.

Two weeks later, our ship entered upon a vista that, when I recall it, still catches my heart: the beautiful Trowenna Sea, and Van Diemen's Land like a jewel in the middle of it.

I knew I was right to cast my fate to the future. Even as a young woman, even before Gower came into my life, I had dreamt about that sea. I had thought I would find it in New Zealand. Looking across the gloomy roofs of Wolverhampton, I had seen it in my mind's eye. Even then I had conjured up Trowenna as liberty's template, years before I set eyes on it.

What Trowenna represented was freedom, and it was what I considered freedom must look like: impossibly blue, merging into a faraway sky, limitless, going on to the end of forever. After all, isn't that what unhappy people do when they wish to escape the harsh reality of their lives — imagine another place to go to?

When I saw the glorious southern seascape, glittering by day with sun-stars and glowing by night under the gleaming Southern Cross and that arching canopy of a million stars, I knew that I had found it. In that moment, just before dusk, when the sea filled with dark purple spheres like many crystal glasses spilling their rich wine into the sea, I myself overflowed with a great sense of completion.

HOHEPA'S STORY
Wellington, New Zealand

PROLOGUE
Wellington, 1925

'E muri ahiahi takoto ki te moenga . . .' Sighing in my sleep I think of you . . .

The voice calls to me along the windless path I travelled years ago. It is a male voice, chanting through the never-ending darkness.

'My father, you were treasured among your people and we have not forgotten you! You were the kaka feather cloak! You were the neck pendant of transparent greenstone! You were the central post of the meeting house!'

It must be my son Rukuwai, calling to me. His words make me weep with gratefulness that I have been found. Aue te mamae toi whenua e! Alas, the ache for the homeland!

'Father, for over eighty years your people have been trying to find you! On their behalf, as well as for myself, I have searched for you here and there in Aotearoa. My grandfather, Korakotai, was the first one to follow your trail from Whanganui when you left us to fight the Pakeha in the Heretaunga. Aue, he died during the search and could not pass on to me the clues he had found. And I, your only son, was just a babe, orphaned most cruelly, and by the time I grew up, mist and cloud obscured your steps as you were taken prisoner from Wellington to Auckland. But as I grew into adulthood, our people counselled patience. They said to me, "E Rukuwai, don't fret. If you wait long enough at the entrance to Te Reinga the day will come when the mist will disperse and you will see your father's footsteps again." So I have been gladly forbearing, never forgetting, looking into the mist until . . .'

It *is* Rukuwai! Oh, my son, show yourself to me . . .

The clouds break apart and I look for him. But what is this? All I see is an old man, stooped, in his eighties. Where is my boy? I take a closer glance at the old man again and I know, a parent always knows, that although the bloom of youth has long gone from him, he is indeed Rukuwai.

Arrived in Wellington, he steps down from the bus which has brought him from Patiarero, our village on the Whanganui River. Dressed in a suit and wearing a snappy fedora, he is accompanied by a young woman with luminous eyes, in her late twenties. She too is dressed formally in a lovely grey jacket and skirt, hat and gloves. Clutching her by the hand is a little girl of about three. They wait for their small suitcase to be unloaded.

'Then came glad tidings,' Rukuwai calls. 'The gods sent me word of you! But, aue, my spirit almost failed me when the magnitude of the task of bringing you back home was revealed to me. Where are the warriors to assist an old man? This is why I have come to Parliament — because here there may be someone who can help.'

Rain down, oh rain, and be my tears as I weep for all the years I was never able to spend with my son. Why have I been punished like this? Even so, I am proud as I watch him. He has become an indomitable old man ascending toward Parliament Buildings.

'Come on, Pone,' he says to the young woman with him. 'I don't want to be late for our appointment.'

'All right, Dad,' she answers. She picks up the young girl and carries her in her arms. 'Your grandfather, Kui, he's always in a hurry.'

He is also fearless as he cleaves a way through the valley that leads to Te Paremata o te Pakeha. He gesticulates with his walking stick to open the pathway.

'Piki mai, kake mai, homai te waiora ki ahau! I climb towards you! I call you! Make way! Make way!'

He is not afraid of the Pakeha marae.

Even so, Pone tries to calm his racing heart. 'It will be all right, Dad.'

She must be my grandchild! And Kui my great-grandchild! I reach out to touch Kui's face. She senses my presence, smiles, and lifts her cheek to my caress.

'What is it, baby?' Pone asks her.

Aue, te mamae! Alas, the pain! For death has also robbed me of the blessing of knowing all my whanau.

Meanwhile, Rukuwai steps firmly ahead of her, up the stairway to the great doorway of Te Paremata o te Pakeha. 'Nothing will be right, Pone, until we get our tipuna home,' he says to her as she catches up. He is breathing hard as he presents himself, Pone and Kui to the Pakeha attendant.

82

Pone does all the talking. She has better English than he has. 'My father and I have come to see the Minister of Maori Affairs.'

'Mr Pomare? Is the Minister expecting you?'

'Of course he's expecting us,' Rukuwai interrupts. He takes a letter from his pocket and gives it to the attendant.

The attendant takes a few moments to check the letter. He waves them through but when the door closes behind him Rukuwai gives a shout of anger and alarm and begins to chant a haka of defiance.

'Why is he frightened?' the Pakeha attendant asks Pone.

'My father isn't frightened,' Pone tells him with scorn. 'He is just telling the doors they had better let him out when he returns.'

My spirit hovers as Rukuwai is shown in to Maui Pomare. The Minister smiles and extends a welcome to him; he has great respect among Maori, having saved many of them during the flu epidemic.

Rukuwai formally presses noses with him and introduces Pone. 'My wife Noni and I were fortunate to be blessed with four children: Kopeka, Molly, Pone and Wenerau.'

'Who is this little one?' the Minister asks, stroking Kui's cheek.

'My moko, Kui.' He turns to Pone. 'Give the Minister the newspaper article. Titiro! Look, Minister! Nga kupu! Read the words! They tell of my father, Hohepa. I have been searching for him for all these years. Now my heart strings are plucked with hope . . .'

Mr Pomare reads the article. His eyes widen with surprise. The article is very short, and he reads it again. 'This is all about a Maori warrior whose remains have been found in Australia.'

Rukuwai nods his head. 'Not just any warrior,' he says, his voice trembling with grief. 'He is my father. No wonder I could not find him, for he was taken from Auckland across the horizon northwest to Australia! Mauria atu ia ki Poihakena, aue, taukiri e . . .'

The Minister tries to calm him down. 'Leave this with me, koroua,' he says.

'How was I to know I should listen to the voice of the seagull?' Rukuwai weeps. 'Only the seagull would have seen my father taken to a place where none of our canoes have ever travelled. Minister, can you help to bring him home?'

'I will make enquiries,' Mr Pomare answers. 'Where are you and your daughter and mokopuna staying? With relatives? Good.' Gently and warmly he sees Rukuwai and Pone to the door. 'I will do what I can.'

When they are gone, Mr Pomare paces the room, deep in thought. He calls a secretary to his office. When the secretary appears, he dictates an official letter dated 2 July 1925 to the Hon. Premier of Tasmania, Hobart:

Dear Sir,

On 18 April last an article in the *Hobart News* made reference to the discovery on Maria Island of the tomb of Hohepa te Umuroa, who is stated to have been buried there in 1847.

A copy of this article was received in New Zealand and I have been requested by the Maoris of the Wanganui District to ascertain full particulars.

I shall be glad, therefore, to know whether it is possible to obtain a photograph of the grave, and a copy of the inscription upon the tombstone. Any other particulars which may be available bearing on how this Maori came to be buried on Maria Island will be very welcome.

Yours faithfully,
Maui Pomare,
Minister of Health

Any other particulars?

Rukuwai's voice reaches me in Te Po, the spirit world, where I have been restless all these years. Until I return home to Aotearoa, I will never be at peace. I am in limbo, lost, a disturbed spirit. He koputunga ngaru pae ana i te one, tenei kei a au.

A mass of sea foam stranded on the beach, that's what I am.

And yes, I was taken to Australia.

7

Tihei mauriora!
E rere kau mai te awa nui nei e
Mai i te kahui maunga ki Tangaroa
E ko au te awa, ko te awa ko au!
Hui e, haumi e, taiki e!

How I would happily return to the years of my youth, those years of the 1820s, when I was born to the Ngati Hau, one of the great tribes of the Whanganui River.

My kainga was Patiarero; my mountain was Pukehika. The name Patiarero means a smooth or flattering tongue.

Ours was a large settlement on a populous stretch of the river, just up from the Mangaiho Stream, with our back protected by impenetrable wilderness, hilly and inaccessible terrain. Well fortified with palisades, our village occupied a bluff from which you had good views both down and upriver. We were therefore well positioned to repel invaders or to prevent their passage past us.

From the very beginning of our history, Patiarero had a reputation as something of a piratical stronghold. Outsiders would quote a well-known proverb about us, whenever somebody was about to do something risky: 'You want to do that? Haere ki Patiarero! Why not save yourself the trouble and go to Patiarero where you can get eaten!'

The proverb referred to our custom of celebrating our victories with the ritual eating of human flesh. It also acknowledged our ruthless tenacity in holding our part of the river, which we called the Matua Tupuna, the

85

Ancestor Parent. We were a proud, passionate and savage race.

Myth has it that the river was created in legendary days, when mountains were able to move. Tongariro and his brother mountain, Taranaki, fell in love with and fought over a third mountain, Pihanga. Tongariro won the contest, so Taranaki, wild with grief and anger, plunged away from them towards the coast. He then went a little way north to where he stands, solitary, to this day. The long, jagged rift left behind — a furrow of chasms, bluffs, races, confluences, waterfalls and raging torrents fringed with dark forest — filled with water, cooling the pain. Thus the principal sources of the Whanganui River were the western flanks of the triad mountains we called the Kahui Maunga, combining into a single two-hundred-mile-long brawling boulder-filled torrent flowing through the volcanic plateau and winding in a long southwestern descent to the Tasman Sea.

My father, Korakotai, was an emissary of Ngati Hau in those days, during the perilous times of intertribal warfare when all the kainga of the river needed to be unified. The symbol of his office was a tokotoko, a stick carved with Whanganui designs, scrolls and chevrons symbolising the taniwha — the spirit shapes — of the river's supernatural guardians.

The Pakeha and his Christian God had yet to penetrate to the Whanganui region; but tribes all around us had purchased firearms from white traders and were using these to conquer each other. At the time I was born, musket wars broke out and over the next ten years, some twenty thousand Maori were killed.

The Whanganui River was a particular prize that the tribes lusted after. We owned it, protecting it with many forts and other military installations perched high up on green promontories, terraces or out-jutting cliffs along its length. Other tribes, however, were so hungry for it that their mouth juices would spill over at the very thought of taking it.

Why? Easy! Whoever owned the river held the longest and quickest accessway through the heart of the North Island, between the tribes of the north and south. The options — of skirting the river and trying to make passage by hacking through the wilderness, or rampaging through other jealously guarded tribal territories, or taking to the sea with waka — were scorned by strategists.

Twice Ngapuhi swept through the region from the north; we turned them back. In 1819, the expedition of musket-armed tribes led by Te Rauparaha, Tuwhare, Patuone and Nene made an incursion as far as the junction of the Retaruke, just before Tawata kainga. All the way, sentries shouted, 'Kia hiwa ra! Kia hiwa ra!' and warned each kainga about their coming. The invaders were met with resistance — flotillas of waka all the way — and when their leader Tuwhare was mortally wounded, they decided to retire. When the Amiowhenua northern war expedition followed, in 1821–22, the cries of our clifftop sentries rang out again over the mighty river. The expedition was fought off at Mangawere by war canoes captained by the great river chief Te Anaua Hori Kingi, and by a hail of rocks and tree-trunks dropped from our river fortress.

In the early 1820s the Ngati Raukawa people also invaded the upper Whanganui River during their migration from Maungatatari. And Ngati Toa, under Te Rauparaha's formidable leadership, were always a threat. In a daring move, Te Peehi Turoa joined with Te Anaua Hori Kingi and Te Rangi Paetahi to forestall any further attacks by leaving the Whanganui River and making a lightning raid on the Ngati Toa fortress island of Kapiti. The purpose? To kill the formidable chief. When that failed, Te Rauparaha retaliated, laying siege to Te Anaua Hori Kingi's pa at Putiki; we escaped upriver to te koura puta roa, the crayfish's lair, and he could not winkle us out.

The only way to repulse our attackers was to stand together. But the river was ruled by different roistering tribal groups, in over eighty kainga, and that did not make for easy communication between us all.

However, although we were different, our descent lines joined us all to the *Aotea* waka that had brought our ancestors to Aotearoa centuries earlier — and what the ancestors had cleverly done was to divide the river into three sections. The first section was the upper length from its source, through Taumarunui to Retaruke; to support the tribal groups there, the ancestors appointed a supernatural guardian taniwha called Waitahuparae, a river shapeshifter. The tribal groups of the middle section of the river from Retaruke to Ranana were placed under the taniwha-ship of Kouraputaroa. The groups of the lower section were guarded by the taniwha known as Tutaeporoporo. These wondrous taniwha — and they were eventually joined by many others — lived in mysterious dark caves and gashes in sheer rocky cliffs; they were the ultimate protectors of the river, ready to join as one in the defence of our territory against any outsider.

The ancestors further devised a way of governing the river, enshrined in the saying, 'Te taura whiri a Hinengakau; the tribes of the river may have their differences but if you plait them together, the rope will pull together.'

My father Korakotai was one of the plaiters. His role as emissary was to represent the tribal groups of the middle section of the Matua Tupuna at meetings of river chiefs. The main emblem of his office was the carved tokotoko; he needed only to raise it in the air, and all would know, 'Ah, he represents the Ngati Hau.'

He liked to associate our meeting house, Te Whare Whiri-taunoka, the house of plaited rope, with his role. 'All I do,' he would say, 'is take the fibre of the rope from our marae and plait and weave it in with the fibres of the kainga along the river, whiria, whiria, whiria.'

———————

It was during one of my father's visits as emissary to a meeting in the upper reaches of the river at Te Ure O Tamatea that I was born.

My mother, Hinekorako, was accompanying him on this occasion, but when she felt the pangs of childbirth, she told my father that they must leave.

'Why not stay and let your child be born here?' one of the chiefs, Te Mamaku, who was attending from Tuhua pa, teased my father.

'You would lay claim to the child, Topine,' he retorted, using the chief's first name, 'and if the child is a boy I would much rather that he was born among the river rats of Patiarero.' My father spoke saltily, making witty reference to Ngati Hau's swashbuckling qualities as opportunistic fighters.

With swiftness, he took Hinekorako downriver on a slim racing canoe known as a kopapa. The night sky was studded with the sparkling eyes of heaven, and it made of the river a waterway of stars.

'However,' my father liked to tell me, 'when we reached Te Wahi Pari, the place of the cliffs, your mother and I heard this great roar coming down the canyon behind us.' It was winter, and the kowhai flood tide was upon them. When the kowhai were in bloom, that was a sign that the snows were melting on the Kahui Maunga, sending huge flows of water into the river.

Upon hearing the roar of the rising current my father began shouting commands to my mother: 'Kia uta! Go towards the shore!' or 'Ki waho! Now go outwards!'

Somehow, they managed to keep the canoe stable as they were swept down the staircase of pools and precipitous rapids until, with a cry, Hinekorako gave birth to me on the crest of that huge flood.

'I didn't know which was worse,' my father would jest, 'the tide trying to overturn the waka or your mother making the boat rock! But I managed to paddle it into calmer waters. Meanwhile, your mother severed your birth-cord with her teeth and, because you were still covered with the birth sac, tried to uncover your mouth so that you could breathe. That's when a deep following swell arose and tipped us over.'

The current rolled me away and sent me tumbling along under the moonlit water, surrounded by my mother's birthing skin.

It was at this time, as my afterbirth trailed like gossamer wings around me, that the taniwha appeared. Noting the disturbance in their waters, they came undulating through the currents to preside over my future.

The first breath I took was water. *Kia mate? Shall we let him die?*

The second breath was when the river decided I should live. *Kia ora. Let it be life.*

Ashen-faced, my parents found me wailing and washed up in an eddy of broken branches and timbers. When they splashed closer, the blind eels that were licking the veil of foetal mucus from my face scattered away in a spray of water.

My father swears that he saw our guardian shapeshifters blessing me, *Haere mai, e tama, ki te Ao o Tane; welcome, child, to the World of Tane, God of the Maori*, before, in a shivering of silver across the river, they disappeared.

At least that's the story of my birth as told me by Korakotai and, let's face it, he liked to weave fanciful stories.

8

Thus was I, in 1821, a brat born of the Matua Tupuna, no different from any other child whelped out of Patiarero except in one respect: when I was one year old and took my first steps on land, I was seen to be very unsteady on my feet; they were so big that I was always tripping over them. I was still awkward at four, and other children laughed and taunted me as I stumbled my way along with them.

Put me in the river, however, and all the awkwardness disappeared. For some reason I took to water as others took to land, diving and swimming with a swiftness and sleekness that allowed the surface to maintain its calm perfection.

'E tama!' the people said. 'You are not a man. You are a taniwha, a merman.'

My father liked to say that this was a gift given to me by the Ancestor River. 'In the water you move with extreme grace. But out of the water, aue, you are a stumblebum.'

Stumblebum or no, when I was seven Korakotai decided to take me with him whenever he was called to service as emissary of the iwi. As the youngest child, I was freer than my older siblings, Marama, Rangi and Te Pae, who were already involved in tribal and family duties such as fishing, gathering food, and protecting Patiarero. But that wasn't the main reason for my father's decision. Given the manner of my birth, which he never stopped marvelling about, I suspect he divined that the Ancestor River had marked me out in some way for leadership.

I became his constant companion as he travelled from one kainga to another, plaiting Ngati Hau into the fabric of the rope. He gave me his tokotoko to hold up whenever we were approaching a new landing place, and in time I too became known to all the iwi of the river.

'Tena ra koe, e Korakotai! Is that your son with you?'

And because we spent so much time together, it was only natural that our affection for each other ran deep, true and strong. I cannot convey to you the pride that burst around me whenever he would reply, 'Yes, it is me and the boy.'

————

The river was glossy as polished greenstone, with bordering treeferns that towered forty feet high like guardian sentinels across the sky; travelling it with Korakotai was my greatest joy. To see the tribes on the river filled my heart with pride and gladness.

Each village had its own fleet of waka taua, war canoes, ready at the instant to be paddled out to confront any interloper. But there were also those days when danger did not threaten, and hundreds of fishermen were about; some would be setting eel weirs, others netting the shoals of migrating whitebait that stippled the water like foam. Villagers on shore would wave to us as they worked on their kumara cultivations, and from the distance would come the echoing greeting of birdcatchers as they snared the succulent Maori pigeon to bring back to the kainga: 'E te rangatira me te tama, tena korua!'

I always looked forward to reaching our destination — some palisaded fortress along the river — and listening as my father spoke with the great chiefs who guarded the Matua Tupuna.

One such chief was Hemi Topine Te Mamaku of Ngati Haua i te Rangi. His kainga was called Tuhua, and it occupied a highly strategic position, the importance of which was enshrined in the proverb, 'Unuunu te puru o Tuhua, maringiringi te wai o puta. If you withdraw the plug of Tuhua you will be overwhelmed by the flooding hordes of the north.' All the tribes of the river respected Tuhua because so much defensive fighting had taken place there.

From the very beginning, Te Mamaku took a shine to me. 'Because the father, Korakotai, is my friend,' he once said, 'the son will be also.' He had shining eyes in a dark complexion. Tattoos scrolled across his face and left arm.

Te Mamaku admired my eagerness to be involved in the korero of chiefs, even when my father was wont to reprimand me for speaking out of place. 'No, don't do that,' he would tell Korakotai. 'How will the boy develop his own opinions and his independence?' Te Mamaku soon became as important an educator as my father was. One day, he detained Korakotai just before we were to leave Tuhua. 'I well remember the evening when we chiefs were all at Te Ure o Tamatea on the night when Hinekorako had her birth pangs. I tried to persuade you to have the boy here among the upper river tribes! You were lucky you didn't because, otherwise, I would have claimed him.'

Of particular interest to me was the korero Te Mamaku had with my father about the new white trespassers to Aotearoa, whom we called the Pakeha.

Korakotai had had some dealings with them when, as a youth, he had gone south visiting our tribal allies of the Ngati Rangatahi. I knew that they had been coming to our southern islands for some time, as explorers, whalers and traders. They had even dared to claim the land for their own sovereign Queen Victoria, and were governing us as a British colony from New South Wales, Australia. And now, those Pakeha originally confined to the northern reaches of the North Island had begun to penetrate southward.

Indeed, the year after I became my father's travelling companion, I saw my first Pakeha. He was a white trader called Joe Rowe, and we came across him and his four companions while we were paddling upriver. The water was flecked with the silver of rough currents when we noticed a hubbub on shore.

'We'd better see what's happening,' Korakotai said.

When we landed, I saw that Rowe was trying to purchasing moko mokai.

'European collectors pay top prices for high quality preserved heads,' my father said.

Rowe was holding one up as an example and gesturing to his pile of blankets and beads, indicating that they were the barter. His skin was as pale as a fish.

Wonder of wonders, one of the other men with him was as black as he was white!

The warriors were making threatening gestures at Rowe and his friends. My father, who could be merciful, intervened and spoke to him in Maori. 'What is a Pakeha doing here? No white man has ever dared to trespass upon the Matua Tupuna. You are lucky you got this far. Go back.'

Rowe gave a barking laugh. 'I know how to handle the Maori,' he answered. His tongue was unsweet and his pronunciation of Maori loud, rough and abusive.

My father was offended by Rowe's remark. He spoke to the assembled warriors. 'This is a stupid man, and his companions are foolish also and not worthy of our attention. Beyond the next bend is their destiny. Let them go to meet it.'

The last we saw of the group, they were headed upriver. Not long afterwards we heard that another tribe had cut off Rowe's head and preserved it for his transgression, killed three others, and kept one prisoner.

'You seek moko mokai? Let it be your own.'

'The river is eternal,' Te Mamaku said to my father when they subsequently met and talked about Rowe's trespass. His words were fiercely protective. He was one of the river's great guardians.

'But times are changing,' my father replied. He knew other Pakeha would soon follow.

One was unshakeably loyal to the Ancestor River, wishing to maintain its purity; the other was aware that even a river could be affected by other torrents flowing into it.

———

So I grew up in a world where the age-old patterns of life were shifting.

By the time I was fifteen, I was no longer taunted for my stumbling ways. Having spent so much time in the company of my father and other chiefs, I had also assumed an air of authority. And, while modesty forbids me from talking too much about my appearance — after all, a man should not look into a mirror, as does a woman, to seek pleasure in his reflection — I was told by many a young girl that I was attractive to look upon. I was already the height I would attain as an adult — at least six inches taller than most of the other men of the river, including Korakotai himself. This reinforced the impression of command.

'Ah,' Te Mamaku would laugh, 'but you also present a bigger target for enemy muskets.'

My contemporaries, who accepted that I was a leader among them but did not want me to get too whakahihi, liked to cut me down to their level by saying, 'You may be tall but your ure tangata is no bigger than ours.'

Well, anybody's ure tangata would be small if he spent as much time in the water as I did! My friends would have been somewhat shattered, though, to realise that it could treble in size when aroused.

Then there was my physique. Constant swimming and practice at holding my breath while underwater had sculpted me in a different way from the other young men. My broad shoulders tapered to taut stomach muscles, slim waist, thick thighs, and knotted calves — and those big feet which were made for propelling me through the river.

Not that I liked the villagers to know about my love of the water. In fact, I tried to conceal it by swimming only at night. I would flip backwards into the river, 'Yahoo!' and strike out for midstream. The currents were often treacherous, but I liked to pitch myself against them, diving deep, responding to their buffeting with elation, keeping pace with the ika and tuna that shoaled around me.

I swam with the Matua Tupuna, not against it.

One early morning, however, I returned too late from my swim, and came upon Korakotai bathing with some of the old chiefs in a small eddy. The river was misty, and the group took fright as they heard me splashing ashore and saw me covered in mud. My father was the only one to recognise me. 'You look like you've been bathing in shit,' he said.

The old chiefs had a different reaction, stepping back and asking, 'He taniwha koe? Are you a merman?' Old chiefs being what they are, and my father being such a teller of tall stories — all involving, now, my swimming prowess — I was soon the subject of a wager among them as to whether I could beat a one-paddler waka across the river to Pukehika settlement, on the riverflat a little downstream and alongside our sacred mountain.

I jested, 'A one-paddler waka? You'd better put two men in it to make the competition fair.'

The day arrived, and both sides of the river were lined with spectators. People had already taken bets on who would win — and the majority were against me. But paddlers take some time getting into their canoe and, with a running dive, I was a quarter of the way across from the Patiarero side before they had even left the shore. By the time the waka reached Pukehika I was already waiting with the jeering crowd, ready to greet them with a hail of well-aimed mud.

Not that my victory met with unanimous approval. My own father had bet against me and was cross that I had won. And when I came up the riverbank with the paddlers, a young girl with sparkling mischievous eyes suddenly shouted, 'Hey! You! Son of Korakotai! The one with feet as big as paddles! Why should you be oh so clean?' Next minute, splat! came her well-aimed missile, followed by a merry bout of laughter.

Insouciant, the girl turned her back and joined her female friends — and so was unprepared for my retaliation. Shocked, and shivering with anger, she flicked the mud with distate off her shoulders and neck. She was lithe and slender and, need I say it, her whole demeanour was not at all submissive. Who was she? I knew most of the girls of Pukehika by sight, and this girl was unfamiliar to me.

With a scream of rage she ran at me. Propelled by the impetus of her onslaught, we both fell into the river.

'Get him, Te Rai!' her friends laughed as we tussled with each other. She soon got the better of me — well, I let her think she did, and pretended to be winded when she hit me in the stomach. Satisfied, she bent over me.

Ka patupatu taku manawa! My heart started to beat strongly. The Earth Mother, Papatuanuku, had graced her with skin the colour of the wattle of the tui. Her hair was curly, black and lustrous as that of the huia. Her lips were red like the pohutukawa. Nor were her eyes as other Maori eyes, either, but hazel and flecked as with shards of the precious greenstone we call pounamu.

And she? Her eyes widened, her nostrils flared. She looked at me, troubled. 'It's not that simple,' she said as stood up. Then she ran back to her friends.

———

Of course the old chiefs wanted to recoup their losses, so they insisted there be another race. This time, they decided I should compete against a four-man waka.

The odds were against me but, being a bit arrogant, I accepted the challenge. Korakotai was impressed with my confidence. 'This time I will bet on you to win,' he said.

I had an ulterior motive for this race: I wanted to see the girl again. Thinking about her brought a rush of desire to my loins; my ardour for her made me toss and turn in my sleep. I knew that her name was Te Rai, and I discovered that she was from Taranaki. I made sure that she knew of my interest but, puzzlingly, I had no word it would be reciprocated.

I wasn't accustomed to rejection.

For a second time the banks on both sides were lined with onlookers from Patiarero and Pukehika. The bets were equally distributed. I had my reputation at stake and, of course, I wanted to impress Te Rai. When the race began, I dived full of confidence and bravado from the riverbank and, to great cheers — whether for me or the waka, I don't know — found myself abreast of it when I surfaced.

The race was on. I thought I would win it except that a drifting log suddenly surfaced in front of me and, by the time I had cleared it, the canoe was in the lead. This time the waka won and received the applause. As for me, only mud. Crestfallen, I submitted to the missiles.

'You may be tall and blessed by taniwha, but you are only a man after all,' the old chiefs shouted.

As for my father, he clipped me over the ears. 'The only time I place a bet on you,' he scolded, 'and you lose.'

I saw Te Rai stepping out from the crowd and coming towards me. She had a cloth of soft muka in her hands and, laughing, dipped it in the river and began to clean the mud off me. 'I am glad you lost,' she said. 'You would have been insufferable otherwise!' Then her lips trembled. 'It would serve no good purpose for you to pursue me,' she continued. 'I am already betrothed.' Her words were not without kindness, or sadness.

My heart sank but I pressed my suit regardless. 'Tell me that you do not feel the same way as I do about you.' I took a step towards her.

She stepped back. 'I must keep my promise,' she said.

The river is eternal, but times are changing.

I resumed my duties with Korakotai. As we journeyed the river, I became aware that the great korero of the chiefs was constantly about the Pakeha now. The new white transgressor was not only explorer, whaler and trader; having found Aotearoa to his liking, he was also arriving as settler.

Te Mamaku was incensed by their coming. 'First the Pakeha claims Aotearoa as his, and calls it New Zealand, and now he establishes himself as a new white tribe? We of the Whanganui River have never given them our consent to do so.'

'But others have,' Korakotai observed. 'It is because of them that the Pakeha have gained a foothold in the north and east, as well as to the south. The Chiefs of the Northern Tribes have sold land to the white man.'

'Do they retain their mana? Are they still higher than the Pakeha intruder? I do not trust the new invader without tattoo.'

'Other tribes benefit from their Pakeha acquisitions,' my father answered. 'Te Rauparaha, for instance, gained advantage from the musket, and continues to trade with them. If we don't take the same path, we might be left behind. Perhaps being in our mountain wilderness works not only for us, but also against us.'

'We are the greater people,' Te Mamaku said. 'As sun dazzling on the river sometimes blinds the paddlers of a waka, so some tribes are dazzled by what the Pakeha offers.' He paused, and then, 'What other tribes do is their business,' he said. 'Our concern must always be the Matua Tupuna. If the Pakeha come to us, will they not be like any other tribe that has tried to take our river? I don't care how powerful they are, if they do this, we must fight. We are renowned for our ferocity. Should they wish to challenge it, so be it.'

I sat listening to my father and Te Mamaku put both sides of the argument of what to do with the new Pakeha tribe. While they talked, all the while, the Pakeha was encroaching closer and closer upon our river world.

Then I heard that Te Rauparaha, the Ngati Toa chief, had invited the Anglican missioner Octavius Hadfield, as the first missioner in our part of Aotearoa, to settle among his iwi on the Kapiti Coast. Not only that, but the wily leader had even sent his own son to the Bay of Islands, where Hadfield had been living, to fetch him!

No wonder my interest was piqued. You had to be careful of Te Rauparaha. Ae, he had got the musket from the Pakeha and, yes, he now traded with them. What new advantage could come from acquiring a 'talking bird', as the missioners were known as? It was certainly not Christianity, as that was only of incidental interest to Te Rauparaha.

I discussed the question with my father. 'Te Rauparaha may still have ambitions to conquer the Whanganui River,' I said. 'Let me journey to the Kapiti Coast to find out what the new taonga, the next Pakeha treasure, is that he wishes to acquire for his benefit.'

It did not take long for my father to agree. 'Find out what you can. Who knows? We may gain some of Te Rauparaha's treasure for ourselves.'

And so I travelled by canoe down the river to where it spilled into the sea; my only weapon was a spear.

You must remember that I had lived all my life on the Matua Tupuna and that this was the first time I had set foot outside it. Was I afraid? No! My questing heart sought only to venture further into the world beyond.

At the river mouth I saw a caravan of Pakeha traders preparing to set off southward along the beach. Anchored offshore was a Pakeha sailing ship; I thought it was a large white-winged seabird sitting beyond the breakers! Men were struggling in the surf to bring cargo to shore. One of the traders came galloping towards me: I thought he was a taniwha — he looked like a monster with two heads!

I picked up my spear and threw it at him.

Laughing, the trader dodged the spear and reined up beside me. 'You haven't seen a horse before, eh?' he asked in our language. He dismounted and the horse nuzzled me and spoke to me in a strange, sighing, whinnying way.

Ka mau te wehi! Surely the world was filled with marvels!

'You look like a strong lad,' the trader continued. 'The tide is running against us, and I need more men. I will pay you. What do you say?'

I was unsure at first, then I nodded. For the next four hours, I battled the surf with the other men and, once the cargo was onshore, helped them lash their crates on packhorses.

'Thank you,' the Pakeha trader said. 'Here are some coins for your work. You can use them to trade with. So where are you off to?'

'Ki a Otaki,' I answered. 'Ki te kite au i te Pakeha Hadfield.'

He nodded. 'Ah, ka pai. Why not join us? We are going that way.'

Trust was not something which was given easily but, after all, there was safety in numbers, so I nodded. Very soon, I was accompanying the caravan as it skirted the edge of the grey and turbulent sea.

When we arrived on the Kapiti Coast, I parted ways with them.

'You will find Hadfield at the church,' the trader said.

The land was dotted with Pakeha whare the likes of which I had never seen. I couldn't believe the number of them. I wandered among them and, as night was falling, I finally came to a large white house with a cross, rather than a koru, on its gable. The moon was full and the bush was filled with the noise of calling owls. I was uncertain whether I should wait in the darkness for morning, but there were candles lit inside the house. I looked in through the door and saw a thin Pakeha man with a straggly beard instructing a group of Maori students, as if in a whare wananga.

The Pakeha saw me — he must have been expecting somebody else, but he came to me and said, 'Haere mai ki roto. Come inside. We've only just started.' He thrust a book into my hands. 'This will be yours,' he smiled. 'But first I will teach you how to read it.'

It was the New Testament in Maori and English.

And I knew why it was that Te Rauparaha welcomed the Pakeha.

Knowledge.

———

Six months later, when I returned to Patiarero, I could speak, if haltingly, in English. More important, I could read in English and Maori.

'Took you long enough,' my father scolded. He was amused when I shook hands with him in the new Pakeha way I had learned, called the hariru.

'We have to get a Pakeha missioner for ourselves,' I told him. 'There's a boat arriving soon at the Kapiti Coast from Waitangi, bringing supplies, including holy books, to Reverend Hadfield. I have coins for our passage. If we hurry, we can catch it and return with it to Waitangi.'

'Then let us go and snare such a talking bird,' he said.

'One more thing.' I bowed my head. 'I have a confession to make.'

'What is that?' my father asked.

'I have been baptised a Christian. I have a new name now, Hohepa, after Joseph, the father of the Pakeha Saviour.'

9

In January 1840, Korakotai and I left the Matua Tupuna.

We journeyed to the Kapiti Coast, where we boarded an American whaling schooner, the *Belfagor*, southbound to the new settlement of Britannia and then, rounding Raukawa, up the east coast to the Bay of Islands.

The first leg of the voyage was a revelation. Yes, my father had met Pakeha before, but what astounded him now was that they were everywhere. 'This is not the Maori world of my ancestors,' he whispered in awe. 'Where have all the Pakeha come from that they can change it like this?'

On the horizon, Pakeha sailing ships, with canvas belling large, came speedily towards land. Shoreward, the sky was stained with the smoke of whaling stations, and of bush being cleared. We saw signs of the transactions that were taking place between Maori and Pakeha: at Kapiti Island, also known as Entry Island for its position commanding the entrance to Raukawa — which the Pakeha had renamed Cook Strait — our schooner was required to pay tribute to the wily Te Rauparaha for the privilege of passage.

But only when we rounded Raukawa and entered the landlocked harbour, Te Whanganui a Tara, did my father fully realise the extent of the Pakeha migration to New Zealand. There, on Pito-one beach, a great crowd of English men, women and children had landed with ploughs, trunks and belongings. Armed with a deed of purchase which Colonel William Wakefield, the brother of Edward Gibbon Wakefield, had made with Maori chiefs of the region, they were laying their claim.

'Te Mamaku was right,' my father said. 'The Pakeha *is* a new white tribe. Now that I see him, my heart trembles for the Maori people.' He was clearly bothered by the clear physical presence of the white man.

'Britannia is the first location bought by the New Zealand Company for settlers from Britain,' I told him. 'Reverend Hadfield, who gave me the information, says the company offered almost one hundred thousand acres for sale at one British pound an acre.'

'Who sold it to them?' my father asked.

'Wharepouri, Te Puni too, and fourteen other Maori chiefs, mainly from Te Atiawa. Te Wharepouri held a celebration after the signing; his men performed a peruperu in honour of the event. The *Tory*, the ship which brought William Wakefield, fired its guns in victory as the New Zealand Company hoisted their flag on the beach.'

'Did nobody speak in opposition?'

'Te Puwhakaawe said to his brother chiefs, "What will you say when many, many white men come here and drive you all away into the mountains? How will you feel when you go to the white man's house or ship to beg for shelter and hospitality and he tells you, with his eyes turned up to Heaven, and the name of his God in his mouth, to be gone, for your land is paid for?"'

'So the Pakeha are here to stay?'

'Yes—' I hesitated, and my father noted my silence. 'There's something you haven't told me,' he said.

'The settlers also have their sights set on the Heretaunga,' I answered.

'It does not belong to them,' Korakotai said. 'That is the land belonging to our kin, Ngati Rangatahi, and also Ngati Tama.'

'According to Te Rauparaha and other chiefs, *they* are the landowners and they have signed over their interests.' You could understand why the New Zealand Company was interested in Heretaunga. Situated a mile north of Pito-one, it stretched for a considerable distance inland. As such, it was ideal for the future expansion of the settlement.

'Were Kaparatehau, chief of Ngati Rangatahi, and Te Kaeaea, chief of Ngati Tama, consulted?'

'No,' I answered.

———

So the Pakeha are here to stay?

Following our very quick call at Britannia, the *Belfagor* departed, sailing north up the eastern coast. I made myself useful with the Pakeha crew and, in the process, practised my English on them; I was improving all the time.

One evening I stayed topside to watch the millions of stars scattered above me like the sparkling eyes of heaven. Every now and then a comet or shooting star would thread its way among those strands of stars. Strange lights sometimes flooded the sky from the south.

'What are the ahua?' I asked a seaman.

'They are called aurora,' he answered, 'and they ascend from the great ice palaces of Antarctica.'

Korakotai joined me. I knew that he was troubled by what he had seen at Te Whanganui a Tara, and what he had heard about the settlers' intentions to move into nearby Heretaunga. And, too, he was bewildered that I had become a Christian. I was reading the New Testament in English every day and had invited him to read passages with me from the Maori translation. 'Will our people be able to retain power in Aotearoa?' he asked. 'Or will it go to the Pakeha and his new God? After all,' he continued, 'if my own son can be changed, so can the rest of the Maori world.'

I thought about that for a moment. 'E pa,' I answered, 'it is not a matter of choosing one or the other. Both can exist in the same new world.'

'But which world will need to change the most?' he pondered.

———

We began our second leg northward. The coast was draped with violent wind and heavy rain. Impenetrable forests and high fern spread from the beaches upward to majestic mountain peaks wreathed with mist. Every now and then was a spectacular waterfall pouring down a ravine, as if the land was still rising from the sea.

Sometimes we made out a fortified pa on a rocky outcrop or beach. The captain would order the small cannon to be fired so that the kainga would know who we were; occasionally, a war canoe would come out to challenge or greet us.

More schooners and ships appeared, plying the eastern coast, and again Korakotai was amazed by what he saw. Landing briefly at Turanga where another Pakeha settlement was being established, he wondered at their boldness. 'Where are their palisades?' he asked. 'Where are their warriors to challenge us on our arrival? Truly they must believe in their own invincibility.'

We continued northward, the *Belfagor* leaping around the East Cape towards the Bay of Islands. I loved to watch the sun come up in the mornings. Dolphins and whales surfaced from the glorious crimson water, while from the land came the stunning, clattering, trilling sound of birdsong. But in the twilight, when the dark fell as swiftly as a tui's wing, I became aware of the profound tension of Aotearoa.

Something psychic, something alien had already come this way and slipped into the land while we had not been looking.

When we arrived at the Bay of Islands, Korakotai and I had clear example of what happened when two worlds collided.

The *Belfagor* anchored at Kororareka. The town had the largest concentration of Pakeha anywhere: sealers, whalers, American traders, and convicts escaped from the penal colonies of New South Wales, Van Diemen's Land and Norfolk Island. As at Turanga, there were no sentries, no palisades and no warriors to defend the kainga. And in Kororareka was an example of what happened to Aotearoa once the Pakeha got hold of it: an ungodly collection of ramshackle drinking places frequented by sailors, whores and drunkards.

My father and I disembarked, and immediately I was the centre of attention. I was taller than most Pakeha, or at least could stand eye to eye with them. My youthful beauty was a liability and not a blessing. I was angered at the lewd invitations from women — and men — to share some obscene pleasure with them. I don't think they realised that I understood every lascivious word; I restrained myself from hitting out at them.

Instead I turned my mind to the matter at hand. I was excited to realise that many 'talking birds' had made their headquarters at Kororareka. The Church Missionary Society's Henry Williams and his wife Marianne, Richard Taylor, William Colenso and other Anglicans and Wesleyans had set up at Marsden Cove. Their main rivals were the Roman Catholic Mission, led by the French vicar apostolic, Bishop Pompallier — they were like the colourful red kaka to the somewhat austere Anglican tui with his black coat and white collar.

'Te Rauparaha has already snared an Anglican missioner,' Korakotai said. 'We can do better than that. Let us try to catch a kaka.'

The hour was late, however, so we decided to leave that task for the morrow. We made our way to the local pa where we waited outside the gateway to be welcomed. The local people were busy but soon noticed us.

'Tihei mauri ora!' I raised my father's tokotoko.

The great chief Hone Heke greeted us. 'Haramai nga rangatira,' he said. He was well built and as tall as I was. 'We are not often host to an emissary from the Whanganui River,' he said to my father. 'Welcome among us.'

The next day, 29 January 1840, our search for a talking bird was delayed again as something much larger claimed our attention. It announced itself with the majestic sailing of the British man-o'-war, HMS *Herald*, into the Bay. Neither Korakotai nor I had ever witnessed a more impressive demonstration of

Pakeha power. We asked Hone Heke what was happening.

'The Pakeha have been represented so far in Aotearoa only by a British Resident, Mr Busby, but Captain William Hobson comes to take over from him.'

An eleven-gun salute roared across the Bay, announcing that Hobson had landed.

'His ariki,' Hone Heke continued, 'Queen Wikitoria, wishes him to talk with the chiefs of the United Tribes of the North. The business of the meeting is to sign a treaty acknowledging our prior rights and our lands.'

'The timing cannot be more fortuitous,' Korakotai answered. 'May we join you to see how the negotiations play themselves out? Perhaps they will offer lessons that we can take back to our own iwi.'

My father's interest mounted when, the next day, two proclamations were posted by Captain Hobson in the township. 'What do they say?' he asked me.

'The first confirms that Hobson is now Governor of New Zealand,' I paraphrased. 'But listen to the second one!' Haltingly, but carefully, I read it. 'Victoria does not deem it expedient to recognise as valid any titles to land in New Zealand which are not derived from nor confirmed by her. All purchases of land in any part of New Zealand made from today are null and void and will not be confirmed by her also.'

Korakotai's eyes widened. 'The proclamation would cover Whanganui and the Heretaunga too?'

'It would seem so,' I answered.

'Ka pai!' my father exclaimed. 'Wikitoria acts like a true chief in trying to control her iwi.'

We walked on through the streets of Kororareka. Rounding a corner, we came across a large crowd. In the middle was a group of Anglican missioners. The crowd comprised the same riff-raff I had taken an intense dislike to the day before, and they were objecting to the governor's presence, the proclamations — and the missioners' roles in supporting the Treaty.

'Tell Governor Hobson to fuck off home,' one shouted, 'and stuff your treaty with the Maoris up your arse! They are perfectly willing to negotiate directly for the sale of their land.'

'Why should we bow down to British law and order?' another yelled. 'We're getting along well enough without it!'

One of the convicts added, 'New Zealand is the last free country of the south. Damned if I want the long arm of the law to haul me back to Van Diemen's Land.'

Tempers were spilling over. 'We had better intervene,' I said to Korakotai.

Immediately we pushed our ways through the crowd. Some of them began to harangue us instead. 'Bloody Maoris!' one burly man said. 'What do you need with all the land anyway, eh? You're all a pack of uncivilised savages!'

I charged him angrily, pushing him to the ground. I was carrying the tokotoko and put its point at his throat. 'One more word from you,' I said in English, 'and I will *push*.'

He gave a cry of fear. I let him up. The crowd backed away. I rushed at them and, cowards that they were, they dispersed.

'I thank you both for coming to our rescue,' one of the missioners said. 'I am Henry Williams.'

'My father is Korakotai,' I answered, 'and I am his son Hohepa. I am a Christian baptised by the Reverend Hadfield. We are from the Whanganui River.'

Reverend Williams' eyes lit up. 'Are you here to witness the Treaty signing?' he asked. 'It will be the great Maori Magna Carta for it will extend the British rule of law, civilisation — and God — to the United Tribes of the North.'

He shook our hands.

'Let us hope that it can be also be taken southward to your own people of the Whanganui River.'

———

The proclamations gave notice to the Pakeha. The Treaty was for the Maori.

On 5 February, therefore, from a very early hour, the chiefs started to arrive by their decorated waka taua into the Bay of Islands to meet with the new governor.

'Me haere tatou hoki,' Hone Heke said. 'Let us also go to the signing.'

My father and I joined him in the swift passage across the sparkling water to Waitangi. 'Toia te waka!' the paddlers chanted. 'Ki te urunga! To the landing place! Ki te korero mo Aotearoa! To talk about the destiny of Aotearoa!'

We threaded through the number of sailing ships that were anchored in the bay — the HMS *Herald*, whalers and other vessels of all nations, all come to witness the Treaty negotiations. In a state of heightened expectation we landed and made our way to a white house, the home of Mr Busby, atop the hillock looking over the sea. A large marquee had been erected close to the house; above the tent the English banner streamed in the capricious wind.

Korakotai and I were welcomed by other chiefs of the north — Rewa, Tamati Waka Nene, Kawiti and Patuone among them. Some had adorned their glossy hair with crimson cloth and red feathers; others were ornamented with the long white feathers of the kotuku. A few were clothed in dogskin cloaks made of long alternating strips of black and white doghair; a number wore splendid-looking woollen cloaks of foreign manufacture in crimson, blue, brown and plaid — indeed every shade of striking colour, such as I had never before seen. There were chiefs dressed in plain European dress, and rangatira in flax kilts and fighting capes. Hundreds of other Maori sat in tribal groups, smoking and talking; many carried guns.

The spectacle mounted. War waka continued to glide to shore from every direction on the sparkling water of the Bay. More settlers' ships jostled for a place to anchor. The cadences of the canoe songs became competitive.

'Ki te takotoranga i takoto ai te waka! Speed onwards to the landing place, speed on!'

Meanwhile, on the hillock, a sergeant and four troopers of the New South Wales mounted police paraded in their scarlet uniforms. Pakeha settlers applauded and chatted to each other.

Governor Hobson arrived at around 9 a.m. in full uniform. He was accompanied by Captain Nias, who had brought him from Sydney on HMS *Herald*, and followed by officers of the man-o'-war and the suite of the governor. There arose a huge buzz of expectancy, like the sound of a thousand excited cicadas, as Mr Hobson greeted the Reverend Williams and Mr Busby and began to look over the translation they and others had made of the Treaty.

The buzz increased with the arrival of Bishop Pompallier, in canonicals, his massive gold chain and crucifix glistening on his dark purple habit. Closely followed by one of his holy attendants, he brushed past the guard at the door of Mr Busby's house and walked without the least hesitation into the room where Governor Hobson was privately engaged with the Anglican missionaries. His manner was so striking that my father could not help but mutter, 'Ko ia ano te tino rangatira! He, indeed, is the chief gentleman!'

The governor and the official party moved in procession from the house to the marquee. Again Bishop Pompallier and his holy attendant showed their mana by briskly following close on Captain Hobson's heels, shutting out the Anglican missionaries unless they stepped out of line with the procession — which the Reverend Taylor did, exclaiming, 'I'll never follow Rome!'

Then, 'Haere mai koutou nga rangatira,' Reverend Williams called.

Chanting, gesticulating, proud and in stirring processional, the vanguard of the chiefs went into the marquee; at Hone Heke's insistence, my father and I joined them. The sunlight streamed down from the top of the tent, lighting us as if with some holy benediction as we entered. As we took our places, the Pakeha residents, settlers, traders, visitors and sailors pressed in around us.

'Let us begin,' Reverend Williams said, giving way to Governor Hobson.

'Ae,' I whispered under my breath. 'Timata.'

The governor began his address. 'Her Majesty Victoria, Queen of Great Britain and Ireland, wishing to do good to the chiefs and peoples of New Zealand, and for the welfare of her subjects living among you, has sent me to this place as governor. But as the law of England gives no civil powers to Her Majesty out of her dominions, her efforts to do you good will be futile unless you consent. Her Majesty has commanded me to explain these matters to you, that you may understand them.'

He turned to the Pakeha present and delivered what seemed to be a reprimand. 'The people of Great Britain are, thank God!, free; and as long as they do not transgress the laws they can go where they please, and their sovereign has not power to restrain them. The Maori have sold them lands here and encouraged them to come here. Her Majesty, always ready to protect her subjects, is also always ready to restrain them.'

Some of the Pakeha were unhappy at his words and looked disgruntled.

The governor turned back to us. 'Her Majesty the Queen asks you to sign this Treaty, and to give her that power which shall enable her to restrain them.' He began to read to us the English text of the Treaty. Henry Williams translated what he was saying into Maori.

It all sounded like the right solution for Maori. How I wish it had been as simple as that! The problem? The powers that Her Majesty sought, to enable her to go about her business, required the Maori to give up our sovereignty to the British Queen.

———

Te Kemara of Ngapuhi was the first of the northern chiefs to reply, and my father and I received our first testimony to the huge, disturbing, horrifying mess that the Pakeha had brought to the United Tribes of the North.

'I will greet you, kia ora, Governor,' he began diplomatically, 'but I am not pleased towards you. I do not wish for you. I will not consent to your remaining here in this country. If you stay as governor, then perhaps Te Kemara will be judged and condemned.' He continued with more energy now, accompanying his remarks with pukana, quivering hands and stamping feet. 'Yes indeed, and more than that — even hanged by the neck. No! No! No! I shall never say yes to your staying. Were we all to be equal, then perhaps Te Kemara would say yes. But for the governor to be up, high up, and Te Kemara down low, a worm, small, a crawler — no, no—'

He made a remark that was a revelation to me and my father.

'My land is gone, all gone; the inheritances of my ancestors, fathers, relatives, all stolen, gone with the missionaries. They have it all.' He pointed at Reverend Williams and Busby. 'Those men there, they have my land. Oh, Governor, give me back my lands . . . Go back, go back to your country, Governor, we do not want you here in this country.'

Missioners, were they land grabbers along with other Pakeha? And would they return the land once the Treaty was signed?

Rewa followed Te Kemara: 'Let my lands be returned to me which also have been taken by the missionaries. I have no lands now — only a name, only a name! Foreigners come; they know Mr Rewa, but this is all I have left — a name. What do the Maori want of a governor? We are not whites, nor foreigners. This country is ours, but the land has gone. We are the governor — we the chiefs of our fathers' land. Return, Governor, go back.'

After Rewa came Moka: 'Let the governor return to his own country. Let us remain as we were. Let my lands be returned to me.'

———

'Go back. Don't stay. Give our land back.'

My father and I looked at each other, alarmed. Even when Tamati Waka Nene of Ngapuhi spoke up for the Treaty, our concern did not diminish.

'It is too late to tell the Pakeha to go back,' he said. 'Many of his children are also our tamariki. He makes no slaves. The Pakeha will bring plenty of trade and it would be best if Maori and Pakeha could be friends together.'

'Is "It is too late?" a valid argument to use, Father?' I asked Korakotai.

'I fear that it is,' he answered. 'Waka Nene has been baptised Anglican and taken the name Thomas Walker. When that happens, how can you choose for one side or the other?' His glance penetrated me. I knew he was drawing my attention to my own situation.

Te Ruki Kawiti of Ngapuhi, however, was in opposition. 'No. No,' he said to Governor Hobson. 'Go back. What do you want here? We native men do not wish you to stay. We do not want to be tied up and trodden down. We are free!'

In this manner did the korero continue, with the Reverend Williams translating the Maori into English so that Governor Hobson could understand what was being said. Following this, the governor replied in English — and the Reverend Williams translated his words into Maori for the chiefs.

The process was fraught with inaccuracies of interpretation, and nuances of meaning were also lost. But one thing was clear: the division between supporting the Treaty and not supporting it had split the North apart.

Tamati Pukututu stood quickly to urge the governor to stay and govern them.

Tamati Waka Nene pleaded, 'Remain for us a father, a judge, a peacemaker.'

Hone Heke, who was the last in the speaking order, also affirmed that he was in favour of signing the Treaty.

The Treaty hung in the balance. Even by the following day, my impression was that most of the chiefs were against signing! However, instead of asking for a consensus, Mr Busby called each chief forward by name — and they picked up the pen and put their moko to the paper.

Reverend Williams suggested to Governor Hobson that this would be an appropriate moment to offer encouragement.

'He iwi tahi tatau,' the governor said in halting Maori.

Forty-six signatures were harvested. That, apparently, was enough to give legal force to the document.

At the request of the governor, blankets and tobacco were distributed to those who signed.

———

Deeply disturbed by the event, Korakotai and I were unprepared when, the next day, Reverend Williams sought us out.

'Governor Hobson has confirmed,' 'he began, 'that I am indeed to take a copy of the Treaty to Gisborne and further south so that chiefs of all the tribes who were not present at Waitangi may put their moko on the paper. We will be visiting the chiefs of Te Whanganui a Tara — among them Te Rauparaha and Te Rangihaeata — and others including your own of the Whanganui River. Would you consider helping us?'

My father asked him to give us a moment in private together. 'Son,' he began, 'you have been at my right hand all my life. For the first time ever, I have the sense that you know more than I do! I cannot, therefore, answer this question without your advice.'

I was overwhelmed by my father's trust.

'I don't want what has happened to the people up here in the North to happen to us,' he continued. 'Tell me, what is best for the Matua Tupuna and for the people of the river?'

I had been thinking upon this question all night. When the words came, they were as I had thought them into existence during the evening. 'The Pakeha God is a just God but the Pakeha himself can be unjust,' I began. 'In the matter of Maori land, for instance, the sale of it must be stopped. It has been the main concern of the United Tribes of the North; for them, the return of the land, despite the governor's intentions, may be too late. But for our kin of the Heretaunga, for instance, perhaps not.'

My father nodded. 'Ka tika,' he agreed.

'The future settlement of land must also be addressed,' I continued. 'Who knows what lies in the future as the Pakeha approach the Whanganui River? The governor and his Treaty offer us the way to regulate the expansion of the new white tribe, but on our terms.'

'To do so, however,' my father argued, 'what must we give up? What about the mana of the Maori?' It was the same question he had asked on the *Belfagor* when strange lights had flooded the sky. 'Will we be higher or lower than Wikitoria?'

Oh, the gods forgive me, but that was when I made my mistake. The chiefs at Waitangi had signed the Maori version, not the Pakeha version, accepting the benefits of governance but not signing over their sovereignty to the Queen.

'The British Queen will have kawanatanga but we will retain our tino rangatiratanga,' I said.

My father closed his eyes. He was leaning on the tokotoko, gripping it so tightly that the veins of his hands threatened to break free of the skin. Then he relaxed.

'Who would have thought,' he smiled, 'that a young stumblebum of a boy could become a tall man to whom, when the time comes, I will happily pass on the tokotoko of leadership?'

We returned to Reverend Williams. 'We will help you in taking the Treaty to our peoples in the south.'

'Thank you,' he answered.

'Now,' Korakotai said, turning to me, 'we should do what we came for and snare a talking bird for the Matua River. We may need one sooner than we think!'

We went to see Bishop Pompallier. Although his reception suite was crowded, his holy attendants allowed us to see him. 'Ah,' the Bishop greeted us, 'you are the travellers from afar?'

'We represent the Whanganui River,' Korakotai began. 'E te rangatira, lord, send someone to mission and teach among the people of Patiarero.'

Bishop Pompallier was puzzled. He spoke to one of his aides. 'Où est le fleuve de Whanganui? Où se trouve le village de Patiarero?' His eyes widened when he was told how far away the Matua Tupuna was. And none of his aides had heard of Patiarero. He pondered my father's question, stood up and spoke to the aide again. 'Répondez à ce néo-zélandais qu'on arrivera un de ces jours.'

My father thought our suit had been rejected.

The aide reassured him. 'The Bishop wishes me to tell you,' he said, 'that one day someone will come.'

IO

My father and I had come to the North as emissaries of the Whanganui River.

Now we became emissaries in the procession of the Treaty to the tribes of the south. With Reverend Williams, Governor Hobson and other officials we boarded the *Ariel* and sailed via Auckland and Gisborne bound for Britannia. During the journey, my father joined with Reverend Williams and me in our daily prayers. While praying, I often felt as if the schooner were some angelic herald, skimming with its white-winged sails fully unfurled to the wind.

As we approached Te Whanganui a Tara, the afternoon turned grey and dull. Clouds hurtled across the sky before a cold front from the south as we bore past Palliser and closed quickly on the entrance to the harbour. With a deft navigational move the skipper evaded contrary winds and, with the southerly pushing us, we sailed into calm water.

Much to our surprise, once we had landed we discovered that the New Zealand Company had not raised Britannia at all. Finding the land around Pito-one Beach too marshy, they had moved the town of bustling waterfront hotels and shops slightly to the westward.

'The Company thinks that possession is nine tenths of the law,' Reverend Williams muttered.

Immediately the Treaty was put to its first test, Pakeha against Pakeha. Not only that, but Reverend Williams discovered that Colonel Wakefield and a number of others had attempted to pre-empt the discussions at Waitangi by appointing themselves a colonial government! As such, they had persuaded Maori chiefs of Te Whanganui a Tara it was unnecessary for them to sign the Treaty and that they would be their agents.

We accompanied Reverend Williams to confront Colonel Wakefield in the offices of the New Zealand Company. 'This will be interesting,' I said to Korakotai. 'Which Pakeha will rule in Aotearoa?'

Reverend Williams went straight on the offensive. 'How dare you, sir!' he thundered. 'Your actions are a direct provocation of what the Government decreed at Waitangi.'

Wakefield was undeterred. 'Our jurisdiction was in place before such a decree,' he answered. 'Our council and magistrates have been placed on commission by the authority of the chiefs of the Port Nicholson District. Therefore, talk to us, not to them. Sign your Treaty with us.'

We were shown a large map of New Zealand with a coloured portion of twenty million acres representing the Company's property, from the 38th to the 42nd degree parallel of latitude. Korakotai and I exchanged looks and, noting our reaction, Reverend Williams' lip curled in disgust. 'Who was your medium of communication with the chiefs of this *coloured* area?' he asked.

'Our agent, Dicky Barrett,' Colonel Wakefield answered. 'He is well liked by the Maori. Sixteen chiefs signed the deed here in the Port Nicholson region. As for the second deed, Kapiti, the main signatories were Te Rauparaha and Te Rangihaeata; who, with seventy-two other chiefs, also signed for the region from Mokau to Cape Egmont and inland to the upper reaches of the Whanganui River.'

To the upper reaches of the Whanganui River?

Korakotai became dangerously still.

Turning to Reverend Williams, I said, 'This is news to us.'

Reverend Williams nodded. 'Your agent has talked to some chiefs,' he said to Colonel Wakefield in a tone that would brook no argument, 'and not to others. As to whether or not you have jurisdiction, you do not. There will be no independent republic in New Zealand.'

My father and I took heart from the outcome of the meeting. 'Wikitoria has won over Wakefield,' Korakotai said. 'If this is the case in Port Nicholson, it will be the case throughout Aotearoa.'

Not without a fight! For ten days Company officials dissuaded the chiefs of the region from seeing us.

During that time, however, Korakotai and I were able to visit our kinsman, Kaparatehau, chief of Ngati Rangatahi. They were sheltering at Kaiwharawhara Pa with Te Kaeaea and his people of Ngati Tama. Dogs rushed out to meet us when we arrived, and some Maori who had been sitting outside the precinct ran in, as if afraid of us. Puzzled, we followed them.

'Aue, taukiri e,' Korakotai whispered. The pa was overrun with refugees. We could hardly make our way to the meeting house, as people were virtually sleeping at our feet. When we arrived at the doorway, both Kaparatehau and Te Kaeaea greeted us.

The first word that sprang to mind when I met Kaparatehau was patriarch. 'Do you see what has happened?' Kaparatehau asked my father.

The New Zealand Company, well along with the marking out of the settlement according to a plan devised in London, had rolled their map entirely over the Maori living at Te Aro, Kumutoto, Pipitea, Waiwhetu, Pito-one and Ngahauranga. Kaiwharawhara, however, on the outskirts of the growing settlement, had so far escaped the map.

'Where could the displaced iwi go?' Kaparatehau continued. 'Into the sea? They had no option but to come here. It's a big job caring for them but, when they are hungry, we go to the pataka, our storehouse.' He was referring to the Heretaunga, the fertile, rich resource of pigeons, waterfowl, fish, eels and berries that had traditionally been reserved as a place of food supply. Ngati Rangatahi and Ngati Tama did not traditionally live in the Heretaunga: they only went there to tend their kumara, yam and vegetable plantations and to replenish their kai. 'But how long will the pataka be ours?' Kaparatehau continued.

'The Treaty will prevent the Pakeha from taking it,' Korakotai assured him.

'Will it?' Kaparatehau answered. 'Ngati Rangatahi have held central and northern Heretaunga for over twenty years, ever since I supported Te Rauparaha and Te Rangihaeata against the Kahungunu who originally owned it. I do not plan to give it up, and nor does Te Kaeaea, who owns the southern end.'

My father gave me a look. 'Should you need my help,' he said to Kaparatehau, 'Hohepa will come to give it.'

———

The show of Wikitoria's higher power finally broke the impasse.

Chiefs came aboard the *Ariel* at Port Nicholson on 29 April. Greatly encouraged, Reverend Williams set sail on 4 May for Totaranui, called Queen Charlotte Sound by the Pakeha, and, on 11 May, to Rangitoto ki te Tonga or D'Urville Island.

The chiefs agreed to governance. Kawanatanga, yes. Sovereignty, no.

Then came the second test for the Treaty when the *Ariel* set sail for Kapiti

Island on 14 May to obtain the signature of Te Rauparaha. The greatest chief in the region, he had conquered and held for Ngati Toa all the lands below the Taranaki Bight and Whanganui, including Te Whanganui a Tara and Heretaunga and across Raukawa to the top of the South Island. Nevertheless, other tribes still disputed his overriding ownership and, certainly, the tribes of the Whanganui River had always held our own autonomy from him — as had our kin of Ngati Rangatahi at Heretaunga.

Thus to have Te Rauparaha's signature would be to achieve a stunning coup, for it would enable the new government to revisit all the agreements he had made with the New Zealand Company.

The *Ariel* approached Te Rauparaha's impregnable island stronghold. I saw the sun flashing off spyglasses on the lookout on Tuteremoana summit. As we anchored offshore I wondered if Te Rauparaha, whom the Pakeha called the Maori Ulysses, would receive us. It was with a great sense of relief, and no little elation, that Reverend Williams got notice that he would.

But would he sign the Treaty?

We waited nervously. Korakotai, who had met the great chief — or, rather, they had been on opposite sides of marae whenever there were negotiations between Whanganui River tribes and Ngati Toa — saw him from a distance and inclined his head. 'Te Rauparaha comes,' was all he said.

He was seventy-two years old at the time, stocky of build and very short — people say he was only about five foot two. Spaces opened up in the air like gateways to allow him entry. When he arrived, I felt his mana vibrating the world. When he strode into the room, it was difficult for me not to feel eclipsed.

With him was his blood nephew, Te Rangihaeata, also known as Mokau. Tall and untamed, he was Te Rauparaha's Ajax. My father had a stronger relationship with Te Rangihaeata because our kin of the Heretaunga came under his, not Te Rauparaha's, protection. What was interesting was that the Pakeha feared Te Rangihaeata more than his uncle! The whaling communities who lived under his aegis disliked his constant exacting of tribute; they thought him a bully and an extortionist. Those of the New Zealand Company and some of its settlers considered the Devil walked beside him.

'Tena koe, e te rangatira,' Reverend Williams greeted Te Rauparaha. 'Greetings to you also, Mokau.' He opened the meeting with formal preliminaries about the Treaty and its principles. While he was speaking, I saw Te Rauparaha's eyes alight on Korakotai. He did not appear to see me, but I was pleased to note, by the flicker of his eyes and a nod of the head, his acknowledgement of my father.

114

I observed Te Rauparaha more closely. He was wearing a fighting cape over a flax-woven tunic and wrap. His striking facial tattoo was incomplete — the lower spiral on his cheek was missing. Still, his charisma, even with half moko, was profound.

Reverend Williams completed his remarks. Te Rauparaha began to question him. 'You represent Wikitoria, the British ariki?'

'Yes,' Reverend Williams answered.

'To her I send my greetings,' he continued. 'She has already put her name to the paper?'

'She has,' Reverend Williams confirmed. 'She invites you to join her in governing the people of Aotearoa, both Pakeha and Maori.'

'It is good that I talk as an equal to her representative. I am a chief, she is a chief. The matters we are to agree upon are matters for chiefs.'

A series of probing questions followed, evidence of Te Rauparaha's intellect as he weighed up the situation. Most of his questions were about his current relationship with the New Zealand Company.

'Your land dealings with them will be recognised if you wish them to be,' Reverend Williams said.

He nodded. 'And if I don't want them recognised?'

'Queen Victoria's mana is greater than theirs. The agreements will be rendered null and void.'

'Ah,' Te Rauparaha nodded, pleased. He unleashed a stream of irritations about what had occurred since he signed with the New Zealand Company. 'I have no real issues with the Port Nicholson Deed,' he began, 'but when I signed the Kapiti Deed, I did not give them all the land that they say I did — and they have not paid for the land that I excluded from the deed! They only showed me the deed in the English version, too. Already Colonel Wakefield here at Port Nicholson tries my patience as he insists he owns Parirua and Heretaunga, and his brother Captain Wakefield at Nelson thinks he owns the Wairau! But those three regions are exempt.'

Up until now, Te Rangihaeata had been smouldering at Te Rauparaha's apparent interest in the Treaty. His intense hatred of the Pakeha was confirmed in his whole demeanour. And then his rage was unleashed. 'So why do you sign the Treaty?' he asked. 'You are only exchanging one Pakeha for another, whether she is an ariki or not! How do you know if she will be better? I have no taste for a treaty or any kind of relationship with the Pakeha.'

Te Rauparaha looked at my father. 'E Ngati Hau,' he called in Maori. 'Kia tuhituhi ahau taku moko?'

He picked up the pen. Held it poised in the air. Continued to ponder.

'He will sign,' my father whispered. 'He is teasing us — and his nephew.'

With a flourish, the signature was done. Like all the other chiefs, Te Rauparaha signed in the assumption of maintaining his sovereignty. Bow down to Queen Victoria? He would never have considered such a thing! Was he not the greatest fighting chief in the world?

He started to cajole Te Rangihaeata into signing. Furious, his nephew shook his head and, with a laugh, Te Rauparaha indicated that the meeting was over.

Reverend Williams stepped forward to shake hands with him. I didn't see what happened next but I presume that Te Rangihaeata, whose anger was still mounting, felt people pressing against him. 'Keep away from me!' he shouted.

A scuffle broke out. I was getting to my feet when Te Rangihaeata raised his fist in a titanic fury at Reverend Williams and then, whirling, raised it again at *me*. He could have killed me with his blow.

Astonished, Te Rauparaha shouted to him, 'No, don't touch him!'

Te Rangihaeata and I were eye to eye. He paused, lowered his fist, gave me a fierce glance and strode from the room.

And Te Rauparaha approached, looking up at me from beneath his furrowed brow and deep eyelids — I was almost a foot taller than he was. He began to sniff me with his aquiline nose and graze my skin with his long upper lip. His movements were fluid, mesmeric, taking me off guard. I was completely unprepared, however, when he pounced like a tiger, took my cape from me and loosened my trousers.

Before I knew it, I was entirely naked before the assembly.

'Is this your son?' he asked Korakotai.

'Yes, my youngest,' my father answered.

'He is flawless,' Te Rauparaha said, cupping my genitals, 'and tall, like my nephew! He is the kind of stock we should put to all our women!'

He roared with lecherous laughter. Although I was embarrassed, I tried to take it in good humour. 'Then tell your women to expect twins,' I answered.

He gasped with surprise, then started to laugh again, choking back tears. 'Well done, Son of Korakotai. Well done!'

With relief and elation we left Kapiti Island and, with Reverend Williams maintaining the helm, took the Treaty to Waikanae on 16 May and Otaki on 19 May. Apart from the Anglican presence of Octavius Hadfield, there was now at Otaki a competing Roman Catholic mission, headed by Father Comte.

'Perhaps we can capture this red kaka for the river,' Korakotai jested, 'instead of waiting for one to come from Bishop Pompallier.'

His jocularity masked his nervousness.

The reason was apparent later that month when our party crossed over to the Whanganui River. Waiting was the third — and, for my father and me, the most personal — test in the southern pilgrimage of the Treaty.

My father felt the enormity of the challenge. 'When we face our people,' he said, 'it is not Reverend Williams who will bear the brunt. It will be you and me, son.'

Would they support the Treaty?

We didn't have long to wait to find out.

———

We led Reverend Williams and Reverend Hadfield towards Putiki, at the mouth of the river. A number of canoes — some of them carved war waka — were drawn up on the riverbank, and one appeared to be from Taranaki. Over two hundred people were waiting at the hui. As we approached, the women called in the high-pitched karanga, and the warriors began a ferocious haka.

Because we were from the river, Korakotai and I were sensitive to the atmosphere; it was foreboding, unlike any that we had come across before. And while the lower river chief Te Anaua Hori Kingi looked as if he was prepared to listen to Reverend Williams present the Treaty for signature, Te Mamaku and other chiefs of the middle and upper river appeared hostile.

Not a good sign.

Thus it was a relief to see the warm faces of my mother, Hinekorako, my whanau and other kin of Patiarero. And was that Te Rai standing with them? Our eyes met, I held her glance, and my heart leapt. I *knew* that, no matter her betrothal, she had been thinking of me.

For the moment, however, I had to pay close attention to the matter at hand: promoting the Treaty, carrying the burden of it, to the iwi of the Whanganui River.

No sooner had Reverend Williams begun the korero than the attack started — for, in endeavouring to advise the benefits of signing, he made a bad choice of words. What he said was, 'It will extend the British rule of law, civilisation — and God — to the Maori people of Aotearoa and place you under our care.'

Te Mamaku leapt to his feet and cut him short. 'Why should we need the care of the Pakeha?' he asked. 'We have always been our own sovereign people. We have our own laws. Our own lands. Our own civilisation. Our own gods. We don't need yours.'

Shouts of agreement followed his words. And then Te Mamaku turned to Korakotai and went for my father's jugular.

'You, emissary of Ngati Hau, is that really you? It must be, for I see the tokotoko of leadership in your hands! All these years you have been on our side, the side of the river chiefs charged with keeping invaders from the Matua Tupuna. Why do you sit with the Pakeha now! Why!'

My father's face was wan. As for me, I was grief-stricken that his dearest friend would attack him in such a public way. Corner him like this. Give him no quarter. As the other river chiefs joined with Te Mamaku in condemning him, I wondered how my father would ever survive. But he has always been a man of great resources, hidden reserves and strength. As the attack mounted, he gripped the tokotoko and levered himself up into the sky.

'Yes, I am Korakotai, emissary of Ngati Hau,' he began, 'and my son and I sit with the Pakeha, yes; but never doubt our loyalty to the Matua Tupuna.' He went on in placatory mood, reaching out to the iwi with gestures of conciliation. 'Indeed, it was because of love of the Ancestor River that we left it to find out what was happening beyond it.'

My father walked backwards and forwards before the chiefs. Suddenly he paused, and his voice shifted, gained strength. To Te Mamaku's attack he responded with like attack. 'You! Chiefs of the river! It's all very well for you to heap scorn on me and my son, you who sit safely behind the palisades of your kainga! Have any of you ventured to the dangerous horizon and looked beyond it? No! While you have been sitting warmly beside your fires, thinking you own the Matua Tupuna, it has already been stolen from you! Stolen by the Pakeha who claimed Aotearoa for Great Britain and who now owns all of it — including the Whanganui River! Stolen, yes, even by these Pakeha who have come today to ask you to sign a treaty with them!'

Consternation greeted his words. 'Stolen,' he continued, with great deliberation, 'also, by those Maori tribes whom we have traditionally fought against and who have now found a way of finally defeating us — by saying *they* own us and, as the owners, have sold all *our* land.'

He let this sink in. Tino pai rawa atu taku pa! He was terrific!

'They didn't even need a musket,' he cried, 'nor to fire a shot. All they did was sign a piece of paper and all the land from Mokau to Rahotu and inland to the upper reaches of the Whanganui River has gone. And we are not the only ones to suffer. The same has happened to the lands of our kin of Ngati

Rangatahi at Heretaunga. Sold not only by Te Rauparaha, but also by other tribes who have always wrongly disputed Ngati Rangatahi ownership.'

By now the marae was in an uproar. My father turned to Chief Te Anaua Hori Kingi. 'Rangatira, you who guard the gateway of the lower river, you already know that what I say is true! You have seen the Pakeha approaching, and you know that he can never be stopped. He will keep coming and coming. He is the enemy, yes, but he can also be our ally.' My father was transfigured. 'Chiefs of the Matua Tupuna, do not continue to turn a blind eye to what is happening around us. My own son Hohepa—'

He looked at me, and I realised that this was the first time he had ever used my Christian name.

'—taught me that both Maori and Pakeha can exist in the same new world.' His eyes were shining with pride. He nodded at me in acknowledgement. Then he turned back to the chiefs and made a direct entreaty to Te Mamaku. 'E te rangatira, can't you see that we have been isolated for too long? We *must* be at the table when others debate our river, our people, our ownership, our sovereignty. We will have to sit beside the Pakeha, yes, but their Queen, Wikitoria, has promised to act on our behalf and restrain and even cancel land dealings that have already taken place.'

Korakotai uttered the ultimate heresy. 'Let us welcome the Pakeha in partnership and plait him into the rope of Hinengakau.'

My father stood resolute and firm. Even when the patai, the questions, began to hail down upon him, he maintained authority and clarity in his replies. During the long day he continued to field patai and, sometimes, insults. While the chiefs were impressed at the number of other tribal rangatira who had signed — some of them women ariki like Kahe Te Rau o te rangi, Rangi Topeora and Rere o Maki — in the end, they made their individual decisions.

The hui ended with fourteen chiefs signing the treaty. Not many, but a beginning. They were mainly from the lower reaches of the river and included Te Anaua Hori Kingi and his brother Te Mawae.

Te Mamaku did not sign. 'Tell the Pakeha that he comes up the Matua River at his peril,' he said. His entire demeanour was angry as he confronted my father. Although his words were punitive, there was still love in them. 'You, Korakotai, who was like a brother to me—'

This time he pointed at *me*. 'And you, Son of Korakotai, whom I regarded as my son too—'

His words were drenched with sadness.

'Come no more to Tuhua.'

The gathering began to break up. Quickly, I greeted my mother and family, and then I went to find Te Rai.

Where was she?

People were rushing here and there, most of them returning to the many canoes on the riverbank. The captain of the war waka which had come from the Taranaki, wishing to take advantage of the offshore winds to enable him to traverse the shifting currents of the river mouth, was shouting hurried commands to his people. 'Kia tere! Kia tere!'

Finally I saw her. She was standing on a small mound, panic-stricken, searching in the crowd. When our eyes met again, gladness was there. I approached her. A greeting trembled on my lips.

'Te Rai, I thought I would never see you again.'

All around, people were bustling and shoving past us.

'You should have pressed your suit on me when we met in Pukehika,' she said. 'Instead, you left me quivering with need for you. Why have you sent yourself only as a dream to hold me during the nights?' She took my left hand and put it to her beating heart. She closed her eyes and lifted her face to the sun. 'At least I will have your touch to remember you by.'

A strong voice called to her. 'E Te Rai! Haramai! Kia tere!'

I clasped her to me. 'No, don't go.'

'It is too late,' she answered. 'My uncle and other kinsmen return to Taranaki and they will deliver me to the man who will be my husband. Alas, Son of Korakotai, the tides have always flowed against us.' She touched my face tenderly, turned, and was gone, racing down to the waka.

My heart was aching. I watched as her canoe pushed off from the shore and moved through the tangled mêlée of other departing waka to the main channel. I ran down to the water's edge. 'E Te Rai,' I called. 'Kei te aroha ahau ki a koe! Do you love me?'

Laughter and good humour greeted my confession of aroha. 'Why would such a beautiful girl love a river rat from Patiarero?'

She stood in the waka and returned my call. 'Son of Korakotai! He kanohi ou? Where are your eyes?' Tears stained her face. 'Titiro mai ki ahau! Look at me!'

I needed no further invitation. I sprang from one departing waka to the next. My progress was greeted with great hilarity by people both on the canoes and the riverbank.

'That can't be Stumblebum! Love has given him fleet feet!'

'Watch it, Son of Korakotai! You will have us all in the water!'

By the time I reached the outer perimeter, Te Rai's canoe was already out of reach and moving swiftly away. I did not hesitate. I plunged into the water and swam to bridge the water between us. But the captain of the waka had already put up a sail and the gap widened. With grieving heart, I called to Te Rai:

E hine tangi kino, kati ra te tangi . . .
Whakarongo ki ahau . . . Oh my sweetheart, crying
so bitterly, cease now your weeping,
I will try to come to you soon and bring you
back to me . . . e taku wahine e . . .

Suddenly, across the expanse, I heard somebody laughing. I saw a burly man — Te Rai later told me he was her uncle — pick her up in his arms.

'I will not stand in the way of true love,' he laughed as he threw her into the river.

The procession of the Treaty around Aotearoa continued. I heard that the raging taniwha that was Te Rangihaeata signed in June, but would not put his mark to the document until Te Rauparaha had done so for a second time.

Why did he sign? Like Te Rauparaha, he now saw the Treaty as a device by which the Pakeha could be kept in check — by the Pakeha.

Not only that, but when he had signed the Kapiti Deed he had not been fully informed that the words 'land purchase' meant the permanent alienation of the land. The conviction that he had been duped corroded his soul. From that time forward, if you were a Pakeha, and Te Rangihaeata was approaching, best to step aside. Even then you might not escape harm, for the whirlwind that accompanied his passage could flay the skin off you.

Meanwhile I returned to Patiarero and Te Rai to Pukehika where we awaited the nuptials that would make us man and wife. I swam to Pukehika often but was always turned back by clucking kuia, protective of Te Rai's status.

She was a puhi, a virgin.

By the time the marriage ceremony took place, my desire for her had mounted to the point where my body, soul and heart craved for possession. The entire day of the wedding, I felt, delayed unfairly my claiming of her.

Korakotai roared with humour at my ardour. 'It is not Te Rauparaha's women who should be worried about having twins,' he said.

I was taken by canoe to Pukehika, and there, Te Rai and I pledged ourselves to the other. Maddeningly, I had to wait while she was accompanied by old kuia to a special bridal whare prepared for us. The old chiefs, seeing my impatience, called to the elderly women, 'Hurry up in there! Her husband is already spilling over in need of her!'

At long last, I was shown to the whare. Te Rai was waiting, trembling and naked beneath fine flax mats. 'I do not shiver from the cold,' she said as I joined her, 'but because you are the first man that I will have known.'

The touch of her skin ignited mine as I embraced her. 'Te Rai,' I answered as I pulled her close so that was no space between us.

She began to whimper, her arms reaching up and around my neck. She lifted her face; our noses touched. Then gently, she began a beautiful waiata of farewell to her girlhood.

> Kia tapu hoki au ki a koe, e tane!
> Kia tapu hoki koe ki ahau!
> I make myself sacred to you, husband
> You are sacred to me, your wife—

I waited, honouring her, stroking her hair and trying to sing the rangi — the melody — with her.

Oh, how delicious was the waiting!

Her waiata turned to an address of welcome to me, and a declaration that she would be faithful all her life. A profound sense of gratefulness came over me, something greater than love or desire.

'Haere mai,' she said. 'Now take the precious gift I offer to you—'

With a sudden, startling, unstoppable surge, my ure tangata planted its seed.

I knew that I would love her forever.

We settled in Patiarero. Te Rai and I delighted in each other. My parents Korakotai and Hinekorako watched, patient with us both.

One day, my father presented himself at our whare and coughed diplomatically. 'Son? Could you come to see Octavius Hadfield with me? I am anxious that, since the Treaty, we have had no news about how the governor is implementing it.'

It was time to resume my duties.

Te Rai pushed me out of the whare. 'Go with your father. Let me have rest from your constant loving.'

When we arrived at Reverend Hadfield's he gave us two government proclamations to read. 'The Crown has claimed sovereignty over the North Island by virtue of cession by the Treaty of Waitangi,' he began. 'Sovereignty has also been claimed over the South Island on the grounds of discovery.'

I was bewildered. 'But Maori already have sovereignty,' I answered.

Reverend Hadfield tried to assure us that we should look at the larger picture — the Crown taking control over *all* its subjects, including Pakeha. 'The Treaty will be honoured in word as in deed,' he said.

Even so, my father and I returned to Patiarero greatly disturbed.

'Father,' I asked him, 'have we unwittingly become agents to the intentions by the Pakeha to control us all along? Is the Treaty now being used against us?'

Then the news came that, instead of stopping land sales, all Governor Hobson had done was to establish a commission of enquiry into land titles! He was delegating one of the commissioners to specifically investigate the New Zealand Company's claims as set out in the Port Nicholson Deed and the Kapiti Deed. The commissioner's name was William Spain, and he was on his way from England to take over the job.

More alarming was that the governor had agreed to forgo the Crown's right of pre-emption to land claimed by the New Zealand Company in Port Nicholson! What was especially grave was that, where that land was in disputed ownership between Maori and Pakeha, Mr Hobson had agreed to the New Zealand Company settlement of it meantime, pending Commissioner Spain's arrival.

That was at least a year away.

———

My head was whirling. 'What else have we not known about the intentions of the new white tribe?' I asked Korakotai.

We had trusted in the goodness of the Pakeha; instead he was reneging on the Treaty. He was turning out to be devious, deliberately out to exploit and control us.

I thought of my kinsmen of Ngati Rangatahi. The words of the patriarch, Kaparatehau, swelled in my memory.

Heretaunga is a pataka, a storehouse.

My father and I had assured Kaparatehau that the Treaty would save the pataka.

Alarmed, I made a decision.

'E pa, I ask you to release me. I must go to the Heretaunga.'

II

Ko te Pakeha kei runga o te Maori?
E kore! E kore! E kore!
Ko te Maori kei raro o te Pakeha?
E kore! E kore! E kore!

Korakotai had once asked the question: 'So the Pakeha are here to stay?'

He had himself partly answered it by saying at the Whanganui River signing that the Pakeha could never be stopped. Indeed, as he had forewarned, not long afterward, in February 1841, New Zealand Company settlers arrived on the *Elizabeth* to set up the township of Petre — named after one of its directors — at the lower section of the river. The New Zealand Company later renamed the town Wanganui (the settlers could not hear our silent 'h') and said that they were acting on the Kapiti Deed by exercising their right as 'owners'.

Was it foolish for us — let alone all the tribes of Aotearoa — to even hope that the Treaty would guarantee us sovereignty in our own land? Would Aotearoa ever have reached the point where Maori predominated in Parliament and Pakeha were subjected to *our* laws rather than those of Westminster?

Is the Pakeha above the Maori?
No! No! No!
Is the Maori below the Pakeha?
No! No! No!

Te Rai and I travelled to Heretaunga. I was twenty-one, a young man and a husband — and, much to my joy, Te Rai was three months pregnant.

124

'Why are you so surprised?' she asked. 'You have been planting your seed so vigorously in my garden with your ko, your digging stick, no wonder I am with child.'

Korakotai and Hinekorako were reluctant to see us leave. As he said farewell, Korakotai's eyes were blinded with tears. 'Would you not prefer to wait and have your child born a river rat of Patiarero?' I knew it was more than that — he would have liked my help in managing and controlling the Pakeha who had arrived at the river's doorstep. Both he and Chief Te Anaua Hori Kingi were alarmed at the rapidity with which trade by small sailing vessels was developing between Whanganui and Wellington — the new name for Britannia — carrying passengers and cargo. Plans were also under-way for an overland mail service linking the settlement to Wellington.

But my father also realised that he had promised my services to our kin of Ngati Rangatahi. With reluctance in his heart, he was finally able to let me go.

'Haere atu koe ki runga o te reo aroha,' he said. 'Take leave of me, with the cloak of my love surrounding you. From our meeting house, Te Whare Whiri-taunoka, take the fibres of the rope from our marae and plait and weave it into the fibres of our kinsmen, whiria, whiria, whiria.'

I took Te Rai by canoe to Putiki, skirting the budding Whanganui town-ship, and went overland along the Kapiti Coast to Reverend Hadfield's. On the way we came across Pakeha travellers coming across country from Wellington, all intent on swelling the numbers at the new river settlement. Reverend Hadfield welcomed us with open arms and when he saw Te Rai's swollen condition he could not help but quip, 'So here is Joseph with his Mary, come to seek a stable for the night!'

From the Kapiti Coast we made our way to Parirua and, from there, down into Te Whanganui a Tara.

Wellington had grown larger. The sides of the ringing slopes were dotted with houses mounted along tiers cut through the thickly wooded heights. Along the beach below the hills were a number of good substantial brick buildings, including the main mercantile houses.

When we arrived at Kaiwharawhara I was pleased to see that, so far, although Pakeha settlement was now at its gateway — Te Rai herded cows from it, 'Haere! Shoo! Hoki atu koutou ki to whanau!' — the pa was still standing. But for how long? And it was a relief to see that the earlier crowd-ing had gone.

But I could not find the patriarch, Kaparatehau.

'Where is he?' I asked Te Kaeaea.

'The New Zealand Company sends settlers into the Heretaunga when it does not belong to them. Kaparatehau has had enough. This day he leads two hundred of the people to take the pataka back.'

'We had better follow quickly,' Te Rai said.

———————

We hastened after the patriarch and his Maori followers. From Kaiwhara-whara we skirted the shoreline towards Pito-one Beach. At one point, Te Rai had to rest, exhausted.

'Are you all right?' I asked.

'Yes,' she answered, 'but don't forget that there is another traveller with us—' she patted her stomach '—and I am that traveller's feet as well as my own.'

We passed Pito-one pa and I saw that Te Atiawa had accommodated the Pakeha settlers, with portions of land settled by Pakeha. As we skirted one of their houses, a Pakeha came out with a musket and fired off a shot. 'What are you natives doing here? Fuck off.'

Angrily Te Rai eyeballed him. She was always so spirited!

'No, don't provoke him,' I said to her. 'You have two to protect now.' I turned my attention back to the task. 'Kaparatehau will have followed the Heretaunga River. We will follow it also.'

Pursuing the people, I saw their tracks leading past the Pakeha cottages dotting the valley. Settlers continued to warn us off. But a mile further inland, blessedly, the signs of their habitation ceased; nothing except dense forest.

My heart leapt when I came across Kaparatehau's boundary marker.

'The patriarch already marks out the land, claiming it back.'

We wound through marshes filled with ferntree trunks. From the branches of rimu and rata came flights of birds. In the river, I saw the flash of teeming eels. The bushes were laden with berries. The valley was truly the fabled storehouse.

Suddenly we came across the travelling tribe. Some of the men were on horseback; others were sitting around an earth oven, finishing lunch. Old kuia were tending to pigs, fowls and other livestock. Young boys were herding cattle to drink at the bank. I saw some of the elderly on litters, having been carried on the journey.

A stocky young man was on guard. Whooping, he leapt on his horse and came thundering towards us. 'Ko wai korua?' he challenged. Man oh man, he was cocky, relishing the opportunity to show his mettle!

'I am Hohepa, a kinsman from the Whanganui,' I answered.

I heard a voice calling. 'Let them through, Kumete!'

It was Kaparatehau. 'You must forgive Kumete,' he said as Te Rai and I approached him. 'His keenness sometimes gets the better of him.'

I nodded. 'They should call you Moses,' I said as I greeted him.

A laugh wreathed his face. 'But my people have not yet reached the Promised Land,' he answered. He motioned to Kumete and the other guards in explanation. 'The Pakeha didn't like us marching through what they consider to be *their* land now,' he said. 'They menaced us with their muskets.'

'Yes,' I answered, 'we were shot at too.'

'Did you see my southern boundary marker at Maraenuka?' he continued. 'I still have to plant the northern one.' He looked up at the sinking sun. 'Time to go,' he called to his people. 'We have another mile to travel and we must get there before nightfall.'

We came to the place called Motutawa. The patriarch called a stop to the pilgrimage.

'This whole valley is ours,' he announced. 'Until now we have never needed to reside permanently. But times have changed and we must change with them.' He drew himself to his full height and took up the second boundary marker. 'From Maraenuka to Motutawa, in the area of the Taita, this day I mark out where we will make our gardens and put up our houses.'

His voice rang across the air. He pushed the marker into the rich soil.

'We are here to stay.'

———

Ngati Rangatahi's occupation of the Heretaunga began.

Our first step was to raise a settlement. The men constructed the whare and the women gathered flax and reeds for the wall coverings and mats. Te Rai soon proved herself to be a leader among them.

'That wife of yours,' Kaparatehau said, 'she is strong-minded.'

I knew he was being polite. 'Some would call her bossy,' I smiled.

Meantime, Kaparatehau also gave me a role similar to the one I had held with my father, as an advisor and negotiator for the tribe. While we awaited Commissioner Spain, I was to be the link with the government, particularly on developments relating to the land question; I was also to maintain surveillance on the New Zealand Company, establish links between Ngati Rangatahi and other Maori tribes, and consider how to develop reasonable links with the Pakeha in the valley.

All this meant regular visits throughout Te Whanganui a Tara and, to ensure my safety, Kaparatehau assigned the keen young Kumete as my right-hand man. In the process we soon became fast friends.

One matter worried Kumete: when we rode around the foreshore at Pito-one, I would take the opportunity to have a swim. I missed the tugging and playful down-currents of the Matua Tupuna; the Heretaunga River just wasn't the same — shallow and sluggish most of the time — and the better alternative was the ocean. 'Yahoo!' I yelled as I dived in.

The first time I did this, poor Kumete thought I had lost my mind, and plunged in after me! I ended up rescuing *him*. 'You don't have to be so keen on your job,' I said as he coughed up water.

He looked at me, puzzled. 'Where you go, I follow,' he answered. And that was that.

As for Te Rai, she kept up her leadership of the women. And to enable them to enjoy their work she encouraged them to sing while they were about their tasks.

'Your wife is always singing,' Te Kaparatehau marvelled. 'She sings lullabies to the baby inside her, she sings songs of encouragement to the other women as they work, she never stops!'

And at night, Te Rai still sang her songs of love to me. 'Remember, my husband,' she would sing, 'a woman is a precious gift.'

A gift, I might add, she sometimes withheld from me.

No wonder I was deeply in love with her!

———

No sooner had we raised our settlement than Matariki — the small star cluster that the Pakeha called The Seven Sisters — began to shine in the sky, heralding harvest time. We hastened to uncover the potato crop from seeds that the people had planted in an earlier visit to the valley. With great relief, we saw that the crop was good and bountiful.

'This will keep us going,' Kaparatehau said, 'but we must now leave the plantations fallow and find other good earth to plant new seeds in.'

Over a week we crisscrossed the valley floor, marking out a number of good, large areas for new kumara plantation. Suddenly, we came across a small temporary shelter on the east bank of the Heretaunga River. A lone Pakeha, wiry and of medium height, was working outside it. He waved to us as we approached.

On behalf of Kaparatehau I asked him, 'Are you aware that you are on Ngati Rangatahi land?'

He replied in our tongue, puzzled at the question. 'I bought this acreage from the New Zealand Company,' he said. 'The land was purchased in

England for a fair price. Are you my neighbours?'

I roared with laughter. 'No,' I answered, 'you are ours.'

A small woman with honey-coloured hair and brown eyes came out of the makeshift whare to watch. Like my Te Rai, she was heavy with child.

'I hope our relationship as neighbours will be agreeable?' He put out his hand in the hariru. 'My name is Thomas Mason.' His jaw set with determination.

'Tell the Pakeha he should join his own people and leave the Heretaunga,' Kaparatehau said.

'It is not his fault,' I answered. 'He was not to know his purchase was illegal.'

Kaparatehau pondered the dilemma. 'All right,' he added. 'I will be lenient and allow him to stay.'

'We *will* be neighbours?' Mason asked again. He extended his hand a second time.

This time, Kaparatehau took it. Smiling, Thomas Mason turned to the small woman. 'Jane,' he called, 'we have visitors!'

We started clearing the various large areas of land we had marked out for plantations, including some three hundred acres, close to Mason and his wife. I discussed with Kaparatehau the possibility of planting not only subsistence crops for ourselves but also a cash crop for sale to the Port Nicholson market.

He liked the idea.

I got into the habit of stopping by to talk to Mason. In just a short time, he began to earn my respect. He was up early and already at work himself, clearing his own small acreage, when I arrived. As I soon discovered, watching him planting his own potato and other root and vegetable crops — and then some orchard trees on a trial basis — he knew what he was doing.

Seeing him labouring with his single set of hands, while we had many workers to the task, led me to sometimes work beside him on his work. From there we proceeded to korero, and he told me his story.

'I was a Quaker,' he began. 'My community is in Yorkshire but when I married Jane, I resigned from the Friends to avoid being disowned, as my mother had been, for marrying an outsider. Jane and I both came to Maoriland because, here, we could begin a new life that was without the restrictions we were facing. All we want to do is to contribute to your country.'

'You are a pilgrim?' I asked.

'Yes,' he nodded. 'It appears that I have been the victim of the New Zealand Company's fraud. I would therefore like to make my own private arrangements of payment with Ngati Rangatahi.' He offered us the use of his plough and stock of seeds, and his wisdom with animals and plants. Jane gave bible lessons from the New Testament.

After clearing the land, the tribe set to preparing it for planting. Often there were up to ten families working on the plantation. Again, my and Te Rai's aroha — our sympathy — went out to Mason and Jane.

'I will go to korero to the Pakeha woman,' Te Rai said. 'After all, we are expecting a common joy.'

Jane was nearer to delivery of her baby than Te Rai, and Mason and I felt stronger bonds between us as we watched them talking.

'You love your wife?' he asked. It wasn't so much a question but, rather, an affirmation of the emotion we were feeling towards the women. 'So do I love mine.'

Not long afterward, Jane Mason gave birth to her first son.

Our child, Rukuwai, was born during the early hours of the morning a few months later. He slipped easily from Te Rai's whare tangata, her house of birth where he had been lovingly kept warm and safe. 'This is the treasure I give to you,' Te Rai said. 'Count yourself lucky, Stumblebum, that I fell in love with you!'

Tearful but proud, I showed my small, blood-smeared, squalling son to all the sparkling eyes of heaven. As the taniwha of the Whanganui River had blessed me, so I uttered the same words over my son.

'Haere mai, e tama, ki te Ao o Tane! Welcome, son, to the world of Tane, God of the Maori.'

Aue, the world was no longer Tane's.

The promises that Wikitoria had made us at Waitangi could not be maintained. Everywhere her own subjects were moving among us and I began to hear of troubles in the Maori world from all points north, west, east and south as Maori tried to resist settlers — and the reprisals that were taken against us when we did.

Wikitoria also could not control Wakefield. Even in her own country, good friends of the New Zealand Company convinced Parliament to err on the side of the settlers. Even so, I hoped that our dispute over the Heretaunga would be resolved when, in May 1842, Commissioner Spain finally arrived in Wellington. I went with Kumete to ask him about the situation for Ngati Rangatahi. I was pleased when he affirmed that the New

Zealand Company's claims in Nelson, Whanganui and Port Nicholson —
including the Heretaunga — did not hold up.

I was perturbed to discover, however, that he would not declare the land
sales invalid! What was he planning to do?

We would have to wait to find out.

Meantime, the New Zealand Company continued to move settlers
into areas they did not own. Despite Te Rauparaha and Te Rangihaeata's
objections, for instance, Pakeha crossed the hills from Port Nicholson into
Parirua and the Paremata. Maori of course resisted, having long held to the
proverb, 'He who owns Paremata owns the gateway between the north and
the south.'

Then, during a visit to Kaiwharawhara, Te Kaeaea told me he had
decided to join Kaparatehau in the Heretaunga.

'I have had enough of the Pakeha assuming the land is his,' he said.

———

Nothing was going right for us.

For instance, Governor Hobson died in September 1842. He was succeeded by an acting governor, Lieutenant Willoughby Shortland, but this
change of leadership further delayed Commissioner Spain's deliberations.
The New Zealand Company deliberately translated their settlers' squatting
rights into land ownership. It was increasingly clear to Kumete and me, on
our horseriding missions around the valley, that the settlers' houses were
multiplying, along with their own plantations.

By the end of the year, the number of Pakeha settlers in New Zealand
reached ten thousand.

I was drawing water from the river when, splat! Somebody threw mud at
me. It was Te Rai.

'Why did you do that?' I asked.

'Do something,' she said. 'Save our world for our son.'

———

Then, at the beginning of winter, in May 1843, I saw a man arriving in the
valley by way of the track from Pauatahanui.

It was Korakotai! Of course my father had visited us as regularly as he
could; and although he had other grandchildren, Rukuwai was a favourite.
'One of these days,' he would say to him, 'I will take you with me on the
Matua Tupuna and you can hold up my tokotoko just as your father did, eh?'

As my father approached, I knew from his gait that he wasn't well. He
was shivering with a fever. 'Aue,' he said when he had recovered a bit, 'I think
I will have to rest.'

I took him to Te Rai. 'What are you up to?' she scolded him. 'You're getting too old for all this travelling!' She covered him with blankets and administered a herbal potion to alleviate the coughing that racked his body.

Until then I had not noticed my father was aging. His hair was entirely grey. No wonder, with all the work as emissary taking him up and down the Matua Tupuna, and from Whanganui to Wellington and to us in the Heretaunga.

'I have to get to Wellington,' he began. 'I am to meet Te Rauparaha at the harbour tomorrow. He wants me to go with him to Nelson to act as an interlocutor in the dispute he has with Captain Wakefield over the Wairau.'

I knew the background. Having distributed the town sections, the New Zealand Company had decided on the 150,000 acres of fertile Wairau Valley, abutting on the shores of Cloudy Bay, as suitable for country lots. The trouble was, the Company hadn't bought the land and it wasn't theirs to distribute; it was Te Rauparaha's and Te Rangihaeata's.

Korakotai had another paroxysm of coughing.

Alarmed, I told him, 'I'll go for you.'

'You will?' He looked relieved. 'I can't let Te Rauparaha down. Ever since he signed the Treaty at Kapiti he has held me personally responsible for its failures!'

Then he thought he had better obtain permission from Te Rai for me to go; we both knew she was the boss.

'If you don't go,' she said, 'I will and *you* can look after Rukuwai.'

'I think that's a yes,' I said to Korakotai.

He thrust his tokotoko into my hands. 'Take this with you — you might need its protection. Let it be both talking stick and taiaha to give power to your words and, if ever you are in physical danger, strength to ward off any evil.'

When I took it from him, I could sense the taniwha within, coiling, at the ready.

———————

I made my way to Wellington. Kumete accompanied me to the harbour, disappointed that he was not coming further.

'I will be here waiting, two weeks from now, for your return,' he said.

I joined Te Rauparaha, Te Rangihaeata and his wife Te Rongopamamao, Te Ahuta of Ngati Haua i te Rangi from the upper Whanganui River, his son Te Oro, and a number of warriors, along with their women and children, all crossing from Wellington to the Wairau — about fifty in all.

'Ah, welcome, Son of Korakotai,' Te Rauparaha said when he saw me.

He noted the tokotoko. 'Come to stand on behalf of your father, yes? Te Rangihaeata and I have only just left the Court of Commissioner Spain,' he briefed me. 'He promises to follow us to Cloudy Bay in a few days to settle the dispute about the Wairau. When we land, I want you to go to Nelson to speak with Captain Wakefield. Try to talk him out of his illegal intentions. Meanwhile, we will stop the surveying. Kua pai? All right? Good!'

Te Rauparaha would never forsake the habit of command. No Pakeha had seriously challenged his control over the region; he was not about to let them do that now.

12

I boarded Mr Joseph Thom's schooner, *The Three Brothers*.

The trip across Raukawa was slow, mainly because of the baffling winds that swirled and shifted through the strait. But that gave me opportunity to talk to Te Rauparaha and Te Rangihaeata about my concerns relating to the Heretaunga — and about the slowness of Commissioner Spain in his decision-making.

'Ngati Rangatahi!' Te Rauparaha spat. 'They are a vagabond tribe. I might sell Heretaunga.'

'You can't,' Te Rangihaeata answered with good humour. 'They live under my protection, Uncle, you know that.' He turned to me. 'As for Commissioner Spain, you must be vigilant, Son of Korakotai.'

Since the slight altercation at the Treaty signing in Kapiti, Te Rangihaeata and I were on good terms now, with a grudging respect for each other. 'The New Zealand Company are Pakeha,' he continued, 'the settlers are Pakeha, Commissioner Spain is a Pakeha. Do you think a Pakeha government will seriously kick Pakeha off the land? No!'

The Three Brothers stopped at Totaranui and then went on to Ocean Bay, where we all disembarked.

'Now we wait here a few days for Commissioner Spain,' Te Rauparaha said. He pointed to a small canoe with a young Maori man waiting beside it. 'Meanwhile, Son of Korakotai, go to Nelson, and do what your father was to do.' Quixotic as ever, he pressed the hook of his nose against mine. 'Tell Captain Wakefield that Te Rauparaha has come to the Wairau. Persuade him to withdraw.'

My young companion — his name was Tamati — launched the small craft into the heavy surf. Once we had made deep water, he raised a sail and we were soon heading northwest, bound for Nelson.

Mist and squally rain shrouded Te Tauihu o te Waka, where we stopped overnight. The following morning we skirted the jagged perimeter which, so Korakotai had told me, had once been the prow of a giant Canoe of the Gods. The waka had carried Maui and his brothers across the ocean and, here, Maui had fished up Te Ika, The Great Fish, the North Island. But his jealous brothers capsized the waka, and now only the shattered prow remained, the sea thundering through its latticework.

Would the great culture of the Maori triumph over the Pakeha? Yes, oh yes! Exhilarated, I gave a karakia to the uplifted prow. 'E te Waka o te Atua, tu mai, tu mai, tu mai ra! Oh, Ancestors, arise! Speak to the Pakeha and show him what can be his, if he will honour you!'

Some hours later, Tamati informed me that we were approaching Aumiti. Ahead was a turbulent stretch of water, racing through a narrow gap between Rangitoto and the mainland. 'Good!' Tamati said. 'The tide has turned, rises and flows westward.' He began to take the sail down.

I felt the quick tug of the floodstream, ready to pull us through. Aue, taukiri e! The seething tide was roaring, forming a staircase of whirlpools and clashing currents.

'Hold on!' Tamati cried.

The floodstream spun us along. *Kia mate?* I prayed for safe passage. *Kia ora.*

As if to provide a sign, a school of dolphins leapt with us through the race, silver heralds shining in the spray, escorting the canoe through to the Tasman Sea.

Tamati raised the sail, and headed to shore. 'We sleep again in the bosom of the land,' he said. 'We will reach Whakatu tomorrow.'

———————

The next morning, we skimmed quickly down the coast to Nelson. Tamati dropped me off on an isolated point north of the settlement.

Anxious to introduce myself to Captain Wakefield, I hurried up towards the township. There was a bustling, festive air around the town, and I soon made my way to Trafalgar Street with its hotels and shops.

It was hard to believe the settlement was only two years old! Tradesmen were going about their business at the forges and workshops. Young children skipped to school under the stern gaze of a schoolmaster, who drew them back as I passed by. Once again it was clear to me that, where the Pakeha roosted, he quickly made his nest.

A public house was doing a roaring trade, with bluejackets and other sailors crowding around its bar. I asked a sea captain going in if he could give me directions to Captain Wakefield's office. He pointed to the New Zealand Company's depot on Church Hill. 'He won't see the likes of you, matey,' he laughed.

True enough, when I arrived at the depot, a supercilious male secretary in the outer office looked me up and down before telling me Captain Wakefield was busy. 'I will wait,' I answered.

'Not in my office, you don't,' he answered, and shoved me into the street.

Several hours passed. Setting my chin in determination I walked back into the depot, pushed the male secretary aside — he was like flimsy wood — and bearded Captain Wakefield in his den.

He looked up from his desk. 'I can't recall inviting you in,' he said.

'Sir, I could delay no longer,' I answered. 'I come on behalf of Te Rauparaha. He has arrived at the Wairau with Te Rangihaeata.'

Captain Wakefield received this information with a mere raising of his eyebrows. Then he said, somewhat offensively, 'The chiefs are nothing but drunken rattles.' Truly his self-confidence was overweening.

I tried again. 'The chiefs have come with women and children. Te Rauparaha asks me to assure you that his intentions are peaceful. Will you not withdraw your surveyors? Surely this would be the best path to follow. After all, the Commissioner of Land Claims' arrival is imminent, and he will issue a ruling under the Treaty of Waitangi.'

I do not know what it was — the mention of Commissioner Spain or the Treaty — but Captain Wakefield's temper flared at this. 'Ruling? We need no ruling. Under the Treaty? When will you Maori ever learn? The New Zealand Company has a bill of sale for Nelson. Go back and tell Te Rauparaha that no matter what Commissioner Spain rules, the surveyors are there to stay. He touches them at his peril.'

He strode to the door. His secretary had gathered reinforcements of two other men. I was unceremoniously thrown out.

Angry and shaken, I picked myself up from the street. It was no use trying to talk to Captain Wakefield again. Better to return to the Wairau as soon as possible.

With this in mind, I walked down to the harbour. A number of vessels were at anchor, taking in or discharging cargo, including sheep, herded off by barking dogs. Among them was the government brig, *Victoria*.

What surprised me was the large shantytown of displaced Maori that had been set up on the beach. Men sat on their haunches, blankets wrapped close against the cold. Families gossiped and tended fires and, when anybody passed by, put out their hands and asked for coins. Hawkers selling fish, meat and potatoes moved among the group. Maori tamariki, mostly naked, ran hither and thither among the makeshift tents.

A group of Maori prostitutes, powdered white like Pakeha, were importuning sailors as they disembarked from rowboats. One of the women accosted me, cheekily saying, 'I give you special rate, eh? Half price for you, cute Maori fella!' Among the women was also a red-headed Pakeha woman with their aged kui procurer.

I picked my way through the shantytown, saddened by the sight of it. For the rest of the afternoon I enquired of every sailor I came across whether they knew of any vessel that was going in the direction of Ocean Bay. I was becoming very disheartened, when I was told of a whaler that was heading for Port Underwood — but not until the morrow. I spoke with the captain and arranged my passage. Deciding to stay overnight on the beach, I went back to the shantytown. I bought three fish from one of the hawkers and a couple of bottles of rum from another and, seeing a group of old koroua, asked if I might join them at their fire.

'Any man who comes with even one fish is thrice welcome,' they jested. 'And one young man like you could not possibly drink all that liquor by yourself.' They spoke to me of their travail, and who was responsible for it. Some blamed Te Rauparaha for having sold land which, they claimed, was not his to sell. Others blamed their own chiefs, whose land it was indeed their right to sell. Others again argued that some of their rangatira had not sold the land, and yet it had been taken.

While they were talking, I noticed the red-headed woman again, speaking with her aged pimp. How odd it was to see a Pakeha woman talking to the kuia. And this time I saw that a small boy was with the woman; he had been playing with a group of Maori children. She brushed the sand off him and put on her bonnet — and that was when I realised that she was not a prostitute at all!

What was such a woman doing down on the beach? I laughed with surprise and, hearing me, she gave me a withering glance. Deciding to ignore me, she kissed the old woman. 'E Mahuika, e noho ra. Until tomorrow.'

As for Mahuika, once the Pakeha and her child had left, she beckoned me over to her. 'E noho, sit.' She took my left hand and traced the scrolls of the palm. She stiffened, and then she suddenly began to weep.

'E tama, you will soon go on a long journey,' she said. 'Did you see the Pakeha woman? Your destiny and hers are intertwined.'

I had no idea what she was talking about.

I spent the night in a shelter on the beach, enjoying the hospitality of the old men. The following morning, I was woken by the sound of running feet and voices shouting, 'Te Rauparaha has taken the Wairau!'

Taken the Wairau?

I sat up, squinting into the early dawn. A ship had come to harbour and a small group of men, carrying what looked like surveying equipment, had come on shore.

One of the old men pointed to them, saying, 'That's Mr Cotterell, one of the surveyors.'

I felt a sense of alarm. What had happened?

I joined the press of citizenry gathered at the Company Depot around the office of Captain Wakefield. A young man rushed in; he was the police magistrate, Mr Thompson. Mr Cotterell recounted to him what had occurred. It seems Te Rauparaha and Te Rangihaeata had waited at Ocean Bay, but there was no sign of Commissioner Spain. Te Rangihaeata became furious and insisted that the party wait no longer. 'Let us go on to the Wairau,' he said, 'and clear the surveyors off.' Their number had swelled to close to ninety people as they were joined by local Maori, including Rawiri Puaha, a local Christian chief. They travelled to Cloudy Bay in a whaleboat and eight waka, and then went upriver to where the surveyors were carrying out their work.

'We were told to leave,' Mr Cotterell said.

A gasp of anger greeted this pronouncement.

'Our hut was burnt down, as were my wooden survey poles and the wooden frames of my tent.'

'Was it Te Rauparaha who did it?' Mr Thompson asked. At the mention of the great chief's name, a murmur of dread circled the crowd. *Te Rauparaha, Te Rauparaha, Te Rauparaha . . .*

'I didn't see,' Mr Cotterell answered, 'but I have no doubt that it was done under his and Te Rangihaeata's direction.' *Te Rangihaeata, Te Rangihaeata, Te Rangihaeata . . .*

'We were taken by boat down to the river mouth,' Mr Cotterell continued.

'What of the other two surveying parties? Those led by Barnicoat and Parkinson?' asked Captain Wakefield.

'They were further upriver than me and my men,' Mr Cotterell answered. 'I do not know what has happened to them.'

There was a huge outcry. Both Captain Wakefield and Mr Thompson had become highly excitable and belligerent. 'Will you swear a formal deposition?' Mr Thompson asked.

'Yes,' Mr Cotterell answered.

'Then I will issue an arrest warrant, on the charge of arson, for the apprehension of the two Ngati Toa chiefs,' Mr Thompson said.

Tempers were at a fever pitch as Captain Wakefield and Mr Thompson discussed leading a special expedition of police constables, New Zealand Company officials and citizenry, including an interpreter, a storekeeper and labourers. Mr Thompson made a great show of carrying the handcuffs.

'Once the Maori see our dread array, they will yield quietly,' Captain Wakefield boasted. 'We will set out in the *Victoria* tomorrow to execute the warrant.'

Then somebody in the crowd spied me. 'There's a Maori over here!'

I tried to get away, but was captured by three burly men. I struggled as they pulled me towards Captain Wakefield and Mr Thompson. 'So you are a lynching party now?' I asked. 'You are in the wrong, not us.'

'A spy! throw him in gaol,' Mr Thompson ordered.

'No,' Captain Wakefield said, recognising me. 'Let him carry a message back to Te Rauparaha.' He was so confident of his power and authority. 'Tell your master and his *familiar*, Te Rangihaeata, that Captain Wakefield will arrive tomorrow. And then we shall see who owns the Wairau.'

My heart thundering, I rushed down to the harbour to board the whaler to Port Underwood. As I passed through the shantytown, a hand clutched at my shoulder and detained me a moment.

It was Mahuika. 'Haere ra, e tama,' she said tenderly. 'Goodbye.'

She added in a puzzling, mysterious way:

'And so it begins.'

———

With mounting anxiety, I returned to Port Underwood. From there I made the journey by foot to Cloudy Bay. On the way I met a man, Reverend Ironside, who saw my agitation and asked what was troubling me.

'A party of Nelson magistrates is coming to arrest Te Rauparaha and Te Rangihaeata and take them into custody,' I told him.

He wouldn't believe it. 'That would be the height of madness,' he said. 'The chiefs will never suffer themselves to be made prisoners.'

Cloudy Bay was an extraordinary place of small deep coves, deep water and steep land. I went upriver in search of the chiefs. I came across a group, which at first I thought was Te Rauparaha and Te Rangihaeata's — but no, it was Rawiri Puaha and his people.

'The chiefs have gone further up the valley,' Rawiri Puaha said. 'They are laying down cultivations.'

I thanked him and proceeded onward.

I found Te Rauparaha and Te Rangihaeata at the Tua Marina Stream where it joined the Wairau River. They had set up camp on a grassy hillside. The camp was fronted by the deep, narrow stream, and the flanks and rear spurs were backed by dense bush.

Most of the party were out planting potatoes. They were singing and laughing. Even the two chiefs were in a good mood, and this was not dispelled by my news.

'I didn't think you would have any luck with Captain Wakefield,' Te Rauparaha said, 'but we had to try, eh? Ah well, if they are coming, they are coming.'

The next evening, Maori at the river mouth reported that Captain Wakefield and Mr Thompson had landed, bearing firearms. The following morning came more reinforcements. All in all the party numbered forty-six men.

Rawiri Puaha turned up, extremely worried. 'The Pakeha threatened to shoot me,' he told us.

And then a group of boys alerted us. 'The Pakeha war party is coming.'

———

I often wonder whether the events at the Wairau on that Saturday 17 June 1843 would have happened had Commissioner Spain not taken so long to come to a ruling.

I also puzzle at the provocation of the arrival of Captain Wakefield's party at the Tua Marina. The size and official appearance suggested that it had been sanctioned by the Government, which of course it had not. To all intents and purposes, it looked much more than a war party — bigger, like a Pakeha army.

'I still wish for peace,' Te Rauparaha said, 'and we have only nine guns between us. How can nine defeat a militia who must have at least forty guns between them?'

The Pakeha war party approached on the opposite bank of the stream. I heard Mr Thompson call the men to ready. 'Act if called upon,' he instructed, 'and show your willingness to uphold the law.'

Trying to maintain an atmosphere of reason, Te Rauparaha sat in front of a fire eating a meal of kumara; Te Rangihaeata and other chiefs sat with him. Women tended to cooking fires.

Rawiri Puaha took out his Bible. 'We must make a last effort to stop this,' he said. He watched in alarm as, under Mr Thompson's instructions, the Pakeha taua formed into two divisions.

'Captain England,' Mr Thompson called, 'I leave one division under your control. Mr Howard, you are in the control of the other. No one is to fire without orders.' He then called to Te Rauparaha, 'We approach you, sir.'

Te Rauparaha indicated a large canoe athwart the deep and swift-flowing stream. 'You are permitted to use that as a bridge,' he called. Then he looked at me and spoke in Maori. 'Hohepa, this quarrel is not yours. You have done your job. Stand clear.'

I was grateful for his words, but, 'No,' I answered, 'I join with you.'

———

There is no doubt in my mind that the Pakeha started the argument.

Te Rauparaha approached Mr Thompson with his hand extended in friendly greeting. The magistrate pushed it aside and, with Captain Wakefield and another man leading, tried to maintain what they thought was their control of the proceedings. Mr Thompson took out his bogus warrant and, while the group's interpreter translated it, read, 'I call upon you, Te Rauparaha, to accompany me to the government brig to talk about the houses you have burnt down.'

'Why so?' Te Rauparaha asked. 'I have burnt down nothing but a hut of rushes. And is that not my own property, made as it is from the grass and wood that grows on my land?' Then he added, 'And the Land Commissioner Mr Spain will be here shortly.'

'The burning is not in his jurisdiction,' Mr Thompson said, displeased. 'I have led this large, armed party on a long journey to arrest you.' He flourished the handcuffs. 'If you resist I will compel you to come. I have the means, you see—'

He pointed to the divisions across the stream.

'Will you come to your trial on the *Victoria*?'

Te Rauparaha was not provoked. 'I will not go, nor will I be bound,' he growled. 'I will not board the ship and be tied up like a slave for nothing. If you are angry about the land, let us talk it over quietly. I care not if we talk till night and all day tomorrow, and when we have finished I will settle the question about the land.'

'Be careful!' a couple of Mr Thompson's men warned him. 'Mind what you are about, for God's sake!'

Rawiri Puaha made his desperate intervention. 'Kati!' he cried, holding the Bible in his hands. 'Stop!'

It was too late. Mr Thompson stamped his foot with rage and seized Te Rauparaha's wrist. When he was pushed away, he flew into a passion, rolling his eyes. He turned to his interpreter. 'Brooks! Tell them the armed party will fire on them all.'

The Pakeha taua made ready to fire.

It was at that moment that Te Rangihaeata claimed the scene, with warriors bearing muskets. 'You come here on our land and try to arrest my uncle? I do not go to England to interfere with the Pakeha! I'm the same as Wikitoria, a monarch, like your Queen.'

'It was only a threat, not an order to shoot,' Mr Patchett tried to explain.

Mr Thompson tried again to handcuff Te Rauparaha.

Captain Wakefield cried out, 'In the name of the Queen, men forward! Englishmen forward!'

Mr Thompson joined the din. 'Advance Captain England, come at the Maoris!'

Six members of the Pakeha taua crossed over the canoe-bridge.

At this, my frustration at the events taking place overcame me. Like every other Maori present, I leapt to my feet with a defiant shout. But my own defiance turned to anxiety when I saw that the women and children were vulnerable. I began to shepherd them to a safe place.

Seeing my action, Te Rangihaeata turned to the Pakeha taua: 'No, do not fire—'

I heard a shot.

With a plaintive cry, like a bird, Te Rongopamamao fell down dead. I looked at her, dazed. What was this? But she was alive only a second ago. And now shot in the breast?

'Aue, taukiri e . . .' Te Rangihaeata wailed. His heart-rending cry split the world.

Then another shot, and the chief, Te Ahuta, went down.

———

I am certain that the first to fire were the Pakeha.

My sympathy was, therefore, with Te Rangihaeata.

Grieving, he gave a cry of agony and then, 'Patua!' he cried. 'Kia ngaro me te puehu e piua ana e te hau. Kill them that they disappear as the dust that is blown by the wind.'

We exchanged a rattling volley with the Pakeha war party. 'We must take utu! Let us avenge our great lady's death.'

Captain Wakefield, Mr Thompson and the others who had come over the stream panicked, retreating back across the Tua Marina; all of Captain

Wakefield's confidence had evaporated. Was it at that moment that he realised his dreadful mistake?

Some of the party fell into the water but, hanging onto the side of the canoe, managed to return to the east bank.

Led by Te Rauparaha and Te Rangihaeata, we pursued them. I saw Captain Wakefield and Mr Thompson vainly trying to marshal their army.

'Rally round us!' Captain Wakefield cried.

A bullet struck one of the constable's powder flasks and it exploded. With a cry he grabbed his waist, looking incredulous at the blood seeping from the wound.

Mr Thompson's shoulder was shattered by a bullet. And the man who had led the charge with Thompson suddenly screamed in agony; shot in the groin. When he fell to the ground, I heard him say to a companion, 'You can't do any good for me, Richardson. I am mortally wounded. You must make good your escape.'

Seeing the distastrous turn of events, the Pakeha taua stampeded and ran for their lives.

Their turn of speed made us laugh and laugh. Oh, in the middle of bloodshed, with the world whirling around us in grief and rage, tears of laughter were coursing down our faces. And then we chased after them.

'Hold your ground,' Captain England called. Thirteen did.

'For God's sake, men,' Mr Thompson cried to the rest of them. 'Come back! The Maoris are upon us!'

Captain Wakefield called to those who remained: 'Surrender!'

The men threw down their arms.

Mr Thompson, holding his shattered shoulder, called out to Te Rauparaha, 'Let there be peace now.'

Te Rauparaha came to a halt. Surrender? Peace?

Indeed, someone did wave a white handkerchief. But after that came a volley of musket fire.

Aue, te matauranga a te Pakeha! The foolishness of the Pakeha!

Te Rangihaeata stepped past Te Rauparaha. 'I will not allow their surrender, do you hear me? Why save them? They have shot Te Rongopamamao! I claim the right to take utu for my wife! And others of our kin have been murdered by Pakeha in the past, do you not remember?'

The sun stopped in the sky. The whole world stopped.

Te Rauparaha weighed the problem in his mind. 'Did I not warn you how it would be?' he said to Mr Thompson at last. 'A little while ago I wished to talk to you in a friendly manner and you would not. Now you say, "Save me." I cannot save you.'

He turned to Te Rangihaeata. 'Take your payment.'

'We lose our lives for this poor work?' Mr Cotterell asked as he and his companions were marched a little further down the hill.

Te Rangihaeata approached Captain Wakefield. 'My wife was a chief; you are a chief,' he said. 'You are the utu, the payment for her death.'

Next to die was Mr Thompson. 'Spare my life,' he pleaded.

Very soon Captain England, too, was gone unto death.

The Pakeha had begun the action; the Maori made a finish.

The blood of both Pakeha and Maori soaked into the earth. Four of our people died that day: Te Rongopamamao, Te Ahuta and two others — Hopa and Te Whiunui. Nineteen Pakeha lay dead and three were wounded. The rest, firing repeatedly, retreated back to the *Victoria*.

Te Rangihaeata came to me. 'I am in your debt,' he said. 'I saw you trying to save Te Rongopamamao.'

As one husband to another, I held him as he grieved for her.

After that, we made due and proper mihi, farewell, to the Pakeha who had died also. *All* dead should be mourned.

Finally, making a karanga of farewell to the land, Te Rauparaha and Te Rangihaeata led us away from the Wairau.

Te Rangihaeata wanted to make a clean sweep of the entire Pakeha population of the area.

Rawiri Puaha pleaded against it, and he prevailed.

The weather turned bad.

Heavy rain delayed our departure back across Raukawa.

After we left, the thriving Maori community at Port Underwood fled to Totaranui in the Queen Charlotte Sound; they feared that the Pakeha would come and take revenge on them.

What had Mahuika said?

'And so it begins.'

13

Kumete was waiting at the harbour when I returned to Wellington.

He was frantic with worry. 'We had better stay clear of the township,' he said as we mounted our horses. 'The Pakeha are baying for blood. Maori blood.'

As we skirted the shore, I heard a crier with a bell parading the town, calling all those who wished to be sworn in as special constables and avenge the massacre at Wairau, as they called it, to meet at the Town Hall.

With a great sense of relief I arrived back at our kainga in the Heretaunga.

'Did you do your job, husband?' Te Rai asked.

'Yes,' I answered as I embraced her. I remembered the death of Te Rongopamamao.

'That's all that matters,' she said.

I held Te Rai close and my son close; Rukuwai was already three years old, a strong and handsome child.

I wanted to hold them forever and ever.

———

The pa was now a permanent settlement. Looking upon it, I was proud of what had been achieved since Ngati Rangatahi had come to this Promised Land. The houses were no longer makeshift, and the marae was tidy. We had even raised a Christian chapel, a beautiful building that had a carved pulpit and a baptismal font; Thomas and Jane Mason's second child had been baptised in it. In the fenced graveyard we had buried our first few dead. It's only when people are born and their afterbirth is put into the land, or when they are returned to the land at death, that you can truly claim it as your own.

Korakotai, of course, grieved over the Wairau episode. He was disturbed that the mission had ended so disastrously for the Maori, the Pakeha, for Aotearoa, for New Zealand.

'The Pakeha could not be turned,' I told him.

————

Te Rauparaha and Te Rangihaeata were marked men.

Rumours were rife that they were rising from Kapiti and Waikanae, their two kainga. Te Rangihaeata was called 'The Tiger of Wairau'.

Thomas Mason, on his return from a trip to Wellington, told me, 'Hohepa, I am most concerned. Wellington citizenry have raised a volunteer militia numbering four hundred. They parade every morning at eight. A rifle corps and cavalry corps have been formed, and two eighteen-pounders are up at Clay Hill. There are other gun positions scattered on the perimeter of the town.'

This was not enough for the settlers. They petitioned Acting Governor Shortland and he appointed Major Mathew Richmond, a captain in the 96th Regiment, as police magistrate and chief government agent for all the Southern Districts, including Wellington. He arrived on the *Victoria* with a detachment of the regiment.

However, even *that* could not quell the settlers. Their incitements to action against Maori 'rebels', as we were now called, escalated throughout Aotearoa; and they reached Great Britain.

Did the British Parliament take our side?

They sided with the settlers.

Worrying about what was happening, I knelt one day in the chapel of our kainga and prayed. 'Kei whea koe, e Wikitoria? Where are you, Queen Victoria? Oh, white Queen, why don't you speak against your own politicians? Why don't you honour your promise that Maori will retain our sovereignty in Aotearoa? Instead, you stand to one side and let your people take our mana!'

Te Rai came with Rukuwai to keep me company. 'It will work out,' she said. 'It has to. We have to make it work.'

It didn't. The British Parliament approved the military plan for the protection of settlers in New Zealand. They were the ones who affirmed Major Richmond's position as Superintendent, Southern Division, in charge of the troubles developing from Taranaki down to Wellington.

From then on, there was a build-up of regiments come on active duty from Britain to Aotearoa.

We called them Ngati Hoia, 'The Soldier Tribe'.

Even when Commissioner Spain finally issued his preliminary report on the New Zealand Company's claims in September 1843 that the survey of the Wairau could only be regarded as an attempt to set British law at defiance, the settlers' anger could not be dispelled. They still kept petitioning the British Parliament to send more troops or to affirm the New Zealand Company's rights to possession of the country.

Thus it was with hope in my heart that I welcomed the arrival of the new governor, Robert FitzRoy, when he arrived from England in December. On 12 February 1844 he met with Te Rauparaha and Te Rangihaeata at Waikanae. The meeting was of such importance that Te Rai virtually pushed me out the door to go to it.

'After all,' she said to Rukuwai, 'it's your father's job, eh, son! He doesn't only belong to us, does he! He also belongs to the iwi.'

Yes, I belonged to the iwi.

———

I journeyed to Waikanae. I liked FitzRoy and, for a brief moment, I thought that Wikitoria had heard my prayer.

'The Maori were hurried into crime by the actions of the Pakeha,' he said. 'Although I am saddened by the killing of the Pakeha prisoners that followed their surrender, I will not avenge their deaths.'

'Ka tika!' the people on the marae thundered. 'Why should you want revenge? They were the ones who started it.'

How were we to know that Governor FitzRoy's judgement would further outrage the Company and settlers throughout New Zealand? From that moment, he became a target too.

I returned to the Heretaunga elated. But what I did not know at the time, although I discovered it later, was that at the same meeting at Waikanae, Commissioner Spain's attempt to get *around* the land dispute over the valley was mooted in private talks with Te Rauparaha and Te Rangihaeata; it would be made public at a later meeting.

'You must go back to Parirua,' Kaparatehau urged me. 'You must speak on our behalf.'

I again made the trek over the hill track with the faithful Kumete accompanying me, and joined two hundred other Maori at the meeting.

Commissioner Spain said, 'I have decided that the Maori who disputed land described in the Port Nicholson Deed are entitled to a further payment.' In other words, he wasn't going to declare the land sales invalid; cooperating with the New Zealand Company, he had decided to arrange further compensation, which would complete their transactions!

Some Maori applauded the decision.

But I spoke on behalf of Ngati Rangatahi. 'We don't want any money,' I said. 'Ngati Rangatahi want to keep the Heretaunga.'

Commissioner Spain took no notice. 'The Protector of Aborigines,' Commissioner Spain continued, 'will decide the proportion of payments you are to receive. When you are agreed I will hold another court, and finally decide. Meantime, your pas, cultivations and burial grounds have now been reserved for your use, in addition to the native reserves.'

I returned to the Heretaunga. Nothing had changed.

———

'Mama is always singing,' Rukuwai would giggle.

'Yes,' I nodded. 'We need no forest birds at the kainga while she's around, eh?'

Even Te Rai's singing, however, could not keep away the relentless pursuit by the Pakeha of the Heretaunga. Not long after the meeting with Commissioner Spain, the axe fell. He began negotiations with Te Rauparaha and Te Atiawa for ownership of the Heretaunga.

Kaparatehau of Ngati Rangatahi or Te Kaeaea of Ngati Tama were not involved in the korero.

The patriarch was outraged. 'While Te Rauparaha was once our over-lord, and Te Atiawa believe they have rights in Heretaunga, it has always been ours. Our eel weirs are here, our plots for growing early kumara, our bird snares and plantations where we have traditionally picked the berries of the karaka and the kahikatea. The Pakeha thinks the valley has always been *empty* — but it never was. We are the rightful people with whom they must negotiate.'

Te Kaeaea took immediate action. He cut a boundary line across the valley floor at Rotokakahi. To make sure the Government got it, it was a mile in length and forty yards in width.

'The land to the south of the line,' he said, 'I don't care what is done with it. But the land north of the line is ours.'

Commissioner Spain kept pushing the envelope towards Te Rauparaha and Te Rangihaeata. 'Take it as payment for the Heretaunga.' I heard rumours that, just as was done to other chiefs who were parties to deeds of release, he let it be known to the two chiefs that if they did not agree to signing the land over, no higher offer would be made and their land would go to the settlers without the consent of Maori.

Eventually, Te Rauparaha succumbed. A receipt was issued. When I received a copy of it, via Reverend Hadfield, my spirit burned with anger.

148

Let all men know the contents of this document. We two consent to surrender Heretaunga to the Governor of New Zealand on behalf of the NZ
Company. We have received 400pds in payment. Hence our names and
marks are written below, on this day, the 12th day of November in the year
of our Lord, One Thousand Eight Hundred and Forty-four.

Na Te Rauparaha X his mark
Na Te Rangihaeata X his mark
In the presence of —
Henare Matine Te Wiwi
Tamihana Katu

But Te Rangihaeata's signature had been forged.
'If the Pakeha attack Ngati Rangatahi I will come to support you,' he told
us. 'I am still your protector.'

———————

Te Rauparaha's signature was apparently enough.

Just south of Te Kaeaea's boundary line was Fort Richmond, built by
Captain George Compton, commanding the Hutt militia. I remember once,
taking produce to the Wellington market — Te Rai and Rukuwai were with
me — how Te Rai had spoken to our son as we passed under its parapets.

'It'll take more than a fort,' she said to him, 'to frighten us, eh son.'

Captain Compton had lived in the Americas and modelled Fort Richmond
on the same lines as those erected as a defence against the Red Indians. The
stockade was arranged in the form of a square of nearly one hundred feet,
with towers of defence, or blockhouses, at two of the opposite angles. Two
storeys high, the blockhouses commanded the bridge and river on both
sides. The picket was composed of sawn slabs of timber and enclosed military quarters, a sleeping dormitory, stable, kitchen and messroom, hospital
and a magazine. It was musket-proof.

Under the protective surveillance of Fort Richmond, settlers began to
cross over into the Heretaunga.

———————

Aue te mamae! Alas the pain!

You cannot imagine what it was like to live in an occupied territory.
Heretaunga was just a valley like any other valley but to us it was the
Promised Land. It was the only land left to us. Where else was there to go?

Our people entered into a time of terror, conflict and bitterness. Certainly,
Thomas and Jane Mason had lived among us, but now settlers were cutting
roads all the way up the valley and even past Motutawa where we had our

149

kainga. They began to replace our forest with their orchards; our plantations with their crops. And just to make sure that there was peace in the valley, small outposts of militia were stationed at Boulcott's Farm and Taita, close to our kainga at Motutawa.

Was the Taita Stockade erected to ensure that we would retain, as Governor FitzRoy had promised us, our pas, cultivations and burial grounds and native reserves?

No. It was to restrict our movements in and out.

We were prisoners in our own valley.

Then Te Rauparaha himself arrived to kick us off the land! Was he trying to show the Pakeha he was still to be reckoned with as the dominant landowner in the region?

If so, he failed. When he arrived at our pa, he was jeered with expressions of contempt: 'You may be Ulysses, but we are Ngati Rangatahi and Ngati Tama. Get off our land.' It was a shocking blow to his mana.

As he left, he saw me. 'Even you, Son of Korakotai? You reject me too?'

'Yes, rangatira,' I answered. He was an old bull whale and to be admired for his great deeds. But his powers and his control of Maori — and Pakeha — were drawing to an end.

Major Richmond ordered our complete evacuation by May 1845. We refused to comply — after all, our kumara crops were due to be harvested.

Instead, we planted more kumara.

'The work we have put into the kainga should not go for nothing, husband,' Te Rai flared. 'This is our home now.'

In all this, I tried to reconcile what the Pakeha were doing to us with the teachings of their Saviour. I was no different from many other Maori who had become blended into a world where choosing for one occasionally meant choosing against the other; and because I had come to love the Bible, I found my inspiration for any decisions from it.

Thus, while some Maori people chose to find exemplars of how they should respond to the Pakeha in the Old Testament — an eye for an eye, a tooth for a tooth — I chose the New Testament. There, Christ's messages of repentance, resurrection, redemption and of love for all one's fellow men were paramount.

As I prayed in our small tribal chapel, I affirmed that, in the case of the Pakeha, I was still prepared to offer the greatest of Christian virtues: forgiveness.

In November 1845, George Grey came to New Zealand as our third governor, replacing FitzRoy, who was a marked man, not only in New Zealand but in Great Britain, for appearing to be overly sympathetic towards us. Grey was directed by the British Parliament to assist the New Zealand Company.

He did not tell us this. Instead, at a meeting of Wellington chiefs at Parirua, he promised us, 'Maoris and Europeans shall be equally protected, and live under equal laws; both of them subjects of the Queen, and entitled to her favour and care. The Maoris shall be protected in all their properties and possessions, and no one shall be allowed to take any thing away from them or to injure them.'

False words! By this time, the great Treaty aspirations had shredded. The war in the North, led by Hone Heke, had already begun and, still fearing Te Rauparaha and Te Rangihaeata, the Pakeha in Wellington feared a war in the south also.

In February 1846, forced out, but with the promise of compensation, Te Kaeaea and his people left the Heretaunga. The enthusiastic Pakeha settlers moved in to take possession of the lands they had vacated. However, we of Ngati Rangatahi stayed, appearing from the hills to discourage them from further penetration.

The patriarch, Kaparatehau himself — as Te Kaeaea had done — cut a boundary line across the valley on the northern side of Boulcott's Farm. While we remained in our kainga, we would retreat if we had to, to the northern side of the line.

Te Rai held Rukuwai in her arms. 'See the line?' she asked him. 'We will not be pushed further.'

Despite her valiant words, the military presence in the area became ominous.

———

Ah yes, we called them the Ngati Hoia, the pretty, parading, red-coated soldiers.

It was mid February, and this is how I became fully aware of their build-up in Wellington, Parirua and Heretaunga. Kumete and I were on our way back from seeing my father, Korakotai, at Patiarero on my beloved Whanganui River. We had planned to take the hill track at Pauatahanui over to Heretaunga but, on impulse, I said to Kumete, 'Let's keep on going through Parirua to Wellington.'

'What for?' he asked.

'Isn't it a lovely day for a ride in the sun?' I laughed.

We made our way along the beach, keeping close up among the sandhills.

On a couple of occasions the wind assailed us with the terrible stench of rotting whales on the shoreline. When we arrived at Parirua we saw that two companies of the 99th, one company of the 58th known as the 'Black Cuffs' Regiment, and a six-pounder gun detachment of the Royal Artillery had taken possession of it. A small force, with tents pitched on Paremata Point and at the large whare near Thoms' whaling station, had set to work on the Paremata Redoubt.

We passed on by, and the roaring sea was at our backs as we ascended towards Wellington. There were no tracks and the forest began to close around us.

'You want to go up there?' Kumete asked. 'The bush is impenetrable!'

'Not for two strong and determined fellows like us,' I said. I took a small axe from my sidesaddle and, whenever we came to a thick and tangled mass, started to hack at it. We made good progress and, near the top of a ridge, had a good view across the ocean.

'Taipo!' Kumete gasped.

Two men-o'-war, *Castor* and *Driver*, were plunging through the swelling sea; I recognised them immediately and grinned at Kumete's imagery for, assuredly, the *Driver* looked like a taniwha, a dragon, as it made triumphal procession over the waves. A paddlesteamer recently arrived from China, wreathed in smoke, it seemed supernatural in its power to defeat even Tangaroa, the sea god.

We came across the road that Captain Russell's Black Cuffs were constructing from Parirua to Wellington. Staying in the shadows, we watched as Pakeha and Maori crews built bridges. Guards were posted to ensure they were not molested.

'Why do they persist in their wish to take Parirua and Pauatahanui?' I asked Kumete.

I calculated the extent of the work that was occurring. A string of stockades, blockhouses and redoubts would eventually span the way from the Paremata Redoubt to Elliott's Stockade to Leigh's Post on the Tawa Flat to McCoy's Stockade to Lieutenant Middleton's Stockade higher up and to the Johnsonville blockhouse, known as Clifford's Stockade, at Johnson's Clearing.

As we proceeded along the line of outposts, I saw that some were already protected by trenches and bristling walls of timbers; and all had firing apertures in their walls.

'We should avoid the sentry post,' Kumete said, when we came to Box Hill at Mount Misery.

152

'I didn't know you were acquainted with where the Pakeha had his emplacements.'

He shrugged his shoulders. 'I have ears,' he answered. 'I overhear things.'

And so we made our way down from the outer hills and gullies into Wellington. At anchor were the HM *Calliope*, the transport *Slain's Castle* and the familiar-looking government brig *Victoria*. The town itself now numbered nearly four thousand settlers. All grown up, it boasted a strong gaol, a bank, four churches of various sizes and the imposing principal residence belonging to the New Zealand Company — nice green lawn, with a pretty garden at the back — shining prosperous in the sunlight.

It also boasted the new Thorndon barracks. The 96th, as well as small garrisons of the 58th and 96th companies, one hundred and eighty men in all, were stationed in Wellington. Another two hundred redcoats and militia were posted in the Hutt Valley, keeping Maori rebels out of Wellington.

A group of soldiers had set two dogs against each other and were making wagers as to which would win. As we went by, three of them stood warily, their arms at the ready.

'We should leave,' Kumete said. He was always nervous of Wellington.

'I want to take a closer look at Fort Thorndon first,' I answered.

The fort was imposing: a ten-foot-wide ditch sloped to a depth of seven feet. The high parapet of earth and sods was breached with splayed openings for two mounted cannon. An even higher gate and drawbridge spanned the ditch. Two lengths of palisaded traverses added further protection. If I remembered rightly, there was another fort like this at Te Aro, but covering a larger area and containing places of refuge and supply for any who sheltered there.

'Altogether,' I mused, 'almost a thousand troops to protect four thousand settlers, together with Maori allies Te Atiawa and others.' I paused. 'I've seen enough.'

Kumete scouted ahead as we journeyed back to Heretaunga. I didn't even want to look the way of Kaiwharawhara Pa as we passed it. Abandoned to Pakeha encroachment, it was now just a bunch of isolated palisades letting in the wind.

Fort Richmond cast its usual shadow over the landscape at the entrance to Heretaunga. As we took the road built by the Pakeha up the valley, a group of five soldiers came up behind us on their horses.

'Come on boys,' one of them said, 'let's have some fun.'

War-whooping, they surrounded us, shoving their horses against ours, trying to intimidate us. Wanting to protect me, Kumete reached for his axe.

'No,' I told him. 'Don't.'

Tiring of their game, one of the soldiers yelled at us, 'Get the fuck out of the valley!'

Another responded, 'That's telling them, Hinton.'

They made one last circle around us and then rode ahead, bound for their quarters at Boulcott's Farm.

We arrived in our occupied territory. Wherever I looked there were now well established Pakeha farms. The houses were roughly trimmed dwellings of sawn timber and shingled roofs; most, however, were made of wood slabs and thatched with broad palm leaves and marsh reeds. Close to the dwellings were crops — wheat, oats and potatoes — and men working with horse and plough or women tending gardens. At a couple of farms settlers took fright and called out as we rode by: 'Mary, take the children inside!' Others stood by, muskets at the ready.

I heard gunfire ahead.

'It's coming from our kainga,' I said to Kumete.

We spurred our horses to the gallop and arrived just in time to see the five soldier boys leaving, laughing like demons.

At the gateway, I saw Te Rai. She had a musket in her hands. 'They said they would be back,' she said. 'We had better mount a guard, husband.'

It all came to a head for me. The Pakeha had come to take over our Eden, and in the taking of the land was written our death by his hand. We were being overrun. This wasn't just a settlement by Pakeha of New Zealand.

It was an invasion.

———

And now my heart almost fails me.

Te Rai, my strong-spirited wife. She was always singing, singing, singing. But I will gather my strength and tell you how I lost her and, oh, the silence that descended on the world.

Yes, they did come back. Whether or not they were the five soldier boys or some other settler boys does not matter. Whoever they were, maybe they were just out to have a bit of fun. Or perhaps they were serious. At that point in the history of the valley, the Pakeha and the Maori were always sniping at each other.

Aue te mamae, keep the tears from my eyes as I tell you what happened.

They came back, they came back, at twilight. I can still hear the horses' hooves thrumming in my memory, thrumming, thrumming through the

154

closing day, when the light was gold and pink. They were whooping and yelling, firing off shots, bang, bang, bangbangbang, and laughing as they circled the settlement.

Kei te tata te mate nei. Death was coming. Why didn't I foresee it?

Te Rai was coming back through the dusk from hoeing the plantations. Rukuwai was beside her. I had just reined in my horse at our whare.

'Stay where you are,' I yelled at her. 'Some Pakeha are shooting up the place.'

Suddenly she gasped. She willed me to look at her. Oh, maybe she had a premonition that she would die, I don't know, but she was so beautiful, her beauty took my breath away. The flickering light of the flaming whare limned her profile.

She said, with such love pouring out of her, 'Hohepa, Son of Korakotai, he kanohi ou? Where are your eyes?'

I smiled, remembering. The waka had been taking her away from me. How glad I was that her uncle had thrown her into the river!

'Titiro mai ki ahau.'

Yes, she must have known death was on his way. But did she try to run from him? No, instead, she went to meet him. Stay where she was? Not her! She pushed Rukuwai towards me and ran to the whare. She picked up the musket and came to the door just as the horsemen went riding by.

There was another volley of shots as our intruders departed laughing, laughing, laughing into the twilight: 'Come on Dockrill, move your arse out of here.'

———

Yes, sometimes when death comes, it doesn't announce itself.

Te Rai fell. Rukuwai looked at her and cried, 'E ma . . .'

I ran to her. 'They've gone now,' I told her.

I lay down beside her and that is when I saw she had been struck down by a bullet.

'But they've *gone*,' I repeated. I couldn't believe that she could be dead. 'They've gone . . .'

The rage built up in me. I knew how Te Rangihaeata had felt that day at the Wairau.

I picked up my musket, lurched outside and, tears streaming from my eyes, began to fire it off into the night. Loading and firing. Loading and firing. Loading and firing.

'Te Rai . . . No . . . Te Rai . . .'

———

That is how the singing stopped and the world went silent.

The next morning, the women prepared Te Rai's body and laid her in the chapel. They were wailing over her as I sat beside her with Rukuwai in my arms. 'Aue te tama! Aue! Aue!'

Through the dazzling light I saw Thomas and Jane Mason coming to pay their respects. Jane Mason had three children now. Although I had grown to love them, and I accepted their condolences, my voice rose to give them bitter warning.

'Thomas Mason,' I began, 'Bad times have come to the Heretaunga. You are a man of peace and, among all the Pakeha, have been my friend. Depart the valley before you are caught up in the whirlwind.'

He nodded his head. 'I thank you for the warning,' he said.

Oh, I don't know how long it was before I rose from beside Te Rai. Maybe it was noon, the sun hotly spinning, spinning, spinning. I took Rukuwai's small hand in mine and made my farewell to the patriarch Kaparatehau.

'It's time for Rukuwai and me to take his mother back to the Whanganui River,' I said.

Kumete wanted to come with us. 'No,' I told him. 'My son and I will do it. You stay here and protect the iwi.'

I asked Kaparatehau if I could borrow one of the packhorses. He said, 'Of course.' I wrapped Te Rai's body in fine mats and strapped her tightly to it.

I saddled my horse and mounted it. 'Haere mai, son,' I said to Rukuwai, reaching down for him. 'Let's take your mother back home now.' I settled him in front of me and gave him the reins.

Somebody passed me the reins of the packhorse, I don't know who it was. As we left Heretaunga, the old women cried a farewell to Te Rai.

'Moe mai ra, e hine. Moe mai, moe mai, moe mai . . .'

From that day, I turned against the Pakeha.

14

E timu ra koe e tai nei,
Rere omaki ana ia ki waho ra
Ebb then, oh tide,
Withdrawing swiftly outwards,
Guardians of the Tupuna River
Receive her—

Tap tap tap, the days were filled with the tapping of the mallet against the tohunga's implement as he began to give me my face moko. The uhi, the chisel he used, was made from albatross bone; it flew steadily through the skin, engraving the deep cuts. His voice, chanting as he performed his work, echoed through the sacred hut where I lay.

Painful though the tattooing was, I looked forward to the distinction of having a ta moko. At intervals, leaves of the karaka tree were placed over the swollen cuts to hasten the healing, and every now and then, burnt gum stored in ornate vessels was tapped into the skin.

Tap tap tap. The tattoo symbolised my transformation. It was a sign that I had turned from the Pakeha back to my Maori ancestors.

The next few months passed by in a daze of grief. In the sanctuary of the Whanganui River only my son offered any solace. I would hug him tight and weep for him. He was five years old and already orphaned of his mother.

Occasionally I heard news from the Heretaunga. The main source came from a visit by the Reverend Richard Taylor to my father. Some time after

I had left, Governor Grey decided on a military display of power by marching contingents of the 58th, 96th and 99th Regiments from Wellington to Fort Richmond. Surely this was an act of war against us! Reverend Taylor himself took a major part in persuading Kaparatehau that bloodshed would eventuate. Under threat of military attack, Ngati Rangatahi were compelled to leave, sheltering just beyond the Heretaunga.

No sooner had they withdrawn than settlers plundered the deserted kainga and desecrated the chapel, overthrowing the pulpit. Two days later, troops burnt down the pa, including the chapel and the stake fence around the graveyard. Settlers rushed in to claim land, crops and livestock.

In response, the patriarch declared war and our people began to make lightning raids on the settler houses.

Because of the troubles, on 3 March 1846 Governor Grey proclaimed martial law in the Wellington District — south of a line drawn from Wainui in Cook Strait to Castlepoint on the East Coast.

During the to and fro of raids and settler reprisals, Kumete was seized and charged with robbery. He was tried before the Supreme Court, held under the rules that governed martial law and convicted and sentenced to ten years' transportation. But when Kaparatehau threatened utu, and new evidence established an alibi for Kumete, he was released.

Next I heard that some Ngati Rangatahi warriors had surprised and killed an elderly settler, Gillespie, and his son, north of Boulcott's Farm. The warriors withdrew over the hill track to Pauatahanui where Te Rangihaeata had built a stronghold.

Aue, Te Rangihaeata had always been a target!

Governor Grey used the pretext that the warriors were being harboured by him to raise a strong detachment of troops of the 58th and 99th Regiments to make a surprise dash on the pa. They arrived on the *Driver*, the *Castor* and the transport *Slain's Castle* and, when Te Rangihaeata could not produce the warriors, the governor decided to establish a garrison of two hundred and twenty men at the Paremata Inlet.

Shortly afterwards, I heard that Te Mamaku from the upper Whanganui River planned to support Kaparatehau — and Te Rangihaeata — in a major push against the settlers both in the Heretaunga and at Parirua.

He was moving downriver from Tuhua with his fighting men, en route to the Pauatahanui Inlet where he planned to meet up with Te Rangihaeata.

I knew I had to join him. I asked my parents, 'Will you look after Rukuwai while I am away?'

Then I watched daily from the bluff at Patiarero for Te Mamaku to pass by.

My vigil was rewarded one morning when I heard chanting from upriver and saw the fleet approaching. Quickly I said goodbye to Korakotai and Hinekorako.

Rukuwai woke and put his arms around me. 'Look after your grandparents,' I said as I farewelled him. His arms around my neck were so warm.

I sped to the river. The imposing flotilla of eight war waka, each one hundred feet long, reared like ghost taniwha through the mist. Each was paddled by fifty warriors. When the fleet had rounded the bend I slipped into the water. I felt the swirl of taniwha, the ancestral shapeshifters, surrounding me in phosphorescent coils of destiny. The water sparkled, shimmered and glowed.

Suddenly I heard a voice. 'Hohepa! The tokotoko—'

It was Korakotai. He had the staff in his hands and threw it.

I reached up and caught it. Waved to him.

His voice was strong and full of love. 'Try to forgive, son. No matter what has happened to you, and what will happen to you, always remember that your job is to take the fibres from our meeting house, Te Whare Whiritaunoka, and plait and weave it in with the fibres, not just of the kainga along the river but all kainga wherever you are, whiria, whiria, whiria.'

I replied to him, 'Stay safely in the care of the Matua Tupuna.'

I truly believed I would see him and my mother — and my son — again.

———

I swam out to the nearest canoe, holding a flax rope in my hands. I knew that Te Mamaku would be in the lead canoe and, treading water, quickly positioned myself in front of it. He must have seen me because I heard a voice calling to the paddlers, 'Run the river rat down.'

I evaded the prow and, as the waka swept by, I threw my flax rope over the tall carved sternpiece. Dragged along in the wake of the canoe, I pulled myself hand over hand towards it and, at last, clambered on board.

I approached Te Mamaku and gave him greeting. 'Tena koe, rangatira.'

His face was impassive. 'I've dragged many a fish in my net,' he said, 'and thrown some of them back, gutted.' Then he melted. 'Even though I was estranged from your father, my heart is softened to see the merman son from the river.'

All the warriors had muskets in shoulder holsters and bandoliers of ammunition across neck and waist. They were oiled for battle, their skin gleaming like silvered eels.

'So what do you want, Hohepa?' Te Mamaku asked. 'It must be important to have been out there waiting all morning.'

'I have come to join you. I no longer take the side of the Pakeha.' The paddles, dipping in the water, splashed through my words. 'Since the Pakeha killed my wife I cleave only to the Maori.'

He looked at me. 'Kei te pai. You must take utu.'

At Pauatahanui, the warrior force moved swiftly into the bush and set up a camp. Kaparatehau joined us. With him was Kumete.

'Ah, my companion,' I smiled as I embraced him.

Kaparatehau and Te Mamaku were talking about news of a catastrophic landslide near Lake Taupo which had buried the powerful Tuwharetoa chief Te Heuheu.

'It is a sign,' Kaparatehau said, 'but what does it mean?'

Te Rangihaeata approached me. He was typically direct in his welcome. 'I heard about your wife. I am sorry for you. The Pakeha are a murdering people.' He turned to Te Mamaku and Kaparatehau. 'I wish you well,' he said, 'I would come with you but the Pakeha have spies and they would alert them to the war party. Even by coming to you now, I place you at risk. Go with my blessing and my support.'

'Rangatira,' Kaparatehau answered, 'we know you love us.'

Even so, it was with extreme reluctance that Te Rangihaeata heeled his stallion. Three times he stopped, making as if to return to us.

Once he was gone, Te Mamaku turned to Kaparatehau. 'So where will we make our attack?'

'This is war. We are soldiers of war and we will make war on the soldiers of the Pakeha.'

'At Boulcott's Farm?' I asked.

'Ae,' he answered.

We climbed the hill track from Pauatahanui over into the Heretaunga. As we exited, we slipped quietly through the bush overlooking the sunlit river and reined our horses in among the shadows.

'There it is,' I said to Te Mamaku.

Boulcott's Farm was situated on the opposite side of the Hutt River in a beautiful grassy clearing. Built by pioneer settler Almon Boulcott, who still farmed the land, it had been converted into an army stockade. Stationed at the outpost were Lieutenant George H. Page and men of the 58th Regiment. Grazing paddocks fringed with half-burned logs and stumps characterised the other three sides of the farm; the paddocks blended into dark, heavy-timbered, steep hill forest beyond. The buildings included Boulcott's cottage, a few outhouses, tents and a large barn, around which a stockade was built.

'The barn is loopholed for muskets,' Kaparatehau said to Te Mamaku. 'Most of the men are billeted there. A few are in the outhouses—'

'See there?' I pointed to the riverbank where a guard tent was erected. 'Normally, five soldiers are on duty.'

At that moment we heard shouts as the soldiers, little more than boisterous boys, made their way from the barn to bathe in the river. Watched over by the picket on duty, they shucked off their clothes and, white arses twinkling in the sun, dashed into the water.

'How many militia are in the valley?' Te Mamaku asked.

'Maybe twenty police and two hundred regular soldiers from Wellington to Fort Richmond,' Kumete said.

'And here at Boulcott's Farm, on Ngati Rangatahi land?' Te Mamaku continued.

'No more than fifty. Half the force is quartered in the barn.'

One of the boys started singing. His voice was clear and strong, and I was very moved by his song.

The minstrel boy to the war is gone
In the ranks of death you'll find him—

The other boys and men laughed and, as they were dressing, joined him.

His father's sword he has girded on
And his wild harp slung behind him!
No chains shall sully thee!
Thou soul of love and bravery,
Thy songs were made for the pure and free
They shall never sound in slavery—

I thought, 'They are just young men.' Even Kumete was taken by the rangi, the tune of the song. He began to hum along.

But young men like them had killed Te Rai. Yes, they may have been just boys, but boys could be murderers.

We completed our reconnaissance and left along a trail up the rocky bed for about half a mile to a place where the stream forked. From there, an ascent up a steep and narrow forested spur took us to a lofty ridge known

161

as Te Raho o Te Kapowai. On either side the ground fell precipitously away for several hundred feet into the valleys. We descended to Paekakariki, back to our warriors.

When we joined the war party, Te Mamaku and Kaparatehau were in sombre mood. Te Mamaku drew in the sand a barn, huts and a tent by the river.

'We will attack at dawn,' he said.

———

It was 16 May 1846 when we began the raid.

Te Mamaku set up a diversionary tactic. He instructed Kumete and me to return to the hills overlooking Wellington, to light a Maori campfire, and walk backwards and forwards in front of it.

'The Pakeha will think we are gathering for an attack there, instead of the Heretaunga,' he said.

It was cold on the ridge, but Kumete and I were glad of the chance to be together again.

'Now we are brothers in war,' I said to him.

We kept up our ploy until well after midnight. Then we returned to Te Mamaku and Kaparatehau and the war party. As we made our way across a hill track, Te Mamaku heard the distant sound of gunfire.

'It is only the soldiers at Boulcott's Farm,' I explained to him. 'They like to fire into the bush now and then.'

Our party rode on through the coiling mist. Below, a white band of denser vapour rising above the tree-tops showed us where the Heretaunga River was.

Half an hour before dawn, we reached its banks.

———

'Timata,' Te Mamaku and Kaparatehau said. 'Let us begin.'

I led a small squad through the thicket fringing the river. Holding muskets high, we crossed the cold rushing water to do a reconnaissance, leaving the main body of warriors to wait on Te Mamaku's signal to attack. 'Haere ngoki tonu e,' I whispered. We crept up and out of the river, the droplets steaming like mist from us.

For a brief moment I was in a quandary of conscience about the forthcoming battle against the Pakeha. But I steeled my heart. No, I was a Maori. I should serve the iwi.

Such a different atmosphere surrounded the moonlit scene — so sombre and menacing, compared to the sunny sojourn of the laughing boys bathing in the river.

At the picket tent the sentry was changing over with his relief; we fell to the ground. As the two men changed they marked the occasion with a volley into the forest. A string of good-natured complaints came from the three other men in the tent.

'Must you wake the dead, Hinton?'

'Or me,' added another. 'I almost had my cock in Molly!'

A boyish scuffle ensued and one of the boys farted.

The first sentry gagged. 'I'll not sleep here with you, Dockrill! I'm off!' He made his way to the barn where he knocked for entry; the door opened and a lantern showed.

'All's well, Private Brett?'

'All's well,' we heard him report. 'I shall be thankful for a quiet night's rest.'

'Matakitaki,' I whispered, 'wait until they settle down again.'

I was surprised at myself. My coolness. My control. I had become a warrior trained to kill. I looked forward to taking utu for the death of Te Rai.

I told my squad to gather shrubbery from the riverbank to use as camouflage, holding the brushwood and branches in front of us. A corporal — Dockrill, as we had heard him called — took up his duty.

———

The stars began to pale.

The forest fell quiet, the stillness intensifying, the silence full of suspense.

Corporal Dockrill beat to the left, in front of the inlying tent, his musket and fixed bayonet at the slope. 'Bloody cold bloody hole,' he muttered.

Some of our party had advanced to within only a few yards of him. But something alerted Dockrill. Maybe he noticed that the low bushes seen through the curling mist were nearer than they had been before. Or perhaps one of the warriors disturbed some small nesting bird and it whirred across the river.

As he turned to pace his beat, he was instantly on guard. Suspicious, he held his rifle at the ready.

'Hell's teeth,' I heard him say as he spied our advancing grove, 'the forest is moving!' His nerves were straining as he cocked his musket. 'Who goes there?' He saw one of our warriors peeking from behind his camouflage. He shouted a warning — 'Maoris!' — and levelled his Brown Bess and fired the first shot.

Stars flickered out low upon the horizon.

I rose and, setting aside my camouflage, threw myself toward Dockrill.

163

His nerves let him down. He fumbled as he tried to snatch another cartridge from his pouch in the reload. He ran back to the picket tent.

Overtaking him, I felled him with my tomahawk.

Then the lad who had sung the song — scarcely more than a boy — leapt out of the tent to alarm the camp. 'The daring Maoris are on us!' he cried. He seized his bugle and sounded the call, but Kumete tomahawked him three times in the right shoulder. He fell to the ground.

I saw him struggling to rise, and admired his courage. He took the bugle in his left hand and again attempted to warn his comrades, but more blows — four on his left shoulder and three on his forehead — rendered him sense-less. As he lay there, Kumete claimed his bugle as a prize.

Warriors surrounded the tent, raised their rifles and fired low to rake the floor. It was soon riddled with musket balls.

'Brett, matey, I'm done for! The Maoris have got me!'

I ran into the tent. The acrid smell of gunpowder pricked at my nostrils. The remaining sentries were writhing in pain. 'Help,' they cried. 'Spare us.'

I was not long alone; behind me, other warriors entered, brandishing short-handled patiti, and hacked the sentries to death.

Blood was on the guy ropes of the tent; blood spattered the canvas.

One of the sentries was still alive. In a moment of sympathy I gave him a look, *Pretend that you are dead.*

He closed his eyes and went limp.

'Kua mate ia?' someone asked. I lifted the sentry's eyelids.

'Yes,' I nodded. 'He is dead.'

———

That was my only lapse. On leaving the tent, the blood lust came upon me.

Warned by the bugle, the Pakeha outpost was fully alert. 'Awake! Awake! Lieutenant Page, we are under attack!'

In the sullen grey light a man rush out of Boulcott's cottage. He bran-dished a sword and loaded pistol. Two other men followed in support.

'Lieutenant Page,' they cried, 'we are with you.'

They ran straight into the midst of our squad.

I signalled to Te Mamaku and Kaparatehau and our main body of war-riors: 'Haramai! Come to battle!'

The darkness on the other side of the river yielded to our men. The water rose like silver jets around them as they forded the river.

Meanwhile, other soldiers were running from the barn to join Lieutenant Page and his two men. Seeing the strength of the warrior contingent, he called to them, 'Give us cover!'

Two soldiers took up a position behind trees that had been felled near the barn. They fired volleys into us as fast as they could. Other men, now roused in the barn, amplified the Pakeha firepower.

Te Mamaku joined me. 'I had hoped for complete surprise,' he said. 'Instead we meet with strong opposition.'

A woman ran out of a nearby hut and into the barn. Within a few moments she reappeared with a cask of cartridges, knocked the head off the cask and handed the cartridges to the soldiers behind the trees; I admired her bravery.

The barn was the only building that was palisaded with slabs and small logs, defensive enough against us. Page and his colleagues tried with sword and bayonet to make for its safety.

'Don't let them through,' I yelled.

Our warriors forced them back to the cottage. However, Page noted that there was another group of soldiers and farmers trapped in the nearby outhouses.

'Join up!' he called.

The two groups fought their way to the barn; two soldiers fell down dead. The survivors, firing at close quarters, hacked and shot their way and, breaking through, made a concerted dash for the safety of the rest of the command.

We advanced on the barn. The soldiers had regrouped, and began to operate according to long-practised drills. Three sections, each under a sergeant, took turns in firing through the light stockade and in returning to the shelter of the barn to reload. Under covering fire, a section would appear outside the barn — 'Ready! Aim! Fire!' — and then fall back. Another volley of covering fire, and a second section would appear: 'Ready! Aim! Fire!'

Ka mau te wehi! They were well drilled! They knew they had to keep open ground so as not to allow us to advance and overrun them. Keeping up a continual volleying from all sides, they prevented us from gaining ground.

For the next hour and a half we killed no more soldiers. Their steadiness and their discipline proved its worth.

Daylight was breaking when Lieutenant Page decided to organise a sortie and counter-attack. He led half his command out of the barn and into the open. Under covering fire from the barn, they marched in extended order with fixed bayonets and firing to plan.

'Fix bayonets! First rank, on my order, fire! Kneel and reload! Second rank, fire! Kneel and reload! First rank, fire! Kneel and reload! Second rank, fire!'

Arranged in a skirmishing line, the command advanced on us. As they came forward, a party of seven Hutt militiamen rode up to the rescue.

The horse-riding militia was enough for Te Mamaku to order us to withdraw.

'Hoki mai tatou i te taha o te awa!' he commanded.

We fell back across the river. Te Mamaku and Kaparatehau looked over the field of battle, talking about our raid. Had we made sufficient utu?

Kaparatehau decided yes. 'Kua mutu,' he said. 'Enough.'

He raised his rifle in acknowledgement, fired a shot and called to the soldiers.

'You, Soldier Tribe, Ngati Hoia, have fought well!'

A soft rain fell as dew, like mercy from heaven.

We blended into the bush.

15

We killed seven soldiers. Later we heard that a Sergeant E. Ingram and a settler named Thomas Hoseman both died of wounds a few days after the attack; on 21 May, Private Jas French of the 99th Regiment also died. Three other soldiers who were wounded lived.

We lost ten men. Although we had been repulsed, the blood fever was still upon us. We turned to plundering farmhouses; and some of our warriors went further up the valley, where we attacked the stockade at the mouth of the Taita Gorge: the soldiers held us off.

One family, down from Boulcott's Farm, escaped by crossing the river.

Throughout the rest of the battle Kumete blew on William Allen's bugle. I had not wanted him to take it. The mournful sound, drifting across the desolate sky, was like a mockery of Gabriel's trumpet. It almost made me wish to repent of my part in the attack.

Kumete came up to me and put his arm around me to ask, 'Are you all right? You are not regretting the battle?'

'No,' I answered.

I had avenged Te Rai's murder. Now that the account was squared, I could return to Patiarero.

———

Wellington feared that Te Mamaku and Kaparatehau would attack there next. Strong lines of pickets from the regulars, volunteers and militia circled the town and patrolled the outskirts. Captain Stanley landed seventy sailors from the *Calliope*. Even Te Atiawa of Petone joined the Pakeha to defend the town: a hundred stand of arms was given to the clans headed by Te Puni, Wi Tako and Ngatata.

Governor Grey never liked being on the back foot. He went on the offensive in what became known as the Horokiri Campaign. He had long wanted to make a move on those he thought were the leaders of the southern Maori attacks and, by showing British might, quell any further uprisings.

A month after the attack on Boulcott's Farm, he had his bluecoats seize Te Rauparaha.

Te Rauparaha, you ask? He had nothing to do with the attack! Nearly eighty, and asleep stark naked between his two wives, they surprised him at his Plimmerton pa. He was kept captive without trial on the *Driver*, where he was locked in the engine room.

———

Governor Grey then pursued Te Rangihaeata and Te Mamaku.

Te Rangihaeata, you ask? But he had nothing to do with the attack either!

Grey thought otherwise and went after him.

Kumete and I joined Te Rangihaeata as he withdrew in pelting, freezing rain from his Pauatahanui pa. With us were three hundred warriors, as well as women and children, all climbing through the rain-enshrouded hills to a hogbacked spur in the wooded ranges high above the Horokiri. There, in the place the Pakeha dubbed Battle Hill, we dug in behind a breastwork of logs roofed over with earth and timber.

The advance of the British troops — regulars, sailors, military police and Maori allies — on our pa commenced on 3 August. The troops sheltered for the night at a recent camp of our own and — so they said — they found William Allen's bugle hanging from the roof of one of the whare. From there, they made their assault on us.

Our position was on the summit of the high, steep range to the right of a narrow gorge where the flooded Horokiri came pouring into the valley. We were under siege for six days under irregular but heavy fire, including two small mortars.

Kumete and I were still with our leaders during that attack. We finally abandoned the position under cover of darkness and rain — the weather was exceedingly wet and stormy — and retired northwards. Grey's pursuit was delayed some days by the bad weather, but there was one sharp engagement inland; there, some of our warriors decided to make a stand so that the rest of us, slowed down by the women and children among us, would have more time to get away.

Grey withdrew his troops, but we continued to be harried relentlessly by the militia and their Maori allies. We withdrew with the women and children over the rough terrain — it was a confusion of sharp and lofty ridges and narrow valleys — through the bitter and howling southerly squalls. We were fatigued and exhausted by the weather and the chase, and also short of ammunition and food — but we were determined to make no submission.

Aue, while still more or less besieged, we saw the approach of our enemy and, to enable out women and children to escape, Kumete and I created a diversion so that they could slip by into freedom.

We found an unoccupied whare and lit a fire; the smoke would attract our pursuers. Then we went into the whare, laid our arms against the walls and waited. With us were six other Maori: Te Waretiti, Matiu Tikiaki, Tope, Mataimu, Te Rahui and a young boy, Te Korohunga.

Our captors were a party of Te Atiawa led by Aperahama Ngatohu and Nepetarima Ngauru, part of a force of over a hundred, assembled by Wiremu Kingi Te Rangitake to assist the Government in searching for us.

When they arrived we shook hands with them to show our peaceful intentions. They put us in handcuffs and marched us to Waikanae, where we were met by Sergeant R. B. Sayer of the Armed Police Force. He took us to the police station and handed us over to the British military forces.

Two other Whanganui prisoners joined us: they were half-brothers of Te Rangihaeata; their names were Matini Ruta (Martin Luther) Te Wareaitu and Te Rangiatea.

———

From the police station we were taken on board the *Calliope* and put into the brig for a month; we were kept below deck for most of the time, but allowed topside at intervals, chained to the deck like dogs.

I was sad to see Te Rauparaha, having been transferred from the *Driver*, imprisoned on the ship with us. He was wearing an loose army jacket and a sailor's cap as clothing. Angry, he blamed Te Rangihaeata for his arrest.

'Aue, Hohepa,' he mourned. 'Look what they have done to me.'

This was how I, Hohepa, came to be captured.

16

Governor George Grey was known to Pakeha as 'The Fighting Governor'.

I never liked him. He was a liar, a cheat and as far as Maori were concerned, devious.

Let me begin this part of my narrative with this: the Colonial Office in London considered that he had the record to bring order to New Zealand, having been Governor of South Australia. They treated FitzRoy unfairly: he had no money and no military to protect the Pakeha; accordingly, the country was almost bankrupt and the troubles between Maori and Pakeha had reached explosion point. When FitzRoy refused to resign, he was removed from office and Grey became governor — and he was given the money and militia to finally bring the country to order.

Soon after his arrival at Auckland on 14 November 1845, he quieted the financial panic and then moved to quell the troubles in the North: Hone Heke and Kawiti were still in arms, but the governor's troops won the battle at Ruapekapeka — and then Grey offered them assurances their land would not be confiscated. By diplomacy he therefore gained control.

In the south, however, as I have earlier shown — and indeed saw with my own eyes — his method was more questionable: he arrested Te Rauparaha, and confined him for ten months on the *Calliope* without trial and another eight months in Auckland. Te Rangihaeata continued to elude him, withdrawing even further into the Manawatu.

Te Mamaku returned to the upper reaches of the impregnable Matua River.

I did not know Governor Grey but I think he was two men: one who ruled by law and also one who put himself above the law.

In my case, he regarded me and my fellow prisoners as rebelling against the Queen's authority. He wanted to continue the lesson against the Maori by trying us, not before a civil court but before a military court. We were really prisoners of war, to be held until the end of hostilities, but he deliberately chose to treat us as rebels against British rule.

Thus were we landed at Paremata from the *Calliope* for court martial.

Not only did Grey do this. He also directed the court that we were to be found guilty. For this offence, we should be hanged.

Not for nothing did we call him Te Kerei Te Turekore.

Grey the Lawless.

―――――――

At Governor Grey's instructions, therefore, and under the authority of Major Last of the 99th Regiment, dated 12 September 1846, Major Arney, 58th Regiment, presided over a court at Paremata consisting of six officers from 58th, 65th and 99th Regiments.

On 14 September, the proclamation of martial law was read. Maori witnesses, sworn in if they were Christian, were called.

Te Rangiatea was the first to be tried. He was charged with being found in possession of a spear, and with having helped and taken part 'in an attack and Massacre of Her Majesty's troops' at the Hutt on 16 May.

No one was appointed to represent him.

His plea was guilty on the first charge and not guilty on the second.

The finding was guilty on the first charge and guilty of helping, but not of having taken part in, the raid on Boulcott's Farm.

He was so ill that the court drew back from sentencing him to death and instead pronounced imprisonment for life on the grounds of insanity.

Insanity?

―――――――

On 15 September, Martin Luther was tried. The charge, though not the military report of the operation, said that he had resisted and wounded Tamati Ngapuna of the friendly Te Atiawa. A second charge accused him of aiding in rebellion and taking part in the skirmish in the Hutt Valley on 16 June.

Again, no one was appointed to defend him.

After the evidence of two Maori women, the court found him guilty of being taken in open rebellion on 1 August, and of aiding, but not taking part in, the skirmish of 16 June.

He was sentenced to be hanged. Did his being a half-brother of Te Rangihaeata have anything to do with it?

'I am not afraid to die,' he said, 'but I regret with deep emotion that I was

171

not killed when I was captured. Instead, I have been reserved for this cruel and disgraceful death.'

Some difficulty came in finding someone willing to carry out the sentence, and a purse of gold had to be provided for a soldier who finally agreed to act as hangman.

A gallows was erected close to the military stockade at Parirua. Martin Luther was allowed to see his wife, who was pregnant.

'When the child is born,' she said, 'the name that shall be given will be Rupeka, or the Hanged One, in remembrance of this bitter day.'

On 17 September, the Rev. Mr Govett accompanied Martin Luther to the scaffold. The entire military camp was assembled to witness the execution. A Christian, Martin Luther left this world praying, 'I am in God's care.'

A drum roll, a click as the trapdoor opened, and he fell, his neck snapping.

Officials and soldiers looking on his lifeless trunk, with its swollen agonised features, doubted the necessity of such a tragedy.

Dr Arthur Saunders Thomson, a surgeon with the 58th Regiment and witness to the execution, said, 'Justice repudiates the name of rebels applied to the Maori prisoners. Luther's death is a disgrace to Governor Grey's administration, and he probably thought so himself, as there is no published despatch on the subject. Luther was tried with all the forms of military law and with all the substance of injustice.'

———————

Almost immediately after the hanging, disquiet erupted about the continuation of the court martial, and of any further executions in particular.

The alarm compelled Ensign Servantes, the military interpreter, to come and see me on behalf of Major Last. He had noted that the other prisoners looked upon me as a leader and, aware of my fluency in English and former dealings with Pakeha, sought my opinion.

'The major, as chairman of the court martial, is concerned at the public reaction,' he said. 'A correspondent of a Wellington newspaper has written that to try the rest of you and then hang you . . . would be a gross act of barbarity. But Governor Grey wishes just such an example to be made to show all Maori rebels of the power of the Government.'

'Governor Grey wishes wrongly,' I answered. 'Were there any Maori at Martin Luther's execution? And now that he is dead, what will they do? They will take him back to his kainga where he can be buried and farewelled as a chief. Governor Grey will therefore get no benefit from his death.'

Indeed, as I was speaking, I heard the loud wailing of Martin Luther's wife and saw the black-garbed women take possession of his body. Such a piteous sight overwhelmed me with anger.

'You tell Major Last,' I continued, 'that what Maori will remember is the unjustness of Martin Luther's death. If we who remain on trial are to die, they will remember the same unfairness. They already know the charges are faulty. Te Rangihaeata and Te Rauparaha were never involved in the attack on Boulcott's Farm. And even if we, your prisoners, were there, were we the ones who killed the soldiers? Where is the proof?'

I don't know what the ensign conveyed to Major Last, but I understand that the major agreed. The bitter irony of having sent a Maori named Martin Luther to the gallows was not lost on him, and he wanted to wash his hands of the entire proceedings. How could he overturn the process?

He found a way.

Ensign Servantes came to tell me the news. 'The trial cannot be stopped,' he said, 'but it can be tried in another court. Major Last has recommended that the proceedings be shifted to Wellington where you will come under the civil court, the town not being included under the proclamation of martial law. There, Major Mathew Richmond will chair the proceedings. I cannot presume the result, but it is likely to be not guilty and then you may all be acquitted.'

Hope rose quickly in my heart — only to be dashed just as quickly.

'I refuse civil jurisdiction,' Major Richmond said. 'The declaration of martial law has abrogated my authority.'

He acted with complete correctness. I do not question his integrity.

He was acting as the law obliged him to act.

By so doing, however, Major Richmond placed us back at the mercy of Governor Grey. I wonder whether it was at this point that the governor realised he had gone too far, and that he was becoming caught up in a situation that was spiralling out of control?

Whatever the case, the matter needed to be resolved quickly to avoid further damage to the Government's image and prevent questions of legality being asked.

Major Last received a direct order from Lieutenant-Colonel McCleverty, senior military officer commanding the troops in the Southern Districts. Whether he received his instructions from Governor Grey I do not know, but I suspect it.

'Sir, convene a fresh court under your own presidency and proceed to try the eight prisoners on charges of rebellion and of helping Te Rangihaeata.'

Before the trial, Major Last was able to discharge one of our number, Te Korohunga, who was, after all, a boy. 'I will not try the young lad,' he said. 'If he were to be found guilty along with the others, and were to be executed with them, our court would be thoroughly despised.'

I was relieved at Te Korohunga's freedom. I had not met him until we had all been imprisoned together and, although he stoutly faced up to his charges, he was too young to be hanged. Oh, yes, that's what we all expected would be our fate. Governor Grey intended to have his pound of flesh.

The young boy was so staunch! He wanted to stay with us to prove he was a man.

'Live to fight another day,' I told him. 'When you get back to the Matua Tupuna, would you pass a message to my parents and my son? Tell them that I love them.'

I was in no doubt that the rest of us would not survive the trial.

Te Korohunga went to Patiarero and told Korakotai I was awaiting sentencing. My father had been under the impression that I had been killed in the raid on Boulcott's Farm. He told my mother and family that he would come to the court hearing and plead for my release.

Apparently, he could not be stopped.

The day of our court martial, 12 October, arrived.

'Mr Grey, today, you will have your way at last,' I thought.

Kumete, my other companions and I were nervous as we filed into the room before Major Last, president, with the other members of the court: Captain I. Armstrong, 99th Regiment, and Captains R. D. Newenham, R. O'Connell and Lieutenant I. R. McCoy of the 65th Regiment.

Major Last nodded to Ensign Servantes. 'Let us begin.'

Ensign Servantes read the charges in Maori. 'Prisoners, you have been arraigned for the following. The first charge is for having on or about 14 August 1846 been taken in arms, and in open Rebellion against the Queen's Sovereign Authority and Government of New Zealand at or near the Pari Pari in the neighbourhood of the Panaha Mountains and within the limits of the district wherein Martial Law was at the time proclaimed; the second charge is for acting, siding and assisting the Rebel Chief Te Rangihaeata in the said rebellion and in being unlawfully present at, and taking part in, hostilities against Her Majesty's Troops stationed in the proclaimed District between the periods of 15 May 1846 and 15 August 1846. The third charge for having unlawfully at the time and place specified in the first charge been in possession of a firelock, the property of Her Majesty the Queen, marked

58th Regiment H. No. 62 the same being loaded at the time of your capture. The said firelock having been so unlawfully detained since 16th May 1846 at which time it was in the possession of Private Thomas Bolt 58th Regiment who was shot in the attack of the rebels on 16 May 1846. Are you each and severally guilty or not guilty of the crimes laid to your charge?'

The proceedings of the court martial record that we severally answered, 'Guilty.' But I had tried to speak. 'Why do you charge us together and not separately? And why are we not to answer each charge as a separate charge?'

My words went unheeded.

———————

The trial proceeded with the first evidence of Aperahama Ngatohu, who gave details of our arrest at Pari Pari.

'In the evening,' he said, 'we were leading the prisoners to Waikanae when we met the Police to whom we gave them over. I know the prisoners to be rebels from their belonging to the Wanganui Tribe and from their appearance, and that they belonged to Rangihaeata. The musket now produced marked 58th Regt. H. No. 62 was one of those taken from the prisoners.'

'Did the prisoners make any resistance at the time of their capture?'

'The prisoner Mataiumu made some resistance but I did not see any others do so.'

The second evidence came from Nepetarima Ngauru. 'The whole eight had arms and they were loaded — the one marked 58th Regt. H. No. 62 was one of them. The prisoners now before the court were all captured — we secured their hands with flax and led them down to the Pa at the Pari Pari where we lived. In the evening we were conducting them to Waikanae when we met the Police and gave the prisoners over to them. When they were taken they made some resistance — Tope particularly. I know them to belong to the rebel Chief Rangihaeata from their being in arms, and from what I have heard I believe them to have been with him for some time previous and I know them to belong to the Wanganui Tribe from their dialect. I heard that the prisoners now present were with Rangihaeata when the fights took place with the soldiers in the Horokiri Valley.'

The third evidence of the woman, Roka-Pekatahi, followed. 'I belong to the Wanganui Tribe. I know all the prisoners before the court. I have been living at Pauatahanui, the Pa of Rangihaeata, the seven prisoners now present were living there at the same time. I recollect the attack of the Maoris on the camp at the Hutt when some of the soldiers were killed —

I accompanied the party that made the attack, it was led by Karamu. Hohepa Te Umuroa accompanied us from Pauatahanui but I do not recollect any of the rest being there. All the Maoris with Rangihaeata were armed with fire-arms but I cannot say whether these now produced are any of theirs.'

I was beside myself with frustration. What specific evidence had been presented against us individually? The only evidence against us was that we were all from the Whanganui and that we may or may not have been involved in any attack in the Heretaunga or any other military action. And the woman Roka-Pekatahi had specifically denied knowing whether any of the firearms were ours. She was from the Whanganui and had been at Te Rangihaeata's pa — why wasn't she on trial with us!

Were we to be hanged on such flimsy evidence? It seemed so.

The fourth evidence came from Te Witu. 'I know three of the prisoners before the court,' he began, 'Te Waretiti, Te Kumete, Te Rahui. The musket marked 58th Regt. H. No. 62 I took from the prisoner Te Kumete and it was loaded at the time. I saw the other guns but I cannot say if those now shown me are the same. The prisoner Tope made some resistance and seized a musket but it was taken from him.'

'Do you know the prisoners taken at the Pari Pari,' the court asked, 'to belong to the party of rebels with Rangihaeata?'

'Yes,' Te Witu answered. 'I know such to be the case from their belonging to the Whanganui Tribe which I discovered by their dialect.'

At this point, my companion Te Kumete objected. 'Are you positive that you took the musket marked 58th Regt. H. 62 from me?'

'Yes, as you took hold of it when you were captured.'

The evidence of the friendly Maori having been heard, the court called their fifth evidence from Corporal Sett Davall, 58th Regiment. 'I was one of the detachment quartered at Boulcott's Farm under the command of Lieutenant Page on 16th May 1846 when we were attacked by the Maoris and Private Thomas Bolt of 58th Regt. was killed. I know that the musket now produced marked 62 Letter H was in his possession at the time. He was one of the picquet. The firelock was taken away at the attack and has not been seen since until taken from the prisoners.'

Burgess Sayers, Sergeant of the Armed Police, gave the sixth evidence. 'I know all the prisoners before the court, they were delivered over to me by a native chief named Aperahama Ngatohu and other friendly natives on or about 14 August last as rebels who had been captured on the hills above Pari Pari. I took them to the Police Station at Waikanae and they were after-wards sent on Her Majesty's ship *Calliope* for safety. I saw the firearms in possession of one of the friendly natives who said they had been taken from Rangihaeata's men.'

This was the end of the evidence against us.

I looked for any person appointed for our defence.

There was none.

Instead, Ensign Servantes presented a statement. It was a fair statement but, in English, does not make it clear that we did not say we were 'rebels' — we said we were Maori Tuturu, True Maori:

'The prisoners being put on their defence have nothing to urge except their acknowledgement of being rebels and also of being Rangihaeata's followers but deny having killed anybody. They have nothing further to add.'

Major Last nodded. 'Please then clear the court for the purpose that we may deliberate on the whole of the proceedings.'

My heart was beating with fury as I was taken with my companions to a holding area. I don't know how long we waited for the verdict.

When it came I was not surprised.

'The court,' Major Last began, 'having maturely considered the evidence in support of the prosecution together with the prisoners' pleas of guilty as well as the acknowledgement in their defence is of the opinion that they the prisoners, Te Waretiti, Hohepa Te Umuroa, Matui Tikiahi, Te Kumete, Tope, Mataiumu, Te Rahui are all and severally guilty of the whole of the charges preferred against them.'

What *was* surprising was the sentence.

'The court having found the prisoners guilty of the whole of the charges preferred against them do now sentence them, the prisoners, Te Waretiti, Hohepa Te Umuroa, Matui Tikiahi, Te Kumete, Tope, Te Rahui to be transported as felons for the term of their natural lives.'

Not hanged?

Governor Grey had decided against our execution and, instead, recommended that transportation should be the preordained conclusion.

Major Last signed the Order. It was approved and confirmed by Lieutenant-Colonel McCleverty on 13 October 1846.

———

On 17 October Kumete and I and our companions were embarked on the naval steamer *Driver* bound for Auckland. Te Rauparaha was also with us; it was Grey's intention to remove him from Wellington and meantime gather more information for his trial.

As I was taken aboard, I heard a voice calling to me. I knew the voice: it was my father Korakotai.

E Hohepa e tangi, kati ra te tangi
Me aha taua i te po inoi, i te po kauwhau?
Me kokiri koe ki te wai Horana
Kia murua te kino, kia wehea te hara, e tama e . . .

You're crying Hohepa, but don't cry any more
What must we do on the night of prayers, the night of preaching?
Leap into the waters of the Jordan
So that evil can be forgiven and the sins removed, my son . . .

My world went crazy for a while as I tried to free myself of the shackles around my ankles and the chains on my wrists. Helpless, I pleaded with the officers in charge to let me have one moment with him. They would not let me go to him.

Korakotai had come alone. I saw him staggering along the beach, reaching out for me. 'Don't worry, son,' he called, 'I will free you soon.'

Then he crumpled to the sand, 'Whiria, whiria, whiria,' kneeling there, trying to regain his breath.

'Move on!' an officer shouted at me.

In a frenzy, I tried to lash out at him. 'Will you not let me go to my father? Korakotai! E pa!' With my brute strength I lunged at the officer. He fell to the ground. I got as far as the railing of the ship before other guards grabbed me.

'E pa,' I cried. 'E tangi, kati ra e tangi . . . Don't you weep, Father. Wherever I go I will take your strength. It will comfort me—'

Kumete grabbed me, saying, 'You will only make it worse for yourself.'

'Oh, friend,' I sobbed, 'if I am to be transported, at least it is with someone from my own iwi.'

A guard raised his rifle butt and clubbed me. As I went down, I saw people running to offer my father help.

That was the last I saw of Korakotai. I didn't know that his heart stopped and that he had collapsed, dying.

When he didn't return to the Whanganui River, a small group of people from Patiarero set out to find him. They searched among the kainga of Paremata for many weeks until the local people realised who they were seeking and took them to his grave. They disinterred him and his body was taken back to the Matua Tupuna, the river that he had served.

Fate played a cruel trick. Nobody knew that he had found me, and knew where I was being transported.

———

Meanwhile, Te Rauparaha, my companions and I arrived at Auckland.

There, we were put in prison. Oh, the lamentations and the groans of that grey stone building and all the Maori imprisoned within! This was what happened to Maori when you fought against the Government. You were thrown into an open-air compound and, every now and then, someone fed you scraps that the guard dogs had not eaten.

Governor Grey took the step of detaining two of us for use as witnesses in the coming trial of Te Rauparaha: Tope and the prisoner who he thought was Matiu Tikiaki, finding him amenable — after all he had accused me wrongly and could well be relied upon to falsely accuse again.

This further hardened my heart. 'No matter what happens,' I told Kumete, 'from now on, let us take the side of the other.'

The *Castor* arrived to take us to the penal colony — Van Diemen's Land had been chosen as our place of punishment — and the five of us went aboard.

With the first fair wind, we left Aotearoa. We only had sufficient time to call out, 'E te whenua, tu mai, tu mai, tu mai! Oh Aotearoa, stand, stand, forever stand!' before we were bundled in chains below. For the rest of the voyage, that is where we remained except for short times above deck during the evening.

Poor Kumete was beside himself with fear. Where were we going? Were we bound for Rarohenga, the Place of the Dead, which was said to exist just beyond the horizon?

As for me, I felt no such fear. No matter that I was being transported, I had regained my sovereignty. I had gone down fighting for it. What more could I have asked of myself as a Maori patriot?

You will understand, therefore, that I felt no pity for the Pakeha of Whanganui when, in late 1846, tensions arose between them and the Maori of the Whanganui River. They garrisoned the town with soldiers of the 58th (Rutlandshire) Regiment and raised the Rutland Stockade seventy feet above the level of the river at the most commanding ground in the town.

When four members of the Gilfillan family were killed by Maori at Matarawa in 1847, again, I had no sympathy for the Pakeha. Four of my kinsmen were hanged for those killings, but I fully supported Te Mamaku when he took utu, blockading the settlement for two and a half months, burning, plundering, killing cattle, and skirmishing on outlying settlers' homes. Many women and children had to be evacuated, and reinforcements arrived in May and June, by which time there were nearly eight hundred soldiers and fewer than two hundred settlers.

On 20 July 1847, the Pakeha regiments fought four hundred upriver Maori at St John's Wood, about a mile distant from the stockade.

Even though the tensions were alleviated the following year when the Government effectively repurchased the Wanganui block, paying 1000 pounds for 34,911 hectares, 2200 of which were reserved for Maori, the seeds were sown for continuing dissension between Maori and Pakeha that would never be resolved.

Pakeha, the unstoppable tide, were everywhere. By 1860 they were already outnumbering us.

The great last civil war of defiance was just around the corner.

———

As for Governor Grey, he may have been frustrated in his desire to hang us all, but he continued to pursue his vendetta against us. Accompanying us to Van Diemen's Land was a despatch, in his handwriting, for the Officer Administering the Government of Van Diemen's Land, which read:

> I think it necessary to state that these five prisoners form a portion of a band of men who came down to the British Settlements from their own country for the purpose of pillaging and destroying the Europeans, and who did actually commit several murders and many robberies.
>
> In accordance with their own law, these men ought to have been put to death immediately they were taken, but the more merciful punishment of transportation was ultimately decided on. I beg further to observe that a great advantage would result to this country if these men were from time to time really kept to hard labour, and if they could be allowed to correspond with their friends, their letters passing through the Government of New Zealand. In this manner many of the turbulent chiefs would ascertain that the Government really intended to punish severely all those who connected themselves with murderers and robbers, and would find from the letters of their friends in Van Diemen's Land what the nature of the punishment of transportation really is.

Then one dazzling morning, my four Maori fellow prisoners and I were led on deck, blinking in the sun, and told: 'We dock in Hobart Town today.'

We were stripped naked and buckets of seawater were thrown over us. Then we were given our clothes.

One of the sailors teased me with my tokotoko, offering it to me but, when I reached for it, he pulled it back. Every time I lunged for it, the manacles on my feet would tear my ankles. Finally he relented and threw it high over my head.

I would have dived into the sea for it if I had to!

Fortunately, my hands grasped it and it immediately assumed an attack position. The sailor backed away.

———

I was one of twelve convicts from New Zealand: seven civil and military convicts, and me and my four Maori fellow prisoners.

Does it surprise you that there were others transported with us?

Never forget that in the first twelve years after New Zealand was annexed, ninety-eight men were sentenced in the colony's courts to transportation to Van Diemen's Land.

———

And then land was ahead, and the long sail into Hobart Town. The surface of the sea was shimmering as we approached our destination: shoals of sparkling fish leapt as barracouta attacked them. Then, petrel, gannets and other diving birds were spearing at them; there was no escape. The surface broiled and seethed with blood.

With this presentiment as prelude, we arrived.

'Prisoners! Attention! At my command, *move.*'

Oh, I did not expect so many citizens there to witness my shame. Hundreds were gathered on the dock. Come to mock me and my friends as Jesus and the robbers were vilified before they were taken to the hill to be crucified.

I stumbled, tears of humiliation falling from my eyes. I prayed, 'Let me die now! Do not nail me to the cross! Aue, aue . . .'

My spirit was in despair. But, suddenly, I heard a woman's voice calling in the traditional manner of the Maori.

Haere mai nga tangata o Niu Tireni e . . .
Welcome, brave men of Maoriland . . .

At first I thought it was a seagull calling from the sky above.

Haere mai nga tangata toa ki runga o te reo aroha e . . .
Welcome warriors, alight to the call of love . . .

No, the call was coming from the earth below.

I searched the crowd for the source of the sound. It was a woman with red hair. As my companions and I shuffled from the ship onto the dock, I knew I had seen the woman somewhere before. But where?

A great roar erupted from the crowd. It surrounded me, lifted me up.

I kept my eyes on the woman.

I remembered her; she was the woman with a small boy on the beach at Nelson, and with her had been the Maori kuia, Mahuika. She had three children with her now. Beside her was a tall man, dressed like a gentleman. He took off his hat as I approached.

With gratitude, I approached the woman. 'He aha to ingoa?' I asked her. 'What is your name?'

'Ko taku ingoa, ko Ismay,' she answered. 'My name is Ismay, and this is my husband, Gower McKissock.'

Her eyes were glowing with aroha.

'Come to land now.'

GOWER MCKISSOCK'S STORY

Rhodesia, Africa

PROLOGUE

Rory McKissock-Gloyne, Rhodesia, 1980

My wife Alison thinks I am crazy to risk my life like this.

I have left her with our two children, Tom and Errol, at Silverstream airport, among the hundreds of other white refugees trying to flee Rhodesia — and driven back to the farm.

'Please don't go,' Alison pleaded. 'It's too dangerous.'

And so it is. The country roads are lit on either side. Crops and homesteads have been set ablaze, burning ragged red holes in the fabric of the night. I've managed to get through all the operational security checkpoints so far; and the last one before the farm is just coming up.

When I slow down and stop, the pint-sized officer in charge doesn't want to let me through. We know each other; his name's Harry, we served in the Rhodesian Army together and his folk had a farm not far from ours. His attitude is understandable; the darkness is full of gunshots.

'The rebels are taking over everywhere,' he says. 'They're rolling onward from one farm to the next, destroying everything. They could be back at any time, Rory. I can't take the responsibility.'

I am insistent. 'Let me through, Harry. I can look after myself.'

'Do you have a rifle?'

'Yes.'

He nods reluctantly. 'You've got an hour at most, but then . . .' He shakes his head. 'Good luck.'

I drive through the checkpoint. The country is in the final throes of the war of liberation. The blacks are cheering Robert Mugabe and his Zimbabwe African National Union. From tomorrow, Rhodesia will be known as Zimbabwe: we Rhodie whites have lost. And although Mugabe has promised us, 'We will not seize land from anyone who has a use for it,' I do not believe him. Nor have I been persuaded by his, 'Stay with us, please remain in this country and constitute a nation based on national unity.'

That's why I'm getting out now with my family.

———

I drive through the main gates of the farm and, as I approach the house, my skin pricks with fear and sadness. The three Rhodesian ridgebacks that guarded the property lie quivering on the road, the froth of poison foaming from their mouths. The perimeter of the garden is utterly destroyed. The whitewashed stone walls are daubed with red paint: VIVA CHIMURENGA! Fire still rages in the barn and stables: all the horses have been shot, and lie still in the dark dust.

I stop the jeep and look out the window. Although the McKissock family have owned the farm since 1906, it was the right decision to leave now. And since 1965 when Ian Smith took Rhodesia out of the Commonwealth, fifteen years of war with the blacks has sapped me completely. I've had enough of national service as a soldier; I didn't expect to see so many of my friends killed. If Mugabe and his mates want the land back, well, they fought hard for it.

Sorry, Nanna Georgina. I know this day would have broken your heart. Best to let the farm go.

Time is running out. I should do what I came back to do.

I step out of the jeep but, suddenly, over to the right I see some blacks silhouetted against the flames.

'Who's there?' I shout.

Thank God they aren't guerrillas returning to burn the farm down completely. I recognise four men who used to work for me. I hope like hell that I can rely on their goodwill, but they are carrying machetes and one of them, Samuel, gives me a mirthless grin.

'Why did you come back, boss? This is no more yours. It's ours.'

I've come too far to go back empty-handed. I reach into the jeep and pick up the rifle.

'Stay out of my way, Samuel.'

I let off two shots in rapid succession and Samuel and his friends scatter. But I know if I don't hurry they'll be back with more men and, if there's enough of them, not even my rifle will save me.

———

I take the farmhouse steps two at a time, run through the front doorway and down the hallway. As I pass each room I look in. The place is a shambles and I'm totally pissed off. I thought I was inured to such destruction by now, but it's different when you've been the target. The walls are smeared with shit, and it smells as if a whole army has urinated on the floor. Furniture has been smashed and sofas and armchairs slashed.

But I can't let the rage get to me. Just get the job done and then get out of here.

There's something stopping me from opening the door to the large drawing room. I have to push and push before I can squeeze through. It's the grand piano, smashed to bloody smithereens. And the chandelier's been pulled from the ceiling, its crystal-like tears scattered over the carpet. Somebody has heaped all the books from the bookcase on the floor and tried to set fire to them. The paintings on the walls hang in cracked glass. The alcohol cupboard is empty.

Quickly, I go into the room that had once been Great-grandfather Gower McKissock's old office. How Grandmother Georgina had loved her father! She always kept the room as a memorial to him and woe betide any of us — her grandchildren — who went in without her permission.

The room hasn't escaped the soldiers or looters but, when I look up at the doorway my heart lifts with relief. There's a locked space above it, and it escaped their attention.

I pull a stool of sorts beneath the doorway and lean it against the wall. The key is already in the lock. A quick turn, yank, and I am able to put both hands into the gap.

Inside is a small, battered tin trunk. It contains Gower McKissock's journals. He began them when he came to Rhodesia with Nanna Georgina, in 1906. When I was a young boy Nanna Georgina — and my father, Lindsay, too — painted this heroic vision of him inscribing by lamplight through all the dark nights while, outside, lions and elephants came to the window to watch him. He kept it up for eleven years until 1917. He was ninety-seven when he died.

I should have remembered to collect the journals when we fled the farm this morning but I was focused more on getting Alison and the children out. Bloody hell, we left more or less in the clothes we were standing up in and I didn't even think of the journals! How sick at heart I was when, at the airport, I remembered the conversation I had when I was sixteen with Nanna Georgina.

'Rory,' she had said, 'whatever happens, you must keep the McKissock journals safe. They are our only link with the past. Will you do that?'

'Okay, Nanna.'

I had to come back. I wouldn't have been able to live with myself if I had left the journals behind. Nanna Georgina would have haunted me for the rest of my life. Oh, why did I always have to be so responsible?

I hoist the trunk down from its hiding place. Small though it is, it's tightly packed with the journals and so unwieldy that I almost fall off the stool as I pull it down. The sweat is pouring from my face as I heft it through the drawing room and along the hallway to the front door.

None too soon. Samuel and more men have returned — maybe twelve or thirteen — and a couple of them are hacking at the tires of the jeep.

I put the trunk down and take up my rifle. I fire over their heads. But Samuel is not daunted. 'What you got there, boss? Is it gold?'

They begin to advance on me, machetes and clubs in their hands. I might be able to shoot some of them but if they rush me, I'm a dead man. Alison was right: it was foolish of me to come on a sentimental mission.

What's worse is that I hear the sound of a rebel truck approaching the farm. My goose is well and truly fucking cooked.

But it's not a rebel truck at all. It's Harry from the checkpoint, the little beauty! His vehicle roars through the front gate and he aims it straight for Samuel and his cronies. When they scatter, he slews to a halt. He is red-faced with anger. 'Count yourself lucky that I have a conscience,' he yells. 'I've had orders to withdraw from the checkpoint but I couldn't leave you behind. Now get in your jeep and let's both get out of here.'

I throw the trunk in the back. In convoy, with Harry leading, we make it back out of the gateway and onto the main road. In the rearview mirror, a sudden brilliant mushroom dazzles my eyes. Samuel or one of his men has put some petrol on the homestead to hasten it on its way to oblivion.

As we escape, I think about Gower McKissock. I wish I could have a conversation with him. According to Nanna Georgina, he always believed that however complicated and messy the relationship between black people and white, there was always hope. Well, maybe that was the case in New Zealand and Australia, but in Africa? Here, the continent is so black, and white Africans don't have the numbers.

Ah well, it's irrelevant now that Mugabe and his mates have taken over. With all my heart I wish them well in creating their own vision of a goodly country.

At the checkpoint I thank Harry for his help.

'Tell me,' he asks, 'why was it so important for you to go back to your farm?'

I smile and shake my head. 'Harry, you wouldn't want to know.' He'd probably knock me down if he knew I had gone back for a battered tin trunk that had in it only a bunch of journals.

But as I drive on to the airport, my oath, I feel so fan-fucking-tastic. 'Nanna Georgina, can you hear me up there? I did it, Nanna, I did it.'

Nanna Georgina always said that the journals carried the *memory* of the McKissock family, its successes as well as its failures in its passage through a volatile and turbulent world. Without memory, how could we know whether or not we had left anything of value?

She had also mentioned something about a secret — and the need for some act of reparation.

GOWER MCKISSOCK'S
JOURNAL

Rhodesia, 1906

17

It was my granddaughter Georgina who told me I should begin a journal.

And because she was the one who suggested it, perhaps I should begin with her, Georgina, whom Ismay always thought pestilential with her prying and badgering about the old days in Van Diemen's Land.

If it wasn't for Georgina, I would still be living in my small pensioner flat in Hobart. Instead, last year, she turned up at the door and said to me, 'Sweetie—' she always called me that '—Austin wants to emigrate to Rhodesia. We won't have any family out there. Please come with us.'

The aforementioned Austin, her husband, had had a love affair with Africa ever since he was there six years ago to fight in the Boer War; he volunteered for the First Tasmanian Bushman Contingent serving with the Australian Expeditionary Forces. After the war, he came back to Tasmania on the SS *Harlech Castle*. Georgina first set eyes on him in a pub in Hobart. You had to watch that girl; anything or anybody she got in her sights was hunted down and, well, Austin was a dead drake.

There was no doubt what the attraction was: sex. Georgina had no qualms about admitting one day to me that 'Austin's a hot toddy, Sweetie.' She was terribly modern and always a saucy one with her salacious teasing. 'Just like you must have been once, eh?'

I will not deny it. Although I am eighty-six (I cannot believe that I have lived this long!), my body still daily wheezes into life and my heart still goes tocka-ta-pockita, pushing the blood around my pipes and regularly into regions where the influx brings sufficient movement to prove Georgina's point.

The flesh is, as ever, willing.

Shortly after their marriage Austin, by telegraphic negotiation with a Dutch couple in Rhodesia, bought a large estate near Silverstream at the foothills of the romantically named Mountains of the Moon.

'Please come with us,' Georgina pleaded. 'You know you're the only other man in my life.'

She knew how to get around me with her flattery, did Georgina! She refused to take any notice of her mother, Clara, who told her, 'Father is much too old to go to Africa.' Instead she kept on pestering me about it. She was ever the buzzsaw, wearing down my resistance in the persistent way that Ismay found irritating.

'Oh come on, Sweetie, don't you want another adventure?'

When she said it like that, I remembered that Ismay had teased me with those words too — and I felt the call of the wild stirring in me. Besides, Clara's objections always made me want to prove her wrong. Too old to go to Africa? Poppycock.

I had been feeling, too, that I was becoming irrelevant to the children. They had always loved their mother more than me — Gower Jr, Rollo gone to England, and Clara — and I'd had nothing to look forward to after she died. There I was, circumscribed by four walls, with other old pensioners dying off on all sides —what kind of life was that?

I said yes to Georgina, much to the children's dismay.

Perhaps by leaving I was also endeavouring to bury Ismay under all my heart's scar tissue.

Foolish thought.

———

I transplanted myself for the third time, from New Zealand and Australia to Rhodesia.

When I arrived my first thought was that Ismay would never have liked the country; she always preferred sea-girt islands like New Zealand or Van Diemen's Land. More to the point, she would have absolutely hated the manner in which the British and Dutch settlers went about establishing their supremacy and ownership over the people and the land. The sprawling farms proclaimed their triumph; they were oases of European shrubbery, flower beds, rolling lawns and arboretums in the middle of the great African veld, crowned by grand homesteads. Teams of servants ironed the grass each morning. Guests arrived for drinks and dinner in the mindless, arrogant evenings.

They were the Great New White Tribe of Africa, having assumptions of superiority to the backward and primitive Shona people in their kraals.

Wasn't that the colonising assumption everywhere? One of these days, however, these same primitive people — like the head gardener and his smiling little son Abraham — may surprise us all.

I immediately liked the big spaces here. Georgina decided to call the homestead Trowenna, which some people thought was an African name; how offended they were when we told them it was Tasmanian! Meanwhile, Austin began straight away to develop a large ranch running beef cattle on the veld, and I helped Georgina to put down a citrus orchard and a sideline in arable crops; I have to hand it to her, she wasn't afraid to get her hands dirty, and she was very fair with her black workers.

Austin was never home early in the evenings, so Georgina and I had many dinners together watching the sun go down. One evening, she said to me, 'Okay, Sweetie, I've got some work to do and I am going to leave you alone now. But I've got a journal for you to write in. And here's a pen. You owe it to all of us to tell us the great, grand story of the McKissock clan. A couple of hours a night.'

She kissed the top of my head.

'And don't you dare leave anything out!'

———

It wasn't as easy as that, of course! In fact it's taken me over a month before I have picked up the pen and put it to paper. My handwriting is still as strong, clear and confident as it has always been; some people might say it looks arrogant as it slants its way boldly across the page.

Wonder of wonders, the memories have rushed upon me like a flood tide. Who would have thought that a young Scots boy would see so much of the world and pilgrimage over so much of it? Even now I gasp when I think about it.

Tonight, the auguries are auspicious. The Mountains of the Moon are glorious. The lawns with the last of the sun on them look like a mirrored, glittering wall. Bordering them are the carefully planted glade and orange plantation, and not far away I can make out the smoke from the native kraal. Beyond, Africa is sovereign: savannah, flat-topped thorn trees and the protective forest spreading to the horizon.

It is in this spirit of wonder that I shall start where it all began:

In Edinburgh, Scotland, where I was born last century, to a father who gave his grievously misshapen body to science.

And to a mother who was, from the very beginning, an enigma.

———

18

The misshapen nature of my father Ramsay McKissock's physique was caused by a curvature of the spine which so bent and warped him that, whenever he was ambulatory, he looked like a hideous dwarf out of a Hans Christian Andersen fairytale. From his back sprouted a gigantic lump which made onlookers shiver and wonder at what mess of bone, blood and tissue was entangled beneath it.

God had played a cruel joke on him.

Perhaps if his face had been attractive, that might have compensated. However, his domed forehead and hooked nose, which must have come from some Jewish ancestry — McKissock being the contemporary variation of McIsaac — doomed him to be forever loathsome to look at. He was saved from utter ugliness only by merry eyes and a disarming, if withering, wit.

Ramsay was the firstborn of a wealthy Ayrshire family. Most creatures with a deformity like his had a short life expectancy; indeed, his parents, Laird Harold McKissock and Geraldine McKissock, could scarcely bear the plaintive cries of a babe whose body, as it grew, tried to unknot and stretch itself beyond the horrible mix of its skeletal architecture. Nothing would give, and Ramsay scarcely grew beyond the stunted four feet of height he achieved at fourteen. In this he was fortunate; other children similarly afflicted cracked apart like eggs.

Again, fortunately, Ramsay had the kind of parents who, when he reached his majority, did not lock him up in an attic or put him into an asylum — or have him suffocated or drowned in a wine vat. I am of course jesting — or perhaps I am not, people having always found my humour unsettling, as if I am laughing at them. But Ramsay's impediment could not belie his ferocious intelligence. Educated by a French tutor from childhood to the age of fifteen, he used his formidable powers of persuasion on his parents, to wit:

'You don't want me around, when the very sight of me is an affront to you both,' he said to them. 'If you support me with a respectable annuity until I am twenty-five, I will exile myself. I will forgo any patrimonial title to the legacy that would, by rights, come to the firstborn and, instead, I will assign all such rights to my brother Dougal.'

Ah, the bitter irony. In royalty one could still become a king, like Richard III, hunchback or no. But in the Scottish Vale of Doon, Ramsay's offer was accepted with relief and not a little alacrity.

He left forever the ancestral lands of the McKissock clan.

My father preferred to gloss over the vilification that surrounded him as he made his independent passage through life. Being a laird's son he was able to obtain entry to one of the most prestigious boarding schools in Scotland, where his young schoolfriends cruelly, if affectionately, nicknamed him 'McCrookback'. The joke was on them when he proved, crookback or not, that his intellectual prowess was equal to theirs. Subsequently, in spite of his deformity, he was invited to take a place at the University of Edinburgh where he decided to major in medical studies. He used to tell me that he did so because he wanted to learn more about the affliction he was hampered with.

'The problem was that there were no cadavers with my special kind of skeletal malfunction to investigate,' he said, 'unless I killed myself.'

Ramsay roomed with a shy young Wolverhampton student, Rollo Springvale, who was bemused rather than horrified to be sharing with someone whom, on first encounter, he almost tripped over. But, after all, they were both committed to their studies, and they appreciated the beauty of each other's minds. They soon became close friends.

On graduating, Dr Springvale returned to a practice in Wolverhampton. My father, however, was not able to find employment — what hospital would accept someone of his appearance on its staff?

By this time the McKissock annuity had ceased, and Ramsay urgently needed a job. He took to the teaching profession.

'If all else fails,' he wrote to Rollo Springvale, 'I can always find some employment in the Highlands where, with a dearth of teachers for their brats, the people would have no option but to accept me as dominie. Beggars, as are the Highlanders, can nary be choosers.'

Indeed, it was not long before Ramsay found himself journeying, in 1818, to the shire of Sutherland, owned by absentee landlords, the Marquess of

Stafford and the Marchioness Elizabeth Stafford: the Ban mhorair Chataibh, the Great Lady of Sutherland.

As soon as he set foot in that misshapen land extending from Cape Wrath to the Dornoch Firth, a wasteland of glacial hostility beset by Arctic winds and the sea raging on all sides, he began to laugh: surely there was no crueller setting for a hunchbacked man than such a crookbacked, punishing land.

He was still laughing as he walked into the moonlit Strathnaver Valley, crabbing sideways — which was the only way he could walk — and sending the old women into wails of terror. God was playing a huge joke on him by setting him down amid superstitious crofters who, believing in the Evil Eye, thought the Devil had sent some spawn of evil among them.

I was born in Edinburgh some two years later, in January 1820. By that time Ramsay had returned from his sojourn in the Highlands with, surprisingly, a wife, Ailie Mackay, whom he had met in Achness, the village in the Strathnaver Valley where he was the schoolteacher.

The Gaelic form of the village's name was Achadh an Eas, the corn paddock by the cascading stream. It was one of a dozen small townships northward down the strath to the sea and westward along the shore of Loch Naver. The villagers lived in long, primitive, stone houses roofed with sod. One end of the house was a byre, the other was where they ate and slept. There was no glass in the windows, the uneven earth was the floor, and the smoke of the open hearths wound its uncertain way through a hole in the roof. Scattered about such houses were drystone barns, outhouses and drying kilns — and natural shelters where sheep, goats or cattle could find protection from the icy wind and rain.

My mother lived in one such shelter in a fold of earth. It had an upjutting stone slab for its roof and was set close to the stream. Her companion was an old woman, Mad Meg.

They were the orphan and the madwoman — who was also regarded as a witch — on the edge of the town.

Ramsay was twenty-seven when I was born. He bonded with me immediately. My mother, however, against the natural expectations of maternity, turned away and, not wishing to nurse me, insisted that my father hire a wetnurse to perform that function.

It is therefore not to be wondered at that I adored Ramsay, but felt nothing for my mother.

Shortly after Ramsay returned to Edinburgh he was marked by good fortune. One of his colleagues at medical school, Sinclair Abbott, called upon him. 'Why, McCrookback,' he said, bending down and slapping him on his hump. 'How are you, you human tortoise? You've fathered a son, eh? Miracles will never cease! But hear this — I've come to offer you a job. It is not a senior lecturing position; rather, I am offering you employment as a docent. You may not wish to accept it — after all, none of us who are lecturing could touch you at medical school! But at least it is a foot, if you call your ambulatory appendage that, in the door, eh?'

Professor Abbott set up a haw-haw-hawing. He was not being unkind; he was merely surrounding in jocular language the embarrassment of approaching my father with such a paltry offer. I was having my napkins changed, at the time, and I'm told that when the professor bent down to chuck me under the chin I showed my disgust at his humour by sending an arc of urine into his face.

Ramsay leapt at the opportunity. 'Thank you, Sinclair,' he said. 'The opportunity to work in a teaching environment, with theatre and other hospital facilities, is too good to miss, no matter how menial the occupation. One man's Abbott is another's McKissock, eh?'

He left Professor Abbott pondering as to his meaning.

———

By the time I was six it had become my greatest joy to accompany Ramsay to his office at the university. In those days I did not take offence at the strange glances people gave us — I must have looked like a baby stolen by a gross Rumpelstiltskin — for I adored the company of my fascinating and interesting parent; I did not think his deformity unusual at all.

Not until I reached my teenage years did I begin to perceive the oddity of it — or, rather, decide that other boys' fathers looked stretched out and strange. And, unlike me, who enjoyed my father's company, they preferred to herd with their peers.

Young people can be cruel. Some of them — louts that they were — jeered at Ramsay, especially when I was within earshot. Luckily I had developed a strong body, had facility with fisticuffs, and was occasionally able to emerge victorious from a mêlée; but I must not be too boastful — most often, I did not.

In other words, I was Ramsay's passionate defender. I did this because my father unreservedly loved me; his attitude to me was always one of ineffable and tender sweetness.

As for Ailie, she was a tiny pudding of a woman with a furious red face and midnight-black hair, whose Gaelic tongue was almost indecipherable. It forever enclosed her off in a world in which nobody could understand her and she could not understand others, unless my father or I interpreted for her. Why ever did she not learn to speak English?

Ailie seemed to have such a grim disagreement with the world! She braced herself fast against it, fists bunched and leant into it as it turned against her; she didn't care for it or for any involvement with it. She had brought with her to Edinburgh a world of superstition, of talking stones, giants, supernatural warriors, and spells taught her by Mad Meg, all of which, surely, must have tried Ramsay's patience. They certainly tried mine — like my father, I developed a greater interest in science and medicine than in religion or superstition.

I was often puzzled as to why on earth had my father married her. Apart from their physical contrast, which I overlooked — I never thought of him as deformed — and the age difference between them, there was no meeting of minds, no mutual sharing of intellectual or cultural interests. Frankly, having supped very early on the female form and its vivacity (I was barely seventeen when a young prostitute inveigled me into her clutches and proceeded to ravish both my body and my pocket money and leave me gasping with shock), I found the relationship puzzling. Yet they honoured one another, and he was patient with her.

But I must adjust my comment above by at least giving her credit for some wifely sympathy. Ramsay was oftentimes assailed with pain as his bones cracked and settled into new positions, causing a pinching of nerves and blood vessels, and when his piteous howls and moans emanated through the house, Ailie loved him enough to give him solace.

I remember once, putting my hands to my ears to stop the sound of his cries. I ran to the bathroom where I knew he would be; immersion in hot water sometimes helped alleviate his pain.

'Father, I'm coming!' I cried.

Upon opening the door I saw Ramsay, half naked, hair displaced all over his body like a hideous ape, being cradled by Ailie. Still dripping wet from the bath, he was suckling at her open breast. She was singing one of her wild Gaelic songs. Perspiration beaded her forehead as she towelled his ridged backbone with one hand and, with the other, stroked his rigid loins.

I don't think they saw me as I closed the door. I wasn't embarrassed by this sight of intimacy between my parents. Instead, I thought it the most humane encounter I had witnessed and, for some time afterward, I respected my mother all the more because of it.

I was eighteen when I heard at last the story of how Ramsay and Ailie first met. I remember the occasion for another reason too: I had just enrolled to study medicine at his university and he responded with undisguised joy. 'I'll even leave my skeleton to you when I am dead,' he said, before clasping me around the waist and doing his best to pat me warmly on the back.

By that time, I had grown into what most people considered to be a fine-looking young man. I was not handsome, but had a strong physique and a sufficiency of looks, with white-blond hair that was already receding at the temples — alas, it is now long gone. I must admit I also had bountiful confidence, which some observers took for arrogance — but, surely, one must excuse such a trait in a young man.

We had a celebratory dinner that evening, and Ramsay and I were discussing in an animated manner some scientific or medical issue — I can't remember what it was — and Ailie, as usual, sat silent at the other end of the table. I had a potato on my fork and was waving it about, laughing with excitement — and the potato went flying off it.

I took little notice of it, but my mother picked it up herself.

'Gower McKissock, are you going to eat the potato?' she asked in Gaelic. Her voice glittered like razors, sharp and dangerous.

I was still in full flight with Ramsay but I looked at her. 'It has been on the floor,' I said.

She gripped my wrist, forcing me to watch. With a swallow, she ate the potato herself. Then she slapped me hard, accompanying the action with a pummelling of fists and a hail of Gaelic. With a whirl of black skirts she marched from the dining room, slamming the door behind her.

It was as sudden and violent as the storms that must have descended on the Strathnaver Valley without warning.

In the shocked silence, Ramsay gently gave me a glass of red wine to drink.

'Why is she always like this?' I exploded.

'Gower, a potato is not just a potato to your mother,' he began. 'It can make the difference between living another day or dying, and for want of a potato your dear mother often wept, being close to starvation. So you must not blame her. She is still damaged from her time as a young girl. She has seen such inhumanity as you and I have no comprehension of. To begin with, she lost both her parents during the initial years of the Highland Clearances.'

He began to narrate those terrible times when the great Highland chiefs, wishing to raise on their properties the hardy Cheviot sheep — the only breed capable of withstanding the harsh weather and terrain of the Highlands — forcibly removed the villagers from their lands. Ailie's parents resisted the eviction and led an insurrection; they were tried and hanged. While they still swayed in the wind, she was taken away by Mad Meg, who raised her.

That was just the beginning, for during her teenage years Ailie was caught up in the Sutherland Clearance and what came to be known as Bliadhna an Losgaidh, the Year of the Burnings.

'I first met your mother,' Ramsay said, 'shortly after I arrived in the Strathnaver Valley. I was already aware of the long history of eviction notices served there, and resisted by the people — a long-running battle of many years. Some people paid with their lives, others had already been removed, but most remained in the valley — tenants, tenants-at-will, cotters, tinkers and vagrants — living on both banks of the river and along the loch from Achness to the water's end at Altnaharra.

'At the time, I was immersed in encouraging students to come to the schoolhouse where I taught them the rudiments of the alphabet, reading and writing. I was also trying to understand Gaelic, which is a difficult language, but I had some facility in it. Your mother, Ailie, was one of those who would stand at the window to listen and copy what the others inside were doing, but she refused to come in through the door. Indeed, she was my greatest tormentor, always darting out of the heather when I was in the open and pelting me with some animal turd, or shouting some obscenity about my hunchback. "What do you carry underneath? What shit and muck and piss is under there, eh?" Whenever I approached her, she would run away.

'The first warnings of the removals reached Strathnaver in October 1818, when a man came running across the hills, shouting, "Dominie McKissock! Master!" He told me that the rent for the half-year ending in May the next year would not be demanded, as it had been determined by the Marquess and Marchioness of Stafford that they would lay the districts of Strathnaver and Upper Kildonan under sheep. For five months the land lay fallow before then but, all of a sudden, fifteen hundred summons of ejectment were issued and despatched all over the district. They were handed in at every house and hovel alike — the summoners even found Ailie and Mad Meg in their place by the river. Although your mother had learnt a little of reading skills she did not fully comprehend the import of the notice. She brought it to me to read, and that was the first occasion on which we spoke directly to each other. "Is this summons the same as everyone else in the valley has received?" she asked me in Gaelic. "Yes," I replied. She nodded and then spat in my face. "That's all I need to know from you, you ugly spawn," she said, and she was off, running like the wind away from me.

'Then, thirteen days before the start of the May term, the burners — sheriff officers, constables, foxhunters, volunteers and others warranted to do the burning — came.'

The destruction was begun in the west at Grummore. Ramsay was on his trap, making some house visits, when he came across a messenger who had been sent ahead to all the other townships. 'They have an hour,' he told Ramsay, 'in which to leave their homes and take away whatever furniture they can.' He could already see that Grummore with its sixteen houses was on fire and the burners were moving on Archmilidh. There, all the houses were set alight, with the exception of one barn.

Ramsay knew some of those families; they were good people. The widower William Mackay was burnt out of Grummore and walked far from his wife Janet's grave to die alone in Wick. Robert Mackay, whose whole family were sick with fever, escaped by carrying his daughters on his back for twenty-five miles, piggybacking first one and laying her down in the open air, and then doing the same with the other, till they reached the seashore. There was a boy, Donald Mackay, who was driven from his home along with his parents; he ran naked and terrified into some bushes and stayed there, watching the flames and refusing to come out until the burners had passed him by. By the lochside an old man, also of Clan Mackay, crawled into the ruins of a mill unseen. His dogs kept the rats from him and he survived for a few days, by licking the dust of meal from the floor.

Ramsay stared at me, haunted.

'I have often felt helpless, but never more so than that day. I turned the trap quickly in the direction of Achness to warn them. The sunshine was thin but already the smoke from the fires was circling in the air. The valley was beginning to fill with a terrible noise: the crying of women and children, and the hysterical barking of the dogs the burners had brought with them. No muskets or swords were used, but even so, the swiftness and barbarity of the removals angered me.

'By the time I reached Achness,' he continued, 'the whole valley was on fire. "Prepare yourselves!" I yelled as I drove like a madman through the village. "Take your families and get out. Out! with whatever food you can carry. They have dogs with them." I came across the Reverend Sage, who cried, "But the great Ban mhorair Chataibh would not allow this to happen!

These are her subjects and they love and honour her." I told him, "If that is the case, then why does she visit upon her loyal people fire and destruction?" Already, the smoke was a heavy dark wreath above the valley.

'I drove back to the entrance to the village to await the burners. I had the insane hope that somehow, if I stood there, I could stop them. How foolish a gesture! I heard them coming, raised my crop, and one of their dogs leapt and had me down in the ground in an instant. I could not get up.

'"It's the hunchback," I heard one of them laugh as the burners surrounded me. "Is there nobody else who wishes to defend Achness?"

'They played skittles with me, standing me up and knocking me down until, at last, they tired of their game and left me unconscious. By the time I was revived, it was night and the clearance was over. The first person I saw was Ailie, yelling and throwing rocks at me. "Crookback, how do you think you could have saved the valley? Look at you, you loathsome evil toad."

'Much later that evening I climbed to the high ground above the strath. From the summit I counted two hundred and fifty buildings on fire in a long line for more than ten miles from Grunmore on the loch northwards to Skail. The fires were still burning six days later. The wind sucked great clouds of smoke down the funnel of the glen; spiralling, it curled out to sea.

'Nearly two thousand souls were utterly burned out. Even Ailie and Mad Meg, who were found by three men and their snarling dogs. Your mother held a sharp pointed stick in front of her to keep them at bay.'

My father concluded his narrative. 'She's been holding a sharp stick at life ever since,' he said.

From that moment, I had more appreciation and respect for my mother. I tried to love her, but Ailie really was an unlovable woman. Instead, and indeed for the rest of our lives, we kept our distance, skirting each other belligerently and confining ourselves to polite but careful conversation whenever it was required.

19

I continued my medical studies, enjoying the company of an academy of excited and enthusiastic students. One of them was a young man named John Jennings Imrie, five or so years older but only a class ahead. Our friendship began because we shared a similar schedule and were always bumping into each other.

'Hey! McKissock!' he would call if there was a seat next to him. 'Over here!'

John Jennings was tall, athletic and with the wiry body of a whippet. He liked to keep in shape by running long distances and swimming, and I soon joined him in these activities, often in the mornings before class.

Our friendship developed at such a pace that I soon planned to involve John Jennings in my escapades at the local pubs where young women were available. But he cocked a knowing eye at my intentions and said, 'A fit body and an active mind keep the Devil away.'

I discovered that he intended to become a missioner and, as far as women were concerned, he was adamant that he would keep a vow of chastity until he was married. Edinburgh University was for him just the beginning of a career in the ministry. From here he hoped to go on to Oxford for further training before shipping out as a clergyman-doctor to the colonies.

If only he had not been so religious-minded!

It was John Jennings who discovered my voice had a lovely quality. 'A tenor,' he said, 'is just the kind of singer that a congregation loves to follow.' He persuaded me to join the choir in his Anglican parish.

Who would true valour see 'gainst all disaster,
Let him in constancy follow the Master

There's no discouragement shall make him once relent,
His first avowed intent to be a pilgrim . . .

Now it was *his* intentions that were transparent! I knew he felt I would make a fine missioner myself, but the real reason why I agreed to sing at his church was that Anglican girls were so pretty!

Who so beset him round with dismal stories,
Do but themselves confound — His strength the more is,
No foes shall stay his might, though he with giants fight:
He will make good his right to be a pilgrim . . .

What cemented our friendship was that John Jennings divined very early in one of our tutorials that, while our tutor might have been only a lowly docent, he was peerless in his knowledge of anatomy.

'His surname is McKissock, like yours,' John Jennings mused.

'He is my parent,' I answered.

His eyes widened in surprise. Then he punched me on the shoulder. 'Surely not, Mr McKissock! He is much more handsome than you, sir!'

———

My medical studies advanced successfully, and good fortune attended my every whim. My pathway was without impediment. I had an excellent memory and, aided by analytical acuity, was able to respond accurately to questions put by the professors — or, if not, I could fake it.

The only blemish was Ramsay's attitude to having me in such close proximity. I thought I would be able to spend more time with him, rather than less, and was puzzled whenever I encountered him while I was in the company of my academic peers.

'Hello young masters,' he would say. He would not look at me directly. 'Get you all to class where your superiors await to uplift you in your understanding of your profession.' Then he would turn and shuffle away.

One day, one of my companions asked me, 'How do you know the dwarf?'

'The dwarf, as you call him,' I said, before I threw a blow at him and knocked him to the ground, 'is my father.'

The corridor was crowded with students. I pushed through them, ran after Ramsay and surprised him by picking him up as if he was a naughty child.

'Put me down, Gower,' he whispered as I brought him to eye level. 'Put me down.' His feet were kicking me in the stomach.

'Are you ashamed of me?' I asked. 'What have I done to deserve such coldness?'

He kept on struggling in my grasp, but I didn't care. As for the students, let them look!

Finally he realised I would not let him go until I had an answer.

'Gower,' he said, 'it would be better for you if you would permit me to admire you from afar. If your friends knew I was your father what would they think?'

'Why should I worry about that!' I answered. 'If I see you in the corridor I wish for us to greet each other as father and son. As I do now—'

I kissed him on both cheeks. Then I turned to the gawking students. 'Can a son not greet his parent without the whole world looking on? Go about your business.'

'Alas,' he sighed, distressed. 'I am most grievously unmasked.'

Unmasked? I had only just begun!

From that moment I was determined that everyone in medical school was aware of Ramsay's superior training — whether he liked it or not. I had had enough of the lack of recognition given to him as some professor gave the lecture and he stood in a corner, a mute functionary obliged to fetch, carry and perform practical tasks on their instruction. So convinced was I of my father's rectitude, I soon brought an argumentative spirit to the classes, interrupting the lecturer if I felt he contradicted what Ramsay himself might argue. My father, realising my rebellion, took my interventions with stoicism and tried to curb my impetuosity.

'Gower,' he said, 'I know you feel frustrated about my lowly position, but I am happy enough. Can't you let matters be?'

I could not and would not. Matters came to a head at a medical examination conducted before us by the illustrious Professor Abbott. In his view the patient's symptoms indicated he was prone to brain seizures; he proposed a surgical intervention to relieve pressure on the patient's frontal lobe.

'Nonsense,' I called from my seat. 'Your docent would confirm that the fellow has only a mild form of epilepsy — but go ahead with your operation if you want to kill him.'

My intervention threw the entire lecture theatre into chaos, but I didn't care.

I was called in to Professor Abbott's office; Ramsay was there with him.

'I will not have a student overrule any diagnosis I make,' he thundered, 'or my proposed treatment for it. I insist that your attitude, which has latterly bordered on the surly and the arrogant, must change. Do I have that assurance, Mr McKissock!'

It was not a question; it was a demand. 'I cannot give it,' I said obstinately. 'My private tutor—' I saw my father flinch '—lets you get away with it. I will not.'

Professor Abbott compressed his lips. Without a word, he showed me to the door. As it slammed behind me I heard him say to Ramsay, 'Talk to the boy. It is only my friendship with you that prevents me from throwing him out of the university.'

My father was waiting for me when I returned home that evening. He got straight to the point. 'While you were correct in your diagnosis — Abbott always rushes in where angels fear to tread — what you said to him was impertinent. After all, he is your elder. Your wish to have me recognised is bringing me embarrassment. Even worse, you are risking your entire medical career by pursuing it. I consider it best that you transfer to another medical establishment to complete your studies. I will write to my old friend Rollo Springvale, and ask if he will take you. He lectures now at the Wolverhampton Dispensary.'

'You are sending me away?' I asked, disbelievingly.

'Abbott plans to have you appear before the disciplinary committee and you could well be expelled,' Gower rounded. 'If you are, this will bar you from obtaining entry to any other medical school in the country. I think it best to pre-empt that possibility.'

'I will not go.'

He raised his voice at me, the veins in his forehead almost popping out of his skin. I had never seen him in such a state.

'You try my patience,' he shouted. 'You force me to disclose something that a parent never wants a son to know.' He keened the words: 'I need the position, son! My savings as a teacher have long gone. If you were expelled I would feel morally obliged to resign. Without the income, how long do you think your mother and I — and you — would all survive?'

I was horrified. Was this where my selfishness had led? Crestfallen and ashamed, I nodded my head.

'No, do not apologise, Father. Of course I must go.'

———

Within the fortnight, Ramsay had news from Dr Springvale that he would be pleased to admit me as an intern to complete my practicum studies with him. Just before I was due to leave I had dinner with John Jennings Imrie and other friends; John Jennings had along with him one of his Anglican pretties, a rather lovely blonde girl with grey eyes called Gwen, and I suggested that we should continue the evening revels by adjourning to a local pub. Perhaps

I might inveigle a kiss — or more — out of her. However, they had a prior engagement.

'Come with us,' Gwen said. She took my elbow and, before I knew it, I was being firmly led through the streets and propelled into one of the large university halls used for public lectures. The notice outside read:

TONIGHT: EDWARD GIBBON WAKEFIELD ON THE
EFFICACY OF EMIGRATING TO NEW ZEALAND

Gwen spurned my precipitate advances that evening, but the occasion was not entirely lost: Edward Gibbon Wakefield's address was spellbinding.

'New Zealand is a land of great beauty,' he said, 'and while it is true that there have been problems between settlers and the native Maoris, peace and tranquility have reigned since the signing of a treaty between them and Queen Victoria.'

Five minutes later and I was utterly captivated.

'The New Zealand Company offers to any of you who wish to emigrate the most opportune of terms to improve your personal situation and your wealth. The most certain advantages and successes would be to those who have been accustomed to agricultural pursuits, if such persons, having families, would be content with having small farms of from twenty to fifty acres.'

'What about those in the professions?' I asked, emboldened.

'Certainly! The Company has established a settlement at Port Nicholson and it is now in a most thriving state. Any man of professional bent would be on the ground floor, as it were, within a town that is already seeking men to assist it to develop governances relating to public works, business, commerce and culture.'

'And doctors?' John Jennings asked on my behalf.

'Yes, they are in short supply at the moment,' Wakefield nodded. 'We are opening new towns at Nelson and Wanganui, and they are already petitioning for medical practitioners.'

When I arrived home I couldn't wait to tell Ramsay about New Zealand. He was somewhat astonished. 'I make plans to send you to Wolverhampton,' he smiled, 'and you talk of going even further, to the other side of the world?'

I realised that my enthusiasm was intemperate. Instead I decided to store the possibility away for the future, once I had finished my study.

———

I moved to Wolverhampton. Although I missed Ramsay dreadfully, I soon made good friends among other students who had come, like me, to work under the guidance of Dr Springvale.

'So you are Ramsay's son,' he said, appraising me on our first meeting. 'Did you know I was the best man at his wedding to your mother?'

And no wonder Ramsay sent me to him; he was second only to my father in the precision and care of his diagnoses. His surgical philosophy was brief and to the point: to conduct an operation without any fuss and as quickly and with as much humanity as its complexity would allow.

What was even better was that he had a daughter, Sybil, the eldest of three — the two others also being young ladies: Isobel and Ursula. Sybil was the pick of the bunch, with the kind of petite beauty that marked her out from the crowd. A poet would have apostrophed her pale milky skin and the haughty beauty which marked her out as unattainable. An artist would have sat her against some Arcadian background, garlanded her golden hair with flowers, and painted her in the guise of Spring or Summer; and a composer, noting her lilting voice, would have composed songs expressly to show off the trilling lyricism of it.

In other words, as soon as I met Sybil, at a small function at the doctor's house for his students, I was totally besotted; my sojourn in Wolverhampton might not be so bad after all!

Happily, Sybil reciprocated my admiration.

'May I call on you, Miss Springvale?' I asked at the end of the evening.

'Yes, of course you may,' she answered, lowering her eyelids and blushing. To give me a further hint of her reciprocity, her face lifted and an inviting smile dazzled my eyes.

————

From that moment, I took every opportunity to put myself in her way, presenting myself at subsequent soirées at the Springvales and even pursuing her to Sunday parish services at Grocott's Bradley Bridge Church. There I was ever the ardent Robin Redbreast, singing my heart out to my turtle dove!

And she, fair Sybil, responded with the light touch of her hand on mine or, pretending to adjust an ill-knotted tie, caressed my neck.

Very soon we were stealing precious moments to embrace each other and, at long last, to kiss in a curtained alcove of Dr Springvale's house. How I remember the touch of her soft lips on mine! The way they parted slightly and I was able to explore, albeit briefly, the sweet moist recess within! While I felt like a thief stealing a diamond from my mentor's house, the theft was worth it.

'Mr McKissock, that was wrong of me,' Sybil whispered.

I was put totally in a spin. My love became a longing to possess her in ways that did not exist on the higher plane; I longed to unpin her fair hair, release her bosom from its cradle of stays and confinement, and ravish her.

Our growing infatuation, however, did not go unnoticed by Mrs Springvale; she had other plans for her eldest daughter.

'I cannot offer you any hope,' Sybil said to me when I tried to steal a second kiss.

That only increased my determination to have her. I was so confident that I would; after all, I had enjoyed a certain success with women albeit not the kind one would wish to marry.

Marry?

There, I own up to my developing intentions! The ardent swain in me saw in every coquettish look, every blush and palpitation of the object of my desire, that — her mild rejection notwithstanding — her emotions indicated otherwise. I considered that we were well suited and, not having had much experience with women of my own class — with a hunchback father and a mother without social graces, I had scarcely been able to make the acquaintance of the young daughters of Edinburgh's gentry — I was not about to retreat from the field of battle without her.

Perhaps this wish to possess her made the ardour with which I pursued her appear overzealous. And my poor Sybil began to fret about the fact that our love appeared to be doomed.

'My parents have a different future mapped out for me,' she told me. 'It would perhaps be best if we remained friends.'

Indeed, as I discovered, Mrs Springvale planned an escalation of her eldest daughter to the echelons of the upper class via marriage to a certain milksop of a man, Marcus Wrenn. He may have had a title but he looked as if he would not know what to do with his male equipment — if he possessed any.

I began to panic. I had to claim Sybil before she spiralled beyond my reach. I hastened to make my intentions perfectly clear. The occasion was yet another dinner at the Springvale house for me and my fellow students, and the subject that advantaged me was immigrating to New Zealand — a matter which I had briefly remarked on to Dr Springvale.

'So, Mr McKissock,' he began. 'New Zealand?'

'Yes,' I nodded. 'Although the possibility is not in my immediate future, ever since I heard Edward Gibbon Wakefield at a lecture in Edinburgh extolling the advantages of immigration to that country I have established an interest in going there.'

And then, I fear, I overplayed my hand. I twinned Sybil to that notion and let my impetuous fantasies run away with me. Oh, my intemperate enthusiasm!

'I understand that it is preferable that the male immigrant take a wife,' I continued. As I uttered this broadside, I looked steadfastly at Doctor and Mrs Springvale — and then at Sybil.

For a moment there was a shocked silence.

Mrs Springvale executed a move which would have been envied by Sir Francis Drake. 'Gentlemen,' she smiled stiffly, 'the ladies will retire.' She gathered up her charges and, like a female armada, they made a tactical withdrawal.

From that moment, Sybil's presence was denied me. In desperation, I discovered she would be attending the Wolverhampton Dispensary Ball.

I decided to go myself and, there, ask her to marry me.

———

The ball was a glittering occasion, intoxicating to all the senses.

Sybil was looking ravishing; she made my heart stop. I am afraid I acted in a most ungentlemanly way by snatching her from Marcus Wrenn — he had been promised the next dance — and spinning her onto the dance floor.

'Sybil,' I said to her, 'I intend to visit your parents tomorrow and ask for your hand. Will you marry me?'

Pleasure greeted my words, but then tears sparkled in her eyes as she turned her face away. Her neck was swan-like, offered sacrificially.

'You may ask,' she said in a trembling voice, 'but I fear that it is already too late.'

20

Sybil was the love of my life. I wanted no other.

The accursed Marcus Wrenn had enough gumption to take his dance back and, while he whirled Sybil away, I sought solace at the punchbowl. Never mind her response, I was determined to follow through on the action I had outlined to her.

You can imagine, therefore, my surprise at noticing a very attractive young woman who smiled at me as if she knew me.

'Miss Glossop,' I said, 'I hardly recognised you.'

When I had first met her at the Springvales, I had understood her to be a companion to the three sisters.

'That is because previously you have not paid me any attention.' Her voice was merry and teasing, and I was pleased that she bore no grudge.

My earlier lack of interest in her can easily be explained by the fact that she was not the kind of light-haired and fair-complexioned woman that I found attractive. My preference was not to wondered at; such women were as far away in looks from my brooding mother as one could possibly get. Not only that but, ashamed as I am to admit it now, I thought Ismay too tall — she was my height — somewhat buxom and forthright. I liked my women to be pliable.

We made polite conversation for a few moments. Then, 'Would you pour me a glass of punch?' she asked, 'and perhaps we can adjourn to the terrace.'

I saw no harm in her request, even though it was somewhat forward. After all, she was looking beautiful, her hair was threaded with rubies and her figure was extremely flattered by a ballgown of shimmering green. I could not help but make a comparison with Sybil: whereas she was bright like a summer's morning, Ismay was a mysterious evening lit by a glowing moon.

Yes, I will admit to a slight acceleration of interest!

Much to my surprise Ismay brought up the subject of New Zealand. 'Miss Glossop,' I said, 'I am astonished that you are so well read about the country.' I decided to take her into my confidence: 'I have intentions towards your cousin, Sybil,' I told her.

That's when she unleashed her first thunderbolt. 'What if my dear cousin is unavailable?' she asked.

I was somewhat puzzled by this. Did she know something I was unaware of?

Then she said, 'Mr McKissock, there are other women who would go with you to New Zealand.'

'Others?' I asked. The conversation was going in a direction that was rather disturbing.

'The woman who stands before you is one of them.'

What?

I remember gasping like a fish stranded out of water. Had I not known better, I would have suspected that I had just been accosted by some trollop in broad daylight in the middle of a crowded High Street! The thought was not entirely without a frisson of sexual excitement. For a moment I didn't know whether to laugh — or take her in my arms and kiss her until she was breathless.

'Miss Glossop,' I said finally, 'please do not embarrass yourself or me any further. The berth that you speak of is already taken.'

I took her back to the ballroom. When she was whirled away by a young military officer, Lieutenant Harry Forsythe, I watched her in wonderment.

However, I was furious with her when, the next day, I went to the Springvale household and there met Dr Springvale and his wife. They advised me that Sybil was in no position to accept my offer of marriage. 'She has already accepted the hand of Marcus Wrenn,' Mrs Springvale told me, with some satisfaction.

My mind went back to the previous evening. Why had Sybil not told me? Had she perhaps been leading me up the garden path?

And then it occurred to me that Ismay had known all along that I would be rejected.

The thought of this double duplicity was deeply humiliating. Thus when, on exiting the Springvales', I encountered Ismay — Sybil was fortunate not to make an appearance — I took out all my anger on her. 'Come to gloat?' I asked her.

I have to hand it to her: Ismay was no shrinking violet. With humiliation in the offing, and Dr and Mrs Springvale as audience to it, she said, 'My offer still stands, Mr McKissock. I am serious.'

'What offer!' Mrs Springvale asked.

'You are not even attractive to me, Miss Glossop,' I intervened, 'and I am quite capable of choosing another wife, should I go to New Zealand.' My knuckles were white, and I did not care that my comment was like a slap in the face to her.

She swayed slightly and then recovered. 'I offered to marry Mr McKissock,' she answered her aunt. 'I wish him well in his search.'

Given that that formidable lady had done her utmost to thwart my marriage to Sybil, it was at least some compensation to see her faint clean away.

I stormed from the Springvales' house. As I left I could not stop the rage that was building up in my heart. I felt I could have committed murder most vile on some poor, unsuspecting local, and was only saved from taking such a course when, on return to my student apartment in Wolverhampton, I found a letter awaiting me from Ailie.

Ramsay was ailing.

———

I rushed back to Edinburgh immediately.

When I arrived, I was assailed by a cloying mixture of smells: of perfume to mask the putrid stench of organ decay, and the heavy, sickly tinctures of the laudanum to alleviate my father's dreadful pain. Upstairs in his bedroom, I ignored Ailie's appeals and straight away opened a window.

'Ramsay will die of the cold,' she said.

He waved aside her objections. 'Gower, you have brought the breath of fresh air with you,' he quipped.

Only then did I look at him directly. His face was gaunt and tinged with green. Fearing already what I knew I'd find, I went to his bedside and, again despite Ailie's protestations, pulled back the covers.

'Let your father be,' she said. 'There's nothing can be done for him now.'

'Oh dear God . . .'

The sheets and mattress were soaked in blood, pus and other liquids. And my dear father . . . his backbone . . . had pushed itself entirely through his skin so that I could see the ridge of it, with gristle and tissue still attached, and blood pulsing through the veins. His entire back was mottled black, red and yellow.

It was as I'd suspected: gangrene had set in.

'Why haven't you changed his bedclothes?' I yelled at Ailie.

'Why?' she answered sharply. 'He will only soil them again.'

'Please,' Ramsay asked. 'Won't you both stop arguing?'

There was clearly no hope for him. The realisation of it was suddenly overwhelming. I burst into tears, and cried for a long time before I felt my father's loving hands stroking my shoulders.

'Gower,' he said, his voice filled with purpose. 'There is something you must be told.'

Ailie was standing by the window, grim, her arms folded. '*Why*, my foolish toad? Why tell him?' She spat a stream of Gaelic at him. 'Take our secret to heaven with you — or to hell.'

He looked at her, silhouetted as she was like some dark angel that had flown through the window. 'I know you do not want your part in it disclosed,' he said, 'but I feel the burden of truth. For too long now, Gower has lived with an assumption that is false. I cannot allow him to continue in it.'

'He might walk away from you,' she said. 'As for what he does to me, I care not one jot.'

'All these years he has not been given that choice,' Ramsay answered. 'If he does turn his face from me, so be it.'

He was having difficulty speaking now — his lips and mouth were severely ulcerated. Gently, I applied some ointment to the ulcers. Even so, exhausted, he motioned to Ailie to begin.

She told me the following story.

———

'The whole of the Strathnaver Valley was on fire,' Ailie began, 'when Mad Meg and I joined the clan walking northward to the coast. We carried everything we owned. There we had been told we could resettle if we chose. Who would want to live on that barren, rocky stretch of coast with the wind coming freezing from the Arctic? And the land was already occupied anyhow by others who had been evicted in earlier years.'

Ailie turned to stare out the window.

'It was so bitter that we instead made our way down to Bettyhill and settled around the quay. We huddled there like frightened children wondering what to do, and our food running out. I took to stealing, just to get some scraps for me and Mad Meg.'

With some effort, Ramsay joined Ailie in the telling. 'And then the clan leaders established, with Mr Thomas Dudgeon, a Sutherland Transatlantic Friendly Association. As dominie, I joined the association which, in July 1819, decided the best option was for the clan to abandon their native country and emigrate to America. Other displaced Sutherlanders had already begun settling the plains of Canada along the Red River Valley.'

Ailie turned to me, her eyes glowing. 'America? America! We wanted our leaders to find some way so that we could return to the valley! What did we know about America? A godforsaken, heathen place! And how were we going to get there! Walk on water?'

Ramsay smiled at her simple mind. 'The Association hired a ship which would set sail, along with other migrant vessels from Wick. Your mother resisted the idea at first but then realised that there was no alternative. It was agreed that the passage would be ten pounds per person.

'Ten pounds?' Ailie laughed humourlessly. 'Who among us had that kind of money? But the association told us we didn't have to come up with the lot. We could work out the rest of the passage by being indentured to farmers in the new land. I put down my name. I wrote Mad Meg's name for her, too. Having signed on, Mad Meg and I travelled with the rest of the clan to Wick to await the sailing.' She darted an angry glance at Ramsay. 'Now, my sweet crookback, go ahead and disclose our secret to the boy—'

Ramsay closed his eyes. His breathing was erratic but with a huge effort he got the words out. 'Your mother was beginning to show.'

'To show?' I echoed.

'Don't play the ignoramus,' Ailie shrilled. 'I was four months pregnant.'

Ramsay calmed her down. 'Frankly, your mother's condition had already become the subject of debate. How serious it was did not become clear to her — or to me — until the evening when the tickets came for all the passengers. Everyone crowded into the community hall. There was a big table in the middle, and at it were seated the ship's agent and the clan leaders, among them Factor Roderick Mackay, your mother's uncle. One by one he called the names of the people in the hall. And family by family, the villagers collected their tickets and moved to the other side of the hall. Gradually, all crossed over—'

Ailie began to double up with laughter, but there was no humour in the sound. 'Even the paralytic Bean Raomasdail had a ticket,' she said. 'But for me and Mad Meg? Nothing.'

'I thought there had been some mistake,' Ramsay continued. 'Then I knew, from the silence, that the clan had no intention of taking Ailie and

Mad Meg with them. Factor Mackay simply said, "The ship will come in one month from today and, when it goes to America, all will be on it. Prepare for the journey."'

————

That's when Ailie spoke up.

'Uncle, I have not been called,' she said.

'Your name was not on the list,' Roderick Mackay answered. He would not look at her.

'Mad Meg's name has not been called either,' Ailie continued.

Roderick Mackay nodded. 'Is there someone who will speak for Mad Meg and take her with them? Is there any such person in the hall?'

For a long moment there was silence. But in a small group there was reluctant conversation. 'I will take her,' a middle-aged man said. 'She is my grand-aunt and I will not have her on my conscience by leaving her here. Come across to me, old woman.'

The gathering began to break up. Ailie claimed everyone's attention by walking to the table and eyeballing Roderick Mackay. 'Uncle, what about me?' she asked.

'The meeting is over,' he said.

'Is it now?' she answered. Eyes ablaze, she moved towards the door, closed it, and stood in front of it. 'Is there not one person who will take me to America?'

'Rid yourself of your bastard child first,' came a shout.

'It is too late for that,' Ailie said, 'and don't blame me for something that was done to me against my will.' She asked again. 'Will nobody speak up for me then?'

'Not if you come with an English whelp inside you.'

'The child is also half Mackay,' Ailie defended. 'So a mad woman has a place in the New World, but not me?'

'You've heard the consensus,' Factor Roderick Mackay said.

Suddenly, there was an interruption. A whirling angry shape approached the table and slapped down ten pounds.

'I will pay for Miss Ailie Mackay's ticket,' Ramsay said.

Roderick Mackay paused, looked at the money and then levelled an arrogant glance at Ramsay. 'The account is twenty pounds,' he said. 'After all, the bastard child inside her will need a ticket. You might care to add another ten pounds on top of that as an inducement for any family who would take care of both.'

Disgusted, Ramsay reached in his pocket. 'Take two pounds on account

218

and you will have the balance in the morning.' He made to throw the money in Factor Mackay's face.

With a cry, Ailie ran from the doorway and wrenched the money from Ramsay's fists. 'You, you loathsome spawn of the Devil,' she screamed. 'You do this for me? Who taunted you for your ugliness?' She was quivering with disgust as she shoved the money back at him. 'I will not shame myself by taking it.'

She made a swift farewell to Mad Meg and then, shoving through the crowd, left the meeting. 'To hell with the lot of you,' she said.

Alone and on foot, she battled the wind and rain and made the long return to the Strathnaver Valley. There, she hid in a small ruined house in Achness. Whenever she was hungry she foraged among the black ruins of the towns for food.

A few days later, Ramsay found her. When she saw him scuttling sideways towards her, she knew with a terrible certainty that he was to be her penance and her destiny.

———

I could barely breathe. I think I knew what news would come next.

But Ramsay began to moan. Beads of perspiration popped on his forehead. Ailie quickly went to him and administered some laudanum. While she held him, she continued her story.

'Our bargain was that we would get married and, after you were born, he would look after us both until death us did part,' she said. 'For this,' she continued with a crooked smile, 'I would be his wife and perform all my wifely duties, eh, my crookback lover?'

Blood seeped from Ramsay's lips. 'Your mother and I exchanged our vows in the church at Wick on the same day the clan's ship was due to leave. After the wedding — there was only my friend Rollo Springvale there — we went lochside and watched the people boarding. The old women were clutching at the earth, not wishing to leave. The clan filled the deck, hold and every part of the vessel. Many had never been on the sea before, so that when the ship left port there was a sudden rush to get off it, and the vessel almost overturned. And the screaming! I will remember it for the rest of my life — the screaming fading away as the ship cleaved a way through the loch.'

'I couldn't have cared less,' Ailie interrupted. 'Let them all sink to the bottom of the sea! After all, they were leaving me and my unborn child into the care of . . . of . . . *this* hideous excuse of a man . . .'

Her voice was hushed, surprised, disturbed, loving.

'I hated giving birth to you,' she continued. 'I didn't want you. But, like Rumpelstiltskin, your father claimed you and gave you his name. Who was your real parent? He was one of the three men who found Meg and me in our hut by the stream. My pointed stick could keep the dogs at bay, but not them. "There's nothing here worth burning," they said. "But at least we might have some sport, eh?"'

Ailie turned to Ramsay. Her voice became vicious, spitting the words out. 'Are you satisfied now, my darling hunchback? Is this what you wanted?'

Suddenly there was a cracking sound and Ramsay began to howl.

I had heard that sound before but never like this, in extremis.

Ramsay's backbone leapt completely out of its confinement, ripping through his skin.

'Leave us,' Ailie wailed. She was already unbuttoning her vest, wishing to suckle him and give him solace. How he must have savaged her nipples when he was like this!

'That's not going to help him now.' I pushed her aside and took Ramsay in my arms. 'Please do not make an orphan of me,' I pleaded.

He was making plaintive gasps of pain.

'You are not orphaned, Gower. Instead, you are well loved. From the day I first cradled you, you were mine. All the happiness in my life has arisen from you — and Ailie.'

He doubled in pain again, fought against it, and in a calm moment that followed, gripped me fiercely.

'I have left my body to the university for the sake of scientific research — and, of course, your mother needs the good money they will pay for my cadaver.' He smiled weakly. 'You are not to oppose it.' And then he said, 'Don't lose your humanity, Gower, as your mother has done. There is always hope.'

The pain came surging back and this time it was on him before he had time to scream.

'Give the gnome to me,' Ailie hissed. 'Foolish boy, get out.'

I knew, or sensed, that she intended to be merciful and, somehow, kill him and stop his agony forever.

'No, Ailie! I will do it.'

I pushed her away again. The blood vessels in his eyes were rupturing. Blood was gushing from his lips.

I clamped the fingers of one hand around his nostrils and pinched them tight.

Ramsay's bloodied eyes widened with surprise, but he nodded at me: *yes*.

With the other hand, I clamped his jaw together so that he could not breathe. Even so, the blood still seeped through, staining my fingers. I was perspiring, my heart hammering with grief.

The natural reactions of Ramsay's body made him struggle against my hands.

'No, Father, take good release.'

'Father?' he whispered.

'Yes,' I nodded. I kept staring into his eyes and he into mine while the tide of blood rose in them. Finally, his entire face was bejewelled, as if with rubies.

One final shudder and he ceased breathing.

Ailie set up a demonic Gaelic wail.

21

Although Ramsay and Ailie had lived quietly, I was heartened at the number of people who visited the house during the two-day wake, to pay their respects to him. Whenever the doorbell rang, I would open it and offer a greeting, 'Thank you for coming.' Ailie, dressed in severe black, accepted their condolences. Once they had viewed him — he was laid out in the front room — I invited them to take a drink and refreshments.

John Jennings Imrie, who came with some of my student friends, was a welcome visitor. 'I am departing for Oxford,' he said. 'We will keep in contact? Good.' But I wondered if I would ever see him again.

Another visitor was Professor Abbott who, with a touch of embarrassment, wanted to know what the most suitable arrangement would be for the collection of Ramsay's cadaver.

'You may come in the afternoon two days hence,' I told him. As he left, I saw him give a bank letter to Ailie. She accepted it without a word.

Rollo Springvale came from Wolverhampton, a surprise visitor who, after viewing Ramsay, drew me to one side. 'I never had the chance to say how sorry I was that Sybil rejected you,' he began, 'and what a pity that my niece, Ismay Elizabeth, is so forward. Perhaps if she had not been so bold, you may well have come to view her as an alternative. The girl is so impatient! I hope you do not hold that against her.'

Most curious of all was a carriage which I saw from the window approaching the house. I went to the front doorstep to greet the occupant. Instead of stopping, I heard an elderly voice give an order to the driver, 'Drive on.' As it picked up speed and passed I saw an old gentleman inside, dabbing at his eyes. I wondered if it had been Ramsay's father.

Then the afternoon of the second day arrived and, with it, Sinclair Abbott. He was accompanied by a group of university assistants.

'I will come with you,' I said to them.

I told Ailie it was time for her to take final leave of Ramsay.

'He is already gone,' she said. 'I have no sentimental attachment to his body.' She was dressing as if to go out, and while she was tying her bonnet, she addressed me. 'I kept my bargain, Gower. Now that it is discharged, my obligation to my darling toad is over. I am leaving.'

Leaving?

'I was never a mother to you,' she said. 'It was Ramsay who performed that duty, as well as being a father.' Her face creased into an unaccustomed smile. 'He was an uncommon man. Had he possessed a breast with milk in it, he would have given you suck. All I ever did was to give birth to you, but I could never bear your smell.' She paused. 'The house has been sold—'

'When did you sell it!' I felt hollow, eviscerated.

'Ramsay arranged the sale while you were in Wolverhampton,' she answered. 'We had been living on credit for such a long time! But there are no bills. And you have a small legacy — but you must vacate within thirty days. Sell everything you don't want yourself. I have no desire to take anything.'

'But . . . what will you do?'

'I've got enough money set aside to buy land in the Strathnaver Valley. It is the only place I have ever been happy. I shall become—' she gave a wry grin '—the next witch of the valley, like Mad Meg was.' She looked at me hard, and then tentatively touched both my cheeks and caressed them. 'I tried my best, Gower—'

'Tried?' I asked. 'That was the last thing you did.'

She swayed at my accusation. 'Well, you don't owe me anything, then. It is better that I take my dark brooding presence out of your life for ever.'

———

I saw my mother's grim face for the last time at the window as I helped Sinclair Abbott and the university assistants carry Ramsay's coffin from the house. The day was grey and overcast, and it started to rain on our approach to the university building where dissection of cadavers was carried out.

When we arrived, we stopped in an adjoining room to the viewing theatre. Ramsay's naked body was placed on a stretcher and covered with a sheet.

'I will accompany my father into the theatre,' I told Sinclair Abbott.

We wheeled Ramsay in. I was surprised at how crowded the room was and stiffened — I could not bear that they might laugh or mock him.

Sinclair Abbott was respectful. He asked if I wished to absent myself now.

'Not yet,' I said. Instead I turned to the gallery and waited until the sheet was taken from Ramsay's body.

I heard the murmurs of dismay from the assembled students when they saw that poor, pitiful frame with the backbone arcing out of its skin. Oh, the marble, translucent sheen of him, the matted hair and rude loins, the broken, humiliating beauty of my parent!

'This man was my father,' I addressed the room. 'He was one of the most courageous and loving men that anybody — you or I — could possibly have known. When I was a young boy I wanted to grow up and be exactly like him. Instead, I look like *this*.'

A murmur of amusement rippled among the students.

I could not go on. I was still sobbing when Professor Abbott put an arm around me for comfort.

'Goodbye Ramsay,' I said.

Tenderly, I kissed him.

I left the viewing theatre. For a moment there was silence. Then, as I was halfway down the corridor, I heard the stamping of many feet and huge applause.

Ramsay deserved their acclamation.

But I was already stumbling away from there. I ran, bereft, back through Edinburgh, colliding with people on the rainswept crowded streets. A number of them, concerned, asked me if I needed help.

I pushed them aside, 'Stay away from me!'

When I reached the house I went from room to room, calling, 'Ailie? Mother?' I hoped against hope that I would see her dark whirling skirts, teasing me to follow across the floor or up the stairs. Even though we had never got on in life, maybe she had changed her mind about leaving. Perhaps she had felt some sympathy for me. Maybe she was still there. Maybe . . .

'Mother?'

But she was gone.

———

I think I must have fainted.

When I woke up the house was cold, dark and silent. I remember going upstairs to Ramsay and Ailie's bedroom, taking the coverlet from the bed and wrapping myself in it: I suppose I wanted to have the smell of my parent on me and to surround myself with what was left of him. There was a bottle of whisky and a glass on a bedside table. I filled the glass, sat on a chair by the bedroom window, looked out upon the wintry world and began to drink.

I felt like I had been thrown from a cliff into a dark abyss, denied, disowned and disinherited. Up until a few days ago, I had believed the story of my birth and that Ramsay was my natural father. Instead I was the bastard son of some English lackey who had raped my mother.

That same mother had never loved me — and now she had left me. She had walked away, just like that; and even the house I had lived in would be gone soon. I looked around it and tears of self-pity came to my eyes.

I had been rejected, too, by the woman whom I regarded as the love of my life. As I thought about Sybil, bitterness invaded my heart. I vowed that I would never again allow myself to love another woman with the same strength of feeling. I would keep my heart to myself.

During the week that followed, people came to the house. Among them were Ramsay's lawyer, Sinclair Abbott and a couple who may have been the new owners; the only person I opened the door to was a clerk I knew by sight from Ramsay's bank. He came to advise me that my legacy was available. I went with him to collect it in cash.

I stayed in the house, drinking and eating until the food ran out. Hunger forced me to venture to the market for provisions. Every time I returned I locked the door and continued to watch callers from behind the curtains as they came and left.

The couple were making regular visits and their knocking was more insistent. 'Open up! We know somebody is inside. We will be taking possession soon.'

There came a time when I sought company. I would leave at night and go to places where I could continue to drink myself into a stupor. I didn't change my clothes, shave or bathe. Every now and then there was some poor lass who didn't mind my stench or my wretched treatment of her as long as I paid her the money for it. All I wanted was somebody to punish.

One morning I passed by a mirror and saw somebody reflected in it. I had fallen so far that I did not recognise myself. I wrapped myself again in Ramsay's blanket. It was my only comfort.

A notice of eviction was slipped under the door.

It did not surprise me, therefore, when the next week I heard angry voices. I looked out the upstairs window and heard a well dressed man say to another, 'Go for a policeman. I know the boy is inside.'

When the policeman came, I watched the men force the door open.

'No, no, nooooo . . .' I whimpered, cowering in the bedroom.

Then I heard a voice saying, 'Oh my poor, dear boy.'

It was Rollo Springvale.

That fine gentleman, my father's friend, saved me.

'When you did not return to Wolverhampton to complete your studies,' he said, 'I became anxious.' He had me admitted to hospital where, over a space of a week or so, the staff brought me back from the brink of the abyss.

I was on the road to recovery when he asked, 'And now, young McKissock, what do you intend to do with your life?'

Lying in bed, I had had plenty of time to think that question over. I had come to the conclusion that, with nothing to anchor me to Edinburgh, there was no reason why I should not think of emigrating to New Zealand.

'I will make a fresh start there,' I told Dr Springvale.

'It is a good proposal,' he said, 'but do place it in abeyance until you have graduated.'

I valued the wisdom of his words and nodded.

Then he said, 'Of course, you need not go by yourself.'

I shook my head, realising what he was hinting at. 'I will not humiliate myself by contemplating your niece's offer.'

He sweetened the deal. 'Ismay will not come entirely without compensation. A respectable dowry will be attached to her.'

A callous thought came to me. My financial circumstances were not the best, so why not ponder an offer that would increase my capital? And take someone who had offered herself to me on a plate?

By degrees Dr Springvale whittled away at my pride and persuaded me of the efficacy of considering Ismay as my wife.

'All right,' I said to him. 'I will visit her again and discuss her offer.'

I returned with Dr Springvale to Wolverhampton. My arrival as a prospective groom to her niece was greeted with cautious enthusiasm by Mrs Springvale. But Sybil appeared to take pleasure in the fact that I might be marrying her cousin. 'Do you forgive me?' she asked.

Although I said I did, nothing like forgiveness was in my heart.

Dr Springvale took me to meet Ismay's father, Lowthian Webster. 'You'll not get a penny out of me in dowry,' he said.

'Why do you assume that we seek such a gift from you?' Rollo Springvale answered.

That took the wind out of his sails. 'Am I to presume that you will provide the dowry?' he asked Dr Springvale.

'It will come from the Glossop inheritance left to Eleanor,' Dr Springvale said, referring to his wife. 'Will you allow the marriage?'

Lowthian Webster drove a hard bargain: 'Whatever the dowry that is settled upon Ismay, I will expect an equivalent,' he said.

I could barely restrain Dr Springvale from striking his brother-in-law; I felt like doing so myself.

'You shall have your money,' Dr Springvale seethed.

He made me promise to never disclose to Ismay the conditions of her release.

I remember the day when, accompanied by Rollo Springvale, I met Ismay again. Now that the prospect was nigh of taking her to wife, I took a keener interest in her looks than I had on previous occasions. There was no doubt that she was a fine figure of a woman, even if she was still not my type. Her face was strong rather than pretty but she was almost a beauty and, as such, I would not be embarrassed in polite company.

I must say I was almost persuaded to diminish my coldness to Ismay when she said, 'I am so sorry to hear about your father.'

Instead I hardened my heart. 'Thank you, Miss Glossop,' I answered. 'I have come to ask whether or not you wish to pursue the matter of marriage and emigrating to New Zealand.'

I thought she would fall immediately into my lap, but she did not. 'Have you come of your own volition?' she asked.

'No,' I answered, 'I have been persuaded by your uncle to call on you.'

She countered with, 'You are not marrying my uncle. You wish to marry me, don't you?'

I was vexed by her attitude! After all, she had been the one who had taken the lead — normally the province of the male of the species — and now she was playing the female role. Well, she couldn't have it both ways.

I saw Dr Springvale's face — he had moved off a short distance but could tell that matters were not going well between us. He approached us both.

'While your niece showed interest in me by jumping the first hurdle,' I said to him, 'she baulks at the second and wants me to entice her over with carrots. I shall show willingness.'

'If that is the case,' Ismay responded, 'do improve your dressage and come bearing roses, and not only a desire to call on me, but also to woo me.'

'Woo you?' I asked, trying to keep the anger out of my voice. 'Surely we both understand that if we agree to marry, it will be a contract and not an ardent declaration on my part or yours. Should that not be clear between us?'

Yes, clarity. And I didn't care that poor Dr Springvale could hear every word I uttered. 'Mr McKissock,' he said, 'your tone is uncalled for.'

'Isn't it better, Miss Glossop,' I continued, ignoring him, 'that we both know where we stand so as not to leave any false expectations?'

I well remember the look of regret in her eyes. 'I had hoped,' she began, 'that we would start our negotiations on a more personal basis, but if expectation and sentiment are not to be part of it, then let us settle for a business relationship.'

'Agreed.'

'Are you sure that is what you want?' Dr Springvale asked Ismay. Now that I had made my perspective clear, he was having second thoughts himself.

'I am furious with Mr McKissock,' she told him, 'but yes.'

The next day, with her mother, Selina, as chaperone, Ismay and I began our negotiations. Selina was a retiring woman of faded charms who must have been, once many years past, very attractive.

Ismay suggested that she pay for her own passage; I accepted.

I asked whether or not her dowry would become entirely my possession. 'I understand that as an investor in the New Zealand Company you will be required to purchase a hundred acres of farmland and one town acre,' she answered. 'I will, of course, pay for half of that investment.'

I went quickly on to the next matter for her consideration. 'Will our marriage, though a business relationship, include a conjugal relationship, Miss Glossop? May I expect your fulfilment of those obligations?'

She reddened. Then, stiffly, she said, 'I will be a partner in all things, but I set greater store by my intelligence. Nevertheless I will not turn away from wifely duties if you wish to contract them.'

I don't know why, but her words aroused me and I pulled her close and attempted to kiss her. She was not pliant, and pushed me away.

'My price for your pleasures,' she said in a temper, 'will be that any child of our union will bear the Glossop name, not yours. My own father did not leave me his surname and, under the circumstances, I will not expect you to do the same.'

Her request took me by surprise; I had not thought of children. I gave the matter quick reflection and my own vanity won out. 'I do believe a child's passage through life is better negotiated, madam, if he bears the family name of the male parent.'

She thought this over. 'While I seek equality with the male species,' she began, 'I acknowledge the truth of your argument. But what will you give me as recompense?'

'I will take financial care of the child until he reaches his majority.' I paused. 'Are we done, Miss Glossop?'

'Not quite yet. My mother is to come with me. I will pay all her costs.'

I looked across at Selina. Paused. Nodded.

And then she slapped me! Hard! 'Mr McKissock,' she began, 'were it not for the fact that a single woman could not go to New Zealand by herself without a male superior, I would not go with you. I agree to marry you but although I will say on our marriage day that I will love, honour and obey, the first and third promises I will *not* keep. And you bear the blame for that, sir, for the unforgivable way in which you have treated my open heart and my generosity.'

She turned and left me. I realised that I may have appeared cruel but, after all, the events of the past month had destroyed any idealism I ever possessed.

22

As it happened, Selina Glossop could not come to New Zealand with us.

Ismay was bereft. 'This is all my father's doing,' she fumed. 'Although he has no use for Selina, he will never let her go. I will never forgive him, never.'

Soon afterwards, we were married at Grocott's Bradley Bridge Church. On my side, Sinclair Abbott kindly attended. I had tried to get word to John Jennings Imrie to be my best man, but Sinclair stepped into that position when I received the news that he was on his way to New Zealand himself — with a bride, too!

Ismay's mother and aunt represented the Glossop family; Lowthian Webster did not attend. Ismay was given away by Rollo Springvale, and Sybil, Ursula and Isobel were bridesmaids.

Ismay was beautiful — but my eyes were on Sybil. Indeed, as I was slipping the wedding ring on Ismay's finger, I could not help but glance at her cousin. *You are the one I should be marrying.* I saw Ismay intercept the glance, and the sharp glint of irritation reflected in her eyes.

After the wedding, we changed into travelling clothes for our coach journey down to London prior to our sailing. The farewells were heartrending between Ismay and her mother.

'It is not too late to come with me,' Ismay wept.

'You know I can't accompany you,' Selina answered kindly. 'Oh, but *you* are free now!'

Then Aunt Eleanor stepped forward, fussing over her niece. 'Oh, what will become of you, Ismay Elizabeth?' she asked.

Dr Springvale presented Ismay with his medical briefcase, whispering in her ear, and holding her. They did not want to let each other go. 'God be with you both,' he said as he kissed both her cheeks and shook my hand.

The coach arrived and we boarded. For most of the journey, Ismay looked out the window, watching the world recede behind us.

We stayed in London for a week. I waited for Ismay to give me sign that our conjugal relations might begin, but she gave no such sign. On our fourth evening in the capital, I took her to see Gluck's *Orpheus and Eurydice*. For some reason, one of the arias brought back painful reminiscences to her.

> What is life to me without you?
> All my joy, alas, has flown
> What is life to me without you?
> All my joy, alas, has flown
> What is life, life without you?
> Why remain on earth alone?
> Why remain on earth alone . . .

She began to weep so loudly that she interrupted the opera! She got up from her seat and swept up the aisle and out of the theatre.

'Do not touch me!' she said.

In our hotel we undressed for bed. I held her and stroked her, and she started to weep on my shoulder.

'There there,' I said, comforting her. 'Hush now.'

Her sorrow ebbed away. Silence fell between us. I ventured a kiss. Her eyes held mine.

'You're supposed to close them . . .' I said, 'for the full effect . . .'

Ismay finally allowed me to make love to her.

I was surprised at the strength of my passion, gasping out my climax when it came. Afterwards I kissed her all over and we held each other as our brief union ebbed away from us and we reclaimed our selves.

A few days later, the *Esmond Hurst* set sail for New Zealand. As the ship weighed anchor and slipped away from England, we stayed topside, watching the dark coast until we could see it no longer.

I think it was my own loneliness that made me say to Ismay, 'Well, Mrs McKissock, we are on our way.'

Her face was wan as she looked at me. 'Indeed we are, Mr McKissock,' she replied.

Almost immediately, Ismay became pregnant with our first child.

However, as the ship neared the equator, the foetus detached itself and in a rush of blood slipped from Ismay's womb; a fellow doctor on the vessel, Dr Nigel Carruthers, attended to her repair. Only recently married, and not by my choice, I was at a loss as to how to comfort Ismay.

Nevertheless, when the babe's body was committed to the sea, I admit to a sudden surge of pity for him — and for Ismay. I held her in my arms.

'Let us be friends,' I said.

'Thank you, Mr McKissock,' she answered.

From that moment, I do believe we were able to find a better accommodation with one another. Indeed, I felt as irrevocably committed to Ismay as I did when, on 10 June 1841, we crossed the line and entered the southern hemisphere.

For the rest of our lives neither of us ever crossed that line again.

————

Happily, Ismay conceived again. This time, to insure against a second loss, we settled in Adelaide and waited until the birth. When he arrived, we named him Gower Jr and resumed our onward travel. He was a bonny babe, looking like his mother, and he took his first shaky steps on the soil of Nelson where we set up our home and I began my surgery.

Surprise, surprise, on our arrival I was hailed in a most familiar way. 'Mr McKissock! Mr McKissock, sir! Over here!'

It was John Jennings Imrie, waving to me as if he had just located two seats together in a lecture hall of Edinburgh University.

I was overjoyed to meet him again. He had not known that Ramsay had died and, with great gentleness, he gave me an embrace of fellowship. 'This is my wife Etty,' he said, 'and our two children, Henry and Eliza.'

I introduced him to Ismay and Gower Jr.

'Look at the two of us now, eh?' he smiled, slapping me on the back. 'Husbands and fathers, who would have thought it possible!'

Watching him with Etty and at play with their children over the ensuing weeks, I sometimes wished I could borrow some surfeit of the love he had for them.

I think Ismay considered her new friend a little too puritan in her thinking but, otherwise, they found each other's company congenial. As for myself, I always felt that Etty suffered me because of my longstanding friendship with John Jennings. Otherwise we were perfectly polite to each other and, all in all, we became a fond foursome, meeting socially at least once a week.

John Jennings admired Ismay immensely, especially her intellectual acumen. 'You have a fine wife, Gower McKissock,' he told me. 'What she ever saw in you I will never understand!'

I did not tell him the circumstances of our contract.

———

We eased ourselves into the settlement, building a small cottage and establishing ourselves in the eager, excited community. I soon developed a thriving surgery and was especially pleased when Maori patients began to arrive; if they did not have money to pay for their treatment, I would arrive home with a little pig trotting after me for Gower to play with, or some fish, or a brace of fat woodpigeons.

But I could not understand their rapid and complicated language! I was therefore pleased when Ismay struck up friendship with an old Maori lady who agreed to give her lessons; Mahuika thereafter considered her status as language tutor an entitlement to come by the surgery whenever she wished, oftentimes smoking us out with the horrible smell of her vile topeka.

It was worth it: Ismay proved an excellent helper in translating the ills that vexed the Maori patients who then flooded in.

I only wish the settlement's political relationships with the Maori were as amicable. During our second year troubles escalated between the New Zealand Company and the chiefly landowners in an alarming, frightening way.

———

Then came the Wairau Incident of June 1843, when Te Rauparaha and his nephew, Te Rangihaeata, killed a number of settlers who had gone to resolve the situation. The affair was so horrific that it was no wonder the whole township took fright, especially since among those murdered had been the very popular Captain Wakefield, head of the settlement. When we heard that the chiefs were on their way to sack Nelson, there was an exodus from the port of settlers seeking the safety of Wellington.

Ismay and I stayed until the last moment. We were reluctant to leave but, under persuasion of town officials, boarded the *Aldred Leith,* the last vessel left in the port.

How were we to know that, instead of going to Wellington, it was bound for Van Diemen's Land!

'Ah well,' I said to Ismay, 'it will take us just a little longer to return.'

Imagine my surprise when she looked at me and said, 'Why don't we consider staying in Van Diemen's Land, when we get there?'

I was dumbfounded. I had truly expected Ismay, our son Gower Jr and

I to grow, prosper, and live our entire lives in New Zealand. I assumed we would have grandchildren who would be New Zealanders and that Ismay and I would eventually be put to rest in the rich, dark soil of Aotearoa, as the Maori called their land.

'What about our house in Nelson?' I asked Ismay. 'And our furniture and belongings? What about my surgery? We did not sign up for Australia.'

Once the idea took hold, however, Ismay was away with it like a mare who had bolted. 'We can always send instruction to a New Zealand Company agent to sell our house and the surgery and have the money sent on. We cannot turn back now, can we? Why not go forward? Don't you want another adventure, Mr McKissock?'

'I thought we were to be New Zealanders!' I said, shaking my head.

'Who is to say that Fate does not have a hand in this and has chosen differently for us?'

I laughed out loud. 'Your uncle always told me you could never be curbed!'

We danced a jig of acceptance on the boat, with Gower Jr dashing in among his mother's skirts.

———

Four days later, on a bright sparkling morning, I came across Ismay on the prow, staring ahead. The sea was dazzling with sun-stars like a bright shining pathway. I had to shade my eyes against the glare. The light shimmered all over Ismay, clothing her with an extraordinary glowing sheen.

'You won't believe me, Mr McKissock,' she said, 'but when I was a girl in Wolverhampton I dreamed of this sea.' She snuggled herself into my arms. 'Hold me, Gower McKissock. Hold me just once as if you really meant it?'

Her voice was fearful and the way she spoke made me shiver with apprehension.

23

I write those lines above in the certain knowledge that they do not portray me in a heroic light. However, Georgina had said, 'Don't leave anything out!' and let me confess that, looking at the young man I was then, I would not have approved of myself either.

In my own defence allow me, as the older edition of Gower McKissock, to take a walk on the deck of the *Aldred Leith* as it approaches Van Diemen's Land. Let me gently confront my younger self as he stares ahead at a new horizon.

I tap him on the shoulder and he turns. I am so envious of the strong, virile, masculine youth that I once was!

'It's a big world out there,' I say, as I join him at the railing.

'Yes, aged sire,' he answers, 'it is.' His voice is pleasant and his demeanour, while serious, indicates that he is not without a sense of geniality.

'It's not too late to turn back,' I tell him. 'Why don't you return to New Zealand or even to Scotland?'

He looks up at the sun, bursting across the ocean. He closes his eyes, taking in the warmth and brightness, but I see pain etched there. 'The past offers nothing for me, and what would I go back to Scotland for?'

'Must Ismay and Gower Jr be obliged to accompany you?' I ask him gently. 'Why not release them now? Would that not be the kind thing to do? Ismay could find herself another husband.'

'She herself chose to become my wife,' he answers, 'and came of her own volition. I did not force her.'

'Your taste for prostitutes?' I press him. 'In Nelson you maintained your interest, do not deny it. The guise you wear of moral probity is false, sir.'

He accepts my reprimand but states his case. 'I am not the first man, nor will I be the last to make love to his wife without loving her. Nor am I the first husband to enjoy female company outside of marriage. Regarding the former, did not my own parents marry without love and, lacking that commodity, yet sustain the marriage over twenty years? Like my father, Ramsay, I will accomplish the same. As for Gower Jr, his destiny is already yoked to ours. Therefore it is much too late to uncouple ourselves. Best to keep on going forward, together, whether we like it or not, in our desire to find . . .'

He is at a loss for words.

'Find what?' I prompt him.

'A home in the world,' he adds. 'While love does not impel that desire, others have begun with less.'

———

And so Fate took us to Van Diemen's Land.

'It looks smaller than I thought it would be,' Ismay said as we looked at a map of our unexpected destination.

'The illusion is caused by the whisky gut above it,' I answered, gesturing to the Australian continent looming over the island. 'In fact, Van Diemen's Land is half the size of England and Wales combined, rugged, forested and similar to New Zealand.'

Ismay laughed at my jest. 'Perhaps we can make the continent disappear like Jonathan Swift did in *Gulliver's Travels*,' she responded.

'How did he do that?'

'He marked Lilliput on a map as being northwest of Van Diemen's Land,' she answered. 'As for the rest, there was nothing but empty sea!'

Land masses may be made to disappear by literary sleight of hand, but Australia *did* exist, with four scattered colonies to indicate that England had vested interest. The colony at Botany Bay, New South Wales dominated, ruling Van Diemen's Land, Port Phillip at Australia Felix and New Zealand. Other colonies at the Swan River, Western Australia and Adelaide, South Australia, rounded out the sum total of the British presence in our part of the world now.

Then a sailor cried 'Land ho!', and Ismay and I took Gower Jr out on deck to look towards the direction of the afternoon sun.

'Where is it?' Ismay asked me, clutching my arm. 'Oh, show me, Mr McKissock!'

I caught her enthusiasm; we had had enough of the open sea. Peering ahead, I shaded my eyes against the sun. Had I been of a fantastic bent, I might have thought we had bypassed Van Diemen's Land altogether and in fact reached Lilliput.

Ahead was a jewel sparkling in a sea of indescribable beauty; dark purple, streaked with layers of gold and deepening to vermilion. Just below the surface was a layer of pink jellyfish, like a bed of aquatic flowers strewn across our pathway. Then, leaping, spraying high, came a school of great giant whales to create an avenue of arching rainbows.

I saw Ismay close her eyes in bliss. When she opened them she saw me watching her.

'I make a wish, Mr McKissock,' she said, 'for you, me and Gower Jr.'

———

It was with such optimism and a fine breeze — and with the bracing air filling our lungs — that we entered the Derwent and took on a pilot. A grand succession of bays and lovely inlets luxuriant to the water's edge opened up to us.

'Just think!' Ismay exclaimed. 'All this could have been a French possession.'

As had similarly occurred in New Zealand, the fear of a Terre Napoleon so close to Australia — Nicolas Baudin on the corvette, *Géographe*, mapping Bass's Strait and Van Diemen's Land — had caused New South Wales Governor King to checkmate the French. On 12 September 1803 John Bowen, with thirty men of the New South Wales regiment and about a hundred settlers and convicts, duly claimed Van Diemen's Land. The following year, Hobart Town was founded by David Collins.

With this history in mind I looked, for the first time, on the settlement which had been established twenty miles inland. Forty years after its founding, Hobart Town was undoubtedly on its way to becoming one of Britannia's most important southern outposts. Numerous sandstone buildings — government buildings, shops and warehouses — clustered in a commercial area around the port. Behind them was an amphitheatre of forested hills and promontories, capped by the imposing and noble backdrop of Mount Wellington, over four thousand feet high.

All was reflected in the still water.

'A new beginning, Mr McKissock,' Ismay said.

'Yes, a new beginning Mrs McKissock,' I answered.

———

Oh, but appearances were deceiving.

The *Aldred Leith* came to anchor about four o'clock that afternoon. The waterfront bustled with life, its many bars and hotels doing a roaring trade. Around us, ships of all sizes were unloading their cargoes. Among them were two prison vessels recently arrived from England.

Prison vessels from England?

I gave a quick intake of breath. All the beauty and optimism of making a new life in Van Diemen's Land slipped away.

'What is it?' Ismay asked.

'We may have jumped from the frying pan into the fire,' I said.

I had completely forgotten that Van Diemen's Land was no ordinary British colony. Only three years had passed since New South Wales closed as a transportation destination; now, just Van Diemen's Land and Norfolk Island remained as the official recipients of convicts. Indeed, as I watched I saw wretched, yellow-liveried inmates being marched from one of the hulks onto the quay under the supervision of a whip-wielding, red-coated military guard.

The whip cracked and the loud report opened a memory in my mind.

When I had been a student at Edinburgh a Scottish doctor, recently returned from Australia, had described to us the punishment of felons at Port Arthur, the main prison in Van Diemen's Land.

'All the inmates were mustered,' he began, 'to watch the flogging of one of their number. The prisoner's shirt was stripped off to the waist and he was tied, with arms splayed, to the inhuman triangle. The warden took up the implement of punishment, a cat o' nine tails with nine doubled twisted and knotted cords; with each stroke it was therefore possible to inflict eighty-one wounds. He began to lay on to the prisoner, who screamed at each lashing. At twenty-five strokes the poor wretch passed out. He was untied and put in a bath of cold seawater until he revived. Then he received a further twenty-five strokes of the whip. The flogging turned his back into a mangled piece of flesh from which enough blood ran to fill his shoes till they gushed over. And this, gentlemen, is the system that George Arthur, fifth Lieutenant-Governor of the Colony and chief enforcer, hails as "the most humane punishment the wit of man ever devised". The *wit* of man? No, gentlemen, the satanic in man.'

I shook my head to clear the memory and looked around with undisguised dismay. I was struck by the incongruence of it all: the beauty of Hobart Town and its seemingly normal appearance were at odds with the monstrous primary function of Van Diemen's Land.

Heaven and hell existed here together.

But Ismay's face was filled with a quiet hope. 'The Lord cares for sparrows,' she answered. 'He also cares for fallen ones and others like us blown by the wind.'

Even so, I was not reassured when the captain introduced us to a customs and excise official who had come aboard to check his papers and cargo.

'So,' the official joked, 'a family of three from Maoriland, eh? How do I know you have not just escaped from yonder prison ship?'

'Sir, you will frighten the child,' I rebuked him.

'Beg your pardon, sir,' he said, drawing back chastised. 'You intend to stay? Allow me to escort you to immigration. Best get your papers sorted quick and lively as free citizens.'

'Free citizens?' I replied. 'The term is unknown to me.'

'Why,' he explained 'it is to distinguish you from those who have been transported.' He bent down and patted Gower Jr's head. 'We wouldn't want your father mistaken for a felon and taken away in the middle of the night to Port Arthur, would we, little boy?'

On that somewhat disorienting note did Ismay and I disembark with Gower Jr into Van Diemen's Land, Britain's 'Gaol of the Colonies'.

'Are you sure you wish to stay?' I asked Ismay.

'I am certain, Mr McKissock,' she answered.

Following the receipt of our papers of citizenship, I raised a loan from the local bank on the collateral which Ismay had so cleverly brought with her from New Zealand: the deeds of our house and surgery. With that money we moved into a small but comfortable three-bedroomed residence at Arthur Circus.

The cottage was very English in style, separated from the street by iron railings and perfectly set off with beds of hollyhocks and roses.

'I shall order some long white broderie anglaise curtains for the drawing room,' Ismay exclaimed, 'and an oval walnut table and a mahogany-backed chaise-longue, which I shall place by the bay window.'

Close by, construction of the St George's Church was almost complete. Within walking distance, by way of Kelly's Steps was Salamanca Place, an ideal location for my surgery.

However, we were running short of funds. 'We must wait until we receive money from the sale of our house in Nelson,' I said to Ismay. 'Meanwhile, I shall try to find a job assisting in some other doctor's practice.'

'Nonsense, Mr McKissock,' she answered.

As always, she was as much the decision-maker in our relationship as I was, and not always willing to let me have the upper berth. Taking herself off to the local pawnshop, she placed her ruby necklace and earrings under care to purchase a lease on a small office close to the harbour.

'You need a surgery,' she said. 'Do not berate me so! You may do with your property what you will. Allow me the same privilege for mine.'

Thus, after diplomatically introducing myself to the medical practitioners currently operating in Hobart Town and assuring them I would not poach their customers, I opened for business. Proximity to the port brought me a strong flow of casual trade — every ship disembarked sailors who required treatment for accidents at sea, and every hotel always had its quota of patrons seeking alleviation from doses of the clap.

Not quite the business I was looking for, but beggars could not be choosers.

We settled into the unique and disquieting society that made up Hobart Town.

Long gone were the days when the colony was on the brink of famine, saved from starvation only by the meat of kangaroos. Gone also was the menace of the bushrangers, such as Mosquito and other escaped convicts, who had rampaged among the hard-working farmers and terrorised the colony.

Instead, the lineaments of a polite, prosperous and free society were everywhere evident in the settlement. The residential areas were surprisingly clean and their streets long and wide. There were also many very attractive gardens. The houses themselves were built on a universal plan — either of brick or elaborations of the early settler cottages, with walls of wattle and daub or logs of local cedar or eucalypt — but with four rooms instead of two, sometimes an upper storey and frequently a lean-to at the rear. The more handsome mansions — homes of wealthy merchants and rural gentry — occupied the ground closer to the hills. If you did not look too closely you could almost believe that you were in some rural town in England itself.

How odd to see the British aesthetic reproduced so cleverly in this distant land!

Hobart Town could, in fact, have passed itself off as a perfect copy, were it not for the sight and sound of the grey-garbed prison gangs and the soldiers who guarded them as they worked at compulsory service or on loan to settlers. Yes, the townspeople went about their business, and always the sea breeze blew from the rippling ocean and the golden sun shone from a clear blue sky — but at no time were we free from contact and consciousness of the convicts.

There was the rub. It was as if some English landscape artist had painted

240

a bucolic, rustic scene and, in the background, a chain gang was being whip-harried along a country lane.

High overlooking the town and harbour were the Anglesea Barracks, a daily reminder that benign appearance notwithstanding, Hobart Town, with its mix of convicts and free citizens, was not as it seemed.

————

One evening, after putting Gower Jr to bed, and while we were having dinner, Ismay gave me some news.

'Mr McKissock, we are to be parents again.'

There was a lilt of excitement in her voice, and I think she expected me to show some sign of gladness.

Forgive me, but I could not hide the expression of unwillingness on my face. I had grown accustomed to being the father of Gower Jr — but children in the plural? That threatened my equanimity.

The regretful words came to my lips. 'I do not want another child in the house,' I said.

A look of disbelief and then outrage passed over her face. 'You dare to impose your conjugal rights upon me, sir, and yet you do not expect the consequences of that — a child? There's nothing can be done about it unless I terminate it. Is this what you wish?'

I put down my knife and fork and stared hard at her. 'No, madam, I do not.'

'Why are you so adamant?' she asked.

Surely it was obvious why? I did not love Gower Jr. How could I welcome a second child?

A long pause ensued. 'Then what's to be done, Mr McKissock?' she asked, her lips quivering with anger.

Ours was always a relationship where ground was contested and, as always, when Ismay was bearing down on me I countered with undue violence. 'All right,' I conceded, bringing my fist down on the table. 'Bring the new child into our lives. I will keep to my side of our contract and support it. But you look after it! You!'

Why was I so harsh?

We completed the meal in silence. When it was over, Ismay stood up. 'I shall excuse myself, Mr McKissock,' she said, collecting the dinner plates from the table. 'But,' she added, 'I would suggest that if there are to be no further children, you take your exclusive pleasure with the prostitutes I know you frequent. Seek my bed no further for I am sick at heart with you.'

My face burned with embarrassment. So Ismay knew, did she? Why didn't she leave me!

Ah well, better for her to face the reality.

Nor would I apologise to her.

24

Somehow, we managed to patch our lives together.

I committed myself to the surgery and, during the evenings, Ismay and I were civil to each other.

Then in August 1843 — I remember the month for the political turmoil which surrounded the dramatic replacement of Lieutenant-Governor John Franklin with John Eardley-Wilmot — I was delivered a letter from my good friend, John Jennings Imrie. Like us, he and Etty had quit New Zealand the month before on the *Sisters* and were now living in Van Diemen's Land! Not only that, but John Jennings had secured a position as a catechist at Port Arthur, some seventy miles away, on the Tasman Peninsula.

'Why not visit with us, Mr McKissock?' he wrote. 'Etty and I would love to have you, Ismay and Gower Jr come for a weekend.'

The opportunity to give ourselves space was too good to miss. 'It would be so good to get into the country,' I told Ismay, 'even if Port Arthur is not the best hostelry.'

'Yes, I should like that,' Ismay answered, looking up from the note which John Jennings had slipped in with his own letter. 'Etty tells me they've just added a third child, Jessie, to their brood. The change of air will do me good and I feel the need of another woman's sympathy.'

By prompt exchange of letters, John Jennings and I came to an agreement on dates, and we were soon making our way by ship from Hobart Town to Port Arthur.

———

The vessel sailed up to the Peninsula, lofty, rocky, clothed in dense scrub, and turned inland.

For all my excitement at the prospect of seeing my old friend, I did so with some trepidation. It was one thing to hear the bleak stories of men, women and children transported as convicts, but to actually witness their degradation first-hand was another. One hundred thousand people from all over the British Empire had already been sent to Australia; 72,000 had wound up in Van Diemen's Land and 12,500 at Port Arthur.

These were the thoughts that came to my mind as the water became calm and we approached Point Puer and the Isle of the Dead.

Ismay was taken aback. 'I didn't realise it would be so beautiful,' she said.

It was an early afternoon in the middle of winter when we entered the spacious and sheltered harbour of Mason Cove. Situated beside the water, with expansive green sward and agreeable avenues of trees, Port Arthur had a beauty that belied its purpose as a place of imprisonment. In the pale sunlight, the scene was overwhelmed with sombre loveliness.

But into this heaven had been transposed hell. Convict ships crowded the harbour and dockyard. One of the ships, the *Marquis of Hastings*, caught my eye; it looked like an ex-slaver, and I shuddered to think of the horror of being transported below decks in such an old hulk. Stretching behind the harbour was the punishment station: penitentiary buildings, dormitories, work factories and sentry positions. On the low-lying slopes beyond were Civil Row, the Commandant's House, military barracks and watchtowers.

Everywhere were gangs of convicts marshalled by soldiers.

———

John Jennings and Etty were waiting at the dock with their brood and a couple of convict servants.

'Scotland, New Zealand and now Australia,' John Jennings smiled as we shook hands. 'Wherever will we meet next, Mr McKissock?'

Etty showed Ismay the new babe, Jessie. Noting Ismay's delicate condition, she prodded John Jennings to congratulate us both. 'Who's following who, eh?' he asked as he pumped my hand.

Instructing the two servants to take up our bags, he led the way to their cottage on Civil Row. 'We have managed to get you into one of the vacant houses,' he said. 'Normally they're reserved for important personages but—' he looked at Ismay '—one of the officers in charge apparently knows your Uncle Rollo and asked you to dance at a ball in Wolverhampton.'

'Why, that must be Lieutenant Harry Forsythe,' Ismay laughed.

'He's captain now,' Etty answered, 'and has gone up in the world. He conveys his apologies as he is away visiting one of the other penal stations at Maria Island.'

244

We were halfway to our accommodation when, coming towards us, was a small gang carrying bricks to the dock. As they drew abreast I saw a young face among the men — and he saw me. He must have been all of fourteen. With a sudden lunge he reached out and grabbed my right hand.

'Please help me, sir! Please . . . I beg you, rescue me from here.'

A guard stepped up to the lad. 'Get back into line,' he shouted. 'Back!' He used the crop of his whip to strike the boy.

I wanted to take his whip and strike *him*.

John Jennings apologised for the incident. Although I was upset by the encounter, I pretended to be calm. 'Do not punish the lad on my account,' I said to both him and the guard.

In a somewhat shocked silence we continued to Civil Row. Once ensconced, and after a cup of tea, John Jennings looked at me. 'Although it is getting late, would you care to look at Port Arthur? We have just enough time before curfew.'

I took a quick glance at Ismay, knowing that she would dearly love to accompany us.

Etty had other ideas. 'The sights are not for women such as you and I, Ismay,' she said. 'Instead, we will take the children into the Government Gardens. You will so enjoy the flowers! The original plants were brought directly from England or collected by officers passing through Cape Town, India and Rio de Janeiro. It is passing beautiful there, and some of the other ladies will be about.'

I saw the frown of vexation on Ismay's face. The restrictions placed on women, which allocated them to a lesser place than men, never sat well with her. But she managed a nod and a smile. 'Yes, Etty dear, it will be lovely to rid ourselves of the men.'

The women and children went on their way. I followed John Jennings as he showed me the extraordinary complex of the penitentiary and gave me some of its history.

'Port Arthur's so different now,' he began. 'In 1830, when the first convicts and their guards arrived, there was just a prisoners' barracks around a central courtyard with a flogging yard nearby. Now look at it!'

The earlier encounter with the young prison boy had upset and unsettled me, however, and I was not about to let John Jennings obscure the true history of the penitentiary. 'You sound so proud of the place,' I answered, 'but George Arthur signed some fifteen hundred death warrants during his tenure; one hundred were executed in his first year! Wasn't Charles O'Hara Booth commandant for eleven years? Some people consider him to have been a sadist and a monster.'

John Jennings gave me a warning look. 'Best to keep your voice down, Gower. Port Arthur after all was, and still is, a prison of maximum security; there were no angels to be found here.'

'They were flogged, John Jennings, flogged! Some spent their entire term of imprisonment in leg-irons. Others were hanged and . . .'

He stopped me with a stern rebuke. 'What did you expect, sir? They were the most hardened of convicted British and Irish criminals! Certainly they were not pampered, but the penitent did not go unrewarded — and times have changed. The chain gang, the lash and even the death penalty are all considered repulsive, and justifiably so. Port Arthur is a model prison of the Empire now.'

He led me around the perimeter of the prisoners' area and prisoner barracks, moving up the slight incline to the guard tower. Soldiers on duty saluted, asked for John Jennings' papers, and allowed us to proceed. I spied many small convict gangs at work: shovel, pickaxe, wheelbarrow and cart were their implements of toil. Some were returning from cutting timber or quarrying, breaking and transporting rock for roads in Hobart Town.

By degrees we came to a very fine lookout, where John Jennings outlined future plans.

'We've come a long way from the days when convicts were sentenced to transportation for the term of their natural lives,' he began. 'Have you heard of the Molesworth Committee?'

'Yes,' I answered. In 1837 the British House of Commons had appointed a five-year inquiry under Sir William Molesworth into convict trans-portation.

'Then surely,' John Jennings continued, 'you would acknowledge that the system of rewards they introduced is revolutionary?'

The committee had produced the probation scheme: transportation occurred only for sentences greater than seven years. Once transported, prisoners were required to spend between one and two years in a probation gang on government hard labour. If they earned a good character certifi-cate, they could become probation pass-holders, enabling them to work for wages as 'assigned servants'. Continued good conduct might entitle them to tickets of leave. Finally, an absolute pardon might be received enabling them to settle in Van Diemen's Land.

'Port Arthur has become a machine for grinding rogues honest,' John Jennings said. 'Discipline, relentless surveillance and punishment are but one part of their rehabilitation. But trade training is also a function here.

There are workshops for carpenters, coopers, wood turners, foundry men, blacksmiths, painters, tailors, shoemakers and nailers. And look at the dockyard—'

I followed John Jennings' pointed finger.

'At least fifty men are employed on building large decked vessels and smaller eight-oared whaleboats. But the best news, Gower, is that soon solitary confinement, not the lash, will be the ultimate punishment. We're building a separate prison modelled on Bentham's panopticon for that purpose. There, felons who disobey the rules will spend between several hours and thirty days on bread and water. This circular prison, perfectly Benthamite in conception, is the ultimate in penology, the most clever punishment devised. Even when prisoners are taken out for exercise each day, their faces will be covered with face-masks with apertures only for the eyes.'

'It sounds as horrifying as the lash,' I answered.

'Can't you see, Gower?' John Jennings asked, irritated. 'By the time they are rehabilitated all convicts, whether men, women or children, are able to take their place in society.'

John Jennings' words were filled with optimism. I wasn't so sure. I couldn't quite put my finger on the reason for my disquiet about Port Arthur.

Then the dark descended like a raven's wing and the setting sun turned the sky to fire. The moment was so striking that it made me recall a painting I had seen in the halls of Edinburgh University of the banishment of Lucifer from Heaven.

The painting showed twin God brothers. They had been at war all their lives for possession of Heaven. Ranged against each other were their mighty armies of angels with stunning white wings enfolded. It was incredible that one brother would hate the other so much, and want power so much, as to cause war between them.

The war had consumed millions of years. The painting revealed that Heaven had been totally destroyed: the celestial sky was wreathed in smoke and flames. But one twin had managed to defeat his brother. He wanted to be kind and to be forgiving. While the smoke of battle still singed the sky, the artist showed him having just told Lucifer, 'If you will agree to my terms and bow down to me, I will allow you and your armies to stay. But if you will not, I will not execute you. Rather, you will be banished.'

In the painting, Lucifer was shown with his head proudly lifted to the light. 'No, brother, I will not bow down to you.' He was already leading his legions from the battleground, their dark wings unfolding from their backs.

The painter had posed his twin brother in an attitude of appeal. 'I give you one last chance.'

In the rendering of Lucifer was defiance. One of his wings had unfolded, crimson red, jagged as a bat's and veined with a thousand sparkling rivers.

'I would rather reign in Hell than serve you in Heaven.'

Looking at the painting, you could almost hear the sky shrilling and crackling as they departed, swirling down a vortex into Hell.

Watching the darkening sky over Port Arthur, I could almost believe that this was the place where a cohort of their number, diverted by some cosmic disturbance, had fallen.

———————

The following day being the Sabbath, John Jennings was occupied with his responsibilities as a catechist, and Etty in a meeting with some of the other women of the penitentiary. This gave Ismay and me some brief time together, and I was pleased to see that the change of air had indeed done her good.

'Etty has told me of the parties, regattas and literary evenings they have here,' she said. 'It all sounds so normal! I am pleased for them — they are happy here, and the children play and go to school despite being enclosed within the prison environment.' There was such a yearning in her voice as she made comparison of the Imrie family situation with our own.

Normal?

Port Arthur was an inescapable prison. There was a fence of guards at the main exit point of Eaglehawk Neck, which connected the Tasman Peninsula to Forestier Peninsula; a line of lanterns kept it lit during the night. The isthmus was so narrow that only eighteen dogs, mainly deerhounds and mastiffs, chained and kennelled along the roadside, were sufficient to stop a man passing between them. Let him try, if he wished to be seized and torn to pieces!

———————

Around mid morning, John Jennings, Etty and the children came to collect us from Civil Row to accompany us to church. The building, with its lovely wooden spire, stood on the high ground.

As we neared it I happened to look seaward and, in the distance, saw a small vessel loaded with convict boys approaching the dock from Point Puer.

How could Britannia justify the sending of young boys, some scarcely ten years old, to imprisonment in Van Diemen's Land? I remembered Ismay's remark, when we had first arrived in Hobart Town, about God looking after fallen sparrows. These little sparrows, having been blown by winds far from their family nests — for stealing a watch or picking pockets — did not look as if God even knew they existed.

Convict women were also coming to church, disembarking from the *Marquis of Hastings*. And from the men's dormitories, parties of convicts with their respective guards began to converge for the service too; among them was the lad who had made his brief plea to me the previous day, walking as if in considerable pain.

'It is compulsory for all the convicts to attend,' John Jennings told me. 'Religious and moral instruction have their place in their rehabilitation.'

He introduced us to the Reverend Hastings and other free citizens living at Port Arthur. I wondered why we could not go inside.

'Must we be spectators to the convicts' shame?' I asked.

'Mr McKissock,' he answered, 'there are rules to be observed. We will not go in until they are all marshalled by their guards and brought to silence. Be patient, sir.'

The boys from Point Puer went in first, followed by the adult male convicts and the women. John Jennings signalled we could follow. He showed us to raised wooden pews to the left, behind a curtain.

———

The Reverend Durham ascended the ornate three-tiered pulpit; it had been carved by a convict craftsman. He announced the first hymn:

> He who would valiant be 'gainst all disaster
> Let him in constancy follow the Master
> There's no discouragement shall make him once relent
> His first avowed intent to be a pilgrim . . .

A playful wind parted the curtains. It was momentary, but sufficient for us to see the convict women. Close up, the coarseness of their attire — white calico caps, brown serge skirts and jackets of brown and yellow gingham — could not diminish their femininity.

Suddenly Ismay grabbed my right elbow. She looked across at one of the young women.

'I know that girl,' she said.

She went to get up, but received a warning look from John Jennings. 'Mrs McKissock, you must sit down,' he whispered.

'But that girl . . .'

'Explain the situation to me after the service,' he answered. 'Meantime, maintain some semblance of serenity?'

Serenity? I would have thought by now John Jennings knew Ismay well enough to realise that serenity was not one of her primary virtues. Wishing to obtain a better view of the girl, she said to me, 'Will you swap places with me, Mr McKissock?' and, regardless of the displeasure she caused, parted the curtains further.

'It *is* her!' I heard her whisper. 'It is Sally Jenkins!'

For the rest of the service, Ismay could scarce contain herself. Upon its conclusion, protocol required that the convicts waited while their betters exited the church. Immediately we were outside, she gripped my arm.

'Mr McKissock, I have not asked much of you in all the time since we became man and wife, but would you support me? I must ascertain Sally Jenkins' circumstances.'

I was puzzled — who was Sally Jenkins? — but I nodded. 'Very well, Mrs McKissock,' I answered.

She therefore approached John Jennings. 'I must speak with the girl,' she insisted. 'Please, Mr Imrie, will you do all within your power to assist me in this?'

'Mrs McKissock, the regulations are quite clear on banning such contact,' he answered.

'Perhaps, on this occasion, the regulations could be relaxed?' I asked him.

He frowned, but was not without sympathy. 'I shall obtain permission from the deputy in charge of the women,' he answered, 'but do be careful. It would do neither you nor the girl any good if the deputy suspected some former relationship between you.'

'Ordered forward, Sally Jenkins,' the deputy commanded. 'Tie your cap, young missy, and curtsey to the lady.'

Up until that time, Sally Jenkins had not seen Ismay.

'Look at me, child,' Ismay said.

Sally Jenkins looked up. She gave a gasp: 'Miss!'

Ismay gave her a warning look. 'I am seeking a young girl such as you to work in my household. You might be able to fill that position.' She looked at the deputy. 'Can you recommend this girl, Madam Deputy?'

To work in our household?

Ismay cast me a pleading look: *Mr McKissock, humour me, I beg of you.* Under the circumstances I could not deny her, and gave her a nod of assent.

The deputy could have said no and hastened her charges on their way. But there was always something about Ismay — her breeding and her authoritative manner — which made women of lower social status submit to her. Instead, 'We do not recommend it, ma'am,' the deputy answered. 'There are several women eligible but—' she looked at John Jennings '—they do not afford much choice, Mr Imrie. Even so I am not sure whether any prior claim on any of my charges may be made until Hobart Town?'

She was giving the responsibility of decision-making to him! Although he was nervous about our inquisitive onlookers, I knew that he would do his best to accommodate our request, precipitate though it was.

Etty was also on our side. 'Mrs McKissock will need a servant,' she said to the deputy, 'with a new babe on the way. Does this young girl still have her innocence?'

'Yes, ma'am,' the deputy answered. 'She is not tainted.'

The deputy, confused, looked at John Jennings — all these strange people hounding her!

'In that case,' John Jennings said, 'for Mr and Mrs McKissock, an exception may be made. They are known to me as persons of upstanding character. I will organise the papers assigning this young girl to be released to them on her arrival at the settlement.'

The gathering dispersed. John Jennings mopped his brow. 'Well,' he said, 'if I have to say so myself, that went very well, didn't it!'

In the evening, Ismay, Gower Jr and I embarked on the vessel returning us to Hobart Town. With profuse thanks, we farewelled John Jennings, Etty and their brood.

When the ship cleared the peninsula, I asked Ismay, 'Who is our new maid?'

'She went with me into the mines when Uncle Rollo was underground. I made her a promise to help her, no matter what the circumstances. I intend to keep it.'

A few days later the *Marquis of Hastings* rolled into Hobart Town. Ismay and I drove down to the dock in our trap. In the free-for-all that developed there were many requests for Sally Jenkins, including a few from single men who should have known better — women, even if they were convicts, could not be taken into service to bachelors.

I strode forward and showed our papers. 'Sally Jenkins is already signed for,' I said.

The deputy recognised me and Sally Jenkins was released to my care. 'Follow me, Jenkins,' I said to her. 'Your mistress awaits you on the dock.'

Carrying her bundle of belongings, the girl obeyed me. I saw her eyes shine with gladness when Ismay greeted her.

'Welcome, Sally,' she smiled, pressing Sally Jenkins' palms with hers. 'How old are you now?'

'I am thirteen, miss.' Sally was shivering uncontrollably.

I will admit to a little envy at the piteous tears when they embraced each other. 'You are safe now,' Ismay said, 'but what are you *doing* here?'

I helped Sally Jenkins into the trap. 'You remember my father, miss?' Sally asked. 'He couldn't get much work after his leg was taken off and, well, I lost my job at the mines and the family fell on hard times. I was charged with having broke into the household of Mrs Ellen Goddard and stealing a loaf of bread. I have been transported for ten years, miss. Who will look after my family?'

'I will write to my Uncle Rollo to ask him to take them in his care.'

I stepped into the trap. 'You know, Sally Jenkins,' I began, 'that the law says you can never go back to England, even when you become free?'

Sally looked at Ismay, horrified. 'Oh, miss . . .'

Ismay calmed her. 'We will be sisters, and Mr McKissock and I will be your family.'

Not until the evening did I recognise my own relationship with the girl — I had assisted Rollo Springvale in removing her father's leg.

———

Of course, with only three bedrooms in the cottage, that meant that Ismay and I were compelled to share the same bedroom again.

In an attempt to make matters better between us, I went to the pawn-shop. I had managed to accrue some savings and therefore redeemed her ruby necklace and earrings.

Ours was always going to be a relationship which, from time to time, would veer wild and dangerously off course. Would one of us be willing to bring it back to magnetic south again?

As Ismay was undressing for bed, I took the necklace from my pocket and placed it around her neck.

'No, Mr McKissock.' I knew she was weeping.

I put her earrings in her hands. Her fingers closed on them.

I pulled her close to me, her back nestling against my chest, and kissed the nape of her neck.

'I will do my best,' I said.

25

Our second child, another son, was born in February 1844.

At Ismay's request, and I was only too happy to oblige, we called him after her Uncle Rollo. I was now the father of two sons and, despite my earlier reluctance, I discovered within myself a happier acceptance of parenthood. Gower Jr was two years old, the bonny baby having grown into a boisterous boy. Because Ismay had been his primary parent he naturally sought her out when he wanted love and attention. Of course I had only myself to blame for that; it was what I had preferred.

With Rollo, however, it was a different matter. From the very beginning he made it clear that he was biased towards my affections. Children care little for a parent's boundaries; innocent, they push them aside as they reach for you and, well, I was ambushed by Rollo before I had the opportunity to close my heart to him.

It was through his persistent expectation of my attention that I began to discover what it was to be a father.

———

With some relief, I received the proceeds of the sale of our house and surgery in Nelson. I was able to pay off our bank loan and move Ismay, the children and Sally Jenkins to a larger house not far from Arthur's Circus at Battery Point. Instead of three bedrooms, we now had four, and a sunroom.

As soon as we moved in, Ismay came straight to the point. 'Are we to continue to share the same bedroom, Mr McKissock?'

'I would like to maintain my conjugal rights,' I answered. 'And you, Mrs McKissock?'

'We are husband and wife,' she answered with a small smile.

Our move came none too soon, as John Jennings wrote to tell me he had been appointed on promotion to replace a Mr Tomlins at the Darlington Probation Station on Maria Island. Could he, Etty and the family come and stay en route?

We were delighted, of course, but oh, with their three children and our two, John Jennings and I felt it necessary to escape the confines of the house. Like cowards, we left the women to the children's mayhem.

It was while we were walking through Hobart Town that John Jennings asked me, 'How did you meet Ismay?'

Compelled to admit the circumstances, I told him, 'She was not my first choice. In fact, she was not my choice at all. I wanted to marry her cousin Sybil.' At the mention of Sybil's name, I felt my heart fill with yearning and that led me to my confession. 'I did not love her when we wed.'

John Jennings was dismayed. 'Does she know?'

'Yes,' I answered. 'Our marriage is a contract.'

'I wish I hadn't asked the question!' he said. He was trying to be affable about my disclosure. 'Your children must surely be compensation.'

'I am their father, yes,' I answered.

'That is all? Your attitude borders on self-indulgence, my good man.' He was becoming perturbed.

'Do not be anxious on my account or Ismay's,' I said. 'Many couples, I am sure, live in worse relationships than ours.'

'Are you happy?' he asked, persistent.

'I am not unhappy,' I answered.

He looked at me carefully. 'Gower, you are the only friend I have from Scotland. And we will always be friends. I will pray for you.'

Not long after John Jennings and Etty departed, my career as a surgeon received a most welcome escalation when Dr John Stephen Hampton, Controller-General of Convicts, asked me if I would accept work at the Hobart Town Penitentiary.

'Whenever transported prisoners arrive to be processed,' he explained, 'the house surgeon is often hard-pressed to examine them all. Would you like the contract?'

I jumped at the opportunity. First of all, it would boost the income received from my private practice and, second, it could lead to greater opportunities within the prison system.

Thus one or two days a week, I found myself being called to the walled compound — 'The Paddock' — where convicts cleared immigration. I undertook full body examinations, reporting on general health and, where necessary, made recommendations for treatment prior to the placement. If there was any suspicion at all of brutalisation by their guards — or other prisoners — that was reported also.

Under the circumstances, perhaps it was not surprising that closer contact with the transportation system at the Hobart Penitentiary would confirm my total opposition to it.

It was on this subject that I first made the acquaintance of a fashionably dressed gentleman at the Hobart Town Royal Society — the first such society for the advancement of science outside of Britain.

I had just become a member (one example of the manner in which Ismay and I were establishing ourselves within Hobart Town's society) and I overheard him arguing with a visiting English historian, who referred to transportation as an example of Australia's infamous convict history.

'Nothing will rid Australia of this, your most shameful stain,' the pompous ass opined.

'Australia's shame?' I heard the gentleman reply. '*Australia's*? This country had nothing to do with the transportation of convicts to the southern hemisphere! If any nation needs to be ashamed, it is your own Great Britain for instituting such an inexcusable and monstrous system! The sooner transportation is abolished and the convicts emancipated, the better.'

The historian was like many of his kind, preferring to conduct his arguments among polite 'yes' men; he stood on his dignity and, no doubt, on his return to England, would comment on the boorish behaviour of the colonials. To wit, he retired from the field of battle when all that had been fired was an opening volley.

I introduced myself to the gentleman who had vented his spleen. 'I commend you, sir,' I began. 'Australia has been stigmatised for something that is not its fault. May I ask your name?'

He gripped my hand in appreciation. 'I am Eion Gascoigne Gault,' he answered. He was slightly older than I, a fine example of manhood, tall and well built. 'Are you a convict-emancipist?'

I hadn't thought of myself in quite that way. 'I think perhaps I am,' I answered. 'Yes.'

'Splendid,' Eion said. 'Then join us.' His eyes were glowing. 'Join the organisation of free settlers who wish to establish our own governance in Van Diemen's Land.'

He invited me to adjourn with him to a nearby eating house for supper. The main question on his mind was: How could Van Diemen's Land establish a society of moral and ethical standing if transportation still persisted?

'When we became a separate colony in 1825,' he began, as we sat down to a meal of meat, potatoes and two jugs of dark ale, 'Van Diemen's Land was assuredly more convict than free, six thousand to three thousand. By 1836, however, we outnumbered the convicts by twenty-six thousand to fifteen thousand. We've had the majority ever since, but have we been able to make our own decisions? No!'

He was on fire with his passion, quaffing down ale and potatoes one gulp after the other.

'Mother England has granted us a council, but her lieutenant-governors remain the supreme authorities, and they are autocratic administrators fully committed to the efficiency of Van Diemen's Land as a gaol.'

I paced Eion. 'They also keep an iron grip on you, Mr Gault!'

'You mean *us*, don't you?' he answered.

We were becoming more animated by the minute and, I must admit, just a little drunk.

I nodded, accepting my inclusion. 'We challenge the authority of their jurisdiction and they don't like it, do they!' I was waving my fork around. If I didn't watch out, my potato would go flying off it!

'Indeed they do not,' Eion answered. 'The prison regulations apply to us too. We are all inmates in the same gaol.'

He leaned over conspiratorially and took my fork with the potato on it, and ate it. 'What do you suggest we do?'

Seditious though the thought was, the answer hit me like a bolt of lightning.

'Get rid of the gaoler,' I said.

———

I joined Eion Gault in the political movement to untie Van Diemen's Land from the umbilical of England.

When I told Ismay of my intentions her eyes shone with pride. 'You have so much to give, and we should invest in the future. After all, the children will inherit it and . . .'

She bit her lip. Seemed hesitant. 'Yes, Mrs McKissock?'

'. . . I am with child again,' she said.

This time, my response was moderate. I suppose that the habit of father-hood had inured me to the problems of coping with two boys — Rollo was now proving to be as much a tearaway as his older brother — but along with them had come joys that sneaked up on me with such stealth that I would be left gasping. Perhaps Gower Jr asking me a question about his grand-parents. Or Rollo needing a splinter of wood extricated from his foot; I put it to my mouth and sucked it tenderly.

Whatever it was, it illuminated our relationship with personal intimacy and made me realise, 'Yes, these *are* my sons.'

I enfolded Ismay in my arms and said to her, 'Now that we have two, we may as well have three.'

And one of the most forgiving and fulfilling phases of our lives began. We opened ourselves to each other and, in this mood of acceptance, also widened our horizons as a couple.

It was Ismay, for instance, who suggested that we invite Eion Gault and other convict-emancipists to meet, whenever they were of a mind, at our house to discuss the politics of the day. As a consequence, our lives became crowded with some of the best and most independent thinkers in the colony.

Among them were two particular groups whose strength and determination were without parallel.

The first was the extraordinary set of independent newspaper editors, who fearlessly engaged with the question of the British governance of Van Diemen's Land, often at considerable personal cost.

George Arthur had tried to muzzle them — in particular Andrew Bent, Evan Henry Thomas and Robert Lanthrop Murray of the *Gazette* — and even threw some of them in gaol or closed them down. When he was recalled and left Hobart Town, the *Colonial Times* published a Supplement celebrating the 'blessing' of his departure by calling it 'deliverance from an iron hand and acts of abomination'.

'Rejoice,' proclaimed the headline, 'for the day of retribution has arrived.'

The newspaper editors continued to attack the rules of lieutenant-governors Franklin and Eardley-Wilmot. No colonial paper ever carved out so relentless and persistent a course of opposition to Government and its abuse of patronage as the *Colonial Times* and its editor, Henry Melville. Few exceeded it in the use of forcible English. It was to the *Colonial Times*, more than any other paper, that Australians were indebted for their subsequent civil liberty.

The roll call of fellow newspaper dissenters — including Gilbert Robertson of the *True Colonist,* who was prosecuted for libel; William Gore Ellison, the anti-transportation editor of the *Hobart Town Courier;* and the great dissenter editor John West of the *Launceston Examiner* — comprised an academy committed to the democratic ideal and the freedom of the press. There they all were, crowding into our house in Battery Point!

Ismay made a strong impression on the newspaper men. After having played the dutiful hostess and ensured that they had imbibed good wine and sweetmeats, she took off her apron and, ever the wilful spirit, came into the room before we had begun our discussions.

'Gentlemen,' she said, 'women and children are also affected by government practices. Pray allow me to listen in and, from time to time, comment on the matters on your agenda.' She was a foxy one with her 'Pray allow me'! Even if she hadn't been so allowed, nothing would have stopped her from taking part!

Fortunately, Eion accepted her argument. 'Please, Mrs McKissock,' he said, 'do take a chair.'

During the discussions, Ismay's interventions were of such quality that very soon she had the men all at their mettle, a challenge they delighted in. 'By Jove,' Henry Melville averred, 'you have a mind, Mrs McKissock!' From then on he called by often to read to her the latest of his blistering editorials before it was put to press.

Eion was also star-struck. He was unmarried, and when Ismay discovered this fact she asked him, 'Why do you not have a wife, Mr Gault?'

'You were already taken, Mrs McKissock,' he answered.

The second group of extraordinary men who came to our house were Quakers — Hobart Town having the proud distinction of being the site of the oldest community in Australasia. Prominent among them was George Washington Walker.

No greater praise than the use of the word 'remarkable' can be associated with the Society of Friends — and their magnificent history of involvement with Van Diemen's Land. Of them all, Mr Walker's history was exemplary: he had come from Britain on a nine-year mission to the Australian and South African colonies with the express purpose of investigating convict and Aboriginal conditions and generally trying to arouse a social conscience among the inhabitants of every colony.

'I left London,' he told me, 'in the company of Mr James Backhouse, a Quaker of greater reputation than mine and a former York nurseryman and amateur botanist. Mr Backhouse obtained in 1831 the concurrence of his monthly and quarterly Quaker meetings in York to pay a visit in gospel to the British settlements here in Van Diemen's Land, New South Wales and in the south of Africa. He also obtained the approval of the Yearly Meeting of

Ministers and Elders in London, and we sailed from the Downs in the barque *Science*. As Exodus 10:26 says, "We knew not with what we must serve the Lord, until we came hither." We wrote eight reports for George Arthur on the penal settlements of Macquarie Harbour and Port Arthur, the Aboriginal establishment on Flinders Island, the condition of road gangs and chain gangs, assigned servants and their masters, the state of prisoners generally and prison discipline in Van Diemen's Land, with observations on the general state of the colony. I am always prepared to bear witness and to take up the cause of any man, woman or child suffering under transportation.'

Mr Walker was one of those admirable men who possessed the enlightened leaven of a Dissenter, the care for humanity of an Evangelical, and the gentle methodical persuasion of a Quaker resolved to effect change in a vicious, brutal world.

———

Eion asked one of us consider nomination to political office.

'We must obtain a seat on the Legislative Council,' he said. 'It is the only way to get further leverage in the vexed matter of abolishing transportation.'

He was on the point of nominating me but I finessed him and proposed him for the position instead! The decision was unanimous. It was worth it just to see him gasping like a fish.

At the time, I did not understand why he was panicking so. His eyes were filled with fear and he said to me, 'You don't know what you're asking.' But he accepted the nomination and, when he was successful in taking a seat, oh the jubilation!

Ismay and I held a party for him where, with tears in his eyes, he thanked us all. 'This is not the end,' he reminded us. 'It is a beginning. Now the battle truly begins.'

He seemed to be over his fear.

———

Ismay gave birth to our third child, a daughter we named Clara, soon after.

A daughter! How did you raise a daughter? My only experience had been with sons!

The birth was protracted and difficult, as if Clara was unwilling to face the world. I was surprised that so much effort had to be expended by Ismay and, in the end, Clara was expelled forcibly from her womb.

I don't think Clara ever forgave her.

———

And then a letter came for Ismay from Wolverhampton.

I often marvelled at the epic four-month or longer journeys made by correspondence. It always seemed to me to be only by great fortune that they ever reached their destination. Somewhere, there was always someone to pass the letter on to, from ship to ship, country to country, sailor to sailor and, on arrival at port, some kind soul to deliver it.

Family correspondence had managed to reach us at irregular intervals — usually from Ismay's mother or aunt. I had come to recognise their handwriting on the envelopes — it was somewhat circular and perambulatory, like the letters themselves, which often began with one piece of news but developed an alarming tendency towards complex narrative darting off at all tangents: family news (all the cousins, including Sybil, were now married with children), news concerning Queen Victoria, interspersed with health advice, recipes and dress patterns.

I did not recognise the handwriting on this envelope at all: functional, sober and clear.

'Why, it's from Uncle Rollo!' Ismay exclaimed with delight. She moved to a dresser to take out a letter-opener.

Immediately I was on the alert. Dr Springvale always left it to the women to correspond. I turned to Sally Jenkins and told her, 'Take the boys to the park.'

Ismay opened the letter. She began to read it and then, with a loud moan, she fell to the ground. I knelt to her and took her in my arms.

She gave me the letter to read.

My dear Ismay,

I have begun writing to you at least six times but on all occasions have been betrayed by the opening strophes which have showed, in the inconsistent lettering, too much undue emotion. I had rather hoped your dear aunt might have been the bearer of this news but that noble lady has found it beyond her capabilities; she will write soon to follow the sympathies that are extended within.

My dear, I will start with the assurances that one usually ends with, namely, declarations of affection and love for you and, as calmly as I can, advise you that your mother Selina Cassia Isoleen Glossop died on 10 June in the Year of Our Lord 1845. As I write these words my preference is to gloss over the circumstances of her death but I know from experience that you would wish the facts and I will therefore honour you by giving them.

My sister-in-law died of smoke inhalation from a fire which has gutted Webster Hall completely. Your father, quite unnaturally, bemoans the loss of his estate more than he does his dear wife, your mother, but you and I would not have expected otherwise from him. One of your brothers, St John, the cause of the fire, also died in it.

As you will recall, my brother-in-law and his disreputable sons were known to visit inns of ill repute of an evening and, there, consume large quantities of spirits. On the evening of 9 June last they returned to Webster Hall. St John, who had taken to smoking opium, fell into a stupor and, while in such a state, did not notice a coal which, being spat from the fire in his room, lit on the carpet. He was incinerated in the blaze.

Your father and remaining brother, of course, thought only of themselves and managed to get out of the fiery furnace which developed, with their lives. Were it not for Matron Baines, who has been your mother's loyal keeper, Selina would have herself perished in the fire. Alas, the strain on her heart from the smoke inhalation was too much for her.

I tried my best, Ismay, but I could not save my dear sister-in-law. She was buried at Grocott's Bradley Bridge Church on 12 June in the Glossop family graveyard.

I was with your mother when she took her last breath. I can assure you that her last thoughts were of you. Her final words were, 'Tell Ismay that . . .' — but alas, no more.

Again, accept these condolences, which are sent not only on my behalf but also for your aunt and cousins. I end by also conveying my regards to Gower McKissock.

Your loving uncle,
Rollo Springvale.

Tell Ismay that . . .
Knowing how the death of Ramsay had affected me, I held Ismay tight.

'I should never have left my mother behind, Gower,' she wept. 'She will be forever on my conscience.'

I kissed her and tried to soothe her. 'Your father would never have released her. At least she got you away from him. She was so glad at your escape. She sacrificed herself so that you could have your freedom. It was the one great victory of her life.'

'I have no parent now,' she said.

'You have a family,' I answered, 'and you have the children.'

But grief must take its course. Comforting words are just the beginning of that painful process of acknowledging there will forever be an empty space in your world.

I tried my best. The children, not fully comprehending their mother's loss, would clamber onto her lap and try to give her solace. Sometimes she accepted them. Other times, she would look at them — and push them away.

Our friends gathered around her: John Jennings and Etty Imrie made a special visit from Maria Island; Etty stayed for a few days and I was grateful that she was able to divert Ismay, albeit briefly, from her depression.

Eion Gaunt was a regular visitor with his flowers — 'Oh, Eion, roses!' she said one day, and that reminded me of her love for them. George Washington Walker and Mrs Walker also called, as did Henry Melville, still bringing his editorials for her to look over and comment on.

In bed with Ismay, I offered myself as comfort; making love had always been a way of forgetting one's pain. She pushed me away.

Please do not judge me too harshly in what I am about to disclose here. I have never been a man who was able to do without female company. I met a woman of good class, Kate Wilkinson, owner of a haberdashery and of a friendly disposition, and we began an affair.

Sally Jenkins kept the house running on an even keel. Sometimes I heard her scolding Ismay, albeit in a plaintive way, 'Miss, you must come out of the coalmine. It's dark in there.'

I had no idea what she was referring to.

'Follow me, miss,' she continued. 'We have to get above ground, where the light is.'

Slowly but surely, Ismay ascended.

———

We began to piece life together again.

As the months passed, I thought Ismay was getting better. Sometimes, however, I would catch her watching me in a curious way. The children assumed that she had come back too, as did our friends.

My career as a surgeon, working both privately and for the Hobart Town Penitentiary, absorbed my energies again. So too, did the uplifting involvement with Eion Gault and our fellow convict-emancipists.

Indeed, Eion came to call with alarming news. 'The Legislative Council,' he began, 'has been advised by the lieutenant-governor that England has decided Van Diemen's Land is to be the main destination of all convicts. All! Not only that, but Downing Street doesn't want to pay for them. Instead, Van Diemen's Land is to provide for the upkeep of the penal system from our own taxes.'

'The colonial secretary is going too far,' I answered.

Then a bill was proposed by the lieutenant-governor to raise duties on tea, sugar and foreign goods. The good citizens of the council opposed it with the slogan: NO TAXATION WITHOUT REPRESENTATION.

From that moment, the slogan became our calling card and, with help from our newspaper colleagues, it was publicised throughout the colony. It was at once the beginning and the culmination of the movement which was to carry the colony to freedom.

The council next decided to challenge the estimates of expenditure presented to them from the Colonial Office. When the challenge was over-ruled, Eion and other opposing members resigned in protest and made up what became known as the 'Patriotic Six'.

'We will not vote on an expenditure which the colony cannot bear,' they said.

Our group of convict-emancipists became nationalists.

When I remember our actions, how my blood is stirred again! And, because I was so taken up with the work — I had become the leader, with Eion, of our informal activist group — it was not surprising that I did not notice that Ismay, in ascending from the grief over her mother had, during that mourning period, come to a decision about herself and the children.

There came an afternoon, following my day at the surgery, when I was at a meeting with Eion at the home of George Washington Walker. We had discussed strategies to raise our citizens to vociferous indignation about the resignations of the 'Patriotic Six'. Mr Walker suggested that we should send petitions to the British Parliament and to all our influential friends in England. Henry Melville and the other newspaper men at the meeting agreed they should rouse their fellow editors in the English press to support us.

We rose from the meeting in the early evening. We were high-spirited and excited.

'Capital work,' Eion said to me as we took leave of each other.

I was humming as I made my way home to Battery Point. The night was balmy and families were still strolling about the streets before turning in for the evening. As I approached the house I saw a carriage outside it, suitcases loaded on top. Beside the horses was a driver; he doffed his hat as I approached, 'Ev'ning sir.'

At first I wondered who our visitor was. And then the driver added, 'I'm just waiting for the missus.'

Sensing something amiss, I stepped quickly through the front door. 'Ismay?' I called.

'We are in here,' she answered from the drawing room. When I joined her, I saw that she was in her travelling clothes: a long velvet dress, hat with veil — and, as soon as she saw me, she began to draw on her gloves. Beside her was Sally Jenkins, also dressed for travelling, holding the sleeping Clara; she was wrapped up in warm blankets.

When Gower Jr and Rollo saw me, they ran to me. 'Father! Father!'

Gower Jr jumped onto my back and Rollo wrapped himself around my legs.

'Say goodbye to your father,' Ismay told them.

Goodbye? Surprised, I felt the boys kiss me on my cheek.

'Take the boys and Clara to the carriage and wait for me,' Ismay said to Sally Jenkins. 'Tell the driver I will be out soon.'

'You will come and see us, won't you, Father?' Gower Jr asked.

I watched as they all left the house. From the front window I could see how excited Gower Jr was, wanting to pat the horses and asking the driver if, when they went, he could sit beside him.

'What is this all about, Mrs McKissock?' I asked.

'I am leaving you,' she answered. 'I shall take the children with me.' There was a mirror in the drawing room. She went to it and began to arrange her veil. She had never looked more desirable to me! 'We could have left before you arrived home but I am not a coward. I owed you the courtesy of saying goodbye to the boys.'

'Where are you going?' I asked. 'Are you returning to England for a visit?'

'No, Mr McKissock,' Ismay answered. 'I am leaving *you*. Our marriage. Everything. I have booked rooms at a hotel in Hobart Town. Tomorrow I will go on to Launceston. Perhaps, later, to Melbourne.'

'A hotel? Launceston? Melbourne?' My head was reeling. 'Mrs McKissock, think of your reputation—'

'I never expected you to be so conventional,' she flared. 'You know that my reputation is the last of my worries.' She gave me a sad smile. 'Goodbye, Mr McKissock.'

I grabbed her.

'Unhand me, Gower,' she said.

'I forbid you to leave the house.'

'Forbid?' She extricated herself from my grasp. 'It was a mistake for us to marry. I will send you word of where we are so you may continue to see the children if you wish.'

'Wish to see the children?' I began to panic. I had already been abandoned three times: by Ramsay when he died, Ailie when she left me in Edinburgh

264

and Sybil when she refused me.

Ismay set her face with determination. 'I will not be like my mother, living in a loveless marriage all her life. I thought I could do it but I know now that I can't.'

'Please don't go.'

'Isn't this what you want, Mr McKissock? Now you can be free.'

Free? Yes, I would be free! But did I want to be free?

I looked at Ismay and knew I had to choose. I realised that I had been holding something tight inside me for such a long time.

Something to do with Ailie. Something to do with not wanting to make myself vulnerable. Something to do with not wanting to love anyone again. Ever.

I let *go*; and a dam burst inside me.

'I need you, Ismay,' I said.

Not love you. Need you.

'Need me? Leave me some pride, Gower. Please.'

'You are my wife.' I answered, kissing her. 'I should never have bound you to me. I am so ashamed.'

I cupped her face in my hands and bade her look out the window at Gower Jr, Rollo and Clara in Sally Jenkins' arms.

'They are my children. *Our* children. We are each other's family now. We have no other, do we?'

We looked at each other, frightened.

'Oh, Gower,' Ismay sighed after a while. 'What is to become of us?'

———

After some further persuasion, Ismay agreed to reconcile.

Heart pounding with relief and joy, I paid the driver for the fare he would have received; he helped me to bring the luggage back into the house. Gower Jr was disappointed not to be able to help the driver with the reins; I promised to take him to a nearby stable where he could ride a pony.

After the family had gone to bed and Sally Jenkins had also retired, Ismay and I went to bed. We held each other for a long time. When I went to make love to her, I discovered tenderness in myself sufficient not to take my own pleasure but to give it.

Something had changed.

I wondered what it was. Later that evening, still tossing and turning over the question, I rose from Ismay's side and went into the back garden. I looked up at the stars, so many, many stars in carousel, moving to some music of the heavens.

Then I sighed with gladness.

I had asked the heavens a question: If ever I were lost in the stars, would I be able to find my way home?

The answer was yes.

I had found my humanity again.

I could hope again.

26

And so, as a family, we began to flourish.

The following year, 1846, Gower Jr celebrated his fourth birthday. Rollo was two and Clara was one. Rollo insisted he also have a cake on the day.

We were like any other family of migrants who had left England, Scotland, Ireland and Wales and, like dandelions, were blown by strong winds to all four corners of the world. We chose to come to the colonies.

Other migrants, however, were forced out by an uncaring Mother England — whether they wanted to or not. I could not help but think of the Highland Scots displaced by their owners from their lands. I knew only too well from my mother Ailie's experience, how bitter such banishment could be. Those kinds of settlers may not have had shackles around their ankles but they were dumped out in the colonies all the same — and assisted with their passage so that they would go.

Here in Van Diemen's Land, we had all come, willing, unwilling or transported, to intertwine with each other in the growth of a new varietal genetic stock.

From such hardy plantings, we hoped, a sturdy people would grow.

Then, one day, we were reminded that we were not the only citizens who required to be accommodated in the growing.

———

The reminder came about when Ismay and I were taking the children for a walk around the port. Gower Jr became most excited. His eyes grew as wide as saucers as he spied, ahead of us, a small native man, square and muscular, with remarkable woolly hair. 'Mother! Mother!' he yelled. 'Is that a Maori?'

Ismay gave a peal of laughter. 'Gower is remembering the times in Nelson, at the beach,' she explained to me, 'when I took lessons in Maori from Mahuika.' She bent down to him. 'No, darling, the man's a Trowennan. He must be a sailor from one of the ships in port.'

Indeed, at that moment, he was grabbed by a rollicking group of seadogs.

'William!' they yelled, 'William Lanney! Come and have an ale with us, you little black booger.' They pulled him into a nearby inn.

'Trowennan?' I asked, puzzled.

'I call the natives Trowennans so as to distinguish them from the taller Aborigines of the mainland,' Ismay explained. 'They have a different physique and nature. Where did they come from, I wonder? How came they here? Surely they are remnants of a more ancient race.'

'Some people consider they are castaways blown by severe storms across from their home on the East Africa coast,' I answered. 'Others think they are the same as the Moriori of New Zealand, reaching Van Diemen's Land from a long land-bridge from New Zealand, now submerged. There are a few, even, who think they migrated northward from Antarctica!'

'Why not Lilliput, in that case?' Ismay smiled.

'The most logical explanation,' I went on, 'is that they were a remnant of an earlier aboriginal tribe who arrived in Van Diemen's Land when it was attached to the mainland. When sea levels rose and glaciation retreated southward, creating Bass's Strait, they developed separately.'

'I shall continue to call them the Trowennans,' Ismay answered firmly, 'as tribute to their own sovereignty.' She paused, reflective. 'Do you realise that the Trowennan is the first of his people that we have seen since we arrived in Van Diemen's Land?' The observation was disquieting. 'Where are the rest?'

'They've been shipped off to Flinders Island for their own protection.'

'Against whom?'

'Us, Mrs McKissock, us.'

———

Then, in that same year, when Ismay and I had long assumed that New Zealand had retreated well into our past, news reached us about the Hutt Valley Incident — and, in particular, the hanging of Martin Luther.

The reaction in Hobart Town was extraordinary. An initial lengthy report in the *Hobart Town Courier* was carried under the caption:

ATROCIOUS MURDER!!! EXECUTION OF
ONE OF THE REBELS

Indeed, according to Henry Melville, the *Hobart Town Courier* and other Australian press appeared to be more concerned about the matters involving the rebels than the newspapers in New Zealand were!

I have kept some of the clippings from those days. The *Colonial Times* had this to say:

> It is impossible to characterise in terms sufficiently expressive of abhorrence the detestable crime of Governor Grey (Captain as he is, to the disgrace of the army, called), in the murder of the gallant New Zealand chief Wareitu ... We should not be sorry to see him delivered up to that brave chieftain Heki, to practise upon him, whatever return he might please. As to his capture by the noble people so bravely defending, at the loss of their blood, their country from a set of mercenary ruthless invaders, this abominable cold-blooded murder proves him to be too great a coward to trust his miserable carcase within the possibility of reach. But while there could be found an Englishman capable of so dark a deed, how will Europe account for his finding five British officers capable of lending themselves to become instruments of his butchery? The 58th, the 99th, and the Royal Artillery are disgraced until they have removed the poor tools of a coward's vengeance from among them!

Imagine, then, the popular reaction — and especially that of all convict-emancipists like our action group — when we were told that five other Maori chiefs, who had escaped hanging, were being shipped to Van Diemen's Land!

It is not too strong to describe it as an 'uproar'.

Why should the news bring forth such vigorous protests in a community which was conditioned to large-scale imprisonment as a normal fact of existence?

Eion, at one of our meetings, laid the reason before us. 'The Colonial Office and Sir George Grey are using transportation as the means by which *anybody*, not only convicts, can be punished. Will we see more nationalists like the Maori chiefs being transported? We must protest predations of this kind. Let our protest be another nail in the wooden coffin of transportation.'

The protests spread, fuelled by our editor friends. 'Newspapers in Van Diemen's Land,' Henry Melville explained to me, 'have always shown a great strain of admiration for the Maori of New Zealand. They are of a different order to our own native species, having many of the qualities of a higher position in the human family. They have learnt to trade with us.

They are becoming capitalists. They are a superior native people not easily overwhelmed by the might of European material and spiritual culture and technology.'

I have another clipping to hand from the *Cornwall Chronicle* of 1 February, which shows this sympathy:

> According to the latest information received from New Zealand, it appears that the native chiefs are not disposed to submit quietly to the forfeiture of their lands to suit the scheming of the London Company. A general slaughter will produce, of course, a general feast; a general roasting of white flesh, which from rather unusual fasting of late, will render a little blood-letting among the Europeans more than usually palatable to the sable anthropophagi.

The word spread about the impending arrival of the Maori chiefs.

Of course, when the time came, on Monday 16 November, there was no question in my mind — or Ismay's — that we should go down to the New Wharf to show our sympathy for them. The Maori troubles in the Wairau may have been the cause of our hasty withdrawal from New Zealand, but we held no personal animosity towards them.

'And Mahuika would be cross with me if I did not welcome them,' Ismay said. 'Sally Jenkins, will you get the children clothed?'

I remember that when we were about to leave the house I looked up. The heavens were flashing with silver, as if the sky was a giant luminescent blue sea and something was chasing shoals of fish across the southern horizon towards us.

Ismay noticed the sky too. 'Nga rangatira kia haramai,' she said. 'The chiefs are coming.'

———

We hurried to the harbour. As we got closer, we joined a steady stream of other citizens. Some were dressed formally, as if they were going to greet royalty. There was an atmosphere of expectation among us all.

No sooner had we arrived at the New Wharf than Eion Gault, Henry Melville and John Morgan hailed us. 'Have you come to join the welcoming party?' Eion asked. 'Just look at the crowd!'

Indeed, the entire population of Hobart Town must have been present: gentry and servants; business men and sailors; shopkeepers, prostitutes and convict servants. Two artists, William Duke and John Skinner Prout, had set up easels, planning to sketch the Maori chiefs on arrival.

A number of other vessels were at anchor. Sailors were on lookout amongst the rigging. Then one of them pointed, 'There it is!'

Coming up the Derwent was HMS *Castor*, like a huge angry white swan pecking at the smaller skiffs that whizzed about her. Immediately there was loud booing, and cries of 'Shame! Shame! Shame!' The protest escalated as, from the Hobart Penitentiary, came a small contingent of armed guards. Arms at the ready, they shouldered through the crowd.

The guard began to secure the wharf. 'Clear the way,' they ordered. 'Clear the way.' When they came to where I was standing with Eion, Ismay, the children and the newspaper men, the officer in charge saluted me, 'Dr McKissock,' and allowed us to remain while they moved the rest behind us.

'Rank does have its privileges,' Eion remarked.

As the HMS *Castor* came to anchor, the crowd grew silent. A gangplank was laid between the ship and the dock and port authorities, including customs and immigration officials, boarded. The crowd was restless.

Someone called out, 'Where are the Maoris?'

At last, disembarkation — but of free passengers, startled at the huge crowd. They walked swiftly past us and into the town.

Then a sailor cried out, 'There they are! Three cheers for the Maoris!' Seamen could always be relied upon to take the side of the persecuted. 'Hip hip—'

'Hoo-*raa*!' came the cry from the crowd.

The first two Maori were wearing traditional dress: long woven kilt to the ankles, woven bandoliers and short doghair capes. Fully tattooed on the face, they appeared to be dazed by the commotion.

'Hip hip—'

'Hoo-*raa*!' came the roar from the sailors in the riggings. The second two Maori had no facial tattoo and wore red blankets over their shoulders. None could doubt the fervency and support of their reception.

'Hip hip—'

'Hoo-*raa*!' came the acclamation, rolling around the wharf. That was when the final Maori showed himself:

Hohepa Te Umuroa.

———

In profile he was truly the chief that the crowd had been waiting for.

He was tattooed, taller than the others and had an arresting bearing that demanded attention. He held a beautiful carved stick, a tokotoko of the kind that Maori chiefs used when talking on a marae. Even though he was shackled at the wrists and ankles with the others, the cruel arm- and leg-irons only added to the power of his appearance.

He was Atlas in chains.

Then he turned his face and body full upon us. His face was only half tattooed, the other side unblemished. The effect was striking. It was as if he were two people, part human, part god. His eyes were dark green, glowing.

They were ancestor eyes. His ancestors were arriving with him.

And his body was extraordinary, with wide shoulders tapering to a thin waist and long slender limbs. The sensory impact was such that a prostitute yelled out, 'Wotcha doin' tonight, fella? Come spend some time wiv Stella!'

'Yes,' Eion muttered, 'you are a pretty fellow.'

I was surprised at Eion's remark. I looked at him and caught him unguarded, his face etched with desire. I wondered: Was Eion a man who loved other men? Wishing to keep his secret, was that why he had been reluctant to accept nomination to public office?

Quickly, before Eion could see that I had fathomed his depths, I turned away.

I saw Hohepa stiffen with anger. Then, unfazed and unbowed, he raised his tokotoko high. 'Karanga mai ki au,' he cried.

Perhaps this was why Ismay was compelled to step forward to welcome the Maori chiefs in their own tradition. I had never heard her do this before, but nothing she did ever surprised me.

Haere mai nga tangata o Niu Tireni e . . .
Welcome, brave men of Maoriland . . .
Haere mai nga tangata toa ki runga o te reo aroha e . . .
Welcome warriors, alight to the call of love . . .

A great roar erupted from the crowd.

The Maori exchanged glances. Where was the call coming from?

Ismay was always unconventional, impulsive and, on that day, breathtaking. She didn't care a jot about the impact she was causing.

'Come to land now,' she called.

In a gathering hush, the Maori advanced. The guards had been as taken by surprise as everyone else on the wharf, and let them approach us. The Maori's irons clanked as they made their painful progress towards Ismay. They were proud more than penitential, refusing to bow their heads.

And Gower Jr suddenly started to do a childish haka! He looked so funny, thumping his little chest with his fists, stamping his legs and poking his tongue out!

272

The Maori men began to smile at his antics. But Rollo and Clara, seeing Hohepa's fearsome tattoos, grew frightened.

Clara gave a shrill cry, lifted Ismay's dress, and crawled under it. She grabbed Rollo's little hand, and he followed quickly after her.

The Maori gaped at the sight. One minute there were three children. Next minute two had disappeared. Hohepa began to laugh, his laughter pealing joyously over the crowd. It broke the spell but also the tension and, soon, the entire crowd was laughing with him. 'You are the mother hen and your children are your chickens!' he said.

He knelt down in front of Ismay. Rollo's face emerged, followed by a fist as he punched Hohepa on the nose.

'Why did you do that?' Gower Jr asked his brother. 'They are only Maori.'

The officer in charge approached, concerned. 'Do you wish me to restrain the prisoners, Dr McKissock?'

Hohepa had begun to play a game of peek-a-boo with Rollo and Clara as they peered from under her dress, shrieked and disappeared again. 'Hei tama! Tu tama! Hei tama! E!'

'No,' I answered. 'Let the Maori have a moment with the children.'

The whole crowd watched on, entranced, as Rollo and Clara lost their fears. They came out like little chicks and pecked at his hands. Two of the others — I later knew them to be Kumete and the young Matiu Tikiaki — began to stroke them.

Hohepa smiled at Ismay. 'Your chickens find safety in your nest! What is your name?'

'Mrs Ismay McKissock,' I heard her reply.

———

The officer in charge stepped forward again.

'Sir,' he said, 'the prisoners should be forwarded to The Paddock to Mr Gunn's depository of men of all castes.'

'Yes, of course,' I answered. 'We will accompany you.'

The sailors began to raise loud cheers again and the crowd to applaud the Maori — and boo the guards. Halfway along, however, the press of people was such that Eion, John Morgan and the other newspaper men became separated from us.

'We'll see you at our next meeting, Gower!'

Their places were taken by George Washington Walker, who stepped into our path. With him was a young gentleman who was unknown to me.

But Hohepa and Kumete gave great cries of joy at the sight of him. They reached out for him as we passed by.

'Tamati, e! Atae te miharo! Mr Mason! Kia ora!'

This Mr Mason paced us and began to speak in Maori to them. He had about him the air of a thoroughly plain and honest man; there was in him also a sense of great determination.

George Walker had an urgent word. 'Mr McKissock, could you authorise my companion and me to accompany the Maoris into The Paddock? Mr Thomas Mason is a friend.'

'All right,' I agreed.

'Thank you,' he said. 'Mr Mason is also a Quaker. He is recently arrived from New Zealand and came down to the dock to express his solidarity with the Maori.'

'You know the prisoners?' I asked Mr Mason, shaking his hand.

'My wife Jane and I were once their neighbours in the Hutt Valley,' he answered. 'When we arrived in New Zealand we were the first settlers to take possession of our allotment which, as we later discovered, was on Ngati Rangatahi land. They permitted us to stay. They themselves forewarned me of the troubles, so I brought my family here, temporarily, to Hobart Town.'

'Is your wife here?' Ismay asked.

'She is feeling poorly,' he answered. 'We have another child on the way.' Then, 'Do you speak Maori also?' he asked.

'Ae,' she nodded. 'Kei te korero ahau te reo o te iwi Maori.'

'Ko koe hoki?' he asked me.

Ismay shook her head. 'Mr McKissock does not know the language.' Then she patted my arm. 'I will take the children home now while you attend to the chiefs.'

She was just about to leave when Hohepa addressed her. 'Who taught you?'

'An old Maori kuia,' Ismay answered, 'in Nelson.'

They were looking at each other with such alarm.

Then, 'Come, children,' Ismay said.

———

I approved Mr Walker and Mr Mason coming into The Paddock with me and the Maori. It was a good move because, as soon as we arrived, they began to show signs of anxiety and resistance.

Mr Mason calmed them down. 'No, you will not be separated,' he said.

I watched as they were processed according to the Indent of Convicts:

Prisoner No. 765, Te Waretiti. Single. Laborer. 5 feet 3 and a half inches tall. Aged about 25. Dark brown complexion, with all over blue marks on his face as well as on both arms. Not able to read or write.

Prisoner No. 766, Hohepa Te Unmroa, correction Umuroa. Single. Laborer. 6 feet 1 inch tall. Aged about 25. Dark brown complexion, tattooed on the left side of his face. Can read and write in the native language.

Prisoner No. 767, Te Kumete. Single. Laborer. 5 feet 5 inches tall. Dark complexion, and possessing a large scar on both arms, as well as having blue marks all over his face and also on his left arm.

Prisoner No. 768, Mataiuma or Matiuma. Single. Laborer. 5 feet 3 and a half inches tall. Aged about 20. Dark complexion, possessing a native mark on his left arm. Able to read and write in the native language.

Prisoner No. 769, Te Rahui. Single. Laborer. 5 feet and a half inches tall. Aged about 25. Dark complexion, with a scar on the centre of his forehead. Not able to read or write.

Te Rahui asked for some water. 'Aue, ka kino!' he cried. 'The water tastes bad.' He spat it out as soon as he'd taken a sip.

Kumete grabbed Mr Mason and, when guards came to separate them, he started to call out in a frenzy, 'Kua ngaro matou i te Po!'

Upset, Mr Mason opened a satchel he was carrying. In it were copies of the New Testament in Maori.

'The Book of All Books will bring you solace,' he said.

'I will read a chapter a night to the others,' Hohepa promised. 'But will you pray with us before you leave? We will need angels to guard us as we go into the stomach of the dark night.'

'What will happen to them now?' George Walker asked.

'They will await the decision as to where they are to be incarcerated. The likelihood is Port Arthur or Norfolk Island.'

'We must act quickly,' Mr Mason said. 'My friends should not be sent to a prison of maximum security. They should not be here at all.'

I looked at George Walker. 'I will call a meeting tomorrow night at my house. Will you and Mr Mason attend?'

'Of course,' he answered.

———

When I arrived home, Ismay had dinner ready.

'How are our Maori friends?' she asked as we sat down together. She had prepared a lovely roast, potatoes and vegetables.

'As well as can be expected,' I answered. 'I've called a meeting for tomorrow night to discuss their situation. Meanwhile, they have fortitude and courage — and they have a leader.'

'The one called Hohepa?' she asked.

I took a sip of rich red wine. 'Yes.'

———

Later that evening, when we were in bed, Clara began crying in her room.

'I'll go to her,' I told Ismay.

I cradled Clara for a while. 'Why so fractious, little one?'

I realised I too was sleepless and affected — nay, disturbed. Just before drifting off to sleep I realised why. Hohepa, coming down the gangway of HMS *Castor*, had lifted his head and stared at the crowd.

They may have been ancestor eyes. But I wondered why, on seeing them, my first thought had been of my father, Ramsay.

27

'The plight of the Maori chiefs has clearly struck a chord,' Eion whispered to me when he arrived the following evening.

The house was crowded with around twenty-five of our colleagues.

'And our stalwart friend Henry Melville,' he continued, 'has corralled John Morgan, Andrew Bent and William Gore Elliston to come along!'

Some new faces arrived at the meeting. Arriving with Mr Walker, Mr Mason brought his pregnant wife, Jane. As soon as she and Ismay began talking, they recognised in each other a kindred spirit. For one thing, Jane Mason was not about to absent herself from a meeting of men! Thus Ismay invited her, 'Come sit by me, Mrs Mason, and let us offer our own opinions so as to advantage the male species.'

Another New Zealander turned up. His name was George Clarke, and he was in transit on his way to London.

I called the meeting to order. But order wasn't what they wanted. Passion ruled the night!

'Were you able to see the Maori chiefs today?' Mr Walker asked.

'They have been separated and placed in their own cells,' I answered. 'Their leader, Hohepa Te Umuroa, is beside himself with anxiety. "We have been together throughout our ordeal," he told me. "When we go from here will we be imprisoned together? It is our Maori way. If we are separated, we will die."'

A murmur of sympathy greeted my description.

'I hear privately that the Colonial Office considers that George Grey has overstepped the mark,' George Clarke told us. 'They are deeply embarrassed about this entire situation.'

Again there a ripple, this time of disgruntlement.

The meeting progressed. Diplomatically, I let everyone have their say. After all, these were businessmen, politicians and editors accustomed to being heard!

'The Maori have been subject to injustice,' Henry Melville said. 'They are not like the great majority of Anglo-Celtic convicts, transported for larceny or other common-law offences. They are people to shake hands with.'

After further strong discussion, we came to two decisions which I recorded as a resolution:

1. Mr Thomas Mason, knowing the Maori chiefs personally, will write a letter to the Lieutenant-Governor testifying to the Maoris' good character. He will make detailed recommendations concerning their treatment while in incarceration. Once the letter is written it will be delivered by Messrs Mason, Walker, McKissock and Gault to the Lieutenant-Governor at the earliest opportunity.

2. The meeting urges Messrs John Morgan, Henry Melville, Andrew Bent and William Gore-Elliston to publicise the plight of the Maori through their newspapers insofar as their independent opinion allows.

Two days later, Mr Mason having written his letter, we made an appointment with the acting lieutenant-governor, Charles Joseph La Trobe, and presented it to him at Government House. Stately and palatial, the residence was everything you would expect of a building symbolic of England's control over the colony.

Our meeting fortuitously coincided with a report on the arrival of the Maori chiefs published in the *Britannia and Trades' Advocate*:

The subject is one painful to contemplate, and it is too serious to treat upon lightly. We have hitherto refrained from all remarks on the execution of one of the New Zealanders, referred to in other public Journals, because we know not all the particulars of the case . . . Our unjust occupancy of his country is another matter altogether . . . It was an act worthy of the Buccaneers of former days, an act by which the British name and character were tarnished, and that the human blood shed in consequence will rise up in judgement on the aggressors, cannot be doubted.

We were shown in to Governor La Trobe and, I must say, I was impressed. Reputation held that he was a highly cultured individual. I saw also a man's man clearly at ease with his role.

'Thank you for coming, gentlemen,' he said. 'I understand you are here to discuss the Maoris?'

'Yes,' Eion began on our behalf. 'We believe they should receive a full pardon and be released.'

'I have already promptly informed the Colonial Office in London of their most unusual arrival,' he said 'and also questioned the severity of their sentences. Perhaps, gentlemen, if you lay out the parameters of your case?'

Mr Mason took the floor. 'The land at Wellington was most wrongly and illegally acquisitioned by the New Zealand Company. They collected signatures for a Deed of Sale without properly outlining the agreement and without due consideration of which chiefs actually owned the land. No chief had complete authority to sign for all. Given that the British Government was yet to sign the Treaty of Waitangi, the deed was a highly disputable document. As well, no communication had been held with places included in the pretended purchase, except at Port Nicholson, Kapiti and Taranaki, where neither party understood the other. Regarding the tribe, Ngati Rangatahi, from which the Maori chiefs have come, they had every right to feel aggrieved. Governor Grey knew that driving them off their land by force was illegal, but he ignored this and went ahead anyway.'

'The settlers of Wellington simply took the law into their own hands,' I added. 'Similarly, the Company and settlers are themselves entirely responsible for the events at Boulcott's Farm, the inciting incident which caused the pursuit of the Maori rebels including the Maori chiefs who have been transported. Any landowner who has their land taken by force is bound to retaliate.'

'All that is context,' Governor La Trobe answered. 'What I need is to be able to refer to a specific New Zealand law to argue the case to the Colonial Office for the Maori's release.'

'Sir,' Mr Mason intervened, 'it is in the questionable application of martial law enabling civil offences to be tried by military courts. Martial law is, surely, an extreme remedy, to be used only when the civil power has collapsed, or is in imminent danger of collapse. It is incredible that any such state of affairs existed in the Wellington district.'

The governor pursed his lips. 'I shall receive your letter from you, gentlemen, and if there is any recommendation in it which I can implement with regard to the Maori chiefs' incarceration, I will do it.'

———

Matters moved faster than Governor La Trobe perhaps anticipated.

On 24 November the *Colonial Times* once again voiced its outrage at Governor Grey's conduct:

There is capital notice in the *Cornwall Chronicle* of the 14th of the murder of the New Zealand Chief, Wareaitee, by Captain Grey. It embraces the whole points of the case; and if we do not very much mistake the British feeling which will arise when the subject is canvassed in England, Governor Grey will not only be recalled immediately, but stand a very good chance of being treated a la mode of Governor Wall. The poor wretches whom he did not murder have arrived . . . in H.M.S. *Castor*. There is general feeling of abhorrence of Governor Grey's conduct throughout the island. It is considered the very quintessence of tyrannical cowardice. Why did he not go at the head of the troops, and fight the New Zealand patriots like a man? But it will be avenged. England will never suffer with impunity such a disgraceful act. There is one part of the subject we are ashamed to touch — the Court-Martial!

The very next day, Wednesday 25 November, *The Hobart Town Courier* delivered a second broadside in an editorial under the heading:

NEW ZEALAND PRISONERS

We forbore to comment on the proceedings of the recent Court at New Zealand, denounced though they have been by a portion of the press as sanguinary and atrocious, until we might obtain more explicit information as to the grounds on which its extreme measures were based. Failing in this, we still withold all animadversion on the legality of its decisions, as well as all censure of the decree which subjected a native chief to the heaviest penalty of the law. But if we have nothing to say of the dead, we have much to plead for the living. Not that we mean to impugn the justice of policy of the sentence which exiled men in the earliest stages of civilisation from the land which they claimed, by natural right, as their own, and on which, from some error of judgement or principle — under all the cirumstances almost venial — they seemed to regard their British co-occupants, though settled with the sanction of compacts and treaties, as strangers and intruders. But we cannot but view the order or the recommendation which accompanied the sentence, for the transmission of these 'children of nature' to Port Arthur, as repugnant to every feeling of humanity, to every impulse of benevolence, and to every precept of the Gospel.

We have visited and, with the aid of an interpreter, have conversed with the five Maories, now in the Penitentiary, under sentence of transportation and of transmission to Port Arthur. They seem to be simple-minded men, with apparently but an imperfect conception of their real position, and with none of the humiliating consciousness of crime. They are by no means deficient in intelligence, though unwilling to express freely any opinion on the hostilities in which they were engaged, or on the justice of their sentence: except so far as to assert that they were only 'fighting those who came against their country,' and to disavow all participation in the murder with which they were charged. They have all been under Missionary instruction, and seemed to feel a grateful exultation in announcing that they could read the 'Book of Books,' copies of which, in their own language, they possess.

It will be recollected that when the Pentonville exiles were sent to this colony, it was understood that they came under strict instructions to be detached from all probation assemblages, and to be removed as far as possible from all deteriorating associations. If then the Pentonville exiles were considered objects of such considerate regard, because, however steeped in previous guilt, they had undergone a purifying process of seclusion, how much stronger a claim on philanthropic care have these unfortunate New Zealanders, who transgressed British law rather from ignorance and the force of habit than from viciousness of disposition or cherished propensity to crime. We doubt not His Excellency the Administrator of the Government will give the matter full consideration before he allows the harsh and injurious appendage to the sentence to be carried into effect. If we mistake him not, an appeal to His Excellency in this behalf will not be made in vain. We are glad to learn that the order for their immediate transmission to Port Arthur has already been countermanded or suspended. We trust that this is but the prelude to a more benevolent arrangement.

We visited Government House again.

Governor La Trobe was in good humour. 'Gentlemen, the Colonial Office is furious with the headlines and the way in which this matter continues to embarrass them. Their file of correspondence grows daily and anxiety mounts concerning the legal position. Mr Grey is being asked some very uncomfortable questions about his actions. It's becoming a huge scandal.'

'I'm glad to hear it,' Eion said. 'What with his hanging, transporting and slaughtering the native race, there has been no lack of employment since His Excellency's arrival in New Zealand.'

'The whole business smacks of a vindictive personal vendetta,' Governor La Trobe agreed. 'I am clearly unhappy about New Zealand's use of transportation to someone else's territory as a sanction for Maori prisoners of war.'

'You must petition for a pardon, sir,' I said.

Governor La Trobe pondered the suggestion. Finally, 'All right,' he said. 'I will write to the Colonial Office to report these perplexities. Meantime, we cannot keep the Maori chiefs in the Hobart Town Penitentiary while awaiting consideration. That could take months. A year, perhaps.'

'They should not be sent to Port Arthur,' Mr Mason insisted, 'or Norfolk Island.'

I thought of John Jennings and Etty Imrie. They had been to New Zealand and would be sympathetic.

'Why not . . .' I ventured, 'the Darlington probation station on Maria Island?'

A light gleamed in Governor La Trobe's eyes. How heady to have him on our side in this way! He turned to Mr Mason. 'They could be kept separately from the other prisoners . . . with their own supervisor . . . somebody who could speak Maori . . .'

Mr Mason appeared hesitant, but, 'Yes,' he said, 'I could go with them.'

'In that case,' Governor La Trobe said, 'let me see what I can do.'

———

Two days later, Governor La Trobe called us together again.

'Thank you, gentlemen,' he began, 'for your patience in this matter.' He took up a letter. 'May I read to you my letter today written to the Colonial Office. The relevant portion is:

. . . Were these prisoners to be disposed of in a similar manner to others arriving in Van Diemen's Land, from the neighbouring Colonies, under sentence of Transportation for Life, it would be my duty to direct their conveyance to Norfolk Island; but viewing the peculiar circumstances of their case, the acts of commission of which they have been convicted and sent hither, the object in view of awarding punishment as well as the character of the individuals, I cannot resolve to send them either to Norfolk Island or Tasman's Peninsula, to be classed and associated with the transported felons congregated in those settlements, more particularly under present circumstances, and with a full knowledge of the degraded state of moral feeling prevailing against them. Nor can I indeed feel justified in admitting of any arrangement whatsoever, under which they would be brought into close contact with the prisoner population of any class, before their case has been submitted to Her Majesty's Government, and your Lordship's opinion as to the course to be pursued shall have been received.

I have taken steps to secure them during their temporary detention at the Penitentiary at Hobart Town from association with the common herd of Prisoners, and have further directed that they shall be removed to Maria Island and placed under the special charge of an overseer expressly provided to secure their isolation and their employment in any manner consistent with their powers and habits . . .

Signed, C.J. La Trobe, this 30th day of November, 1846'

We crowded around Governor La Trobe, shaking his hand and thanking him.

Can one divine a pattern here in the efforts of the Quakers of Hobart Town and the strong vigorous support of the newspapers? And now the sympathetic hand of Governor La Trobe?

Not until later did I become aware of the serendipitous coincidence of his involvement. Acting as lieutenant-governor for only four months, he had come from a family long involved in the campaign for the abolition of slavery — indeed, he himself had been sent by the British Government to the West Indies to report on measures to enable the slave population to gain their freedom! Would another lieutenant-governor of less humanitarian interest have intervened to such a strong degree?

However, a problem arose.

Thomas and Jane Mason called at the house. They were most upset.

'We can't accompany our Maori friends to Maria Island,' Mr Mason said. 'Jane is not well and although I could go by myself I am loath to leave her. I therefore ask, Mr McKissock, if you would go in our stead.'

'Me?' I answered. 'I don't speak Maori.'

Ismay said, 'The Masons are speaking diplomatically, Mr McKissock.'

Mr Mason was patient. 'If you say yes,' he said, 'I am sure the governor will obtain your release from the Hobart Town Penitentiary and Mr Walker's Quaker mission will compensate you for loss of income from your surgery.'

I looked at Ismay.

'The decision is yours,' she said. Her diffidence surprised me. Under normal circumstances she was always so decisive.

I knew I had to say yes. There was no doubt that this appalling sentence should be seen to its rightful judicial end.

'All right,' I answered. 'We will go.'

Ismay and I, the children, Sally Jenkins and the Maori left Hobart Town on the *Mary* the following week.

To show that this was a transfer to which the Government attached great sympathy, Governor La Trobe and the Controller-General of Convicts, Dr Hampton, accompanied us.

Gower Jr began to chase Rollo all over the deck and, alarmed, Ismay and Sally Jenkins scooped them both up.

'You boys will be the death of me,' Sally Jenkins said. 'If one of you fell overboard I'd have to save you — and I would sink to the bottom of the ocean.'

Ismay smiled at me, 'We'll take the children below deck,' she said.

Governor La Trobe joined me as we exited the Derwent and made open sea. 'Thank you, Dr McKissock,' he said, 'for enabling Mrs McKissock and yourself to perform this most important service of caretaking the Maoris on behalf of the Government.'

We stayed chatting for a while and then he was called away by his secretary. 'No matter where I am,' he laughed, 'there are always papers to be signed.'

I remained on deck. I have always loved the swelling motion of the sea, the sense that somewhere far below the bellows of the ocean are blowing the currents hither and yon. I noticed that a guard had brought the five Maori up from below.

'Tena koutou,' I said to them.

'Ah, Mr McKissock,' Hohepa Te Umuroa answered. 'Mr Mason told us of your and Mrs McKissock's kindness in replacing him. Thank you.'

'Ae,' the other Maori said. 'Ka nui te pai.'

We stood together, embarrassed at first but united in the brotherhood of man.

'In which direction lies Aotearoa?' Hohepa asked.

I pointed and Hohepa turned to look into the distance, his profile etched against the heavenly swirl of transluscent pink, purple and lambent ivory and pearl.

I realised what it was about him that reminded me of my father.

———

When I had left Edinburgh in 1840 I tried not to think of Ramsay's skeleton being looked upon and discussed by students year after year at the medical school.

I had since learned that instead of being ridiculed and reviled, the intricate nature of his framework incited awe and reverence.

Although he might have been a joke of God, in the end the joke was on those who had only seen ugliness. For, according to my father's colleague,

Professor Sinclair Abbott, in a letter to me from Scotland, there was a perfect, extraordinary symmetry in that twisted physiology, like a double spiral in Gower's bones that made him look almost . . .

'As if, at one further unfurling, unbending and straightening and arching and springing upward and out,' Professor Abbott wrote, 'he would have emerged from that misshapen chrysalis of shining bones as an angel.'

Like Hohepa, standing there, silhouetted against that turbulent sky, almost as if he was on the moment of leaping, wings extended, from that extraordinary heaven, and plunging below into the dark purple spheres of the sea.

THE SECOND BOOK

ISLAND AT WORLD'S END

ISMAY'S STORY

Tasmania, Australia

PROLOGUE
Tasmania, 1903

Do you know the old Van Diemen's Land legend of how Trowenna was created?

The old ones say that in the Dreamtime, when the world was in darkness, Trowenna was a sliver of sand in the sea. Then Parnuen, the sun, came up, up, up from the sea and into the sky with his wife, Vena. They travelled across the sky together and sank into the sea on the other side of Trowenna.

This was the first day.

The second day came and, this time, as Parnuen and Vena passed across Trowenna, they dropped from the sky some seeds on the sandbank.

Came the third day, up, up, up rose Parnuen and when he crossed above Trowenna he sprinkled the seeds with rain. From them grew tar monadro, the first gumtree.

On the fourth day, he blessed the sea circling Trowenna with shellfish. They fell into the water and burrowed into the sand.

Then came the fifth day when Parnuen and Vena mated and their first child, Moihernee, was born. That's Moihernee up there, can you see him? He is the great South Star who watches over Trowenna.

On the sixth day, Vena gave birth to the gentle Dromerdene, a son. Parnuen set him in the sky as the star Canopus, to be the second watcher over the land.

All throughout the Dreamtime trees grew from tar monadro. When their leaves fell, they mixed with the sand, and out of the mixing came the good rich earth. In the sea, generations of shellfish gave up their shells to make the stones and rocks from which came Trowenna's great mountains.

The old ones say that Moihernee, when he reached adulthood, dug the channels in Trowenna's soil and, when it rained, the water made the rivers. It was Moihernee who cut Trowenna into pieces to form our islands.

He also created the first human. He named the first man Parlevar, but he was not like we are today: he could not sit down because he had no joints in his legs and he had a tail, can you imagine?

It was Dromerdene, Moihernee's brother, who saw the problem — he cut off Parlevar's tail, rubbing grease on the wound to heal it, and made joints at his knees! That's why humans can now sit and make ourselves comfortable.

Alas, later, the brothers Dromerdene and Moihernee quarrelled with each other. During their battle, they both fell from the sky. Dromerdene fell into the sea and Moihernee fell to earth: he became the tall stone which stands in the southwest of Trowenna.

When the first white creatures came to Trowenna, the local people thought they had fallen from the sky too. They saw Captain Cox of the *Mercury* making his survey in 1789 and sent up smoke to tell others of the arrival of the sky people who had come down to earth.

Then they saw the French expedition under Baudin in 1802, and they grew suspicious. They prodded and poked the white creatures and, when one of them took off his outer skin and they realised he was just a man after all, with an unnatural white organ, they laughed and laughed and laughed.

But the sky started to fall all together, white creatures falling out of the sky with great rapidity like shooting stars, until the whole of Trowenna was writhing and wriggling with them. Wherever they hatched, Trowenna browned and wilted.

The Trowennans knew that their world would never be the same again.

———

I come now, by reluctant degrees, to the particular memories that Georgina so badgers me about for the book commemorating Tasmania's Fiftieth Anniversary: the history of the five Maori prisoners on Maria Island.

Perhaps it is not as interesting as the territory her colleagues have staked out — the stain of convict ancestry or the relationship between the colonials and the Trowennans is somewhat more controversial — and I will await with interest to find out whether those researchers will gloss over the embarrassments and injustices of the past to attain the celebratory tone of their book.

The problem is, however, that Georgina doesn't want just the public history of the Maori. She also wants the personal memories of my relationship with my dear Hohepa and what happened to the three of us — Hohepa, Gower and me — on Maria Island.

She has sniffed something out. She always did have a long nose, like the proboscis of a kiwi — the flightless bird of New Zealand — wielding it like a sword and slashing through the undergrowth of history to find the seed beneath.

I must have revealed my hand to her. When was it? How did it happen?

Perhaps it was that day in 1877, the year Port Arthur was finally closed. I was fifty-five that year and Gower was fifty-seven. Our son Gower Jr was thirty-five and had a good wife in Claire; their four children, David, Harry, George and little Ismay were a joy — I don't think Robina had been born yet.

Rollo, of course, had already left Van Diemen's Land for England, turning his back on me and his father, walking away without a backward glance. I heard he married a German girl; he was an ungrateful son and she is welcome to him.

With Clara I was always disappointed. Even as a child she played games, pretending that she was frightened of everything so that other people would protect her; but she didn't fool me one bit. Or perhaps I was too strong an influence on her and she never became accustomed to independence. I have to hand it to her though: as a woman she managed to attract big bulky men — like her rich banker husband Phil, who was more than happy to provide the requisite protection.

But to return to Georgina, who, by the way, is Clara and Phil's only daughter.

On that occasion marking the closure of Port Arthur, Tasmania stopped entirely for the day. Clara told me that Georgina was taking part in a school pageant. The child wanted to go as a fine lady; might she borrow the ruby necklace and earrings?

I said yes, so Clara turned up at the house with Georgina in tow. I was making a cup of tea for us, and I had a glass of milk ready for Clara, when they arrived. I put the teapot down to go to my dresser to get the jewellery, but Georgina said, 'I can get them, Nanna,' and upstairs she scooted before I could stop her.

Clara and I have never been able to converse about politics or the state of the nation; we get by on unthreatening topics like gardening or cooking. She loves jigsaw puzzles, and showed me one she had purchased earlier in the day. What a waste of time trying to fit five thousand pieces into assorted spaces that would, on completion, give you a portrait of the Mona Lisa or the Tower of London!

I didn't hear Georgina come back downstairs until Clara said to her, 'Georgie dear, what have you been doing!'

She looked such a sight! She had put on lipstick, a hat and a pair of my high heels, and somewhere she had found a long satin slip that trailed along the floor.

She was also wearing the earrings and necklace.

She had a clever look on her face, and held her hands behind her back.

'What else have you got, Georgie?' Clara asked.

'I want to take *this* too.' She showed what she had: Hohepa's tokotoko.

The child had been rifling through the baize-lined chest where I kept my most personal possessions.

I saw Clara looking at me. I'm sure my expression had changed, but nary a drop of tea spilled from my cup. 'No, darling,' Clara told the scheming child. 'Nanna wouldn't want you to take that. It belonged to her special friend.'

My special friend?

Clara gave me another of her looks: the one that pretended innocence and yet came with a slight smile from her thin, painted lips, creased above with little lines that would, in a few years, give her the air of having suffered.

'Why can't I take it?' Georgina asked. Although she had inherited the same wishy-washy, waxy appearance as her mother, I must admit that she had more passion to her. She had a habit of pushing back the wings of her tendril-blonde hair and she did so now, exposing her devious grey eyes.

I was not about to be conciliatory. 'How dare you go rifling through my belongings!' I said to her. 'That carved stick was at the bottom of the chest. Return it, you naughty girl, now.'

Clara sat bolt upright: I could almost hear every joint in her backbone crack.

Georgina, however, just looked at me, appraising me in that clever way of hers. But she knew she had overstepped the mark. 'Sorry Nanna,' she said as she picked up the hem of the satin slip and, balancing on the high heels, pecked my cheek. 'I'll go and put it back.'

Sorry? The child wasn't sorry at all! She was off up the stairs.

I said to Clara, 'What did you mean, "Nanna's special friend"?'

Whenever Clara was found out, she always tried to retreat; she was such a coward. 'Mother dear,' she began, her face crimson, 'let's not dredge up the past, shall we?'

'The past?' I asked her. 'What do you know of the past?'

'Mother,' Clara answered, 'I was there. I saw. I know.'

'You were only a child,' I snapped. 'Two years old when my—' I could barely say the words '—*special friend*, as you call him, came to Van Diemen's Land.'

'That may be so,' Clara answered. 'But I was your accomplice when . . . when . . .'

'When *what*?'

Clara knew she was digging her grave. 'Please, Mother, don't get upset. I know that you . . . that . . . Father wasn't happy with you either . . . that . . .'

I grabbed her delicate wrists. 'What do you *know*? None of you know anything about me and Hohepa. I will not have you sully with your dirty thoughts my memories of him.'

I was so upset I slapped her.

The action shocked us both. I had never bonded with my daughter but, even so, that was no excuse to hit her.

She gave a cry and put a hand to her cheek. That's when I saw that Clara had returned. She was watching us from the bottom of the stairs, pushing back her hair again, her eyes lit up, fascinated.

'Georgie, dear,' Clara said. 'Say goodbye to Nanna.'

Like a martyr she departed, without speaking.

———

The memory exhausts me.

And now Georgina has come again, twenty-six years later. She thinks that because I am older (and, in her eyes, weaker) and she is stronger, she will be able to dominate me and find a way to get at a story — she must have heard it from her mother and, perhaps, others — that has always held a fascination for her.

She may slash all she wishes. Let her rattle the skeleton she thinks is in my cupboard. I am onto her and my resolve is the same.

Some things I will tell her.

Others I will not.

28

Yes, I will tell Georgina some things. But not others. To those questions I will respond with evasive circumlocutions.

I will not tell her, for instance, that my sighting of Hohepa Te Umuroa at Hobart Town was not the first time I had seen him. There had been another occasion — a cold afternoon in Nelson as I was leaving Mahuika after one of my language lessons. 'E Mahuika,' I said, 'e noho ra. Kia haere au ki a koe apopo. I will see you tomorrow.'

A brisk wind began to blow as I turned and walked up the beach. I stopped to tighten my scarf and button Gower Jr's coat. I happened to look back and there, silhouetted between land and sky, I saw Mahuika talking to a tall young Maori. She pointed in my direction; I saw him stand up and shade his eyes — and then he raised his tokotoko in acknowledgement.

The next day, when I was with Mahuika, she said to me, 'You saw the Maori warrior?'

'Ae, e kui.'

Before I could stop her she grabbed my hands and looked at their palms. She had already read my future once and now she read it again. 'The warrior begins his long journey today. You begin yours soon. What I saw the first time in the lines that scroll across your palms are also in his.'

However, when Gower and I left New Zealand, why, I completely dismissed what she had told me. I never expected that I would ever have anything further to do with Aotearoa. That is, until the Maori prisoners arrived in Hobart Town. When Hohepa made that gesture of raising his tokotoko, I remembered him. I therefore welcomed him and his friends, in the manner that Mahuika would have wanted.

Haere mai nga tangata o Niu Tireni e . . .
Welcome brave man of Maoriland . . .
Haere mai nga tangata toa ki runga o te reo aroha e . . .
Welcome warriors, alight to the call of love . . .

Then Gower asked me if I would mind our escorting Hohepa and the prisoners to their temporary — we hoped — incarceration on Maria Island. When I said yes, I couldn't help but hear Mahuika's words echoing in my ears.

'Your destiny is intertwined with his.'

And so Hohepa came into my life, that day of 20 December 1846, when I went northeast from Hobart Town to Maria Island on the *Mary* with Governor La Trobe, Dr Hampton, Gower, the children, Sally Jenkins and our five Maori charges.

I remember it as if it were yesterday. The ship left just before dawn and, as we were departing the Derwent, the sun rose above the ocean and ignited it. The sea that I had often dreamt about, looking over the rooftops of Wolverhampton, opened its arms to me. It filled with dark purple spheres like many crystal glasses spilling their rich wine into the currents. Swelling to the brim, it stilled for a moment. Then the sun, ascending further, transmuted those empurpled swirls into a shimmering pathway of gold and crimson.

I heard Hohepa and the Maori greet the new day, 'Ka ao, ka ao, ka awatea! It was dark, it was darkness, and now the dawn has arrived!'

The invocation was also a greeting to me: Would this be my dawning, too?

Gower spent most of the trip in the company of Governor La Trobe and Dr Hampton. Poor Sally Jenkins had her hands full as the children ran hither and thither over the tossing deck. I spent my time below, reading the material I had been provided with on life at Darlington Station: prison rules and regulations. I also came across the letter which Mr Mason had written to Governor La Trobe about the Maori:

Four of the New Zealanders in custody are from Wanganui & the fifth from Taupo (boiling springs) — I have known E'Opa I think since 1841, the Taupo native E Ware since 1843 — Pitama and Matiu since about the same time, and was in the habit of seeing and conversing with them almost daily — and during that time I do not recollect having a complaint against any of them, they were good neighbours. I felt myself perfectly secure, both as regards life and property also, and although at a considerable distance from a fellow settler, could leave my wife and children with confidence under their care, if business compelled me to leave home.

I read again Mason's words, 'They were good neighbours . . .' I prayed that that relationship would be maintained.

My mood of anticipation increased as we approached our destination. The world around me was changing. Van Diemen's Land was always to port, an ever-changing coastal forest vista merging into mountains beyond.

I went up to await the first sighting of Maria Island and joined Gower, Governor La Trobe and Dr Hampton. The governor acquainted us with the island's history.

'The original inhabitants were the Tyreddeme,' he began, 'and they called their home Toarra Marra Monah. First landfall in Van Diemen's Land was actually made here when Abel Tasman arrived in 1642. It was he who named it Maria Eylandt, after Maria van Aelst, the wife of the colonial governor-general of the Dutch East Indies; of course, the mainland is named after her husband. If I remember rightly, I think it was from here that Tasman journeyed further south and discovered and named Nieuw Zeeland.'

Sally Jenkins was still having some difficulty controlling the children, so I edged away from the conversation. 'Oh I shall be glad to get them on land!' she said. 'I'm so afeared they will fall overboard!'

Gower Jr saw Te Umuroa, Kumete, Te Waretiti, Rahui and the young Matiu Tikiaki; they were further along, manacled and guarded by two soldiers. Children are oblivious to chains and guards, and Gower Jr ran towards them calling, 'Kia ora! Kia ora!'

'No, don't—' Sally called. She followed after him, just in time to see him scooped up by Tikiaki.

'Ki a koe?' he asked Sally. 'Do you want him?' He was grinning from ear to ear as he said to Gower Jr, 'Haere koe ki te wahine ataahua.'

She blushed, thanking him, as he returned Gower Jr to her charge. The other Maori cheerfully poked fun at Tikiaki for his chivalry. 'So you think the girl is pretty, eh?'

Hohepa joined me. 'Are you enjoying the day, Mrs McKissock?'

I inclined my head, 'Yes.' I was still trying to come to terms with the coincidence of our meeting again. Had he recognised me from Nelson? We'd not had an opportunity to ask it of the other. What was more disturbing, perhaps, was that I had not told Gower about the earlier Nelson encounter.

I banished further thought from my head. Oh the warmth of the sun! I lifted my face to it. Those were the days when my skin loved to absorb the strong Trowenna rays. How I have paid for my exposure — in my old age, my English rose complexion has long faded and is gone now. Then I heard a sailor shout, 'Starboard ho!'

The first sight of Maria Island made me catch my breath. Large and dark green, it looked like an ancient uncut pounamu slab resting against the lustrous sky.

I recall the movement of the government schooner as it approached Cape Peron and made to enter the broad channel of Mercury Passage between the island and the mainland. Standing as a striking sentinel was the isolated granite rock known as The Pyramid, rising almost two hundred feet out of the water. The sea was racing into the Passage. The *Mary* ran on its surging breast, keeping to the eastward side of the flow, and I had to hold tight to the rail to keep my balance.

We were not the only ones impelled into the channel. From behind the vessel, dolphins began to appear. No matter how many times I had seen them on my voyages — from England to New Zealand and then to Van Diemen's Land — my heart still gladdened to see them again. They came abreast like a royal escort and I laughed out loud at their antics; they always brought such a spirit of joy and playfulness, pacing each other and sometimes rising on their fins to greet us.

'Nga tamariki o Tangaroa na,' Te Waretiti said. 'They are the children of Tangaroa, god of the ocean. Greetings, you silver heralds of the sea.' At last they outran us, speeding ahead to announce our coming, leaping from the water into the sun as if it were a silver hoop to jump through.

And then appearing on our right was Maria Island's isthmus, the narrow neck of land where the sea almost met within a few yards on each side. A little lower, and the isthmus would have made the one island into two: the large pendant above, and a smaller jewel below in a setting of sparkling sand. I felt a shiver of apprehension, for it had been at the isthmus that first contact with the white man had occurred.

They fell from the sky.

Now, only ghosts inhabited that place, heavy with eucalypts and she-oaks and shifting with shadows.

———

I was jolted out of my thoughts. As the vessel shifted to accommodate the currents a crisp and playful wind contrived to loosen my bonnet and send it spinning across the deck towards the Maori.

Rahui tried to scoop it up, but he got into a tangle of shackles with Te Waretiti. More nimble on his feet, Tikiaki made a dive for it.

'Kaore! Ko ahau etahi atu o nga mea ra!' I called, laughing. 'I have other caps and bonnets.'

Even so, Tikiaki made a further quick five-step lunge before being brought short by the chains. The bonnet flipped up and over the side. Hohepa saw the bonnet drift past him. 'E hika!' he exclaimed as he jumped onto the rail, reaching for it.

I gave a cry of alarm — and he stopped where he was. He looked across at me and shrugged his shoulders, smiling, 'Ae, etahi nga mea.' He stepped down from the railing. I was so relieved he hadn't jumped. With the weight of his leg-irons, he would have been drawn down into the depths to his death.

This time, Hohepa was the butt of remarks from the other Maori about *his* chivalry. 'Matiu Tikiaki isn't the only one to be swayed by a pretty lady,' they laughed. Kumete scowled at the implication. As for me, my cheeks burned a little and Mr McKissock leant to me and said, 'You have an admirer.'

I wanted to reply, 'The only admirer I wish is *you*.' Instead I pushed him away. 'Nonsense,' I said.

The crew of the *Mary* busied themselves bringing the boat about and I was soon occupied with gathering the children together for disembarkation. We fast approached the northern tip of Maria Island. Ahead was the open-ing of a flat valley between hills, watered by a small rivulet, and a sandstone quay.

The soldiers began marshalling the Maori for disembarkation.

Seabirds squealed above and around us, whirling and weaving in the glit-tering sky.

With our arrival my future was sealed.

29

There are times in life when one is both within and without the moment.

I can see myself on the tossing deck, a tall woman of pale complexion, dressed in a black travelling outfit and with a domino cape lined with red silk. 'I am twenty-four years of age and was born in Wolverhampton, England. I have come to an island at world's end. I never knew that one day I would leave England and journey to Aotearoa, and from there to Van Diemen's Land.'

My red hair tumbles loose as the pins are prised out by the same capricious wind that took my bonnet. Laughing, I put my hands to my hair to keep it out of my face — and that is when I see Hohepa staring back at me.

Then I hear a voice inside my head, addressing him. 'Tena koe, Mr Te Umuroa, who are you? Why do you bother me so! Here we are, strangers to each other but there is already a bond between us.'

And I see Gower too, and the children. They are smiling at me, and Gower teases me. I hear my voice again, asking, 'And you, Mr McKissock, how well will we negotiate this Vale of Tears? Will we do so with grace and goodwill towards each other? We are all pilgrims.'

Indeed, would love leaven Gower's and my days? As the *Mary* approached the jetty, I was unsure of the answer.

Darlington Station was seated on a gentle ascent, about a quarter of a mile from the shore. I was relieved to see that it possessed a neat and dry appearance. The Union Jack fluttered from a flagstaff, and close by was the prison precinct itself: the imposing penitentiary, barracks, cottages and other buildings. On a hill to the rear of the wharf was the hospital; the pottery and brick fields stood nearby, as did the civil cemetery. Everywhere, prisoners were at work.

'Here we are then,' Gower said. 'Another surprising adventure, eh? You don't seem to be so keen this time, Mrs McKissock!'

How could I tell him why I was feeling ambivalent! 'Why have we put ourselves out like this?' I asked him.

'Who else but you could speak to the Maori prisoners in their own language?' he answered. 'And are we not both committed to the cause of their freedom? Long after the Maoris have been released the fight will go on to free Van Diemen's Land of all convicts and, in the process, ourselves too.'

There were moments when Mr McKissock made me aware that in spite of the lack of love in our marriage he was to be admired for his noble political views. 'You are a good man,' I said, leaning back in to him.

———

I saw John Jennings and Etty Imrie waving to us; in my changing world they might ensure constancy.

'Mrs Imrie!' I called. 'Oh, Etty!' It was a comfort to see them and to realise we would have friends here and good companionship.

I saw Hohepa and the other prisoners were showing signs of anxiety. 'I had best be about my duties,' I said to Gower. 'Sally?' I called, 'could you obtain a replacement bonnet from the travel chest?' I tied it on my head and approached my Maori charges. 'Do not be afraid,' I told them. 'Darlington Station is not like Port Arthur.'

'How many prisoners are here?' Hohepa asked.

'About six hundred, and nearly five hundred at Long Point, the other station on the island. All are in the first stage of probation, and have come directly from Great Britain and Ireland, along with their military guards.'

'Must we always be in leg-irons and manacles around our wrists?' Rahui asked.

'I will see what I can do,' I answered, 'but prisoners when travelling are required to remain in chains.'

'Will we be separated?' Kumete asked, his voice rising with fear. 'E kui, please make sure that we won't be.'

'I give you my word,' I answered.

———

I joined Gower, Sally Jenkins and the children, and with Governor La Trobe kindly offering me support, stepped onto land.

'Well, well, Mr McKissock,' John Jennings said to Gower. 'Still following me around eh?'

302

'Yes,' Gower answered. 'I have come to some accommodation within myself of the matters we discussed when last we met.' Overhearing, I could not help but wonder what they were talking about. Whatever it was, John Jennings was very glad to hear it. 'In that case,' he answered, 'let us embrace in true fellowship.'

Meanwhile, Etty Imrie and I were making our own greetings. 'John Jennings and I are overjoyed to have you with us,' she said. 'The situation is so much more relaxed than at Port Arthur and the ladies are all very friendly. You are especially welcome, Ismay.' She spoke with such warmth, I couldn't help but be moved.

The next few minutes were a whirl of formalities, as Mr Lapham greeted Governor La Trobe and Dr Hampton; he appeared to be a person of benevolent disposition, mild and unassuming. His wife, Susan Lapham, had clearly been schooled in her duties, because she edged us away from the menfolk to enable them to continue some discourse which should not admit of women. Such segregation always irritated me, and I was not mollified by her kind invitation to join the ladies — they were preparing luncheon at the superintendent's residence — as soon as I had settled the children into our lodging.

How typical! The men went about their higher duties and the women made cakes, sandwiches and tea.

Clara was beginning to complain, but I kept her in check. Behind us Hohepa, Kumete, Te Waretiti, Matiu Tikiaki and Rahui were waiting. Some convicts, meantime, were unloading our luggage, eyeing us all with open curiosity. Sally Jenkins seemed a particular object of their interest. She took my arm and leaned in to me as if for protection. 'It's all right, Sally,' I said. 'There cannot be many young girls on this island.'

Then Governor La Trobe, mindful of the younger ones' discomfort, intervened. 'Gentlemen,' he said to the other men, 'we cannot leave the ladies and the children standing by in the hot sun.' He bowed to Mrs Lapham. 'Would you excuse us? Dr Hampton and I must look over Darlington with Mr Lapham. Mr Imrie? You will no doubt want to settle your Maori charges into their accommodation. Mr McKissock, would you care to join me in my inspection of the station?'

'Mrs McKissock?' Gower asked, his eyes twinkling. 'May I take my leave?'

Oh, it vexed me — and vexes me still — this separation of men and women as if there were some aspects of life too harsh for the gaze of the female of the species! However, I gave a nod, whose sourness I did my best to disguise, as we split up.

'Come,' Etty said, taking my elbow, 'let's get you and the children to your new home.'

Imagine my surprise when John Jennings and the two guards marshalled the Maori prisoners and began to follow us! Using his smattering of missionary Maori, he attempted to engage Te Waretiti and Tikiaki in conversation. When Te Waretiti showed John Jennings his New Testament, his pleasure knew no bounds. 'I wasn't aware that the Maoris were Christian,' he said.

We headed along a small, well kept road. My puzzlement increased: I had expected John Jennings to divert with the Maori to Darlington Station, which was on our left now. 'Mr Imrie,' I asked. 'Where are we going?'

'We will all be living approximately a half mile away from the station,' he replied.

'The prisoners too?' I asked. Oh this was happy news!

'Didn't you know?' Etty asked. 'Mr Imrie and I have been charged with being their overseers. You and Mr McKissock have a cottage next to ours, and the prisoners have a hut as accommodation nearby. It's ideal, considering that should they require any assistance, you will be close at hand to interpret for them.'

I couldn't help myself. I told the armed escort to halt and advised Hohepa of the arrangement. 'Despite your being convicted of rebellion against Her Majesty, and Governor Grey's recommendation that you be kept in harsh detention, you are to be treated with dignity and respect away from Darlington Station.'

'Kei kora? Away?' Hohepa asked. A convict gang was approaching. 'You mean that we are not to be treated like them?'

The gang drew up beside us. The men were wearing caps marked in front with their police number and at the back with the station number. They eyed the Maori men with interest, pointing and taking particular note of their tattoos.

One of them, a sunburnt boy, raised his voice. 'It's the Maori chiefs,' he said. 'Welcome, mateys.'

'Keep your silence, Seamus Keelan,' an officer reprimanded, 'or you will have a spell in solitary.'

Hohepa acknowledged the convict lad with a nod; so did Rahui, who scowled at the officer in command. I, too, took an instant dislike to him.

'No,' I answered Hohepa, 'you are not to be treated like them.'

The children skipped ahead yelling, 'Hurry along, Mother!' Very shortly, we came upon two large cottages abreast a point overlooking the sea; views were to be had of both the Mercury Passage and Darlington Station.

Immediately below the cottages, about twenty-five yards separate, was a smaller, more rudimentary dwelling.

'You will be all right,' I said to the Maori as John Jennings and the two guards shepherded them towards the hut.

I accompanied Etty to one of the cottages. There was no fence but a small, pretty flower garden in front. 'The geraniums are beautiful,' I said.

'They grow like weeds,' Etty answered. 'Here we are!' She opened the door, shepherding us in.

'Etty, you shouldn't have,' I said. She had already been busy with the furnishings, for there were drapes on the windows and cushions on the couches, and the beds were made up. Flower posies were in each room.

'It's been a pleasure, my dear Ismay,' Etty answered. She bustled over to the windows and opened them to the cool welcome sea air.

The cottage was surprisingly large. On one side of a central hallway was a spacious living room that looked out over the water; it had a fireplace and furniture made by the Darlington convicts. There were three bedrooms: one for me and Gower and two smaller bedrooms: one that would be suitable for Sally Jenkins and Clara — there was even a cot for Clara; and Gower Jr and Rollo would share the other. A side door from the kitchen led to the Imries' cottage next door.

'Ten steps,' Etty said, clapping her hands, 'and we are in each other's cottages. It will do us all good to live as if we are in normal society,' she continued, 'and I am pregnant again, expecting my fifth.' She spoke with dismay as well as exasperation.

Then the Imrie children — Henry, Eliza, Jessie and John — burst in through the side door, followed by their scolding convict minder.

'Oh,' Etty laughed, 'I am so grateful that our little ones will be able to expend their energies on each other — my brood are so boisterous!'

So we arrived. I could not go back. From now on I had to go forward. Convicts arrived with our luggage on a cart. Sally Jenkins and I supervised the delivery. I heard voices floating up towards me from the Maori's hut. How cleverly the arrangement for keeping them under surveillance had been established! They were close enough to be supervised yet far away to allow the discreet dissemblance of independence and freedom.

Rahui and the boy Matiu Tikiaki walked out to a pump to take a drink.

'Ka pai te whare!' Rahui shouted.

I acknowledged his praise of the hut with a friendly wave. I was pleased and not a little relieved that he and the others were not harbouring any grudge against us — after all, we were in a sense their gaolers. The only one among them who appeared to be at odds with our friendliness was Kumete; I had no idea why he was like that, but I hoped to win him over.

Tikiaki grinned at me — or the object of his attention may have Sally, who was nearby. Yes, it was! 'Kei te wera te ra!' he said to her in Maori. 'He wai?'

When she didn't understand him, he looked at me in despair. 'Mr Tikiaki is asking whether or not you would like some water to drink,' I translated for her, amused.

Sally shook her head, 'Oh,' and took a step back. 'Could you thank him for me, miss?'

Etty appeared beside me, and she was all business. 'Today we must not tarry,' she said. 'Are you ready to go to Mrs Lapham's? It will be good for you to meet the other ladies.'

———

And what did my new world look like? I was eager to find out. The walk to the Laphams' house gave me the opportunity to get my bearings. I had not expected Darlington Station to be so busy! Convicts and guards were everywhere, working in gardens and repairing the road. As we passed, they stopped and doffed their caps.

We approached the guardhouse to the station. 'Afternoon, Mrs Imrie,' the corporal of the guard greeted Etty. 'Please pass through.'

On the other side was the substantial and formidable brick penitentiary. The military barracks and gaol were also nearby. The sight of the penitentiary depressed me and I thanked God that Hohepa and the others were not incarcerated within.

'Six large wards contain sixty-six men each,' Etty said as she hastened me by. 'Mr Imrie tells me that they are clean and orderly and the ceilings are high and lofty.'

Well they might be, I thought, but, oh, the sleeping conditions were most inhumane. I had read about the station before we arrived, and had noted that the beds were built of wood in three tiers. They were only two feet wide; and all that separated one prisoner from the next were open battens. The convicts slept like bottles in a bin.

Etty saw me look across at another block. 'Those are the separate apartments,' she said. 'A hundred and two cells thus far, and the convicts sleep on the floor.'

Convict bricklayers and carpenters were adding another storey. One of them, a red-headed, solid man, doffed his cap as we walked by.

'That's Mr Liam Connor,' Etty said. 'He's the husband of my children's minder, Patricia Connor.'

'They were transported to Van Diemen's Land together?'

'No,' Etty answered. 'Patricia Connor was — for stealing from her employer. Mr Connor could not bear the separation, so came out as a free man to be with her. She was initially at one of the factories in Hobart Town but I wished to hire her to look after the children and so she accompanied us here to Maria Island. Mr Connor came too and now works as a master builder, living within the station.'

———

'Mrs McKissock, you are most welcome here among us.'

Mrs Lapham was all warmth when Etty and I arrived at the superintendent's residence. It was an excellent brick cottage surrounded by pleasure gardens: an extensive garden in front, and a cornfield adjoining it.

In quick succession, Mrs Lapham introduced me to her daughter, Mrs Frances Dobson; Mrs Elizabeth Brownell and her daughters; Mrs Bayly and her daughter; Mrs McNeill, and others. Mrs Lapham herself reminded me of my dear Aunt Eleanor, being one who insisted on ceremony and, in particular, the acknowledgement of her status as the senior lady of the station. Perhaps among the company of such good women I might find protection against my errant heart.

Eventually Governor La Trobe, Dr Hampton, Mr Lapham and Gower arrived for luncheon. 'We have been waiting for half an hour,' I said to Gower.

'Is that not the lot of women?' he answered. 'To wait for their menfolk?' Oh, I could have hit him!

Mrs Lapham presided over the luncheon's progress so as to enable speeches and responses between all the officials while, at the same time, ensuring that the visitors were supped and fed. I must admit to changing my initial opinion; I was beginning to admire her. At one point, I intervened on my own behalf. 'Thank you, madam,' I said, 'for making me so welcome on my first day.'

She pressed my hand. 'I am aware,' she began, 'that you are of gentry from Wolverhampton. You should know, therefore, how much I appreciate your compliment — especially here in Van Diemen's Land where, whatever our class, women must support each other.' She may have appeared confident, but I understood then that she felt what all women of duty felt: the loneliness of her position.

Halfway through luncheon, Governor La Trobe advised us that he had to leave. 'Regretfully, Dr Hampton and I must make inspection of our station at Long Point before I return to Hobart Town.'

'We will adjourn and accompany you to the *Mary*,' Mr Lapham said.

It was a merry band who walked to the jetty.

On arrival, Mr La Trobe was pleased to see that John Jennings and the armed guard had brought the Maori to say farewell. The Imries' children were there too, and our three with Sally Jenkins.

The government schooner was not yet fully loaded. Governor La Trobe was a kind man: he could see that the children, fully dressed in the hot sun, were looking longingly at the water. 'Mrs Lapham,' he began, 'with your permission, may the children take the opportunity to swim? In fact, when I was a young officer sent to the West Indies I loved the water — and I wouldn't mind a paddle myself.' With that he divested himself of his boots and coat, rolled up his trousers and waded into the water. 'Well, it is rather hot,' he said, and he sat down completely in it!

Mrs Lapham's mouth dropped open with astonishment. Gower Jr and Rollo giggled with hilarity. 'Look at him, Mother,' Gower Jr said. 'He has wet his trousers.'

'Come on, children,' Mr La Trobe called to the two boys. 'If it's good enough for me, it's certainly good enough for you. Come, everyone!'

Well, an invitation like that, coming from a representative of Queen Victoria, was like a command from the throne itself. There was only a moment's hesitation before Gower followed the governor's example. He undressed to his singlet and breeches, and dived into the water.

Would that I could have done so too!

'Come on, Mr Imrie,' he challenged John Jennings. 'I'll race you out into the channel.'

Mrs Lapham recovered from her shock. 'I do believe that what is good enough for the gander is good enough for the geese,' she said. She took off her shoes to trip sedately in the shallows. Oh, how I liked her then!

Within moments, all decorum was abandoned as the rest of us waded into the sea, splashing and wallowing in the shallows. The water was so cool and liquid, simply delicious.

Governor La Trobe called to Mr Lapham, 'What about the Maoris, sir?'

'But they are in chains . . .'

'Oh, take them off,' the governor said. 'We don't want them to drown.'

'But what happens if . . .' one of the guards spluttered.

I imagined what he was thinking: innocent English men and women massacred by Maori prisoners on a lovely day.

It was too late. Although Matiu Tikiaki and Te Waretiti hung back, Hohepa put his arms out for release and also slipped out of his leg-irons. Kumete and Rahui followed, and all three divested themselves of their native skirts.

'But — they are naked,' Mrs Lapham gasped. 'Ladies avert your eyes!'

I heard Hohepa give a whoop of joy as he ran past. Laughing, I looked as he plunged into the sea. Indeed, we were *all* looking: Hohepa was such a magnificent sight. With his powerful arms he pushed himself from the water, almost flying across it like a magnificent skimming ray. Every now and then his feet sent up a jet of spray and, with this propulsion, he surged ahead.

He caught up to Gower and John Jennings. The three men appeared to be in conversation; then Hohepa powered out beyond them into the channel.

I shaded my eyes from the sun. Ridiculously, I heard myself call, 'Don't go too far.'

Kumete reassured me. 'He taniwha ia,' he said, shaking his head. 'Hohepa has always been a merman.'

Onward and onward he swam.

Meanwhile, Gower and John Jennings turned back to shore. On their return I heard Mr Lapham ask John Jennings, 'Is the fellow trying to escape?' Perhaps he was thinking of the famous incident years earlier when four convicts constructed a canoe from stringy bark and made it to the mainland, where they committed robberies until apprehended.

'Oh goodness,' John Jennings replied, his face blanched. Only one day on the job as the overseer of the Maori prisoners, and one of them was making a bid for freedom.

Hohepa looked more than capable of swimming to the world's edge. Where was he going?

'Don't worry,' Gower said, shaking his head like a puppy. 'He asked permission to stay out there longer. I said yes.' Then, 'There he is!' he pointed. 'He's on his way back. I'll go out to meet him.'

Together, they returned to shore. Sleek, and with the water runnelling off him, Hohepa emerged from the water.

'Oh my goodness, ladies,' Mrs Lapham warned us again.

Etty and I giggled like little children and waited until Hohepa had tied on his native skirt. When we looked again, he was thoroughly decent. I could not help but appraise him and Gower. One was sable, the other fair. They were both handsome men, with strong bodies. Hohepa's, however, was startling: it was exquisitely and powerfully shaped, with broad shoulders like wings, taut stomach muscles, and thighs and legs that, yes, were entirely suited for a merman.

Gower Jr ran at Hohepa — not at his father — and almost bowled him over. 'Would you take me out there, Mister Te Umuroa? Into the deep?'

He looked at me — not at Gower. 'Is that all right?' he asked. 'I will not harm him.'

Before I could say yes or no, he hoisted Gower Jr onto his shoulders and headed out to sea again.

'My son has defected to the other side,' Gower said, bemused.

They looked so lovely frolicking in the shimmering sea. 'Mr Te Umuroa will never get any peace from Gower Jr from now on,' I answered.

After a few more minutes, Mr La Trobe laced on his boots, rolled down his trousers and put on his coat. 'Duty calls,' he sighed. Immediately, we followed suit, and Mrs Lapham realised that her clothing — some parts of it — had been made, well, *transparent* by the water.

'I am as naked as the natives,' she whispered, horrified. She pulled Mr Lapham's coat from him to drape around her 'nakedness'.

I called out to Hohepa and Gower Jr, 'Hoki mai korua. Come back to shore.'

Very soon we were all returned to the usual semblance of our normal selves. With the putting on of our clothes, we reassumed our dignity and our English culture.

Our idyll was over. My trial, however, was only beginning.

———

We accompanied Governor La Trobe from the beach to the *Mary*. We were thankful to him for having given us the opportunity to desport ourselves in a way that was beyond our usual decorous behaviour. Our farewells, therefore, were deeply felt. None more so than the Maori's goodbyes to him. Realising that it was his kindness which had brought about a relaxation in their conditions of incarceration, they one by one kissed his hands.

Rahui raised his wrists to him. 'Te taima kua tae mai,' he said.

'What is he saying, Mrs McKissock?' the governor asked.

'He is reminding you that their chains must be put back on.'

His eyes brimmed. He motioned to John Jennings, 'Would you do our duty, sir?' He saluted us all and went on board.

We waved and waved as the *Mary* left the dock, turned and, swiftly catching the flowing tide, soon disappeared.

30

Time to reflect.

I was alone at the cottage, changing my clothes which were damp from the sea. Gower had returned to the hospital with Dr Brownell, who was the medical officer at the station, John Jennings resumed settling the Maori into their new abode, and the children were playing at the Imries'.

Taking up a hand mirror, I looked into it. My image stared back at me, my eyes bold and fringed by unruly hair; it was me and it wasn't me. Pondering myself, I could not believe that only five years ago I had been unmarried, assistant to my uncle and at risk from my father and brothers at the hated Webster Hall. Now I was married and had travelled to the other side of the world.

What on earth had possessed me! Why was I so wilful? Would my mother, Selina, ever forgive me for leaving her?

I now had three children; three souls had been added to my life — the same three innocent lives were Gower's too. For me they were an astonishing blessing; for him they were a burden. Ah well, a mother always fought for her cubs and there was no question that I loved them and would fight for them against any enemy, even their own father. After all, that was what my mother had done as my maternal example.

I began to brush my hair. 'Will we be happy?' I asked my reflection.

I immediately castigated myself for the question. Happiness was such an abstract notion. The more you pondered it, the more you questioned the foundations of all your decisions. Most of mine had been sensible, though there was caprice in having approached Gower and offered myself on the altar of matrimony!

Should I have regretted the action?

I inspected my reflection again. My uncle had once called me a stupid, wilful, vexing, troublesome girl, for having gone down to him when he was trapped in a mine. 'Oh why, oh why, Ismay, are you so . . . independent!'

No, there could be no looking back, or indulging myself with sighing after happiness; such introspection was against the grain of my current condition. Let those with the luxury of choice ponder their happiness or no.

'You have always made your own way through life,' I said to myself. 'Better to keep stepping forward and living in the moment — and take all those whom you love with you. And they now include five Maori!'

I smiled at the thought.

Even so, apprehension settled upon me. Although my marriage to Gower had returned to its customary balance, something *else* was pressing upon it. Some would have called it destiny, but that was such an unscientific proposition.

'Stuff and nonsense,' I said to myself. 'Pull yourself together, Ismay Glossop!' I was not about to succumb to foolish notions of the kind that my dear female cousins in Wolverhampton liked to frighten themselves with.

I had made my bed. I would lie in it.

———————

However, that very evening brought with it the first real test to my resolve.

The pearly sky was streaked with pinks and purples stretching all the way to the horizon when Gower returned from the hospital. He was very pleased about the regime which Dr Brownell had established for the patients. 'I will be very happy working with him,' he said. As for the children, they were exhausted after their long day and, once they had had dinner, I sped them off to bed.

Then the wind began to blow cold from the sea and, shivering, I went to close the windows — and saw Hohepa staring towards the probation station. He was watching the work crews returning from their daily activities. Some were bringing fresh water from the reservoir; others, who must have been working on the farm to the north of the station, were driving a bullock team before them.

The intensity of Hohepa's gaze made me wonder what was bothering him. I heard him call Kumete and the others out of the hut. 'Haramai! Titiro!' They conversed for a while and nodded in agreement.

At the sound of their voices, John Jennings came out of his cottage to investigate. He saw me and walked over to enquire what was happening.

312

'Let's go and find out what has engaged Hohepa's interest,' he said.

Etty and Gower came to join us.

'I have watched the men in the distance, walking back to Darlington,' Hohepa began.

'Yes,' I answered. 'Their work for the day has ended.'

'Haere ratou ki a ratou moe i te po? They are returning for the night?'

'They will eat, say prayers, and after that they go to their dormitories for the evening.'

'They will have karakia?' Hohepa asked.

'Yes,' I answered. 'The Anglicans meet in the muster ground.'

That is when he asked, 'Mrs McKissock, although we are outside the station, we are prisoners too. Please tell Mr Imrie we wish to join the inmates in fellowship. We will take our Bibles.'

When I advised John Jennings he pursed his lips. 'That shouldn't be difficult,' he said, 'but I had best obtain the superintendent's permission. In the event that he gives it would you accompany us, Mr McKissock?'

'Why, yes,' Gower answered.

I wasn't about to be excluded! 'The Maori consider we are all one in God's eyes,' I said, raising my voice.

John Jennings reflected on my observation. Conceding, he answered, 'That they are, Mrs McKissock,' he said.

'Are you of the same view, Mr Imrie?'

'Indeed I am.'

'Good,' I said. 'Then I shall come to the service too.'

'But you're a woman, Mrs McKissock!' he answered.

At that, Gower gave a chuckle. 'I warn you, Mr Imrie, on that score Mrs McKissock will never be curbed.'

John Jennings did not give ground so easily. 'The Maoris are one thing; a woman is another, especially if unaccompanied by another of her sex.'

Etty, just as she had done once before at Port Arthur, took my side. 'In that case, Mr Imrie,' she said, 'I will accompany Mrs McKissock.'

'You are pregnant, Mrs Imrie!' John Jennings interjected.

'I will take Patricia Connor as my attendant,' she said simply. 'Now go and seek Mr Lapham's permission for all of us, the Maoris *and* the women, to go to the church service. Off with you now.'

She fluttered her apron at him.

Poor John Jennings! He knew he had been bested. Off he went to see the superintendent.

———

Etty and I were watching out the window when, an hour later, we saw him Jennings returning. He was walking quickly and in an agitated manner.

'The Maoris' request has stirred a hornets' nest,' Etty giggled.

Their request, however, was not the issue. Rather it was Etty's and my having stated our intention to accompany our husbands.

'The superintendent was most bothered about this,' John Jennings told Etty, 'but he has agreed—'

'He has agreed?' Etty asked. 'Oh, well done, Mr Imrie!'

'—on condition,' John Jennings proceeded sternly, his eyes twinkling, 'that you, Mrs McKissock and Patricia Connor are dressed in your most sober and modest attire, with bonnet and shawl.'

'Thank you, Mr Imrie,' I answered. 'I am always dressed modestly when I go to church and—' I teased him '—I am not about to break out a red gown.'

Hohepa was grateful for the permission. When we set off, I noted he and the other Maori had taken special care of their appearance. They remained shackled at wrists and ankles, but all were wearing tunics and trousers, with red blankets around their shoulders for warmth. Hohepa's hair was in a topknot, and he was holding his tokotoko.

Imagine my surprise when, on rendezvous with the superintendent at his house, I discovered that both Mrs Lapham and Mrs Bayly, the wife of the magistrate, were to join us!

'Mrs Lapham,' the superintendent said in hasty explanation, 'as senior woman of our establishment, has considered the circumstances and has decided that two junior women cannot go unattended.' It was apparent that Mrs Lapham had given her good spouse a dressing down for his lack of consultation with her. She looked ready to give us a lecture, too.

'Thank you, madam,' I said to her with as much meekness as possible.

She maintained a look of severity. 'You ladies are to stay close beside me at all times, and do remember your demeanour.'

Mr Lapham tried a jest. 'Ah well, we should be off then, eh? Protocol has already been breached once today, by allowing the prisoners to swim. We may as well go the whole hog.'

'Mr Lapham,' she remonstrated. 'Your choice of imagery is most unbecoming.'

Dusk gave way to dark as we approached Darlington.

Mr Lapham had arranged for a small detachment of soldiers to meet us.

314

I recognised the officer in charge immediately: James Boyd, the senior assistant superintendent, had disciplined Seamus Keelan for spontaneously greeting us on our arrival. I had disliked him then, and saw no reason to change my opinion now. He was waiting with the Reverend Charles Dobson and Mr and Mrs Brownell.

'I am not at all in agreement with this matter,' he said. 'I have no concern for the Maoris, but for the ladies, who may inflame indecent passions and be subjected to the worst vocal observations upon their sex. The felons have been warned that any misbehaviour will not be tolerated.'

I spoke out of turn, I know, but I thought his comment insufferable. 'I hardly think that prisoners attending a church service would be of a mind to rudeness or lewd behaviour, sir. After all—' I turned to Mrs Lapham '—we are certainly not women of *that* kind, are we, madam?'

Mrs Lapham's eyebrows lifted at the suggestion.

The superintendent glossed over the tension. 'The prisoners have been waiting already far too long. Sir,' he said to Mr Boyd, 'perhaps you might report to me after the service to explain your comment. Let us go to prayer now.'

We made our ascent into the station, through the entrance and into the muster yard.

The evening was beautiful. A cool breeze was blowing from the sea. The stars had come out. As we approached, we saw a congregation of around a hundred and forty men sitting in two groups on either side of the aisle. A guard gave a sign and, as one, they stood up and removed their caps. How young they appeared to be — between eighteen and twenty-five, perhaps — with only a sprinkling of grey-haired men among them.

We walked down the aisle, and I knew that there would be no jeering or shouting of lascivious words. These were men who had been churchgoers in their home countries. Many of them would have left behind wives or sweethearts or even daughters in the Mother Country. Among them I recognised Liam Connor — Patricia Connor's husband, who had so lovingly, as a free man, accompanied his convict wife to her incarceration in Van Diemen's Land. I also spied Seamus Keelan, and seated beside him a third man, whom I later came to know as Kieron Moore. Mr Keelan escorted our party to our seats in the front.

'Evening ma'am, evening,' Liam Connor said to Mrs Lapham. He dusted down the seat with his handkerchief before she sat down.

'May I offer you my prayer book?' Seamus Keelan asked Etty.

Etty looked at me, and smiled. 'It's going to be all right,' she said.

'Yes, Mrs Imrie,' I answered. 'We have nothing to fear.'

'Mrs Connor?' Liam Connor asked his wife as she took a seat behind Etty. 'Here is a hymn book.' I saw their fingers touch and linger. 'Thank you,' she answered in a barely audible whisper.

Mrs Lapham saw the exchange. 'Do join us, Mr Connor,' she said. She turned to Mr Lapham, 'After all, Mr Connor is a free man, is he not?'

'Thank you, ma'am,' Mr Connor said with gratitude.

As I took my own seat in the front with Gower I leant over and whispered to Mrs Lapham, 'That was a most Christian act, madam.'

'So many odd things have happened today,' she sighed, 'that I scarce know what is right or wrong. I shall ask for forgiveness in my prayers this evening.'

———

Hohepa and the other Maori took their places just across the aisle from us. Behind them a man was coughing very loudly and had to be excused from the service.

The Maori caused a stir because of their striking appearance. 'The New Zealanders,' came the whispers, 'the Maori chiefs.'

'Settle down,' Mr Boyd reprimanded.

Reverend Dobson walked to the makeshift pulpit in front of us. He coughed, and nodding to Kieron Moore asked him, 'Mr Moore? Would you lead the singing of the opening hymn?' Mr Moore took up an accordion, played the opening strophes, and we stood and began to sing.

> He who would valiant be 'gainst all disaster,
> Let him in constancy follow the Master
> There's no discouragement shall make him once relent
> His first avowed intent to be a pilgrim . . .

It was such a surprise to hear those male voices singing their hearts out. How proud I was to hear Gower's beautiful tenor voice winging its way among them to the stars. I pressed his arm.

'So far so good,' he said.

With a great sense of peace and relief, we sat down. On the perimeters of the service, other men were looking on — perhaps they were not of the Anglican persuasion. Silent sentinels, they held their caps in their hands and, whenever Mrs Lapham or any of the women happened accidentally to catch their eye, they bent their heads in deference to us.

Reverend Dobson began the sermon. 'Gentlemen,' he smiled, 'and ladies, let us start with a reading from the Gospel according to Saint Luke, chapter one, verses twenty-six to thirty-three, when happy tidings filled the earth about the coming of the Saviour.' There was a rustle as those men with Bibles turned to the place.

I saw Hohepa murmur agreeably to Kumete about the reading. He spoke to me across the aisle, 'Ka tika, Mrs McKissock, ka tika tenei korero mo Ruka.'

Reverend Dobson began. 'And in the sixth month the angel Gabriel was sent from God unto a city of Galilee, named Nazareth . . .'

That was when the Maori suddenly stopped the sermon.

———

Of course, having seen the way that their people conducted themselves at church in Nelson, I should not have been surprised as, led by Hohepa, they began to chant the next verse.

'Ki tetahi wahina i taumautia ma tetahi tangata, ko Hohepa te ingoa, no te whare o Rawiri; ko te ingoa o te wahina ko Meri.'

The sound was strong, passionate and guttural. It swooped and soared above our heads like the sound of wounded doves. The entire congregation seemed struck by the power of those alien sonorities. At the end of the verse, the Maori stilled, waiting.

Reverend Dobson was perturbed, to say the least!

'Mrs McKissock,' Mrs Lapham whispered, 'whatever is happening?'

'You had better advise the reverend,' Gower said.

I approached the pulpit. 'The Maori will alternate the reading with you,' I told him. 'It is their custom.'

He mopped his brow. 'Thank you, Mrs McKissock,' he answered, and he proceeded to the next verse. 'And the angel came in unto her, and said, Hail, thou that art highly favoured, the Lord is with thee: blessed art thou among women.'

'Otira he nui tona oho ki taua kupu,' the Maori interpolated, 'ka whakaaroaro ki te tikanga o tenei ohotanga.' They were swaying, their eyes closed; they knew the verses off by heart.

The power of the New Testament, released from its Anglo-Saxon constraints, began to make its presence felt through the musical cadences of the chanting. So plaintive was it that I saw Mrs Lapham was moved at its beauty.

'And the angel said unto her, Fear not, Mary: for thou hast found favour with God. And behold thou shalt conceive in thy womb, and bring forth a son, and shalt call his name Jesus.'

Hohepa and Kumete nodded at one another, and embraced. 'Ka nui ia, ka kiia hoki ko te Tama a te Runga Rawa: a ka hoatu ki a ia e te Ariki, e te

Atua, te torona o Rawiri, o tona papa.' They stood up and began, to everyone's consternation, to circulate among the convicts.

'Sit down! Sit down!' Mr Boyd ordered. He made a gesture to the guards to intervene. 'Restore order,' he called, 'quickly!'

'No,' I commanded. 'They are only greeting their fellow men as brothers, even if they are all enchained.' I looked at the superintendent. 'Sir, do order Mr Boyd to desist.'

'But what are they *doing*!' he asked.

'They are inviting the congregation to the hongi, the pressing of noses. They mean no harm. It is their custom.' Indeed Matiu Tikiaki, Rahui and Te Waretiti had followed suit, after Hohepa and Kumete. There was a great hubbub, a loud murmur of surprise, but Seamus Keelan and Kieron Moore obliged in responding to the invitation.

'I am going to trust, Mrs McKissock, in your knowledge of the customs of the Maoris,' Mr Lapham said. 'Mr Boyd, withdraw!' He signed to Reverend Dobson, 'Sir, do continue.'

The Reverend was in a state of high apoplexy. He managed to get the words out: 'And he shall reign over the house of Jacob forever; and of his kingdom there shall be no end, Amen.'

Hohepa and the Maori returned to their seats.

'Amine,' they responded.

The danger was over.

———

I will remember that evening as long as I live. The sky was hung with millions of stars. The night was rich with black velvet. The Trowenna Sea murmured beyond.

I don't think that the Reverend Dobson had ever given a better sermon, surprised as it was into splendour by the Maori interjections.

'Ka tika!' they called. 'That is true! Ka pai! That is good! Kei te tautoko! That is what the Holy Book says!'

Most of all, I will remember Hohepa, dramatic, gesticulating with his tokotoko as if it were a staff of God.

That evening, we were transported out of the customary and into the unusual. So much so that at the end of the service, everyone was elated and joined in a way which none of us had anticipated. Mrs Lapham stood like a queen as a line of convicts assembled to bid her farewell. Liam Connor introduced them as they came forward to bow and gingerly kiss her hand. One of the poor souls had tears streaking down his cheeks, and called her 'Mother'.

The convicts also reached out to Hohepa and the Maori, shaking their hands.

'Come again, mateys, eh?' Keiron Moore asked.

'Ae,' Hohepa said. 'After all, we are all felons together.' He was watching as Liam Connor took tender farewell of Patricia Connor.

The formalities over, our party turned and moved toward the gateway. As before, the Maori followed a little behind. At the last moment, however, Hohepa paused, raised his tokotoko and turned to the assembled convicts. He spoke quickly to the other Maori.

'What are they planning to do *now*!' asked Mr Lapham.

'They may be considering a haka of farewell,' I answered, 'or a waiata of departure. It is a custom among their people.'

In truth, I had no idea!

I was therefore taken by surprise when, instead, Hohepa led the Maori in an altogether different kind of waiata.

The minstrel boy to the war is gone,
In the ranks of death you'll find him—

Liam Connor gave a great laugh of recognition. Seamus Keelan and Kieron Moore were dumbstruck. After Mr Connor's laughter came a moment's silence — and, from some quarters, choked cries of emotion. Then there arose a huge swell of sound as the convicts raised their own voices and joined in.

His father's sword he has girded on
And his wild harp slung behind him—

Oh, and then did I remember a young bugler boy with a sweet voice — what had been his name? William Allen, that was it — and how he had sung this same song on the boat from England. I wondered what happened to him? 'I am going to fight the daring Maoris!' he had said with pride.

I couldn't help but hope that all had gone well with the young bugler.

Hohepa raised his tokotoko again, this time in farewell. There was something valiant about the gesture. The convicts kept singing. They raised the roof, rhapsodic, rapturous:

No chains shall sully thee!
Thou soul of love and bravery,
Thy songs were made for the pure and free
They shall never sound in slavery—

We walked away into the darkness. A clattering roar and the sound of many hands clapping followed us.

The moon shone full in the firmament as we left the penitentiary.

'Thank you, ma'am,' Patricia Connor said to Mrs Lapham as we were taking our leave at the superintendent's residence. 'Mr Connor and I scarce get a chance to be at prayer together and . . . well . . . it meant a lot to both of us.'

From the Laphams' we made our way back with the Maori to our own cottages. There John Jennings and I escorted them to their new abode. After prayers had been read, John Jennings had a surprise for them — and me. 'Could you tell the men,' he asked, 'that Governor La Trobe has ordered that they are no longer to be kept in chains? He advised the superintendent before he left Maria Island today.'

I gave them the news. 'Ka tika? Is it true?' Te Waretiti asked. They scarce believed it until Mr Imrie unhooked the bunch of keys at his belt and began to unpadlock their wrists and ankles. Once freed, they fell on each other with excitement.

'Mrs McKissock, do you know that we have met before?' Hohepa asked me.

The others were too busy with their joy to notice us. 'Yes,' I admitted. 'But we did not meet exactly, sir. Rather, our paths crossed.'

He nodded. 'The old kuia . . .'

I smiled at him. 'We are both pilgrims, Mr Te Umuroa,' I said. 'How blessed we are if we are able to share part of our journey.'

He pulled me in to the hongi. The tingling as our foreheads met. The touch of his nose grazing mine. The outward sigh of breath from his nostrils. The smell of his skin. It lasted only a few seconds. But it was like an eternity before Kumete's voice separated us. 'E hoa . . .' he said to Hohepa.

Hohepa opened his eyes. Wide. Surprised.

Turned away.

I returned to the cottage, checked on the children, and made Gower some supper: a couple of ham sandwiches and tea.

'I will come to bed soon,' he said. 'I have some prisoners to look at when I go to the hospital tomorrow and I want to check their medical records.' He smiled at me, 'You did well today, Mrs McKissock.'

I basked in his compliment. So much so that when he came to bed and pressed his insistent body to mine, I did not deny him. Never having known another man in the intimacy of conjugal relations, I had no idea whether the frequency of his desire was inordinate; I suspected that it was. Nonetheless, ever since we had made our marriage arrangement in Wolverhampton I had honoured this aspect of my wifely duties, and indeed did not find the requirement lacking in pleasure. The depth of satisfactory completion created a sense of union which was as significant in its own way as love was to the heart.

'At the station . . . something extraordinary happened tonight, don't you think?' Gower asked.

'Yes,' I said.

'I've tried to put my finger on it,' Gower continued. 'It's something to do with the common humanity and companionship between the Maori and the other prisoners; something to do with fellowship. But it also spilled over upon us all. I feel quite . . . *blessed.*'

As Gower and I lay there in the great encircling darkness I thought our lives were not without warmth and affection.

My final thoughts before drifting off to sleep, however, were of Hohepa.

31

You may well wonder how a woman of my sensibilities and morality could so easily become a-swoon like this.

If you are a woman, look deep into your own heart and dare to tell me that there has not been, in your own life, someone you longed to be with, someone for whom you would gladly have transgressed all boundaries of culture and class. Someone whom, perhaps, you loved, but you kept your love cloistered and unspoken.

Dare to tell me that there has never come a time for you when you have wished to speak your love!

But could I do that? My moral world was not as my granddaughter Georgina's is. Proximity between the sexes today has fostered equality — which is excellent — and also an independence of spirit that allows young lovers greater licence to be able to conduct both licit and illicit relationships.

I could not have done then what I suspect Georgina would do under a similar circumstance — which would be to act on her love, even if only for self-gratification.

Although the world had been shifting around me for some time and all the old verities were disestablishing themselves, a woman did not bring disgrace upon herself, her husband, family and children. And while leaving England had given me a sense of freedom and my mother's death — terrible though it is to say it — meant that I had no parent to answer to, when *I* was a young woman, one valued character and self-sacrifice. One was impervious to temptation and, instead, chose the maintenance of an honourable standard of behaviour.

I had thus perfected in myself the difficult art of surviving as a woman. But, oh, the cost!

————

Meantime, life had to be got on with and that, in its own way, maintained the moral probity between me and Hohepa. Early the next morning, I was woken by a sharp rapping at the door.

Gower got up to answer it, and I heard him talking to somebody before he came back to bed. 'It's for you,' he said, before returning to sleep again.

Mystified, I put on my dressing gown and went to the door. John Jennings was there in the darkness. 'You are not yet dressed, Mrs McKissock?'

I looked at the clock in the hallway. 'It is four-thirty in the morning!' I answered. 'Not even dawn.'

'Were you not advised,' he continued, 'that although we are living outside the station we will be observing penitentiary hours?'

'Definitely not!'

He grinned at my discomfiture. 'The first bell is at 4.45 a.m., and I will require your assistance to explain to the Maoris their daily routine. May I wait inside for you?'

I hastened back to the bedroom. I dressed in a dark blue outfit and, as I exited, contemptible woman that I am, made as much noise as possible to vex Gower's peaceful slumber.

When I rejoined John Jennings he had the impertinence to inspect me! 'As prison officers . . .'

'I am not in Darlington Station's employ!'

'. . . we are expected to be sober and set an example to our charges at all times,' he continued, with a mischievous glitter in his eyes. 'Would you be so kind as to put a shawl over your *colourful* dress and tie a bonnet to contain your somewhat wilful red hair?'

As he led the way to the Maori's hut in the cold and dark, I heard the bell in the distance, coming from the penitentiary, and then a sound that was as strange as it was unsettling — I shivered when I heard it — a mournful moan as of lost spirits.

It was the sound of six hundred men being woken by their guards to a new day.

'Wait here, Mrs McKissock,' John Jennings said. He knocked on the door of the Maori's hut and, without waiting for an invitation, walked in. I heard him rousing them and asking them to get dressed. Then his head appeared and he said, 'Please come in now, Mrs McKissock. Would you be so kind as to translate the instructions to the men?'

I stepped through the opening. 'Morena,' Hohepa said. 'You can't sleep in either?'

John Jennings coughed for attention. 'This will be the daily routine . . .' He was talking so fast I hardly knew what I was translating! 'From 4.45 a.m., first bell, you have time to wash and change into prison clothes. At five o'clock, we shall muster for inspection and prayers before allocation of duties and beginning of the work for the day under my direction. 7.45, we return to the hut for breakfast but at 8.45 we recommence work duties. Midday, we break for lunch. At one, we return to work duties until five when we come back to the hut where we will wash and muster for light tea or supper. From six, the activities will include reading, writing, ciphering lessons and bible discussion. Then at eight o'clock you shall return to the hut for the evening.'

When he had completed his instructions, John Jennings turned to me. 'Thank you, Mrs McKissock. You may be excused now until 7.45.'

'Excused?' I spluttered.

'I assume,' he said, 'that you will not mind assisting Mrs Imrie to prepare breakfast for our return? The superintendent and I would also appreciate an assessment in writing from you on the five Maoris under our joint charge. Please have it completed by the end of breakfast so that I might take it to Mr Lapham. He wishes it on his desk at 8 a.m.'

He was delighting in teasing me, but I vowed to myself that I would oblige him to the letter. And although I had to get the children out of bed and breakfasted, force Gower to dress and depart to his duties at the hospital by eight — not to mention assist Mrs Imrie and Mrs Connor with making breakfast — I managed to make the required notes, to wit:

Hohepa Te Umuroa is clearly the leader among the Maori, and their spokes-man. He is from the Whanganui River. His physical height and his tokotoko give him natural status, but with these also come an authoritative demean-our. Te Umuroa has the best understanding of the English tongue; he is able to communicate any instructions or requirements to the group. In their hierarchy, he is the mangai, the mouthpiece for us to them and them to us.

Kumete and Te Umuroa have the closest relationship among those in the group. Kumete is of a Hutt Valley tribe; Hohepa's tribe assisted them in the recent Hutt Valley conflict. Kumete and Te Umuroa apparently fought side by side, and Kumete regards himself as Hohepa's protector. While he respects the Pakeha (the Europeans), he is also wary of us. He has some understanding of English.

Te Rahui and Te Waretiti know no English at all. They appear to be from a different tribe to Te Umuroa, Kumete and Matiu Tikiaki. Because of their lack of English, they are prone to becoming suspicious and excitable and must be placated. Te Umuroa is the best person to call upon to do this.

As for Matiu Tikiaki, I am puzzled why he, rather than Mataiuma — whose name is on the indent — is among the prisoners. Has a mistake been made and Tikiaki sent in error? When I asked him for his own explanation, he answered, 'Perhaps all Maori look the same.' He is the youngest of all the prisoners and has a boyish and light-hearted demeanour.

The five Maori share a sense of fatalism about their plight. Coming to Van Diemen's Land has been ordained. Indeed, it is fortunate they have all been transported as a group. I suspect that had any of them been sent singly they would have pined away. The Maori are a tribal people, not the kind to exist without the aroha, or love, of kin. They hope soon for release and return to their beloved Aotearoa.

With the above in mind, it is my view that they offer no danger to the security of Darlington Station. Any fear that they might try to escape is minimal. They came together and they will leave together. They would hardly jeopardise their positions by doing anything foolhardy.

I was most put out when, after handing the report to John Jennings, he put a line through my final paragraph.

'Mrs McKissock,' he said, trying to keep a straight face, 'that is an observation that is best left to me, as their *male* overseer, to make.'

'Mr Imrie,' I retorted, 'my evaluation should not be related to my gender. I would have made it whether I was a woman or a man.'

———

Indeed, for the rest of my time on Maria Island I strove to prove to John Jennings that I was as good at my work as he was.

If the truth be known, pioneer women had greater fortitude than the male of the species, and I proved it to John Jennings by pacing him every morning. Indeed, young women like Georgina, living in these permissive times, may lay about all morning in pretty frilly clothes reading fashion magazines, but we women of our generation knew how to get on with it; there was no option for us.

Thus I soon grew used to Darlington hours although, I must admit, I would never have managed without Sally Jenkins. She took the children off my hands completely in the mornings, giving them breakfast while I assisted John Jennings and then got Gower ready for his day at the surgery.

Would the man of the house have ever got to work without the woman to push him out the door?

Once that was done, Sally and I joined Etty in taking the children to the station school. There, Mrs Lapham had dragooned me into taking a class!

'Without a schoolmaster,' she said, 'and no matter that we live in the colonies, an English education must be pursued.'

I saw that the other ladies were already instructing their charges most competently in reading and writing and, much to my distaste, the girls were taken for needlework while the boys kicked a ball outside. That would never do.

I remembered how I had loved Uncle Rollo's capacious library. 'May I suggest philosophy and history for all the children, girls as well as boys.'

Mrs Lapham surprised me with a grateful sigh. 'Ah, the intellectual pursuits normally reserved for gentlemen?' She patted my hands. 'Why, Mrs McKissock, am I not surprised?'

But, yes, Sally was a godsend. As far as the children were concerned, she was as capable as she was lovable, spooning out codliver oil and malt — which they hated — and persuading Clara to swallow the flat white iron pills, the size of a halfpenny, that Gower sent down from the surgery for her. From the very beginning she was a pallid wishbone of a child.

'Oh, Sally,' I remarked one day, 'I could not have done this without you!' Hugging her, I realised she was filling out, growing from a girl into a fine-looking young woman. Why had I not noticed before? Absurdly I had not, even though, when her menstrual bleeding had begun, I had been like an elder sister and instructed her on how to manage that monthly inconvenience. I appraised her womanly curves, lovely face and lustrous hair. Yes, the skinny child who had guided me through the darkness of a coalmine was gone for ever.

No wonder, then, that Tikiaki was smitten by her.

———

I must admit, however, to irritation that my sex limited me in the eyes of those who were supposed to be my betters. With regard to Darlington Station, for instance, I would think, 'If only a woman such as I could be superintendent!'

As it was, I took a keen interest in the construction of the second tier for the separate prisoner apartments; I liked to talk to the foreman, Liam Connor. I also made a firm friendship with Kieron Moore, who was in charge of the gang constructing the windmill and miller's cottage to grind all the grain and convert it to wheat. I do believe that there was nothing that Mr Lapham did that I could not equal or improve upon!

For instance, I would have eagerly embraced the challenge of making the station not only self-supporting but also profitable. Darlington had over three hundred acres of land under cultivation — I saw the books — three hundred acres of wheat, plus another sixty-two acres of hops, potatoes, turnips, and sundry other vegetable crops. In addition, a flock of two thousand sheep and sixty pigs were kept for prison consumption.

Convict tradesmen like Seamus Keelan produced some four thousand pairs of shoes annually for the Hobart Town market. One hundred yards of cloth was woven every week from wool and yarn spun by women convicts in Hobart Town. Turners and carpenters made furniture: chair legs, mallets, mop handles, spokes, stools, tubs and wheelbarrows. Weavers and basketmakers made baskets, rope mats and prepared hemp. Hides and kangaroo skins were tanned for exportation.

Every day I passed by labouring gangs on their way to cut down timber or quarry stone. The lumber yard was constantly busy. A team of bullocks helped to cart the timber to sawpits and from there to the quay. Nor was the convicts' labour confined to Maria Island. Prison hulks regularly travelled back and forth, carrying special crews to road-building projects all along the mainland coast.

I will give Mr Lapham his due. He maintained the station well and was fair to the convicts. However, I recall that my ebullient views on how *I* would run Darlington Station earned gentle chiding from Gower.

'You and I, Mrs McKissock,' he said, 'are committed to this system's demise. It is only a little higher than slave labour, and that is no compliment. There is no justice in Britain's having sent men, women and children to their incarceration on the other side of the world — for what? Stealing a piece of bread? And they are exiled forever, denied a return to the Mother country?'

I was instantly shamed — but Gower understood my impetuosity. 'Never forget,' he said, 'that this very colony, which the children will inherit, will be built by the convicts' industrious labour.

'Never.'

———

And then Christmas Day arrived.

It reminded us — Etty, John Jennings, Gower and myself — that no matter the prison society that we administered, we should never forget the fellowship of man.

The Christmas festivities also forced me to acknowledge, despite my success in resisting any overt emotional thoughts about Hohepa, my conflicted position.

I had come to consider him as a most extraordinary being. Close observation had uncovered so many felicities in his fine character. He led not by domination but by inculcating trust. He worked hard at the labours John Jennings had for them — building fences, cultivating gardens, chopping wood, drawing water — and when he took up the implements of labour, they did too. When he put them down, they followed. He did not eat until they had eaten. If there was some reprimand to give, he gave it quietly.

There was also a mystery about him that made him intriguing to me. It was a special sadness. I wanted to fathom his depths and swim down into his soul — even if there was nothing there for me to find.

———

John Jennings and Etty Imrie invited us to their cottage in the morning for the opening of presents. The Maori were already there waiting when we arrived. On the pretext of being required at the hospital, Gower absented himself from the Christmas preliminaries.

Leaping and yelling, Rollo asked the Imries' Henry and Eliza, 'Has Father Christmas been yet?'

'No,' Eliza said sorrowfully. 'I think he's lost his way from the North Pole and can't find us.'

Lo and behold, there was a loud 'Ho! Ho! Ho!' from the door and Gower appeared, in the guise of the jolly old fellow. Rollo looked at Eliza. 'I told you he would get here! I knew he would find us! I knew it, I just knew it!'

Oh Rollo, I thought, although your future lies in the Antipodes, I pray that Father Christmas will always find you.

The children literally *shredded* the wrapping from their presents! In Hobart Town, I had thought to buy kaleidoscopes for the children — crystals within formed and reformed into beautiful patterns — and Etty had lovely picture books for them as well. The Maori had brought gifts for the children also. They had made swift Maori fighting kites for the older children — I was pleased they did not discriminate between the boys and Eliza — and poi, pretty balls on string, for the younger children.

'You don't mind, Mrs McKissock?' Hohepa asked. He had Gower Jr on his knee and was showing him how to operate his kite; it was crafted with the silhouette of the Maori hawk. 'I have a boy his age.'

'A son?' I asked. Why had I not expected that he was married?

'His name is Rukuwai. He will be wondering why I have not returned home yet.' His eyes began to well with tears. 'He is a good boy . . .'

I couldn't help myself. I bent down to him and put my forehead to his. 'E te rangatira,' I said. 'Kaua koe e te tangi. Hohepa, please don't weep.'

'We are always looking at each other, aren't we, Mrs McKissock?' Hohepa said.

Then Gower appeared again. 'Did the children guess that I was Father Christmas?' he asked.

'No,' I answered.

'Good,' he sighed. 'It's best that children keep their illusions.'

I couldn't help but reflect on the ironic turn of his phrase; it could well have applied to the camouflage of our marriage.

Etty clapped her hands. 'Now that the children have been attended to,' she said, 'we must hasten to the station.'

————

It was the tradition for Reverend Dobson and the Roman Catholic catechist, Thomas Champney, jointly to take a midday Christmas sacrament for all, including the convicts at the Darlington chapel.

Trailing the kites in the sky — for the children soon got them up — we made our way to the service. There, we joined Mr and Mrs Lapham, the prison officers, staff and wives of the station, wishing each other the greetings of Christ's Day. I even managed to utter such a greeting to Mr Boyd. By now, a fond rapport had grown between the convicts and the Maori; Liam Connor, Seamus Keelan and Kieron Moore sat with them. How extraordinary it was to gather in the hot Antipodean sun and listen to Reverend Dobson and Father Champney as they read of the arrival of Joseph and Mary to Bethlehem, and the birth of the Christ child! All credit to Mrs Lapham, she had marshalled the women to create an atmosphere of thanksgiving. But although we sang 'Deck the halls with boughs of holly, Fa la la la la! Fa la! la! la!' there was not a bough of holly in sight.

'The convicts are thinking of a different kind of Christmas,' Gower said. 'Falling snow, sleighs in the streets, children throwing snowballs and — alas — this Christmas their families will be sitting down to dinner with an empty chair at the table.'

Indeed, when Seamus Keelan began to weep, Rahui gave him a comforting embrace. 'Kia kaha, tama,' he said. 'Have strength.'

After the service, we tried to raise the convicts' spirits. Mrs Lapham and the ladies had been busy making Christmas plum pudding and, as the prisoners filed past us, we pressed a piece into each hand together with other gifts of tea, tobacco and sugar. Etty and I gave the Maori an extra gift of gilded bookmarks for their Bibles.

We returned with the Laphams to the residence where they had invited all the station personnel to have supper. Convicts had cut down a small tree

— so unlike our English fir — and it was decorated with lovely candles and ornaments. We had for dinner some roast goose, legs of boiled mutton and caper sauce, boiled fowls, roast duck, pigeon and giblet pies, gooseberry tarts and little cinnamon sweets for the children.

'We don't have a mistletoe,' said Gower, holding a sprig of native wattle above my head, 'so this will have to do!'

He gave me a lovely, thoughtful gift: a glass ornament which, when you shook it, swirled snow around an English cottage. In return I had purchased him a waistcoat which he immediately put on; he looked very dashing in it, and he knew it!

I had a special gift for Sally. A parcel of presents for the children had come from Aunt Eleanor in Wolverhampton — she had got the seasons entirely wrong and sent mittens and scarves — and in the same package were also her letter to me and, for Sally, a letter from her father as dictated to Uncle Rollo.

Sally was now able to read, and when I gave her the letter her eyes lit up. 'The family are well, miss! They send their love to me!'

Then, as the children were tiring, I asked Mrs Lapham if we might be excused. 'You have a lovely family,' Mrs Lapham said as she farewelled us.

Our brood and the Imries' children were almost asleep on their feet, and I wondered how we would get them home.

That is when Hohepa nodded to the others, 'We will help to carry the whanau.'

Before I knew what was happening he put Gower Jr on his back, Gower picked up Rollo and Matiu Tikiaki took Clara. John Jennings had his Henry, Kumete picked up Eliza, Te Waretiti put Jessie on his back and Rahui carried John.

We all laughed, astonished at how every child had a male to carry them.

And as the first evening star appeared, Gower was inspired to sing.

What child is this, who laid to rest,
On Mary's lap is sleeping—

Nostalgic thoughts rose unbidden, swamping me with memories of my dear mother Selina.

Tell Ismay that . . .

They had been her last words before she died. What had she wanted to tell me? 'Tell Ismay that I love her?' Or 'Tell Ismay that I miss her?' Or 'Tell Ismay that I want her to be happy?' If she had been in Hobart Town on the evening that I had proposed to leave Gower, what might she have said to me? 'Don't wait for his return. Go now, Ismay, darling. Now, while you have the opportunity.' Instead I had stayed, and Gower had persuaded me to honour my marriage vow. And, yes, we were kinder to each other.

Tell Ismay that . . .

I felt that those three words would haunt me for the rest of my life.

So bring him incense, gold and myrrh,
Come peasant, king, to own him—

Etty linked arms with me. I looked at her, John Jennings, Sally Jenkins, Patricia Connor and Gower, and I knew I wasn't the only one thinking of the past. Gower's father would not be far from his own thoughts. Nor Sally's family from hers. No doubt the Maori and the prisoners at Darlington were remembering loved ones too.

And Hohepa his little boy.

I took Sally's elbow — and Sally linked arms with Patricia Connor. We walked in female fellowship. I felt at an extraordinary peace with myself watching our men, yes, *our* men — and Maori magi come from afar — carrying our children and babes home.

'What was that Maori word Te Umuroa used?' Etty asked, 'when they offered to carry the children — whanau?'

'It is the Maori word for family,' I answered. Indeed, that's how it felt that evening. Like a family, a whanau. Crucially, the constraints to my heart were sundered when I realised how much I wished Hohepa was at its head:

The chief; my rangatira.

Joy, joy, for Christ is born,
A babe, the Son of Mary.

Later that evening, I opened the envelope from Aunt Eleanor.

A couple of recipes and remedies for chilblains and whooping cough were enclosed, plus the letter itself.

The sight of her writing, with its clarity and evenness on the horizontal, made me smile; she and my tutors had tried hard to obtain from my stubborn hand the same clarity as well as the maintenance of parallel equity between one line of writing and the next.

'My dear Ismay Elizabeth,' she began. 'Is it summer there in the Antipodes? Oh, this odd world in which winter has come to our northern hemisphere but is bringing the sunlight to yours, I shall never get used to it! Apropos of which, the gifts I send you may not be in season but, after all, I am a creature of habit.'

Aunt Eleanor's letter was filled with circumlocutions and asides as she wrote about my cousins and their lives as mothers, like myself.

'Your cousin Sybil, married to Marcus Wrenn, now has a son and daughter of her own,' Aunt Eleanor wrote.

Oh, I remembered how Sybil had been such a minx, leading Gower on! Why had she not been truthful to him and admitted that she had never intended to marry him? Instead, she had marked his heart forever.

Ursula had taken a trip with Aunt Eleanor to the Continent and was now engaged to a German baron. 'What is good enough for Queen Victoria is good enough for me,' Aunt Eleanor wrote, referring to our own Majesty's marriage to Prince Albert. 'But, oh, how vexatious it is to realise that, like you, Ursula will be spirited away from me!'

As for Isobel, she was still single but being courted by some clever accountant, 'Which,' Aunt Eleanor wrote, 'will be very good for her as, if they marry, at least he will ensure the sensible financial running of the household, Isobel having no head for figures whatsoever.'

Aunt Eleanor's letter continued, 'My dear, I miss my sister Selina dreadfully.' I felt hot tears as she described her faithful visits to see my dear mother in the graveyard at Grocott's Bradley Bridge Church. 'But you must regard me and Dr Springvale as your parents now. We both send you and Mr McKissock our fond wishes and felicitations at this Christmastide.'

And then Aunt Eleanor ended with the following news of my father:

'Poor Lowthian,' she wrote. 'Tragedy continues to dog his footsteps. Having lost one son, he has now lost the second, your brother Alfred, in an accident at one of the Webster Mills. Rollo tells me that he warned my brother-in-law many times to protect his workers from machinery, whose many parts could snag the unwary and pull them into its maw. Sadly, Lowthian did not take any notice.

'I perform my Christian duty by visiting him in his new home. He is much changed, my dear. Your heart would go out to him.'

My heart go out to the father who never gave me his name? And who treated my mother as his chattel all her life?

Never.

32

Ka Ao! Ka Ao! Ka Awatea!

It was dark! It was darkness! And now the dawn has arrived!

There is one other matter that I should broach about me and Hohepa. It is the issue of my being an English woman and his being a Maori. Certainly, I had never been a person who admitted to the hierarchical roles of women to men. The years assisting Uncle Rollo ministering to the poor of Wolverhampton had similarly predisposed me to see past the boundaries of class and social position. Were we not, now, in a new world where such verities could be challenged?

Why, therefore, should colour and race matter to one such as I who has never let convention intrude upon my relationships with others? Let others consider themselves the betters of native peoples.

I would not.

———

New Year came ascending over the bright Trowenna Sea.

For some reason, while Hohepa had known that word of any release would take some time, the others needed convincing. 'Would you tell them?' he asked.

I called them to a meeting. 'The letter Governor La Trobe has written to the Colonial Office will take at least four months, and possibly longer, to get to England. By the time they consider your position, that could take another four or five.'

Te Waretiti counted the months on his fingers. 'We could be waiting a year then,' he said. 'That is a long time indeed.'

———

It was at the New Year celebration that Hohepa and I finally admitted our attraction for the other.

At fellowship that evening with the Laphams and the staff of the station, we all joined in a merry jig. Gower took me in his arms and whirled me around the room. Emboldened, Matiu Tikiaki put his arm around Sally's waist and tried to imitate us. How we laughed at his efforts!

Then it was midnight.

Should auld acquaintance be forgot
And never brought to mind!

I saw Hohepa and the others standing to one side. I called to him, 'Haere mai!'

He beamed a smile, motioned to Kumete to follow him, and joined us. We linked arms — Gower on one side of me, Hohepa on the other.

I tried to be gay. 'You must be thinking about your wife, Mr Te Umuroa.'

He looked quickly at me. 'My wife is dead, Mrs McKissock. She was murdered by Pakeha soldiers.'

'Oh I am so sorry,' I answered. 'I didn't know.'

Fortunately, John Jennings' exclamation, 'It's 1847 now!' saved us both. People began to hug each other. Gower was whirled away from me by Mrs Bayly and Mrs Brownell; he was always a hit with the women.

Leaving Hohepa and me, drowning.

Then he smiled with extraordinary tenderness. 'Mrs McKissock . . . Ismay . . .' It was the first time he had used my Christian name. I closed my eyes, relishing the way he pronounced it: *Is*–may. When I opened them and looked into his, it was not I who fathomed his depths but he who fathomed mine, swimming down into my soul.

I stepped back. 'No, Mr Te Umuroa.' I was trying so hard to hide the loud beating of my heart. My lips were trembling. The words of the song burst all around me.

For auld lang syne, my dear,
For auld lang syne!

A ghostly echo came from the prisoners at the station, singing to each other in their dormitories and cells, like some mockery of our own celebration.

We'll take a cup of kindness, dear,
For the days of auld lang syne.

No matter my emotions, I still tried to contain them. When 1847 began, I started to drop in on Gower at the hospital as if such resuscitations would help. For a while the ploy was successful.

The faculty was an excellent brick building and well appointed with beds for thirty men. It had attached a surgery, cookhouse and pharmacy. The windows of one room were stained to admit moderate light for patients suffering from opthalmia.

'Dr Brownell and I,' Gower told me, 'have two convict medical assistants helping us and our main job is to do medical checks on convicts on their arrival and when they leave Maria Island. Otherwise prisoners are admitted for the usual accidents while working or for respiratory and other bronchial ailments; these peak in the winter when sometimes the men come down with pneumonia.'

One prisoner, by the name of Jaimie Craddock, had been ill ever since arriving on Maria Island; he was in and out of the hospital and for him Gower had a special sympathy. 'I fear that Mr Craddock has brought with him a sickness that cannot be treated. The best we can do is to alleviate his pain.'

One day Gower paid me a compliment. 'Would you come regularly, Mrs McKissock? There is something about a woman's visit that lifts the spirits of men who are so far from home and lack the sympathies that only women can provide.' Then he added, 'My spirit is lifted too.'

On another day I saw Gower in all his strength. On that occasion he was the acting chief medical superintendent — Dr Brownell having left on his regular visit to the convict hospice at the Long Point station — and the unlikeable Mr Boyd came marching into the hospital. He went to the bed of this same Mr Craddock, threw back the blanket and ordered him up. 'You are a malingerer,' he said, 'but today you *will* work.'

Gower came at the run and confronted Mr Boyd. 'Get out, sir.'

'You are only a civil officer at this establishment,' Mr Boyd answered. 'I hold rank. Move aside.' He took Mr Craddock by an arm and pulled him from the bed. With a cry, the poor man fell to the ground.

Gower pushed Mr Boyd back.

'Are you assaulting a British officer, sir?' Mr Boyd asked.

'I am the acting chief medical superintendent,' Gower answered. 'The hospital and the men in it are under my care. Get out now before I have you thrown out.'

Mr Boyd turned on his heels — but he did not like being made a fool of in public and, in particular, in front of prisoners. 'We will settle this in our own way, Dr McKissock,' he muttered.

It was not an idle threat. I was not privy to what occurred, but I understand that two evenings later, Gower and Mr Boyd met to settle the account in the boxing ring. John Jennings was Gower's second and when he delivered Gower back after the bout — he was bloodied and bruised — he was as white as a sheet.

'Gloves were worn,' he reported, 'but the combatants are both the worse for wear.'

That evening I bathed Gower's wounds and nursed his bruises. 'I got some very good blows in,' he said. 'Mr Boyd won't be barging into the hospital again in a hurry.'

———

You will understand therefore why I was so incensed when Mr Boyd submitted a private undercover report to Dr Hampton, controller-general of convicts. I wonder whether it was partly written in spite because of his altercation with Gower?

He complained that under Mr Lapham's supervision, underpatrolling of the watch meant prisoners' crimes were frequent. The use of convicts as overseers and watchmen contributed to lax discipline.

Mr Boyd further made claims, without evidence, of offences including attempting to murder the military sentinel, sheep-stealing, housebreaking, theft, robbery, plotting and conspiring to steal the station's boat, absconding with violence, disobedience of orders, insolence to officers, and riotous and irregular conduct in the wards and mess-room.

He also noted the light application of punishment, his evidence being that within a six-month period, while there had been upwards of thirty cases requiring corporal infliction, on only two occasions had the hoary villains uttered the slightest cry of agony!

No wonder I disliked the man.

———

I myself came into head-on conflict with him.

It happened that one afternoon, when Sally Jenkins and I were taking the children to school, we passed a work crew — a group of men dragging their clanking irons and yoked to carts like brute beasts — and one poor creature fell in our tracks.

'Mother!' Gower Jr cried in sympathy.

I rushed to the convict's aid. My intemperate action stopped the convoy entirely. The abominable Mr Boyd happened to be their overseer. He put a hand on my shoulder and grasped me roughly. 'Mrs McKissock,' he said, 'kindly allow us to go on our way.'

'Take your hand off me, sir,' I answered. 'I am only doing my Christian duty.' I took a flask of water and poured it down the poor wretch's throat. 'This man should be taken to the hospital as soon as you arrive back at the penitentiary.'

'You are a doctor now?' he asked. 'That will be my decision, madam.'

'I will advise my husband—' I took note of the prisoner's number '—to expect this prisoner, to ensure that you do so.'

Of course, Mr Boyd reported the incident to Mr Lapham, and John Jennings was asked to convey the station's censure. 'You were out of line, Mrs McKissock,' he said.

His remarks went in one ear and out the other.

———

Yes, and sometimes there was punishment by the lash.

How I would have got rid of that!

Even Seamus Keelan had to submit: the nocturnal aggregation of males bred behaviour considered unnatural between one man and another, and he was discovered in such an infraction.

Gower and I were at the cottage the day of the punishment. I could hear the singing snarl of the whip and Seamus's plaintive cries sobbing on the wind. The Maori listened, horrified. Rahui had his hands over his ears. When the sounds of the punishment drifted away, Hohepa called to Gower: 'E hoa, and you call *us* savages?'

I know the remark hurt Gower deeply. 'Mr Te Umuroa,' he responded. 'Don't you ever dare associate me or my family with punishments such the whip. Ever.'

———

One morning, Gower arrived home without warning.

He was depressed and sad. 'One of my patients has died,' he said. 'You may remember him? Mr Craddock?'

I nodded.

'He is being committed to the convict graveyard,' Gower continued. 'I would be most grateful if you were able to come along.'

'Yes, of course,' I answered. I dressed in a black gown and put on my hat and veil. Gower and I walked to the Burying Ground, the name given to the convict resting place. It was a bare, dusty area with nary a cross or headstone anywhere.

Mr Lapham was there with the Reverend Dobson and four convicts — I presumed they had been friends of the deceased. His bare coffin lay beside the open plot.

337

'Mrs McKissock,' Mr Lapham greeted me, 'there was no necessity for you to attend.' I had brought flowers hastily picked from the garden but, when I went to put them on the coffin, Reverend Dobson whispered, 'That will cause a precedent.'

Mr McKissock looked at him. 'Precedent or not, the man *will* receive Mrs McKissock's gift of flowers.'

The sun was hot, burning the sky almost white. I was pleased I was wearing a veil as the wind was whipping up the dust; it was swirling around us.

I felt most uneasy and perturbed at the perfunctory nature of the Reverend Dobson's service to the dead. I knew Gower was feeling the same way. I think Reverend Dobson's farewell remarks at the end of the service were what set him off.

His words were: 'God have mercy on your soul.'

The diggers came forward, lowered poor Mr Craddock into the grave, and were about to shovel the dust over him when Gower stepped forward.

He addressed the coffin. 'Is this poor work all you obtain at the end of your days, Mr Craddock? Should your life end like this, in an unmarked grave so far from England, with strangers attending your farewell? And with words to send you on your way to meet your Maker that still judge you? No! I will not let you go this way! I fare thee well, Craddock. I fare thee *well*.'

I felt so proud of Gower. On that day he proclaimed his outrage at a system which maintained a man's guilt throughout his life, and also stamped him guilty in his passage to the world after death.

———

Then events conspired against my struggle to maintain moral compass in the matter of Hohepa when the regimen organised for the Maori by the superintendent and John Jennings was altered.

'Would you translate for me, Mrs McKissock?' John Jennings asked. 'Mr Lapham has agreed that the Maoris' days may be conducted free of the penitentiary schedule. Instead, they are to be granted considerable freedom of movement and association.'

The relaxation of the Darlington hours was like the opening of a door to the gaol. While I welcomed the news — and so did the Maori when I told them — I looked at Hohepa with some alarm. The freedom would be welcome, yes, but it could also be dangerous, tipping the scales toward closer intercourse with him.

———

The Maori worked daily until half past twelve, supporting both our households, carrying out outdoor tasks such as building fences and digging the garden. In the afternoons, John Jennings took them to collect firewood from the grove of she-oaks just south of the station, or on expeditions even farther towards the Fossil Cliffs to the northeast.

'Mr Imrie is ecstatic,' Etty confided. 'While in Van Diemen's Land, he has developed a fondness for birdwatching and now has the opportunity to pursue it.' Indeed his binoculars, the small official publication of sketches of birds found in Van Diemen's Land and a notebook were the first items he packed in his knapsack.

And of course, he and the Maori could not return to Darlington Station in time for lunch. So lunch had to go to them!

———

The new world of Maria Island beyond Darlington, in all its natural beauty, suddenly opened up to all of us.

Etty and I developed the habit of taking the children immediately from their school lessons so that we could join the men. Sally Jenkins and Patricia Connor came with us, to help carry Clara and Etty's babe, John — and, whenever Liam Connor could make it, he came too. We would pack a picnic lunch of boiled eggs accompanied by generous slices of bread and penitentiary-made butter, and fruit and water.

Wherever they were, John Jennings would despatch Matiu Tikiaki, the youngest of them all and the fastest runner, to come to collect us.

'Here he comes!' Gower Jr and Henry would shout, watching through the schoolroom window. And off we would go with him.

If John Jennings had taken the Maori to the northeast, we headed away from Darlington in that direction, ascending the slope and following the rivulet straight up the gully where the vegetation opened out into grassland. From there was a good view across Bass's Strait to the mainland with its cupped hands reaching for Van Diemen's Land. To help us find them, Hohepa often put up one of the Maori fighting kites. The children enjoyed watching out for it and, when they saw it dancing in the wind, would yell and scream, 'There it is! There it is!'

Continuing in a northeasterly direction over the hills took us to the edge of the magnificent layered Fossil Cliffs plunging sheer to the sea. We descended by a precipitous and slippery path to the base of the cliffs where, at low tide, the colours simply glowed. Swell pounded the rocks, with dangerously large waves washing over the top. The layers showed sea fans, coral-like creatures, scallop shells and sea lilies.

On other days, we struck out in the direction of the Painted Cliffs south of Darlington.

'Don't go so fast, Mister Tikiaki!' Etty would call. 'You forget that I am with child.' Truth to tell, although Etty sometimes laboured up the slopes, the exercise was good for her and brought out the blush in her cheeks.

We followed the curve of the hills through groves of tall stringybarks and blue gums, passing the sandy expanse of beaches and the impressive Hellfire Bluff to Hopground Beach. The Painted Cliffs at the end of the beach were so beautiful, with sandstone in stunning patterns of orange, gold, beige and rust; they were notched with potholes and sprinkled with crystals of salt that sparkled in the sunlight.

Sea eagles glided on the wind currents above; Hohepa was always loath to put up a kite among them. 'The eagles are sovereign here,' he said. 'Let them remain that way.'

Generally, it took only an hour or so for us to reach the men, wherever they were. But Etty and I enjoyed each other's company and the children loved doing as children do, racing ahead and crying out with delight at the abundant birdlife.

At some point we would hear the sound of men chopping wood. Or see the Maori silently crowding around John Jennings as he drew the bird species he was observing.

'Mr Imrie,' Etty would shout — and the birds would scatter. He didn't appear to mind, except on one occasion: 'Oh no,' he said. 'That was a forty-spotted pardalote!'

Rahui nodded, lugubrious. 'Thirty-eight,' he corrected, in his minimal English. 'I count them in the binocular.'

We fell about laughing.

However, Etty made accidental recompense when, one afternoon, on arriving, she told John Jennings we had seen a most curious creature on our way. 'It was a small dog,' she began, wrinkling her nose, 'and it was eating something dead. It had black fur, looked like a little devil, and the horrible thing was very smelly and screamed at me!'

Well! You should have seen John Jennings literally fly back to the spot where we had spied the creature. When we caught up with him he was lying in tall grass watching it.

'Oh, Etty,' he said in awe. 'It's a *Sarcophilus harrisii*.'

———

As for Gower Jr, Rollo, Henry and Eliza, they loved the trips most if the men were working close by the sea. They would yell out to Hohepa, 'Mister Te Umuroa! Mister Te Umuroa! Will you take us in the water? Will you?' Racing at him like puppies, they leapt into his arms.

Watching them splashing together, I felt a great happiness.

'The children are getting as brown as the Maoris,' Etty said one day.

I often wondered how Gower felt when he returned from the hospital in the evenings and they spoke so volubly of swimming with Hohepa.

'We each had a turn going under the water,' Gower Jr would enthuse. 'We had to hold onto his neck, take a deep breath, and then, down we went, down and down and down! We were very brave!'

'Weren't you worried about them?' he asked me.

'No,' I answered.

When they were with Hohepa, floating among the luminous emerald grottoes encrusted with sea lilies, I knew that they would be safe from all evil and harm. Sometimes I yearned to be with them, swimming through large ribbons of sea kelp, necklaces of feathered crimson seaweed, playing hide and seek with playful seals — and Hohepa and I with each other.

33

I strove, with all the last vestiges of strength I could muster, to maintain appropriate distance between myself and Hohepa. Surely it was possible for us to respond to one another without entertaining overt inclinations or emotions towards the other?

Indeed, Hohepa himself offered a way.

One evening, the Maori were reading the Maori version of the New Testament at the Imries' when Mrs Lapham — she and Mr Lapham had joined us — picked up on a familiar word: 'aroha'.

'Oh, what *is* that word!' she asked.

'It means love,' John Jennings answered. 'But that translation seems much too narrow, referring to love in its physical or secular or romantic dimension without—' he was fumbling now '—acknowledging the spiritual dimension.'

'I agree, sir,' Gower said, after pondering the question. 'In my short experience of the New Zealanders, I became firmly of the opinion that the Maori words are like the old rune stones of our Celtic races. They are . . . talismanic, having many meanings, sacred as well as profane.'

I was surprised by his insight.

'Perhaps our own English words have lost their runic quality but the Maori words still retain theirs?' Mr Lapham asked.

John Jennings turned to Hohepa. 'Would you like to shed light on the discussion?'

'Ka tika,' Hohepa said, nodding at Kumete and Rahui. 'This is a good korero on the translation of words. I do not know about your Celtic races, but I do know that words can have different meanings for my people and for Pakeha. The word "kawanatanga" as written in the Treaty of Waitangi is an example.'

'Ae,' Te Waretiti agreed, asking me to translate for him. 'Pakeha wrongly thought we had signed over our sovereignty. We had not. We had agreed only to Pakeha governance but not to his taking Aotearoa away from us. That is why we had to fight him. Because of one word we are imprisoned and exiled.'

'With the word aroha,' Hohepa continued, 'the case is similar. It does not have one meaning but many — and it cannot be considered by itself in isolation. It has to be associated with our other words like "awhinatanga", to support, and "manaakitanga", to offer hospitality, and "whanaungatanga", to honour kinship.'

Etty tried to be helpful. 'Are your Maori words more layered, then?'

'Ae,' he nodded. Then he looked at me. 'If I was to use the Pakeha word "love" and say to Mrs McKissock that I love her, I would mean that I love her as a man does a woman—'

Gower gave a surprised cough. I felt myself going crimson.

'But if I was to use the Maori word "aroha", I would be telling her that although I love her I also have sympathy for her and for her other great qualities as a mother, a wife, a member of her iwi, for her hospitality and friendliness to others, and her love of her husband. My love for her would be both selfish and unselfish.'

Mrs Lapham looked somewhat disconcerted by Hohepa's observations. Etty gave me a sharp look.

Hohepa took in the uncomfortable silence and was puzzled by it. 'This is also the way that Christ taught us to love one another, is it not?' he asked.

I saw John Jennings give a hesitant nod. 'Why, yes, of course,' he answered. 'Surely we must all agree with you.' He turned to Mrs Lapham. 'Madam, does that satisfy your question?'

'Yes,' she nodded. 'Do carry on with our reading.'

Relieved, we turned to less complicated matters. But as we did so I was able to offer Hohepa a smile of appreciation for his words unspoken as well as spoken. We could enjoy our feelings for each other, yes, but in the spirit of aroha. That would enable us to both go on with the rest of our lives.

As we were leaving each other's company, however, Etty detained me a moment. 'I know you are diligent in your care of the Maoris,' she said, 'but in the case of one of them, Hohepa, perhaps more distance is called for?'

She was correct in her evaluation but, 'I don't know what you mean, Etty,' I answered.

'I am a woman, Ismay. Men do not see what one woman sees of another. Remember who you are.'

Gower similarly confronted me as we were preparing for bed.

I was brushing my hair — it was always so unruly — when he asked, 'What was all that about, Mrs McKissock? Does the Maori presume to entertain feelings for you?'

I turned to look at him. 'Gower, that is an unfair accusation. He feels aroha for me. I feel the same for him and for the others, too.'

'It sounded like a declaration of love, madam.'

Oh, I don't know why I did it, but I was so angry that I threw my hair-brush at him. 'And why should that worry you, sir? *You* do not love me!'

He looked at me, surprised. Came up to me and held me in his arms. Peered closely into my eyes. 'What is *wrong*, Mrs McKissock? We both came to our marriage knowing fully our attitude to each other. And since the occasion in Hobart Town when you planned to leave me, I have taken audit of my attitude and have tried to be the best husband that I can under the circumstances. There has been no other woman in my life since. I don't want to lose you.'

'It's not a matter of other women,' I answered.

'Then what *is* it!' he asked, the frustration showing in his voice. 'Our life is a good one, isn't it? And we have the children.'

'Yes,' I said. 'We have the children. And I know you have done and continue to do your best. I am not unappreciative, Mr McKissock.'

He calmed me down. He made love to me — it was what he wanted and, I think, he assumed that it was what *I* always wanted.

———

Life crept on apace.

One very hot day, while Etty and I were with John Jennings and the Maori — they were diving for shellfish along the western coast of the island — the sun sizzling in a frying pan of a sky led me to make an impetuous request.

'Bother this!' I said to Etty. We were expiring from the heat and had taken shelter under shady trees.

I walked down to the edge of the sea and called to Hohepa. 'Mister Te Umuroa!'

He came immediately, stepping out of the water, a cloth wrapped around his thighs. 'Yes, Mrs McKissock?'

'I would like to learn how to swim,' I said.

'This is most irregular,' John Jennings interrupted.

As always, however, Etty was my accomplice. Coming across the sand, she called out, 'A few strokes might benefit me also.'

From that time on, we would strip to our petticoats and join the children in the water and — I think I may boast — I attained a modicum of prowess in the aquatic art, sufficient to enable me to dive, albeit shallowly, and to keep up with the children when they stroked from one rock to another. As for Etty, she relished the opportunity to float, with the baby inside her, buoyed up by the water.

It was on one of our walks home after a swimming lesson that Etty threaded an arm through mine.

'I want to say how sorry I am,' she began, 'about you and Mr McKissock.'

'Sorry?' I asked.

'Mr Imrie told me that in conversation with Gower he had ascertained that . . . that . . . well, the circumstances of your marriage.'

'My back stiffened. 'Kindly explain.'

'Oh, now I have made you angry,' Etty said, 'and that was not what I intended at all. Should you at any time want to talk about it . . .'

If only I had been able to! But I had always made my own way through life and, as far as female friendship was concerned, had never been one to confide my personal thoughts to another.

I decided to keep it that way.

———

As it happened, that evening our brave cavemen brought back muttonbirds for dinner. And who was to cook the game that they proudly displayed to Etty and me?

We were, of course!

'You may pluck them, Mrs McKissock,' Hohepa said imperiously.

I looked at him aghast. What impertinence! I might expect such a command from Gower or John Jennings, but for Hohepa to act the lord of the manor! However, he began to laugh then, and I realised he was teasing me. 'Rahui,' he said, 'is already on the job.'

Etty and I offered to give Rahui a hand with the work.

'Kaore,' he said in Maori. 'Ko au te kuki. I am the cook. I will pluck and then boil and boil and boil in one pot. In another pot I will cook us some potatoes and puha to go with the birds.' He didn't mean 'puha', of course; rather, some edible weeds he had collected on the way home.

'Where did you find the titi?' I asked.

'Near the Fossil Cliffs,' Hohepa answered. 'Kumete couldn't stop himself. He was down on his face in the dust, putting his hands in every burrow nest, pulling them out. We were all doing it. We will have a good kai tonight. We want you and Mr McKissock and Mr and Mrs Imrie to be our guests.'

We duly presented ourselves at five o'clock and, when we were shown in, were given four of the five chairs in the hut. The Maori had made a fire in the middle of the hut. Two pots were boiling on top of it.

The whole room was filled with smoke and steam, tinged with the somewhat tangy and thick smell of fat. 'I'm still boiling the birds,' Rahui said from the middle of the fug. 'Not long now. You will like them I bet.'

'Perhaps a drink, then?' Gower suggested. He had brought some bottles of ale with him.

As the birds boiled and boiled, we drank and drank. Very soon we thought, oh, we're not in polite society, so we really imbibed much too generously and, by the time the birds were ready to eat, I am afraid we were somewhat the worse for wear. Just as well, because the muttonbirds were much too salty for our English palates but . . . well, we were away with the fairies and too happy to care, taking one mouthful of titi and dousing it with the beer.

'Very nice?' Te Waretiti asked. 'You like the titi?'

'It is like a tiny little turkey,' Etty slurred.

Gone was any distinction between gaoler and prisoner. All decorum disappeared.

———

We ate every small bird before we left that evening.

'I thought Pakeha didn't like titi!' I heard Rahui say grumpily to Hohepa. 'From now on, when we have titi, we don't tell them.'

I went to bed feeling quite merry. I suppose I should have encouraged a spirit of forgiveness in myself but my mind went back to Etty's disclosure earlier that day that she knew Gower and my marriage had been one of convenience.

The more I thought about it, the more it rankled. I felt a need, no matter how hard I had tried to repress it during the day, to turn to Gower. 'It was wrong of you,' I said, 'to tell Mr Imrie about our marriage. I am a proud woman, Mr McKissock.'

He was silent a moment. Then he clasped me gently. 'I acknowledge my error, Mrs McKissock,' he said. 'I am sorry.'

———

The next day I had the opportunity to think of the remarkable success the Maori were having at Darlington Station — more so since their special separation and treatment caused no ill feeling among the bulk of the prisoners at Darlington.

346

Indeed, like the free citizens of Van Diemen's Land, the convicts of Maria Island felt, 'These are Maori chiefs! Shame on you, Governor Grey! Return them to New Zealand!' Even among convicts was a moral and ethical attitude that saw injustice and did not want to be a part of it.

Possibly, too, the sheer force of the Maori's magnanimity for the prisoners themselves — their aroha — won them deep gratitude and respect.

Then there was their generosity. Most afternoons, after a successful hunting or fishing expedition, they would start singing, 'The minstrel boy to the war has gone . . .' as they approached the station.

This was the inmates' signal. Mr Imrie would turn a blind eye as Hohepa or Kumete tossed over the wall a couple of gamebirds.

'Thanks Hohepa!' someone on the other side would cry. 'We'll give the birds to the cook! The boys will eat well tonight.'

If they came abreast of a work gang, Te Waretiti would engage the overseer while Rahui flipped a fish over to them.

What the convicts appreciated most was that, according to Maori custom, the game bird or fish was the best catch of the day. Not just any old offering but, as Hohepa liked to explain it, 'The finest ika of the sea or bird of the forest is always given to the chief.' It was their way of saying that the convicts, and not they, were the royalty of Darlington Station.

———

I now turn to the duality that existed in the world of Maria Island and made it both a paradise and a hell.

Assuredly, Nature had formed of the island a paradise, one of the sweetest spots in Van Diemen's Land; it was Eden. Why then, had she allowed it to also be a place where man could imprison man?

Oh, Maria Island was a place of such contradictions! It was paradise and prison. It was inhabited by free man and convict. Good resided here, but also evil. Humanity and inhumanity.

Symbolic of this was that paradise possessed a heart of poison. By this I mean Maria Island seethed with snakes, many of which could cause instant death.

God had left the serpent in Eden.

I remember the day when I heard Te Waretiti give a strangled shout as he was digging in the front garden of the cottage. I rushed to the doorway and saw that he was standing quite rigid with his spade in front of him.

Immediately, I wiped my hands on my apron. 'Shut the door,' I commanded Sally, 'and under no circumstances let the children out.'

Fear made beads of perspiration pop on my brow. I grabbed a garden hoe and approached Te Waretiti. The snake was no more than a couple of yards in front of him. It was a copperhead, coiling and uncoiling, hissing.

'Don't move.' My throat was so dry I could barely get out the words.

The copperhead caught my movement. In a flash it turned, raised its head and *struck.*

I brought the hoe down upon it, pinning it into the earth. Its tail was lashing back and forth. With compressed lips I bore down with all my strength and broke the snake's spine. When I was sure it was dead, I took a deep breath and then another. I realised that I had been holding it during the entire episode.

Te Waretiti began to howl. He would not stop, even when I cradled him. Matiu Tikiaki, Hohepa and the others came rushing out of the hut to investigate.

'He aha te mate?' Rahui asked. 'What is the matter?'

'We have been cast out,' Te Waretiti cried, 'and are now in the place of Satan, in the dwelling place of serpents.'

Even Hohepa blanched when he looked down at the dead copperhead. I had no idea that snakes should cause such deep and utter terror. 'Hatana,' he said. 'Satan.'

From then on, whenever Matiu Tikiaki came to fetch us, he would borrow Hohepa's tokotoko so that he could defend us from any snakes in our pathway.

————

There is another reason for remembering that event so keenly. Just before the Maori returned to their hut, Hohepa must have noticed that for all my decisiveness in dealing with the copperhead, I was in need of some comfort myself now the danger had passed.

'Are you all right?' he asked. He put his arms around me, a simple warm gesture. When he did that, I had a sudden image of the copperhead coming to life to give one last strike at my heart.

I was done for. From now on I would never be able to maintain my unmerited deception.

'Oh . . . Hohepa . . .' I wept.

I looked at his face. I barely noticed his tattoo. Most in English society would have considered him a savage, but — had I been able — I would have exclaimed, 'It is beautiful!'

I saw *him.*

————

That evening I tossed and turned in my sleep. Eventually I left Gower sleeping, put on a dressing gown, and went outside to take the air. I gratefully breathed it in.

A pod of whales made its spellbinding way through the Mercury Passage. They were whales such as I had never seen before, with long horns, as unicorns have, on their heads. The moon flashed on the horns and I suddenly felt a longing to reach out and touch them.

I made confession to myself.

Gower would never understand that, from the moment I had first seen him, I had been in love with him. Yes, he had given me a life, a family and children, but I had given *him* those too.

All I had ever wanted him to do was love me back.

Then I saw a shadow outside the Maori's hut. It was Hohepa, watching me.

I felt a rush, a yearning, to cross the gap between us and . . . and . . .

'Mother?' It was Rollo crying out.

I stepped back into the cottage to attend to him. The piked whales cracked on, splintering through the moon-drenched mirroring sea.

HOHEPA'S STORY

Maria's Eylandt

PROLOGUE

Maria Island, Wellington, Hobart & Canberra, 1985

Voices are calling me again, waking me from my eternal sleep.

I see two lovely young girls looking at my headstone on Maria Island. They are puzzled as they read the inscription:

> HERE LIE THE REMAINS OF HOHEPA TE UMUROA, NATIVE OF
> WANGANUI, NEW ZEALAND

That evening, they tell their father, a New Zealander by the name of Chris Heald, what they found.

———

'Piki mai, kake mai, homai te waiora ki ahau! Aue e te koroua e . . .'

The voices are louder, and my hope grows. It is 1985, and I go to the entrance of Te Reinga, the Place of Spirits, to look out upon the world below. It is much changed, but I see Te Paremata o te Pakeha in Wellington again.

This time the Minister of Maori Affairs is Koro Wetere, and he has received a letter from Chris Heald. 'The people of the Whanganui River will be interested in this,' the minister says to his private secretary. 'Write to them and ask them if they would like me to take any action.'

———

Ka mau te wehi! Ka pai e te minita!

Stronger are the voices now. They remind me that sixty years have passed since I was last woken by my son Rukuwai, sixty years since I was lost again. Why am I still here, in limbo, awaiting my return to the ancestral river? The clouds break apart and my spirit, eagerly floating, beholds again the world of humankind.

I see an old kuia climbing the steps of Parliament. She has bright shining eyes; and with her are a group of four elders from the Whanganui River. They are unafraid as they seek entrance from the doorkeeper.

'We have an appointment with the Minister of Maori Affairs,' the old lady tells him.

He looks into his appointment book but the old kuia doesn't bother to wait. Too many years have been lost and she is not about to lose another by pausing for some functionary to see whether her name is in any stupid book. The other elders, however, wait to receive name tags.

I overhear one of them saying, 'I'll sign Kui in.'

Kui? Rain down, oh rain, because I recognise her now! She was only a young girl, not more than a babe, when I last saw her, climbing the steps of Parliament Buildings with my son Rukuwai and Pone, his daughter!

The elders catch up with her. An usher is with them, and he says to Kui, 'Would you follow me, madam?'

'Aren't I going the right way?' she asks.

'Yes, but we wouldn't want you to get lost now, would we!'

She purses her lips. 'No,' she says in droll manner, 'I suppose *we* wouldn't. Okay, after all, it's your building, not ours.'

The usher guides them through Te Paremata o te Pakeha. He knocks on a door and Kui and the elders are welcomed in to take a seat. Not long afterward Mr Koro Wetere greets them. He is a big man of great sincerity with a grin that encompasses them all.

To him, Kui addresses her words. 'E te Minita, we come because of your letter.' She takes a large handkerchief from her kete and blows her nose loudly. 'You have found Hohepa? He was the kaka feather cloak! He was the neck pendant of transparent greenstone! He was the central post of the meeting house! He was wrongly taken to Australia! We want him returned to us. Will you help us?'

Mr Wetere soothes her. 'Leave it with me,' he says.

He begins to dictate a letter. He koputunga ngaru pae ana i te one, tenei kei a au. For so long I have been a mass of sea foam stranded on the beach.

When I look again upon the bright world, what is this?

The scene has changed! I see a different parliament building, the Parliament of Tasmania, Hobart. Mr Wetere's letter is being delivered by messenger through the halls of that august building. It is like a poi spinning this way and that way.

———

Kokiri, kokiri, kokiri! Whiri atu whiri mai, taku poi porotiti!

The letter is delivered to Mr Chris Batt, an endorsed Labor candidate for the state seat of Lyons. He reads it, thinks on the contents and then asks his secretary to take dictation: a telex which, once it is completed, he sends to the Premier of Tasmania, Robin Gray:

> Mr Premier, I have been contacted by tribal elders from New Zealand who have requested the release of the sacred remains of their honoured ancestor, Hohepa Te Umuroa, who is buried on Maria Island. The elders might find some difficulty in travelling to Tasmania, and I have advised them that any application for funding assistance may be met favorably by the State Government.

Hei ha hei ha! Taku poi kaue kawe aroha!

The poi flies to the premier's office. There, on receipt of Mr Batt's letter, the premier too ponders the matter. What will he do with it? Will he take any action?

Yes! He communicates with the National Parks and Wildlife Service — they control all matters to do with Maria Island now — and also the Health Department:

> May I refer the matter to you of the disinterment of the remains of the Maori warrior whose bones lie within your two jurisdictions? In your considerations, do further investigate the use of funds to support the venture.

Whirinaki, whirinaki, poi porotiti!

I grow impatient! The National Parks and Wildlife Service's consideration of the matter is so complex and time-consuming. My return hinges on the principle of whether or not material of any kind may be removed from a national park. Usually this refers to wildlife; it also refers to archaeological or other material at historic sites and — in my case — to the remains of the dead. The same principle has vexed other museum and conservation institutions internationally, when they have been asked to return mummies or shrunken heads or even koiwi, Maori tattooed heads. Some have policies that allow it. Some have regulations that do not.

Which way will the decision go?

A year passes, despite the expression of sympathy for my repatriation from the Australian prime minister, Mr Bob Hawke, himself.

———

Poi porotiti tapua patua!

I send a second poi spinning to see where the case rests.

Look! My poi flies back to Mr Chris Batt. He reminds Mr Gray and other principals in a letter that 'as the Tasmanian Government has recently returned the Crowther collection to the Tasmanian Aboriginal community, I feel it would be appropriate to make a similar offer of returning these remains to the man's home country.'

Taku poi! Taku poi!

I must keep my two poi spinning in Tasmania. One follows Mr Gray who, at long last, receives a reply from the National Parks and Wildlife Service and other bureaux of the Tasmanian Government. He writes to the Minister of Maori Affairs:

> The remains can be repatriated on certain conditions: the expense of the operation is to be met by either the New Zealand or the Commonwealth Government, including the cost of the archaeological excavation as well as the conservation and curatorship of any remains or artefacts.

Oh, my heart leaps! But I need a third poi, and send it flying through the air to Canberra, the capital of Australia. The place where the Parliament Building rests was once sacred Aboriginal ground. Not far from the building is the Australian Department of Foreign Affairs. There the director of diplomatic relationships between Australia and New Zealand has a briefing with his desk officers. They make an assessment:

> Given the warm relations between our two countries, and if there is unanimous agreement on returning the remains, the Department will assist.

Ka nui te pai! Poi e, poi e, poi e . . . e poi e!

I send a fourth poi spinning back to Wellington where the news from the Department of Foreign Affairs is communicated to the Australian High Commissioner in New Zealand. I watch as High Commissioner Penny Wensley climbs the steps of Te Paremata o te Pakeha to discuss the matter with the Minister of Maori Affairs. Red-headed and beautiful, she evinces a formidable spirit and a great love of both Australia and New Zealand.

And my four poi join together. They tap against each other as the Australian High Commissioner speaks to the Minister of Maori Affairs. They wait as the negotiations begin between Mr Tamati Reedy, Secretary of Maori Affairs, and his counterparts in the Tasmanian State Government. They hover. They spin. They twirl.

Mr Batt waits. Mr Wetere waits. Penny Wensley waits. Mr Christopher Heald, the expatriate New Zealander living in Tasmania, waits. Doubts are voiced about my resting place; graves have been robbed and my actual remains might be nowhere near my headstone.

A year goes past. Another and another.

My heart fails me for the clouds break apart again and I see my village of Patiarero, tena koe! The sacred mountain Pukehika, e tu mai! The meeting house Te Whare Whiri Taunoka, greetings!

The old woman, Kui, stands on a rise overlooking the Whanganui River, waiting, waiting, waiting. She is an eternal sentinel as she looks up at me. How my spirit longs to dive down from Te Reinga and into the bright strand below.

All I seek is the embrace of the Matua Tupuna.

'Oh, ancestor,' Kui cries, 'I *will* come to get you. Let nobody stand in my way.'

———

What will be the outcome?

When will I be gathered up by loving hands and taken back to my homeland before strong winds scatter me again?

Hei ha hei ha! Hei ha hei ha!

34

Taku tamaiti e
E karanga to papa ki a koe e
Noho mai koe i te taha o te Matua Tupuna e
Ki Patiarero te kainga, Pukehika te maunga
Aue te mamae toi whenua e . . .

In Maori mythology, the world of the living was known as Te Ao Turoa.

There was also the world of the dead. Sometimes it was called Te Po, the Underworld. At other times it was called Te Reinga, the Place of Spirits. And, again, people who had died were often farewelled to Hawaiki, the Original Homeland.

Another world was also associated with the spirits. It was known as Rarohenga, the World Beyond. Whether or not it was the same world as the world of the dead I do not know; perhaps it was one of the many kingdoms in which the spirits lived. But in the old days, man was able to journey back and forth to Rarohenga and commune with the spirits and mythical beings which lived within: the ponaturi, for instance, goblins who lived beneath the sea by day, or turehu, albino folk, and other shapeshifters.

Thus, when Kumete, Te Waretiti, Rahui, Matiu Tikiaki and I were tried, sentenced, and transported from Aotearoa to Van Diemen's Land, for us it was like being sent to our deaths from our World to the World Beyond. To Purgatory, if you like.

We stepped off the HMS *Castor*. Disoriented, I saw ponaturi, the hordes of Tangaroa, pressing in on us from all sides. The daylight was supposed to be fatal to them but these Pakeha ponaturi had developed immunity to the sun — and they were malevolent.

There were turehu among them also, so white they had no faces.

That is why, when Ismay stepped forward and called to us, 'Haere mai nga tangata toa o Niu Tireni e, welcome, you brave warriors of New Zealand,' it was as if she was our rescuer. She was like Niwareka, the beautiful turehu wife of the human chief, Mataora. Having married him in Our World, she left him when he struck her, and returned in tears to her father's house in Rarohenga. Bereft, Mataora navigated the ocean to the Outer World, sought entrance from Kuwatawata, the guardian of the gateway between both worlds, and found her. He asked her forgiveness and she returned with him to Our World again.

I had understood that the gateway had subsequently closed. But when Thomas Mason, our neighbour from the Heretaunga Valley, also stepped forward, my fellow Maori prisoners and I realised it was still open.

We could go back.

Indeed, not a day had passed that I did not think of my kainga, Patiarero, my mountain, Pukehika, and my beloved Matua Tupuna, the Whanganui River. I had been born in its waters and, graced by the taniwha of the river, proudly travelled it with my father, Korakotai, as he maintained his duties as emissary.

Did the villagers still set their eel weirs and net the shoals of migrating whitebait? Did they continue to work on their kumara cultivations? And were the birdcatchers still snaring the succulent Maori pigeon to bring back to the kainga?

And my father, Korakotai, did he now take my son with him as he travelled the river?

'Kia ora rangatira! Is that Hohepa with you?'

'No, he has been taken to Australia. This is my mokopuna, Rukuwai. We wait for his father's return.'

Aue, i aku rangi mate. Alas, the days of my misery.

Despite the gladness and hope of our arrival, despair surrounded me and my fellow prisoners during the dark nights we were incarcerated in the Hobart Town Penitentiary. We had known prisons before, but not such a one as this with its living and its dead occupying the same sinister space.

The living crowded the cells: the penitentiary was the first call for all convicts sent from England, Ireland, Wales, Scotland — and from the Africas, Australia itself, and New Zealand too. Thousands of frightened and bewildered men awaited distribution to Norfolk Island or Port Arthur, Macquarie or one of the other institutions in Van Diemen's Land.

'Let it not be Port Arthur,' men moaned. 'Please God, anywhere but there.'

We were like animals caged, shackled and herded together. The stench of unwashed bodies, shit and piss was overwhelming. We stood tightly together; if you fainted you would be trampled. The food stank, the water was bad.

'We have indeed come to the World Beyond,' Te Waretiti shivered.

It was a world crowded with ghosts and spirits of the dead too. The souls of men who had been flogged to death still hovered all around us, seeking a way out.

Rahui, who was always sensitive to their presence, gibbered with fear.

'Where is the tohunga to exorcise this place of its sadness and release them?' he asked. 'Must they remain in limbo forever?'

The prison guards taunted and humiliated us. The slightest infraction and the offender was thrashed or beaten. When that happened, the groans that otherwise afflicted the penitentiary were silenced. There was only the song of the whip and the sobs of the poor soul, before merciful unconsciousness claimed him.

———

We could have borne the imprisonment were it not for the fact that, for the first time, we were separated.

The guards came to take us to separate cells — I don't know why, perhaps they thought we would be less dangerous if we did not remain together. Kumete, who always considered himself to be my protector, fought to stay with me. 'E te rangatira,' he cried, 'I fail you, forgive me.'

Rahui, Te Waretiti and Matiu Tikiaki also struggled with the guards, but to no avail. 'Will we ever see each other again?' they asked as they were taken away into the hungry mouth of the night.

We were a male tribe with such loyalty to each other that I doubted whether Tikiaki, the youngest, could survive without the rest of us.

Distraught, I sank down to the cold stone. My thoughts turned to hopelessness, and I would have given myself up to them had I not heard a voice calling:

'E Hohepa, he kanohi ou? Titiro mai ki ahau!'

It was the voice of my dear wife, Te Rai, and at the sound of it, memories of her streamed through the dark; she had been so beautiful when the old women had brought her to me at our marriage hut! 'Tu tapairu, e, tenei haramai nei,' they sang. 'A princess, indeed, is she who comes!'

I cried out, 'Wife, where are you?' I saw her shimmering in the dark, but when I went to embrace her she disappeared.

In her place I saw a young boy wandering beside the Whanganui River.

My son Rukuwai, and he was weeping.

Oh, he had been so young when Te Rai was taken away from him. When she died I wrapped her body in fine mats and strapped her to the packhorse. Then, pulling the horse after us, Rukuwai and I rode from the Heretaunga back to the Whanganui River. The world had become drenched with tears and the mountains were crowned with misty funeral wreaths. We negotiated the chill, windswept track over the hills to Pauatahanui. In the evening, we found a place to rest and eat, and to keep vigil over Te Rai. Throughout the night, stars were falling, unpinned from the breast of heaven. Rukuwai had fallen asleep in my arms; his warmth comforted me as I wept for my dead wife.

The following morning, we continued down the Kapiti Coast. I hadn't wanted to stop by Reverend Hadfield's; I would have killed any Pakeha I came across. Rukuwai looked back at his mother's body. He called to her, 'Are you all right, e ma?'

When we reached the Whanganui River, I went to Putiki and asked Te Anaua Hori Kingi for the use of a canoe. He gave one to me and I placed Te Rai in it. Together Rukuwai and I paddled her upriver to Patiarero.

'Almost there now, e ma,' Rukuwai said. 'Almost home.'

My heart burst with emotion when I saw Pukehika on one side of the river and Patiarero on the other. Both banks were lined with people, crying out to us. 'Karanga atu ra e te tama!' the women called, 'Oh come, Son of Korakotai! Come in the sadness of the day! Come with your beloved Te Rai! Haere mai—'

Korakotai and Hinekorako were waiting for us. How had they known we were coming?

I told Korakotai what was in my heart. I had tried to reconcile what the Pakeha were doing with the teachings of their Saviour.

I had been prepared to offer the greatest of Christian virtues: forgiveness.

Not any longer. 'Father, I was wrong to support the Pakeha. From this day forward I am against him.'

I willingly submitted to the tattooist. By the time half my face was tattooed, I had joined Te Mamaku and returned to the Heretaunga. There I fought the soldiers at Boulcott's Farm. I also took utu, revenge, for Te Rai's death.

Then I was captured.

Aue te mamae! In the Hobart Penitentiary, longing for Rukuwai over-whelmed me. Did he go daily with my father to the bluff overlooking the river to watch for my return?

In unbearable grief I called out to the guards, 'Let me out! Let me go to my son!'

When they came they could not pacify me; I knocked them down. In retaliation they clubbed me with the butts of their weapons. I raised my arms to protect my head and face. My blood was everywhere.

It was hopeless. I began to sing a waiata to Rukuwai from my prison cell.

Taku tamaiti e . . . overcast is the sky above,
over my heart is the pall of my sadness!
From mine eyes the tears do pour out!
Keep looking northward, my son, to Rarohenga!
With all my strength I will make my way to the gateway
I will ask its guardian Kuwatawata to let me pass!
And l will come to you, for what is life without you?

From the memory of Rukuwai I was able to lift myself out of the pit of darkness. Yes, I would survive, for his sake. I would not let myself go into despondency.

Then came the sound of Kumete singing back to me. 'E te rangatira, e tu te mana . . . Oh, Hohepa, do not weep . . .'

From other parts of the penitentiary, I heard also the voices of Matiu Tikiaki, Rahui and Te Waretiti. Together we sang waiata to each other, offering comfort and strength, singing through the turning darkness.

I sank into unconsciousness. I sensed the coming of dawn but remained in oblivion. Occasionally I felt the hands of kind prisoners washing my wounds. Then I heard someone speaking to me. 'Hohepa? My God, man, what has been done to you?'

The voice belonged to Gower McKissock. I had only met him briefly — he had been by Ismay's side when she had welcomed us at the port — but he had observed us as we had been processed for imprisonment. He was about my height and had an air of authority about him. Some people thought him arrogant, but I knew this to be a shield; some damage had been done to him in the past and, because of it, he raised the shield so that it could never happen again.

It was he who, in his kindness, raised me out of my prison cell and had me transferred to the penitentiary hospital. I drifted in and out of consciousness. I saw Thomas Mason. I heard the voices of others whom I later came to know as George Washington Walker and the newspaperman, Henry Melville. One day I heard Gower upbraiding the staff. 'Why haven't you changed the sheets?' he asked.

'He will only soil them again.'

He ordered the changing forthwith, holding me in his arms until it was done.

'I am here, Te Umuroa,' he said to me as he laid me back onto the bed.

I know now that it was because of Gower, Thomas Mason, George Washington Walker, Henry Melville and other good men and women of Hobart Town that the malevolence of Sir George Grey's wish to punish us was denied.

Indeed, from the moment of my beating I was visited regularly by friends. 'The entire population is up in arms about your imprisonment,' Mr Mason told me. 'Look! Look!' He showed me newspaper reports decrying our transportation.

As for any official report on the brutality, there was none; the authorities argued that I had brought the punishment upon myself. News of the beating was also kept from Ismay and Mrs Jane Mason, so as not to upset them.

'Moves are afoot,' Mr Mason said, 'to try to have your sentences overturned and for you all to be returned to New Zealand.' Mr Mason and Gower managed to persuade the authorities to reunite me and my four companions. When I was fully recovered, I returned to the cells to a joyful reunion with them.

'Forgive me,' Kumete wept, 'for leaving you at the mercy of the guards.'

'We are again one,' I said. 'He whanau kotahi tatou.'

But hope was so difficult to hold on to!

Two convicts were hanged at the nearby gaol. People gathered to watch and, as their bodies kicked and struggled at the end of the rope, I thought to myself that it would not be long before we, too, felt the hangman's noose.

Meanwhile the days came and went. My companions and I tried not to think of our beloved Aotearoa, but it was impossible.

'The last time I saw my wife and three boys,' Rahui said, 'was at the gateway of the pa. Do they still wait for me? Who is looking after them?'

'My mother begged me not to go on the raid on Boulcott's Farm,' Te Waretiti added. 'I told her, "Hei aha! Stop your crying, old woman! You were always possessive! I will be back tomorrow."'

Finally, Thomas Mason brought the news. 'Governor La Trobe has agreed to petition the Colonial Office in London to have the charges dropped,' he said. 'You are all to be moved from the Hobart Town Penitentiary — not to Port Arthur or Norfolk Island, but to a less punitive institution to await the outcome.'

Soon afterwards, we left the penitentiary. I felt a great sense of aroha for the convicts, and guilt that *we* had been spared. 'But you are Maori chiefs,' they said, as if that explained everything.

I did not know what to say in reply. When I and the others had left Aotearoa, I had made a vow that I would forever set myself against the Pakeha. I expected only to be humiliated, dishonoured, punished and, finally, put to death by them.

Instead, even in Rarohenga, I discovered aroha.

———

We boarded the *Mary* with Governor La Trobe, Dr Hampton, Gower and Ismay and their three children, and the young servant Sally Jenkins.

Governor La Trobe had only our best interests at heart. Just as the ship was approaching the dock at Maria Island, I asked him, 'Why are you doing this, rangatira?'

'I am not averse to questioning the British Government's policies,' he began, 'and certainly I am not afraid of Mr Grey. He may intimidate lesser fellows, but let him try it with his equals, if he dares.' His voice softened. 'I assume that you, a Maori chief, love your native land as dearly as an Englishman — as I am — loves his. But I will not seek to punish you, as Mr Grey does, simply because you were fighting for your own land, even if—' he paused, smiling ironically '—my own countrymen were your opponents.'

And then there was Mrs McKissock . . . Ismay.

From the time she welcomed us at Hobart Town, I knew our destinies were intertwined. The old kuia, Mahuika, in Nelson had hinted at this when she had studied the scrolls of my palms.

At the first opportunity, I reminded Ismay of that earlier meeting. I did not mention, of course, that I had mistaken her for one of the prostitutes on the beach among the dwellings of the Maori shantytown!

'Haere atu pokokohua!' she had said to a sailor as he tried to grab her skirts. 'May even your tiny ure tangata fall off!'

The other prostitutes had shrieked with laughter.

'We are both pilgrims, Mr Te Umuroa,' she said, 'traversing this Vale of Tears. How blessed we are if we are able to share part of our journey.'

Darlington Station was such a bleak settlement! There, hundreds of young men like us were in shackles, with overseers to keep them at their hard labour. They slept in overcrowded cells. They worked from dawn to dusk. They were punished if they did not keep to the rigorous Darlington hours. It astounded me that the Pakeha did this to their own, as well as to us. Not until then did I realise the full extent of the savage Outer World. Even so, what was the convicts' response when they discovered we would not be incarcerated with them? It was the same as that of the prisoners at the Hobart Town Penitentiary. 'But you are Maori chiefs.'

Even among the imprisoned of Rarohenga, good men like Seamus Keelan and Kieron Moore, aroha.

I will never forget the moment when John Jennings Imrie took us to our hut overlooking the Mercury Passage. We were all astonished, more so when Ismay, translating for Mr Imrie, told us Governor La Trobe had ordered that our shackles be removed.

I was so overcome that I pulled her into the hongi.

I was unprepared for the impact of the gesture. The tingling as our foreheads met. The touch of her nose grazing mine. The outward sigh of breath from her nostrils. The smell of her skin.

It lasted only a few seconds. But it was like an eternity before Kumete's voice separated us. 'E hoa . . .' he said.

Later, I told Kumete, 'You don't have to worry.'

'You look at each other,' he accused.

'She has a husband,' I answered, 'and I still mourn Te Rai. And one day news will come of our freedom and, when that happens, our aroha for one another will be fulfilled.'

'Aroha?' he asked puzzled.

'Our lives are intertwined,' I answered.

35

I remember the first time I saw the nankeen night herons.

It was just after New Year, 1847. We had worked hard that morning fixing fences for Mr Imrie and he was very pleased with us. 'As a reward to ourselves,' he said, 'let's go southward beyond the she-oaks and do some fishing.'

Te Waretiti's mouth began to water. He had a special place where he could fossick for oysters — their size and flavour were similar to those of Aotearoa — or dive for crayfish among the rocks of Tangaroa's kingdom. On an earlier visit, we had also left a small boat in a sheltered cove which we could row out to a place where mullet thrived. I wanted to take a good ika back for Liam Connor and our convict friends.

'We leave the binocular behind?' Te Waretiti asked, winking at us.

'Oh no,' Mr Imrie answered. 'We will take them just in case we spot something.'

When he said he wanted to reward us, what Mr Imrie really meant was that he wanted to reward himself, too, with his favourite pastime: birdwatching.

———

The day was bright and clear as we set off along the coast. Matiu Tikiaki ran ahead through the lagoons, disturbing flocks of cormorants and oystercatchers, which took flight. The sea cliffs teemed with silver gulls and terns; this was their kingdom, not ours, and they ignored Tikiaki's antics as he shouted at them.

'He's happy,' Rahui said. 'Sally Jenkins must have smiled at him.'

Albatrosses glided overhead and out across the Mercury Passage. As they reached the channel, where the water turned from green to blue, they swooped low over a school of ever-present killer whales; not for them the boisterous leaping of the black right whales but, rather, the sleek sliding through the sparkling water.

'There is a story,' Mr Imrie told us, 'that once the whale pods were so large in the Passage that, whenever they were in processional, they filled the entire bay's width. If you wished to, you could walk across their backs from Maria Island to the mainland.'

His story sounded just like one my father, Korakotai, would tell me when we travelled the great Matua Tupuna. How I missed him! And how I wished it were true — that all the whales from every sea would come to form a bridge back to Aotearoa.

We came to the she-oaks and continued south through more lagoons. Mr Imrie cautioned Matiu Tikiaki, 'From now on, turituri, be quiet.'

'Yes,' Tikiaki answered, 'sshhh,' and he wagged a finger at Te Waretiti as if *he* had been the one making all the racket.

It was when we were crossing a very deep swamp that a beautiful rich cinnamon-coloured bird, of the crane kind, black-crowned and white-breasted, rose gracefully from the mud among the reeds. As it slowly passed us, two others also lifted in slow and flapping flight.

'Oh my goodness,' Mr Imrie said. '*Nycticorax caledonicus.*'

We looked at him blankly.

'Nankeen night herons,' he explained. 'They're also known as the rufous night heron or, in the islands above Australia, the natives call them the melabaob. They're summer visitors and not at all common in Van Diemen's Land.'

His voice was hushed with awe as he got out his binoculars. The herons hadn't flown very far and were perched on a large tree above the sedgy swamp. 'They're breeding!' he exclaimed. 'See? They have three long slender plumes on their heads. There must be a colony somewhere. The male and female both incubate the eggs, and they share in raising their young. They build their nests together, too, high in trees, and pairs don't just feed their own young. If there are other chicks that are hungry, those mouths get fed as well.'

One of the night herons took wing again. It flew straight at us.

'That's most unusual,' Mr Imrie said. 'They're usually very shy.' Then he sighed with happiness. 'Van Diemen's Land must surely have been where Noah anchored his Ark to let all of the birds off, eh?'

I could not tell him that as the heron had flown past, it had stared at me with its large yellow eyes. It had reminded me of the hokioi, the spirit bird of the Maori. Known as the messenger of the gods and of immortal life, the hokioi communicated between all the worlds; it was regarded by the god Tane as his favourite bird companion.

Hello, Hohepa Te Umuroa. We will meet again.

Why do I recall the nankeen night herons? The sighting of them coincided with Te Waretiti's encounter with the serpent.

I was in the hut when I heard him give a yell. In three steps I was outside. Ismay had come to rescue him.

There are times in life when one is both within and without the moment.

I see Ismay at the doorway of the cottage, her face drained of colour. In the dust between her and Te Waretiti something sinister slithers, coiling and recoiling in front of him.

You don't have to do this, kui. You have three children. You could turn back inside if you wanted to.

Instead, Ismay looks at me. 'Don't come further,' she says. She reaches for a hoe, leaning against the outside wall. Her forehead is beaded with sweat and concentration.

Hatana. Satan.

She takes a step and the serpent, sensing her, whips its head around, watching her. Another step. This time, Satan tightens, poises, lifts its head.

That's when I shout to her. 'Kui! Na.' Ismay. *Now.*

My shout diverts the copperhead's attention. In that moment when the snake hesitates, Ismay brings the hoe down on its head with a scream.

I run to her and catch her before she falls. I gather her in my arms. Oh, my aroha for her pours out, my unsurpassing gratefulness for what she has done. After all, what is Te Waretiti to her? What am I to her?

Death has passed our way and it could have taken her with it.

'Kua mutu te he, kui,' I say to her. 'The danger is over now.' But I cannot tell her that the serpent, like the heron, has also looked at me.

Te Umuroa, next time you may not be so lucky.

Ismay and I were a man and a woman trying to negotiate that strange Outer World. Gower was also making a traverse of his own; for him I held no animosity, but as soon as I had seen him and Ismay together I knew theirs was a union without aroha. Although I was grateful for his kindness, my overwhelming aroha, sympathy, was with Ismay because of his cool heart.

Rarohenga, Rarohenga.

Both real and unreal, there were moments when the Outer World was absolutely savage and demonic. At other times it was benign, filled with a radiant ecstasy.

And always, conflicting forces surrounded us. They seemed to come from a huge dark whakapapa, a genealogy, that had always eluded me.

That is, until late February 1847, when news came that Governor La Trobe and his wife would be visiting Darlington.

It was through his visit that I discovered the terror of Van Diemen's Land's dark history.

The visit made Rahui and Te Waretiti instantly expectant. Not a day had passed that we had not looked across the Mercury Passage hoping for the ship to come to take us back to Aotearoa.

'Are we to be freed?' Rahui asked.

'If so,' I ventured cautiously, 'it won't be because of the letter the governor has written to the Colonial Office. Not enough time has lapsed.'

'Perhaps there have been other developments that we don't know of,' Te Waretiti said. 'Who knows? Governor Grey may have relented.'

I did not want to engender false hope. 'We will have to wait and see,' I answered. 'If the Lord wills our freedom, then it will be so.'

The small military contingent of the 96th Regiment was at drill morning and afternoon. Mr and Mrs Lapham ordered a spruce up on the penitentiary for, isolated as they were, the visit from the governor was like a visit from Queen Victoria herself. A bugler was posted to watch out for the governor's arrival and, one crisp morning, we heard his bugle blowing, *Tara tara! Tara tara!*

'Te rangatira kei te haramai,' Kumete said. 'The governor comes.'

The *Mary* sailed swift as a gull landing on the Mercury Passage. We gave a loud 'Hoo-*raa*!' when it glided to anchor.

'Well, well, well,' Governor La Trobe said.

He was most affable as he introduced Mrs La Trobe to Mr and Mrs Lapham and then to the rest of the official party. He saw Ismay with Gower and the children and whispered something to Mrs La Trobe.

'The governor has told me so much about you,' Mrs La Trobe said to Ismay.

'Greetings, Maori chiefs,' Governor La Trobe said. 'I trust I find you all well?' Then he gave us his dismaying news. 'This is both a happy and sad occasion: happy because I am so very pleased to see you all, but sad because this will be my last official visit to Darlington and Long Point.'

Ismay translated the news to the others.

'My place as lieutenant-governor is to be taken by Mr William Thomas Denison,' he continued. 'I am to become the first Governor of Victoria, now that it has separated from New South Wales.'

We all offered Governor La Trobe our heartiest congratulations but he must have seen from our faces how disappointed we were — and not simply because he'd not brought good news for us. That he was leaving Van Diemen's Land was also a blow.

'How will we become free,' Te Waretiti asked him, 'if you are not there to obtain our liberty for us?'

'Let us hope,' the governor answered, 'that Mr Denison will continue to prosecute the tragic miscarriage of justice that has befallen you. New Zealand will never become truly great if there is not a judicial and equitable balance of power ensuring the flourishing of both its peoples.'

But our fate must have weighed heavily on Governor La Trobe's mind because, after he had completed his official visit, I saw him in discussion with Mr Lapham, Mr Imrie, Gower and the arrogant Mr Boyd. 'Superintendent, as you know, I must still go to Long Point before I return to Hobart Town. I would be personally indebted to you if you would allow your Maori charges to accompany me? I find myself reluctant to leave them so precipitately and would appreciate a longer farewell. They will be obliged to return to Darlington by foot, but I am told that it is not difficult.'

I stepped forward. 'My friends and I would dearly wish the opportunity of an appropriate farewell to you, Governor. We honour you deeply.'

'Then it's done?' Governor La Trobe asked Mr Lapham. 'Good! And perhaps Mr Imrie and Mr and Mrs McKissock will also accompany us?'

'As it happens,' Gower said, 'I am due to make an inspection of the hospice at Long Point. Mrs McKissock could return to the children with Mr Imrie while I remain there for a few days.'

'Excellent. But the return overland, Mrs McKissock,' he cautioned, 'will you be up to it?'

'Sir,' Ismay answered, 'although I am a woman, I am not a decorative appendage!'

Mr Boyd assigned two guards to accompany us.

———

We were a large party boarding the *Mary*. Once we settled, the captain headed north on the tide and then west, circumnavigating the top of Maria

Island into Bass's Strait. I kept company with Governor La Trobe and Gower on the deck, close by Mr Imrie as he pointed out to the governor the islet known as Ile du Nord; flocks of titi clouded the nesting colony.

I took the opportunity to talk to Gower. I wanted to know why he had put himself out by agreeing to take Thomas Mason's place at Maria Island.

'I believe in your innocence,' he answered. 'Apart from which I owe something to my father.'

I was puzzled by his remark. I think he, too, was surprised by it! He smiled, 'What is it about you, Te Umuroa, which makes me want to confess my innermost thoughts?' Then he explained his answer. 'I couldn't save my father,' he said. 'Perhaps I can save you.'

'You loved your father?'

'Yes,' he answered.

I began to warm towards him.

———————

The *Mary* rounded Cape Boulanger and skirted down the eastern side. Ismay was speaking with Mrs La Trobe; there was a shining ecstasy about her. I remembered Niwareka again, the turehu princess, and thought, 'Yes, Ismay, this is your kingdom.'

Maria Island possessed a rugged, alluring beauty. To our right rose the perpendicular walls of Mount Pedder, high basaltic rocks like an ancient fortress. 'In our country,' I said to Governor La Trobe, 'we have a saying: if you must bow your head, let it be only to the highest mountain. On maunga such as this we put our defensive pa.'

'I would love to visit Maoriland,' Governor La Trobe answered. 'Tell me about your home, Mr Te Umuroa . . .'

The *Mary* came upon Cape Mistaken. Looking back, Mr Imrie pointed out Mount Maria, higher than Mount Pedder, its summit cloaked in a layer of cloud. 'We're almost there,' he said, as we approached the narrow land bridge that created of the island one teardrop from which another just below it was forming.

For a few minutes, everyone was silent, looking at the shore. Seals basked among the rocks. Some dived and ventured out to see who we were, escorting the *Mary* past Cap des Tombeaux and into an inlet in northern Riedle Bay.

Once we landed, it was a short walk across the forested isthmus to the Long Bay Station. Kumete, Te Waretiti, Matiu Tikiaki, Rahui and I made our farewells to the governor. Rahui grabbed his hands and kissed them.

Governor La Trobe was affected. 'And now,' he said, 'I have been too proprietorial and really must let you go!' Trying to hide his emotion, he shook our hands vigorously. 'May we rub noses in the manner of your people?' We obliged him. 'An interesting sensation,' he laughed, 'but I suspect you would prefer a flatter proboscis than mine, eh? I leave you to God's mercy.'

Gower turned to Ismay. 'I'll return to Darlington as soon as I can. Mr Imrie, would you look after Mrs McKissock?'

For a moment Ismay looked at me. Panicked. 'Gower, no . . .'

But he was already gone.

36

With Mr Boyd and Mr Imrie leading and the two guards bringing up the rear, we started out along the rough bush track that connected Long Point and Darlington.

Fifteen minutes into our journey, however, the guards stopped. One of them pointed out something.

'Smoke,' Kumete said to me drily. 'They've taken long enough to see it.'

I suppressed a grin.

'My training obliges me to investigate its source,' Mr Boyd said to Mr Imrie. 'Although we have had no notification, it may be an escaped prisoner.'

'Sir,' Mr Imrie answered, 'we have a lady in our midst. Perhaps it would be better not to engage with any dangerous individual?'

'I'm sure Mrs McKissock would not want any leeway given on the basis of her sex,' he said.

'Precisely what I was going to say,' she answered, irritated that he had pre-empted her reply.

———

We moved up the neck of the valley. It was not an escaped prisoner at all; rather, we came upon a strange, leathery-skinned individual sitting beside a tent in a shady clump. He wore a wide-brimmed hat, two coats, thick trousers and leather gaiters up to his knees. Around him were a number of sticks of assorted lengths, leather sacks and cages covered with canvas.

Mr Boyd was most officious. 'Do you have papers, sir? Are you a free man?'

'As free as you, my strutting poppycock,' the man answered. 'The name's Harry, as you will see from my dockymint.'

Mr Boyd frowned. 'What are you doing on Maria Island, Mr . . . Campbell, is it? Visitors are restricted.'

'I have a pass, young rooster!' He fished in his pocket for another paper. 'See? Here's me licence given by the guvnor himself.' He looked at us, one after another, enjoying his audience. 'Apart from which, who would not wish to sit here on Maria Island and appreciate Nature? The vast sheet of water embosomed in the passage between this glorious isle and the mainland yonder! The hills covered in noble forest trees, truly grand, while above we are blessed by the warmth of yon journeying luminary, the sun, to gild us with its warmth!'

Ismay laughed with delight. 'You have a gift for the poetic utterance, sir,' she said.

'Would you like a cup of tea, ma'am?' he answered, flattered. 'Me billy's just been a-boiling over the fire.'

'Thank you, Mr Campbell, I will.'

'Good,' he said. 'I don't see many ladies and it would be a pleasure to have your lips impressed on me very own mug.' He started to clear a seat for her. 'Just let me move my staff of office.' He picked up a long walking stick, grand, polished and gnarled, twisting into a fork at the base. Then he saw me and my tokotoko. 'Ah! One of Nature's true gentlemin!' he said. 'Mowry, are ye? And with your own staff of office, eh?'

Mr Boyd was irritated. 'What do you hunt?' he asked, insistent, without looking at the licence.

'Wanna look-see?' Harry said, squinting cunningly into Mr Boyd's face. He reached over and, opening up one of his leather sacks, spilled its wriggling contents onto the grassy sward. Ten snakes slipped out, golden lines which raised their heads, spitting, hissing and striking. Blinded by the sudden sun they coiled, recoiled and stabbed at each other.

Mr Boyd gave a cry and stepped back. As for Te Waretiti and Matiu Tikiaki, they yelped, 'E hika ma!' and climbed into the lower branches of a nearby tree.

'No good getting up there, mateys,' Harry said. 'The boogahs will still get ya!' He pinned the creatures with his staff of office and lifted them back into the sack. 'These ones aren't poisonous, though,' he reassured us.

Mr Boyd was taking no chances. Pale of countenance, he stepped back, his legs bumping against Harry's covered cages.

'I wouldn't go further back if I was you,' Harry said. There was a hissing sound beneath the covers. 'These are . . .' he continued. He lifted the canvas: inside were venomous tiger snakes. 'Don't they have such tyrannic

374

insolence?' he asked.

As soon as the light struck them they reared up.

'However,' Harry said, giving a low sweeping bow, 'before my staff of office, like the rod of Aaron which Moses used in the court of the Pharaoh, they are brought down.' He began a nimble dance. 'Harry Campbell is my name and catching snakes is my game. Welcome to my base camp. Once I git enough of the snakes, me mate Stan comes from the mainland with his boat and off we go back to civilisation.'

I smiled, enjoying the old man's performance.

'I sell them to museums, zoos or an apothecary, and sometimes I show my pretty ones in Hobart Town city! I catch little snakes, big boogahs, poisoned ones too, copperhead five foot, tiger snake six foot, whoo hoo! One bite and you're dead, mate, an antidote's too late mate! But me? They don't like my stink and slink away because I drink a bottle of rum a day!' He leaned into Mr Imrie. 'You must mind out for snakes. Some are very poisonous, especially the black ones. One of them beauties kisses you, rather than the missus here, and you will never see your own country again.'

Mr Imrie laughed out loud. 'Here you are, Mr Campbell,' he said, passing him his hip flask.

'Thank-ee,' Harry answered, taking a swig and transferring the rest of the rum into a bottle. 'I was running low and to be bit by a poisonous snake in my prime would be a blow.'

Clearly put out, Mr Boyd said, 'Mrs McKissock, once you have finished your tea perhaps we can move on?'

But we were all fascinated by Mr Campbell's snake-catching paraphernalia and didn't want to go quite yet. I looked at a large pile of thick hemp ropes.

'I use them to fence the boogahs in,' Harry explained. 'They have soft underbellies and dislike the tickle of the fibres. Sometimes it works, sometimes it don't. So if a tiger snake gets out, don't confront it. If you do, it's likely to get so riled up it'll come after ya and it won't stop until it's got ya. Have you heard the story of the man on a horse pursued by a tiger snake? It pursued the horse, brought it down, and when the man ran off it caught him too.'

Te Waretiti and Matiu Tikiaki came down from their tree and crowded around, fingering Mr Campbell's impressive staffs of office — forked sticks, hunting sticks and kylies, some of them painted with aboriginal tribal designs. 'What is this one?' Te Waretiti asked.

'Ah,' Harry answered, 'it's a bou-mar-rang.' V-shaped, the wing curved in towards the centre of rotation. 'I got it from the Turuwal people when I was in New South Wales coupla years back. I'm a lefty so they made it for me, a long-distance flier, travelling clockwise. Watch—'

He threw the boomarrang sidearm. Spinning rapidly, it made a wide rotation above the trees where some birds, startled by the sound, panicked into the air. Astonishingly, the boumarrang came back to where we stood. With great nonchalance, Harry plucked it from the air.

Kumete clapped in astonishment. Harry's throw was like a marvellous conjuring trick.

'Yes, my darksome sons of Sycorax,' Harry said, 'I've seen your aboriginal brothers bring down a kangaroo with a boumarrang. Emus too with broken necks and—' he looked slyly at Mr Boyd '—doubtless some unfortunate humans . . .'

Mr Boyd gave him back his papers. 'They appear to be in order.'

Ismay shook Harry Campbell's hand. 'Thank you for the tea,' she said. I heard her whisper privately to him. 'And you put Mr Boyd in his place, too!'

'It was my pleasure, dear lady,' he answered. Then he turned to all of us. 'Life is sweet, brothers and sister! There's night and day, both sweet things! There's sun, moon and stars, all sweet things! There's likewise the wind from the sea and, if you're lucky, somebody to lie down beside and sport with during the night! Oh, missus, if you were lying beside me, never would I wish to die!'

Mr Boyd slapped the side of his left thigh like a cross child. 'Mrs McKissock,' he said. 'We wait upon you.'

For all that the walk into the valley had been a detour, we were in good humour when we left it. From that moment on, however, it was as if we had passed through a veil from a world of laughter into a world of pain.

As we continued to traverse the world, the balance moved from the real into the unreal.

———

Rather than return down the valley's neck, Mr Boyd suggested climbing over the side and down to the sea to make up some time.

Harry Campbell shouted a warning. 'I wouldn't take that shortcut if I was you.'

It was too late. We were already committed.

We reached the top and saw before us a large sinkhole covered in sparse brush. Mr Boyd and Mr Imrie descended into it. Ismay followed them and then, suddenly, something rushed up and into my nostrils, a terrible smell of rotting bodies, and I knew why Harry had tried to stop us. 'Mrs McKissock, e tu.' I raised my tokotoko in warning.

'What's wrong with you?' the soldiers asked. 'Move.'

Ismay turned and came back. 'He aha te mate?' she asked.

I looked at her. 'Death has already passed this way, hasn't it.'

Rahui sensed it too. 'Nga tangata whenua kua mate kei raro i tenei wahi. There are over a hundred people lying in an unnatural grave. We should not disturb them.'

I swayed, almost passed out, and began my vertiginous, spiralling descent to the murderous heart of Van Diemen's Land's memory.

I felt such self-loathing.

Why hadn't I noticed it before, the entire absence of tangata whenua, the original inhabitants of the land?

———

When I opened my eyes the landscape was glowing. All the trees were shining, as if rain had suddenly and quickly cleaned them — they shimmered and, when a breeze whispered among them, scattered the raindrops like sacred tears.

I felt as if I had walked into a world made of pounamu, with sun refracting through the depths of the stone. Whenever I looked around, the facets of the greenstone shifted the view so that it was constantly fading in and out of focus. Right in the middle of the greenstone was my father, Korakotai, sitting on a log. 'E pa,' I said, astonished, 'what are you doing here?'

'All things are possible in Rarohenga,' he answered, opening his arms in welcome. 'Waiting for you, of course,' he continued, 'and enjoying the sun.'

I went to him with such yearning in my heart. We pressed noses in the hongi. As soon as they touched, however, I began to weep — no breath came from my father to warm and mingle with mine to him. Our greeting was the hongi ki te tupapaku; not a greeting at all, but the ritual farewell that Maori give to the dead person before he is enclosed in earth.

He waited until I had finished grieving. 'Once I was the holder of the tokotoko,' he began, 'and my job was to bind all the tribes of the river together.' His spirit form was luminous, transcendent. 'You are now the tokotoko's guardian,' he continued. 'Your job is still the same as mine but bigger. It is to bind the worlds together, the inside to the outside, the past to the present, whiria, whiria, whiria.'

He pointed to other luminous shapes among the trees: the spirit forms of the tangata whenua. They were small, dark, sparsely dressed, with glowing eyes. They moved silently, blurring in the sunlight, coming to whisper in my ears.

'White ghosts fell from the sky,' one said.

'At first they fell slowly,' another continued, 'but then they were like shooting stars falling all over us.'

'Until the whole land writhed and wriggled with them,' said a third.

'Wherever they hatched,' a fourth continued, 'maggots came forth. Look at us.'

I cried out because all I could see were tangata whenua, flyblown, rotting.

I shook my head to clear it of the vision and the stench. Korakotai was already walking away into the depths of the pounamu. He pointed at the spirit forms. 'They are tangata whenua. Once they were nine tribes. They had whanau groups. Now they are almost all gone.'

Then he pointed at me. 'You are tangata whenua too, son.

'You know what you have to do.'

———

'I want to know what happened to them,' I demanded of Ismay.

We backtracked from the sinkhole and circled towards the coast.

'It's been more than twenty years,' she began, 'since anything has been seen of Trowennans on Maria Island. And, on the mainland, well, there was conflict as soon as Europeans began to occupy it.'

As she spoke, I had a vision of a tribe of men, women and children on a kangaroo hunt, bursting upon the settlement at Risdon. Panicking, the soldiers fired and a cannon was aimed directly at the tangata whenua; fifty were slain.

'The Pakeha did the same thing in Aotearoa,' I answered.

'No,' Ismay said, shaking her head vigorously. 'Here, it was just the beginning of a war that the Trowennans could never win. Not like in Aotearoa where, from the beginning, Pakeha have always regarded Maori as equal.'

Rahui came up to me. 'The dead follow us. Can't you see them?'

———

Rarohenga was a place where the past and present conjoined. The real and the unreal met and collided. The rational and the irrational both existed within the same space: human, spirit, non-human.

Disturbance was all around us as we passed a patch of bulrushes; some, had I noticed, showed evidence of regrowth — as if they had once been cut and fastened in bundles, perhaps as makeshift rafts for fishing.

Never win? The tangata whenua had no hope at all. For yes, the spirit forms of the tangata whenua kept on darting up to me, always whispering, whispering, whispering.

'Did you know we were more than twelve thousand? The settlers preyed on us . . . the convict bushrangers, too . . . the soldiers . . . Our babies were murdered . . . our women raped . . . our wives stolen. And then, ask the kui, ask her . . . ask her about the Black Line . . . ask her, her, her, *her* . . . ask her how many of us are left . . .'

Disoriented, I turned to Ismay. 'I am sick at heart, kui. It may not be the same history as that of Pakeha and Maori in Aotearoa, and Pakeha may think that Maori are their equal — but could *we* be hunted?'

'Hohepa,' she said, 'it is so easy to become disillusioned with what man does to his fellow man. We must rise above our human condition.'

'Rise above it?' I answered. 'How?' Her words made me angry.

'By forgiveness of the sins of others.'

Coldness overcame me. I thought of Te Rai, murdered. 'There are times, Mrs McKissock,' I answered, 'when forgiveness is not enough. When I am sent back to Aotearoa and a Pakeha attacks me or mine, I will kill again.'

'If that is the case, Hohepa,' she said, 'I hope you never go back.'

———

And in that realm of Rarohenga was a freshwater lagoon.

I heard Rahui talking in a low voice to Kumete, Te Waretiti and Matiu Tikiaki. 'They are gathering,' he said.

Wherever I looked, there were spirit shapes everywhere, wraith-like, insubstantial, the spirits of the dead still following us.

Ismay stopped to rest. Steadying herself, she put a hand to a red cliff. When she removed it I saw that her hand was covered in red mud. Whimpering, she tried to wipe it off. 'What is it! Is it blood?'

'Tangata whenua lived here,' I answered. 'They used the ochre to paint their hair and bodies. We must retreat again. We should not go further.'

It was too late. A cry from one of the guards split the air. He had discovered large tree trunks hollowed by fire to form shelters. 'Look!' he shouted. He bent to the earth and found further evidence of the tangata whenua's habitation: stone tools, middens and shell beds.

His colleague had meantime wandered further, to a large patch of green sward against the side of the red cliff, protected from wind and sun and covered by protecting ancient she-oaks. Among a spreading profusion of wildflowers stood four decaying conical structures roughly made of pieces of eucalypt bark. They rested on four branches, each curved in a semicircle and, with one end planted into the ground, fixed in the earth below and bound together above by a large band of the same material. From such an arrangement there resulted a kind of four-sided pyramid of such symmetry as to produce a graceful, haunting effect.

'Stop,' I called to him.

He thrust his hands down through one of the pyramids. When he drew it out, he had in his grasp a burnt human jawbone. With a laugh he held it aloft.

I caught glimpses of the tangata whenua beneath — skull and skeleton fragments all profoundly altered by fire and reduced to bone and powder.

A huge, sad weariness came over me.

The spirit forms of the tangata whenua began to sway and shift before being scattered by the wind. 'See them? Even when we are dead, they do not leave us to rest . . .'

'We are in their graveyard,' I said.

———

The mood was sombre as we moved on. Dusk was drawing a curtain on the day, the red sun falling close upon the sea.

We reached the beach. Rahui, Te Waretiti, Kumete and Matiu Tikiaki already knew what they had to do. They waded into the waves, praying and sprinkling themselves with the water. 'Forgive us, spirits, for our desecration. Rest for ever, takoto, takoto, takoto.'

I called to Ismay, 'Haere mai.' I picked her up and carried her out into the water. 'Mr Imrie? Mr Boyd? You too, and your soldiers. We must all be purified by the sea.'

Mr Boyd and the two guards sat on the sand. 'We will not indulge ourselves in your mumbo jumbo,' they said.

I remembered how my father, Korakotai, had responded when we had met Joe Rowe and his four companions on the Whanganui River those many years ago. Rowe had wanted to acquire preserved heads, and refused to listen to my father when he told them they should turn back from their quest. 'Mr Boyd and his companions are foolish men and not worthy of our attention,' I said to Kumete. 'If they do not wish protection, then let them go forward without it.'

I sprinkled Ismay with water to cleanse her.

'I am so sorry,' she said. 'I didn't mean what I said earlier — about hoping that you would never return to Aotearoa.'

'Sorry?' I asked. 'No, you meant it.'

Then I had to ask her, 'How many tangata whenua are left, kui?'

380

'Almost none,' she answered. 'They live in exile now on an island named Flinders.'

I let her go. Grief drove me to plunge through the surf, breasting each wave as it advanced upon me. On and on, where the ocean turned from luminescent green to indigo.

There, I stopped, treading water.

'You are tangata whenua,' Korakotai had said. 'They are tangata whenua.'

I turned back to the beach.

––––––––

When we arrived at Darlington Station, I asked Mr Imrie if I could have a word with him.

'I want you to put the shackles back on me,' I said.

He was startled. So were my Maori companions.

'I am not one of you,' I said to Mr Imrie. 'I am one of *them.*' He thought I was referring to the convicts. 'And from tomorrow, I wish to work with the other men.'

'You were to be kept separate from them,' he frowned, 'but I will see what I can do. I will have to ask the superintendent . . .'

'Whether he says yes or not,' I interrupted, 'I *will* work with them.'

I did not ask, and did not expect, my fellow prisoners to follow my lead. But when they did, my eyes were blinded by tears.

And Kumete divined my other reason. Ismay was not of Our World.

'We will join you in your penance,' he said.

37

Of course it wasn't as easy as that.

Mr Imrie was dismayed. 'This is a backward step,' he said. 'I am very sorry that you wish to take it.'

'We will be comfortable in the company of other men,' I answered. 'Nor are we afraid of hard work.

At first, Ismay was puzzled. 'Why are you doing this? Voluntarily taking on the leg-irons? Why?' Then her face grew pale. 'Oh, Hohepa,' Ismay said. 'Is this all my fault?'

'Let us be as the pilgrims,' I answered, 'and, as pilgrims do, let us support each other when the noonday sun is high and hot and, when the winter comes, let us take shelter, the one shading the other from the wind and rain.'

Most difficult of all was Gower. He had the job of checking the irons, once they were fitted to our ankles and wrists, and the chain that linked us together. Halfway through, he threw the shackles down in a temper. 'This is so wrong,' he said. 'I am an emancipist and I refuse to do it.'

He was kneeling in front of me. I lifted his head. 'Titiro ki ahau,' I answered him. 'Look at me. I am glad you have found your humanity.'

He stared at me. He refused to acknowledge my insight and looked away.

———

Then two incidents happened that tested my resolve.

The first occurred when the superintendent, uneasy about our working with gangs led by Liam Connor or Kieron Moore, sought out a separate job — just for us.

'The Reverend Cox, chaplain of the Church of St John the Baptist near the Brushy Place rivulet,' he told Mr Imrie, 'has asked for the most reverent of the prisoners at the station to help him in a particular task; I thought of the Maoris. Could you get them across to Triabunna, where they are to await the arrival of a most precious cargo due for installation?'

'What is it?' Mr Imrie asked.

'I don't know,' he answered. 'Reverend Cox was most secretive about it.'

The morning mist was coming off the sea when we left Maria Island, but by the time we arrived at Triabunna the haze had burnt away. The morning was bright and clear. The Reverend Cox was there to meet us. He had with him four local men on a cart pulled by two bullocks. The reverend seemed agitated, and paced up and down, nervous, while we waited for any sign of the *Mary* approaching across the passage.

At last the vessel arrived, and Reverend Cox rushed over to sign for a large crate. 'Careful, oh, please be careful!' he kept calling as we placed it gently on the cart.

The bullocks, though, were spooked and uncontrollable. The driver tried soothing them — 'Steady! *Stea*–dy!' — but they threatened to bolt.

I made a quick decision. 'My friends and I will carry the crate to the church,' I told Reverend Cox. 'It is not far and it will be safer.'

Well . . . the walk was much longer than I had thought it would be, and the crate was heavy. We were all sweating by the time we arrived at the church. Reverend Cox was profuse in his thanks.

'Here is your reward,' he said. He carefully prised the crate apart. 'Praise the Lord, it is not broken!'

Inside was a most beautiful stained-glass window. It depicted, in the style he told us was called white grisaille, the Crucifixion of Jesus Christ during the period of His agony. Over the head of the Christ was the inscription *I.N.R.I. Jesus Nazarenus Rex Judaeorum*. As man had judged the Son of God; so the Son of God will judge man.

'I didn't think it would arrive safely and in one piece,' Reverend Cox said. 'It has come such a long way, from Battle Abbey, built by William the Conqueror in the latter half of the fourteenth century. It was buried for safety during the Cromwellian Revolution.'

As soon as I saw the window, I fell to my knees in prayer:

'Help me, Lord, to know what is the right thing to do in your Outer World.'

No matter all my resolutions, my conflicting heart still wavered on the question of forgiveness.

The day after we helped with the stained-glass window, the second incident occurred.

The morning started in the usual way. We arose at 4.45 a.m., washed, dressed and waited for Mr Imrie to advise us of our duties for the day.

'We will spend the morning chopping firewood,' he told us, 'and, after breakfast, you will join the convicts working at the mill.'

At 5.30 we gathered up our implements, and we were on the road with two handcarts soon after. We spied Liam Connor with his work gang travelling in the opposite direction. 'Kia ora,' I waved to him with my tokotoko.

The men waved back. I know that they never understood why we Maori had put on our shackles when we could have been free of them forever. I hoped they respected us for it.

We travelled to one of our usual firewood-gathering spots in the forest south of the Painted Cliffs, and worked solidly until 7.45, when we stopped for breakfast: water and some thick sandwiches that Mrs Imrie had made for us. The sun was up and it was good to sit looking over the gleaming Trowenna Sea as we rested from our labours.

Half an hour later we got up to resume work, but Mr Imrie was keen to walk on to do a reconnaissance of another part of the forest. I don't know how long we walked for, maybe for just under an hour, but we arrived at a densely wooded place where we had never been before: a ridge, with the land sloping steep to marshland. We took up our axes, and very soon the forest resounded with our chopping.

The day suddenly darkened. A strong wind began to blow from the Mercury Passage.

Kumete looked out. 'E hika! Where did that come from?'

We were accustomed to summer squalls, but this one was different: in one spot on the sea's surface, the wind was sucking up the water into three twisters, which danced and spun and then joined into one twisting spout, like the whirlwind of Enoch, heading towards the land — heading towards us.

We ran for our lives down the ridge. The squall was around us, and over us thundered the water spout, pulling up trees into its core. The noise was ear-shattering, and the circling winds threatened to suck us up into the heart of the spout.

No sooner had the twister begun than it ended, passing to the east and there collapsing. The sky filled with gentle rain, and out of the rain emerged a soft, gentle rainbow.

'Titiro ki kahukura!' Rahui laughed.

384

Yes, just another summer squall coming out of nowhere and then disappearing into nowhere.

Only then did I see that the storm had driven us into the same valley where, in our journey from Long Point a few weeks earlier, I had sensed the massacre of the tangata whenua, and had farewelled my father's spirit form. My first reaction was to yell, 'Haere atu! Get out of here—'

But then I saw the Tree of White Flowers in the middle of the grove, still shivering and sending blizzards of white petals through the air.

It was a tree out of the Dreamtime, having blossomed from seeds of the great gumtree, tar monadro, dropped on the second day of creation by Parnuen, the sun, and his wife, Vena. 'Surely it is the Tree of Trees,' Te Waretiti whispered.

Towering over two hundred feet tall, the tree was supported by an ancient trunk of deep-brown furrowed bark. From its outspreading boughs it bore other branches, strong and interwoven. Each branch was filled with leaves made glowing by the gentle rain. And from the leaves burst bouquet clusters of creamy-white blooms like offerings.

The blooms were both sun and moon. They alternately sparkled and gleamed; at their centres were thorny crowns. They garlanded the tree with dazzling light and, when the breeze blew softly on them, they released a heavenly scent.

I thought of the tangata whenua, dead in this place. But I also thought: Where there was evil there was also good.

And then I came out of my reverie. Two nankeen night herons, black-crowned, white-breasted, humbly bibbed in soft cloistered shades of brown, were shrieking and flying around the Tree of White Flowers.

Below, at the bottom of the trunk, was a tiger snake. It was slithering up to a group of herons' nests and their helpless fluffy chicks. Then, not one serpent but seven or eight were sliding across the grass towards the Tree. They were following their leader in a group assault.

———————

Where there was good there was also evil.

A deep rage came upon me. Matiu Tikiaki and Te Waretiti held back, but 'Haere mai! Come!' I yelled to Kumete and Rahui. Mr Imrie too, without thought for his life, came yelling and screaming, diverting the attention of the attacking serpents.

'Don't get too close,' I said. 'Let them see us. Let them back off by themselves.'

The snakes were startled at our intervention. Some of them had curled within them the bodies of herons they had struck while protecting their young; one was still alive, putting up a sterling fight, spitting at the snake that held it, trying with its beak to pierce the snake's brain.

The serpents reared and displayed their venom. We kept on yelling at them, 'Haere mai! Come to us instead.'

My eyes were bulging. 'Hatana,' I hissed. My body tensed. I feathered my tongue in and out of my mouth in the action the Maori call the pukana. 'Satan!' It was the same action the tiger snakes were making.

Meanwhile, the two remaining nankeen herons flapped frantically above the leader of the serpents — it had reached the tree's trunk. They slashed at it with their claws, trying to dislodge it. But it kept up its relentless ascent, coiling closer and closer to the chicks in the nests.

In desperation, I threw my tokotoko at it. 'E tu, Hatana!' The throw was too high and my stick hit some branches two feet above it. But as it clattered downward, it wedged itself in the fork of a branch, upright, between the heron chicks and the serpent.

The tiger snake saw the tokotoko — its Whanganui carvings and the representations of the spirit shapes within.

The one stared at the other.

Kanohi ki te kanohi. Eye to eye.

Angered, the tiger snake struck at the tokotoko. Coiling and recoiling, it kept on striking, striking, striking again. Finding no victory, it turned its ugly head, reared and launched itself from the branch. As it hurtled through the air I knew with dread that I would not be able to escape its fangs.

This time, Te Umuroa, you will not be so lucky.

———

The bou-mar-rang came out of nowhere.

All I heard was the swish swish *swish* of it as it came clockwise, skimming over my head. It moved from spinning on a vertical plane to spinning on the horizontal. It caught the tiger snake in its whirling hook with enough force to snap the serpent's neck. Lifeless, it fell at my feet.

'If I have to say so myself,' Harry Campbell said, 'not even one of my Aborigine mates could have done better.'

———

Ten minutes later, we were sitting below the Tree of White Flowers, recovering with a cup of Harry Campbell's bitter tea. The two nankeen herons that had survived the assault were alternately mourning their dead clan and soothing the orphan chicks.

'How will they manage?' I asked Harry Campbell.

386

'Nankeen herons share in raising their young,' Mr Imrie told me, repeating the information he had given us when we had first seen the herons. 'It doesn't matter whose young it is — that mouth gets fed.'

Harry nodded his head. 'It'll be a big job for those two blighters,' he said, referring to the two adult survivors. 'It looks like they are males, too. But I guess they'll get by—' he took a sip of his tea '—until the next attack.'

'Is there no way we can protect them?' I asked.

He scratched his head. 'Snakes can't be stopped from seeking their prey. The tree and the birds in it will continue to draw them. They will be back again. But . . .'

'There's got to be some method,' Mr Imrie said, his passion for these birds flaring in him. 'Nankeen night herons are a rarity in Van Diemen's Land.'

'We can't stop the boogahs,' Harry Campbell said, 'but we can delay them. The chicks are hatchlings at the moment and can't fly. If we give them time to grow, they'll be able to fend for themselves. Here's what we have to do . . .'

He outlined his plan. Mr Imrie agreed to it, as did Kumete, Te Waretiti and I. Although Matiu Tikiaki and Rahui blanched, they nodded their heads. 'Kei te pai.'

Armed with nets and a supply of Harry Campbell's staffs of office, we left the Tree of White Flowers and headed for the marshland. One of the night herons followed us. *What are you doing?*

'We're looking for Hatana,' I told it.

The heron waited while we searched this way and that. After a while it gave a scolding shriek: *Oh, you are all looking in the wrong place!* It flew into the hot sun, out of the immediate vicinity of the marshland, to a dusty rise where titi had once nested.

'Yup,' Harry Campbell said. 'They'll be in there, all right.'

Matiu Tikiaki paled. 'I put my hands down in holes like that to pull the muttonbirds out.'

'Count yourself lucky, mate,' Harry Campbell said. 'Now we have to flood or smoke the boogahs out. Let's first make a fence so they can't get far. Then I'll pour a bit of oil down there and light it, and when they come out, pin 'em quick with your sticks.' He wagged a finger. 'Don't miss.'

A puff of smoke at one hole, another puff at the second, another at a third, and the tiger snakes came writhing out.

Harry was overjoyed. 'I do you a favour,' he danced, 'and you do me a favour! With this lot, I'll reach my quota. You boys wouldn't like to have a job, would you?'

Matiu Tikiaki shook his head vigorously. He had been terrified by the entire experience.

'All right, my mateys,' Harry resumed. 'I think we got the lot. But just in case there are other beauties around, back to the tree we go.'

The heron followed us again. It watched as Harry Campbell took up a scythe and began to clear the grass around the tree, establishing a zone of barren earth. Its companion came down to join us.

I looked at them both. 'You have to keep the area clear yourselves now, so that you can see the snakes and get your chicks to fly off before they get to you.'

Then Harry drew from his bag a long coil of hemp rope. 'Just as well I have a lot of this stuff,' he said. 'It may keep the snakes away . . . for a little while, anyhow. You, Hohepa, would you give us a hand here?'

I looked at Kumete. 'I think the rope will be stronger if we plait it together.'

'Ka pai,' he answered.

I had then a sharp recollection of my meeting house, Te Whare Whiri-taunoka, the House of Plaited Rope. What had my father said of his role as Ngati Hau's tribal emissary? 'All I do is to take the fibres of the rope from our marae and plait and weave it with the other fibres of the kainga along the river.'

I remembered again the visit by his spirit form. 'Your job is still the same as mine but bigger. It is to bind the worlds together, the inside to the outside, the past to the present.'

'Yes, rangatira,' I addressed him tenderly, 'but you never said anything about birds!' I laughed out loud, and began to sing to myself, 'Whiria, whiria, whiria.'

Whiria, whiria, whiria?

'Yes,' I nodded, 'whiria, whiria, whiria!'

'The trouble is the hemp will have to be kept clear and spiky,' Harry Campbell said when we had finished. 'Otherwise the snakes will be able to cross over.'

'Did you hear that?' I asked the herons.

Like this? One of the herons plucked a fallen leaf off the rope.

'Yes, don't leave a pathway for Hatana to cross over.'

And like this? Pluck, and the other heron was dressing the hemp, drawing out its rough fibres to spiky needles.

'Yes,' I said. 'It's the best I can do. You'll have a lot on your plate, a lot of chicks to look after.'

What's mine is yours. What's ours is theirs. We carry on. So what's new!
They came to me, caressing my fingers. One cocked a stern eye.
I nodded. 'Protect your iwi,' I answered.

38

The next night, I tossed and turned in my sleep, dreaming of the Tree of White Flowers and the tiger snakes. I saw myself throwing the tokotoko, and the way it lodged in a bough. But *I* was the tokotoko, defending the chicks.

Along the branch Hatana came sliding. He raised his head ready to strike.

Kumete awoke me, frightened. 'Hohepa, are you alright?'

I sat up, streaming with sweat. I closed my eyes. 'Yes,' I answered. 'It was only a dream.'

Where there is evil there is good. Where there is good there is evil. Every person is offered the same choice between sin and salvation.

————

A few days later, there was much excitement when Gower received a letter from Mr George Washington Walker and our fellow New Zealander, Mr Mason.

'He aha te korero?' I asked, overhearing Gower talking to Ismay about the contents of the letter.

'Our good friends the Quakers,' he said, 'have advised us that they are with the last free group of Trowennans. They were under the care of their Methodist protector, George Robinson, who was appointed by the Government to gather them up. He transferred them to what was supposed to be their sanctuary on Flinders Island in Bass's Strait. They have a new protector now, Superintendent Robert Clark.'

He took out a map of Van Diemen's Land and spread it on the table. 'This is where Flinders is—' he pointed to an island at the very top northeast corner of the mainland '—but they are now being moved by boat to a new home.' He traced the map again. 'The boat will come down the coast, past Maria Island, and continue southward and then around the bottom of Van Diemen's Land to their new sanctuary at Oyster Bay.'

Ismay was excited and proud. 'Mr Walker has sought the permission of Governor Denison for Mr McKissock to board the boat at Maria Island and undertake a medical examination of them.'

'Nga tangata whenua?' I asked. 'They are coming home?'

'Yes,' Gower nodded. 'I will be going on the boat—' he turned to Ismay, who had that *look* on her face '—and of course Mrs McKissock will come with me!'

'Mr Walker and Mr Mason have also suggested you should come also,' Ismay added. 'Mr Mason, in particular, is adamant that you attend. He feels that the Trowennans would feel much uplifted in spirit to see a member of the Maori race among them.'

'Just me? Not the others?'

'Yes.'

———

I explained the situation to my Maori companions, and told them I was sorry they weren't coming along as well.

Although Kumete was disappointed, the others soon brought him around. 'Kei te pai,' he said after a while. 'We can take the day off, eh boys? Go fishing or put our hands down holes for titi, eh?'

In the early morning, I waited with Ismay and Gower on the Darlington jetty for the arrival of the Trowennans. Gower had come fully equipped for his medical inspections, and Ismay had with her a large leather briefcase that I hadn't seen before.

'You didn't need to bring Rollo Springvale's medical kit,' Gower said her, looking at it askance. 'I feel as if he's looking over my shoulder now.'

'Nonsense,' she answered. 'You never know, it may come in handy.'

I sensed the coming of the boat. 'Nga tangata whenua, haramai ratou,' I said to Ismay.

———

Mist lay across the Mercury Passage, but at last a whaler emerged in full sail. Gulls were circling above it, crying like lost children. As the craft came nearer, I saw clustered aboard it a colourfully clothed band of dark men and women. In their midst were the familiar figures of Mr George Washington Walker and Thomas Mason, along with a couple I did not know — I presumed them to be Mr and Mrs Robert Clark.

They were tangata whenua. I was tangata whenua. I could not help myself. I broke into a Maori waka-hauling chant:

Toia mai! Te waka! Ki te urunga! Te waka! Ki te moenga!
Te waka! Ki te takotoranga i takoto ai, te waka!'

I was not surprised when Ismay joined in on the final lines:

Pull the boat in! The boat! To its resting place! The boat!
To its landing! Pull it in to its harbour, the boat!

The whaler came to the jetty, a little too fast, hitting it; the tangata whenua on board cried in alarm, steadying themselves and then laughing.

I saw the captain come to look at the damage; his name was Captain Falwasser. He shook his head, looked at us and said, 'This bloody morning tide.' He motioned a sailor to put down a plank so that we could board. 'Come quickly now,' he said.

Gower went first, then held out an arm for Ismay. But the tide was contrary and widened the distance — the plank fell into the sea. Quickly, I gathered her into my arms, jumped across the gap and delivered her to him.

'Thank you, Te Umuroa,' Gower said.

The boat made way again.

———

'Hohepa,' Thomas Mason greeted me. We embraced in the hongi, and then he made way for me to make my greeting to Mr Walker.

I expected both Mr Mason and Mr Walker to be in good spirits. After all, weren't they returning the tangata whenua to their ancestral homeland? But one look at their faces told me a different story. 'Welcome to you,' Mr Walker said. He seemed curiously subdued, his face pale and drawn. 'Look you, Maori chief, upon the sad remnants of a bygone race.'

I began to grieve then. 'Is this all of them?' I asked. They were such a small group, becoming unsettled at my gaze and moving away.

'Yes,' Thomas Mason answered. 'They are the surviving remnants of a nation's dead. They tread upon their nation's tomb and are merely exchanging one burial place for another.' His words were chilling.

'How many are there?' I asked.

'Fourteen adult males,' Mr Walker began, 'twenty-two adult females, three boys and five girls.'

'Forty-four in all,' Thomas Mason continued. 'Yet they were here for tens of thousands of years before the arrival of Europeans.'

I could not believe it. When I looked at them again I wondered: Was I staring at the fate of my own Maori race? Then I saw that *they* were staring at me!

'They are surprised by your height,' Mr Walker said. 'You are much taller than most of the Europeans on board the ship.'

The tangata whenua also appeared fascinated by my half-tattooed face. Little by little they became bolder, coming close to me and exclaiming with excited voices in a tongue that sounded like a babbling river.

Most of them were small with spindly legs and protruding abdomens; the tallest reached only to my chest. How could Pakeha ever have thought they were dangerous? They looked well enough for a people who had been in exile, but their eyes lacked light, as if whatever spark of resistance had died years ago. All wore conical woollen caps on their close-cropped heads. One woman wore a blue woollen dress with a bright leather strap around her waist; another wore a printed dress. Their body smell was musky but not unsweet.

They had dogs with them; small and mangy, they held back as if they had been as whipped by life as their owners.

Four of the women pushed themselves through the crowd to stand in front of me. 'Introduce us,' one of them asked Mr Walker. She was smaller than the rest, just a little over four feet. She was probably in her forties, but her beauty was still clearly apparent. Her eyes were enormous.

Mr Walker nodded. 'These ladies are Emma, Flora, Wapperty and—' he turned to the small woman '—this is Trucanini. She and her husband Woureddy helped Mr Robinson in his mission of persuasion.'

I saw a flicker of defiance blaze in Trucanini's eyes as he spoke.

'But we've forgiven her,' the woman called Wapperty said with a laugh. 'Eh, girls?'

———

The winds were capricious and contrary and the sea frothy as Captain Falwasser sailed the whaler out of the Mercury Passage and into the stretch of open sea. The sylvan coast was clothed in magnificent forest.

Gower set up a tent with a private canvas inner room as a medical inspection post at the stern of the whaler. Ismay was with him, sitting with Mrs Clark at a desk. I leant against a railing, watching as Mr Clark, Thomas Mason and Mr Walker moved among the tangata whenua, trying to encourage them to come to the inspection. Whenever they engaged someone, that person would move away; sailors were standing by, laughing at their attempts.

'They'll never get anybody that way,' a male voice said. It was one of the tangata whenua; he joined me at the rail. 'You must be a Maori,' he continued.

'How can you tell?'

'I've met a coupla you fella,' he answered, 'and only you fella does the war dance like the one at Maria Island. My name is William. My surname is Lanney. You rub the nose with me?'

I pressed my nose to his, and Wapperty, sitting nearby and puffing on a clay pipe with Emma, Flora and Trucanini, called out, 'Give us the Maori kiss, too.' Emma and Trucanini almost choked, roaring with earthy laughter.

'Our people are not so nervous of you now,' William Lanney said. 'You one of us, eh. But as for the white fella . . .' The rest of the women and the children still held back from the Europeans on board. 'And you have the Maori talking stick,' he continued, pointing to my tokotoko.

'Yes,' I answered. 'It belonged to my father. Now it belongs to me.'

He nodded, satisfied. He saw me watching Ismay; she had joined Thomas Mason and Mr Walker in attempting to encourage the people to accept inspection by Gower.

'Is that your woman?' William Lanney asked.

'No,' I answered, surprised. 'She is Mrs McKissock.'

He shook his head. 'She might belong to him but she supposed to be yours. You and her sing well together. Both of you are one soul.' He put his hands together in a tight clasp.

'But she is not one of us,' I said.

'No,' he answered. 'Bloody bad luck eh?'

'Yes,' I said. 'Bloody bad luck.'

I saw Ismay give a sign of exasperation.

'Listen,' I said to William Lanney, 'the doctor wants to examine your people. Could you persuade them to let him?'

'I dunno,' he answered. 'Every time white fella poke and prod and measure, we wonder whether they measuring black fella's head or bones to show in a glass case.'

'I can vouch for Mr McKissock,' I said. 'He is a good man.'

William Lanney paused. 'All right,' he said. 'I will go first and maybe the others will follow but if my head end up in a white fella's museum, my ghost come after ya.' Thus my new friend, William Lanney, provided the example. He strolled up to Ismay and asked, 'Looking for me, missus?'

Gladly she took him to the makeshift medical post. She sat down and, with Mr and Mrs Clark assisting, began to ask William Lanney's details for the medical register. 'Your name, sir?'

Mr Clark had a tape measure in his hand. He started to take William Lanney's height and chest, hip and buttock measurements. But it was only when he looped the tape around William Lanney's skull that I felt a sense of alarm.

Somebody had just walked across William Lanney's grave.

William Lanney rolled his eyes — and the tangata whenua all laughed. The merriment mounted when Gower asked him to poke out his tongue, and looked into his eyes and ears. He had always appeared to me to be such a dour man that it was a pleasant surprise to see him getting into the spirit of things. He started to make faces at William Lanney, opening his mouth wide with his fingers and poking out his tongue, and then pretending to look in his own hair for nits. And when he asked William Lanney to move into the private canvas anteroom for an internal inspection, well, he farted . . .

Loudly!

'Mr McKissock!' Ismay exclaimed, 'we are in polite company!'

Mr and Mrs Clark mimed their own dismay as they dashed for fresh air. And then Gower's wind floated downwind to where I was standing with the tangata whenua.

He had definitely had beans for breakfast.

After that, *all* the barriers came down. The tangata whenua submitted for inspection, and I saw that when they disrobed, some were tattooed in a very curious manner: the skin was raised so as to form a kind of relief. One man, called Binggo, had a burnt patch in the centre of his chest and fourteen parallel slashes on his right side and left. 'They were given to me,' he said when I asked how he had got them, 'to mark my passage from boy to man. After, I was allowed to have my first woman—' He looked over at one of the women and laughed. 'Eh Ruby!'

'Was that your cock that sneaked into me that night?' the woman called back. 'Honestly girls,' she said to some of the others, 'I hardly felt it.'

Gales of laughter ricocheted around the group. I saw that Ismay and Gower took the ribald repartee in good part; Mr and Mrs Clark, and Thomas Mason and Mr Walker, being Quakers, reddened slightly, but then smiled in acceptance.

I moved to Mr Clark's side. 'They are laughing,' I said to him.

'Yes,' he said after a moment. 'It is good to see them enjoying themselves.'

Indeed it was — for what violent history, not known to me, had they endured?

Even Gower was disturbed as he catalogued not only their own tribal scarring but also the scars caused by whips, knives and, in some cases, bullets.

'The white fella did this one,' another of the tangata whenua, Reggie, said to me, pointing at one wound after another. With deep shining eyes he pointed at Captain Falwasser and the sailors. 'Not You-Fella,' he said, to distinguish me as one apart. '*Them*-Fella.'

———

When at last Gower's inspections finished, he joined me at the stern.

'It was certainly the best suggestion to bring you along,' he said. 'You are earning your keep!'

We stood together watching the tangata whenua. Then he turned to me and, hesitating, began to speak. 'The last time we talked, you said something to me that I haven't been able to get out of my mind . . . about vulnerability. Why did you say that?'

'I have great aroha for you, Mr McKissock,' I began, 'but I also have great impatience. You are a good and decent man but, like all the rest of us, you are lost in Rarohenga.'

'Rarohenga?' he asked.

'It is the World Beyond,' I began, 'the Outer World. Indeed, you remind me of Mataora who, while living in Our World, mistreated his wife Niwareka. She fled across the ocean to Rarohenga and he was obliged to go after her. He sought entrance from Kuwatawata, the guardian of the gateway between both worlds, and found her. He asked her forgiveness and she returned with him to Our World again.'

Gower took in my words. 'Do all Maori speak . . . obliquely . . . as you do?'

'Yes,' I answered. 'Our korero is like our reo, our words, having many meanings.'

'We have a story that is similar to yours,' he continued. 'It has to do with a man called Orpheus who is separated from his wife when she is bitten by a poisonous snake. After his wife Eurydice's funeral, he descends into Hades to bring her back to the world of the living.'

'Does he do it?'

'Alas, no,' Gower answered. 'Although the gods have warned him not to look at Eurydice until they get to the surface, her entreaties of "Do you love me?" make him gaze upon her and he gives the answer, yes. But he loses her forever.'

———

The whaler continued southward. The weather turned unfavourable, and the water treacherous; Captain Falwasser did his best as the ship heaved this way and that. The tangata whenua huddled miserably on deck, and their

396

dogs whined in misery. Only William Lanney, Binggo and the four ladies, Wapperty, Flora, Emma and Trucanini, had their sea-legs.

We changed tack and headed westward, crossing the busy shipping lane where commercial ships, sails straining against the spar-breaking wind, exited the Derwent River. They were having a hard time of the sea too, sailing against the wind to make the open sea.

The day became stormier, and rain pelted the open deck. Captain Falwasser ordered his sailors to unroll a canvas roof and the tangata whenua took shelter beneath it. Some of them were seasick now; Gower ministered to them as best he could. The four ladies, Wapperty, Flora, Emma and Trucanini, joined their whanau sheltering from the weather. Then Wapperty called out to me, William Lanney and Binggo where we were standing, enjoying the elements and each other's company. 'Come and join us, Maori fella,' she said. 'We won't bite.'

'Speak for yourself,' interjected Flora.

'Me and Binggo better accompany you for your protection,' William Lanney winked.

We huddled together under the tarpaulin. I hadn't realised how wet I was until Emma started to give me a rubdown. Then Wapperty slapped her hands as they began to wander further south than they should, and she gave me a blanket to wrap around my shoulders.

I don't know how long it was before I started to speak to them. And when I did, I don't think my question was a surprise to them. 'I want to know what happened,' I said.

They looked at me with glowing eyes. *Don't you know?*

'The same thing that happened to you Maori fellas,' William Lanney began. He pointed at some of the sailors. 'They fell from the sky. They turned our land into a ghost island — full of ghosts, many many ghosts.'

Emma, Flora and Wapperty began to hum, a strange, dissonant, uneasy sound. William Lanney offered me a puff of his pipe. I coughed when I drew the smoke in. He urged me to take another puff. The tobacco was infused with some kind of herb, pungent, acrid — I don't know what it was, but it began to . . . *shift* things. That's the only way I can describe it. I passed it to Trucanini.

'Keep me out of this,' she said.

Wapperty began to speak. Her voice sounded as if it was both outside me and inside me. 'You really want to know what happened to us, Maori fella?' she asked. 'Governor George Arthur happened to us. He was the boss man of Van Diemen's Land, and he was worried — so he said — that we were being killed off by the settlers. Being the boss man, he decided we should be gathered together so that we could be put in a safe place far from trouble, far from making trouble.'

'It was the big round-up,' Emma said.

'But they had to catch us first,' William Lanney added.

He blew smoke over me. I coughed again, tried to wave the smoke away, and when I did I was looking into the past.

'It was Arthur,' William Lanney began, 'who came up with the plan. "We will draw a military cordon over the island, from St Mary's on the east coast of Deloraine, halfway across the island, and then southward to the Derwent. Then we will drive the Aborigines into a corner of Van Diemen's Land where they can't get out."'

Wapperty took up the story. 'Arthur didn't have enough soldiers to form the Black Line,' she said. 'He asked others for help — and two thousand people came. They formed a human chain and began their big drive, pushing us from the north all the way down towards Tasman Peninsula. Then they could shut their gate, quick, and we'd be *in*.'

'I was one of five children in my hearth clan,' William Lanney said. 'I was sleeping beside our campfire. My father woke up. I saw him look at the sky. He saw the birds flying. He put his ear to the ground. He motioned us to do the same. We all heard the same sound: the white fellas were coming. Quickly we broke camp. We got to the top of a ridge and looked back. The bush was moving. The drove had started. The treetops would shiver and then, as whatever was passing through went by, they were still again.'

'Of course,' Wapperty continued, 'many white fellas said they only joined because they thought it was the only way to save the black fella. But other white fellas, why, they thought it was just like a shooting party. They had muskets and handcuffs, and we were animals, like game.'

'That first morning my father told us to move,' William Lanney said, 'was just the beginning of the terror. Every morning we would wake up and listen to the ground. And very soon we could hear the white fellas' dogs barking. Very soon, we came across other black fellas, caught like us in the drove.'

'We weren't the only ones being pushed ahead,' Emma added. 'All nature was disturbed. Not only the birds but the animals moving in the same direction as us: wallabies, kangaroos — and snakes too, slithering through our feet without striking at us.'

'You can't tell me the white fella was not determined to capture us,'

William Lanney said. 'Plenty of horsemen, plenty of soldiers, plenty of big fires on the hills.'

'Do you know how long the Line lasted?' Flora asked. 'Two months, my Maori friend! Two months of headlong panic, with the white-fella beating the brush and making the big noise to frighten us, stretching from the sea on the left to the Derwent River on the right. None of us could escape except through the line of beaters.'

'One day my father stopped our kin group,' William Lanney said. '"We can't run away any more," he told us. He consulted the other hearth clans and kin groups. "Wait. Don't move any further." He wanted to scout the white fella. He made himself invisible and went back to one of their camps as they rested for the night; their dogs almost sniffed him. He heard one of the officers boasting to some of his men: "Once we drive them onto Forestier Peninsula, we will have them." When my father got back he told us the news. "If we keep going forward we will be caught in the white fellas' trap."

'"We can't retreat either," I said. "Can we escape from the sides?"

'"No," my father said. "We will have to go into the ground or into the air." Then he looked at the moon. "There is another way," he told us.'

Into the ground? Into the air?

'It was thanks to my father that we were able to escape the Line,' William Lanney said. 'The moon was waning, and we knew that two nights later it would be just a sickle in the night sky. There must have been about a hundred in our group now. My father told us to smear mud everywhere over our bodies, so that the dogs would not pick up our smell. He told us to cover ourselves with leaves from the bush so that we would become the very forest itself. We were lucky. On the night we broke through the Line, the wind was blowing from the land to the sea — we kept to the seaward side and were able to slip through without the dogs picking up our scent. We were happy and excited, but my father hushed us. "Don't talk. Don't look back," he said. 'Not until midday did he let us stop. He looked back at the Line, the shivering trees, the birds flying before the drovers. I wanted to shout with joy. But my father stopped me. "You don't understand," he said. "This is not the end. This is the beginning of the end. Run, my son. Run as fast as you can. Get away. Keep going. Don't stop. One day the white fella will get you, but be free for as long as you can. Breathe the air."'

Silence fell.

Wapperty began to snort. 'I wish I'd been there when the white fellas closed the Line and joined together at the Tasman Peninsula! All they caught was one old man and a boy!'

As the others enjoyed the moment, I became aware of Trucanini. Silent until now, she stood up and, with a quick movement, went out onto the rainswept deck.

'Was she one of you trying to escape the Black Line?' I asked.

'No,' William Lanney answered. His voice was mysterious. 'She came later.'

39

My head was spinning so much from the effects of the tangata whenua's tobacco that I didn't notice at first that Captain Falwasser had changed the whaler's course; it was tacking towards the shore.

Then I saw Mr and Mrs Clark standing at the rail — a look of absolute dread on their faces — and I knew that Oyster Cove lay ahead. Very soon Ismay and Gower joined them, and I saw Ismay give Mrs Clark an embrace of comfort.

'How will we survive here?' I heard Mrs Clark ask. 'How will *they* survive?'

Gower saw me sitting with the tangata whenua. 'Hohepa! There you are!'

'You had better go,' Wapperty said. She and the others were still in their drug-induced stupor.

———

Unsteady on my feet, I staggered from the canvas shelter.

I had my first glimpse of the cove. It was hemmed in by steep hills to the south, west and north, flat with foothills between. The reserve set aside for the tangata whenua was lightly timbered with a dense, low scrub. Only a small area of it was cleared, and there I could see several buildings, including the bare stone wharenui where the tangata whenua would live. At the western end of the sweeping bay I glimpsed a freshwater creek.

'Well, it's not paradise is it?' Gower tried to joke. 'What have you been talking about with the Trowennans?'

'They've been telling me about the Black Line.'

'Ah,' he nodded. 'You know, we had something similar in the Highland

Clearances. My mother, Ailie, and her clan were moved off their land by the Ban mhorair Chataibh, the Great Lady of Sutherland. The removals came to be known as Bliadhna an Losgaidh, the Year of the Burnings.'

'You are not comparing that pain with this pain?' I asked angrily.

'No,' he answered, taken aback. 'But I can understand the plight of the Trowennans, just as you can. My mother's people were forced to emigrate to Canada. The Trowennans are being shifted from one place of exile to another.'

'So the settlers of Van Diemen's Land have achieved what they really wanted,' I said to him.

'What is that?' Gower asked. He was defensive and as angry as I was.

'Please, Hohepa,' Ismay pleaded. 'You make us sound as if we are on the other side.'

'They wanted—' I began '—no, *you* wanted an empty land to occupy. Terra Nullius, is that what you call it? Congratulations, today you have truly achieved it.'

'That is unfair, Te Umuroa,' Gower said, 'and as hurtful as the other occasion when you associated me and Mrs McKissock with the savagery of the lash. You congratulated me on finding my humanity. I suggest you find yours.'

———

And so one burial place, as Mr Walker had put it, was exchanged for another.

Captain Falwasser moored close by a barque which had come from Port Arthur to collect the convict labourers; over the past six months they had been building the settlement under the supervision of a small military guard of four very young-looking soldiers.

Mr Walker and Thomas Mason joined us all at the rail. 'We should get you off now,' Mr Walker said to Mr and Mrs Clark, 'together with your charges and their supplies.' He would not look them in the eye.

The tangata whenua preceded us. They were pleased to feel the earth. 'Come on, girls!' Wapperty said.

The captain and soldiers and some of the convicts looked at the women with distaste as, with little cries of delight, they began to race about investigating their new home. 'Look at the fookin' black bitches,' one of the convicts, a bald-headed man, sneered. They were agile, leaping and springing and pecking like kiwi, the flightless bird of my homeland. The dogs added to the excitement by running hither and thither among them.

As for me, I felt myself raging. The wharenui for the tangata whenua was grey, bleak and unwelcoming. It stood amid mudflats and coarse grass; a saltmarsh oozed nearby. There was no shelter from the winds of the god Tawhirimatea; only clusters of breakwinds that he could easily sweep aside. Beyond the wharenui, a desolate swamp stretched towards the sea.

I helped Captain Falwasser, the sailors and convicts with the unloading. Captain Worthington, Sergeant Dalton, Corporal Baines and Private Lister introduced themselves to Mr and Mrs Clark, and then escorted them and the others on an inspection. By the time the unloading had been completed, they had finished their tour.

Mr Walker was fuming. 'It is more like a barracks,' he said to Captain Worthington. 'The rooms where the Aborigines will sleep are much too low and uncomfortable. The small windows will give very poor light and worse ventilation.'

The captain muttered his apologies. 'I was not the architect, sir.'

'What are we to do?' Mr Clark asked.

'I will report to the lieutenant-governor and insist on remedial work,' Mr Walker answered. 'Meantime, let's put the best face on the situation and settle the Aborigines in. Ladies, would you be so kind as to supervise the matting and help unroll the bedding . . .'

Mrs Clark looked despairingly at Ismay.

'Let's just do as all women do,' Ismay responded tenderly, 'and make the best of it.'

———

Night was falling by the time we had completed the work.

Captain Worthington ordered Sergeant Dalton to break out the rations which had earlier been dropped off at the cove: beef and pork, biscuits and flour and, as a special treat, tobacco. Mrs Clark, Ismay and one of the soldiers — Corporal Baines, who was a cook as well as a guard — organised the evening meal.

Mr Walker said to Mr Clark, 'Will you offer a prayer of thanksgiving, sir?'

The karakia was like a lost dove trying to find its way to Heaven. After it, we sat down in fellowship to dinner — Captain Worthington, his soldiers, convicts, the captain and sailors, Mr and Mrs Clark, Ismay and Gower and all.

I was sitting next to Gower. 'I apologise, e hoa,' I said to him, 'for my remarks on the whaler.'

'We are all upset about the Trowennans' situation,' he answered. 'But wouldn't friends speak to each other with honesty? Had we been boys in Edinburgh I think I would have sought you out to be such a friend.'

The night fell quickly, as if a dark bird had flown over the cove and spread its black wings completely over it.

After the meal, Corporal Baines took out his fiddle and began to play a Highland reel. By the flickering light of the fire, the Pakeha danced on the beach with the tangata whenua. Or, rather, the soldier scraped to their dancing, the Pakeha hopped to his fiddling, and the tangata whenua dipped and flew with quick, angular movements and gesticulations.

I stayed on the perimeter with William Lanney and Wapperty, clapping our hands to the music. I couldn't keep my eyes off Ismay, enchanted by her gaiety and laughter as she danced with one tangata whenua after another — and then with Gower in a merry jig. When the dance was over, she gave a mock bow and collapsed into his arms.

'I told you before,' William Lanney said, 'she should be your woman, not his woman. She knows, you know, but *he* doesn't know.'

I refused to be drawn into responding.

'You escaped the Black Line,' I asked, anxious to change the subject but also to hear out William Lanney's story. 'How then did the white man gather you all together and take you to Flinders Island?'

'He clever fella,' William Lanney said. 'He tried another way. He contracted a kindly man—' his lip curled '—to attempt by conciliation what the capture parties had failed to do. And most of us had grown tired of running, eh.'

'His name was George Augustus Robinson,' Wapperty said. 'He looked like the pictures of God that the mission stations had on their walls. He had a few friendly Aborigines—'

'Trucanini and her husband Woureddy?' I asked, remembering Mr Walker's earlier reference to them.

'Them two, yes,' William Lanney answered.

Ah, so that was where she fitted into the picture.

'Did you know her mother, Mangana, was a chief?' Wapperty asked. 'No? Well, chiefly status could not save her from murder at the hands of whalers. Trucanini witnessed it. She also saw her sister raped and shot by whalers and her husband-to-be murdered by timberfellers. She too was raped by the white man, when she was still young.'

Wapperty recited all this as if it was to be expected in the life of a tangata whenua woman. Then she added, 'But you should ask her yourself.'

Not that night. It was eight o'clock and the time for celebration, such as it was, was over.

Even at Oyster Cove, prison regulations were observed.

I think we must all have spent an uneasy night. I bunked down with the convicts, sheltering in the barque, the vessel which had come to collect them from the cove. One of my companions was a young Irish boy called Quilter, who groaned so much that Gower had to be called for.

'He has an inflamed appendix,' Gower told Captain Worthington. 'When you return to Port Arthur, it must be seen to immediately.'

Another companion was a bald-headed prisoner — his name was Galvin — who kept on swearing all night. 'Fookin' weather, fookin' cunt of a country, fookin' Quilter shut your groaning gob willya?'

The wind shrieked and shrilled as if demons were gathering. It was not a good place.

The next morning, our departure was perilously delayed. Mr and Mrs Clark were clearly upset at the thought of being left behind and kept pressing Mr Walker to stay longer.

And we were *all* leaving, not just our whaler but also the barque with the convicts along with their guard detachment aboard. The loading of equipment and supplies on the Port Arthur barque seemed to go on and on.

All the while, Captain Falwasser and the captain of the convict barque — his name was Captain Bentley — were watching the weather.

It was during a break in the loading, when I was taking a drink of water at the pump, that I was able to speak, finally, to Trucanini.

'Kia ora, e kui,' I said.

She looked at me. I could not read her emotions. 'They were talking about me to you last night, eh, Maori fella?' she asked.

I felt great aroha for her — for what had happened to her as a young girl and what was happening to her now — and for her guilt at the part she had unwittingly played in the exile of the tangata whenua.

'They still blame me for what happened,' she flared, 'but it was not my fault. When Robinson came to see me and Woureddy he guaranteed that, by treaty, if black fellas moved from the mainland we would be given peace and our own sovereignty on Wybalenna.'

'Wybalenna?'

'That's our name for Flinder's Island.'

'How did you help him?'

'We surrendered to Robinson,' Trucanini said. 'We became his faithful servants in persuading all the other black fellas to give themselves up. Robinson was like the Pied Piper in the story I was told once when I was a girl. We walked over four thousand miles, we reckon, and gradually we won over their confidence. And when we had all the black fellas, we took them to Wybalenna.'

'Was life on Wybalenna good to you?'

Trucanini waved her arms at the others. 'Good? My Woureddy died, along with all the others. Here we all are, and it is twelve years later. Judge for yourself, Maori warrior: most of us died from despair, poor food and the coughing. That's why we petitioned Queen Victoria to get us out of Wybalenna. You think it's easy for me to know I'm to blame for so many deaths, all because I believed in a treaty? Is forty-four survivors a good thing?'

She began to shake. I embraced her. 'It was not your fault,' I said.

'Yes it was,' she answered. 'I should never have believed the talk of a treaty. And now look at us. This will be our last resting place.'

'No . . .' I tried to comfort her.

She stared at me. 'Don't you have eyes, Maori fella? Yes, we have a few children, but how long do you think they will survive here? And when they die, can't you see that all us women have moved beyond child-bearing?'

———

Oh and I began to howl.

I had truly descended to the very depths of Rarohenga and could go no further. I grieved so loudly that Trucanini put her hands over my mouth to stop from attracting the soldiers' attention. The tangata whenua crowded around me.

'I can't leave you here,' I wept.

Wapperty looked over my shoulder and said something strange. 'You and your father can't save us. Go back to your world and look after your own.'

Tenderly, she said to me, 'Fuck off.'

40

It was time to go.

Squally winds were scattering foam across the beach, revealing an onshore wind that would make it difficult to get out of the cove.

There was a new problem. The plan had been for all the convicts to return to Port Arthur on the small snub-nosed barque that was rolling heavily in the surf. It had all the unused slabs of stone and timber aboard, and now there were more convicts than could be safely carried. I counted fifteen aboard and another fifteen to be loaded.

Captain Worthington was clearly bothered by the situation. He called the two ships' captains into consultation with him. After much shaking of heads — and then nodding of agreement — a decision was reached.

'Sir,' Captain Worthington said to Mr Walker. 'Your captain has kindly agreed to take fifteen of our convicts on your ship, with me and Private Lister as their overseer.' He turned to Sergeant Dalton and Corporal Baines, 'Proceed to the barque, gentlemen, and enchain the convicts.'

But another dilemma presented itself. Quilter, the Irish prisoner with the inflamed appendix, had just boarded the barque — and he gave a short cry of pain.

'I had best accompany him,' Gower sighed. 'If his condition worsens, he may need treatment.'

Events unfolded quickly. Gower pressed Ismay to him and hastened to the barque; he was the last man on. We watched anxiously as the ship made way, wallowing in the shifting surf and, finally, forcing through the incoming breakers.

Ten minutes later, it was our turn. As we left, the tangata whenua shrank to small waving figures clustered around Mr and Mrs Clark, waving.

It was then that I turned to Ismay with the question which had been bothering me all morning.

'Ever since my fellow Maori and I have been in Van Diemen's Land,' I said, 'we have been kindly treated by the Europeans. But why — when they treat their own tangata whenua so poorly? *Why!*'

———

Despite the contrary winds, the whaler was able to make good headway through the thundering surf and, once clear, bore away to eastward.

We soon caught up with the barque. It was managing to keep its heading, but it was struggling as the squalls turned to fierce rain.

'What does the weather matter?' Ismay asked, lifting her face to the rain and licking the drops as they ran into her mouth. I knew what she meant. Free of Gower's presence, the elements seemed to charge both of us; they made us tingle. And the swell was like music, crescendo following crescendo, rising and falling in time to the sea's great underwater bellows.

There was nobody to see us when I reached for her hand. She held it. Leant against me. 'Hohepa . . .'

———

Then it happened. The lookout called, 'There they blow!'

Coming up from astern was an undulating mass, a pod of over fifty sperm whales, some sixty feet in length, with smaller calves among them.

'Oh, Hohepa,' Ismay began, 'aren't they . . . ?'

In the face of their magnificence, words failed her.

Very soon, the whales were all around us, tightly packed, mounting the waves. When some rose, others fell. The spray from their spouts spumed upwards, creating rainbows in the air. One ascended right next to the whaler and Ismay tried to reach out and touch it.

'*No,* Ismay,' I said.

I don't know why I stopped her like that.

The ship rocked violently as, like some thundering herd, the whales went ahead of us through illuminated rainbow gateways, their giant flukes propelling them through the sea.

———

The barque lay ahead, in the great pod's pathway.

'Look!' cried one of the convicts.

Through the rain I saw that the whales were crowding the vessel, driving it in front of them. Some quirk of wind, current or fate caused it to turn broadside — and one of the whales, caught in the middle of the rampaging pathway, lifted the barque astride its massive bulk.

Another two following whales crowded under it.

A fourth whale, in exhilaration, breached . . .

Plunging down, the beast struck the barque with its monstrous tail. Amid the quaking sea it rolled, snapping its mast with a sickening crack.

'Gower!' Ismay screamed.

Then we could see no more as the spray of the departing whales obscured the vessel entirely.

Captain Falwasser immediately made full speed for the barque, and we reached the place of the disaster within minutes. The vessel was floating upside down in the agitated sea, but we could see that some of the sailors had managed to jump clear. We pulled them aboard.

Ismay was frantic, her voice loud and insistent. 'Where are the others?'

'They are under the barque,' one of the sailors gasped. He was the only one who seemed capable of speech. 'Sergeant Dalton is trying to unchain them. I think Corporal Baines and three of the convicts are dead, smacked by the whale. So are some of my mates—'

Ismay was frantic. 'What about Mr McKissock?'

'Last I saw of him, he was helping Sergeant Dalton.'

Even as he spoke, one of the convicts, released from his chains, emerged at the surface. 'You're a devil, Worthington,' he yelled, 'for chaining us with lock and key! Good men will go to a watery grave today.'

'Gower?' Ismay called. 'Gower!'

Gower?

Yes, no matter their relationship, Ismay loved him.

I dived into the heaving sea. With a few strokes I reached the overturned barque. There, I dived again, kicking down and under it. Drowned men, sailors, were floating around me, and there was Corporal Baines, his eyes opened, surprised into death.

I saw, like a ghastly drifting branch of seaweed, three drowned convicts. With horror I realised they were attached to the one long chain; their combined weight was threatening to pull the others, still trapped inside in the bubble of air, to drown with them.

I surfaced under the vessel and found Sergeant Dalton and Gower trying to release the remaining ten convicts.

'We're going to die,' cried Galvin, the bald-headed convict, 'like fookin' rats, without ever again seeing the sun.'

'Sergeant Dalton,' I yelled, 'the men, as you release them, must take up the chain's slack for their mates. Once everyone is unchained, then we can go up to the surface together.'

'Fook you, you black booger!' yelled Galvin, 'I'm getting out of here now.'

One of his fellows, larger than he was, grabbed him and snarled, 'You stay, you snivelling coward.'

Oh, it was such a slow job for Sergeant Dalton. He had to unlock four padlocks on each convict, diving underwater to reach their leg-irons, before he could release them from the chain.

The barque's timbers were creaking around our heads; water was pouring faster in; we were all panicking.

'We don't have much time, Mr Dalton,' Gower said.

'I'm going as fast as I can. Do you think *I* want to drown?'

Someone popped up between us and gave a huge gasp, choking and coughing and reaching for a handhold. It was Mr Thomas Mason. 'Captain Worthington had another key; Mrs McKissock ordered me to bring it down. You must hurry.'

'Give it to me,' Gower said. He joined Sergeant Dalton in undoing the locks on the remaining prisoners. His fingers were wet, cold, and shaking and he was screaming at the key, 'Go in, go *in*, you bastard.'

And then it was done. 'At the count of three,' Gower said to the convicts, let go the chain — one, two, *three*.'

Released, the chain that held their drowned comrades curled slowly away into the dark sea, taking the bodies down with them.

'Now can we fookin' leave?' Galvin asked.

'Yes,' Gower yelled. 'You go first, Mr Mason, *now*.'

Sergeant Dalton and Galvin left with him struggling out of the belly of the barque. The others quickly followed, leaving only Gower and me to follow. But just as we were leaving the little space that had been our saviour we heard a great cracking and splintering. Water began pouring in all around us. One of the stone slabs snapped its ropes and, plunging downward, dealt Gower a crushing blow.

'My leg—' he screamed.

A huge swell filled the vessel, and down, down, down it plummeted, stern first. The water came rushing in. I felt the pressure changing in my ears.

———

The bubble of air was no longer.

Gower and I were drowning.

Holding back panic, I signed to him. *Get out before we're taken into the prodigious depths.*

He signed back. On his face was great pain: *Save yourself.*

Oh, I could have done that — left him there, gone to the surface. I made my choice, just as Ismay had done when she cried, 'Gower!'

I grabbed him and pulled him out of the plunging vessel. The currents swirled dangerously around the barque, threatening to pull us down with it into the dark depths of the sea. I steadied myself. The barque disappeared beneath us.

E hoa, me haere taua. Friend, let us arise now.

With Gower in my arms, I began our slow ascent to the shimmering light. Every now and then I signed to him, *E tu,* stop, to let air out of his lungs and wait before we proceeded.

But at some point in our upward flight he ran out of air altogether. *Homai ki ahau.* I gave him short bursts of air from my lungs.

I didn't think we would make it. But I knew I could not leave him, even if I sacrificed myself in the process. I would not abandon him.

It was what Ismay wanted. It was also what *I* wanted.

Then *I* ran out of air.

From the depths came a last broiling of air from the barque. It buoyed us up. And I arose with Gower, screaming in pain, to the surface of the sea.

41

Eager hands plucked us from the water.

Gower was gasping for breath and moaning with pain. 'My leg ... my leg ...' When the sailors hauled him aboard, he collapsed in agony on the deck.

As soon as Ismay saw blood seeping through his trousers, and the unnatural angle at which his leg was splayed, she knew the worst. Grabbing a knife, she cut the cloth away to reveal the damage. As soon as his leg was exposed, she swayed. One of the watching sailors ran to the side of the ship and retched.

From the knee down, the leg was crushed. I could see the bone was entirely fractured in several places. Blood was spurting from the artery.

'Give me your belt,' Ismay said to a sailor. Using it as a tourniquet, she tied it tightly above Gower's knee to staunch the blood's flow.

There was mayhem aboard the whaler. We now had extra convicts on board, and Gower and the other injured men from the barque lying on the deck. Captain Worthington and his soldiers were trying to restore order among the convicts.

Ismay helped Gower to a sitting position. Although he was still disoriented, he wanted to make his own assessment of his leg. 'Let me see the damage for myself,' he said. One look and a terrible expression of resignation came over him. 'The leg will have to be amputated,' he said. 'It's beyond repair. He looked at Mr Walker and Mr Mason, who had gathered next to Ismay. 'Gentlemen, you must take me to Hobart Town.'

'You have already lost too much blood,' Ismay said.

'Then get me there as quick as you can.' He was gasping with the pain.

'Mr McKissock, you won't last the distance,' Ismay said.

'There's nobody qualified to do an amputation here,' he exploded. 'Can you, Mr Walker? Mr Mason? Captain Worthington? Is there any among the convicts who can do it? No. My best chance is to be speedily operated on in Hobart Town.'

He had not reckoned with Ismay's determination. 'Gentlemen,' she said to all of us, 'will you assist me? Hohepa, I will need you to hold Mr McKissock down.'

'What do you think you're *doing*, Ismay?' Gower yelled.

She kissed him on the forehead. 'You can help me with instructions. You know as well as I do that this is the only way.'

He shook his head, but began to groan — and he closed his eyes and nodded. 'All right,' he said.

Different surgeons have different procedures. A surgeon would be well advised to develop a facility in a number of them and apply the one which is most suitable for the surgery to hand. One rule, however, is paramount: the amputation should be done in as quick a time as possible so as to minimise the pain to the patient and the shock to his system.

The wind and rain were howling around the deck as Ismay opened her uncle's briefcase of instruments. I looked at them with horror. I had never seen such a collection of knives, saws and needles before; they looked like tools of torture and not medical instruments at all.

'We must all work as a team,' Ismay said to us, tightening the tourniquet. 'Mr Mason, kindly lift Mr McKissock's leg in the vertical. Mr Walker and Captain Worthington, please ensure that you hold him down; he must not be allowed to move. Te Umuroa, would you sit behind Mr McKissock; grasp him around the shoulders and, if he struggles, do not let him go.'

She clamped her left hand across his thigh and picked up a knife. She closed her eyes briefly, as if saying a prayer. 'Are you ready, Mr McKissock?'

He nodded. 'Locate the place of election,' he said. 'Just above the knee.'

She swayed. 'I will make the election below the knee.' Perspiration was beading her brow.

'No! It must be above the knee. Ismay . . .'

Gower was still arguing when she made a rapid movement — the first cut. Astonished, he gave a loud cry. 'Ismay, wait—'

She ignored him. Frantic, Gower tried to struggle out my grip. 'Ismay, do as I say!'

He kicked with his right leg and both Captain Worthington and Mr Walker went sprawling. She looked around at the other convicts. 'Two of you men, help to hold my husband down.'

She motioned to a wooden mouthpiece in the medical briefcase. 'Put that in Mr McKissock's mouth so that he doesn't bite on his tongue,' she said.

She reprimanded her patient. 'Do behave, Mr McKissock.'

Then she looked at me. 'Do you hold him tight, Te Umuroa?'

Amputation is very rarely a matter of making one simple cut. Although some surgeons advocate making a sweeping incision around the circumference of the limb, in reality it is more complex, and depends on the circumstances prevailing at the time of the operation.

Without a word, Ismay held the knife tight until her knuckles whitened. 'I am now going down to the bone, Mr McKissock,' she said. 'It will hurt.'

He was still raging at her. His resistance was broken only when Ismay, making another, deeper cut with the knife, divided the muscles covering the bone. He clamped down on the mouthpiece and gave a muffled scream.

'Do you have any whisky?' Ismay asked Captain Worthington. 'Yes? Pour it down Mr McKissock's throat. Now please.'

While he was coughing and spluttering on the liquor, Ismay made another sweep and separated the flesh that adhered to the bone. Without a pause, she took up the saw.

Gower bucked and struggled. He looked at us all. 'No! No!'

'You know this must be done,' Ismay said. She looked like a butcher, with blood all over her dress. She began to saw at the leg.

I couldn't watch. I heard the rasp of the instrument as she worked it back and forth through the bone.

Gower gave a sobbing cry: 'Ramsay, my father, help me!' He collapsed backwards into my arms.

Ismay kept sawing. Perspiration beaded her brow and ran into her eyes but she didn't stop to wipe it away. Her eyes were glazed and she was without expression.

Mr Mason, with obvious revulsion, realised he was supporting the full weight of the injured leg. Meanwhile Ismay kept sawing, even though the job was done.

I let Gower's head loll on the blanket and reached for her. Took the saw from her hand. Spoke to her. 'Ismay, it's over.'

She blinked. Saw Mr Mason with the mangled leg in his hands. 'Throw it into the sea,' she said, her voice hoarse and guttural. 'Deep, deep away with it.' She took a thread in her mouth, and began tying off first the main artery of the thigh and then the smaller blood vessels.

'Let me help you,' I said.

'No,' she answered. 'I will do it.' She was sobbing as she threaded a needle and began to stitch the flesh together so that the skin could form a flap around the exposed leg. Shock was carved on her face as she looked at what she had done.

'I think everything's finished now,' she said. 'Loosen off the tourniquet.' She looked at the blood, her implements, tried to wipe the blood off her hands, but it would not come off. Whimpering, she stood up and grabbed at the sky for support. Finding no purchase, she fainted.

It was mid afternoon.

With Gower in delirium, and other men also needing medical attention, the whaler made its way to Hobart Town.

We landed at nightfall. Captain Worthington and his soldiers took their convicts to temporary accommodation at the Hobart Town Penitentiary. Thomas Mason, Mr Walker and I rushed with Ismay and Gower to the hospital, where a surgeon inspected the work Ismay had performed on him.

'You have not taken a leg before?' he asked, amazed.

'Does that matter?' Ismay answered. 'If there is anything further to be done, kindly do it. I want to take my husband back to Maria Island as quickly as possible.'

'Mrs McKissock,' the doctor answered. 'He should remain under observation here. If infection should set in, this would be the best place to treat it. I suggest that you return meantime to Maria Island.'

'My husband will stay with the hospital overnight,' Ismay replied firmly, 'but I intend to take him to Maria Island in the morning. Darlington Station has a perfectly respectable hospital with the excellent Dr Brownell as medical officer and two convict assistants with nursing experience.'

'But . . .'

'It is also well equipped with a good dispensary to alleviate the pain that Mr McKissock is suffering as well as any infection that may develop.'

And that was *that*.

On the morrow, we returned to Maria Island with Gower. He was tossing and turning in agony, but his fever seemed to have dropped.

'That is a good sign,' Ismay said. 'Pray God that his wound heals without any problem.' Meantime, she gave him an opiate against the pain.

Mrs Imrie was waiting at the dock with Sally Jenkins, Gower Jr, Rollo and Clara. The children's smiles of happiness turned to bewilderment when they came on board and saw their father on a stretcher. 'What has happened to him, Mother?' Gower Jr asked.

Her face was wan and sad. 'Your father has had an accident,' she told them. She took a deep breath. 'He has lost his leg.'

'Lost? His leg?' Rollo answered. 'Then we must find it, Mother, and give it back to him.'

They tried to comfort him, crowding around the stretcher but, in a fit of temper, he swept them away — and Gower Jr fell to the deck.

'He didn't mean it,' I said to Gower Jr when he backed away and ran to me. 'The pain is affecting him.'

'But he will be all right?' he sobbed. 'Won't he, Hohepa?'

I embraced him. Rollo ran to join him and Clara wanted to crawl onto my lap. I thought of the nankeen night herons.

It doesn't matter whose mouth it is — that mouth gets fed.

'Your father needs to be left alone for a while,' Ismay said.

Mr Imrie returned from the day's work with Kumete, Rahui, Matiu Tikiaki and Te Waretiti. My friends were all concerned about Gower and went to see him. But he was still raging with pain and his own sorrow. 'I don't need anybody to pity me,' he shouted, and shut the door on them.

One evening, a week or so later, I was woken by the noise of arguing voices from the McKissocks' cottage.

I ran up to investigate and was just in time to see Ismay come running out the door.

'He blames me, Hohepa,' she said. 'I am to take the responsibility for his leg.'

She crumpled to the ground in front of me. Tears spilled from her eyes. 'And I haven't even thanked you for bringing Mr McKissock up from the depths,' she said. 'You saved his life. But he does not want it.'

I knelt down beside her, took her in my arms and stroked her hair. 'Kaua koe e te tangi,' I said to her. 'Don't weep.'

Frustration, desire, longing, *aroha*.

Whatever it was, my face sought hers. Her lips lifted to mine. All the yearning we had for the other rose up in both of us.

We kissed.

———

Rain down, oh rain, fall from my eyes.

Oh, it was a different kiss from any I had shared with my beloved wife, Te Rai. Passion was there, yes, but there was also restraint. Wonder but also fear. Elation as well as sadness. Most of all, I felt a deep, profound and over-whelming love for Ismay. I took the fibres of the rope, whiria, whiria, whiria, and I plaited and wove her into my heart and tightened her within it.

And then I pressed my nose to hers, my forehead to her forehead, and our soft breath intermingled.

She clasped me tightly, weeping, as if she never wanted to let me go. We could have stayed like that forever. 'Kei te aroha au ki a koe, ' she said. 'I will love you always.'

———

That was how Mr and Mrs Imrie found us.

They had heard the commotion, and came to see what was wrong.

'Mr Te Umuroa!' Mr Imrie said. 'What are you doing here? You must return to your hut immediately.' As for Mrs Imrie, it was clear from the expression on her face that she did not think I was to blame for the situation.

The guilt was Ismay's.

———

Not long after, following a morning's work with Liam Connor and his convict gang — we were carting water from the reservoir to Mr and Mrs Lapham's home — Mr Imrie allowed me and the others to go fishing and swimming.

I dived into the water and swam out to mid channel. The water was sharp, cold and glittering.

Suddenly, all around me, seagulls and terns were diving. A shoal of small fish had swarmed nearby and the birds were feasting on them.

I laughed and turned to swim back to shore.

That was when the pain hit me — a powerful blow, as if someone had punched me in the heart. I doubled in agony. Cramp seized every part of my body and I was flung down by it, down into the darkness into the silent sea. I felt my physical strength being sucked away from me. Like a koiwi, a man with no substance, I was tossed about in the swelling tides. When they had finished playing with me, hurling me this way and that, they casually flipped me up and onto the shore.

I coughed and coughed. Blood rose up and out of my throat.

———

I thought of Mahuika.

She had wept when she read my future. 'You are beginning your journey,' she said. What she hadn't told me, however, was that I would never return from it.

I would join the spirits of the tangata whenua on Maria Island, forever wandering in limbo.

I would never leave Rarohenga.

GOWER MCKISSOCK'S STORY

from Gower McKissock's Journals

PROLOGUE

Tockita-pockita, tockita-pockita, so continues my heartbeat.

I cannot believe that I am ninety-seven. I've outlived everybody of my generation. Why *me*?

And it is 1917 now, and World War I still alarms us.

———

I am sitting in my spacious study in the old house in Rhodesia. Georgina has let me have a velvet-covered antique chaise-longue in here, just in case I want to have a nap. She has also provided a small cabinet in which stand an exquisite crystal decanter of whisky and two crystal glasses — though who the other glass is for, I have no idea.

One whole wall is taken up by a glass-fronted bookshelf packed with my medical books; another wall has a collection of objets d'art and artefacts from a surprising life: photographs of Ismay and me, together or with the children; an African mask; the skin of a leopard shot by Georgina in a hunting expedition — its glossy pelt hangs tail downwards and its glassy eyes follow me around the room. I know exactly what it's thinking:

Oh the indignity of being bagged by a woman! How would you like it, when you are dead, to be skinned like this?

Frankly, although I would mind the former, I don't think I would object to the latter. After all, if my father Ramsay could allow his skeleton to be looked at by thousands of Edinburgh medical students, who am I to begrudge the leopard a sense of payback by joining it on the wall?

———

I do wish Ismay and Georgina had got on better. Perhaps it was because Ismay had no interest in her that Georgina found her grandparently affection

421

in me. Oh, I realise Ismay was vexed at Georgina's investigative ways. Georgina always harried everyone, she was always wanting to *know*, and she had that horrible affectation of pushing back the wings of her hair when all she required was a bobbypin or two to do the job.

However, after her marriage to Austin and our arrival in Rhodesia, Georgina became quite chic: the heightened manners of the local expatriates rubbed off on her. I can still remember one family photograph for which she insisted the children — Gower III, Lindsay and Sophie were toddlers then — dress in little velvet frocks and lace collars, even though it was a sweltering day. Nor did Austin and I escape her primping and prodding of us both into suits for the occasion. Georgina wanted everybody to know, if they looked at the photograph, that she had, quite clearly, *arrived*.

Ismay's medical briefcase, the one her Uncle Rollo gave her, is here too — a bit battered, but it still has all his equipment in it, including the saw she used to amputate my leg all those years ago in Van Diemen's Land. She was a brave girl. Not many women could do that, even if she never quite forgave herself the feminine indulgence in fainting immediately after she had finished the operation.

The war, alas, the war.

Georgina has had to be brave too. Last year, both Gower III and Lindsay went off to fight, not on the Western Front, but as light horsemen of the Australian and New Zealand Mounted Division. When the Muslims launched a jihad against the infidel allies, Turkey joined the war — and that's who the boys are fighting now, in the Middle East.

'Why don't you stop our sons?' she raged at Austin before they left. 'You've seen men killed in front of your eyes. Tell them how stupid and futile it is.'

Of course he wouldn't — and, even if he had, I doubt whether Gower III, the more impulsive and dashing of the two brothers, would have listened. As for Lindsay, he was always the follower, shy, with a high-pitched voice and not much self-confidence.

Thank God they survived the tragedy of Gallipoli. Evacuated to Cairo, they are now defending Egypt and the Suez Canal. At least they are with other boys from Australia and New Zealand, and under the command of Major-General Harry Chauvel, an Australian, and not some British military nincompoop. In Lindsay's latest letter, he writes that the Anzac Mounted Division is training and re-equipping for desert operations. Having lost many of their mates, both boys feel they have a score to settle. They are preparing for a battle at some place called Romani.

'This is no country for horses or for men,' he writes in the letter. 'The wind is like a blast furnace and you could cook an egg on the sand in two minutes, if you had an egg. The sun is shocking and fierce. I rely on Jumbuck to get me through all this, even if he is a bad brute! Yesterday, if it wasn't for his temper he would have been one of the poor beasts — and I would have been one of those poor men — dashed and torn by descending bombs. Instead he led the thundering scatter of six hundred horses and men out of the oasis. Ditto when we had to charge the Turks: he was so fast that we were onto the enemy before they could even raise their rifles. A few days ago, on patrol, Jumbuck and I rode into an area of shifting sands, quite by accident, and next moment he was sunk up to his haunches. But he succeeded in throwing himself clear. I shall take him for a good swim in the sea, which is about five miles from here, and I shall have a dip myself. And I shall give him an extra polish when I groom him.

'Tomorrow we are riding to Hill 70, Romani and Etmaler. Up to two thousand Turks are known to be at Bir el Mazar, east of Romani, and aerial reconnaisance has spotted camps containing about eight thousand Turks and three thousand camels between Bir Bayud and Bir el Abd. It looks like we'll be riding to Romani through a hail of bullets. Ah well, I will put my head down and go on, and I'll say to Jumbuck, "If I get a bullet in me, go like blazes and get me away to the nearest billabong."'

A bullet in me . . .

Lindsay's phrase makes me catch my breath with fear. Why should he and his brother Gower die for Britannia? She never did anything for the colonies.

Oh she made it *look* good, I must admit. When was it — 1848, the peak year for emigrants from the United Kingdom? Almost twenty-five thousand were encouraged by assisted immigration to Australia and New Zealand alone, and why? Our dear Mother Country was overburdened with the economic woes of looking after its children, notably because of the potato famine in Ireland. So how to solve the problem?

Stamp them: NOT WANTED BY ENGLAND.

And then turf them out.

———

No, I don't want my great-grandsons shot down in the flower of their manhood for Britannia. Nor can I abide the thought of Georgina mourning their loss, those pale eyes of hers filling with tears.

They must have had their fight at Romani by now. Dear Lord, I pray that they got through it.

42

I must get back to my journal.

It will at least take my mind off my great-grandsons.

I shall also remember Georgina's admonition, 'Tell all of it, Sweetie, and don't leave anything out.' Has she already sneaked a look at my narratives and found herself disappointed in the disclosures?

Well, it's not as if I have left anything out. On the other hand, I haven't put everything in either.

So where shall I begin again? With Hohepa Te Umuroa perhaps and the first time I saw him, on Monday 16 November 1846.

———

The entire population of Hobart Town was at the harbour on that day — or so it appeared — to await his and the other Maoris' arrival on HMS *Castor* from New Zealand.

When the vessel docked, there was an inordinate time until it cleared customs. Then the gangplank was put down and officials and passengers began to disembark.

Finally, a sailor cried out, 'There they are! Three cheers for the Maoris!' Seamen could always be relied upon to take the side of the persecuted. 'Hip hip—'

'Hoo-*raa*!' came the cry from the crowd.

The first two Maoris were wearing traditional dress: long woven kilt to the ankles, woven bandoliers and short doghair capes. Fully tattooed on the face, they appeared to be dazed by the commotion.

'Hip hip—'

'Hoo-*raa*!' came the roar from the sailors in the riggings. The second two Maoris had no facial tattoo and wore red blankets over their shoulders. None could doubt the fervency and support of their reception.

'Hip hip—'

'Hoo-*raa!*' came the acclamation, rolling around the wharf.

That was when Te Umuroa showed himself. In profile he was truly the chief that the crowd had been waiting for, tattooed, taller than the others and having an arresting bearing that demanded attention. He was holding a beautiful carved stick, a tokotoko of the kind that Maori chiefs used when speaking on the marae.

All this, and even though he was shackled at wrists and ankles with the others, the cruel arm- and leg-irons only added to the power of his appearance.

Then he turned his face and body full upon us. His face was only half tattooed, the other side unblemished. The effect was striking. It was almost as if he was two people, part human, part god. His eyes were dark green, glowing.

Ancestor eyes. His ancestors arriving with him.

'Karanga mai ki au,' he cried.

Perhaps this was why Ismay was compelled to step forward to welcome the Maori chiefs in their own tradition.

Haere mai nga tangata o Niu Tireni e . . .
Welcome, brave men of Maoriland . . .
Haere mai nga tangata toa ki runga o te reo aroha e . . .
Welcome warriors, alight to the call of love . . .
Come to land now.

I had never heard Ismay do this before, but nothing she did ever surprised me. She was always unconventional, impulsive and, on that day, breathtaking.

———

Ismay and Te Umuroa . . . when I look back on that sunlit day, I see I should have realised that they would mean more to each other than I ever meant to Ismay.

Why did I not divine it then?

———

So Te Umuroa came into both our lives. I must admit, I admired him. Although he was a native Maori of New Zealand he appeared to be just as good as I was and an equal to many an English gentleman.

Would I have agreed to go to Maria Island to care for him and his Maori colleagues had I known that he and Ismay would be attracted to each other? I think the answer I would give would still be yes. After all, I was a convict-emancipist and I believed strongly that Hohepa and the other Maori prisoners had been transported without the proper legal basis.

But to lose a leg in the process was a high price to pay.

———

'Leave me alone, woman. Get out. *Out.*'

I don't like to think of that month of March 1847 after Ismay amputated my limb. I was confined to my bed, in excruciating pain, and I shouted often at her and the children.

What did she do? Other women might have been kind and consoling — and left the bedroom where I was lying — but not her. She folded her arms, set herself squarely against my anger and refused to obey me. 'Hate me all you like, Mr McKissock, but you've already had long enough to get over losing your leg. You must come back to life now.'

I didn't hate her; I hated myself. How could a one-legged man continue to support a wife, family and career?

While Ismay took my curses and anger with stoicism, the children were ill at ease and frightened. How unfair that was on them — but I was too miserable to see it at the time. 'Father?' Gower Jr asked. 'What is happening to you?'

I couldn't tell him how much I loathed myself. At twenty-seven I was in my prime, but I was also less than a man. Morose and taciturn, I pushed him away.

I pushed *all* of them away, my favourite Rollo too, as well as timid Clara. 'Come *back*, Father,' Rollo wept, as if I was still away somewhere in a distant land.

I refused to see any visitors, except for Dr Brownell, who came regularly to check on me and would not be shut out. With John Jennings and Etty, the Maoris, the Laphams, Captain Bayly or any other friends at the station, I barricaded myself in the bedroom, not wanting people to express their pity or concern.

One day, I was delivered a 'gift' — a pair of crutches made by one of the convicts, I think it was Liam Connor. They were beautifully polished and very handsome but, in a temper, I threw them at Ismay. 'Get out, Mrs McKissock, and take these with you!'

Instead, she calmly placed the crutches just outside the bedroom door.

The only one who understood my despair was Sally Jenkins. She took it in turns with Ismay to dress my stump. She put her hand in mine when I said to her, 'Now I know how your father felt, Sally.'

I was otherwise not the best patient. I was fevered, and I was sick at heart.

In my selfish sanctuary, I was not aware that in the hut, not too far away, Hohepa had fallen seriously ill.

———

It was Gower Jr who let the news slip one day when he came to the bedroom after school. Although I still shouted at him, he was as stubborn as his mother.

'Hohepa? Sick?' I asked Ismay when she came with my dinner tray. 'Why didn't anybody tell me?'

Perhaps something had happened to his lungs during our ordeal in the sinking barque and the long ascent to the surface of the sea. I shuddered, remembering that terrifying moment when I had no more air; I had opened my mouth and the water rushed in.

I was horrified at the news of his illness — I blamed myself. When Ismay put the tray on the bed I picked it up and threw it on the floor.

Ismay bent down to the floor to clean the mess. 'The Imries' and our lives have not been exactly filled with joy,' she said angrily. She looked exhausted. 'Etty, despite the difficulties of her pregnancy, has been caring for Hohepa, while I have been nursing you.'

Guarding Hohepa, more like. Later, when Etty wrote of the relationship between Ismay and Hohepa, she told me she had taken it upon herself, as a Christian woman, to protect the sanctity of my and Ismay's marriage, and had forbidden Ismay from entering Hohepa's sickroom without her express permission. But at the time, I knew none of this; my concern was for Hohepa.

'I must see him,' I said.

'In that case,' Ismay answered, standing and holding the tray, 'you will have to get out of bed yourself because I am not going to help you. Your crutches are in the hallway.'

She watched as I eased myself into a sitting position. Even that simple manoeuvre was enough to make me perspire. 'Please be so kind as to give me my shirt and trousers,' I asked Ismay. I had not been out of bed since taking to it and my head was whirling, the room spinning with it.

'My hands are full,' she said. 'You will find your clothes where they always are, in the drawer on your side of the bed.'

I balanced on my leg and lunged. Propping myself up on the drawer by my elbows, I managed to open it. Pulling it with me, I sat back on the bed again and dressed myself. I felt so weak. My arms wouldn't do what I wished them to do. I was panting by the time I levered myself into the trousers. The empty trouser leg for my left foot flapped ridiculously.

Ismay put the tray onto the chest. Her mood softened. 'Do you wish me to pin the trouser leg up for you?' she asked.

I nodded, exhausted. 'Thank you.'

Did she have to be so cruel as to force me to come to terms with reality?

Once she was finished, she stepped away from me. I took three deep breaths, one, two, three, stood, and tried to hop to the door. I collapsed to the floor before I could reach the safe hand-hold of the door frame.

'I am not going to help you,' Ismay said. 'You can lie there all day and all night, for all I care.'

'You'd like to see that wouldn't you?' I answered. Furious with her, I pushed myself across the floor with my hands, and crawled through the door; reaching for the crutches, I hoisted myself up. I gave a cynical laugh, remembering the times when I had helped patients with crutches in the past. I could almost hear my own voice telling them, 'This one goes under your right armpit, the other under your left, there — that wasn't too bad, was it?'

With a cry of gladness, Ismay came to support me.

'Don't touch me, Mrs McKissock,' I cried. I pushed her away and she almost fell. Walking, stumbling, falling and getting up again, I made my way down to the hut. A large tent was erected close to it; the flaps were open and I saw bedding, rolled up, on a floor of straw.

I stood on the threshold. For a moment, I didn't want to go in. But Etty Imrie saw me from the hut window, came to the door and welcomed me warmly.

'Mr McKissock, you are up at last,' she said. 'Come in, come in, you've arrived at a very good time. Dr Brownell has just left — goodness me, the poor man has been run off his feet looking after you and Hohepa! But Te Umuroa needs round-the-clock care now and it's a two-person job. When I have the children to look after, Patricia Connor is with him. This is my shift and it is time for his bed linen to be changed. Will you help me?'

'Of course,' I answered. Now six months into her pregnancy, she was walking slowly and carefully. 'Are the other Maoris not with you?'

'No,' Etty said. 'Looking after the sick is women's work. They have gone to a job at the brickworks with Mr Imrie. It's better that way; they get upset if they stay, particularly Kumete.'

'I presume they are sleeping in the tent?'

'Yes,' she said. She came to my left side, butted herself against me and took the crutches away. 'Lean on me, Mr McKissock,' she continued as she manoeuvred me into the chair beside Hohepa's bed. 'There!'

The room was dark. It was completely empty except for one bed, a couple of chairs, a table and set of drawers. Hohepa was a shadow on the bed; the stench that accompanied sick men was masked by the perfume of freshly picked flowers.

'Mr Te Umuroa?' Etty said him. 'You have a visitor.' Then she smiled at me. 'You are two invalids in the same room together.' She moved to the windows and, before I could stop her, opened the curtains.

The sudden sunlight took all pretence away. It slashed at Hohepa's skull, showing sunken cheeks and eyes now deeply recessed into dark orbits. I had known what to expect, but even so I was shocked at the sight of the deterioration.

Etty tried again to wake him.

I shook my head, 'No, leave him be.'

While he was still sleeping, I examined him. Carefully, I drew the blanket from him; he shivered. He moaned when I put my fingers on him. His musculature had melted away, leaving only a skeletal frame. His skin was so transparent that I could see his veinous system, pulsing the sluggish stream of blood from a pitiful beating heart. Where his veins had collapsed blood pooled, marked by big bruises and stains.

This was not the same man who had rescued me a month ago. That man had been strong, vital and upright, with the body of a swimmer — a merman. I could only guess at the huge pride which Hohepa had attached to his extraordinary physical health, fitness and appearance. This man bore only a ghostly resemblance to Hohepa, and looked a hundred years older.

I felt ashamed of myself. When I had been in need, Hohepa had come to me; when he was in need, I was not there. For a month he had been like this.

Once, he had been *beautiful*.

'I am so sorry,' I said.

He gave a sharp intake of breath at my words, shuddered, and his eyelids flickered open. 'Mr McKissock, was that you who opened the door and windows? You have brought the breath of fresh air with you . . .'

I looked into his eyes. His ancestors were with him.

———————

There are times in life when one is within and without the moment.

I see, again, my own terror reflected in Hohepa's eyes as, cracking and splintering, the prison barque begins to sink.

My leg, dealt a crushing blow, dangles uselessly as he pulls me out of the vessel. I wish I could scream with the pain but, if I open my mouth, the water will pour in and I will drown. The barque plunges downward, trying to pull us with it. But Hohepa fights against it, steadying us both in the dark depths of the sea.

I sign to him, *Save yourself.* Oh, the pressure of the water!

Instead he smiles, *No.* Gathers me in his arms, breast to breast, and slowly we make our ascent.

I want to go faster. I am panicking, I have never liked the dark, and the shimmer of light above us looks to be so far away, like a dream. But Hohepa forces me to pace him. And every now and then, he lets out a steady stream of air. I know immediately what he is doing and copy him. *Good, Mr McKissock.*

He seems to have an inexhaustible supply; whereas I run out. *Go on without me,* I sign.

No, he returns. He kisses me, putting his lips over mine and breathing his own air into me. *Trust me.*

After a while, there's no air left. *I'm sorry, Mr McKissock.* Even then he will not leave me. I open my mouth and begin to choke as the water rushes in.

It's terrifying, but he holds me tight. Then he himself begins to drown, spasming and kicking, almost screaming under water, *No, no.*

Only the chance irruption of air bubbles from the sunken barque saves us, enclosing us and taking us unconscious to the surface of the sea.

He could have left me there.

He didn't.

43

The sight of Hohepa shocked me out of my selfishness.

I made my way back to the cottage. Sally Jenkins had just returned from school with the children.

'Father?' Gower Jr asked. Instead of running to me, however, he and his brother and sister backed away towards Ismay, hugging her for protection. Clara still had a habit of disappearing under Ismay's skirts and tried to do that again. Ismay stopped her.

'See how your children are frightened of you, Mr McKissock?' she asked. 'You can vent all your anger on me if you wish, but kindly stop taking it out on them.'

With a cry, I put out my arms to them. I forgot that I was on crutches and, unbalanced, I fell to the floor.

'Father! Are you all right?' Rollo asked. He ran to help me up.

I grabbed him in a hug. 'I am so sorry, Rollo,' I said. 'So sorry.'

———

Thus did I make my peace with Ismay, Sally Jenkins and the children. The children skipped around with joy. 'Father's back! He's back! He's back!' they shouted, unperturbed by the empty trouser leg and eager to take turns with the crutches if only I'd let them.

That evening others in our little community came to celebrate my resurrection. When John Jennings arrived with the Maoris after a day's work, I saw Etty giving him the happy news of my visit to Hohepa; he immediately brought a bottle of whisky over to celebrate.

'Gower, my good friend,' he said as he slapped me on the back. 'By Jove, we have missed you!' He invited the Maoris to share in the celebration and they arrived soon after him. Or perhaps it was the attraction of the whisky?

'Ka pai, e hoa!' Rahui said. 'Good to see you up and about!'

Kumete, however, was not among them.

'Where is he?' I asked.

'He always goes straight to Te Umuroa,' John Jennings said. 'He is very upset that this has happened to him. It's almost as if he thinks he could have stopped the illness.'

'Let's go and join them,' I said. 'Bring the bottle. Ismay, can I have two extra glasses?'

John Jennings, the Maori and I all adjourned to the hut. Matiu Tikiaki was a good fellow, helping me to negotiate the steps. When we entered, Kumete shook my hand.

My mouth was dry with emotion. 'Mr Imrie, would you be so kind as to fill the two extra glasses?'

I gave one to Kumete. I woke Hohepa and, although he was dazed, he took the other glass. 'To your good health, Mr Te Umuroa,' I toasted him.

'Ki a koe hoki,' he said to me. 'And health to you also.'

————

From that moment, the two cottages and the hut resounded with warmth again.

I took over the daytime responsibility for Hohepa. I read to him and, together with one of the convict staff, relieved Etty and Patricia Connor of the need to feed him, change his linen or assist him with his bodily functions. I think he was thankful to have our male support and company.

My first command — and Ismay immediately agreed — was that Hohepa should be carried up to the cottage and into our own bedroom, from where he would have a view of the Mercury Passage. It had been a source of comfort to me in my darkest hour; and I suspected it might bring comfort to Hohepa too.

How he loved that! For most of the time he had been alone in the hut, listless and sleeping the day away; no such luck in the McKissock household! With Ismay and me around (we moved into the boys' bedroom; they happily went over to spend the evenings with the Imries' children), he was surrounded by the noise and routine of a busy family. And what with his other visitors, he was tired out by night-time.

His Maori companions visited him every day after work, bearing delicacies such as crayfish and shellfish and urging him, 'Eat! He matekai koe? Eat!' Mr and Mrs Lapham regularly came to see him, as did his old friend

Captain Bayly. A small group of convicts — Liam Connor, Seamus Keelan and Kieron Moore — sought permission from Mr Lapham to visit also.

'Maori chief, what ails you?' Liam Connor asked. 'Get up from your bed!'

One day, Thomas and Jane Mason arrived on the *Mary*.

'Tena korua,' Hohepa greeted them. 'You two still here in Van Diemen's Land like us?'

The Masons were shocked by his appearance. Thomas Mason could only say, 'Dear oh dear, oh, dear oh dear . . .' in a most bewildered way.

After a while, however, the three friends began to talk about their common experiences as neighbours in New Zealand and the atmosphere turned from sadness to gaiety. Even so, when they departed on the *Mary* the next morning, their farewells were deeply affecting.

'E noho ra, rangatira,' Thomas Mason said. 'We shall see each other soon.'

———

Then, far too quickly the weather turned unpredictable and inclement, with sleet and hail storming up through the Mercury Passage on one side and Bass's Strait on the other. It seemed to specifically be looking for Hohepa and, when it found him, it breathed icicles into his lungs.

When I inspected him, leaning to his chest to listen, I knew from his coughing and the heaviness and labouring nature of his breathing that his serious pulmonary condition had worsened. His heart was still valiant but his breath started to rattle as if his ribs had come loose inside his chest.

'He has pneumonia,' I told Ismay.

She almost collapsed. 'Oh no,' she cried.

The Maori kept up constant prayer. 'E Ihowa,' they chanted, 'is Hohepa to die in this strange land? Will you not succour him and lift him out of this place?'

The only light in his life came when Etty Imrie gave birth on 27 April 1847. Hohepa asked to see the babe, a bonny boy swaddled in blankets, his face screwed up in distaste at the chill of the world.

'What is his name?' he asked.

'Charles William,' Mrs Imrie answered.

Looking at Hohepa with the child, all I could think of was the eternal cycle of death and life, and that Hohepa would have found great joy in the coming of a new child representing a new generation.

'Haere mai e tama ki te Ao o Tane,' he greeted him. 'Welcome, child, to the world of man.'

Hohepa rallied for three weeks. On 21 May, I was able to deliver him a message.

'There's finally been a reply from the Colonial Office to Governor La Trobe's despatch of November,' I told him.

'What does the reply say? Are we to be pardoned and sent back to Aotearoa?' In his eyes was a gleam of hope. 'If I am to die, let it be in my homeland.'

'No, it's not the pardon we have been waiting for,' I began, 'but it *is* good news. The secretary of state advises that he has asked for a report from Governor Grey on the circumstances surrounding your imprisonment. In particular, he has sought reassurance of the legality of the court martial that sentenced you all and wants to know whether all statutory and administrative measures were taken to empower New Zealand courts to impose the sentence. Were you all lawfully despatched to Van Diemen's Land? If the answer is no, and I am sure it will be, I can see no option for the secretary but to release you all. Meantime, the secretary has shown mercy.'

I read his words. '"I therefore limit myself to the Instructions that they, the Maoris, should be allowed all the freedom enjoyed by the holders of Tickets of Leave, so far, and in so far, as you may find the enjoyment of that freedom to be compatible with their real welfare . . ."'

'So we are to remain prisoners, like the tangata whenua?' Hohepa asked.

'Yes, but you are no longer convicts.'

'We are still to remain here, Mr McKissock.'

'Let's hope it will not be for much longer.'

'I will pray for the others,' he answered. 'As for me, I am already as a mass of sea foam stranded on the beach . . .'

Then all the ills and spites of the world came from the north, west and east, and hastened Hohepa to his death.

Even he knew it. 'Blows the wind to chill the marrow,' he said. 'Forgive me, Mr McKissock.'

'Forgive you?' I asked. I had no idea what he was talking about, but he drew breath and continued in similarly enigmatic vein. 'Now let me spend my last days among my own people, Kumete, Matiu Tikiaki, Rahui and Te Waretiti.'

'No,' Ismay pleaded, 'stay in the cottage with us.'

'Let me go now, kui,' he answered.

We returned him to the hut. There, his Maori companions kept him constant company, singing, chanting from the New Testament, talking — and often there were outbursts of laughter. I went to bed hearing the Maori chanting and, when I awoke, the first sound I heard was chanting.

'Ka koa te hunga he rawakore nei te wairua: no ratou hoki te rangatira-tanga o te rangi. Blessed are the poor in spirit: for theirs is the kingdom of heaven.'

I thought to myself, how strange the Maori customs were! Whereas English men and women tiptoed around the ailing, they chanted and sur-rounded their dying with song.

A few days later, I came across John Jennings writing in his diary: 'Hohepa very ill — 8 p.m. rallied. At 9 p.m. expressed his desire to see Mrs Imrie.'

They both went in to see him. I was at the doorway when I heard Hohepa thank them. 'I was a stranger and you took me in. I was sick and you visited me. I was a pilgrim and you gave me sanctuary.'

He was failing fast.

———

The following day I woke at around three in the morning with a gasp. It was dark, not yet dawn, and although it was not cold, I was shivering.

I had dreamt of my father, Ramsay, and the way his backbone had cracked through his skin at his death.

Something else was wrong.

I realised that the chanting had *stopped*. I suppose I should have woken Ismay, but I didn't. Instead I dressed quickly, grabbed my crutches and stumbled to the hut where Hohepa was lying. Curiously, John Jennings and Mrs Imrie were also hastening to the hut.

The chanting began again. This time its tone was different, no longer Christian and, instead, invoking traditional Maori strophes.

'Tiwhatiwha te Po, tiwhatiwha te Ao. Gloomy is the night, gloomy is the day.'

When we walked into the hut, the Maori were all kneeling beside the bed.

'Tenei tangata, he is almost gone,' Kumete said. He was most distressed, groaning to himself and beating himself on the breast.

'Niwaniwa te Po, niwaniwa te Ao. Deep dark is the night, deep dark is the day.'

Hohepa's entire face seemed to have collapsed. From the orbits of his skull his eyes stared out. They swivelled across at me. Took me in with a glance.

He beckoned me close. Whispered in my ear. 'Mr McKissock,' he said. 'Don't be a foolish man. You have found yourself a family to love. Don't spend your time growing bitter. Instead, love your family back.'

I was bewildered by his words.

'Hiwahiwa te Po, hiwahiwa te Ao. Deep deep dark is the night, and the day.'

Ismay came running.

'Why didn't you wake me?' she asked me. 'Am I too late?' She went to Hohepa.

'I wish life had given us both quarter,' Hohepa said. 'Ko taku ngakau me to ngakau.'

Ismay sank to the floor. 'Aue, e te tangata aroha e, aue . . . Don't leave me.'

'Mrs McKissock,' Etty Imrie said sharply, 'remember where you are.'

Indescribable grief and loss entered into the room. And suddenly I realised that I was not a part of it.

What was happening? I didn't know! Of course I had joked earlier about the appearance of love between Hohepa and Ismay and had commented on the attraction that they shared for each another. And I had been irritated during a discussion on the English and Maori definitions of love, certainly, but not sufficiently to suspect Ismay and Hohepa of any reciprocal affection.

After all, Ismay was an English woman and Hohepa was a Maori. But this felt like eavesdropping.

'Aroha mai,' Hohepa said. 'I'm sorry, Ismay. Kei te maara o taku ngakau, in the garden of my heart I hear the night herons singing. E toku tino hoa pirihonga, e kata tonu pai ai, ne? Oh, my dear Ismay, keep smiling, ne?'

He shivered. 'I am getting cold now.'

And he unfurled.

One further unbending and straightening and arching and springing upward and out, and he left the chrysalis of his shining bones.

The Maori set up a mournful lamentation. Ismay kept repeating over and over, 'No, no, *no*.'

This was how the Maori chief Hohepa Te Umuroa left us.

From Darlington Station came the groaning sound of six hundred men awakening to a new day.

The dawn came crimson, and dark purple spheres spread across the sea.

436

44

Hare ra, e pa, i runga i te au heke
I te hurihanga o te whenua
Moe mai, e pa, moe mai

I have an indelible impression of Ismay in those first moments of grieving.

Ismay was sitting beside Hohepa, stroking his face and hair. Around her, the other Maori were rocking, exclaiming their sentiments of loss.

She seemed a different person. Somebody I didn't recognise.

Neither the Imries nor I had ever experienced the Maori lamentations for the dead. I was stunned at their passion and uncivilised — nay, pagan — grief. The closest I had ever come to it had been through my mother, Ailie, and the ancient Scottish dirges she occasionally sang.

Thus, when Mr Imrie invited me to accompany him to the superintendent's house to convey the news, I picked up my crutches and went with him, leaving Ismay and Etty Imrie with the Maori and Hohepa.

———

As soon as Mr Lapham opened the door of his house and saw us, he knew that Hohepa had died.

'This is serious and tragic news,' he said. 'We have had a Maori chief under our care, someone who may have been not guilty of any of the charges put to him.'

'Sir, we will need to think about the funeral,' John Jennings answered.

'Yes,' Mr Lapham nodded. 'But should Te Umuroa be buried in the prisoners' cemetery or in the island's civil cemetery for free settlers? Let me think on it, gentlemen.'

Mrs Lapham appeared behind him. 'Surely he was not a prisoner, Mr Lapham?'

It was on the way home to the cottages that I asked John Jennings the question that had been burning in my soul. 'Mr Imrie, was there anything between Ismay and Te Umuroa?'

Startled, he looked at me. 'Mr McKissock, why are you asking me that question?'

'You spent more time with them both than I did,' I answered. 'Did you see anything occur between Mrs McKissock and Mr Te Umuroa?'

'No,' he answered. 'And even if there had been, the man is no threat to you or your marriage, loveless by your own admission.' He could scarce veil his anger. 'He is dead now.'

Etty Imrie was alone in the hut when we arrived.

'Where are Ismay and the Maoris?' John Jennings asked.

'They have taken Hohepa's body down to the sea to bathe and cleanse him. When they return they will dress him.'

I walked to the rise overlooking the Mercury Passage. When I looked down to the shore I saw Ismay and the four Maoris waist high in the sea, with Hohepa between them. The water was shimmering and Hohepa was lying in an aureole of dazzling light.

Half an hour later they returned with Hohepa and laid him naked on the bed. Salt crystals sparkled on his face and in his hair.

He looked otherworldly.

For a moment, there was silence. Then the four Maoris looked respectfully at Ismay and Etty Imrie. 'Ko korua nga wahine,' Rahui said. 'You are the women.'

'What does he mean?' I asked Ismay.

She looked at Etty Imrie. 'He means that it is the role of the women to dress and prepare Te Umuroa. Black-clad women of his own race, his female relatives, would be doing this for him, not such ones as me and Etty who do not even wear chaplets of green in our hair. But in their absence, Etty, would you assist me?'

'Of course,' Etty Imrie answered.

Already, and with great tenderness, Ismay was braiding his hair.

I wondered: When I am dead, Ismay, will you be as tender with me?

Mr and Mrs Lapham came to the hut to pay their respects.

Mrs Lapham was regal and did not mind when Rahui collapsed onto her shoulders and wept.

'Haere mai e kui i roto,' Te Waretiti invited her. 'Come inside.'

Kumete and Matiu Tikiaki were like guards watching over Hohepa.

He was lying on a red blanket. He was dressed in a long woven kilt to his ankles. Around his shoulders was a short doghair cape. The tokotoko was clasped in his hands. Ismay and Etty had returned a semblance of magnificence to him.

'Oh, Mr Te Umuroa,' Mrs Lapham said to him. 'We will truly miss you.'

'Sir,' John Jennings asked Mr Lapham, 'have you decided where Te Umuroa is to be buried? The Maoris and we are anxious to know.'

Mr Lapham looked at his wife — and she nodded. 'The secretary of state gave him the same freedoms as are enjoyed by holders of tickets of leave,' he began. 'I interpret that to mean that although he is still a prisoner with us, he may be buried in the civil cemetery. By heaven, let nobody try to stop that from happening.'

Ismay immediately turned to Mrs Lapham and kissed her hands. 'Thank you, madam,' she said.

'All station personnel have been notified of Te Umuroa's death,' Mr Lapham continued. 'Some will come to the hut to join the cortege to the civil cemetery. The coffin will be delivered by convicts half an hour prior to departure from here. The funeral service will take place in the cemetery.'

———

Ismay and I went up to the cottage to dress for the funeral.

'Sally Jenkins?' Ismay called. 'Will you get the children ready?'

'Do you think that's wise?' I asked. 'The Imries are leaving their brood with Patricia Connor to look after. Shouldn't ours stay at home with Sally Jenkins?'

'No,' she answered. 'They have asked if they may come. They loved Hohepa.'

'Very well,' I said. But I thought as we were dressing, with some irritation, that Ismay was acting like the grieving widow. She put on a black dress and a black bonnet completely covering her red hair. As for the children, they were dressed in formal wear and jackets.

'Are you all nice and warm?' Ismay asked. 'It will be cold on the hill where we are taking Hohepa.' Once they were ready, she knelt down and said, 'And now let us go and pay our final respects to Mr Te Umuroa.'

We went down to the hut. I wondered how they would react to seeing a dead person. But they were not fearful.

'Goodbye, Hohepa,' Gower Jr and Rollo said.

Clara gave him a shy wave.

———————

At midday, Liam Connor, Seamus Keelan and Kieron Moore arrived with Hohepa's coffin on a handcart. It had been lined with a lovely soft mat.

Liam Connor approached Mr Lapham, cap in hand. 'With all due respect,' he began, 'the men at Darlington request that the Maori chief's body rest briefly in the compound so that he can be farewelled by them. They want to pay tribute to him and not let him go into the earth unheralded and nameless.'

'Mr Te Umuroa is not going to the burying ground where no gravestones mark the dead,' Mr Lapham answered. 'He will be buried in the free settlers cemetery.'

'That is good news, sir,' Kieron Moore said, his lips quivering. 'It would be a miscarriage of justice otherwise. But may he still rest briefly in the station?'

Mr Lapham considered the request. He and John Jennings conferred. 'No,' he answered eventually. 'But I am prepared to allow you, Mr Keelan and Mr Connor to represent the prisoners of the station at the graveside when Mr Te Umuroa is buried.'

'Thank you, sir,' Liam Connor said. 'It is much appreciated and I know the men will understand.'

He and Seamus Keelan then carried the coffin into the hut. They were greeted by a tragic cry from Kumete. He began to speak in a torrent of Maori to Ismay.

'What is wrong, Mrs McKissock?' John Jennings asked.

'Kumete doesn't want to have Hohepa buried at all,' she answered. 'He asks that he be embalmed for eventual return to Aotearoa.'

'That is impossible,' John Jennings replied.

Even so, it took Ismay at least half an hour of persuasion. Then, 'You may wrap Hohepa in his shroud now,' she said. As this was being done, she lowered her veil over her face.

Hohepa was placed in the coffin by his Maori companions. They bent to him to press noses in the hongi to the dead person, the last physical farewell.

The lid was placed on him by Liam Connor. Seamus Keelan and Kieron Moore hammered nails in. The sound was shockingly loud. The tokotoko was placed on top of the lid together with a wreath fashioned out of winter leaves and flowers.

I noticed something curious. Whoever had fashioned the coffin had carved an inscription on it: the letter H.

And then Reverend and Mrs Dobson, Dr and Mrs Brownell and Captain and Mrs Bayly arrived with other officers and their wives of Darlington Station. It was a most impressive group of mourners, all dressed in formal black.

'Are we ready?' Mr Lapham asked.

I nodded to Kumete. He signed to Matiu Tikiaki, Te Waretiti and Te Rahui, and they raised Hohepa's coffin and took it out to the cart.

We walked from the two cottages and the hut, following Hohepa. Ismay was immediately behind with the children. Gower Jr and Rollo had brought their Maori kites and let them up into the sky.

'Can you see the kites, Hohepa?' Gower Jr asked.

Whenever we came across any convict gangs, they took off their caps: 'Goodbye, Maori chief.'

We reached the end of the road. The four Maoris lifted Hohepa's coffin onto their shoulders and began to climb the hill to the cemetery. Every now and then one of them would give the task over to Liam Connor, Seamus Keelan or Kieron Moore.

'Okay mateys,' Liam Connor said. 'Onward we go.'

They were all such a strong group of pallbearers. I wished I could help them but I was having difficulty myself climbing the hill.

We seemed to be ascending into the very sky itself. Pearly grey, it stretched over the lustrous sea.

Far away, distant lightning flickered. 'You'd better bring your kites down now, boys,' I whispered to Gower Jr and Rollo.

'All right, Father,' Gower Jr said.

The wind began to blow and the lightning was advancing upon us. Dark clouds were broiling across the sea. Already the water was white-tipped and turbulent.

We all stood around the open grave. Reverend Dobson was with Mr and Mrs Lapham and other officers of the station. Two members of the guard were present at stiff attention. John Jennings and Etty Imrie stood with the four Maoris and three convicts. Ismay and the children were to one side of the grave. At their feet, the coffin lay on ropes, ready to be delivered to its resting place.

Ismay's black dress swirled in the wind and her veil draped across her face. Her eyes gleamed behind the fluttering cloth like moonstones. I stepped forward to stand beside her, stumbling a bit — and she caught my arm and helped me to gain some steadiness.

Four convict diggers stood at a distance; the ground was so hard it must have taken them all morning to dig down six feet into the earth.

'Let us begin,' Reverend Dobson said. In deference to Mr Imrie, he asked, 'Sir, would you conduct the service?'

Mr Imrie nodded. He stepped forward. 'Tena koutou katoa,' he began haltingly. 'Ka haere tatou ki te poroporoaki ki a tatou hoa, Hohepa.'

I had not expected John Jennings to make his opening remarks in the Maori language, but how appropriate it was! The Maoris appeared to be very grateful, standing up straight and acknowledging what he was saying with their interjections.

'Ka tika! That is true! Ae! Yes! Kapai! Good!'

Then John Jennings turned to English and I noticed some relief among our little congregation. I don't remember all that he said, but I shall never forget the opening lines of his address. 'Hohepa,' he said to the coffin, 'like the same Joseph of the Bible, you were a fruitful bough by a well, whose branches ran over a wall. Those branches came even to Maria Island and we have been greatly enriched by the fruits of your aroha.'

I looked up at the sky. I thought the weather should be upon us by now, but it appeared to hesitate, standing off the island and over the mainland. There the clouds billowed black and the lightning began to crack.

We were all nervous. To be caught in a thunderstorm, with lightning flashing overhead, was not to be desired. But John Jennings would not be rushed. He maintained his steady unfolding of the funeral oration. And it was only when he began to speak in Maori again that we knew he was coming to the end.

'Na reira,' he said, 'te hunga mate ki te hunga mate, te hunga ora ki te hunga ora, tena tatou katoa. The dead to the dead, the living to the living, good fellowship to us all.'

He stepped back from the graveside and motioned to the Maoris to come forward and take hold of the ropes. At the last moment, however, Kumete stepped back and began to passionately cry out again.

'I must take him back to the Matua Tupuna . . .'

Rahui spoke to him sharply, and called Liam Connor to take his place at the ropes.

'Wait,' Ismay said. She bent down and took the tokotoko in her hands.

Only then was Hohepa lowered into the ground. As he was, dust suddenly swirled around us.

Slowly the coffin descended. The Maoris began to intone, 'Aianei ka tukua te tinana . . .'

'Now we commit your body . . .'

'He oneone ki te oneone . . .'

'Earth to earth . . .'

'He pungarehu ki te pungarehu . . .'

'Dust to dust . . .'

'He puehu ki te puehu . . .'

'Ashes to ashes . . .'

'I te awaawa o te atarangi o te mate.'

'Through the valley of the shadows of death.'

There was a dull scraping noise as it came to rest.

The children ran to my embrace as Ismay stepped forward to sing a beautiful lament of farewell:

'Haere atu ra te rangatira ki Paerau, ki Hawaiki nui, Hawaiki roa, Hawaiki pamamao, kua wheturangitia ratou. Farewell, Hohepa, to your ancestors and the place of the Maori dead. Become like them a brilliant star in the sky.'

She held the tokotoko in her hands and went to drop the stick into the grave.

Shrill cries came from the air: *No.*

We looked up. Against the backdrop of turbulent echoing sky and lightning came two nankeen night herons. Inscribing configurations of light in the lowering dark, they made several passes over our heads, causing us to duck and, as they did, they glared at us.

'What's wrong with the crazy birds?' I heard Mr Lapham mutter.

Some of the ladies were clearly nervous. I saw Mrs Brownell clutching her veil.

In a flutter of outspread wings the herons landed. They showed their irritation by a noisy display of hoarse bird calls. Then, as bold as brass, they stepped through us to the graveside.

One of them put its head against Ismay's dress and made as if to push her back from the opened earth. All the time it was crying angrily at her: *Back, back. Don't.* Its feathers were ruffled, standing high, but when Ismay had retreated far enough, it was satisfied and seemed to calm down.

Its companion came then to preen it, stroking its beautiful beak through the shimmering feathers. Then, *pluck*, it pulled a feather out of the other bird's plumage, walked to the edge of the grave and let it drop. *Goodbye, rangatira.*

Dust swirled as the herons lifted, and we watched as they disappeared over the station.

'Well,' Mrs Lapham gasped. 'What are we to make of that?'

'Feathers are ruffling among the humans, too,' I whispered to Ismay.

Indeed, the incident, coming as it had within the context of a Christian burial, was causing a rippling murmur in our little congregation.

Ismay put a stop to it. She picked up some dirt in her hands and cast it into the grave. That was the sign for the others; one by one they filed past Hohepa's resting place and followed her example.

Kumete, Matiu Tikiaki, Rahui and Te Waretiti took the spades from the convicts who had dug the hole and began to shovel earth into the grave. As they worked, they called to each other:

Ka mate ka mate! Ka ora ka ora!
Ka mate ka mate! Ka ora ka ora!

It was an old haka composed by the warrior chief Te Rauparaha. Their eyes were bulging, the tendons on their necks were taut, their passion was wild and pagan.

Then Hohepa was completely buried. I saw Sally Jenkins give comfort to Matiu Tikiaki, leaning against him.

Mrs Imrie stepped forward with the beautiful wreath of winter flowers and laid it on the grave.

That's when I heard a strange sound. I thought it was the soft moaning of the sea. Or perhaps it was the whispering wind. The sound gathered strength.

'It is the men of Darlington,' John Jennings said. From the convicts below came the sound of singing.

The minstrel boy to the war is gone
In the ranks of death you'll find him—

Denied attendance at Hohepa's funeral, they were making their farewell tribute in the only way they knew how:

No chains shall sully thee!
Thou soul of love and bravery
Thy songs were made for the pure and free
They shall never sound in slavery—

There came a huge roar and a clapping sound. 'Goodbye, matey Hohepa Te Umuroa! You're freer than you'll ever be! Nobody can catch you now! Goodbye! Goodbye! Goodbye!'

The storm, long held back, rushed over the island and unleashed itself upon us.

Go, lord, upon the ebbing tide
The land is overturned
Sleep on, lord, sleep . . .

45

Following Hohepa's funeral, the days drifted by in sadness.

The Maoris felt the death of Hohepa the most. Once there had been five of them; now there were four — and he had been their leader. They were like a canoe whose captain had fallen into the dark wide sea and, without him to point the direction and call the strokes of the paddle, their waka was foundering.

It was not until Te Waretiti stepped forward and began to lead them that they started to lift their heads to the horizon again.

'Haere mai matou,' he said. 'Piki atu matou i te awatea. Come, let us climb towards the dawn.'

———

As for me, something changed with Hohepa's death.

Oh, perhaps it had been coming for a long time but I hadn't realised it. Perhaps, even, losing my leg had something to do with it.

I watched Ismay with the Maoris and, instead of standing back from their relationship, joined it. They were happy to allow me into their iwi — their tribe — and Ismay herself complimented me. 'I think they would much prefer to talk to you than to me or John Jennings.'

I also realised that I had to rely on other people to help me; I had never allowed myself to be beholden to another person. Yet, when Ismay took it upon herself to encourage Liam Connor to make me an artificial limb, I did not object to the idea. Indeed, when I strapped it to my stump I opened my arms to her and said, 'Would you like to dance, Mrs McKissock?'

I found myself accommodating Ismay in ways that would have been foreign to me even a year ago. When I pressed myself on her in bed and she declined, I did not persist in having my way. Rather, I lay there beside her, stroking her hair and holding her and, in those moments, I felt a different kind of emotion sweeping over me; something more profound than any ecstasy from making love to her.

I discovered myself looking at the children — and I was startled into loving them, especially Rollo and Clara. I sought their company when they played games or flew their kites. I took pride in their achievements at school. When Rollo started to accompany me to the hospital I thought with pleasure, why, he might become the third generation McKissock to enter the medical profession.

I opened a door upon myself, made myself vulnerable, and knowledge blossomed inside me. The words that Hohepa had said to me were the same words which my mother Ailie had said: 'You have found yourself a family to love. Don't spend your time growing bitter. Instead, love them back.'

————

I also made stronger resolve regarding the cause of the Maoris' freedom. No other Maori would die on my watch.

Indeed, I was heartened that, when Hohepa's death became widely known, our Quaker and newspaper friends in Hobart Town, particularly Eion Gault, Mr Walker, Thomas Mason and Henry Melville, were spurred into action. The Van Diemen's Land newspapers again resounded with editorials like that of the *Hobart Town Courier*, which asked: 'Why are the Maoris still imprisoned in the colony? One of the Maori chiefs has already died. Will the others die also in captivity? Release them! Release them!'

My good friend Eion highlighted the plight of all political prisoners incarcerated in Van Diemen's Land in a blistering public speech at the Town Hall. 'Transportation,' he thundered, 'is being used illegally. The Maoris are not the only ones who have been transported simply because they are patriots! Witness William Cuffay, the Black London Chartist! Or non-Celtic prisoners as follows: sixty coloured Mauritius-born convicts, twenty-two of them Afro-Malagasy from Mozambique, Madagascar and Bourbon; over forty Asians of Indian and Chinese origin; and thirty Khoikhoi, Hottentots and Bushmen peoples of the Cape Colony! All transported because they fought for their countries!'

As for Mr Mason he took up the pen again dealt with Governor Denison as he had dealt with Governor La Trobe.

When would the Maoris' imprisonment end?

————

In December 1847, some five long months after Hohepa's death, a report arrived of possible progress.

'In New Zealand,' John Jennings told the Maoris at one of our regular evening meetings, 'Governor Grey has released the two men, Mataiuma and Tope, who had originally been destined for transportation but whom he kept in Auckland, hoping to use them as witnesses in the trial of Te Rauparaha.'

'Why is this good news?' Kumete asked.

'Mataiuma and Tope were charged with the same crimes as you were,' I told him. 'If they are released, that is precedent for your own.'

But it took another two months, until 16 February 1848, for happy news to come from the governor's office. Indeed, George Washington Walker and Thomas and Jane Mason came to deliver it in person, and told us to assemble the four Maoris together.

'After much devious explanation,' Mr Walker began, 'Governor Grey can no longer maintain the fiction of the court martial. Doubts exist about the legality of the tribunal which condemned you. You are all to be returned to Aotearoa as an an example of his clemency.'

Kumete and Matiu Tikiaki could hardly believe it. After all, almost fourteen months had gone by since they had first arrived in Van Diemen's Land.

'Can it be true?' they asked Ismay. 'Ka tika?'

'Ae,' she answered. 'It is true.'

Rahui and Te Waretiti hugged each other and then embraced us. 'We can go home now?'

'Yes,' she answered. 'Haere atu koutou ki a Aotearoa.'

Tears flowed freely between us.

In all the happiness, Te Umuroa was not forgotten.

Mr Mason had also brought with him a substantial headstone to erect over Hohepa's grave; the Quakers again bearing witness in their generosity for a fallen warrior. The Maoris had been up at the graveyard erecting it and, now, the job was finished.

'Tomorrow we have the kohatu,' Rahui said.

'It is the unveiling of the headstone,' Ismay explained. 'It is the final token of aroha for the dead, a fitting end to Hohepa and his achievements on earth.'

The next morning we all went up to the graveyard for the ceremony. We were a happy crowd — the Masons and the McKissock and Imrie clans

— and the children weaving among the Maoris. Gower Jr and Rollo had grown a lot and raced ahead with Henry Imrie, shouting, 'Come on everyone! Hurry up!'

As we walked up the hill, I took Ismay's hand.

'Hullo!' came a cry from the graveyard. Already there were the Laphams, Brownells, Baylys and other colleagues of the station. Mr Lapham had given permission for Liam Connor, Seamus Keelan and Kieron Moore to be present.

The headstone was draped with a black veil. We greeted each other in fellowship and then waited for the ceremony to begin.

'Would you mind, Mr McKissock,' Te Waretiti asked, 'if your son Gower Jr did the unveiling? Hohepa loved your boy.'

'Of course,' I nodded.

I was so proud as he carefully took the veil away! 'Tena koe,' he said to Hohepa. 'E rangatira koe. You will always be a chief.'

We all clapped as we looked at the headstone.

It bore in English and in Maori the inscription:

Here Lie the Remains
— of —
HOHEPA TE UMUROA
Native of Wanganui
New Zealand
Who died July 19th
MDCCCXLVII

Later, we adjourned to the Laphams for afternoon tea. It was there that Thomas Mason took me to one side.

'Passage has been arranged for the Maori to depart by the *Lady Denison* from Van Diemen's Land soon,' he said. 'Arrangements for the payment of their passage is somewhat bothersome. The New Zealand Government will not give over the money until they have arrived! However, the sailors of Hobart Town have guaranteed the tickets and the *Lady Denison*'s captain has said he will wait for his money. I want to thank you and Mrs McKissock for looking after the Maori in Jane's and my place.'

'No thanks are required,' I answered.

'Like them,' he continued, 'we will be leaving Van Diemen's Land too. 'Despite the continuing troubles in New Zealand, our joy is to go back to that beautiful country. In that new world, we will build lives for our children and grandchildren.

I thought of all our various destinies: the Imries', the Masons' and ours. Could we, like the Masons, return to New Zealand and settle there? But no, Ismay had made up her mind. She desired to stay close to the Trowenna Sea.

And what was my desire? I realised that my life had not been one I had sought for myself at all. Instead, I had gone along with it. Would there ever come a time when I would steer my own canoe towards the horizon?

Was it too late to even think of that? And was I, in the event, happy?

Although passage had been arranged, the rest of February went by without a sign of the *Lady Denison*. By the second week in March the boat had still not come. The weather turned miserable, with frequent storms, and the Maoris took to watching long hours over the sea for any sign of the vessel. I could sense how disheartened they felt, and it was difficult to know how to keep their spirits up.

The only one who was not unhappy was Matiu Tikiaki. We had observed his interest in Sally Jenkins from the very beginning of his incarceration and, well . . . they had fallen in love with each other.

Then at last, at dawn on 15 of March, I saw from our bedroom window the long-looked for vessel at anchor. I immediately woke Ismay.

'It's here,' I said.

She dressed hastily and ran barefoot to the Maoris' quarters bearing the glad news. 'Te waka kua tae mai nei,' she shouted. 'Kia tere! Kia tere! The boat has arrived. Hurry! Hurry!'

I knew her heart wasn't in the excitement. She had grown accustomed to the Maoris. They were whanau. She dreaded the moment when they would go back to their lives — and she to ours.

The *Lady Denison* lay at anchor for a few hours while stores from Hobart Town were unloaded, and goods made at the station were loaded to be sold in the town.

There was just time enough for the Maoris to make one last visit to Hohepa's grave with Liam Connor, Seamus Keelan and Kieron Moore.

'Moe mai,' Rahui said, weeping.

'Haere ra, e pa,' said Te Waretiti.

'Aue te mamae,' Matiu Tikiaki said.

The most piteous farewell was Kumete's. 'I should be taking you home with me,' he said. It had been his constant refrain.

We returned to the *Lady Denison*. Mr and Mrs Lapham had come down to farewell the Maoris too.

450

'You will be travelling in steerage,' Mr Lapham said as he shook their hands, 'but I have been assured that you will be treated with dignity and that you will receive a good and sufficient supply of provisions during the passage.'

There was one other passenger to farewell. Sally Jenkins.

She and Matiu Tikiaki had been crying so much during the past few months that Ismay had taken matters into her own hands. 'Would you like to go with Matiu Tikiaki when he departs Van Diemen's Land?' she asked Sally.

'But, miss, who will look after you?'

'Oh, Sally Jenkins! Go if your heart wills it!'

'Yes, miss. Oh, miss, thank you!'

We bought out the remaining years of Sally Jenkins' sentence, enabling her to become a free woman. She and Tikiaki were married by John Jennings Imrie in our cottage.

As a wedding gift, Ismay settled some money on her to ensure she would have a good beginning with her new husband in a new land.

It was a busy departure day for us as well.

Now that the Maoris were returning to New Zealand, our tour of duty was over and, we also were returning with them as far as Hobart Town.

My emotions were mixed. While Ismay, the children and I had been at Darlington Station, our life had taken its course from the job we had come to do — to look after the Maori prisoners. And then there were the Imries, and new friends made on Maria Island. All had contributed to our lives. And now we were leaving.

What lay ahead?

John Jennings and Etty Imrie came down to wave goodbye as we boarded the vessel.

'Where next in the world, eh, Mr McKissock?' John Jennings said.

As it happened, he had been offered a promotion to the Female Convict Establishment at Ross, seventy-three miles north of Hobart Town on the Macquarie River, and he and Etty planned to accept it. He slapped my back. There was a genuine sense of regret at our departure.

Etty was similarly regretful. 'I will write to you, Mr McKissock,' she said. Then she turned to Ismay. 'Goodbye, Mrs McKissock,' she said.

I noted the exchange with some curiosity. I had been conscious of the coolness between the two women since just before Te Umuroa's death, and had expected it to have mended. There was a distance with Ismay that not even the sadness of departure could breach.

All our lives were changing.

———

The *Lady Denison* left shore, and as the distance between boat and dock widened, so the sense of loss increased.

'Goodbye, mateys!' Liam Connor called to the Maoris.

The wind came up, the breeze steady and favourable as we turned southward down the Mercury Passage.

We made midstream and, on the breast of the tide, quickly began to move away. Past our cottage on the rise. Away from Darlington Station and its Union Jack fluttering. Leaving behind the waving figures of our friends.

Above the place where Hohepa was buried, nankeen night herons were circling.

And then all that was left was the phantom moaning of the sea.

———

The *Lady Denison* stopped briefly at Hobart Town to take on other passengers. Ismay, the children and I disembarked with our luggage and waited with a group of wellwishers, including George Washington Walker, the Masons and Eion Gault for the ship to weigh anchor again for New Zealand.

'Haere ra,' I said to Kumete, Matiu Tikiaki, Rahui and Te Waretiti.

We were all beyond words. Pure emotion flowed between us.

Ismay and Sally Jenkins sobbed like sisters. 'Goodbye, Sally,' Ismay wept. 'And you, Matiu Tikiaki, you look after her and be a good husband or else . . . I will come over to Aotearoa with a snake and chase you up a tree with it!' Her threat made us all laugh.

With a flurry of hugs and tears and shouts, they all went on board.

As the *Lady Denison* left harbour, Ismay stood on the dock waving a long white scarf. With some dismay she suddenly stopped and looked at me:

'The tokotoko! Kumete has not taken the tokotoko with him!'

She was in such a state that I had to calm her down. 'When the Masons return to New Zealand they can take it.'

Nodding with relief, Ismay started waving her scarf again. She burst into a song of farewell:

Hoki atu koutou ki o koutou kainga,
Hoki atu ki runga o te reo aroha.
Return, oh chiefs, to your homes,
The voice of love farewells you.

We heard that the *Lady Denison* arrived in Auckland some twelve days later. The arrival was reported on 1 April in the *New Zealander*; Henry Melville received a copy in Van Diemen's Land and kindly gave it to me.

> By this vessel (*Lady Denison*) four of the five natives of New Zealand who were transported to Van Diemen's Land for bearing arms against the Queen's troops during the late disturbances at the southward, are returned, liberated by order of Earl Grey, the fifth having previously died.

On behalf of Governor Grey, the colonial secretary wrote to Governor Denison to advise of their safe arrival and that the fee for their passage had been discharged as arranged with the agents of the barque. In the concluding pleasantries, Governor Grey extended 'the expression of his thanks for the trouble taken by His Excellency (Governor Denison) and the authorities at Hobart Town in this matter'.

What happened to the four Maori after that?

I don't know. Perhaps they fought again against Grey's troops in the wars yet to come in New Zealand. I hope so.

We never heard from Sally Jenkins again.

———

And then it was just Ismay and I and our three children.

We took a carriage to our house at Battery Point. The children were tired and sleepy. Ismay was carrying Clara. I had Rollo in my arms. Gower Jr unlocked the door.

When it opened, all I could see was the dark on the other side.

'Well, here we are, Mr McKissock,' Ismay said.

'Yes, here we are,' I answered.

46

It is another night in Rhodesia.

The stars are dancing over the Mountains of the Moon.

Georgina, her husband Austin and I have been celebrating. Indeed, I might say that I am just a tiny bit drunk, bad boy me. Why? A letter arrived this afternoon from Lindsay.

We live for his letters now. On the day the post is due to arrive, Georgina stands in front of the pot-pourri vase, twisting it. Ismay used to do that too, the pungent perfume filling the room. But no amount of lovely inhalant can soothe Georgina's anxieties and, when the rural delivery van comes, dust billowing behind, she runs to it even before it has stopped.

Meanwhile, Austin and I watch her from the verandah, and we know when a letter comes from her boy, because Georgina doesn't even open it.

'Still alive,' she sobs, crumpling to the ground.

Austin moves quietly to the hallway to pick up the telephone and call their sisters Ida and Sophie. 'Hello? We've had news . . . yes, a letter from Lindsay . . . they will have survived the battle at Romani . . .'

Keep writing, Lindsay. You must keep writing. And you, Jumbuck, good horse, keep him safe, you bad brute, and waltz our two Matilda boys back to us, eh?

Fortified with good news and whisky, I turn again to writing what the family have come to call 'The McKissock Journals'. There's no literary merit whatsoever, so I hope the family will not be disappointed.

I pray I can tell the truth too and, in particular, all those lessons I had to learn about the nature of life and of love — or aroha, the Maori word. They were not easy lessons but, in the end, I hope that Te Umuroa would congratulate me that, at least, I tried my best.

454

The years, oh the accumulation of years!

Our last ties with the Maoris came when Thomas and Jane Mason left Hobart Town for New Zealand, a few weeks after the Maoris.

'We are so looking forward to returning to New Zealand,' Thomas said. 'The grand towering trees there are our friends, and we wish God's green cathedral to be our home. New Zealand's great trees and the rare flowers from far-off shores may, in the fullness of time, live easy together.'

When Ismay went to pass them Hohepa's tokotoko, Thomas Mason returned it. 'I think Hohepa wanted you to have it.'

Ismay thanked him. 'It is good company and the last tangible reminder of Te Umuroa. I will hold it in safekeeping.'

We settled our brood back into Hobart Town, that lovely settlement of handsome freestone buildings nestled beneath Mount Wellington.

I realised that I had come to regard Van Diemen's Land as *my* green cathedral. Symbolic of this was Mount Wellington itself. I loved that mountain with its purple expanses of rock and forest. I watched it smile if the elements were kind, and frown if they were savage. If, on a summer morning, a band grew delicately out of nothing and lay like a fine lace veil across the Organ Pipes, then I knew that by afternoon a sweet steady breeze would ripple the Derwent River and give the yachtsmen the fine weather they knew and loved. On the other hand, a frowning grey mist meant fierce squalls and rattling showers over the shivering city. Until the cloud dispersed it would be a day of gloom.

I reopened my surgery and began work again at the Hobart Penitentiary. As for Ismay, without Sally Jenkins to assist her, she was fully occupied with the upkeep of the house and with the children. I marvelled at her resilience; she gave the impression that she had shut the door on Maria Island and, with that duty satisfactorily discharged, it was time to get on with the rest of her life. It was not until much later that I discovered how false that impression was: for many years, what happened there between her and Te Umuroa remained indelibly imprinted on her heart.

If there was any diminution in the quality of Ismay's affection for me, I did not notice it. Although, from time to time, a shadow cast itself over us, I considered that only to be a consequence of some immediate tension in our lives rather than some more lasting grief.

The next six years were among the happiest of our lives. They happened to coincide with those tumultuous times when Van Diemen's Land rose up against transportation, and against our political dependence on Great Britain; when I rejoined Eion Gault and the coalition of like-minded citizens, who had determined on stronger protest, Ismay made quite sure that she was a part of it.

Indeed, it was Ismay who remarked on the increase in the pauper population of the settlement. 'The children and I were stopped three times today by beggars,' she said. 'What is happening to Van Diemen's Land, Mr McKissock?'

The changing times were the constant discussion point with the group of Quakers and editors — and now, through Eion, the local politicians and businessmen, whom we met either at the Hobart Town Royal Society or, more frequently, at our own house in Battery Point. Again, Ismay became a focal point with her intelligence and perspicacity, and continued to attract admirers. Among them was the up and coming politician, Richard Dry, who, as one of the 'Patriotic Six', had resigned from the Van Diemen's Legislative Council over the estimates of expenditure presented to them by the Colonial Office two years earlier. Now restored to office, and still embattled with Governor Denison, Mr Dry was one of those men with distinctive leadership qualities of whom great things were expected.

'You and Mrs McKissock,' he complimented me, 'are an excellent partnership.'

What increasingly disturbed me was the pressure being placed on the colony.

'Are you aware,' I asked Eion one day, 'that although gangs of probationers are stationed in every direction where roads or bridges are required, there are over seven thousand prisoners still waiting in the Hobart Penitentiary, Port Arthur and other penal institutions for distribution?'

Furthermore, towards the end of 1848, rumours arose that the British Government intended to increase the numbers of prisoners — not only to Van Diemen's Land, but also to other colonies formerly closed to transportation.

It was a matter of weeks before our worst fears were confirmed by the arrival of the *Ratcliffe* from Spithead with two hundred and forty-eight male prisoners aboard. This ship was the forerunner for twenty others which arrived during the year, six from Ireland, five from New Zealand, three from England, two from Adelaide, one from Sydney, one from Port Phillip, and two from India — bearing a total of one thousand eight hundred and sixty convicts.

Then Eion came rushing to our house one evening when I had just returned from the surgery. 'Gower, have you heard?' he asked. 'Earl Grey didn't even wait for replies from the colonies before sending the *Neptune*, with two hundred and eighty-nine Irish convicts aboard, to the Cape of Good Hope! The prisoners have not been allowed to land there and the ship continues her voyage to us now. Not only that, but the *Hashemy*, with two hundred and twelve convicts, is also on her way to us after having been turned away at New South Wales.'

'The British Government pushes us too far,' I said. 'But mark my words, this will rebound on them.'

Indeed, Earl Grey's contemptuous disregard for Van Diemen's Land had one salutary effect. It united the people of the colony — some of whom had earlier argued that the convicts were a source of free labour for farms, roading and public buildings — in a decision to save the land of our adoption from further degradation. There were now few dissenting voices at the meetings that were held in all the chief towns. Petitions were sent to Parliament, to all influential friends and to the English press.

It was then that Earl Grey made a big mistake. During a debate in the English House of Lords, he declared: 'Millions of pounds have been spent in preparing Van Diemen's Land for convicts, and the free inhabitants cannot expect that, when they chose to call for cessation of the imperial policy, we would alter it on their demand. Van Diemen's Land was always and originally intended as a penal settlement and will receive any number of prisoners the British Government chooses to send. The authority of the Crown should be firmly asserted.'

When his words were reported in all the newspapers in Van Diemen's Land, the fire of indignation burned throughout the colony — and it led to the inauguration of the League of Solemn Engagement of the Australian Colonies.

———

I remember the first time I heard Eion talk about the League.

'Will you stand with us, Gower?' he asked. 'The League will be led by the Rev. John West, congregational minister of Launceston.'

Of course I said yes! I knew John West to be one of the most influential men in Van Diemen's Land, co-founder of the *Launceston Examiner*, political activist and one of the great middle-class dissenters of the colony.

I gathered with Eion, Reverend West, Richard Dry, George Washington Walker, Thomas Chapman and other distinguished gentlemen at the offices of Robert Pitcairn, a well-known barrister of Davey Street, Hobart Town, to witness the pledge:

We, the undersigned, deeply impressed by the evils which have risen from the transportation of the criminals of Great Britain to the Australian colonies, declare that transportation to any of the colonies ought forever to cease; and we do hereby pledge ourselves to use all lawful means to procure its abolition.

Rev. West led the meeting in putting his signature to the pledge. 'I like not Downing Street,' he said. 'There the groans of Australia die away in silence.'

What, in effect, were we doing? We were telling the colonial secretary to bugger off! But there was more:

It really *was* time to get rid of the gaoler.

'I haven't felt such a rush of passion since my days at Edinburgh University!'

Ismay laughed at my excitement. 'What happens now?' she asked.

'The League has decided to go to Melbourne to hold a conference of delegates from South Australia, Van Diemen's Land, Victoria, New South Wales and New Zealand. It will be the first time that our southern colonies will ever have been united on a particular matter.'

She looked at me with an impish look on her face. 'Mr McKissock, would you mind if I came along to do a spot of shopping? I'll bring the children. We won't get in your way. Oh please say that we may join you!'

I looked at her, somewhat surprised. Ismay *never* asked! However, she wasn't exactly deferring to me either. I nodded. 'Although the conference is not for women,' I answered, 'I know that wild horses will not prevent you from coming.'

'Is that a yes or a no?' she asked. 'It had better be a yes! After all, women have also been transported. Free or no, women have as much at stake in the future as men.'

I gathered her in my arms. 'Mrs McKissock,' I said, 'I'd quit while I was ahead if I were you. And of course it is a yes.'

Richard Dry was right: Ismay and I were indeed an excellent partnership. In politics we found common ground and a common ambition.

We were an excited crowd of delegates and supporters on board the boat taking us across Bass's Strait to Melbourne. The passage was exhilarating, with the wind coming up from the Antarctic and literally hurtling us before it across the storming sea.

Ismay took the children down below while I stayed on deck with Eion

Gault, huddling at the rail and looking out at the world swirling around us. I was so moved by the rhapsodic movement of nature — the scudding clouds, the hurtling ocean — and felt grateful to be part of God's bountiful immensity. Here at the bottom of the world, surely, He rather than man was triumphant — and I prayed that His kingdom would last forever.

I grinned at Eion and, in that heightened mood of elation, decided to raise the matter which had lain unspoken between us: his revealing remark when he had first seen Hohepa, *Yes, you are a pretty fellow.* I had wondered at the time whether Eion had unmasked himself. I wanted him to know that I had sympathy for him — aroha, perhaps, if I was to use Hohepa's more appropriate word.

'Eion,' I began, 'when you were nominated to the Legislative Council you said something which puzzled me at the time: "You don't know what you are asking." How do you feel, now that we are embarking on yet another enterprise which will put you even more into the public eye?'

'I don't know what you mean, Gower,' he smiled evasively.

'There is still time to withdraw,' I answered. Seagulls were wheeling above us. Higher, myriads of birds in migratory movement skimmed the blue vault of the sky.

He looked at me closely. 'You wish me to admit something to you that not even my closest friends know?' he asked.

'I am already your friend,' I answered, 'and there's no need to tell me. And regardless of any admission, I will always be your friend.'

The sun was so bright above Bass's Strait. Schools of flying fish leapt into it, disappearing into its blinding light.

'Thank you, Gower,' he said. 'And do you think me . . . weak . . . because of it?'

'It is only a weakness if you think it so,' I answered. 'But it can also be a strength. It gives you an understanding, call it compassion if you will, that others may lack when they make decisions that affect all of us.' I remembered something Ismay had said, in another context. 'Free or no, you also have as much at stake as all of us.' I gripped his hand and we embraced.

He was silent for a moment. Then he leant back against the railing and looked cheekily at me. 'You wouldn't happen to be attracted to me, Mr McKissock?' he asked.

'No,' I smiled.

'Not even a modicum?'

I knew he was teasing me.

We lapsed into silence and watched as the mainland grew larger, overpowering. Then I brought forward from my coat a flask of whisky and handed it to him.

'To the future?' he asked, taking a drink.

'Yes,' I answered. 'To the future.'

In the event, only delegates from Victoria and Van Diemen's Land met in the Queen's Theatre, Melbourne. But there, on 1 February 1851, Reverend West read out our manifesto.

> We must engage not to employ any person hereafter arriving under sentence of transportation for any crime committed in Europe. And as far as Van Diemen's Land is concerned, our colony is no longer available.

I was standing on the stage; Ismay and the children were in the public balcony. The applause was thunderous. While it resounded around us, I felt an extraordinary sense that something none of us had expected was about to begin.

The League had created for all colonists a common identity. On that day was awakened a sentiment, a surge for unity.

I later noticed that Ismay had sneaked her signature onto the document. I don't know how she did it: she must have come down from the public balcony while we were all congratulating ourselves.

'One of these days,' she said, 'women will be able to sign such documents and also give attribution to their sex.'

There it is: E. E. McKissock.

Under Rev. West's dynamic leadership, the League met again in Melbourne on 13 February, this time at a greater gathering at St Patrick's Hall. At the conference, the mottoes of the League, 'The Australians are One' and 'Under this sign we conquer', were enthusiastically endorsed. And the national sentiment that was aroused at our earlier conference gained expression when the flag of Australia was unfurled.

A blue ensign. The Union Jack in the upper hoist corner. In the centre, five white stars — the Southern Cross, the familiar constellation of the southern skies, emblematic of the Australian colonies, with an added star for New Zealand.

When the schooner *Swift* returned to Van Diemen's Land carrying the delegates back from the conference, the beautiful silk banner floated from the masthead.

From that moment the banner was copied, manufactured in bunting, displayed at rallies, flown from mastheads, and observed on ships as far afield as the United States.

Australia was born.

———

It was within this context of growing independence and nationalism that, later in the year, a legislative council of twenty-four members was proposed for Van Diemen's Land: sixteen to be elected by the people and eight nominated by Britain. With great cheering, the new council assembled on 30 December 1851. Richard Dry became the first native-born premier and speaker of the House of Assembly in the Parliament of Tasmania.

———

In 1853, transportation officially came to an end.

The last convict ship to arrive in Van Diemen's Land was the *St Vincent* on 26 May. Van Diemen's Land chose 10 August as a holiday to celebrate the joyful event. In Hobart Town the Trinity Church bells ushered in the day with joyous peals. At 8 a.m. public thanksgiving services were held at St David's Cathedral and other churches. Business was suspended; flags waved over the city and harbour and in the evening there were illuminations and a display of fireworks.

Even that not enough for us. It was also time to change the name of Van Diemen's Land to Tasmania.

Thus, after many years of importunity, the people of this land wrested self-governance from Britain.

'Isn't this what we came to the southern hemisphere for?' I asked Ismay.

'Yes Mr McKissock,' she answered. 'Indeed it is.'

We owed England nothing.

47

Our aim, as free citizens of Tasmania, was to create a new society in which all people could live with one another as equals.

Our intention brings to mind a newspaper article that appeared in the *Hobart Times* in 1856, and which I have kept all these years. Here it is, yellowed and creased:

CLERGYMAN BELIEVES TASMANIA
IS GARDEN OF EDEN

———

The headline referred to a lecture given in London by the Reverend Geoffrey Wilson, (M.A. Cantab.) in which he offered 'A Proof against the Atheisms of Geology'.

'The truth of the chronology of the Bible conclusively shows,' the Reverend said, 'that there was a Garden of Eden. I myself have received a new and important revelation of its whereabouts. The Garden of Eden was not, as supposed, located in the region of Arabia, but was, instead in Australia, on the Island of Tasmania.' The Rev. Wilson also included in his lecture a full and extented explanation of 'The Theory of Divine Refrigeration'.

Well, if nothing, it was good for a laugh, eh?

In many respects, we were seeking to create our own Eden, our own Australian Arcadia, where all our flowers, drawn from all countries of the world, could grow, and children of our own could play among them.

———

The years passed by.

In 1860 I was forty and Ismay was thirty-eight. While I no longer had the contract of the Hobart Town Penitentiary to supplement my income, the surgery was doing exceptionally well. In appearance, my blond hair was thinning at the temples and the Australian sun had certainly thickened my skin; it looked like a kangaroo hide that had been hung out to dry. But my eyes were still piercing blue and vanity had kept any surplus poundage off me; I still walked as upright as ever, and flattered myself that nobody seeing me passing by would know that my left leg was a piece of wood. Indeed, I liked to think myself still a fine figure of a man and attractive to women.

As for Ismay, she had hardly changed at all. People always commented on her burnished red hair, such a dark rich red, and her figure; the fuller figure was now fashionable and, while Ismay cared little for such trends, I have a suspicion that she dressed with an eye to fashion anyhow and, in particular, chose gowns that showed off her still slim waist.

However, her views on the relationship between men and women were as sharp as ever. I still remember the absolute fury she flew into on reading Mr Ruskin's essay, 'Of Queen's Gardens'. Her cousin Isobel had enclosed a copy of the essay with a letter from England, with a note: 'You may find Mr Ruskin's views of interest, Ismay dear.'

Of interest? Why, the boys and I had to hastily exit the house before Ismay turned on *us* about Ruskin's views on the separate roles of men and women, to wit: '[a woman's] intellect is not for invention or creation, but for sweet ordering, arrangement and decision . . . Her great function is Praise' . . . Or, '[a woman must be] wise, not for self-development but for self-renunciation' . . . Or, 'Speaking broadly, a man ought to know any lan-guage or science he learns thoroughly — while a woman ought to know the same language, or science, only so far as may enable her to sympathise in her husband's pleasures, and in those of his best friends.'

Not for Ismay the sweet ordering, self-renunciation or learning languages or science only so that she could sympathise with her husband!

On other matters, her child-bearing years appeared to be behind her, as no further children appeared to disturb our family horizon. To tell the truth, I would not have minded another child. The years had rubbed off many of my former attitudes. Life had smoothed me out, and some of the edges which had caused an ill fit between us from time to time had, by some knocking into shape on both our parts, been smoothed to make a better join. I suppose we were rather like an odd jigsaw puzzle, of the kind that Clara loved to put together. Some of the pieces had been fitted into the wrong places but, by dint of sufficient squeezing and shoving, the puzzle achieved some successful completion.

As for the children — goodness, the boys were young men now! I often had to catch my breath when I looked at them. After all, by Gower Jr's age I was married a year to Ismay and we were on our way to New Zealand! Had I really looked that young? How ever had I managed to cope with being a husband, and with all the events of that time? Yet, looking at Gower Jr — taller than me now, but dark, and as confident as his mother — I knew that if the same circumstances faced him he would rise to the challenges and would make the best of them. Recently returned from my old alma mater, Edinburgh University, he had the makings of a fine academic, specialising in the medical sciences. Of course, he had looked at his grandfather Ramsay's bones during anatomy classes. Instead of finding the experience ghoulish, he was instead moved.

'He was *extraordinary*, Father,' he told me.

I could not help the emotion that welled into the pool of my memory. 'Yes,' I answered. 'When I was younger, I always wanted to look like him. Instead, I look like *this*.'

As for Rollo, he hadn't turned out as well as his brother. As fair as Gower Jr was dark, he was the good-looking one of the family. His intellect was not as great as his brother's — nor, dare I say it, as his good mother and father's — and the horizon of his ambition was somewhat lower than I had hoped. I had harboured expectations that he might become a surgeon like me; instead, his inclination was towards an easier passage through life, and he was content to be a clerk in the offices of a maritime insurance company.

But of both my sons, it was Rollo whom I loved more. To treat them with equity was difficult. Whenever I was in that quandary, I tried to remember Hohepa's words about the nature of love — or aroha. 'It does not have one meaning,' he had said, 'but many. It cannot be considered by itself in isolation. It has to be associated with other words like awhinatanga, to support, and manaakitanga, to offer hospitality, and whanaungatanga, to honour kinship. When all its qualities are observed, they ensure that we are in the right relationship with each other and with our world.'

———————

I come now to the episode which neither Ismay nor I could ever have foreseen.

Its harbinger was a letter from Wolverhampton, delivered late one evening in May 1865 by a young English migrant only just disembarked from his ship in the harbour. Addressed to Ismay and myself and marked

URGENT, it came with a request 'PLEASE PAY THE BEARER OF THIS LETTER THREE GUINEAS FOR HIS MOST SPEEDY AND HELPFUL DESPATCH THEREOF.'

'You are Mr Gower McKissock?' the migrant asked. 'I was only to give the letter over to him or his missus.' He saw Ismay behind me. 'You are Mrs McKissock?'

'Yes,' I answered on our behalf. The handwriting belonged to Rollo Springvale. I took the letter from him and gave it to Ismay. 'When did Dr Springvale give you the letter?'

'Ah,' the young man said, relieved. 'So you know the gentleman? He come to the Downs when he heard a ship was sailin' for Tasmania and pressed his urgent request on me as I was boarding. Indeed, he wrote the letter while I waited him and I've been most careful with it all the way across the ocean. I am come post haste from landing to deliver it.'

Intrigued and worried, I gave the young man the three guineas he had been promised. 'Thank you for your safe delivery of it,' I said.

'It will be bad news,' Ismay shivered. 'Oh, I hope nothing has happened to Aunt Eleanor . . .'

The children clustered around their mother. 'Please open the letter, Mother,' they begged.

The news within was not about Eleanor Springvale at all. Rather, Dr Springvale's letter, hastily scrawled, contained an apology, and a warning.

My dear Ismay,

You will forgive me if I forgo the usual pleasantries and news about the family — let me assure you they are well and send their love — but I have little time to write this letter and give it to the person who will deliver it. Dear child, I have recently had news from a fellow doctor who has a patient known mutually to us. Against his doctor's advice that gentleman, who has a congested heart condition, has decided to book passage to Australia. He is Lowthian Webster, he is much changed, and I know not what his reasons are for his voyage. His departure is imminent and, who knows, he may arrive before this letter reaches you! However, I have felt it my duty to alert you to his coming.

I am, as always, your loving Uncle,
Rollo Springvale.

Ismay went very pale. 'What is it, Mother?' Rollo asked.

'Your grandfather is on his way to Australia,' she answered.

465

Five days later, while rain lashed Hobart Town, Ismay received a note delivered by a message boy of the Imperial Hotel. Lowthian had arrived off the *Primavera* and taken a suite. Would we be so kind as to visit him at our convenience?

'Never,' Ismay said. 'Nor can I comprehend why he would want to come all this way to see us.'

'Perhaps he wants to reconcile with you,' I answered her.

'Reconcile? I hold him personally responsible for my mother's death.'

So began a battle of wills between Ismay and her father. Every morning the same message boy would come, battling the cold wind, to deliver Lowthian's message, and every day Ismay would refuse to see him.

Of course the children were puzzled. Ismay had never spoken about their grandfather, preferring to keep her relationship with him to herself. Alas, if only she had done so! Not knowing that history, they could only view their mother's resistance as selfish and unwarranted. 'Why won't Mother see him?' they asked me. 'And why can't *we* see him! After all he is our grandfather and the only immediate relative we have in the world.'

But still Ismay would not detail the punitive regime that had marked her childhood and led her to be brought up by the Springvales. Why, she had not fully explained it to me either! Thus, I am ashamed to say that I was in sympathy with their view. After all, there were no relatives on my side — except for Ailie, and who knew what had happened to her — and the children's only other relatives were the Springvales. In all the wide world, the closest immediate family was Lowthian Webster.

'I will not have any of you standing against me in this matter,' Ismay said, 'and that goes for you too, Mr McKissock.'

A week later, while the stormy weather maintained its fury, Lowthian decided to take matters into his own hands.

I now realise he knew exactly what he was doing. One afternoon, he organised a carriage to bring him to the house. He must have known that I would be at the surgery. He may even have asked the driver to wait until Ismay left to go briefly, umbrella up against the weather, to the fish market on the quay; I would not put it past him to have enquired of her routine.

Clara was home, and when both Gower Jr and Rollo arrived soon after, he made his move. He walked down the pathway, leaning against the wind and rain, and tapped at the door.

Rollo opened it.

'You must be my grandson,' he said to him. 'May I come in?'

When Ismay returned to the house, she found Lowthian settled in an armchair before a blazing fire. He was in conversation with the children. The blood drained from her face.

His eyes swivelled in her direction. 'Well, miss . . .' he began.

'How *dare* you come into my house uninvited, sir,' she said, almost screaming.

The children had been enjoying their grandfather's company. That only made matters worse for her. Why could they not see the evil in him?

'Go and get your father,' Ismay told Rollo. '*Now.*'

———————

I came at the run. When I arrived, Lowthian's carriage was waiting outside. He was esconsed in an armchair by the fire as if he was already master of the house. Gower Jr and Clara were standing by the window and Rollo went to join them.

Ismay was sitting opposite her father; I stood beside her. This was a matter between her and Lowthian, but I would support her.

He was, as Rollo Springvale had intimated in his letters, much changed — piteously so. In his early seventies now, his tall frame had doubled in upon itself. He had a shock of white hair and, when he spoke, half his face was immobile from some stroke he had had as early warning of his heart condition; the incipient sneer of lip was thus camouflaged. But even in his old age he still had about him the aura of power.

The fire was burning, the flames crackling.

'Why have you come?' Ismay asked him. 'Why did you not die on the voyage here?'

The children were shocked. 'Mother . . .' They saw only a defenceless old man.

'I wanted to make peace with you,' Lowthian answered. 'After all you are my daughter . . .' The flames silhouetted him as he spoke, surrounding him with a penitential penumbra.

'You have never called me that in my entire life . . .'

'. . . and you are the issue of myself and your mother . . .'

'. . . whom you abused all her life,' Ismay responded. 'And you would have continued your patriarchal abuse of me as well, had Selina not got me out of the house . . .'

He gave a moan. 'I agree I wasn't perfect,' he began, 'and I acknowledge all my past indiscretions . . .'

Ismay gave a laugh of cynicism. 'Like that? You wish to wipe away all your sins . . . just like that? No, I will not allow it.'

'Won't you forgive me? Now that both your brothers are dead . . .'

Oh, he was so clever with his words: *your* brothers, not *my* sons, playing on her sympathy — and that of the children.

'. . . you and your children are the only family I have . . .'

'Family?' Ismay flared. 'How dare you mock that fine institution. When I was born, you didn't even want me to have your name. I was christened Glossop, and not once did you ever make restitution to me of the Webster surname and lineage.'

She was trembling. I had never seen her so angry. 'Why are you *here*! Why!'

The fire was crackling and roaring in the grate.

It was all so simple really. 'I have no male issue now,' he answered. 'Your children are my only heirs . . .'

'All of them?' Ismay asked, 'or are you referring only to my sons?'

'I will not lie to you,' he answered. 'Yes, I speak of my grandsons Gower Jr and Rollo. Would you not want me to settle upon them the Webster inheritance?'

He laid down his obscene offer. 'All I wish to do, and this is why I have come around the world to see them . . .'

He opened his arms to them: our sons.

'. . . is to make them my heirs . . .'

There was a condition, of course.

'. . . if they take upon themselves the name of Webster.'

With his words, the matter turned from one concerning Ismay and her father to include *me* also.

My gorge rose at that. Oh, I know I had never wanted the children at first. And Ismay had asked me when we were working through our marriage contract whether or not they would take the Glossop or McKissock name — and I had offered McKissock. But never would I have expected to defend an offer fabricated not by love but from circumstance.

My senses were reeling.

I was a McKissock. My children were McKissocks.

Ismay was about to respond to Lowthian Webster. But I pressed her shoulders. 'No, Ismay,' I answered. 'I am the head of the house.' I turned to Clara. 'Clara, would you please fetch Mr Webster's hat and coat. He is leaving.'

I will give him his due. He rose up with dignity. Bowed to Ismay. Put his hand out to me to shake; I would not do it.

Gower Jr and Rollo escorted him to the door.

'Thank you for hearing me out,' he said to them.

The wind whistled past him when he went out the door. I watched him battle down the pathway to the carriage. When it left he turned to the house and nodded.

At the time I didn't know who the nod was for.

And then he was gone.

Of course it wasn't over.

Ismay and I discovered that one of our sons had begun to visit with his grandfather at the Imperial Hotel. Had it been Gower Jr, I wouldn't have minded so much.

Instead, it was my dear son Rollo.

Oh, my son! Why did you do that to me? Why the defection?

Even now, all these years later, I remember how I railed against Rollo's decision, mourned that he would even think of giving up the McKissock name but, most of all, desert me for Lowthian Webster.

He had, at least, the courage to advise Ismay and me of his action. 'You have reached your majority,' she said to him. 'I cannot stop you. But you take your grandfather's side and, therefore you are against me.'

'I hope one day you will forgive me,' he answered.

On the last day, standing on the dock — Ismay refused to come down to say goodbye, but Gower Jr and Clara were with me — just before he was due to sail with Lowthian back to England, I didn't want to let go of him.

'Tell Mother I said goodbye,' he asked. 'And please understand why I have done this. I am not as my elder brother. I will never have a brilliant career as a McKissock. But I will as a Webster.' His words were foolishly chosen and I know he did not mean them.

When I returned home, I vented my anger on Ismay. 'I hope you are satisfied, Mrs McKissock.'

'Satisfied?' she answered.

'Your father has stolen the only child of ours that I ever loved.'

I heard a choked cry. I hadn't realised that Gower Jr and Clara were there and had overheard. Although we managed to maintain our relationship, I know now that on that day I lost *all* my children.

Ah yes, and then three years later, I was taught another lesson about life and how, no matter your expectations, often the reward is bitterness.

On 7 January 1868, Prince Alfred, Duke of Edinburgh and second son of Queen Victoria, arrived in Hobart on HMS *Galatea*. He was the first member of the royal family to visit Tasmania, and Ismay and I were invited to the grand reception in his honour.

We saw at the glittering function a familiar figure, the Trowennan William Lanney. The last time we had seen him was in 1847 when he had been on his way to Flinders Island. He was dressed in a blue coat decorated with gold braid. Later, the two royals — the Duke of Edinburgh and King Billy — the name by which William Lanney had become popularly known — strolled together beneath the public gaze engaged in a regal tête-à-tête on the banks of the Derwent.

I waited for a moment until he was alone and then went up to him and introduced myself. 'Mr Lanney,' I said, 'it is a pleasure to meet you.'

In his eyes I saw his ancestors.

'Mr McKissock,' he answered. 'You must help me . . .'

I now report, with heavy heart, on what happened to the Trowennans.

To do so I will have to backtrack to 1847.

There had been hopeful expectations for the Oyster Bay community, and at first the forty-four Trowennans welcomed their return to their native country and soil. Soon, however, these survivors from Flinders Island started to die from disease, as well as from the effects of strong liquor and depression. At first the number of deaths excited no comment, but between the months of December 1850 and March 1851 five were struck down by various diseases.

That year, too, Mrs Clark, the wife of the superintendent, died. Worn out and heartbroken, Robert Clark succumbed too. He had been the one person who could speak the Trowennans' dialect well. To him and Mrs Clark they had turned for affection and guidance; he had stood between them and the stern administration of the Colonial Secretary's Department.

In Mr Clark's place, two chaplains were appointed to visit and guide the Trowennans, but though both were good, earnest men, they were so unpopular that, on seeing them coming by horse over the hill, the Trowennans disappeared into the bush, hiding until they left for home. Not that any good would have been communicated between them as the chaplains did not speak their tongue.

By 1854 only sixteen Trowennans in all — three men, eleven women and two boys — were left. They were idle and depressed. Twenty-eight of their fellows had died and been buried in the dip in the hills above them.

Ten years later a further major epidemic carried off more Trowennans, and by the end of that year there were only five females and one male alive.

They were sent rations and tobacco each week from Hobart, but they had let their vegetable gardens die, and sorely missed the nourishment they were used to when killing and eating live game.

The solitary male, William Lanney, left Oyster Bay and, because he had friends among the sailors, settled close to the port of Hobart Town.

'Don't hesitate to call if ever you need my help,' I said to William Lanney just before Ismay and I left the reception.

We were both concerned for his welfare. Sometimes we saw him around the docks and were heartened that he had many friends among the seamen of the harbour. By that time only a handful of Trowennans were still living: Maryann, Patty-the-Ringtailed-Possum, Old Wapperty, Trucanini and William himself. They were the last of the full-bloods.

William was often blind drunk. It was in this state that one night he banged on our door. He was in total terror. 'Mr McKissock, sir, I don't dare to go to sleep. I have nightmares. In my bad dreams people come to poke at me, measure my skull, paint my image on canvas and take my photograph.'

He began to drink even more heavily and was to be seen in the lowest hovels of town. He rallied once, in 1869, to sail on the whaler *Runnymede* as a crewman but, on his return, he was afflicted with a terrible illness.

I was at home one night when a sailor banged on the door. 'Mr McKissock, please come. It's King Billy.' I followed the sailor to the Dog and Partridge tavern. William Lanney had been taken to a room. As soon as I saw him, I knew he was not long for this earth. All I could do was to sit with him and make his going as peaceful as possible; he had all the symptoms of choleraic diarrhoea.

'Ah, Mr McKissock,' he said when he opened his eyes briefly and saw me. 'Promise me that when I die, you will bury me deep or burn me up?'

'Yes, Mr Lanney,' I answered. 'I promise.'

He was only thirty-four.

I am not happy with what happened next.

William Lanney's death touched off a macabre dispute between the government and the Royal Society of Tasmania. My scientific colleagues, who up until that time preferred to classify flora and fauna, suddenly discovered that they lacked the skeleton of a Trowennan; they petitioned the colonial secretary for a permit to dissect William Lanney's body.

I spoke up on his behalf. 'I promised Mr Lanney that he would be buried intact,' I said, 'and I mean to keep my vow.'

I could not help but compare the situation with that of my father, Ramsay. My father had willingly allowed his body to be used for the purposes of medical education, but William Lanney had not.

Thus my colleagues were allowed only to measure him and take plaster casts; the government issued an order giving the necessary power to the local authorities to give William a decent burial.

On the day of the funeral, however, a rumour swept Hobart Town. His corpse, it was said, had been mutilated.

Ismay and I were both at the church for the funeral service. I was not surprised when Captain McArthur, on behalf of William's friends, including William's former master, Captain Bayley, demanded that the coffin be opened.

I examined poor William. 'The body appears to be untampered with,' I said.

The coffin was sealed again. Four whaling hands from the *Runnymede* acted as pallbearers, their ship's flag covering the casket. An old possum-skin rug and a handful of native weapons lay on the bright standard.

Over a hundred seamen from all the ships then in port marched behind. Like me, they all wished for William Lanney to rest in peace without being desecrated.

But after the burial the seamen — oh, they were such stalwart friends! — were still suspicious of the members of the Royal Society. They demanded a guard for William's grave. A policeman was ordered to patrol but somehow this order miscarried.

No guard stood over William on the night when he was committed to the earth.

The next morning, soil soaked with blood and grease showed that grave robbers had dug him up. A skull lay close to the disturbed earth, but it was not William Lanney's.

Who had desecrated his grave?

I am pleased to say that my friend Richard Dry was immensely disturbed by the incident. He dismissed Dr William Crowther of the hospital, along with Dr Stokell the house surgeon on duty that night. A popular song swept through Hobart Town when the official inquiry was held:

King Billy's dead, Crowther has his head,
Stokell has his hands and feet,
My feet, my feet, my poor black feet,
That used to be so gritty,

They're not aboard the *Runnymede,*
They're somewhere in the city.

———————

That wasn't the end of the story of the Trowennans.

The decision was made to close the reserve at Oyster Bay. Trucanini and the half-caste known as Mary Ann were the only ones left of that proud race. Trucanini remained there until 1872, and while she received an offer from Lucy Beedon, matriarch of the Bass Strait community, she chose to stay with a family by the name of Dandridge, to whom she was deeply attached. For the last three years of her life she was known as 'Queen Trucanini'. Tiny but stout, she liked to wear a red turban, and was well liked at Government House functions. Sometimes, she would come to my surgery and lead me silently outside to sit in the sun.

We wouldn't say anything to each other. Just hold hands like two lovers — or close friends. Then she would beam a smile and leave.

She died on 8 May 1876, after a day or two's illness. She was the last of the Trowennans. In one generation, all were gone.

The tributes for her were fulsome, but macabre events surrounded her death, as they had that of William Lanney. The Royal Society, as in Lanney's case, made application for her remains in the interests of science. Again the colonial secretary would have none of such barbaric antics. She was buried at a secret ceremony at the Cascades Penitentiary.

The Royal Society was apparently undeterred. Some of its members exhumed her body in 1877, and the society kept the body in their collection until 1900, when it was put on public view, together with remains of Woureddy, her husband, in the Tasmanian Museum.

———————

Ah yes, I had learnt one lesson about losing a son.

Now I learnt another about man's inhumanity to man. We may have desired a Garden of Eden.

There was no place in it, however, for the Trowennans.

48

Another night, another page of the journal.

There's a mirror in the study. I never like to look in it. Why? It tells the truth. It shows the way I have sunk into old age, my blue eyes now smoky and my complexion ruddy. Dressed in my usual shabby tweeds, I've turned into an old fart.

———

By 1884 Gower Jr was forty-two and Clara thirty-nine. I like to think that they forgave me my impetuous and unkind remark about loving them less than their brother. Their marriages to Claire and Philip appeared to happy and their children were healthy and strong. What more could we have asked for?

During those burgeoning years, Tasmania and Hobart had leapt ahead. Princes Wharf was busy with London and overseas traders as well as inter-colonial trading ships from Mauritius, Queensland and New Zealand. The whole wharf reeked of whale oil, which seeped from long barrels on the wooden timbers.

Life seemed to me as surprising as the appearance now and then of English goldfinches, thrushes, blackbirds, yellowhammers and bullfinches, populating the clear blue sky as irrevocably as we were populating the landscape.

———

Then I received a letter from Etty Imrie. Following the cessation of trans-portation in 1853, she and John Jennings had moved from Ross, where they had been overseers at a convict women's factory, to Queensland. I had often thought of them, particularly of John Jennings, who was my oldest friend.

But when Ismay and I left Maria Island I presumed that the friendship had ended, naturally, because we were moving in different directions. Yet, from time to time I had missed John Jennings; after all, it had been because of him and his friend Gwen that I had gone to hear Edward Gibbon Wakefield extolling the attractions of immigration to New Zealand.

I therefore opened Etty's correspondence with anticipation and pleasure.

Dear Gower,

I hope you do not mind my being so informal in my address and pray that this letter finds you in good health and prosperity. I cannot believe that all these years have passed since our former friendship and association in Nelson, Hobart Town and on Maria Island. What extraordinary experiences we shared in New Zealand and in Van Diemen's Land!

Of course we are all Australians now, though John Jennings continues to keep in touch with his family in Castlehill, Parish of Ayr, Scotland, and I with relatives in Cashmere, Ross. Actually, I had assumed that he was still in touch with you when we left our positions at the women's factory. But he tells me that he has been tardy in that respect so you may not know that we purchased Cashmere Station on the Macquarie River and started sheep and cattle farming? Unfortunately, it proved to be unremunerative and, after some consideration of our finances we sold up and came over to Queensland with the family on the *Black Swan*.

However, you may have come into contact with our eldest son Henry — you remember Henry, don't you, he and Gower Jr were very good friends on Maria Island. He married a lovely Launceston girl, Mary Frances Wettenhall, and remained in Tasmania. But Eliza, Jessie and John travelled with us and are all married now as is Charles William this year past. He was the babe who was born on Maria Island just before our dear Hohepa Te Umuroa passed away. How sad that was.

Anyway, John Jennings and I had two further children, both daughters, before we departed for the mainland. We did not know what employ we would find at our age, being in our late forties, but the Lord provided! John Jennings was able to find a position as the postmaster at Laidley and, for the past ten years has been a clerk in the Queensland Public Services. People remark upon his gentlemanly bearing and his kind, gentle disposition. I know that those descriptions will tally with your own estimations.

Indeed, it was because of his gentlemanly ways and kind disposition that John Jennings always had great sympathy for you. He told me of the circumstances of your marriage to Mrs McKissock — you will note that this letter is addressed only to you and I would appreciate your keeping it in confidence — and I know how he agonised when you asked him one day whether there had been anything between Ismay and Mr Te Umuroa. However, dear Gower, the matter has weighed on his conscience for many years and mine too, ever since I saw Mrs McKissock in a passionate embrace with the Maori. But I am sure, and so is John Jennings, that these matters are resolved between couples and I pray that you have subsequently found happiness in each other.

Should you ever travel to Queensland, we would be overjoyed to see you.

I remain your friend,
Etty Imrie

I put the letter down.

It was harmless enough, but the line, 'I saw Mrs McKissock in an embrace with the Maori' began to bother me. Why had Etty waited so long to tell me about Ismay and Hohepa? And why had John Jennings agonised over his advice to me that there had been nothing between them?

Aue e te tangata aroha aue e . . . Don't leave me.

Those words of Ismay's, at Hohepa's death, had been puzzling. Oh yes, I knew there was a deep affection between them, and I had often felt closed out by it.

And what about Hohepa's words as well?

Forgive me, Mr McKissock. And when the time comes, forgive her too.

I felt a great sense of anger. It mounted in me to such a point that Ismay sensed that something had upset me.

'What is wrong, Mr McKissock?' she asked.

I should have confronted her then, rather than wait — the words of accusation often came like bile in my throat — and I know they affected matters between us. But I chose to avoid confronting Ismay directly with Mrs Imrie's letter and my own suspicions.

And then I began to wonder about certain occasions in the past when I was away on business, sometimes overnight, around Tasmania or Melbourne or Sydney, most often to conferences involving gatherings of fellow surgeons.

In the early days, Ismay would say, 'Oh, perhaps I can visit Etty Imrie while you are away and stay overnight with her' — but Etty had not mentioned any of Ismay's visits in her letter!

Where did she go?

A year later, I was no longer able to maintain my composure. Ismay might be able to keep moving forward, but I was finding my anger difficult to live with — apart from which, I was curious to know where Ismay went on her secret excursions. Oh, I think I already *knew*, but I needed confirmation.

I told Ismay that I had a few days' business in Launceston. She had long abandoned the Etty Imrie pretext, but I wondered what she would do with the opportunity. I booked into a nearby hotel, and watched and waited.

Only hours after taking my leave I saw our daughter Clara, with Georgina — she was a teenager now — approaching the house. Ismay appeared at the door in a long brown travelling coat and hat held by a long pearl-tipped hatpin. She kissed Clara's cheeks and made some pretence of affection to Georgina, and then walked away down the street.

As soon as she had gone, I went to the front door and let myself in.

Georgina came smiling towards me, 'Grandpa! Where did you spring from?'

'My business trip was cancelled,' I lied as I kissed her. My greeting of Clara was much colder. 'Where has your mother gone?' I asked as she emerged from the parlour to see what the commotion was about.

She had the decency to look shamefaced. 'I don't know,' she answered. Poor Clara has never been able to lie with any proficiency.

I took her arm. 'Your mother,' I repeated. 'Tell me.'

'To visit her . . . special friend,' she answered in a rush.

Wresting herself free, she ran up the stairs and into the bedroom where she had slept as a child. I could hear her weeping.

'Has Grandma got a special friend?' Georgina asked. Her eyes lit up.

I kissed her again. 'That is none of your business,' I said to her, 'and don't forget, Georgina, that curiosity kills kittens as it does cats.'

Turning away, I proceeded out the door to follow Ismay. I was just in time to see her step up to a light chaise from a stables close by and, taking the reins, urge the horse onward. A quick inquiry of the stable owner, who was at first reluctant to advise her destination, soon got that out of him: 'Mrs McKissock is taking the road northeast along the coast.'

A heavy stone settled in my heart. There was no need to hurry. I knew her destination.

Why then did I follow her? Oh, perhaps because I wanted to spoil her rendezvous. Mess her memorial nest. Let her know, 'You can't hide any more, Ismay.'

I organised my own chaise, hurried back to the hotel, packed my suitcase and paid my bill — and then I followed after her.

The day was a delightful one, soft and mild; I purposely stayed far behind, and to tell the truth I was rather proud of my shadowing skill. Ismay reached Sorell and proceeded towards the east coast to Orford. There was quite a bit of traffic heading east, and as it passed me — horsemen in haste or other carriages and coaches — I wondered where they were all going.

But I was too far behind her. When I caught up at Louisville, it was only to see that the ferry *Papua* had already made midstream in the Mercury Passage.

There were another boat preparing to leave, however, and as I walked towards it I was spied by a political colleague, William Henry Burgess. 'Hello, Gower. Are you going across for the festival? Come with us.'

Festival? Of course! That accounted for the traffic. The prosperous Italian silk merchant and entrepreneur, Angelo Giulio Diego Bernacchi had completely transformed Maria Island. Over two hundred and forty people lived there now, in a small town with the palatial Grand Hotel surrounded by vineyards and plantations and, yes, he sponsored an annual festival. Perhaps Ismay's visit was to do with her indulgence in cultural pursuits rather than for any other reason.

I accepted William's affable offer and was soon aboard the vessel chartered to take him and his guests across the Mercury Passage without having to rub shoulders with the hoi polloi. I took the glass of cabernet sauvignon William thrust into my hands. 'From Mr Bernacchi's vineyard,' he said, 'and already such quality!'

I wandered to the bow, sipping at the wine; the water was as smooth as a millpond. My heart was thudding with nostalgia because, ever since Ismay and I and the children had left Maria Island forty years ago, I had never returned.

It was, as ever, intriguing and beautiful. There was no place like it, purpling in the dusk, edenic, within an iridiscent sea.

———

The boat arrived at the dock. I saw that the *Papua* was there, as well as the steamers *Endeavour* and *Warrentina*, and the *Belle Brandon*. Men and women in gay attire were strolling from the jetty up a pathway lit with a double row of Venetian and Chinese lanterns, to Mr Bernacchi's house. The trees along the beach were illuminated by countless more lanterns, making a magnificent promenade.

I said goodbye to William, who was heading to the house also. 'Be careful of Diego's banditti,' he laughed. 'They like to ambush unwary guests!'

I assured William I would be alert, and made my way to the Grand Hotel.

478

As I did so, memories stirred all around me, for the hotel had been built where the separate apartments of Darlington Station had originally stood.

'It's all vanity,' I said to myself. 'Nothing can cover what happened here.' Even so, I was impressed with the Grand Hotel, which had been based on plans combining the best qualities of Riviera establishments. The building was in the form of a T, with verandahs back and front. There were two fine dining rooms and a large sitting room in the wings on the east and west side, while the north wing boasted a double row of bedrooms and small sitting rooms for private parties. There was also a fine billiard room — a favoured domain of the town's gentlemen.

The air was filled with enchantment. A tiered ornamental garden sent perfume upon the breeze and provided a beautiful foreground for a panoramic view of Darlington Bay. Tonight it, too, was lit up with lanterns. An Italian gondola flitted over the glassy water.

From the lobby of the hotel it was clear that no expense had been spared on the furnishings. Chandeliers hung from the ceiling and, from the desk clerk's position, I could see that all the public rooms were richly furnished.

'Do you have a Mrs McKissock registered?' I asked.

The desk clerk checked. 'Oh yes,' he said. 'She arrived this very evening.'

'If you would be so kind,' I answered, 'could you give me a room near to hers.' I was pleased to have located Ismay so quickly, but apprehensive at having tracked her down to such a lavish hotel. And now that I was here, what would I say to her?

I immediately regretted coming. 'Oh you foolish, *foolish* man,' I said to myself. I turned back to the desk clerk, preparing to cancel my room. Where I would go from here I had absolutely no idea, but my one resolve was to get away as quickly as possible.

Just then, Ismay appeared. I happened to look out the glass doors of the hotel and saw her returning from the beach, walking with her shoes in her hands. The doors were bevelled at the edges, and for a moment she took on a number of reflections as she approached.

My heart caught in my throat. Why, she looked just like she had at the Wolverhampton Dispensary Ball: tall, determined, upright, elegantly coiffed and dressed. *Mr McKissock, there are other women who would go with you to New Zealand.* I must confess I was taken aback by her beauty; it had grown rather than diminished. I felt I was seeing her afresh. Had I taken her for granted all this while? Her hair was pale gold now, the titian in it tempered by silver, and her green eyes were softer, like jade rather than diamonds. The virtues and experiences of her life had added rather than detracted from her appearance, making her more desirable. She was dressed in a pale green dress and looked quite girlish.

Before I could slip away she saw me — she had stooped to put on her shoes, and glimpsed me as she did so. Her eyes widened and her face fell. She recovered quickly, however, came through the doors and approached the desk. 'Gower,' she smiled, 'I thought you were in Launceston. Have you come to San Diego for the festival?'

My frustration and dismay with her returned. 'No, madam,' I answered. 'Have you?'

She swayed, realising from the tone of my voice that I had followed her. 'Ah,' she said, 'so you have found me out. Have you checked in?'

'Yes,' I answered, 'but I have booked into a separate room.'

A sad expression crossed her face. 'Don't you think that is unnecessary?' She turned to the clerk. 'Mr McKissock will not need a separate room unless he chooses to.'

She looked at me; I shook my head.

'In that case,' she continued to the clerk, 'would you kindly take my husband's suitcase to my room. Would you like to dine with me, Mr McKissock?'

'I would — unless you are expecting company?' I answered. 'You are dressed as if you are.'

'What an unfortunate, hurtful thing to say,' she said. 'You know the opposite is the case.'

We dined together, but we were years apart. Indeed, we spent most of the meal in silence, barely savouring the food — fish, if I recall, served on fine porcelain. The table was by the window, with a bouquet of beautifully arranged flowers. We were the only guests in the dining room, the others having gone to the festival. The strains of a brass band wafted through the air.

Then Ismay dabbed at her lips with a napkin and excused herself to go to the bedroom. 'It has been a long day. Why don't you look around San Diego? Or go up to the Bernacchi festival? I understand they are having dancing after the entertainment. There will be some pretty grisettes.'

This stunned me a bit: that she should allude to my appreciation of pretty young women. I went to the smoking room to have a cigar. The concert was ending and I heard the thunderous applause; and then people started tripping gaily back to the hotel. Among them was William Burgess with his party. 'We've returned to change into dancing attire,' he said. 'Are you coming along?'

'Soon,' I answered. Instead, I took up my cane and, taking Ismay's advice, decided to make a short perambulation of San Diego: a butcher, baker, shoemaker, storekeeper, doctor's residence. A school. A spacious clubroom and reading room. The Coffee Palace was still open.

I had hoped that the air, fresh and balmy, would cool my thoughts. Sadly none of Mr Bernacchi's banditti accosted me and took me to a cell. That would have created a welcome diversion.

———

Eventually I could delay no longer, so returned to the hotel. A lamp was on in our bedroom but Ismay was already in bed, her back turned away from me. I changed and slipped in beside her.

That night there was no warmth between us. We were careful not to touch each other. The music from a Palm Court orchestra played a lovely Victorian waltz.

At last, long after I had thought Ismay asleep, she spoke. 'Do not blame Clara,' she said. 'Goodnight, Mr McKissock.'

I lay awake listening to far-off music and the laughter. I don't know how long the merriment went on, but it must have been quite a way into the early hours.

———

I was awoken the next morning by the whistle from the steamer *Warrentina*. The space beside me in the bed was empty. Ismay was gone.

I dressed hastily and went down to breakfast, but by then the steamer had departed.

Was Ismay on board?

———

I checked at the desk.

No, I was informed that she had already eaten but had not checked out. I went onto the verandah and shaded my eyes.

There she was, a solitary speck against the turning sky, at the Maria Island graveyard. As I made my way towards her — strangely, perhaps, I didn't for a minute consider leaving her be — scores of pigeons circled and darted in the pale sky. The terrain was more difficult than I had remembered and I had to grip my walking stick firmly before taking the next step.

The cemetery looked neglected, with boobialla threatening to overgrow it, but Hohepa's grave was clean and weeded. Ismay was arranging red roses in a vase on the headstone as I came up beside her.

She looked up at me, defensive, and then she made her declaration. 'He never knew how much I loved him,' she said. 'In many ways I loved him more than I did anybody else, but it was the kind of love that you would not understand.'

Of course I wasn't surprised at Ismay's admission, but to hear her come out with it so boldly made me want to hit her. I was the injured party, not her.

She knew what I was thinking. She was wearing a buffon of gauze around her shoulders and, as she adjusted it, she stepped back.

'I want you to go home now, Mr McKissock,' she said. 'I myself will return to Hobart soon. I come here only once a year to Hohepa. I made my sacrifices for you. Make this one small sacrifice for me.'

'What sacrifices have you made for me, madam?'

'I have been aware of your occasional affairs,' she answered. 'In particular with a lady named Kate Wilkinson, owner of a haberdashery in Hobart Town. No doubt there have been others.'

Ah, so that was the meaning of her remark about pretty grisettes. But there had been times when Ismay had not welcomed my advances in bed and I was a man, I had manly desires, and celibacy and I had never been comfortable partners.

'They are long over, Mrs McKissock,' I answered.

'And Hohepa is *dead*,' she answered. She was trembling with grief. 'I chose *you*, Mr McKissock. I have always chosen you. My life has been one of self-denial and self-sacrifice. I have lived with you and the children constantly, and never have I taken time for myself.'

'You could have told me,' I answered. 'Why didn't you? I would have understood.'

'Understood?' She sank to her knees then, and I saw tears in her eyes. 'Oh . . .' she began, frustrated, 'leave, Mr McKissock, before I say something I will regret. Before I do something I will regret.'

I was unmoved. Why should I condone her expression of love for another? I could not help but utter the bitter words about her choice of flowers:

'Red roses, Mrs McKissock.'

'Yes.' She nodded. 'Red roses.'

I could think of nothing further to say. Instead, I tipped my hat to her and turned away, stumbling with my cane down the hill. I packed my bag and caught the next ferry from the island.

———

Ismay returned to Hobart late that afternoon. Clara ran into her arms, begging forgiveness.

'It's not your fault,' Ismay answered. 'You should take Georgina home now. She has already seen enough.'

I was seated in front of the fire, my back to her, when she came into the room. 'What do you want me to do, Mrs McKissock?' I asked her. 'Tell me, eh? What are we to do . . .'

I don't know why, but I was cruel to her. I was like a man who, when a cat has soiled the house, rubs her face in it so that she will not do it again. 'You have been unfaithful to me, Mrs McKissock.'

Ismay stared at me, uncomprehending. Then her face twisted with anger. 'How dare you make that accusation. You, who told me even before we were married that you never loved me and, in all the years since, has never said that word, *love*, to me.'

She came to stand beside me. Took my head and cradled it beneath her chin.

I was so full of self-pity. I let her do that. Why?

'You foolish, vain man,' she sighed as she stroked my hair.

I remember it all as clear as day.

'How many years has it been since we both left England to find our way like pilgrims in the world? And how long have we been together now? Over forty-five years? Gower, I can count the nights that I was not at your side in our marriage bed on two hands and, mostly, they were either when I was confined in childbirth or ill or *you* were sick. I was a young girl when you took my virginity and you are the only man I have known throughout my life. You have been a good husband. You are a good father to your children. No woman could have asked for more.'

Should I have believed her?

———————

What *was* there to do?

We resumed our lives as if nothing had happened. And, somehow, I was generous enough every year to let her go to Maria Island. Even so I could not help but feel my heart thudding in pain when she put on her coat and hat and left with her red roses.

Why should I have ever begrudged the red roses? After all, I was the man who, when going to ask her hand in marriage, took only summer flowers.

49

I think this may be my last journal entry. I feel mortality upon me, but am not at all surprised. I have lived a long life and to all must come one's appointment with one's Maker. Perhaps he — or mayhap it will be she (the world no longer surprises me) — might also be as partial as I am to a glass of whisky and join me in a toast to all that has been.

But first, to the business of tying up the loose ends, eh?

———

Regarding the Maori and their transportation to Van Diemen's Land, the words that come to mind to describe Grey's actions are duplicity, deviousness, trickery and deceit. He left a catastrophic mess in New Zealand, and I imagine they'll be cleaning it up for centuries to come. The mistrust. The poison.

Grey was untruthful from the moment he arrived in New Zealand. For the Maori it was a tragedy. He perverted the course of justice they had presumed would follow from the Treaty they had signed at Waitangi. He could not resolve the policy contradictions that had grown between Maori and settlers, and knowingly enabled the Europeans to settle the land by failing to insist on the use of the available arbitration — and instead used force against the Maori to establish settlement. He let slip through his fingers the opportunity of satisfying the aspirations of both Maori and Europeans and, instead, used military expedition to keep the Maori in awe.

A comment attached to a Colonial Office file in 1848 reveals that:

Lord Grey will probably remember that it was doubted whether the Transportation of these men from New Zealand to V.D. Land was legal.

They are now gone back to their friends, and Sir W. Denison's Despatch affords some reason to feel glad that it has been deemed allowable to recall these poor men with the intention of setting them at liberty.

How long will it be before the equality idealised in the Treaty is recovered?

––––––––

Privately, it is with some distaste that I review the explanations Grey made to the Colonial Office. Here he stretched the truth to the point of falsehood, not from ignorance of the facts but from a calculated attempt to mislead. He was very convincing and painted an entirely imaginary picture of military insecurity and the excellent effect of the trial on the tribes.

Thus no good account should be given of the Colonial Office in this matter either. They protected Grey to the end and refused to allow any damaging documentation to be printed or forwarded to the commander-in-chief, the Duke of Wellington, to avoid raising questions as to the propriety of the measures adopted.

Would Governor Grey have continued in his illustrious career? Yes; the Colonial Office protected their own. He had been instructed to set matters to rights for European settlement, and this he accomplished. And for this he now has a bust in the crypt of St Paul's Cathedral, London! It sticks in my craw.

As for the Maori, my prayer is that they are not long in awe. Keep fighting those who come against your country.

––––––––

And now I think it is time for me to admit that, although Georgina calls my writings the McKissock Journals, they have never been about me. They have in fact always been about Ismay and it has taken me all my life to realise this.

You, Ismay, *you* are the spirit who animates these pages.

You and Hohepa.

––––––––

So let me address you personally, Ismay, my dear wife.

I remember the last of our wedding anniversaries, in 1903. The children and grandchildren had decided that there should be a gathering of family and friends for a picnic on the banks of the Derwent River.

Hobart was lovely at that moment. Now known as 'Queen of the Southern Seas' she was poised between spring and summer. It was always an artist's paradise, with rows of new trees surging towards maturity and the blue water of the Derwent dancing so that the town seemed to sparkle. At that time of year there was also the Regatta to watch — how easy it was to be caught in the fun and excitement as the river ketches competed and the brass bands played.

I recall that Georgina, who was always a tease, persuaded you to ride in the dicky seat of her boyfriend Austin's car — the automobile was a common sight now. She had become a student journalist and Austin had recently returned from the Boer War. Georgina always considered him a 'hot toddy'.

I can remember your grim face as he helped you out of the dicky seat. 'That young man is not only a hot toddy,' you said to me as soon as he was out of earshot, 'he is a fast toddy, too.' Nor were you pleased when Georgina, at the height of our festivities, produced a little booklet she had written about us. 'That child has been eavesdropping too close to my life for my liking,' you said.

At that moment I thought our life together had reached a kind of completeness. All the flotsam and jetsam of it had cast us up, this day, beneath the fringing trees — how almost perfect it was! The children played family tennis and had pillow fights before settlng down to the picnic. Eion Gault sat with his partner Jeremy and discussed politics with you.

Then Gower Jr, who had become a founding lecturer at the University of Tasmania when it opened in 1890, proposed the toast and read a tribute which he had penned, beginning:

O Mighty Pater, wise and prudent!
And thou, noblest and most gracious Mater!
Thy family bow to thee on this thy 61st Wedding Anniversary!
But knows the promises for the future will be greater!

We seemed so deeply rooted as a family to Tasmania. How we laughed that neither Gower Jr or Clara had married someone from 'the mainland'. Instead, they — and their children too — had married from good Tasmanian stock. 'Far better that — or somebody from another colony, a Maori even, eh Father?' Gower Jr asked.

I looked at him with affection. I wouldn't have minded at all if he had married a Maori.

But, oh, why did I not get you red roses, Ismay? Even so, you smiled and accepted my Australian native flowers. I still have the photograph of us all, kneeling at your feet under the shimmering trees. You have the bouquet in your lap.

'Your father never brings me roses,' you said. 'And just as well, otherwise I would begin to wonder!'

Wonder what?

———————

That evening, we went on a sentimental engagement, just you and me, to the opera house — all cream and gold elegance with red curtains.

In the foyer, a three-piece orchestra scraped away on popular tunes. The opera was a performance of Gluck's *Orpheus and Eurydice* which we had seen in London in 1841, the year we had left.

You were looking beautiful in a long black evening dress and, while I may have looked somewhat old-fashioned in my white shirt and cutaways, I like to think we presented well when we entered the auditorium.

There was a young girl singing as Orpheus, who followed his beloved Eurydice into Hades. She was a contralto and, oh she could have been you, Ismay, when you were that age!

> Che faro senza Eurydice,
> Dove andro senza il mio ben!
> Che faro dove andro
> Che faro senza il mio ben
>
> What is life to me without you?
> All my joy, alas, has flown . . .
> What is life? Life without you?
> Why remain on earth alone?

I looked at your face as she sang. With alarm, I saw it was blanched with memories. And then you started to sob.

I tried to take your hand but you pushed it away.

'Don't touch me,' you said.

Others sitting in our row looked at us curiously, some frowning because your voice was billowing forth through the opera house.

I knew you were remembering those early years when I was more interested in your cousin Sybil, and had not even thought of you in any romantic way. Why, I had even rejected your suit when you came to me as bold as brass that night of the Wolverhampton Dispensary Ball and pressed yourself upon me. And then, on our marriage night I had told you, 'You know I will never love you.'

How I wished I could go back to that moment and put those words back into the mouth of an untried youth who did not realise what he was saying — and now regretted it.

And then *I* started to weep too, excessively so, at the shameful callow youth I had been. I wanted your forgiveness.

I reached for your hand again and, no matter how hard you fought, I took it in my fierce grip. I didn't care that people were furious with us. You were standing and struggling against me.

Eurydice? Eurydice, oh Dio! Rispondi!
Io son pure il tuo fedele
Son pure il tuo fedele . . .
Eurydice? Eurydice! Make answer!
I beseech thee, alas, are you gone?

And then you let out a huge wail. Oh, the things that matter to women.

'I lost our first baby, Gower. All I've got is three left . . . oh, and I have missed Rollo so much . . .'

'And me too, Ismay,' I said. 'Me too . . .'

We were causing such a commotion in the opera house that the conductor stopped waving his baton.

This had happened before.

People were very cross. One smart aleck yelled out to us, 'Hey, you two, this isn't a variety hall! Do your knees up Mother Brown somewhere else!'

I wanted to keep on holding you, holding on tight. I wanted to tell you what I never did tell you in your life: 'Ismay, my girl, you have been the making of me, look what I have become!'

Then the ushers came to bundle us along the aisle and into the foyer, and ejected us into the street!

I turned to you and laughed. 'My God, Mrs McKissock, after all these years, you can still bring an opera to its knees!'

I was so proud of you!

In 1904, you were taken ill.

You? Ismay Elizabeth, *ill*? I couldn't believe it.

'You are never ill, Mrs McKissock,' I said. 'You will get up and stop this shilly-shallying about. Up! Up with you now.'

Then you had your stroke. That really shocked me. You had always been so strong in body and in will. I had always assumed *I* was the one who would go first.

I felt so powerless. I said to Gower Jr, 'I don't know what to do for your mother, son. I don't know what to do.' I felt so helpless. After all, you were the one who always managed the family.

You asked to be taken to a rest home a little way from Hobart where you could look over the Trowenna Sea that you had always loved. The currents fretted in the coves, crystal clear over golden-syrup rocks, fanned to white wave crests by the sea breeze and turning deeper blue where the sea merged into the sky.

One autumnal evening at dusk, just after the sun had gone down, you saw two nankeen night herons skimming the violet sea. They flew right up to the window and tapped their beaks on the glass.

'Let them in,' you said.

I opened the window wide. The herons settled, preening their feathers, waiting. *So, Ismay.*

You looked at them, nodded, and said to me, 'Call the children and grandchildren.'

That evening we all went in to you. You asked for the baize-lined chest you always kept in our bedroom. When it was delivered to your bedside you opened it and took out Hohepa's carved tokotoko. I saw Georgina's eyes widen at the sight of it.

You put the staff into my hands. 'This belonged to Hohepa,' you said. 'While I was alive I couldn't bear to part with it. Now the time has come to send it back to his people. It should not come into the grave with me. It is theirs.'

At that moment the herons looked at the walking stick, nodded at me, opened their wings and lifted away, away, away.

I gave a gasp of pain, pressed your hand and tried to tell you something.

'Don't go yet, Ismay, I have brought you roses.'

I laid the bouquet in your arms.

───────

And, like Orpheus, I could no longer wait to look at you, no longer stop from telling you what you had always wanted to hear.

Why had it taken me so long to say it? Three words, strung into a sentence. When I think of them they appear so simple really. But never had I uttered words that had so much meaning in them and so many years of our life together to prove their truth.

───────

'I love you, Mrs McKissock,' I said.

───────

Your eyes were closed. I didn't think you had heard me. Then radiance came upon you, and you smiled.

'Yes, I know, Mr McKissock,' you answered.

And then you were gone.

Now the harsh golden globe of the sun is going down.

It's that magical moment when the earth, rhapsodic and in a great cheer, brightens, becomes vivacious with birds circling and wildebeests leaping to celebrate the last rays of the day's sun. Light melts into darkness so slowly and the heat dissipates — not so fast that you can't remember how hot it has been, but maddeningly slow into the slaking coolness.

In the lowering, I see that my handwriting is not so bold now. It is thin, tracing the letters carefully, not like it was when I was a young man and hasty in my handwork.

I've told Georgina that when I die she should not send my body back to Tasmania. It is nice to think of being buried next to you, Ismay, but I am not a sentimental fellow, really. And anyway it would cost too much money to return my dust to Hobart. This practicality will not surprise you.

But, Ismay, I did a terrible thing to the tokotoko, to Hohepa Te Umuroa's talking stick.

Yes, I should have returned it to his people when you died, but in my loneliness I became angry with you again. While I had come to terms with your love for him, my lonely emotions one day got the better of me. Grief makes us unreasonable and, in a fit of pique and jealousy, I gave it away.

A tinker, passing by the house with his barrow, was calling out for old iron, implements, anything second-hand, anything unwanted. I stormed upstairs, took the tokotoko from the chest, opened the window and threw it down at him with such force that I thought it would break, *crack*, when it hit the pavement. 'Take it!' I yelled. 'It is a heathen thing! Get it out of my sight!'

I wish I had not done that, Ismay. Within hours I regretted my action and tried to find the tinker but without success.

Just before I came to Rhodesia, I went to the graveyard in Hobart to say good-bye to you. 'I may not be back in Tasmania, Ismay my girl. The time has come for me to go on alone.' Then, on a whim, I took a last trip to Maria Island.

No, I lie. I knew exactly what I was doing.

I hired a boatman to take me across and to wait for me. The day was hot, and I stumbled on my walking stick up to Hohepa's burial place in the civil graveyard. I was sweating profusely when I arrived and stood in front of his headstone.

'She's gone now,' I told him. 'She won't be coming back. Now it's only you and me.'

I sat on the ground and took off my hat. I had brought a small trowel with me and I started to clean and clear the ground.

'Bloody weeds,' I said. I kept clearing and clearing and, all of a sudden, oh I don't know why, but I couldn't go on. I started to cry.

I finished the job. Love. Aroha. Yes.

'Goodbye, Te Umuroa,' I said.

There was only me now.

Since then, Ismay, I have been happy enough.

I haven't wandered into the past too often. After all, the people who inhabited that time are all gone now, especially those we left in England: your Uncle Rollo and dear Aunt Eleanor are long gone; my mother Ailie must surely be dead — perhaps like Mad Meg she inhabited a cave by the stream in the Strathnaver Valley. I hope she found happiness.

Your cousins Sybil, Ursula and Isobel are gone too, though they had children; one of Sybil's sons came out to see his antipodean cousins — what a little snobby prick of a chinless wonder he turned out to be!

And then there are Ramsay's bones, transcending mortality in a far more useful way than ours could ever hope to do.

My dear, I am happy that we left the Home country when we did, although latterly I have been wondering about that great diaspora of British who spilled across the globe of the world, and endeavoured to fashion continents to our alien ways.

What will they think, the future people of this place, of our vain attempts to impose our brittle English values on the veld? Our whole life here seems as out of place as a bone china teacup.

Here in Rhodesia, unlike in New Zealand and Australia, our society may not be so triumphant. But I find encouragement in my father Ramsay's words to me, those many years ago when I was just a young man in Scotland:

'Don't lose your humanity, Gower. There is always hope.'

Ah well.

Enough.

I will put my thoughts away now with my body, and fold myself up into the long sleep that already gently and lovingly bears my eyelids down.

When Africans bury their dead they begin a very special vigil.

They believe the spirit of the departed is wandering in a forest and needs to be fed to stop it from getting lost. They get a hollow stick, a length of bamboo or a reed, and they place one end touching the body and the other sticking up out of the grave. They come every day and put some food by the grave, until one day they see that the makonye, the maggot larvae, have come up the bamboo and are wriggling about on top of the grave. The larvae represent the spirit which has now successfully navigated its way home. Then the family stop bringing food and end their vigil.

I can hear the quiet thud of jungle drums and, not far away, the smoke from the nearby tribal kraal circles in the air.

I know I will find my way through the forest, Ismay, and home to you.

And far away, the Mountains of the Moon, darkening.

50

The Phantom Moaning of the Sea

Even on a windswept day such as this, the sea, this Trowenna Sea, is so bright, so clear.

From where my gravestone is, I can see down to the beach and my people coming to take me home. My iwi are calling to me:

'E Hohepa e tangi, kati ra te tangi . . . You're crying, Hohepa, but don't cry any more . . . We climb toward you, we ascend toward you, our ancestor, we are here to bring you back among the people.'

It's August 1988.

———

Elders of my iwi, including Matiu Mareikura and Te Otinga Te Peehi Waretini, have come to Tasmania to take me back home. With them are a lot of other people: whanau, supporters of the Whanganui people, two state archaeologists, local Tasmanians, television and press journalists — and tangata whenua too.

I will be reburied at Patiarero, Jerusalem, on my beloved Whanganui River.

They come through the graves of the other dead with whom I have rested: Rosa and Thomas Adkins, Captain Bayly, Diego Maria Tasman Bernacchi, Margaret Boyd, Delvis Cusick, Hilda Ellen, Johanna Glenwright, Sarah Griffiths, Mary Harrison, Joih Hedderly, James Brisbane Jarvis, Charles Lapham and John Purdy.

I recognise among them an old woman, black-clad, with wreaths of greenery in her hair: Kui, finally come to take me home.

She looks at the stone above my grave:

Hei konei takoto ai me tou tinana
O te hoa, Hohepa Te Umuroa,
Wanganui, Niu Tirene,
I mate Hurae 19th
1847

Someone brings a chair for her to sit in.

Maori elders of my Whanganui people start to dig. Their spades cut the earth. They chant as they dig. The ground is rocky. The work is dusty. The sun spins high in the sky, once, twice, thrice. They strike wood. They stop. The world takes a breath.

'Go careful now,' Kui growls as the state archaeologists go into the trench to take off the lid of my coffin. And she gives a cry when she sees the first of my bleached bones. She is unsure but . . .

They are the bones of a tall man, a swimmer with wide shoulders . . .

'Yes, it is him,' she says. 'Hohepa.'

Gradually I am brought from the dark closet of earth into the sunlight. My skull and my bones are placed in a casket — not large, but big enough.

'Wait,' Kui says. She looks upon my bones and addresses me. 'E Hohepa, you were never forgotten. Your son Rukuwai was eighty-two in 1925 when my mother and I travelled to Te Paremata o te Pakeha to petition for your return from this place, Tasmania. When we went through the doors of Parliament, how he feared that he too would be imprisoned and would be sent to Australia! I was his granddaughter, three years old at the time, and he used to whisper to me your story:

'"E mokopuna, there was a man called Hohepa Te Umuroa, my father, who went to help make peace at the Wairau and then with the Pakeha in Te Whanganui a Tara. He was caught up in the wars in the Heretaunga and was imprisoned by the Pakeha authorities."

'Aue, koroua, I am now an old person myself, and it has taken me a long time to fulfil the promise I made to Rukuwai and his daughter, Pone, that I would take up the task! But there have always been faithful whanau to keep your memory alive, and friends in both Aotearoa and Tasmania who have helped to bring about this day of your deliverance. And now, here we are. Here you are.'

She turns to the people. 'If you are born a Maori you die a Maori. No matter what you have done in your life, the one certainty you have in your life is that, as a Maori, your iwi will come for you and take you home.'

One hundred and forty-one years after I was taken to Australia I am going home. I know Ismay will be pleased. Since she died only one other person — Gower McKissock — has come to remember me.

Ismay is buried in Tasmania; she belongs here. She loved this place. Her children are buried beside her, as well as her grandchildren and all her descendants now.

Even her husband, Mr McKissock, lies with her. His granddaughter, Georgina, was always wilful and disobeyed his wish to remain in Rhodesia.

———

The sky breaks open with a pure light and rain comes like a drifting blessing.

In the New Testament, Luke 11:9, the Lord promised that if people sought, they would find. If they knocked on the door, it would open to them.

My people have done this, and they have their reward. Kui leads them back down to the sea.

I am among them, no longer lonely, no longer in limbo.

The clouds are streaked like shoals of silver fish. A warm breeze blows to the horizon.

Across the Trowenna Sea, the shimmering sun is dancing.

HOMEWARD, BEAUTIFUL ANGEL

KUI'S STORY
Whanganui River, New Zealand

PROLOGUE
Whanganui River, 2009

E rere kau mai te awa nui nei
Mai i te kahui maunga ki Tangaroa
Ko au te awa, ko te awa ko au

The river flows
From the mountains to the sea
I am the river, the river is me

You've come all the way from Hawai'i to talk to me?

You want to know the story of how we brought the koroua, Hohepa Te Umuroa, back to his iwi?

Okay, boy, let's go and sit on Patiarero marae. The sun is still shining, and the marae would be a good place to korero. From our meeting house, Te Whare Whiri-taunoka, we will have a view over the Whanganui River to our sacred mountain, Pukehika. Once there was a large settlement alongside the mountain; it was called Pukehika at first and then renamed Kauaeroa; it's on the river flat a little downstream from us. We were so close that even today we still think of ourselves as coming from Kauaeroa too.

Yes, Patiarero is the original Maori name of the village. I am one of the iwi of Patiarero, the Ngati Hau, who hold this place as our papakainga. We acknowledge our lineage from the *Aotea* canoe; in the old days before the Pakeha came Patiarero was one of many kainga along the river, and the plaited rope of our *Aotea* ancestors bound us all together. Whenever we were threatened in the past, by Maori or Pakeha, the strands were woven between us. And today we are still threatened. Did you know that the Whanganui River claim before the Waitangi Tribunal is the longest-running legal case in New Zealand's history? Our petitions for ownership go all the way back to the 1930s, court action since the 1940s, land occupations from the 1950s and, of course, we're still at it occupying Tieke Marae and Moutoa Gardens.

We share kinship with Ngati Rangi; they were here before the *Aotea* canoe arrived. They came down from the Sky to the earth on the backs of birds.

Why do I tell you this? Well, everything connects in the Maori world.

And birds are a part of the story.

———

I love my marae and my river; it runs through my heart like a rich arterial waterway. We had a fearsome reputation in the old days. You've heard of the proverb, 'Haere ki Patiarero!' And you know that Hohepa's surname, for instance, means 'Long Oven'? That could be a veiled reference to the times when we sometimes ate people, but let's not dwell on that, shall we? Not that you have anything to fear. Too skinny, no meat on your bones, no, you would not be a tasty morsel.

E hara! Do I frighten you? What a scaredy-cat to be frightened of a sweet innocent old lady! Come closer. Closer. Gotcha.

You must excuse our Whanganui humour. It's wicked, eh!

It was the early Anglican missionary, Reverend Richard Taylor, who, having arrived in our area in 1843, changed the name of Patiarero to Hiruharama, meaning 'Jerusalem' and recorded our population at two hundred and twenty-two; Pukehika had five hundred and sixty-six. Taylor also changed other Maori river settlement names to Ranana, London, Koroniti, Corinth and Atene, Athens.

Our village of Jerusalem was therefore first associated with the Anglican Church — and Kauaeroa too. Christianity took a strong hold, with Christmas gatherings of as many as two thousand at Kauaeroa.

Then the French priest Jean Lampila moved to the Whanganui River in 1852 and was mostly based at Kauaeroa. *Où est le fleuve de Whanganui? Où est le village de Pati-arero? Répondez à ce néo-zélandais, qu'on arrivera un de ces jours.* He went up and down the river with a lay millwright converting villagers to Roman Catholicism and building mills for us; at the Battle of Moutoa in 1864, despite the valiant efforts by the mission, many of the faithful were killed when the Hauhau came over from the Waitotara and Upper Whanganui intent on driving the Pakeha from the district. But nineteen years later Sister Suzanne Aubert, who had been recruited from France by Bishop Pompallier and was missioning in Hawke's Bay, arrived to re-establish the mission. With her were Father Christophe Soulas and three sisters of St Joseph of Nazareth — Reverend Mother Hyacinth, Sister Aloysius and Sister Teresa — who later withdrew. Sister Aubert remained, became Mother Mary Joseph Aubert and, strong-willed and determined, set up her Sisters of Compassion, a station and convent.

Can you see St Joseph's, our church? When the original church burnt down — the rumour was that a jealous Pakeha set it on fire — the local Maori didn't want to replace it. But Mother Aubert wasn't having any of that! Apparently she set out on a national fundraising tour and, well, the new St Joseph's was the result; the bell still summons us to prayers. Mother Aubert later became famous for her health remedies made from Maori herbs.

You know the poet James K. Baxter? He was a Catholic. We called him Hemi. He's buried in the graveyard.

———————

Timata, let us begin. I will tell you what I know but it may only be part of the story and not all of the story. Some of it belongs to others, like dear old Uncle Joe Wanihi, who was one of two descendants of Te Umuroa who went to Tasmania; he's gone now, but he may have passed some of the korero to his daughter Bernadette. Nohi Wallace, have you met Nohi? He was a young man when he went and now he's such a strong leader, he will have another part of the story. So will Manaaki Rerekura, she's a direct descendant, a lovely and humble lady, you should talk to her too.

They might not want to talk to you though. After all, you might just be wanting to meet with us because you might want to make money out of our ancestor.

You're not planning to do that, are you?

51

The mission all began in Tasmania in 1985 when two young schoolgirls were on a school trip to Maria Island National Park. They happened to come across the graveyard where Te Umuroa was buried and, that night, asked their father, 'Daddy, why is there a Maori grave there?'

Now, Chris Heald was their dad's name, and he happened to be an expatriate New Zealander living in Tasmania. He was astounded to discover that the grave was Hohepa's and that he had died there, right on Maria Island. Imagine his surprise when he discovered that our ancestor had been transported to Australia so many years ago in 1846! He mentioned the discovery to his boss, Mr Chris Batt, who was the endorsed Labor candidate for the state seat of Lyons and recommended that Mr Batt convey news of the finding to Mr Koro Wetere, the Minister of Maori Affairs in New Zealand.

As it happened, there was a strong association between the Labour parties of Tasmania and New Zealand, and perhaps this explains why there was warmth from the very start towards Hohepa. And Mr Wetere was also the Member of Parliament for Western Maori, which includes the Whanganui River. He made enquiries and his first question was, 'Are there any direct descendants of Hohepa Te Umuroa? And do they want their ancestor back?'

The answer was, 'Yes,' and, of course, 'Yes.'

And naturally, we wouldn't want our ancestor to be put in a parcel and sent back by post, would we now! No, we would have to go to get him.

So Mr Wetere's second question was, 'If you want to go personally to bring Hohepa back, who would be the best people for the task?'

That's how Matiu Mareikura, his wife Lei and sister, Hoana, became involved. You don't know about Matiu Mareikura? Gee, living in Honolulu is no excuse for your ignorance! What are you doing over there? Sitting on a beach sunning yourself and drinking maitais?

Where do I start telling you about Matiu? Well, he was a leader of the Whanganui iwi of the entire river. He was also the leader of Ngati Rangi at Ohakune and a committed Catholic. But he was also known far beyond the Whanganui River, especially in Wellington where he often advised government. He walked humbly among the big people of the Pakeha and Maori worlds as well as the small. From a leadership point of view he strode many worlds; such a person would have the experience and determination to bring to the task.

Matiu and his sister Joan were also among the main leaders of the Maramatanga, a very spiritual people. To look at him, you would think that he was just an ordinary man, but he was also a tohunga as well, having great tapu or sacredness. He well knew that bringing Te Umuroa back would entail negotiations not only with the temporal world but also with the Maori spirit world. Only a tohunga would have the appropriate knowledge of the deeper Maori realm of kawa, tikanga and wairua — protocol, custom and things of that world.

Haven't you heard of the Maramatanga? Take a deep breath, boy, and dive with me back into the past and into their history!

To start with, the Maramatanga are generally acknowledged among the wider Whanganui iwi as spiritual leaders. They are like the Ringatu in your area, a Christian Maori movement that comes down from the prophetess Mere Rikiriki, who lived in the early 1900s; today their members include Catholic, Anglican and Ratana too.

Oh, Mere Rikiriki was as famous among us as Riripeti Mahana was among your iwi! Like Riripeti, she established a spiritual centre at Parewanui. Based on the New Testament, she emphasised the unity of Maori under God. Thousands flocked to her, just as they did to Riripeti, to listen to her teachings and, because she was a faith healer, to be healed by her. When she died, her mantle passed to her two disciples: Ratana — who went on to found his own church — and Hori Enoka Mareikura. Hori Enoka was originally Anglican, but his wife Te Huinga was a devout Catholic; it was he who further blended Mere Rikiriki's original teachings and Maori beliefs with Catholicism to create the Maramatanga movement that we know of today. Acknowledged as a visionary, seer and healer, he established in the 1920s Maungarongo marae at Ohakune at the southwestern foot of

Mount Ruapehu. As Rongopai is to the Ringatu, Maungarongo is to the Maramatanga.

The Maramatanga's kaupapa, purpose, was enshrined in the following saying: 'Ko te kawa, he kawa Atua, ko te tikanga he aroha.' The purpose is to serve God, and the way is with love.

From Mareikura, the mantle passed to his granddaughter Lena Ruka, who died suddenly at the age of sixteen in 1935. Oh, this is a beautiful story, boy, even though Pakeha would not understand it. But after she had been laid in the coffin her wairua, spirit, began to communicate with her whanau. And it still does today! Over the past seventy-five years, that beautiful girl, whom we now call Te Karere o te Aroha, The Messenger of Love, has continued to come to the Maramatanga, conveying knowledge and inspiration in the Maori way through korero, whakapapa, pakiwaitara, waiata, tohu, karakia, matakite and himene.

And the Maramatanga, well, its work has extended all throughout the larger Whanganui iwi. They have people serving on hospital boards, social welfare committees and community councils, you name it, they're on it. They don't do it for themselves either. Their mission has always been spiritual, going all the way back to Mere Rikiriki.

The plaited rope, ne? Twisting all together.

Whiria, whiria, whiria.

———

Righto, let's scoot back to the present.

A message was sent to Koro Wetere at Parliament in Wellington. 'We wish to go to Tasmania to bring our ancestor back.'

On receipt of the message, Koro Wetere got in touch with his Tasmanian Labor Party colleague, Mr Chris Batt. Accordingly, he sent a telex to the Premier of Tasmania, Robin Gray. 'Mr Premier, I have been contacted by tribal elders from New Zealand who have requested the release of the sacred remains of their honoured ancestor, Hohepa Te Umuroa, who is buried on Maria Island.'

Of his own volition, Mr Batt added another paragraph. 'The elders might find some difficulty in travelling to Tasmania, and I have advised them that any application for funding assistance may be met favourably by the State Government.'

On receipt of Mr Batt's letter, the premier dictated a letter to the National Parks and Wildlife Service — they had assumed responsibility for Maria Island, which was proclaimed a National Park on 14 June 1972. He also wrote to the Health Department. 'May I refer the matter to you of the disinterment of the remains of the Maori warrior whose bones lie within your two jurisdictions?'

And, because Mr Batt had raised the matter, the premier also added, 'In your considerations, do further investigate the use of funds to support the venture.'

Neat, eh?

Well, that was good news about the possibility of some cash to help the mission, wasn't it? Up to this point, I have nothing but praise for the way the Australians approached the task.

But of course it wasn't going to be as easy as that, was it! Luckily, we had Matiu in the hot seat and his guidance and patience got us through. He was steeped in our rituals and knew how to conduct them, rituals that had to do with life, rituals that had to do with death. You had to be a strong, humble man like Matiu to be able to bear the responsibility of performing your role as a tohunga according to all the tenets of the whare wananga. One wrong step and you could be punished.

Matiu immediately recognised the great burden of the task, for when one dealt with the dead, or matters of the spirit, one was required to walk both realms and divine, find agreement and select the appropriate pathway towards completion with the support of those of this world and that world. From the very beginning of the task, he was constantly at prayer, karakia, opening the gateways for us so that we could progress without harm. He was our cloak of protection and, as in all things, he sought the advice of his wife, Lei, and in particular his sister, our beloved Hoana, in assisting by revelation. It was they who courageously took on the spiritual burden on behalf of the family and who helmed the return of Hohepa, a former 'enemy of the state'.

Guidance was sought from The Messenger for support, protection and for the way to be cleared.

Not even The Messenger, though, could help negotiations go faster.

At the time, the return of artefacts, whether historic or contemporary, to owner countries was, internationally, an extremely touchy matter. For Australia, the issue was one of precedent: what precedent would be set if the remains of Te Umuroa were sent back to New Zealand? Would that open up the cases for other countries to request the return of their artefacts? Another issue was that, legally, no removals of any kind could be made from a national park. I mean, you could be fined if you picked up a rock and took it with you. These two issues have vexed other museum and conservation institutions for years. For instance, the question still causes debate at the Imperial Natural History Museum in Vienna which holds the Reischek collection of Maori artefacts. If we ask for the return of koiwi, will that open a precedent for, say, the Egyptian authorities to request the return of ancient Egyptian mummies? Today, some countries have policies that allow such returns. Others have policies that don't.

What was heartening, however, was that despite the bureaucracy, the Australian authorities remained sympathetic. Even the Australian Labor Prime Minister, Mr Hawke, got himself into the act, supporting the case to the Tasmanian Premier, Robin Gray, for Hohepa's return.

And Mr Chris Batt kept on the case. He reminded Mr Gray and other principals in a letter that 'as the Tasmanian Government has recently returned the Crowther collection to the Tasmanian Aboriginal community, I feel it would be appropriate to make a similar offer of returning these remains to the man's home country'.

How were we to know that the negotiations would take almost three years?

———

Not only that, but such a mission wasn't going to be cheap, eh.

Look at the sums for sending, say, ten elders max. Right, how much for air travel from Whanganui to Christchurch to catch the direct flight to Tasmania? Put that in the budget and go to the next expense. What was the cost to get on the aeroplane for ten people from Wellington via Christchurch to Tasmania return? What about the cost of a hotel when we get there? And meals?

Gee, the cost was mounting up. But go to the next question. How do we get to Maria Island (where the heck is Maria Island!) and what will it cost to dig Hohepa up?

Whoa, and we have to get Hohepa's remains through customs and air freight him back. Well, of course, add that to the bill too.

Luckily, the Department of Maori Affairs did the budget and it came to $32,845.80 total.

Gee, somebody bring us a kapu ti and a biscuit.

———

Meantime, Matiu was continuing his karakia and Hoana told us that she was dreaming of mountains. The Messenger was opening up the way for Pukehika to speak to mountains on Maria Island.

No, I don't know what mountains they were, but it was so appropriate because in our Maori myths, our mountains talk to each other.

Finally, Mr Gray had word back from the National Parks and Wildlife Service and other bureaux of the Tasmanian Government. He wrote to the Minister of Maori Affairs, 'The remains can be repatriated . . .'

However, there were certain conditions. One of these was that, disappointingly, the State Government was not able to meet any costs of the operation — these would have to be met either by the New Zealand or the Australian Commonwealth Government. The other was that we would have to meet the cost of the archaeological excavation as well as the conservation and curatorship of any remains or artefacts.

Okay, so that was another expense. Heck, we had muscles, why couldn't we dig him up ourselves? And what the heck are conservators and curators anyway?

But help was on the way from Canberra, the capital of Australia, where a spokesperson for the Department of Foreign Affairs gave an assessment. 'If there is unanimous agreement on returning the remains, the Department will assist.' This was the wonderful news the Department of Foreign Affairs communicated to the Australian High Commissioner in New Zealand, Penny Wensley.

The Minister of Maori Affairs also contributed to the putea. There was even enough money to provide a per diem for all the elders.

Negotiations therefore opened between Mr Tamati Reedy, Secretary of Maori Affairs and his counterparts in the Tasmanian State Government. Travel bookings were made. Guess what, there was a Maori community in Tasmania (what were they doing there! had they been transported too?) and they agreed to help us on our arrival.

Three years may have gone by, but the red tape was behind us.

We had, as my mokopuna would say, a green for go.

———

I still remember the day the mission left Whanganui.

A Mass was held at St Mary's in the city. Following the service, the mission went to the airport to catch a flight to Christchurch. Our mission was led by the elders Matiu, Lei, Hoana and Te Otinga Te Peehi Waretini. They were the kakahu aroha for the two family representatives, Uncle Joe and Nohi.

At Christchurch, we were joined by David Cresswell, who had been appointed to come with us from the Department of Maori Affairs, and the formidable John Tahuparae, representing the Maori Television news channel of the New Zealand Broadcasting Corporation.

We flew to Tasmania, along with the other New Zealanders with plenty of money that they were no doubt going to lose at the Wrest Point Casino.

Landing in Hobart, we suddenly became aware of the magnitude of what we were trying to accomplish. Heck, we were in a foreign land! I had a vision of Hohepa and the other Maori men with him stepping off a ship in 1846 in shackles and irons, and I looked down at my own wrists and ankles in nervousness.

But when we were on the other side of Customs, we heard a voice in karanga and saw representatives of the Maori and Aboriginal people of Hobart, welcoming us. The news media had discovered our mission and took a photo of Aboriginal leader Dawn Smith at the airport. And I saw a relative from the Whanganui River; I didn't know he was living in Australia! Seeing him and hearing the powhiri and action songs made me feel much, much better and that we were not alone. I saw a Pakeha who was introduced to us.

Then the two Chrises as I liked to call them — Chris Heald and his boss Chris Batt — made a special presentation: a colour copy of John Skinner Prout's painting of our ancestor. Oh, I cried, because when Maori see an image, they also see the person. Chris Heald introduced us to his two daughters, the ones who had found Te Umuroa. 'They are coming with us to Maria Island,' he said, 'to lead the way.' They were such pretty girls.

The tangata whenua presented us with an Aboriginal flag, red, yellow and black. 'The black is to represent our ancestral heritage and the night sky,' they said. 'The red represents the blood that Aboriginal people have spilt for their land. The yellow represents the sun, dawn and, with dawning, hope for our people.'

They waited for us to reply. I was so proud of Matiu and Te Otinga! They spoke of how we had come for Hohepa, the one who had been tuki-notia, ill treated and sent away by the New Zealand justice system. Once the speeches were over, we added our waiata, 'Kiko', a song that was a Maramatanga waiata acknowledging the continuing importance of the past. The encounter was electrifying. There were many tears of greeting, shared loss and pain for the young man who had died and remained unconnected to his family for so long.

Hoana was still dreaming and receiving reassuring messages from the spirit world. The Messenger was continuing to open the pathway, something she had already begun from the time we boarded the plane in Aotearoa, calling the elements to make way, make way.

And the mountains continued calling to each other.

Matiu's karakia continued all the way from Hobart to Louisville, on the east coast of Tasmania. I hadn't realised that the countryside would be so like Aotearoa. It was 31 July and we were to stop at a motel for a couple of nights.

Imagine our consternation when we were advised that our mission had become even more public and that there would be hangers-on! Television cameramen, press reporters, government officials and schoolteachers were planning to join us in our pilgrimage.

'We just have to hold on to each other really tight,' Matiu said. 'This other stuff must not get in the way of what we are here to do.' Both he and Hoana were now living in both the real world and the spiritual world, and I feared for them — but prayed that they would always be succoured by The Messenger.

Indeed, although it was always the practice of the Maramatanga to pray at 7 a.m. and 7 p.m., at dawn of the day we were due to go to Maria Island we had a very special ceremony involving those karakia which are said as you approach the very threshold of the task before you. Hoana told us, 'The road has been cleared of harmful influences. We must maintain the kaupapa, the purpose, of our journey so that we continue on the sacred road, te ara tapu.'

We asked the press and television reporters to respect our mission and stay behind us or out of sight and earshot. Then we embarked on the boat — man, it was packed with hangers-on — and, as we departed Louisville, Te Otinga intoned a prayer, 'Let the waters that lie between us and Maria Island be calm so that we may go safely to our ancestor.'

Once on the boat, Hoana called out in Maori to the Earth Mother, Papatuanuku, linking the sea and the land. The trip was beautiful, the sea bright, glowing and illuminated like a pathway rippling from Louisville to Maria Island.

By the time the boat landed at the Darlington jetty we were all in a state of great emotion. We lost sight of the two schoolgirls who had offered to lead us to where the koroua was buried, but Matiu and Te Otinga were not concerned.

Te Otinga looked up at the mountain on his left and said, 'Te Umuroa is there.' Matiu had not at all hesitated, having had a dream about the location, and was already heading for the gravesite.

Immediately, Hoana began to karanga to him. 'Maranga mai, e koro. Wake up, old one, for in the fullness of time we have arrived to take you home!'

Have you ever climbed a mountain in ecstasy?

'Maranga mai, e koro. E tomo atu nei, e! Wake up! Wake up! Your grand-children come unto you!'

That is how I felt, climbing the slope between earth and sky.

The climb to the graveyard seemed to take forever. Hoana kept up her karanga and, as the group approached the gravestone, Matiu began his kara-kia. It was spellbinding to hear karanga and karakia ringing through the sky. Indeed, it seemed as if the elements were opening up to us, with a warm breeze coming off the sea and then, in a burst of glory, the sun shone down.

We stood around his grave, weeping, yearning for our ancestor. The press and television reporters respected our wishes and did not intrude upon our private time with him. Once we had concluded our tangi to Hohepa, however, Matiu invited them forward so that the world could see our open prayer and weeping.

He nodded his head, indicating that the dig should commence.

The first earth was turned.

———————

The State Government gave us five days to complete the exhumation.

The first day, the excavation was supervised by the archaeologists Richard Morrison and Brian Prince. But Hohepa was Maori, we were Maori, and we did the digging. Our own to our own. Every now and then, however, we had to stop as Richard and Brian got out their brushes and tapes and did what archaeologists do to 'protect the integrity of the site' or whatever they like to call it, putting samples into little plastic bags.

That day, as we left the graveyard, we sprinkled our heads with water to cleanse ourselves.

On day two we were still digging. We were all concerned, especially Uncle Joe and Nohi, that the rumours were right: maybe our ancestor had been removed after all. But Matiu reassured Uncle Joe, 'I had a dream last night. The Messenger indicated where Te Umuroa lies. There is no ambigu-ity about the place. He has not been removed. Nor have robbers robbed the grave of him. He is still here.'

I saw Chris Heald finish a cigarette and drop it to the ground. Then he paused, picked it up and slipped it into his jacket pocket.

'Good boy,' I thought. 'You are honouring sacred ground.'

Richard and Brian were still hopping in and out of the hole, he hoha!

And again, we sprinkled water over our heads at the end of the day.

On the third day we came to fragments of wood.

———————

How can I describe to you the hush that fell?

Even the sky seemed to breathe in.

We still had a crowd of people with us. 'Oh my,' they gasped.

I could hardly contain my tears as Matiu kept up the glorious karakia. Meanwhile, Uncle Joe and Nohi were carefully unearthing their ancestor. The gradual uncovering seemed to take years. The thoughts of everyone were on the binding of this moment with that other moment so long ago in 1847 when Te Umuroa had been laid to rest.

We came to the wood of the coffin lid. Richard dusted it carefully. Still discernible was the letter 'H' carved into it.

It was time to take up the lid. Matiu and Uncle Joe knelt at the edge of the grave. Richard Morrison and Brian Prince carefully lifted sections of the lid and placed them on clear plastic for wrapping.

All present were hushed. I couldn't even see, for I was blinded by my tears. I tried to wipe them away but they still kept coming, streaming down my face, streaming.

Oh, ancestor . . .

And then I was able to see him lying in scraps of his shroud, the beautiful long bones of him.

'Tena koe, e koro,' I greeted him.

5²

'Rain down oh rain from my eyes rain down.'

The tension burst, releasing such emotion.

'Kua kitea to matou tupuna! We have found our ancestor! Hohepa has been found!'

His bones were brought up from the grave, along with remnants of the mat on which he had lain and the cloth in which he had been wrapped. All were placed in a casket for the return home to Aotearoa.

As we left, I turned to Maria Island to say our poroporoaki, our farewell.

'You have looked after our ancestor all these years. I pay tribute to you, oh ancient island, rest always in the sparkling, glistening sea.'

And Hoana said, 'The mountains are talking again. The mountains of Maria Island are saying farewell to Hohepa. Now, our mountain, Pukehika, is calling us back. We must hasten.'

———

Here's the thing.

I have mentioned earlier the pathway between the living and the dead that one must open when you are dealing with tapu, sacred, matters. I have already stated my admiration for Matiu, his sister, wife and family, for taking on this great task.

Now came one of the greatest challenges of all, to agree with the spirit world on the pathway and to define the rituals of Hohepa's return. For although Pakeha culture might have considered that we were taking only the remains of Hohepa, our Maori protocol required us to always treat him as tupapaku, the full dead person, and to therefore accord him all the honour and respect of someone who may have died, say, yesterday.

One of these rituals was that Hohepa should never be left alone. He had already been alone long enough. So I was elated and happy, and glad when everyone began to take turns at watching over him.

Another was to maintain the karakia, the prayers for the dead.

———

The next day, we packed up our bags, left Louisville and began the journey homeward. Matiu told us the plan was to let Hohepa lie in the Catholic St Joseph's Cathedral in Hobart and, there, wait with him until our flight to New Zealand.

On 4 August, we arrived in Hobart. Our Maori people of Tasmania were there to welcome us with powhiri and mihimihi charged with lamentation. We took Hohepa into the body of the cathedral and laid him in the place of honour in front of the altar. Because this would be the last evening we would be with our Maori whanau in Tasmania, there was a huge kai with special Maori dishes — crayfish, shellfish, muttonbird, oh it was yummy — and songs of aroha for each other. We gave gifts to all those who had helped us: woven kete and carved taonga were given to the two state archaeologists and to the two Chrises as well. It was a community ceremony because all had joined in the kaupapa, the purpose of the visit, and thus all had become family to each other.

For the rest of the evening, we maintained our vigil over our ancestor. And towards morning, our local iwi turned to supporting the kaupapa.

'Haere,' they said, 'Go now. Haere e hoki me nga aroha o te hunga e noho ake nei e. Go with our love and blessing. Take our tupuna home to Aotearoa now,' they said. 'Take him to rest in his beloved Whanganui River. Go and return with the love of the people who remain behind. Haere, haere e hoki me nga aroha o te hunga e noho ake nei.'

We were lucky David Creswell from Maori Affairs had come with us because problems arose with the clearance of Hohepa from Tasmania. I said to him, 'Yeah, well, just let them try to stop us now!' And then I added, 'Over my dead body.' How everybody laughed at that!

The next day we were on our way across the Tasman.

———

Oh my giddy aunt, it was cold when we landed in Christchurch.

I am not one to worry but was I glad when our ancestor cleared Customs? Was I what! We were all waiting for him when they rolled him through the gate.

'Took you long enough,' I said. 'But, after all, not every day that some-body comes through Customs who died a hundred and forty-one years ago, eh? It must have been a shock to some of those Customs officers. They probably keeled over when they checked the passport.'

We took him to St Mary's Cathedral where local iwi and some of the koroua's family of descendants welcomed Hohepa back on Aotearoa soil.

Next day, Matiu smiled at me, 'We're on the homeward stretch.'

I tell you, I couldn't wait to get on the plane to Whanganui.

Meanwhile, Nohi had rung ahead to Sister Dorothea of the Sisters of Compassion at their Whanganui retreat at Seafront Road.

'Can you tell Pa Gled we're on our way and to get the people at Patiarero ready for the tangihanga?' Pa Gled was David Gledhill whom we also knew as Pa Rawiri.

Sister immediately asked Sister Walberga to go to Whanganui Airport; usually the Whanganui Sisters went to Jerusalem from Friday to Monday.

We landed in Whanganui and it was such a relief to see everybody waiting for us. The crowd was hu-mon-gous, as my mokopuna would say. Massive! There must have been over a hundred people at the airport. We were most elated and grateful. Auntie Piki Waretini's powhiri welcoming us back was so wonderful; Auntie Moke's too. Their calls to Hohepa reminded us all of the many years that had passed between the time he left the Whanganui River to go to fight with Te Mamaku and his return.

'Warrior, you are among us at last,' Auntie Moke said.

The kapa haka the iwi did for our ancestor, well, it knocked my socks off. They showed such ihi, mana and wehi, with everybody putting their bodies and souls into it.

Now, you know, around this time you're supposed to feel exhausted, ne? Nobody would have blamed us if we had dropped to the ground and gone to sleep. But the most heartening thing is that the tangihanga actually buoys you up. You are carried through everything by the love of the people. Thus, even though the trip and the stress associated with it had been enough to fell ten oxen, I was so proud to be Maori! So proud to feel the unity! So proud to have done this! So proud to be bringing Hohepa back to the Whanganui River!

Of course we had to get going. We had karakia, left Whanganui and by mid afternoon were on the river road to Jerusalem with Hohepa's hearse in the lead.

Some two hours later, we reached Patiarero marae, Jerusalem. At that time in winter, the sun goes down behind the surrounding hills earlier than it does at the horizon, so the light was lovely and soft when we arrived. I felt proud when I saw the iwi, the whanau, all gathered in front of Te Whare Whiri-taunoka for the beginning of the tangihanga. The black-clad women began to wail a welcome to the koroua. The men began to do a haka, pulling us on.

And then there was the weeping.

Chris Heald, whose daughters had found Hohepa, arrived during the tangihanga. I don't know what day he arrived, possibly the second. He later wrote an account of the return of Hohepa whch was published in the *New Zealand Listener.*

Oh, the tangihanga was so beautiful! It was a time when we could all remember our history, our whakapapa, our links with one another. All the branches of our genealogy were sung by the kuia; they had poi in their hands, tapping them as accompaniment as they recited the names of the ancestors. In this way the names of our ancestors remain alive and circulated and repeated. Tap tap tap. Tap tap tap.

Then it was 8 August 1988.

On the third day, with high honour our ancestor's body was borne from the marae with great dignity to his final resting place. There was a big wind as three separate groups of pallbearers carried Hohepa to his grave on the banks of the Whanganui River, in the shadow of Pukehika, the mountain of our ancestors.

The burial ceremony was carried out by Father Te Awhitu.

Lie forever, ancestor, with your family, in the soil of your country
on the banks of the Whanganui River, i runga o Patiarero,
above Patiarero, i raro o Pukehika, beneath Pukehika,
te maunga o Ngati Hau, sacred mountain of the people.

At the end of it, all the members of the mission who had gone to get him were blessed with a special karakia for, in bringing their ancestor back, others who resided in the graveyard had had to be disturbed. Forgiveness had to be sought in a ceremony of purification.

So you see, this was not a journey just to pick up Hohepa and bring him back, no. It was something much bigger than that. It was the making right of a wrong that had been committed one hundred and forty-one years ago, the joining of the dead to the dead as if the past was just yesterday.

Once that was done, the bindings had to be brought together again. The past bound to the present, the inside with the outside, the top with the bottom. The continuum of the world corrected and Te Umuroa put in his proper place in that world. Only then could all the worlds be sealed together again, the dead to the dead.

The living could be released to return to the living.

The mountains stop talking.

———

Oh, there were some people in the community of Whanganui who raised their voices in anger that government monies should have been spent on the repatriation of our ancestor.

One letter writer to the *Wanganui Chronicle* on 8 August said:

> They state it as a matter of mana within the family or tribal group to which they belong. Surely it would have been more fitting to accept an apology from the Governor-General or Prime Minister Lange.
>
> It shatters me to hear of the money that is being spent on wasteful Maori claims and complaints.
>
> I am fully aware of the problems facing all genuine New Zealanders who are being kicked in the guts, but the ones who think it is their God given right to bludge off society should be the ones who should suffer. It could or should be a proud nation of all people.

Matiu was clearly disappointed. His reply, by way of an interview in the *Wanganui Chronicle* the next day, spoke for all of us:

> The general public didn't know about it, or didn't care. And the ones who did know said it was a waste of time and money. But the Tasmanian people were tremendous. We were overwhelmed with their love and generosity.

When are the Pakeha going to get over themselves! Look at the fuss being caused just because we want to get the name of our city correctly spelt — Whanganui like our river, not Wanganui. Was it our fault that the early settlers couldn't hear our 'h'? We're the Maori Cockneys, eh. They don't pronounce the 'h' either, but it's there!

Will there ever be aroha for each other in our own land of Aotearoa?

———

Now.

We have been talking together for quite a while, haven't we? And you probably think the korero is over, don't you? But nothing is ever ended.

518

Something wonderful always happens when you least expect it.

This story occurred after the tangihanga was over.

———

Let's see: the kouroua was buried on the Sunday, yes, that's right.

Well, the next day, Monday, Sister Dorothea at the Sisters of Compassion heard the telephone ringing. She went to answer it. 'Hello?'

There was a strange woman on the phone ringing from Cairns, Australia. Her name was Delphina Crapp.

'I have the old warrior's stick,' she said, 'the old warrior who has just returned to New Zealand. I heard it on the news. Anyhow, I tried to get in touch way before now. The stick's been kicking up a fuss in the house. It wants to go back to him. I'm sending it back.'

Sister Dorothea immediately telephoned Pa Gled. 'Oh,' he answered, 'that must be the tokotoko. We better prepare to welcome it when it gets here.'

Instead of sending the tokotoko, however, Delphina rang again on Tuesday to say, 'I've decided to bring the stick back to you personally. It's quite distressed! It makes me so nervous I won't undress in the same room! So I better bring it to make sure the old warrior gets it.'

That's why Delphina arrived with the tokotoko the following day at Whanganui airport. 'I'm a New Zealander, and a Maori too,' she told us, 'but I've been living in Australia. I have no idea how this stick got to Cairns but when I saw it in a local auction room I knew I had to buy it. I recognised the Whanganui River carvings.'

We immediately took Delphina and the tokotoko to Patiarero. Pa Gled headed the group which brought her onto the marae where Matiu Mareikura, Uncle Pestal Pauro and Ron Hough welcomed the tokotoko back home as an ancestor.

Well, this is what happened. It was a windless day but when the tokotoko was laid on a flax mat, a wind got under the edges. The mat folded itself twice around the tokotoko as it was lying in state — and the tokotoko sat up. We were all moved by the occurrence. With reverence we then placed the tokotoko inside the meeting house, and the wind died down.

———

Then we heard something calling, something coming down the Matua River.

When we looked, we saw two shapes, like angels winging swiftly and low across the water. They swooped up to perch on two poplar trees just behind the graveyard, unfurling, unbending, straightening, arching and springing upward and out—

Ta-raaa!

They were two nankeen night herons, spirit birds. The ones that arrived were mainly light reddish brown, close to orange, crowned with a small black patch on the top of the head and a white bib under their chins. They began kicking up a ruckus.

Where had they come from? *Don't you know?*

Nohi has the tokotoko now.

———————

Today, the two night herons have now become a colony of seventeen. They are such spiritual creatures. Forest & Bird tells us that they have no idea why they have turned up at Patiarero.

They roost together for warmth and they are the only colony in the country. Sometimes I look at them as they glide down the river. Their wings often scatter the surface with sun-stars. Oh, they are lovely birds for many reasons. One of them is that they cannot recognise their own chicks, so they feed any other baby herons around, not just nankeen night heron chicks either. Maybe they're blind. I prefer to think that they have whanau habits like us.

Their lovely appearance can be deceiving, however. Like, they are so hardcase! They like to float downriver on their backs, calling to each other, *Whiria, whiria, whiria.* You see them swimming the way birds are supposed to swim and then, next moment, flip! There they are with wings outspread, like some of our kuia and koroua, black coats unbuttoned, enjoying the sun. *Ae, whiria, whiria, whiria.*

Did you know they are also called quakers?

They're like a blessing from the past.

A blessing for the future.

———————

Well, that's all I can tell you.

Over twenty years have passed since we brought Te Umuroa home and the tokotoko and the birds arrived. The koroua would be proud to see all his descendants — there are many of us now. I have grandchildren myself and I like to gather them around me and tell them the story.

'There once was a man called Te Umuroa who was the son of Korakotai and Hinekorako. He was the fourth of their children, his other siblings being Marama, Rangi and Te Pae. He married a woman from Taranaki named Te Rai. Aue, he was wrongfully imprisoned and taken to Australia over a hundred and sixty years ago. Although they only had one child, a son Rukuwai, he was never forgotten and the story of the wrongful exile was carried down from generation to generation. Rukuwai married Noni, and they had four children: Kopeka, Molly, Pone and Wenerau; and although Wenerau had no issue, the other siblings had children.

They were not the only ones to commit Te Umuroa to memory, for their whakapapa joined horizontally with other descent lines and thus Te Umuroa's extended iwi and whanau always remembered the great wrong done to him. This is why in 1988 a mission from the Whanganui comprising iwi and whanau went to Tasmania to get him. This is the lesson, e moko-puna, it doesn't matter how long it takes, always fight for justice, and always look after each other.'

———————

I like this time of the day, don't you? Looking across the Matua River, every-thing is so peaceful and calm. The river is eternal. It will flow forever.

Sometimes, however, like today, I see a shimmer across the surface. And often I hear a voice in my head as clear as day.

E kui, titiro ki te awa.

Maybe it's my imagination, but I regularly see a young man diving from the bluff into the water. I see him swimming like a taniwha under the river, springing up at midstream, gasping, the water streaming from his head, laughing, 'Yahooooo!' He looks at me, gratefully shakes his head from side to side in ecstasy, and then flips down into the depths again.

You think it might just be a village boy swimming before the sun goes down, or a shoal of fish or a log swirling in the swollen river?

Ah well, humour a sentimental old lady, eh. I like to think that it is Hohepa, happy that he has been returned to the people who never forgot him.

Welcome home, e koro, tama a te awa, child of the river.

Ancestor, you are home now.

Moe mai ra, e koro.

Be at peace.

AUTHOR'S NOTE

The Trowenna Sea is a work of fiction, which I began thinking about when, in 2005, I had the honour of being the second Distinguished Visitor (the first was J. M. Coetzee) to the University of Tasmania. While there I gave a number of lectures and was astonished when, at one of them, the novelist Richard Flanagan introduced me with the following words: 'You will know, of course, Witi, that you are not the first Maori to visit our shores . . .', and then proceeded to tell me the story of the five Maori transported to Van Diemen's Land in 1846. The story immediately arrested me and, during the three weeks I was in Tasmania, I did as much research as I could on the event itself and the remarkable response shown by the colony when the five Maori arrived in Hobart and were kept not at Port Arthur Penitentiary but at the facility on Maria Island.

Thus, I could not have written this novel without the instigating enthusiasm of remarkable Tasmanian friends who, during that first visit of 2005, went out of their way to help me: Professor Jeff Malpas, who nominated me for the Distinguished Visitorship; Professor Ralph Crane, who took a day out of his busy university schedule to take me to Maria Island; Nicki Ottavi, Archives Office of Tasmania; and Eryl Raymond. I am particularly indebted to eminent historian Henry Reynolds, for kindly reading the first draft and providing invaluable advice and correction.

On my return to New Zealand after that visit to Tasmania I was surprised to find that the story had been virtually erased from New Zealand history — almost as if the transportation had never existed. But I was not able to begin writing the novel until December 2008 due to my teaching commitments at the University of Auckland and also my literary commitments, including the rewriting of my first five books (the fourth book, *The Matriarch*, was republished in its rewritten edition in March 2009).

The five Maori were taken under the care of John Jennings Imrie, born 1 June 1813, Castlehill Parish of Ayr, Scotland, and his wife Elizabeth (Etty) Bailey, born 2 June 1815 Cashmere, Ross, Scotland. I wish I had been able to write about them but, in the end, I felt I had to honour the original Imrie and Bailey families and not fictionalise their lives. I therefore created new characters, Gower McKissock and Ismay Glossop, whose stories parallel those of John and Elizabeth Imrie, but acknowledge that the narrative arc of the story — the epic span of it from Scotland to England to New Zealand and thence Australia — is entirely owed to the original John Jennings Imrie and Etty Bailey. I wish to thank the descendants of these two remarkable people wherever you are in Australia, New Zealand and around the world.

I also wish to thank the descendants and wider iwi of Hohepa Te Umuroa who were unaware of this novel until very late in its writing. My first meeting with their representatives, arranged by my good friend Jenny McLeod, took place during a quick visit back to Aotearoa from Hawai'i where I was working at the University of Hawai'i. On 23 March 2009, Jenny and I drove to the home of Sister Dorothea (Mary) Meade, Sisters of Compassion of Mother Aubert's Order, 21 Seafront Road, Whanganui. The sisters have an intimate relationship with Patiarero, where Mother Aubert established her community, and the iwi and family of Te Umuroa. I was grateful to meet Bernadette Wanihi, daughter of the late Uncle Joe Wanihi (one of two descendants who went on the 1988 mission to collect Te Umuroa and bring him home to the Patiarero), the koroua, Te Otinga Te Peehi Waretini, who also went on the mission (he showed me wonderful photographs of the visit), the kuia, Piki, and John Haami, Pastoral Co-ordinator for Maori in the Catholic Diocese of Whanganui, and his wife Pearl. At that meeting I arranged for the draft to be made available through John to the family and iwi. My second meeting with family representatives took place on 3 June 2009, again at Sister Dorothea's home, a week after I returned from Hawai'i, and this time I was thrilled to meet the genial, but staunch, Te Konohi Wallace, more simply known as Nohi, the second of the two descendants who had gone to Tasmania in 1988. I also met Manaaki Claver Rerekura and her nephew Steven Rerekura; in a subsequent telephone call I came to appreciate Manaaki's quiet and modest strength. It inspires me greatly to know that the story of Hohepa Te Umuroa is so strongly protected by the loving hands of his many descendants and his iwi, and I offer my mihi to them and my great respect. I hope that they will forgive me for any errors or interpretations that I have made which do not conform to their own under-standings of their ancestor and their own lives.

I completed the first draft of *The Trowenna Sea* in March 2009. I obtained leave without pay from the University of Auckland to take up the Citizen's Chair at the University of Hawai'i at Manoa. To both those institutions I offer my gratitude. With some gloom, I note that there are as many historians per acre in Tasmania as in New Zealand (and no doubt Wolverhampton), and that they may discover many errors of fact in the manuscript, for which I take entire responsibility. I'd be grateful to be duly chastised and advised so that I am able to make corrections in any second edition.

I owe a great debt of gratitude to Geoff Walker, my publisher, Jeremy Sherlock, and the staff of Penguin New Zealand and the Raupo imprint. My grateful thanks also to my editor, Jane Parkin, for her exceptional skill in helping me to take the manuscript to second draft, and to Gillian Tewsley for assisting to finalise the draft for publication. Finally, my tribute and thanks to my agent and dear friend, Ray Richards, Richards Literary Agency, Auckland.

Texts consulted include: *The First Report of Commissioners for Enquiring into the Employment and Conditions of Children in Mines and Manufactories 1842*, British Parliamentary Papers for 1842; *Down the Mine* and *The Story of Lotte*, Nuffield Primary History, 2000; *For Fear of Pain: British Surgery, 1790–1850*, Peter Stanley, Rodopi, 2003; *Wolverhampton Archives & Local Studies; Wolverhampton Dispensary*, Bev Parker, Wolverhampton Local History Society, 2005; *Story of New Zealand*, Dr A. S. Thomson, John Murray, London, 1859; *Told from the Ranks*, E. Milton Small, A. Melrose, London, 1901; *New Zealand: Romance of Empire Series*, Reginald Horsley, T. C. & E. C. Jack, London, 1908; *Old Redoubts, Blockhouses, and Stockades of the Wellington District*, Elsdon Best, Transactions and Proceedings of the Royal Society of New Zealand, 21 September 1920; *In The Green Canyon: "The Place of Cliffs"*, James Cowan, The New Zealand Railways Magazine, vol. 4, issue 12 (1 April 1930); *Te Rauparaha*, W. Carkeek, *Te Ao Hou*, no. 32, September 1950; *The New Zealand Wars (1845–1872)*, James Cowan, R. E. Owen, 1955; *The Early Journals of Henry Williams*, Henry Williams (edited by Lawrence M. Rogers), Pegasus Press, 1961; *The Shadow of the Land: A Study of British Policy and Racial Conflict in New Zealand, 1832–1852*, Ian Wards, Government Printer, Wellington, 1968; *Te Riri Pakeha: The White Man's Anger*, Tony Simpson, Alister Taylor, 1979; *To Face the Daring Maoris*, Michael Barthorp, Hodder and Stoughton, 1979; *Te Rauparaha: A New Perspective*, Patricia Burns, Penguin, 1980; *Cork of War*, Ray Grover, John McIndoe, 1982; *The Treaty of Waitangi*, Claudia

Orange, Allen & Unwin, 1987; *Waiata: Maori Songs in History,* Margaret Orbell, Reed, 1991; *An Encyclopaedia of New Zealand,* Ministry for Culture & Heritage, Wellington, 2005; *Waitangi Tribunal: Te Whanganui A Tara Me Ona Takiwa. Report on the Wellington District,* Maori Law Review, September 2003; *Hohepa (Opera Libretto),* Jenny McLeod, 2007; *Mukiwa,* Peter Godwin, Macmillan, 1996; *The Highland Clearances,* John Prebble, Secker & Warburg, 1963; *Extracts from the Letters of James Backhouse* (2 vols), Harvey and Darton, London, 1841; *Diary of Dr J. J. Imrie While He Was in Charge of the Maori Exiles on Maria Island, 20 December 1846–25 March 1848,* (Copy) NS1093/1/1, Archive Office of Tasmania; *Life and Adventures of William Thornley,* Charles Rowcroft, J. Walch & Sons, 1846; *The Emigrant's Friend,* J. Allen, 1848; *The Broad Arrow,* Oline Keese, J. Walch & Sons, 1859; *Memoir of James Backhouse,* William Sessions, 1870; *A System of Penal Discipline,* Henry Phibbs Fry, London, 1870; *The Progress of Australasia in the 19th Century,* T. A. Coghlan & T. T. Ewing, The 19th Century Series, W. & R. Chambers Ltd, 1903; *The Early History of Maria Island, East Coast, Tasmania,* Clive E. Lord, Royal Society of Tasmania, 1919; *The Making of Australasia,* Thomas Dunbabin, A&C Black Ltd, 1922; *That Yesterday Was Home,* Roy Bridges, Australasian Publishing Company, 1948; *For the Term of His Natural Life,* Marcus Clarke, Hallcraft Publishing, 1949; *The Life and Times of Sir Richard Dry,* A. D. Baker, Oldham, Beddome & Meredith Pty Ltd, 1951; *The Viking of Van Diemen's Land,* Frank Clune & P. R. Stephensen, Angus and Robertson, 1954; *The Penal Settlements of Early Van Diemen's Land,* T. J. Lempriere, Royal Society of Tasmania (Northern Branch), 1954; *The Tasmanians,* Robert Travers, Cassell Australia Ltd, 1968; *Maoris on Maria Island: Punishment by Exile,* John Tattersall, Hawke's Bay Art Gallery and Museum, Napier, 1973; *Tasmania: The Island Series,* S. W. Jackman, Stackpole Books, 1974; *Victorian and Edwardian Hobart,* Dan Sprod, John Ferguson, 1977; *The Aboriginal Tasmanians,* Lyndall Ryan, Allen & Unwin, 1981; *The Fatal Shore,* Robert Hughes, William Collins, 1986; *Down Home: Revisiting Tasmania,* Peter Conrad, Chatto & Windus, 1988; *Hohepah: A Warrior's Journey Home* (DVD), Peter McKinley, Dodges Ferry, 1988; *Tasmania: The History,* Peter Collenette, D. & L. Book Distributors, 1990; *Edith May 1895–1974; Life in Early Tasmania,* Mary Cree, James Street Publications (date unknown); *Fate of a free people,* Henry Reynolds, 1995; *Aboriginal Sovereignty,* Henry Reynolds, Allen & Unwin, 1996; *Fighting Those Who Came Against Their Country: Maori Political Transportation to Van Diemen's Land 1846–48,* Jeffrey E. Hopkins, THRA *P&P* 44/1, March 1997; *Maria Island, A Tasmanian Eden,* Maggie Weidenhofer, Darlington Press, 1997; *Black Pioneers,* Henry Reynolds, Penguin, 2000; *Along These Lines: from Trowenna to Tasmania,* C. A.

Cranston, Cornford Press, 2000; *Tasmania's Maria Island*, Michael Ludeke, Ludeke Publishing, 2001; *In Tasmania*, Nicholas Shakespeare, Vintage, 2004; *Tasmanian Visions*, Rosslyn D. Haynes, Polymath Press, 2006; *The Other Side of the Frontier*, Henry Reynolds, University of New South Wales Press, 2007; *Maria Island National Park* and *Parks Update*, National Parks and Wildlife Service Tasmania, continuous publication; *Devils on Horses; In the Words of the Anzacs in the Middle East*, Terry Kinloch, Exisle Publishing, Auckland, 2007.

For those interested, Hohepa Te Umuroa and the other Maori prisoners were sketched by two colonial artists while they were in Van Diemen's Land. One artist, William Duke, who spent time in New Zealand during 1844–46, was resident in Hobart in 1846. The other noted artist was John Skinner Prout. Prout painted all five Maori prisoners from drawings he had sketched on the day of their arrival and next, 16–17 November, while the Maori were kept temporarily in the Hobart Town Penitentiary. William Duke's sketch of Hohepa Te Umuroa is part of a private collection; Skinner Prout's five paintings, all 'autographed' by the prisoners, now reside in a collection of twenty-six Skinner Prout portraits in the Museum of Mankind, Ethnography Department of the British Museum, London.

Regarding Trucanini and Woureddy, her second husband, their remains and other artefacts remained on public view at the Tasmanian Museum until 1947. After continuing controversy, they were put into the museum vaults. However, it was not until 1 May 1976, at the centenary of her death, that her skeleton was cremated by the Government of Tasmania and the ashes scattered on D'Entrecasteaux Channel, the waters adjacent to her birthplace, Bruny Island, as she had originally wished.

The Trowennans, as Ismay McKissock calls them in this novel, survive. They did not die out when Trucanini died. Today there are over two thousand Tasmanian Aborigines in Tasmania and elsewhere who trace their whakapapa to their Tasmanian Aboriginal past through blood connection. They are, like Maori, unquestionably jealous of their descent lines from Tasmanian Aboriginal ancestors and retaining their identity with pride and passion.

Maria Island, on 1 June 1971, in recognition of its flora and fauna, was declared a wildlife sanctuary under the control of the Animals and Birds Protection Board. The National Parks and Wildlife Service was formed in November of that year, and assumed responsibility for the island, which was proclaimed a national park on 14 June 1972. It is now managed by Tasmania's Parks and Wildlife Service; it is the only Australian island that is entirely a national park.